New York

*Hearts Are Entwined
in Four Complete Novels*

Kjersti Hoff Baez

Claire M. Coughlin and Hope Irvin Marston

Ginger O'Neil

Ellyn Sanna

BARBOUR
PUBLISHING

Wait for the Morning ©1996 by Kjersti Hoff Baez
Santanoni Sunrise ©1994 by Claire M. Coughlin and Hope Irvin Marston
A Touching Performance ©1996 by Ginger O'Neil
The Quiet Heart ©1995 by Rae Simons (aka/Ellyn Sanna)

Cover image © GettyOne

ISBN 1-58660-714-6

Published by Barbour Publishing, Inc., P.O. Box 719, Uhrichsville, Ohio 44683, www.barbourbooks.com.

Our mission is to publish and distribute inspirational products offering exceptional value and biblical encouragement to the masses.

Printed in the United States of America.
5 4 3

New York

Wait for the Morning

Kjersti Hoff Baez

Chapter 1

Just remember, Jessie, I tried to talk you out of this." Kay, wearing oversized glasses, studied the key in her hand. "I hope this works," she said as she thrust the key into the lock. "You never know with these old houses. So far, so good. It's the right key, Jessie." She turned toward her friend. "Jessie, are you listening?"

Jessie hurried across the length of the porch that swept around the face of the house. "It's perfect, Kay!" she exclaimed. "I just know it will be perfect."

"A realtor's dream," muttered Kay. "She takes one look at the porch and it's a sale." She turned the key in the lock and pushed open the door. "I think it might be wise to see the inside first. . .before you buy," she added wryly.

Jessie strode through the door into the foyer. "A grandfather clock!" she cried. "And look! A marvelous staircase, all carved wood. Wainscoting. I always wanted wainscoting."

Kay picked her way through the garbage that littered the floor. She flipped a switch on the wall and squinted up at the light. "Well, the electricity is still on." A piece of faded wallpaper hung down over the wainscoting. As Kay pulled at it, it crumbled in her hand. "Obviously a fixer-upper, Jessie. Jessie?"

"Oh, wow!" a voice exclaimed from down the hall.

Rushing down the hall, Kay joined Jessie in what appeared to be the kitchen. The pungent odor of decay stunned the realtor's senses. She pulled a tissue from her purse and covered her nose. "Oh, wow is right! That's awful."

"Oh, wow!" Jessie repeated, oblivious to the realtor's discomfort. "Look at those porcelain fixtures on the sink. They're marvelous. Must be original to the house."

"Smells like whatever died was original to the house, too," choked Kay. "Let's get out of here."

"Oh, Kay, it's probably just a dead mouse in the wall."

"Mice in the walls. Definitely a fixer-upper. Come on," said Kay, taking Jessie by the arm, "the smell is deafening."

"That doesn't make sense."

"Poetic license, Madame," sniffed Kay. "You know how creative I am with words. It's my true medium."

"How could I forget?" laughed Jessie. "Oh, look! This is a huge closed-in porch!"

A door at the back of the kitchen opened on to a porch that spanned the width of the house. The windows lining the porch were arrayed haphazardly with occasional glass and tattered screens.

Kay guided Jessie back down the hall. "That must be the living room." She pointed through the archway to the left of the staircase. Jessie nodded and hurried in. It was a large room with a fireplace. Tall windows graced the walls with a quiet dignity, despite the peeling paint and cracked panes. An archway opened into a square-shaped room.

"Maybe a dining room?" queried Kay as she walked through the archway.

"Look! A bay window," exclaimed Jessie. "With a window seat. I—"

"I know, I know. You always wanted one. Too bad someone painted it purple." Kay cautiously stroked the wood with her finger. "And I mean dark purple. . . hideous purple."

"I can refinish it," countered the prospective buyer. "No problem."

"That could take months, even years. Looks like they put on three or four coats," said Kay, shaking her head. "Purple with a vengeance."

"Who would paint this beautiful bay window purple?"

"Years back, in the sixties, some hippies rented this place. Guess purple was in then," said Kay.

A door at the back of the room opened into a narrow hall. The realtor squinted through her glasses. "Must connect with the kitchen."

"You're right!" Jessie passed through the hall and excitedly circled through the first floor again. "This is it, Kay. I'll take it."

Kay pointed up the stairs. "How about we check the bedrooms? See if there's a bathroom or anything useful like that?"

A quick survey of the second floor revealed four bedrooms, three large and one small. The bathroom was large, the fixtures cracked and antiquated. Jessie looked out a hall window onto the yard.

"Two acres of gleaming, unkempt jungle. The natural look," drawled the realtor. "So what do you say? It certainly has a charm all its own." She grinned at her friend.

The women descended to the cellar and discovered a gloomy area cluttered with old trunks and boxes.

"Looks like a dry cellar," said Jessie. "That's good."

"Yep. Real good. And creepy. Let's get out into the sunshine."

The women climbed the narrow stairwell to the first floor.

"I love it! Absolutely!" Jessie turned to her friend. "Please draw up the papers today, okay? You said the bank owns it?" she asked.

"You'll get a great price, Jess. They just want to get rid of this eyesore. . .I mean this stately old mansion. Pardon me."

Jessie brushed off her friend's gloomy assessment of the house and walked toward the front door. "Let's go. The sooner the better. I can't wait to get started restoring this place."

Kay followed her out. She locked the door and stood for a moment, concern on her face.

"What's the matter, Kay?" Jessie asked.

"Let's sit for a moment on the steps here, Jess." She pointed to the front steps.

"Look at these gorgeous stone steps, Kay. They are perfect! Not even chipped."

"Jessie, don't you think you should reconsider? This house needs mounds of work, and it's so big and, after all, it's just you to live in it. I figured at your age it might be wiser to buy a condo or something. It would be easier to manage." Kay said the words quickly, anxiously studying her friend's face for a reaction.

Jessie patted Kay on the hand. "Kay, I know you're concerned about me. But honestly, I love this place. I always wanted to buy an old house and fix it up. But you knew Tom. He was happy in our apartment, happy he didn't have to do things like mow a lawn or repair a roof."

"Tom was a gem, Jessie." Kay's eyes watered. "You were one lucky woman to have had him."

"Luck had nothing to do with it," she said softly. "The Lord was the maker of our marriage. Tom was wonderful, but now he's gone. And it's been three years. Time for me to do what I feel is right for me."

"But Jessie, I can show you some lovely condos. They're new and practically maintenance free. I don't think you should take on this big of a project now."

"Kay! You make it sound like I'm one step away from Happy Vale Retirement Home. I'm fifty-five, not ninety-five!"

"Okay, okay," sighed Kay. "I just thought—" She stopped midsentence. "Would you look who's coming down the walk. My, my, but he's gorgeous!"

Jessie looked up. "Good night, Kay," she whispered. "You sound like a teenager."

A tall man strode up to the house and approached the two women. "Excuse me, ladies," he said politely. "Are either of you a realtor or someone official connected with this house?" The tanned stranger smiled, his gray-blue eyes accented by his sterling gray hair.

Kay stood up and held out her hand. "I'm the realtor. Kay Bantam."

"Nice to meet you."

"I've been a realtor for five years now. Ever since my husband left me. Actually, I quite enjoy being a realtor," the woman chattered. "You meet so many interesting people. It's hard work, a lot of legwork, of course, but there's nothing more thrilling than connecting the right home with the right buyer. After all—"

"Kay!" Jessie stood and nudged her friend.

Kay looked horrified. "Am I babbling?" Her face reddened. "I always babble when I'm nervous," she explained to the stranger. "Can't help it. Ever since I was a child. In grade school, whenever I was called on to answer a question, I would talk on and on about everything but the answer. Why, one time I had a part in the school play, and I started talking and couldn't stop and they had to—"

"Kay!" whispered Jessie. "You're doing it again!"

"Sorry," Kay sighed and adjusted her glasses.

Jessie extended her hand. "Jessie Woods. I'm buying this house," she said firmly, with a glance at her realtor friend.

"Sam. . .Reverend Samuel Taylor. I live across the street." He turned to the realtor. "I thought you should know I saw someone or maybe two someones snooping around this house last night. Looked like they were casing the place."

Kay laughed. "Casing it for what? Dead rodents?"

"Don't laugh too hard, Ms. Bantam. I guess you've never heard the legend, have you?"

"Legend?" Jessie perked up. "About this house?"

"Well, I don't know too many details, but they say the man who built this house amassed a fortune in gold and hid it somewhere in the house. No one has ever found it. Who knows? It may still be hidden in there yet."

Jessie laughed. "All the more reason to buy, right, Kay?"

"Oh, yes," responded Kay. "It always helps to have a treasure legend to make a sale. I'm having a great day, that's for sure." They all laughed together.

"About those trespassers," Sam continued. "I sent Manny over. He took care of them nicely."

"Manny?" inquired Jessie.

"My dog. He's a great watchdog. A few loud barks and a growl and he scared them off."

"Well, thank you, Reverend Taylor," said Kay. "That's a plus, you know. . . having good neighbors."

Jessie nodded. "Yes, I guess I should thank you, Reverend Taylor. After all, this will soon be my new home."

"No problem," he replied. "I'm always ready to help a neighbor." He walked down the sidewalk. Turning momentarily, he smiled at Jessie. "And by the way, Jessie Woods, I'm going to marry you."

Chapter 2

Can you believe that?" Jessie fumed while Kay arranged the papers on her desk. "The nerve of that man! 'By the way,' he says. 'By the way.' Who does he think he is, anyway?"

Kay sighed. "I should be so lucky! A guy as good looking as that, mature, and unattached. Really, Jessie, I've changed my mind about the house. I think it's a great idea for you to buy it. Who knows what'll happen!" She leaned over her desk toward her friend. "He was probably joking. Besides, that was a couple of weeks ago. How can you still be angry?"

"Because he's obviously full of himself, thinking he can just say things like that—to a total stranger, no less! Honestly, sometimes I think I shouldn't even buy the house."

Kay's face blanched. "Jessie, the closing is next week. Everything is moving fast because you're paying cash. You can't possibly—"

"Oh, don't worry," Jessie reassured her friend. "I'm just letting off steam." She sighed. "I'm probably a little jumpy, now that it's really going to happen. You know. . .moving. . .leaving the city." Her lips quivered, and a tear slipped down her cheek.

"Kind of like leaving Tom behind, is that it?" asked Kay softly.

Jessie nodded. "So many memories in that apartment. . .good and bad. Mostly good, though," she sighed. "But I need to move on."

"So you're moving out. I think it's good," said Kay briskly.

"Yes, you're right. It is good," responded Jessie, wiping her tears.

"This is a very moving conversation, my dear," Kay grinned.

Jessie smiled and shook her head. "Kay, you are impossible. Your sense of humor is. . .well, interesting, to say the least."

"Thanks a lot," sniffed Kay. She checked over her paperwork. "That about does it for today. You're all set for the closing."

Jessie stood up to leave. "Thanks a lot, Kay. I'll see you next week."

"By the way," Kay called to Jessie as she was leaving, "it looks like you bought this house just in the nick of time. There was a guy here yesterday inquiring about it. Looked really interested."

Jessie caught her breath. "Luckily I got here first. I can't imagine not getting that house. Do you think anything could—"

"Don't worry! I told him it was a done deal." Kay pushed at her glasses.

"Figure that out. For years the house just sits there rotting, and—"

"Rotting?" said Jessie. "You know the inspector gave that house a clean bill of health, Kay Bantam."

"Sorry. I forgot how sensitive you are about it. Anyway, the house sits there for years, and now, bingo! Everyone wants it." Kay shook her head. "The real estate business sure is interesting. You never know what's going to happen next."

"Kay, you're making me nervous. Nothing can prevent me from getting the house now, can it? I mean, what if the guy comes and puts a higher bid on the house? And what do you mean by 'everyone wants it'?"

"Jessie, get a grip on yourself. It's just an expression. You two are the only ones who've shown any interest." Kay peered over her glasses at her friend. "Between you and me, this guy didn't look like he could afford to buy a cup of coffee, if you know what I mean. Besides, this is it; it's almost over. Just show up for the closing next week."

Jessie smiled. "I'll be there. . .early."

∞

The closing proceeded without a hitch. The bank representative smiled as he handed Jessie the keys. "Congratulations, Mrs. Woods. I hope you enjoy your new home."

Jessie extended her thanks to everyone, gave Kay a hug, and hurried out the door. She could not wait to get to the house.

"But the first stop is the post office," she mumbled to herself.

Jessie hurried across the street, her mind busy with all the details that needed to be worked out before the movers showed up the following week. She did not notice the man leaning against a parked car, reading a newspaper.

The man lowered his paper. He watched the woman cross the street and pull open the glass door of the post office. Years of dashed hopes and bad business deals had chiseled hard features into his face. His dark eyes patiently studied the door of the post office, waiting for the woman to reappear.

Sunlight glanced off the glass as the door was opened and the woman hurried away. The man squinted. He painstakingly folded his paper and put it under his arm. Dodging the traffic, he made his way across the street, pulling along his lame left leg with care.

Once inside the post office, the man eyed a skinny, uniformed postal worker behind the counter, perched over his stamps like a bird. The stranger approached the counter, a smile slowly crossing his face.

The postal worker returned the smile. "Well, hello. Spencer Hart, isn't it? You were in here last week to buy stamps," he noted triumphantly, his head bobbing up and down rapidly.

"Right you are, Sir. You certainly have a good memory," the stranger complimented.

"I never forget a name or a face. Herb. . .Herbert Stamping, at your service." He chuckled. "I know, I know. No one believes that's my real name. But it is!" He tapped his cheek with a long finger, his brow puckered with remembering. "I once knew a butcher by the name of Raw. . .Chester Raw. Called his shop Raw's Meats, as I recall. Really! Truth is stranger than fiction, you know."

Spencer nodded in agreement. "Busy today?" he asked casually.

Herb adjusted the strand of hair that vainly covered his receding hairline. "Oh, yes, busy as usual," responded the talkative clerk. "All my regulars have been in, of course, and then some new faces."

"New faces?"

"Oh, yes. As a matter of fact, there was a woman in here just now who is moving here. Lovely woman. Name is Jessie Woods. Actually, I recognize her from before. She comes here every so often to visit her friend, Kay Bantam, the realtor, you know. They're best friends. Mrs. Woods bought the old Denver house. The closing was today," he added importantly.

"Oh?" Spencer's eyebrows shot up, as if in surprise.

Herb frowned. "I'm sorry. You probably don't even know what I'm talking about. Why, you're a stranger here yourself, aren't you, Mr. Hart? Are you settling here, too?"

"As a matter of fact, I am considering it," Spencer Hart answered, another slow smile revealing his yellowed teeth.

"Well, Carlisle is a wonderful town, friendly and clean. I think you'd like it," Herb chirped. He cleared his throat. "Now, may I help you?"

"As a matter of fact, I would like to procure a post office box. I will be here for some time, if not permanently."

Herb busily complied with his customer's wish. He carefully handed the man a slip of paper. "Here's the number and the combination. It's for your eyes only, of course."

"Of course," Spencer nodded. "Thank you for all your help, Mr. Stamping."

"Any time. Hope you enjoy Carlisle. If you need any information about the town, just stop by here. I'll be glad to help." Herb paused a moment. "What do you do for a living, if I may ask?"

Spencer smiled benignly at the prying clerk. "I'm a writer," came his ready answer. "I write novels. In fact, that's why I'm here. The setting for my next project is in a small town, just like this one. Living here will give me a feel for the small-town environment, don't you agree?"

Fascinated, Herb bobbed his head. "Oh, how exciting!"

"I write under a pen name. To ensure my privacy," Spencer continued. "You understand, don't you?" His words neatly curtailed any further prying.

"Oh, yes. . .of course. Mum's the word," whispered Herb.

"Thank you for your time," said Spencer.

Spencer Hart exited the post office, softly chuckling under his breath. "He's better than a gossip columnist. And real cheap, too." A deliberate look in his eyes, Spencer plodded down Main Street, his sluggish leg scraping the sidewalk with a steady rhythm.

"Welcome to Carlisle, Hart," he said to himself. "May all your dreams come true."

Chapter 3

Jessie laughed at herself as she tried to unlock the door with her trembling hands. "Calm down, Jess," she said to herself. "You're only entering your new home as its owner for the first time!" She turned the key and swung open the door. A burst of color caught her eye.

"Flowers!" she exclaimed. A large vase on the dusty hall table overflowed with a fanciful blend of pale pink roses and blue wildflowers. The surprised recipient hurried over and extracted a small white card from the blooms.

" 'Here's to you, kid,' " she read out loud. " 'Enjoy your new home! Love, Kay.' " Jessie smiled. "What a doll!" She fingered the delicate petals.

The scent of the roses lent a hominess to the front hall. "Thank you, Kay," whispered Jessie.

Standing still for a moment, Jessie listened to the house. All was quiet. There was an air of expectancy, as if the house were waiting to see what this woman was going to do next. She sensed there was history within its walls, but what kind of history she did not know. Was it an ordinary story or were there tales to be told? Who had lived here, and how had they played out their lives?

"Well, I'm here now," said a determined Jessie Woods. She sighed and spoke again, a softness in her voice. "We're here, Lord. You and I. Please fill this house with grace."

She stopped for a moment. Thoughts of Tom flashed through her mind; a twinge of pain stirred in her heart. Suddenly, Jessie felt very alone.

"Pull yourself together, Jess. First things first," she told herself as she strode through the living room doorway. "This place is starving for fresh air." But, try as she might, she could not get any of the windows open. They were all stuck.

A knock at the front door interrupted her struggle with the windows. "Coming," she called out, wondering who was knocking. She did not know anyone in Carlisle, except for Kay.

Jessie swung open the heavy, wooden door. To her surprise, Sam Taylor stood there grinning at her, his arms loaded down with brooms, mops, and dust pans. Behind him stood a handful of people similarly armed.

"Good afternoon," he said loudly. "This is the official welcoming and cleaning committee from First Baptist of Carlisle." He bowed graciously.

For the moment, Jessie forgot the man's previous outlandish statement concerning marriage. Then she smiled and welcomed the crew inside. The committee entered the house and introductions were busily made all around. Jessie noticed one woman still standing in the doorway. She was small of frame, with yellow-gray hair. Standing wide-eyed, she clutched her sponges for dear life.

Sam turned to the nervous woman and smiled. "Come on now, Camilla," he spoke gently. "It's all right. Come on in and meet Mrs. Woods."

The obviously nervous woman entered slowly, and Jessie held out her hand. Camilla responded with a quick handshake.

Jessie scanned the row of happy faces. "I appreciate your kindness," she said hesitantly, "but I really don't think I need help. I'd rather—"

"I know, do it yourself," interrupted Reverend Taylor. "We're not here to redecorate, just do the basics. . .dust, mop floors, and so on. This place hasn't been cleaned in years, as you can see. We want to make the load a little lighter for our newest neighbor in Carlisle."

"We do windows," offered one man shyly.

Jessie laughed. "As a matter of fact, I am having trouble with my windows. Can't get them open."

"Come along then, Henry," commanded Sam with a grin. "That's our department." Sam hurried off into the living room with Henry Lewis close behind.

"Be careful," urged Jessie.

A stout, kind-faced woman named Martha stepped forward. She patted Jessie on the arm. "It's okay. Don't worry. They'll do a fine job. Now, why don't you show us women the kitchen and bathrooms? And we'll get to work!"

Jessie was no match for the insistent woman who stood before her. Nodding her assent, Jessie led the women to the kitchen.

"My, my!" exclaimed Martha. "Something must've died in here somewhere."

"What do you suppose it was?" Camilla asked, her voice faint and trembling.

"Don't worry, Camilla," Martha responded briskly. "I'll find it out and get rid of it in two shakes of a lamb's tail. Where's Mary?"

Jessie shrugged. She was not sure which woman was Mary.

Martha stuck her head out the kitchen doorway and scanned the hall. Mary was bending over the roses, breathing in their sweet aroma.

"Mary T. Benson, get over here!" Martha commanded. "There's work to be done! And we've got to get out of here by five o'clock."

Mary frowned as she reluctantly walked toward the kitchen.

"My sister is the bossy type, Mrs. Woods," droned Mary, "in case you didn't notice."

"The good Lord got our names right," snorted Martha. "I do all the work that crops up at the church. Mary goes to every prayer meeting and Bible study that comes down the pike," Martha continued, her eyebrows arched. "That is, as long as Sam's leading the meeting. I doubt she's there primarily for spiritual sustenance, if you get my meaning."

Mary's face reddened. "Why, Martha Benson, what a horrible thing to say in front of a perfect stranger!"

Words exploded like fireworks between the two sisters, and Jessie was mortified. The sounds of war drew the pastor from the living room.

"Ladies!" exclaimed Sam. "Calm down. You're liable to send Mrs. Woods fleeing from her home."

"Little does he know," mumbled Jessie to herself. "How I wish they would be the ones to flee from my house."

"But she insulted me in front of a perfect stranger!" wailed Mary.

"Shall I tell him what I said?" Martha smirked.

"That won't be necessary, Martha," replied the pastor. "Let's try to do what we've come here for, all right?"

The women nodded; the crew returned to the kitchen. Jessie retreated to the living room to check on the windows; Sam followed.

"Mary was right about the perfect part," whispered Sam. "From where I stand, I'd say you are perfect for me."

"I'd appreciate it if where you were standing was in Idaho," hissed Jessie. "You really are quite rude!"

"Rude?" replied Sam. "You must mean my proposal of marriage."

"Keep it down," whispered Jessie. "Someone might hear you. And I'll thank you to keep your distance. You don't even know me. And I certainly am not interested in you!"

A big bang from the dining room punctuated Jessie's fervent words. "Got it!" whooped Henry. "It's open now."

Jessie and Sam joined the triumphant Henry, who stood at the bay window, pointing out his handiwork. "Just took a little prying with the screwdriver, Mrs. Woods," the man explained shyly as a warm breeze spilled through the old screen into the purple room.

"Oh, thank you, Henry," said Jessie warmly. "I really appreciate it."

"Now that's what I like to see," said Sam, "a nice smile on Mrs. Woods's face."

"You can call me Jessie," she said to Henry, ignoring Sam's beaming comments.

"Okay, Mrs. Woods." Henry cleared his throat. "I mean Jessie. I'd better get back to work."

"Right you are, Henry," said Sam. "Let's try the living room again."

The men marched out of the dining room, and Jessie headed for the kitchen to see how the women were faring. The sudden chiming of a vaguely familiar tune stopped her in the hall.

"The doorbell works?" said Jessie, surprised, as she pulled open the door.

"The doorbell works!" exclaimed Kay, bustling into the foyer. "What a shocker! And whose cars are parked in the driveway?"

"Hello, Kay. I'm fine, how are you?" laughed Jessie.

"What?" said Kay, looking into the living room. "Oh yeah, hi, Jessie. How are—" she stopped and grabbed Jessie by the arm. "Well, look who's here," she whispered. "How did Mr. Marriage Proposal end up in here? I'm surprised you even let him on the porch."

"Kay!" Jessie hushed her friend as Sam and Henry appeared in the hall.

"We're going to check the windows upstairs, if that's all right with you," said Sam. "Nice to see you again, Ms. Bantam. This is my friend, Henry Lewis."

"Charmed," smiled Kay. "You can call me Kay."

Henry blushed and hastily stuck his screwdriver into his back pocket. An ominous ripping sound met the ears of the foursome.

"Go on ahead," said Jessie hurriedly. "We'll go and check on the women in the kitchen." She dragged Kay down the hall.

Jessie and Kay found the crew in the kitchen, busy at work. Martha was scrubbing the faded tiles of the floor. Camilla stood at the stove, her yellow gloves a blur of color as she attacked the stove top.

"You've got quite a job ahead of you, Mrs. Woods," grunted Martha. She swished her rag in a red bucket of hot water and soap. "This place sure needs a lot of work. I'd put a new floor in here, if I were you."

Jessie agreed. "I'm thinking about putting down ceramic tiles," she said. "Cream colored."

"That sounds lovely!" Camilla turned to face Jessie. Her voice was thin and quavery. "My brother does tile work. He's very good. . .a true artist." She blushed at her own boldness.

"Better take his name and number," suggested Kay. "It's almost impossible to find good craftsmen these days. In fact, it's impossible to find good men, period."

Martha laughed. "Sounds like your searching has been fruitless."

"More like futile," muttered Kay.

"Well, that's not for me," declared Martha, plopping her rag into the now-murky water. "I'm happy being single. See it the way Paul did. . .as a gift."

"A gift?" responded Kay doubtfully.

"Now, my sister Mary, on the other hand, sees singleness as a curse from which to flee. She—" Martha sat back, hands on her hips. "Where is Mary?"

A piercing scream from the back porch answered Martha's question. Like a chain reaction, Camilla screamed, her hands flying above her head. "I knew it!" she yelped, running out of the kitchen, down the hall, and out the front door.

Chapter 4

Kay and Jessie looked at each other in wonderment. They followed Martha out to the back porch. Mary stood in the corner, shaking.

"This white thing f–f–floated by that screen there!" Mary pointed, her hand trembling. "Why, it came out of nowhere and fluttered and—" Her hand flew to her forehead. "I think I might faint!"

"Skip it," interjected the ever-practical Martha. "Sam's not back here yet."

Jessie stifled a laugh. Kay peered intently through the screen. "What did it look like?"

"It was a blob, a blur of pasty white," explained Mary.

"You must be seeing things," said Martha. "You know you've got an over-active imagination, sister."

"Don't you sister me," pouted Mary, indignant. "I know what I saw."

"This is so exciting," gushed Kay.

"I don't know about exciting," sighed Jessie. "I think I'm getting a headache."

"But just think!" continued Kay. "What if those stories about the house are true? What if—"

"Yoo-hoo!" A voice rang out from the backyard. "Is anyone here?"

"Now, who is that?" muttered Jessie to herself. "I don't think I can take any more welcome-wagon people."

Martha reached over and pushed open the back screen door. "Over here, Lorena!"

An elderly woman in a blue-flowered apron crossed the yard to the women. Her steps were firm. As she climbed the stairs, her face lit up with a smile. She reached out for Jessie and gave her a gentle hug.

"I'm Lorena Smith, my dear." Her voice was soft and musical. "You must be the new owner of the Denver home. How nice."

Jessie nodded. "Jessie Woods. Pleased to meet you."

"I live right over there." She pointed to the white house behind Jessie's property in the back. "Hope you don't mind my coming through the bushes. There's an opening there in the middle. It's easier for me than walking all around the block to your front door."

The newcomer to Carlisle managed a smile. *Well, I guess I might as well give up the idea of privacy,* thought Jessie. *This place is swarming with nice people.*

"Well, anyway, my dear, this isn't my official welcoming visit. I'll be bringing you a homemade pie for that," she smiled. "Right now I'm looking for Gertie."

"Gertie?" echoed Jessie. "I'm not sure if there's a Gertie here."

"Oh, you'd know her in a minute if you saw her. She's as white as a ghost and flaps about like one, too. She drives me to distraction."

Kay coughed. "Well, I guess I'd better be going."

Jessie grabbed Kay by the arm. "Now, Kay, why don't you stay? You and I can both meet Gertie. . .together."

"Meet her? Meet her?" Lorena laughed. "She's a chicken. I think she's in your yard somewhere. She's always 'flying the coop,' as they say."

Martha threw back her head and belted out a laugh. "Some ghost, Mary! I don't know who's the bigger chicken around here, you or Gertie."

As if on cue, the fugitive bird flew up from beneath the back porch and flapped at the women behind the screened windows. Mary screamed. Kay shrieked. Martha almost fell down laughing.

"There you are, Gertie, you cantankerous old coot," scolded Lorena. She hurried out the doorway and down the steps. "You come here right now."

Jessie watched Lorena disappear around the corner of the house.

"You all had better go out the back way, too," said Martha. "I'm going to finish up the floor and I don't want you tracking it up."

Jessie, Mary, and Kay descended the steps and made their way around to the front of the house. The unkempt grass was long, and it pulled at Jessie's feet. "I'd better get that lawnmower right away," she remarked aloud.

"Better make it a tractor," spoke Kay. "This is a pretty big yard."

They found Camilla, Henry, and Sam on the front porch. Camilla sat on the top step, gratefully clutching a steaming cup of coffee. Sam held up a large thermos. "Anyone else for coffee?" he asked. "It's fresh brewed from the Cafe Taylor."

"A man after my own heart!" exclaimed Kay.

Mary frowned at Kay. "I'll have some, too, Sam," she crooned. "After all, what a scare I had!"

Sam smiled and handed both women their cups of coffee. "Jessie?"

Jessie nodded. Coffee sounded good about now.

"Now, tell me what happened," said Sam. "Camilla's been trying to tell us. She certainly was frightened."

Camilla nodded furiously. "Mary said she saw a ghost. And I wouldn't be a bit surprised." Her voice quavered. "This house is bound to be haunted."

"Why?" asked Kay. She sat down eagerly next to Camilla. "Tell us what you know about this house."

"I don't think we should get into this right now," interjected Sam.

"Nonsense," said Jessie. "I'd like to hear what she has to say. After all, it's my house now."

That was all the encouragement Camilla needed. She took a deep breath, cast a furtive look at the house behind her, and began her story. Jessie caught a you'll-be-sorry look on Sam's face. She chose to ignore it.

"They say the man who built this house, Mr. Carlton Denver, was a wealthy man. He had only one daughter, and he built his world around her. They did everything together. Well, when she grew up, she traveled to the Orient. They say she contracted a severe case of malaria and died overseas. Mr. Denver never saw his daughter again. They say he died soon after of a broken heart." The nervous storyteller's eyes widened. "They say his ghost wanders the halls of this house, mourning the loss of his daughter."

"Ever wonder who 'they' are?" muttered Jessie under her breath.

"Thought they were an advertising group down on Madison Avenue," whispered Sam.

"Fascinating," cooed Kay. "It's so exciting, so auricular."

"So what?" chorused Jessie and Mary.

"Auricular," recited Kay. "It means 'spoken in the ear,' you know. . .secretive."

"Big word," said Sam. "I'm impressed."

"Oh, it's part of my new regimen," explained Kay. "Gymnastics for the brain."

"Don't pull a muscle," laughed Jessie.

Kay adjusted her glasses. "Very funny. I happen to feel it is very important to expand one's abilities to communicate. I'm learning a new word every week. Got the idea from the *Reader's Digest*. You know. . .the 'Word Power' page."

"That's nice," said Jessie.

Camilla loudly cleared her throat.

"Oh, we're sorry," apologized Kay. "Please continue."

"There's more?" asked Jessie.

Camilla nodded. "They say Denver's daughter's ghost has been trying to return to this house all the way from the Orient. And that some day she'll succeed. When she does, this whole house will light up with supernatural light at the reunion of father and daughter."

"Wow," breathed Kay.

"This is making me nervous," shivered Mary. She sidled over toward Sam. "Don't you think we'd better stop talking about this?"

The front door flew open with a bang. Camilla and Kay jumped off the porch.

"Martha, do you have to come busting out of the house like that?" exclaimed Mary.

"I'm done in here," announced Martha. "Kitchen's done. I took the liberty of finding the bathroom, and I gave it a quick cleaning, too. Hope that's all right with you, Mrs. Woods." She stopped and surveyed the group looking up at her. She held out her hand. "Wait a minute. . .don't tell me. Camilla's been bowling you over with her ghost stories."

"Camilla's new to our fellowship," explained Sam. "She's getting acquainted with us and is enjoying our beginner's Bible study on Sunday mornings."

"Pastor Taylor says I'm superstitious," sniffed Camilla. "He says there's no such thing as ghosts. Well, what about today?" she asked. "What about what Mary saw?"

Martha laughed and her sister, Mary, blushed.

"That was the neighbor's chicken," said Jessie.

"So that's what Lorena was looking for when she came by here." Sam rubbed his face. "I think we'd better be going now. We've done enough here, I think." He blushed and looked at Jessie. "Henry sends his regards. He had to go home and, uh, change his clothes. I hope we made you feel welcome," he said.

"It was interesting," said Jessie. "And thank you all for your help."

"No problem," said Martha. She thrust a piece of paper into Jessie's hand. "Here's my phone number and the number to the church. If you need me, just give a holler."

As they all pulled out and drove away, Jessie flopped onto the top step. "What a day! That was the weirdest welcome-wagon experience I ever had."

Kay nodded. "Yes, but it was awfully nice of them to come and help clean up. And I still say that Sam Taylor's one handsome guy."

Jessie got up and headed for the front door. "I'm going to look around some more and see what needs fixing," she said over her shoulder. "I'll be over at your place in another hour or so."

Kay followed her friend into the house. "Are you sure you don't want to come with me now? You don't mind being here alone, after hearing Camilla's stories?"

"Nonsense," replied Jessie. "That stuff doesn't bother me. And by the way, thanks for letting me stay with you until my furniture comes."

"No problem," smiled Kay. "Sure you won't come with me now?"

"Oh, no," replied Jessie. "I've got work to do."

Kay left, and Jessie stood alone in the living room. She breathed in the sweet air gently drifting through the open window. Entering the dining room, she sat down on the window seat. Jessie studied the tall oaks in the side yard. They stood straight and strong.

The next thing she knew, she was weeping.

Chapter 5

Spencer Hart squinted at the screen of the microfilm machine. He grunted and leaned forward. The letters blurred before his eyes.

"Hey!" he called to the librarian seated at her desk. "How do you expect me to read this newspaper when it's so blurry?" He motioned for her to come over to his table.

"Excuse me, Sir," spoke the librarian quietly as she hurried from her desk. "You simply cannot raise your voice like that. This is a library, you know."

Spencer started to say something sarcastic, but he stopped himself. "Oh, yes, of course, I'm sorry," he whispered graciously. "I suppose I just got so excited at the prospect of reading actual newspaper articles about Mr. Denver, why, I just forgot where I was. I'm sure a woman in your position understands such things."

The librarian blushed. "Of course. Research can be quite thrilling, can't it?" she beamed. "Here. Just adjust this knob to sharpen the lettering."

"Thank you so much," replied Spencer. "You've been such a help, Miss. . . ?"

"Mrs. Ruby Clearwater," replied the librarian. "My pleasure. If you need more help or more materials, just let me know."

"Thanks."

As Mrs. Clearwater returned to her desk, a young woman entered the library. She caught sight of Spencer Hart and joined him at his table.

"It's about time," Spencer grunted. "You're late."

"I got lost," the young woman explained. She shoved her long brown hair to the side. "This town is a dump. Are you sure there's anything to this scheme of yours?"

"Keep it down, Stacy!" hissed Spencer. He studied the face of his partner. Her brown eyes and hair were perfect. "Take a look at this." He turned the screen toward the young woman. "Here's a picture of the guy's daughter. You could pass for her in broad daylight!" He turned the screen back. "Just do as you're told, keep your mouth shut, and we'll make the biggest haul you've ever seen."

Stacy snapped the gum in her mouth. "Providing this story isn't just a stupid legend," she retorted.

Spencer's face reddened. "You just wait. I found stuff on this Denver guy in New York. He was loaded!" Spencer leaned forward. "The man had this queer habit of keeping large amounts of his money in gold. Didn't trust paper money or the banks. There's got to be gold hidden in that house."

The young woman's eyes gleamed. "Sounds good. When do we pull this scam off?"

"Not yet," replied Spencer. "The woman who bought the house hasn't moved in yet. She's still fixing it up. Once she's settled in, we make our move."

"How do you know she's living there alone? Maybe somebody's moving in with her."

"She's alone, all right," said Spencer.

"How do you know?" insisted the young woman.

Spencer smirked. "A little bird told me. She's alone. Don't worry about it. In the meantime, you lay low. It's best if we're not seen together. I'll call you. You found the motel in the next town?"

"Yeah. A regular Hilton," snorted Stacy.

"When this is over, you can buy yourself a Hilton!" laughed Spencer. His partner joined his laughter, but the sudden appearance of the librarian at their table cut the laughter short.

"Please, Sir, you must keep it down," repeated Mrs. Clearwater.

"Yes, Ma'am, my apologies," said Spencer hastily. He nodded to his partner. She got up from her chair, smiled at the librarian, and left.

Mrs. Clearwater walked away, pulling thoughtfully at the chain to her eyeglasses.

∞

Jessie plunged into her restoration work with boundless energy. Thrilled with her new home, she attacked each room, one at a time. She hired contractors to revamp the plumbing throughout the house, giving them careful instruction to preserve all original fixtures as best they could. The electricians updated the wiring. Camilla's brother tiled the kitchen and bathroom floors. Jessie had to laugh to herself at the speed with which he completed the job. He was as nervous as his sister, refusing to take his lunch breaks in the house.

"Well, that's one thing good about the legend," Jessie said to Kay when her friend came over to observe the progress. "This floor was replaced in record time!"

Kay reached down and put her hand on the cool ceramic tile. "It's lovely. And he did a great job, too."

"I still can't believe how fast everything is getting done," remarked Jessie. She flipped the new light switch on the wall. "In New York it takes two months to get someone to come and change a doorknob!"

"Well, in Carlisle, people are looking for work. Times have been tough around here. You shouldn't have any trouble getting things finished in record time." Kay followed Jessie into the dining room. "Who's doing the painting?"

"I am," said Jessie triumphantly. "And I think it's turning out beautifully, if I do say so myself."

Kay nodded. "I'd volunteer to help, but you know when it comes to painting, I'm simply maladroit!"

Jessie pressed her hand to her forehead. "Let me guess. All thumbs, clumsy."

"Very good," beamed Kay. "That can be your new word for the week."

"Fine," said Jessie. "But don't drag me into your latest quest for knowledge. I have a hard enough time balancing my checkbook!"

"Learning new things is good for the soul, Jess," said Kay. "Don't knock it. Remember what your father used to say, God rest his soul, and I quote: 'If you're not learnin', you're not growin'.' "

"Oh, yes. I forgot," said Jessie. "He used to say that a lot."

A frown crossed her face. "Isn't your lunch break over?" She shooed her friend to the door.

"I have the distinct feeling you're trying to get rid of me, Jessie Woods. What's the matter?" Kay studied her friend through her oversized glasses.

"Nothing's the matter," insisted Jessie. "You're busy and I've got things to do. Now I'll see you at dinner time."

Shutting the door after Kay, Jessie let out a sigh. "I don't want to learn anything new," murmured Jessie stubbornly. "I just want to fix my house and settle down and. . ." She shook her head. The memory of her father's smile and his wise words nudged her thoughts. "All right, Dad, I admit it. I don't think I'm growing." Her chin trembled momentarily, but she pushed herself into action. "Time to check out the cellar."

The door to the basement was in the kitchen, but before descending the stairs, the new homeowner cast an approving glance at the kitchen. The new appliances gleamed and the porcelain sink fixtures were restored to perfection. "Now from the sublime to the ridiculous," Jessie muttered as she flipped the switch at the top of the stairs. "Why do cellar stairs always have to be so narrow?" Her question hung in the air along with the acrid aroma of must. "Never met a cellar that didn't smell musty," said Jessie, wrinkling her nose.

At the foot of the stairs Jessie paused to survey the clutter. Trunks and boxes were stacked haphazardly around the room. Some piles reached to the low ceiling. The new furnace and phosphorescent lights appeared alien in their antiquated surroundings. An old lamp stooped mournfully in a corner, its dusty olive shade tilted down as if to hide from the shame of it all. Narrow windows at ground level stared dustily at the visitor. The lawn glowed faintly green through the cellar's eyes.

"What's that?" Jessie wondered aloud, observing a black object perched on one of the narrow windowsills. She gingerly picked it up and immediately almost dropped it because of its weight. A vigorous rubbing with a rag removed a slimy coating of dust.

"It's adorable!" exclaimed Jessie. It was a black Scottish terrier statue. "Must be solid cast iron," she mused. She patted it on the head. "You're coming upstairs with me," she announced. "I hereby rescue thee from the confines of thy now former dungeon." Placing it on the bottom step, Jessie smiled. "I dub thee Joseph."

Turning back to face the clutter, Jessie noticed a green velvet hatbox atop a pile of other boxes. She reached over and pulled it down, mindful of the dust and obvious aged condition of her find. It felt heavy in her hands.

"Too heavy for a hat," she muttered. She placed the box on top of her new washing machine. The round lid to the box slipped off easily in Jessie's hands.

"Letters!" The hatbox was brimming with letters. The delicate handwriting on the envelopes was exquisite. Jessie carefully pulled out the top envelope.

"June 23, 1885. Wow! This could be real interesting."

She slipped the letter out of its envelope and began to read it.

> *Dear Father,*
>   *I'm not sure if I can forgive you for sending me to this dreadful school. (You know I don't mean it!) But I do miss you so. And Sophie, too. How is she? I suppose her blueberry pancakes continue to tantalize the neighborhood on Saturday mornings. The food here is perfectly awful. (Actually it's not bad. I'm just homesick and I feel like complaining.)*
>   *I should scold you for sending Miss Nickels a sampling of my poetry. She actually read one of them to the class! I was utterly embarrassed. She says I have real potential. In other words, my poems were pitiful! Ah, well. Really, Father, please let's keep my poetry to ourselves. You and The Professor are my best and only true audience.*

Jessie paused a moment. "I wonder who The Professor is?" She continued to read the letter.

>   *The strangest thing happened the other day. I went down to my favorite spot by the river to read for awhile. I was totally engrossed in my* Pride and Prejudice *until the sun began to set. There's something about the sky that captures my heart. Sunsets are a daily miracle, I am convinced. There was color everywhere, reds, yellows, oranges, tinging the water, the air, the pages of my book. I took it all in, wide-eyed as usual. Suddenly, I saw a woman walking along the riverbank toward me.*
>   *I caught my breath. It looked like Mama! Blue dress, auburn hair, lovely, graceful strides.*

At this point, the writing in the letter was smudged. Jessie held the letter closer to the light. She began to read aloud.

I actually jumped up and was about to call out to her, when I saw the woman's face. It wasn't Mama. Of course it wasn't her. I do miss her so. I can't imagine how lonely you must feel sometimes. Do you believe in heaven, Father? Do you think Mama is there, happy and well? Roscoe says it's all rubbish, that religious stuff, he calls it. I wonder.

It's been lights out for over an hour and my lamp is burning low. Miss Charter will have my head if she catches me up at this hour! I bid you good night, dear Father. Write me as soon as you can.

Your loving daughter,
Amelia Elizabeth

Folding the letter carefully, Jessie put it back in its envelope. She gathered up the hatbox and headed for the stairs. She stooped to pick up Joseph.

"Well, Joseph, did you know Amelia Elizabeth?" she asked the mute little statue as she carried her treasures up the narrow staircase.

Through the kitchen windows the golden light of day's end poured, heralding the impending sunset. Jessie hurried down the hall, and she placed Joseph next to the grandfather clock. Pulling open the front door, she walked out onto the porch to catch a glimpse of the blushing sky.

Chapter 6

Music spilled quietly from the organ in preparation for the Sunday morning service at First Baptist of Carlisle. The stained-glass windows were not elaborate, but their simple blues and purples lent a soft blend of color to the sanctuary.

"I can't believe I let you talk me into coming here this morning," muttered Jessie Woods as she shifted nervously in the hard, wooden pew.

"Oh, come on, lighten up," whispered Kay to her distracted friend. "For once I got you to come to church. Usually it's the other way around. You've been trying to save me for years."

"Oh, hush," whispered Jessie. "Let's just make the best of it."

Kay adjusted her jacket. "Do you think this outfit is okay for church or is it too loud?"

Jessie glanced at Kay's red suit with the flowered silk blouse. "It's fine," responded Jessie. "It's you."

"Good. Hey, look!" Kay nudged her friend. "There's what's-his-name. The shy guy."

Henry Lewis walked up the aisle of the church with several bulletins in his hands. Kay jumped up and hurried over to the man. She engaged him in earnest conversation. They walked to the back of the church.

Jessie sighed. It seemed harder to come to church now. *What is the matter with me?* she wondered. *Probably just tired from all the excitement of moving.*

Suddenly, a little blond head popped out from the pew in front of Jessie. A round face with soft, plump cheeks peered carefully into the newcomer's face.

"Hello," said the girl. "I'm Madeline. Who are you?"

Jessie smiled. "I'm Jessie Woods."

"You have any little girls?" inquired the youngster.

"No, dear, I don't," replied Jessie.

"That's too bad. Got any little boys?"

"No," Jessie answered. "I don't have any children."

"Oh." Madeline thought about that for awhile. Then she leaned over the back of the pew and put her face close to Jessie's face. "Do you have a mister?"

Jessie stifled a laugh. "Well, Madeline, I used to have a mister. His name was Tom."

The little girl frowned. "Is he gone to heaven?"

"Yes." Jessie was beginning to wish Kay would get back to her seat.

"He's probably with my Grandpa Joe. He's in heaven, too. They're prob'ly fishin'. My daddy says Grandpa Joe loves to fish so much he took his poles to heaven. I don't s'pose Jesus would mind, do you?"

"No, I don't suppose He would."

The music in the organ crescendoed to herald the beginning of the service. Madeline's mother joined her daughter, giving Jessie a friendly smile. Kay returned to her seat in a colorful flurry. Reverend Samuel Taylor appeared from a side door and approached the pulpit. He greeted his congregation with a warm smile. Kay nudged Jessie. Jessie ignored her.

The service passed by in a blur for Jessie. Afterward, she made every effort to leave quickly, but her plans failed. Kay insisted on staying for the coffee hour.

"You've got to mingle," urged Kay, taking her friend by the arm. "You've been in that house for a month, and I haven't seen you out even once to socialize. Now, come on." She led Jessie to the back of the church and out onto the lawn. The refreshment hour was being held outside.

Jessie squinted in the bright sunlight. The air was morning fresh and sweet with the smell of newly mown grass. The mild roar of a nearby lawnmower sounded rebellious on the Sabbath morning.

"Ed Jenson," a voice from behind startled Jessie. It was the pastor. "He has a running feud with me. I tried to get him to come to church. Apparently I annoyed the daylights out of him. Now every summer he mows his lawn on Sunday mornings." Sam laughed. "I think the Lord's working on him, though. He used to mow during the sermon. Now he starts during the recessional."

Kay laughed. "That's the most ridiculous thing I've ever heard. Don't you think so, Jessie?" Kay nudged her friend.

"Ludicrous," replied Jessie. "Now, can we go?"

"Now, Jessie, please," said Sam, "I need to talk to you."

"We really don't have much in common, Reverend Taylor," said Jessie coolly.

"I'll go get us some punch," bubbled Kay. She gave her friend a pleading look. "Mingle!" she mouthed to Jessie.

"Listen, Jessie, I wanted to apologize for the welcome committee fiasco over at your house." Reverend Taylor nervously cleared his throat. "I meant it to. . .it was meant to be helpful and make you feel at home. I'm sorry it was so. . .so eventful."

Jessie could not help but smile. "I can still see Camilla, running out of the house. And that chicken!"

Sam sighed with relief. "So you're not angry with me?"

Jessie turned to face him squarely. "Listen, Reverend Taylor—"

"Please, call me Sam," interrupted the pastor.

"All right, Sam," Jessie continued, "you seem like a nice person, and you have a lovely church here. But you really annoyed me when we first met. Do you remember?"

Sam blushed. "Uh, yes. You mean the marriage proposal?"

"Proposal? You call it a proposal? 'I'm going to marry you' sounds more like an announcement, don't you think? It's outrageous!"

"You're right," Sam conceded. "I was being rash. It's just that when I saw you I. . . ," he stumbled for words. "It's like I just knew. I don't know." He ran a nervous hand through his silver hair. "I don't usually come out with crazy things like that."

Jessie sighed. "Look, Sam, let me explain something to you. My husband died three years ago. We were very happy together. I doubt very much if I'll ever marry again. Do you understand?" Jessie tried very hard to control the trembling in her voice.

Sam studied Jessie's face. His gray-blue eyes searched her brown eyes carefully. She felt as though he was seeing into her heart, reading the truth written there, a truth she was not willing to face.

"Okay, Jessie," Sam finally responded. "I'll do my best to behave myself. I promise I'll try not to say anything outrageous to you again." He stopped and smiled at her. "Can we at least be friends?"

Jessie smiled. "That would be fine."

"Hello," yodeled Kay from a distance. "I'm coming with the punch." She bustled over and gave the two their drinks. "I didn't want to disturb you. It looked like you were having a very serious conversation." She stressed the word "serious," dragging it out with great relish.

"You're right, Kay, my dear, sweet, matchmaking friend," said Jessie. She put her free arm around Kay. "I was just telling Sam that I wasn't interested in a relationship such as the one he suggested. We agreed to be friends, didn't we, Sam?"

Sam nodded.

"Oh, Jessie, really," blushed Kay. "You're embarrassing me. I'm not a matchmaker. I wasn't trying to get you and Reverend Taylor to get together. I—"

"Right," smirked Jessie. "I appreciate your concern, but let's all leave Jessie Woods's personal life well enough alone."

"That's all right with me," said Sam thoughtfully. "As long as Jessie Woods doesn't leave it well enough alone. I suggest she deal with it." With those words, he walked away.

Kay's eyebrows shot up, and she looked closely at her friend. "What do you suppose he meant by that?" queried Kay. "Does he know something I don't know?" She looked at her friend. "Hey, are you all right, Jessie? You look kind of flushed."

"I'm fine," Jessie replied. "Let's go." Her heart pounded. Sam's words had stirred something up in her, something dark and painful. "Let's get out of here," she urged her friend. Somehow she thought that if she left the church grounds, she would leave behind the unsettling feeling that was gripping her heart.

"Okay, okay. Hey, wait up, Jessie," cried Kay. She hurried to catch up with her friend. "Where's the fire?" she muttered under her breath.

❧

"Yes, that's her," nodded Herb Stamping, peering over his glasses and pointing in the direction of the harried Jessie Woods. "She's the one I was telling you about. She bought the Denver house over on Lark Avenue."

"She's sure in a hurry," noted Ruby Clearwater. "Wonder what's the matter."

"Maybe she just wants to get home to her new house. Maybe she's got a roast in the oven." Herb took a sip of his punch. "You're always trying to make a story out of everything, aren't you, Ruby? Must be the librarian in you." He laughed.

"Don't be so quick to judge me, Herbert Stamping. I bet I know something you don't know. And I bet there is a story brewing over at the Denver house." She pursed her lips and nodded. "Something's going on."

Herbert was all ears. "What are you talking about?" he whispered.

"Promise you won't blab it all over town?"

"Why, I never," stammered Herbert indignantly. "I never blab things all over town."

"No, you just blab it from your perch at the post office," snorted the librarian.

"I shall choose to ignore your rude accusation," sniffed Herb. He leaned eagerly toward his friend. "What's the story?"

"Well, do you know that new man in town, the one who's got some sort of leg problem?"

"Oh, you mean Spencer Hart. I know him," replied the postal worker importantly. "What about him? Has he been to the library?"

"Yes, he's been to the library several times," whispered Ruby.

"He's a writer, you know. Maybe some big-name writer. He writes under a pen name."

"More likely he has an alias," sniffed Ruby Clearwater. "If he's a writer, then I'm a bus driver and you're a professional wrestler!"

"Ruby! What are you talking about?"

"Mr. Hart is digging up research about the Denver estate. He's been reading all the articles he can get his hands on. He was even asking me if there was anyone in town who could help get him more information."

"So," said Herb, "the man's doing research for a book. He told me himself his latest novel is about life in a small town, like Carlisle. Maybe he's going to put a character like Carlton Denver in his book."

"Doubt it." Ruby shook her head. "He's even got an accomplice."

"What?"

"Some young woman with long brown hair. Looks like she'd sooner sell your soul to the devil than say hello."

"Why, Ruby Clearwater, you've been reading too many Agatha Christie novels. I can't believe you're judging these people by their outward appearance. Accomplice," sniffed Herb, "accomplice to what?"

"They're up to something," insisted Ruby. "I just know it!"

∞

Back at 16 Lark Avenue, a man dressed as a housepainter studied the Denver house, counting windows. He tested a few of the ground-floor windows. He smirked. Most of the windows were open. The screens could be easily jimmied up.

"Easy access," Spencer Hart laughed to himself, and then he used a ladder to reach the second-story windows. He made motions pretending measurements. In reality, he was peering inside the house.

He climbed back down the ladder and walked around to the back of the house, pleased to see a back porch. It would be easy to hide underneath the porch. He squinted up at the second floor.

"Hmm," he licked his lips. "Something's not right." He rounded the house a second time, keeping his eye on the second floor and making measurements in his head. Two windows were covered from the inside with shades. "I don't get it," he muttered. He stopped and checked his watch. It was after twelve o'clock. "Better beat it, Hart. Church is over." He hurried to his car and pulled away from the house. He looked into his rearview mirror and rubbed the red and gray stubble on his face.

"There's something not right about the layout of that house," he said aloud. "And I'm going to find out what it is." He spit out his window. "This just keeps getting better and better, Hart. I have a feeling you're going to be a very rich man!"

Chapter 7

Jessie Woods picked another letter from the hatbox and began to read it.

Dear Father,

I had the most delightful experience this morning! I was going to the kitchen to coax the cook for another cup of coffee. Her coffee is so delicious, and it's a shame to waste it all on the teachers. Perched on a stool next to the stove sat a thin little waif with soft blond hair. She looked so pale next to the black of the cast-iron stove, I thought at first I was dreaming! Cook never lets anyone hang about in her domain. A grimace from Cook confirmed I was not seeing things.

"Who's this?" I asked, giving the small one a smile. She looked so solemn.

Cook shook her head with obvious annoyance. "One of Miss Bristol's charges. Another hopeless case, I say. You can't change those mountain people. They're as stubborn as mules and twice as slow." She harrumphed and stirred her stew with renewed vigor.

I winked at the little girl. She stared at me without so much as blinking her eyes. "My name is Amelia Elizabeth," I said.

Silence. "Don't you have a name?" I asked, smiling and trying very hard to put her at ease.

"You might as well give up, Miss Denver," Cook chimed in. "She wouldn't say boo to a ghost! Stubborn, I tell you. Ornery people."

The little girl looked at Cook, then she turned to me, lifted her delicate chin to me, and spoke. Oh, Father! You would have loved it!

"Rosemary," she said. "Like the plant."

"Rosemary? How lovely!" I exclaimed.

"My mama sets great store by plants. Says rosemary puts her in mind of the woods in the springtime, when the wet of the mornin' mixes with the earth and makes perfume."

I was captivated. "How do you know Miss Bristol?" I inquired.

"She's cousin to one of my kin. Don't know exactly how. Uncle Bo said he reckons Miss Bristol is from the drinking side of the family, seeing how she's all the time turning red in the face."

I choked back laughter. Miss Bristol is the last person I could see imbibing *alcohol. She can barely take syrup for a cough, let alone drink whiskey! And you met her, Father! She's always so easily flustered. She blushes when she's angry, sad, or excited.*

I had to know more. I poured the visitor a glass of milk (much to Cook's chagrin). "Why did Miss Bristol bring you to Charter School?"

"She says I have a talent for describing things," she replied precisely. "Says I should have more book-larning. Mama says it's fitten for me to larn. Says I'm special, like one of those what writes rhymes and such."

"You mean a poet," I said.

The blond head nodded.

"I'll tell you a secret," I said, leaning toward Rosemary. "I like to write poetry, too. Maybe we could help each other. We could read each other's rhymes."

Her lips clamped shut into a thin line. How careless of me. She couldn't read or write.

"Don't worry, Rosemary," I tried to assure her. "I'm sure Miss Bristol will teach you to read in no time. You seem like a very bright little girl."

She relaxed on her stool. "I ain't afeared to larn," she said, half to herself. "My grandpa, he was afeared for me to go. He said I might lose somethin' of the mountains iffen I came to the city. But I don't think so," she said, her eyes no doubt glistening with the thought of her home. "A body can't forget the call of the whippoorwill ridin' the wind, or how your heart runs when you catch the shadow of a deer, racin' slick and easy through the woods."

Really, Father, she is amazing. I must have a talk with Miss Bristol. I imagine this girl could teach me a thing or two about listening and really seeing the world around me. I'm so excited. I would have stayed longer, but Cook practically threw me out of the kitchen.

"Aren't you late for class?" were her parting words. She was right. I was late for Miss Task's class. History. That's why I needed the coffee!

Well, here I have practically written you a book! Give my love to all and write to me soon.

Your dutiful daughter,
Amelia Elizabeth

P.S. I hope Mr. Reardon wasn't too angry about the tulips. Did The Professor really dig up all the bulbs, or are you exaggerating? You mustn't tease me about sending him to jail. Mr. Reardon would be all for it. You must keep a better eye on him, you know.

Jessie slipped the letter into a folder, smiling. She grabbed her mug of coffee and headed for the back porch steps. The early morning sun enhanced the grass and trees with a silver shine. Jessie drew in a deep breath of the new day's fresh air. An old feeling moved faintly in her heart.

"Wow," she thought, "I think I actually felt a glimmer of happiness! It's been a long time."

She got up from the stairs and began to walk around her yard. The oaks and maples scattered throughout the large yard were thick with age and sweepingly tall. Their myriad branches and leaves blended and rose in a harmonious tangle of greens and browns.

"Good morning," a voice rang out from behind the back hedge.

"Good morning, Mrs. Smith," said Jessie.

"Please, call me Lorena," responded the elderly woman.

Jessie walked over to say a proper hello to her neighbor. "How are you this morning, Lorena?"

"I'm fine, Dear. Just fine. And how are you? Getting settled in your new home?"

Jessie nodded. "I love it here. This house really feels like home. It's wonderful."

"What color are you going to paint the house?" inquired Lorena. "I saw your painter over here last Sunday. Are you going to keep it white?"

"Yes, I am," replied Jessie. She wondered about the painter. "I haven't decided on a painter yet. I've gotten several estimates."

"Well, the man on Sunday certainly inspected your house thoroughly. I was home from church with a bum leg. Sometimes my arthritis acts up."

"I see," said Jessie. "I'm sorry." Any question in her mind about the unnamed painter slipped quickly from Jessie's mind. It was probably one of the men who had given her an estimate.

"I haven't forgotten your pie, you know. I've been so busy with my grand-children I haven't had much time. They usually come one at a time to spend a week with me. That way they each get individual attention." Her blue eyes smiled at Jessie. "It's so important to give them a listening ear. The way the Lord is with us, you know. He's always attentive to His children's cries."

Jessie squirmed inside. Lorena's words were fingering her heart, unnerving her. *What's the matter with me?*

"You go to First Baptist?" Lorena asked, ignoring or unaware of Jessie's discomfort.

"I've been there a few times," nodded Jessie. "I'm not sure if that's where I want to join as a member."

"I go to the little Alliance church on the corner of Beech and Main," replied Lorena. "We're small, but we do have a good time singing and praying. That's what matters, doesn't it? Enjoying our Lord and His people."

Jessie smiled halfheartedly. She could not remember the last time she'd actually enjoyed church. Quickly, she changed the subject. "Lorena, do you know anything about the original owner of my house?"

"Carlton Denver? Oh, I know a little about him. My grandmother knew him. She lived on this street back in the late 1800s. She was a neighbor of his."

"How exciting!" exclaimed Jessie. "I found an old hatbox full of letters from Amelia Elizabeth."

Lorena adjusted her silver-rimmed glasses. "That would be Carlton's daughter. How wonderful that you found her letters! My grandmother used to tell us all the wonderful things Mr. Denver would bring his daughter when he returned from one of his trips. A bicycle from England, silks from the Orient, and books. . .armloads of books. I guess he and Amelia were avid readers.

"He traveled a lot," Lorena continued. "He was a businessman of some sort," Lorena recalled. "I would love to have you read some of her letters to me. That would be so exciting. There's a lot to be learned from the past, you know."

Jessie smiled. "My father used to say that if you're not learning, you're not growing."

"Wise man," smiled Lorena. "Well, I better get back to my breakfast dishes," said Lorena, patting the blue-checkered linen towel draped over her shoulder. "I just came out to feed the chickens. Nice seeing you again. We must get together. What kind of pie do you like best?"

"Apple," replied Jessie.

"Apple it is," sang Lorena.

Jessie watched the elderly woman walk back to her house. Her gray hair shone silver in the light. The blue cotton dress she wore was soft and a compliment to her hair. There was something about Lorena that comforted and unsettled Jessie at the same time. It was as if the Lord was in Lorena, reaching out to Jessie Woods. Jessie sighed. Lorena's words had caused her to stop and examine herself for a moment.

She took a sip from her now-cool coffee. "Yuk."

Jessie resumed her walk around the yard. Casting a glance at the house, Jessie considered the roof. The man who inspected the house suggested replacing it as soon as possible. Jessie had to admit he was probably right. The black-gray shingles clung rather precariously to the slanted roof. Some shingles had lost their grip altogether and were dangling out of place.

Jessie walked around to the front and then back to the side again.

A window on the second floor captured her attention.

"Wait a second," she said to herself. "I washed all the windows up there. I remember washing two windows on this side of the house."

She counted. "One, two, three," she said aloud. "There are three windows on this side." Her heart began to pound with excitement. She dumped her coffee and ran around to the front porch and into the house. Patting the rounded knob on the banister, she bounded up the stairs.

Breathlessly she examined the hall and the room on the west side of the house. The first room had one window. "That's one," counted Jessie.

Back in the hall, Jessie noted the wall situated between the two rooms. "No window here," she said, softly running her hand on the newly papered wall.

Jessie slowly entered the second bedroom as if she were sneaking up on a child playing hide and seek. "Window number two."

The room was the smallest of the four bedrooms. Jessie had painted the walls a soft peach and added a flower border. It served as a little sitting room, with an overstuffed love seat, a flowered wing chair, a bookcase, and a table. The solitary window was off-center on the west wall. Light splattered unevenly into the cozy room, creating soft shadows and patches of gold.

She knocked on the wall with the window. "Solid enough," she said under her breath. Then she knocked on the wall facing the back of the house. It sounded different. . .muffled and hard.

Jessie stepped back and surveyed the room, hands on her hips.

"Maybe the room was shortened," she thought out loud. "There's one way to find out," said the explorer, eyeing the window. She pulled aside the lace curtain. The window had already been opened to let in the fresh air. Jessie struggled with the screen. She pulled at the small metal knobs and immediately broke a fingernail.

"Just what I needed," she muttered. Determined to succeed, she pulled at the knobs with all her might. The screen flew open with a bang. Eagerly she stuck her head out the open window.

"Can't see," she grumbled. Jessie leaned out as far as she could.

"A window!" she shrieked, losing her balance. She fell forward and, for a terrifying second, she thought she was going to plunge to the ground, but her hands grabbed the sill just in time.

"Whoa," yelped Jessie. "That was close."

She plopped down on the peaches-and-cream love seat and hugged a lace-covered pillow. "There is a secret room in the Denver house," she whispered, wide-eyed. "Wait till Kay hears about this!"

Chapter 8

Kay, Henry, and Sam stood with Jessie in the side yard, looking up at the second-story windows. While the humans surveyed the building, Sam's dog, Manny, explored the yard. He sniffed his way around the grounds, circling about the grass as his nose led him. When he neared the house, he stopped. A low growl emanated from his shaggy throat. The four turned to look at Manny.

"What's the matter, Manny, old boy?" asked Sam. He petted him on the scruff of the neck.

"Wait a minute," said Kay, pushing her glasses up her nose. "Is this where Manny tells you what's wrong, by barking? And then you decipher the message? You know, Lassie style?" She giggled and leaned over the dog. "What is it, Manny? Is the stock market about to crash? Have aliens landed? Is there hope for the Mets?"

"Pardon me, Madame," responded Sam with feigned indignation. "Are you making sport of my loyal companion? I must demand an apology."

"Sorry," giggled Kay.

Manny continued to growl.

"Why is he doing that?" asked Jessie.

"He's picked up a scent," said Henry. "A scent strange to him. So he growls."

"Maybe it's your perfume, Kay," Jessie teased. "It's a strange scent. What's the name of it?"

"Night in the Bayou, thank you very much," sniffed Kay. "Really! How insulting."

"Now, really," said Jessie, "maybe the dog smells the painter who came by yesterday to check out the house."

Sam's eyebrows shot up. "A painter here? Yesterday? What time?"

"Must have been sometime between eleven and twelve. He wasn't here when Kay picked me up for church, and he was gone when we got back. Why? What's so strange about that?"

Henry frowned and looked at the pastor. Sam caught his eye but shook his head to squelch the discussion.

"Oh, nothing. Now, let's get back to the project at hand."

"Right," said Kay. "We've seen there are three windows on this side of the house. So noted. What's the big deal? You called us here to see windows? What gives?"

"Follow me," said Jessie.

She led the three through the front door and up the stairs.

"The house looks really nice, Jessie," said Henry from behind.

"Thank you, Henry. Glad you like it."

Once upstairs, Jessie pointed out the window in the first bedroom. "There's one," she said.

She entered the sitting room. Her followers stood in the doorway. "Window number two!" she announced triumphantly. "There must be more room with another window on the other side of this wall."

Henry stepped into the room and ran his hand along the wall, periodically knocking with his fist. "Sounds like they've bricked it off and plastered it." He thumped the wall again. He left the room and entered the hallway; it continued to the back of the house. Straight ahead a window overlooked the backyard. An antique half-table stood beneath the window; a vase overflowing with silk flowers was on top of the table.

Henry studied the hallway wall, thumping gently with his fist. He seemed unaware of the others. With precision and ease, mental calculations and measurements issued forth from his lips. He explained the probable makeup of the wall's innards, as if talking to himself. Finally, he turned to his audience.

"Best thing to do is break through here," he said, tapping the wall. "Easier than breaking through a brick wall. Shame, though. We'd have to rip up your nice wallpaper, Mrs. Woods."

"Jessie."

Kay stood with her mouth hanging open. "Incredible."

Henry's face reddened. "It wasn't so hard to figure—"

"No! I mean I've never heard you say so many words at one time," she piped. "Catch me, Sam, I'm going to faint."

Sam laughed. Henry blushed again. Jessie reached over and patted Henry on the arm.

"Don't mind Kay," she said reassuringly. "She feels it is her duty to share her insights and observations at any and all times. She takes some getting used to."

Henry flinched at Jessie's touch. "You two ladies sure know how to make a man's head spin." He looked at Sam. "I'm going to my truck," he said then hurried down the stairs.

Jessie and Kay looked at each other in amazement. "What did we do?" they said practically in unison.

Sam laughed at the shocked look on their faces. "Henry Lewis is just about the shiest person I know," he explained, laughing. "You two have bowled him over with your attention. But don't worry. He hasn't fled the scene. He just went to get some of his tools."

Sam's laughter only served to fluster the two women all the more. "I feel terrible," groaned Jessie. "I'm going to talk to him."

"That might be a nice idea," agreed Sam. "Can't hurt to communicate. It would probably be good for Henry."

"I'm staying here," announced Kay. "I've stirred up enough trouble already. There's room in my mouth for only one foot."

Kay went into the sitting room and plopped onto the love seat.

Sam followed. He began his own inspection of the wall.

"I'm getting a headache from all this tapping, tapping, tapping," complained Kay.

" 'All this tapping on the parlor wall,' " continued Sam. " 'Gently rapping, rapping at my chamber door—' "

"Oh, please," groaned Kay. "No more of 'The Raven,' if you don't mind." She pulled out her makeup bag and began to apply powder with painstaking accuracy. Forgetting to take off her glasses, she managed to get powder all over her lenses.

Jessie found Henry standing in the side yard, looking up at the mysterious third window. In one hand he held a small pickax, in the other, a sledgehammer.

"Henry," Jessie spoke.

Startled, the man dropped his tools. "Jessie—" he said.

"Henry, I came to apologize. I'm sorry about what we said, how we acted. We didn't mean to make you uncomfortable. Kay and I are—"

Jessie stopped. She looked at the man as if seeing him for the first time. His face was tanned from working in the sun. His wavy brown hair was graying at the sides. The laughter wrinkles near his eyes belied smiles and a warm heart. But what captured her attention was his eyes. They were pale green, the color of sea foam. Jessie found herself staring at him. Something in Henry's eyes drew her to him.

Henry held her gaze. He, too, was seeing Jessie in a way he had not seen her before. Her deep brown eyes were beautiful; gentleness and sadness mingled there. He felt his stomach turn inside out. He wanted to say something, but no words came.

Inside the house, Sam Taylor pulled up the window screen. "Yep, Jessie's right," he said, sticking his head out the window. "What do you think of that, Kay? You sold a—" He stopped short.

He could see Henry and Jessie in the yard, obviously involved in earnest conversation. Something about the look of the two stabbed at his heart. Pulling himself in, he abruptly banged his head on the window. "Ouch," he muttered.

"What did you say?" asked Kay. "Are you all right? Hey, who turned out the lights?"

Sam looked over to see Kay vainly trying to see through the film of pink powder covering her glasses. He could not help himself. He laughed until the tears came. Excusing himself, he hurried out of the room.

Kay pulled off her glasses and wiped them clean with a tissue.

"Honestly, what is going on around here? I thought we were going to tear out the wall. Where are Henry and Jessie?"

She jumped up and looked out the window. "Jessie! Come on! Get the lead out. Let's rip out the wall and see what we find. What are you waiting for?"

Kay started out the door. "Sam?" she called. "Are you here?"

The hall was empty. She walked down the hall and stopped at the top of the stairs. Directly across from the stairs was the door to the attic. The closed stairwell of the attic divided the upstairs in half, with a hall and two bedrooms on either side. The bathroom was in the front of the house. Kay hesitated. She put her hand on the round, white doorknob.

"I bet the attic holds some clues to the mystery room," she said to herself. "After all, the attic is above the room, *n'est-ce pas?*"

She turned the knob. "Come on, Kay. It's up to you to do some exploring. Looks like everyone else has abandoned ship."

The heavy steel hinges moaned as Kay pulled the door open. The attic stairs, steep and dusty, swept up abruptly before her. Kay cautiously climbed up the first few steps. She found a light switch on the left and flipped it on. A feeble bulb glimmered at the top of the stairs.

"Here I go," whispered Kay. "Secret, beware. The fearless Kay Bantam is about to disclose you. *'Veni, vidi, vici,* I came, I saw, I conquered.' Oh, lovely Latin. Kay, you're a regular language laureate. Ready or not, here I come!"

Chapter 9

Henry, I—" Jessie suddenly could not think of anything else to say. Her hands were trembling.

Henry picked up his tools. "I guess I. . .we better get back to the house, you know," he stuttered. "I appreciate you. . .your words, Jessie. What you said, I mean."

"Oh, really? I mean it. I'm sorry we were so rude."

"I don't think you could ever be rude, Mrs. Woods. I mean, Jess. . .Jessie." *Oh, man, Lewis, you are blowing it,* he scolded himself. *You are a klutz!*

"Thanks, Henry." Jessie cleared her throat. "You're right. We better get back to the house."

Back inside the house, Kay made her way carefully up the narrow stairway. The bulb of light, hanging from the ceiling, was strung with faint strands of cobweb. Kay sneezed. At the top of the stairs, she stopped and scoped out the room. Boxes cluttered the corners. Piles of newspapers lay about the room, dust covering their faded headlines. The eaves sloped gradually, leaving plenty of space for storage. The attic was large enough for Kay to walk around freely.

"Pays to be diminutive," said Kay aloud. "Now let's see what we can find. The secret room should be underneath this area."

She tapped the floor. "Well, no one tapped back," she said. "No ghosts," she giggled nervously. "Nobody up here but me, right?"

The silence suspended in the close air spoke volumes to Kay's listening ear. The lives that had occupied the house in the past were gone. Only physical fragments remained: the boxes, the papers, and an occasional suitcase. The movement of life was a puzzle, relentless and defying understanding. No matter how one clung to it, life would eventually move out of the physical and beyond to something or somewhere that Kay did not understand.

She scrutinized the floor above the secret room. "Maybe there's a gap near the eaves, where the floor meets the roof," she wondered aloud. "Maybe I could get a look down below!"

She noted the thick film of dust shrouding the floor. "Be brave, Kay."

She knelt down. Then, on all fours, she crawled as close to the wall as she could. There was a slight gap. Kay peered through the crack, but her eye met only darkness. She sighed and stood up slowly, but still managed to bump her head on the sloping roof.

"Youch!" she muttered, rubbing her head. Suddenly, she froze.

"Hey, what's that?"

A small wooden box was snuggled in a corner, resting on a beam. Kay gingerly grasped the box by both ends and picked it up. Forgetting the dust, she plopped on the floor, the box on her lap.

Adjusting her glasses, Kay stared at her find. "I really should wait and let Jessie see this," she admonished herself. "After all, this is her house. She should be the one to open the box and see. . . Oh, well. Jess is not here. And probably there's nothing in it, anyway. What are friends for?"

Kay carefully undid the darkened brass clasp that secured the box. She lifted the lid. To her amazement, there lay a large brass skeleton key.

"Wow," she whispered. "Wonder what this goes to." Kay lifted the key up to the dim light and then put it back into the box. "And what, pray tell, is this?"

Underneath the key, in the bottom of the box, was a folded slip of paper. Kay gently picked the paper up and unfolded it. The message written there sent a jolt through her. She screamed.

Jessie and Henry were on their way through the front door when they heard the scream. They ran up the stairs to the second floor.

"Kay! Where are you?" called Jessie.

Their search of the bedrooms was fruitless. A second scream led them to the attic door. Flinging it open, Henry rushed up the stairs with Jessie behind him. They found Kay sitting on the floor, her face flushed, her glasses crooked.

"Kay, what is the matter? And what are you doing up here?" queried Jessie.

"It's all true," stammered Kay. "The rich guy, the gold. You're rich, Jessie. Filthy rich. All we have to do is find it."

"Kay Bantam, what are you talking about?" demanded Jessie. "You're not making any sense."

"Here," responded Kay as she handed Jessie the paper. "Read it for yourself."

Jessie read aloud: " 'To the one who holds this page, look around. There is treasure to be found. If you have courage, somewhere within the walls of this domain a cache of gold doth remain. Look high, look low. Don't sleep in the moonlight. Signed, the Goldkeeper.' "

"Kind of corny," muttered Jessie, trying to fight the excitement fluttering in her stomach. "But this certainly looks old," she said, fingering the fragile paper. "The handwriting is old-fashioned, too. Maybe it was written by Denver."

"Wow," said Henry. "It's like a treasure hunt. Wonder if there are any more clues."

Kay jumped to her feet. "Oh, yes, a real treasure hunt. Maybe this is only the first clue!"

"What's going on in here?" a voice from behind startled Kay and Jessie. They both yelped in surprise.

It was Sam. His face held a serious look. For a second, Jessie thought she saw sadness or disappointment in his eyes. It tugged at her heart, but she quickly dismissed it.

"We have found a clue. It's a treasure hunt. There's gold!" Kay babbled. "I was looking around the attic to see if I could maybe figure out this secret room thing, and I knelt down there," she pointed, "to see if I could see through the crack, and then I bumped my head and *boom!* There was this box hidden in the shadows. There's a key and—"

"Kay, Kay, calm down," laughed Jessie. "You're making the poor man's head swim, I'm sure. Let's go downstairs and rustle up some tea. Then we'll discuss it like civilized folks."

"I already took the liberty of putting on the teakettle," said Sam. "Follow me, O mighty explorers!"

At the kitchen table, the four sat looking at the box and its contents. Sam shook his head. "It could be a child's game, you know. My mom used to make up treasure hunts for us on rainy days. The treasure was usually a bag of those gold foil-covered chocolate coins. We loved it!"

Henry took a sip of his tea. He agreed with Sam. "It's probably nothing at all, maybe long gone by now. Maybe you should just forget about it. People are always finding strange things in these old houses. It's fun but not necessarily all that mysterious."

Kay frowned at the two men. "And what about the key?" she demanded. "It must unlock something. Like another box maybe."

"Like a treasure chest, eh, matey?" croaked Sam in the best pirate voice he could muster.

Henry blushed, and Jessie choked on her tea. "Now, come on, gentlemen. Let's not burst Kay's bubble altogether. Who knows? Maybe there is something to this." She curled her fingers around the cool brass key. "After all, there is the secret room to consider. We haven't opened it up yet. Who knows what we'll find in there?" Her cheeks blushed with color as she spoke. Both men noted the beauty of her face and the sparkle in her eyes. The ever-vigilant Kay did not miss the staring gazes of the two men.

"Excuse me," grunted Kay, frowning at the men. "I realize this is all very fascinating, but let's get down to business. When are we going to open up the room? And who's going to do it?"

"I'd rather not do it today," said Jessie. "I'm a little overwhelmed."

"Well, I can do it this Saturday," Henry volunteered. "That is, if it's all right with you, Jessie."

"I'll help," said Sam flatly. "I'll be glad to help. Two hands make light work."

"Okay," agreed Jessie. "Saturday's fine. And I'll make lunch."

"Who can think of food at a time like this?" said Kay. "I'm so excited I could scream!"

"You already did, my friend," said Jessie. "Let's keep things to a dull roar, shall we? And Sam's right. This is probably nothing. The poor man probably shut up the room in grief over his daughter's death. That's probably all there is to it."

Kay got up in a huff. "Well, I can see none of you has a sense of adventure. Mark my words, we'll find something in this house, or my name isn't Kay Bantam, ace realtor!"

She turned on her heel and marched down the hall to the front door. "See you all Saturday," she called back. "Jessie, call me tonight."

"Okay," Jessie answered. "She tends to be dramatic," she explained to Sam and Henry. "She's kind of, well, excitable."

The men smiled and rose from the table. They said their good-byes and left. Jessie noticed an awkwardness in the moment.

∞

"What is going on?" she said to herself later, as the earlier events of the day tumbled in her mind. She thought of her conversation with Henry.

"Conversation. What conversation?" she said. "All we did was stand there and stare at each other like a couple of schoolkids." In the tumble of her thoughts, the look of Henry's eyes surfaced. His eyes were so kind.

"I don't like this," said Jessie. Her feelings were running amuck. Feelings she'd thought were long dead were faintly awakening. Thoughts of Tom and feelings for him swirled around in her heart amidst the pull of Henry's green eyes.

A brisk knock on the back door snapped Jessie out of her turmoil.

"Yoo-hoo," a voice called. "It's me, Lorena Smith."

Jessie went to the back porch and opened the door for her elderly neighbor.

"Here's your pie!" announced Lorena, handing the gift to Jessie. "Apple, just as you ordered."

"Oh, Lorena, it's still warm," proclaimed Jessie as she accepted the fragrant gift.

"Just took it out of the oven a little while ago," nodded Lorena.

"Thank you so much," said Jessie. "It smells delicious. Please, come in and sit for awhile."

"Don't mind if I do," smiled Lorena.

Jessie took Lorena into the living room. They sat down on the sofa that faced the tall windows.

"These windows are lovely," commented Lorena. "Let in a lot of sunshine, they do."

"I love looking out into the yard," explained Jessie. "Those trees are so strong and beautiful."

The afternoon sun mingled in the leaves of the old trees, casting golds and greens that shimmered in the air and on the ground below. The fragrance of sweetpea wafted through the windows and decorated the room with sweetness.

"You're doing wonderful things to this house," complimented Lorena. "I was so afraid no one would buy it and that maybe they'd have to tear it down."

Jessie smiled. "It's a real blessing to be here."

"So, tell me how you're doing, my dear. I saw you in the yard before with Henry Lewis. He's a nice man, isn't he?" said Lorena.

"Uh, yes, he is a nice man," stuttered Jessie. She looked at Lorena. Beneath the calm of her soft blue eyes, Jessie had a feeling the woman could look straight into Jessie's soul and read all the secrets written there.

The ringing of the phone snagged Jessie's attention. She jumped up and went into the hall to answer the call.

"Saved by the bell," she whispered under her breath. She picked up the receiver. "Hello?"

"Don't you hello me," sputtered Kay. "Can you imagine such a thing? And what are you going to do about it?"

"Kay, calm down. I was going to call you tonight. Are you still bowled over with the treasure hunt thing? Calm down, woman, before you have a fainting spell!"

"I couldn't wait. Forget the gold. I'm not talking about the treasure hunt. I'm talking about them."

"Kay, what are you talking about? Them? Who them?" Jessie leaned over and smelled the flowers on the hall table. Ever since Kay had surprised her with a bouquet that first day, Jessie had made sure there was a fresh arrangement every week. A tradition, she had decided.

"I mean Henry Lewis and Samuel Taylor, that's who!" exclaimed the realtor. "Didn't you see them both gawking at you when we were in the kitchen? Looked like puppies, both of them."

Jessie sucked in her breath. "What are you talking about?"

"You heard me. Nothing gets past old Kay Bantam, no siree. I know puppy eyes when I see them. And I saw two pairs. Is this great or what? You are in a pickle, and I think it's marvelous!"

"Marvelous," echoed Jessie. Rival feelings were fighting their way to the forefront of Jessie's heart. She felt dizzy.

"Jessie?" Kay's voice sounded in the phone. "Are you there?"

"Gotta go," said Jessie faintly. "Lorena's here."

"Who? Jessie, call me back, okay?" pleaded Kay. "You sound weird. Are you okay?"

"I'm okay," said Jessie. "Bye." She hung up the phone and leaned against the wall for a moment. Taking a deep breath, she returned to her guest, determined not to break down.

But as soon as she reached Lorena and saw her kindly face, Jessie burst into tears.

Chapter 10

My dear! Whatever is the matter!" Lorena exclaimed at the sight of Jessie's tears. She reached over and put her arm gently around Jessie's shoulders. Jessie let her tears flow freely.

When Jessie finally stopped weeping, she raised her tear-stained face to her guest. "I'm so sorry," she said. "I don't know what's come over me."

"Here," responded Lorena, handing Jessie a tissue, "I always carry a packet of these in my pocket. Never know when you'll need them."

"Thank you," sighed Jessie, wiping her eyes.

"Now, tell me what's in your heart," admonished Lorena. "It sometimes helps you sort things out if you just talk about it."

Jessie took a deep breath and looked out the windows. A breeze was tugging at the branches of the oaks and maples. She stared at the place where she had been standing with Henry. *What is happening to me?* she wondered.

"I'm so confused, Lorena," she spoke softly. "Let me start at the beginning. Three years ago my husband, Tom, died of cancer. We had been married for twenty-seven years. We weren't able to have any children, and we never felt the leading to adopt, so all those years it was just Tom and me." Jessie smiled. "The Lord was so good to us. We were busy at church, busy with our jobs, and enjoyed each other's company." Jessie stopped and wiped the silent tears escaping from her eyes. "I guess I thought it would go on forever. And then, *bam!* Tom doesn't feel well, goes to the doctor, and in six months, he's gone." She shuddered. "Just like that. Twenty-seven years and suddenly it's over."

Lorena patted Jessie's hand. Her own eyes had filled with tears.

"Go on, Jessie. Get it all out."

"Oh, Lorena, I just don't know what's the matter with me. You know how they tell you about the stages of grief? Well, I went through all that. My pastor and friends were all kind and comforting to me. I went back to work. Three years went by. I came up here from the city to look for a house. I felt it was time to move on." She looked around the living room. The woodwork gleamed with warmth; the furnishings were at the same time tasteful and comfortable. "This house was perfect. I thought, 'This is it. I'm finally getting on with my life!' Then suddenly I find myself crying for no apparent reason."

"Grief's a peculiar thing," said Lorena softly. "It floods your days at first, and then fades, only to spring up again at unexpected moments. Many months after

47

my Walter died, I'd be going along pretty good, you know, able to do my work. Then the next thing you know, I'd be sitting at the table, not even thinking about him, and tears would spring to my eyes like a fountain."

Jessie nodded. "The worst part is when I can't remember Tom's face. Then I run to the photo albums and try to imprint his image indelibly on my mind." She let go a sad laugh. "It doesn't really work. It looks as though my life has moved on, but my heart hasn't."

Lorena reached over and squeezed Jessie's hand. "The healing will come, my dear. But I'm going to be straightforward with you, Jessie, if I may."

Jessie nodded. "Go ahead, Lorena."

Lorena placed both her hands over Jessie's. "I don't think it's Tom you're grieving for now. I think it's the Lord you're grieving over."

Jessie sat up straight. "The Lord? What do you mean? I haven't turned from the Lord. I still go to church. I still read my Bible."

"That may be so," responded Lorena patiently, "but you're probably just going through the motions."

Her words stung Jessie. She felt as though she had been slapped across the face. "How can you say such a thing?" She vigorously denied her visitor's charge. "You don't know me at all. You can't judge me like that. It's not right."

Lorena gently but firmly held her ground. "You're hurt, Jessie. You think the Lord took Tom away from you. You can't believe the One you trusted would have done such a thing to you! It's shaken you down to the very roots of your faith. Everything you ever thought you knew about the Lord and life was suddenly snatched away. The rug was pulled out from under you."

Jessie lowered her head and began to weep. Her shoulders shook as her weeping turned to sobs. "Why did He do this to me? I trusted Him, followed Him. I served the Lord. How could He hurt me so?"

Lorena was silent for a long time. She simply sat with her arms around her new neighbor. When the sobs dissipated into shuddering sighs, Lorena lifted Jessie's head. She looked into Jessie's rich brown eyes.

"I can't say why Tom died. I can't even say if it was God's hand or God's plan or anything like that. Some people are content to make sweeping statements about such things. Not me. I don't understand why some things happen. But this much I do know: Jesus is here to help us through. He's more than that. He's here to love us, to give life to us. He is our life, if we're willing. No one else can do that or be that for us. No one. Only Him."

"I don't know, Lorena," Jessie said, her voice hoarse from crying. "I just don't know. What you're saying is. . .hard to take."

"Your relationship with the Lord needs to be restored, Jessie. God didn't do this to you. It happened. Maybe it was Tom's time to go, I don't know. I'm not a theologian. But the Lord is still here, loving you. . .wanting to help you and walk with you." Lorena smiled, her white hair catching a glint of afternoon sunlight. "Everybody talks about God's plan for your life. He is the plan for your life. . . for mine."

Jessie leaned back in the sofa. She was exhausted. "Maybe you're right," she said quietly. "Maybe I am a little distant from the Lord. I'll have to think about that one. I can be stubborn, you know. Just ask my friend, Kay. She'll tell you."

Lorena got up from the couch. "I'd better be going. I have chores to do before supper. I'll be praying for you."

Jessie walked Lorena to the back door. "Thanks for listening," she said. "Maybe I just needed a good cry."

Lorena smiled. Wisdom had taught her not to argue when God was working on someone's heart. "Enjoy the pie," was all she said in parting. "Bye, now."

Jessie then climbed her stairs and went into the bathroom. The mirror reflected her puffy eyes and reddened face. "You look terrible, Jessie Woods." She splashed her face with cold water and then dried herself with a soft, blue towel. Heading for her bedroom, she flopped on her bed, grabbed her pillow, and promptly fell asleep.

∞

Several blocks away, Spencer Hart climbed into his car. He checked the rearview mirror and started the engine. Clenching a toothpick between his yellow teeth, he smirked as he drove down the streets of Carlisle. He had scored big in the post office. Earlier that day he had stumbled into an interesting conversation the postal worker was having with one of his customers. He laughed to himself, replaying the scene in his mind.

"Can you believe it?" Herb Stamping had gushed to the woman in the orange-flowered dress and matching hat. "A secret room in the Denver house!"

"I do believe it," the woman had replied, her flowered hat bobbing vigorously up and down with every nod. "That house has always had a mysterious way with it. Everyone knows it, too."

"I'll say," Herb had agreed. "I wouldn't be surprised if there is gold hidden over there somewhere."

"I'd say even better than that," the woman had said, then lowered her voice to a loud whisper. "I bet it's haunted." She had drawn out the last word with a tremulous gasp for emphasis.

Spencer had entered the post office at the moment of the whispering and had stepped up immediately and joined the excited twosome.

"My dear lady, did you say 'haunted'? Whatever do you mean? A house right here in Carlisle?" He had used his meekest, most interested voice.

Herb had piped up in response. "Why, the Denver house, of course. They say the new owner has discovered a secret room."

The woman in orange had nodded enthusiastically. "It's true! I have that information from a most reliable source. And I heard something about a box and a key of some sort." She had quivered at the thought.

"Really?" Spencer had smiled at the woman. "That is most amazing."

"I already heard about it this morning, of course," Herb had said importantly. "And I know for a fact it is true."

"But now, really, that's not too surprising, is it? After all, the house does have an interesting history," Spencer had commented, fishing for more information.

"Yes, it's true," Herb had said. "How do you know about the Denver house?"

"Research, my man, research," Spencer had been swift to reply. "You know." He had winked at the postal worker.

"Oh, yes," Herb had said. "Your book. He's writing a book, you know. A novel about a small town."

"Ooh, a real live author!" she had exclaimed, the flowers on her hat trembling with the excitement.

"Now, Clarabelle, you must keep this under wraps," Herb had directed. "He writes under a pen name, for privacy purposes."

"I would appreciate your cooperation, Miss. . . ?"

"Burton. Clarabelle Burton. Are you going to write about the gold?" she had asked. "I mean, you know about the gold, don't you?"

"Well, I've heard a little about it," Spencer had replied.

"I'm afraid that's just a rumor," Herb had chimed in. "After all, that was years ago. And I don't think they're going to find anything of the kind in that second-story room."

"Which floor?" Spencer had asked innocently.

"The second floor," Clarabelle had prompted. "They're going to open up the secret room they found on the second floor." She had lowered her voice to a whisper. "Who knows what they'll find!"

"Well," Spencer had said, "I wouldn't get too worked up over it. There's probably nothing out of the ordinary involved here. Imagination is a powerful thing! It's probably nothing more than a small-town rumor!"

Clarabelle had sniffed; her shoulders had drooped. The excitement had obviously fizzled out of the conversation.

"Now there's the voice of reason," Herb had nodded. "Secret rooms are rarely anything more than that. . .secret rooms! Why, when they open up that room next Saturday, they'll probably find nothing but dust!" He had sighed. "Still, it would be exciting if the hidden gold was more than a small-town rumor."

Spencer laughed again as he changed gears. He turned right onto Lark Avenue. "So it's on the second floor. Just as I thought. I better get a move on before my plan is spoiled."

He slowed his car when he got to house number sixteen. Craning his neck, he scrutinized the side of the house with the extra window. The diverging branches of the trees obscured his view of the second floor.

"Better not stop," Spencer spoke to himself. "Don't want anyone to connect me or my car with this neighborhood." His lips curled in a grin. "Smart fellow to rent a truck for my paint inspector scam. Hart, you are a genius with a capital G!"

∞

At the post office, Herb Stamping was on the phone in earnest conversation. "I told you, Ruby." He cupped his hand over the phone for effect. "He wasn't all that impressed with the secret room story."

"What did you say?" asked Ruby. "I can't understand a thing you're saying. Get your hand off the phone. Nobody's listening."

"You never know," said Herb, who reluctantly lowered his hand. "I said Spencer Hart wasn't all that impressed with the secret room story, or the gold story, for that matter. He dismissed it as, and I quote, 'a small-town rumor.'"

"Well, maybe you're right. Maybe he is what he says he is, a writer acclimating himself to the small-town ambiance. I could have been wrong suspecting him."

"You've been wrong before," said Herb. "Remember the year Irving Winters moved to Carlisle, and you insisted he was a CIA man?"

"Well, he was always traveling to Washington, leaving his house at all hours of the night."

"Right," snorted Herb. "Then we found out he has grandchildren in Washington. He was visiting his family! I hope you've learned your lesson, Ruby. Why don't you start using that imagination of yours and write a story yourself. To think you used to spy on Irving!"

"I wasn't spying," countered the librarian. "I was simply looking out my window toward the house across the street. It just happened to be Irving's house."

"Ruby Clearwater!"

"Well, I don't care," she replied. "One must be an informed citizen. And I still don't like the looks of that Spencer Hart. I'm going to keep an eye on him. Maybe he's just trying to throw us off his trail."

"Us?" echoed Herb. "His trail? Ruby Clearwater, don't think you're going to drag me into this escapade. I have resigned from the Clearwater Detective Agency, thank you very much."

"That's what you always say," laughed Ruby on the other end of the line. "That's what you always say."

Chapter 11

Stacy, Spencer Hart's accomplice, calmly blew cigarette smoke in his direction. "So when do we make our first move?" she asked impatiently.

"Soon," Spencer responded gruffly.

"But didn't you say they were opening up that secret room on Saturday?" Stacy ran her fingers through her thick brown hair. "Shouldn't we do something before then?"

Spencer frowned and carefully folded the newspaper he had been reading. He pulled a stick of gum out of his shirt pocket and popped it into his mouth.

"Patience, my dear, patience. I'll be stopping by the house before Saturday. See if I can get my hands on some more information about the so-called treasure hunt. I pretty well know the layout of the house. My visit on Sunday was very productive. Amazing what one can learn by peering through somebody's windows."

"When? When are you going over?" Stacy asked excitedly.

"You don't need to know." Spencer rubbed his sore foot. "We'll let them open the room. Then I'll drop by one more time to check out the room for myself. When the time and the weather are right, we initiate our plan."

The young woman sighed. She ground her cigarette into a green ceramic ashtray. "I'm getting tired of waiting. This better work. And there had better be gold in that house." She glared at her partner.

Spencer laughed. "Don't worry. It's there." His eyes gleamed. "And I'll find it."

❧

At 16 Lark Avenue, Jessie settled into the sitting room love seat, unfolded the next letter from the hatbox, and began to read it.

Dear Father,

You will be pleased to know that our little Rosemary is doing famously with her studies. She can read simple sentences and is practicing writing words. She is especially enthralled with writing her name. She writes it over and over again. Miss Bristol told me that the first time Rosemary saw her name written down, she exclaimed, "That's me on paper!" Honestly, Father, she is a delight.

I told Miss Bristol of your generous offer of supplying Rosemary with books and paper supplies, but she politely refused it. She said she was grateful, but that she and Rosemary's family would tackle the expense. Miss Bristol said she guessed the independent spirit of her people has remained in her.

I've changed my view of Miss Bristol altogether. I used to think she was such a prissy, bookworm type. Now I know better. She is full of fire, a passion to educate those who don't readily have the opportunity. I found out that Rosemary is one of a long list of children who have benefited from Miss Bristol's care. Many of them have gone on to become teachers themselves!

On Saturday, Rebecca Thomason rubbed whale oil on all the doorknobs in the school. Everyone had a horrendous time getting a grip on the handles and opening the doors. Some of the teachers failed completely. It was terribly funny. They finally summoned Mr. Grates, our handyman, and he cleaned off all the knobs, sputtering away as he did it. "Ought to lock up the scoundrel who did this. Lock her up for life and swallow the key, I tell you."

You should have seen the look on Headmistress Charter's face. Needless to say, Rebecca was found out, reprimanded, and confined to the study hall for a month. No parties, no visits from her folks. I doubt Rebecca cares. She has always been a little wild. She has strange ideas about life. Says she's going to run for political office one day. Or maybe study to be a doctor or some such thing.

One of my favorite things to do is to watch the lamplighter come to light the street lamps. I sit at my window that overlooks the street and watch for him. He usually hurries down the street, but last night was different. His dark figure (you know they often wear black) slowly emerged through the murky gray of dusk. I watched as he hooked his ladder up to the lamp irons. This time, instead of rushing up to do the job, he climbed slowly, even carefully. He touched his stick to the lamp. Then he gazed intently at the glow, as though seeing it for the first time. I wondered if perhaps he had fallen in love, or perhaps his wife had borne him their first child. Or maybe he had had a dream, glorious and full of wonders, a dream for his life and it had gotten hold of him and he was full of it, wondering what it could all mean. A dream beyond the lighting of the lamps.

I can hear you now, Father, laughing and saying the poor fellow was probably just suffering with a bout of lumbago. But seeing him this way turned the thoughts in my head. I wonder what shall be the path that I take?

There is talk in the school about a group of girls going on a trip through the Orient. Several teachers and guides would be the chaperones. I think I would like to go along. After all, Father, you've had your share of travel. You know I love to hear your tales of the sights you've seen, but now I should like to see them for myself. Please consider letting me go. We can discuss it in further detail at Christmas.

My love to Sophie and The Professor. I am your devoted daughter,

Amelia Elizabeth

Jessie sat back on the love seat. Her eyes followed the soft pattern of flowers on the wallpaper of the sitting room. The lamp on the corner table threw a warm glow onto the walls and the nearby sofa. Jessie tried to imagine what little Rosemary looked like. She was beginning to feel as if she knew Amelia and her circle of friends and family. "I wonder what we'll find behind the walls of the hidden room," she said softly.

Jessie placed the letter on the table. She reached for the box Kay had retrieved from the beam in the attic. Opening it once again, she lifted out the brass key.

"Well," she murmured to herself, "is this all a game between father and daughter? Or is it a real treasure hunt?" Jessie sighed. How she wished she could talk to Tom just now. She knew exactly how he would react. First, he would laugh that deep laugh of his and shake his head. "It's all the result of an overactive imagination, Jessie darling." At the thought of his words, a smile lit Jessie's face, but it faded as the customary feeling of aloneness wrapped itself around her like an all-too-familiar blanket.

"I'm getting tired of this," she muttered aloud. "Time for bed." She put the box back on the table near the lamp then walked down the quiet hallway to her bedroom and got ready for bed.

Light from a glowing half-moon rested faintly on the white quilt on Jessie's bed. She lay quietly, listening to the sounds of her new home. At first it had been hard getting used to sleeping in such a large house after having lived in an apartment for so long. The creaking of the floorboards; the muffled chiming in the dining room of the mantel clock, a gift from Kay; the whisper of the trees consorting with the night wind. All these were becoming songs to Jessie's ears.

She fell asleep.

∞

Just after midnight, Spencer Hart rushed through the darkness toward the house. He swiftly made his way to the side of the building, hiding himself in the shadows. He moved along the side to the back porch and checked the screen door. It was not locked. He pulled it open and noiselessly slipped through the door. One of the kitchen windows was easily pried open. He stuck his head in first to listen. All was quiet and dark inside. Spencer climbed through the window, finding himself on the kitchen table. Feeling over the top of the table, he found it to be clear of objects.

"Lucky for me she's a neat chick," he said to himself. He dismounted the table and made his way through to the hallway. As he stopped in the hallway acclimating his eyes to the darkness, he patted his sore leg. "That painkiller is working just fine," he whispered to himself. Suddenly, the clock in the dining room chimed the half-hour, and he nearly jumped out of his skin. His hand brushed against something, almost knocking it over. It was the vase of flowers.

He quickly grabbed it and, to his relief, immediately righted the vase. Then he listened for any sound from upstairs. Nothing.

He entered the living room. Periodically he turned on his small penlight to search for clues. Finding nothing, he tried the dining room. There were papers on the table, but they were nothing more than bills, receipts, and junk mail.

Back in the hall, he approached the bottom of the stairs. "Now this is the hard part," he said to himself. Bending down, he ran his hand over one of the lower steps. It was covered with a rich, soft carpet. "Perfect!" He took a deep breath. "Now go as quickly and lightly as you can, Hart. You can do it."

He sprinted up the stairs. The steps emitted a few faint creaks.

Jessie turned in her bed.

Spencer stood at the top of the stairs, barely breathing. Minutes passed and, satisfied the owner had not been awakened, he crept down the left hallway. Once inside the sitting room, he flashed on his little light.

"Bingo!" he whispered. His small circle of light landed on the round table with the lamp. There was a piece of paper and a wooden box. He reached over for the letter and began to read.

"Nothing but emotional tripe," he said to himself as he placed the letter back on the table. He clenched his penlight between his teeth. Picking up the box, his hands trembled slightly. Carefully he opened it. An object glistened dully in the narrow light. *A key!*

In his excitement, he dropped the light from his mouth. It fell with a gentle thud. Spencer cursed and listened for Jessie Woods. He picked up his light and looked again into the box. Underneath the key, he discovered the note. He absorbed its contents and restored it to the box. Pulling a lump of clay from a back pocket, he rapidly made an impression of the key.

Suddenly, Spencer heard noise coming from the direction of the master bedroom. Quickly, he restored the key and the box to its original position on the table. He raced down the stairs as lightly as he possibly could and managed to get himself out through the window. Sliding the screen closed with a soft click, he turned toward the screen door. The leg of a chair grabbed at his foot, and he fell on the floor of the porch. He winced. *My foot is going to be sore tomorrow,* he realized.

Sputtering at himself, he jumped up, exited the porch, and disappeared into the shadows.

Jessie froze in her bed. She had heard peculiar sounds, first coming from the sitting room and then downstairs in the back of the house. She reached for her phone and grabbed the receiver. The touchtone pads glowed green in the darkness. Frantically, Jessie dialed Kay's number.

"Hello," a groggy voice responded on the other end of the line.

"Who is it?"

"Kay. It's me, Jessie. I think there's someone in the house."

"What are you talking about?" muttered Kay. "You know I live alone. There's nobody here but me. And the cat."

"I don't mean your house," Jessie whispered fiercely into the receiver. "I mean my house."

Kay sat up in bed and reached for her glasses.

"Well, what are you calling me for? Call nine-one-one, you goose."

"But what if it's nothing? What if it's just my imagination?" stammered Jessie. "What if it's—"

"A chicken?" prompted Kay. "Then send it back over to Lorena."

"But what if someone is in the house?" Jessie began to shiver with fright.

Kay pushed her glasses onto her nose. "Then call Sam, Darling. He's right across the street. Better to be embarrassed in front of one man than the entire Carlisle Police Force." Kay fumbled on the nightstand for her address book. "I've got the number right here. I'll call him for you. Don't worry about a thing."

Before Jessie could protest, she heard a click and then the blaring hum of the dial tone.

Chapter 12

In a matter of minutes, there was a loud knocking on the front door of Jessie's house. She threw back the covers and grabbed her robe. Then she flipped on the light switch in the upstairs hall and hurried down the stairs.

Jessie hesitated. "Who is it?" she called out to the door.

"It's me, Sam Taylor," a voice answered back.

Jessie unlocked the door and let him in. He rushed past her with Manny at his heels. "Kay called me," he said over his shoulder. He first checked the living room and dining room. Jessie followed after him.

"Does anything look like it's been disturbed?" he questioned her.

Jessie, in a daze, looked around. "Well, I don't think so," she said, her voice tinged with uncertainty.

Sam headed for the kitchen. Manny began to whine and whimper. The dog pawed at the back door.

"What's the matter, old boy?" questioned his master. "May I?" he asked Jessie, pointing to the lock.

"Yes, sure, go ahead," she answered. Her head was beginning to clear.

Sam let the dog out, and he went wild on the back porch, yelping and barking. Sam opened the screen door, and Manny ran into the darkness of the backyard, barking.

"What do you suppose that means?" stammered Jessie. "All that barking, I mean."

Sam peered out into the yard. "Could mean nothing. Maybe he smells the guy who reads the electric meters. I don't know."

He stopped and looked at Jessie. She looked pale, and he noticed that her hands were shaking. "Let's sit down, and I'll make you something hot to drink. Have any instant cocoa?"

Jessie nodded and pointed to the cupboard where he could find the cocoa. He sat her down at the kitchen table and put on the teakettle.

"Now, tell me exactly what happened," Sam said, seating himself across the table from Jessie.

Jessie fumbled with her hands. "I don't know. Maybe I just got spooked by the sounds in the house," she said. She was beginning to feel foolish. With the lights on and someone in the house with her, Jessie's feelings of fear were shrinking fast.

"Seems kind of silly now," she sputtered. "Really, what happened was that—"

The piercing whistle of the kettle shot into Jessie's ear. She jumped and let out a yell.

"Hey, hey!" Sam grabbed her arms. "Calm down. It's okay."

Jessie blushed and freed herself from Sam's gentle hold. "I'm sorry," she apologized. "I guess I still feel a bit jumpy."

Sam handed Jessie a steaming mug of cocoa. "Now, why don't you start from the top. Tell me exactly what happened. What did you hear?"

Jessie sat down and dipped her spoon into the cocoa. "Well, I remember turning in my bed, sort of half-asleep, when I thought I heard the stairs creaking. It was very slight, so I decided it was just the usual creaking of the house." She slowly stirred her cocoa. "Then, just a few minutes later, I thought I heard something, as if someone were in the sitting room. Then I panicked. So I called Kay."

"Let's go up to the sitting room and see if anything looks like it's been moved or removed," suggested Sam.

Jessie smiled gratefully at the handsome pastor. "Thanks for taking me seriously," she said.

Sam's gray-blue eyes glistened with warmth. "I try never to jump to conclusions or question another's cry for help. I just try to be there when I'm needed. The rest will sort itself out."

"Oh, yes. Never jump to conclusions. This coming from the man who proclaimed our marriage the first day we met!" Jessie laughed. She was glad she could laugh about it now. "You certainly jumped to a conclusion that day."

Sam's cheeks reddened. "That's, uh, different," the pastor stammered. "It just sort of came out."

Jessie led Sam down the hall to the stairs. She stopped at the table that held her flowers.

"Oh, dear," she sputtered. "There's water on the table." She ran back to the kitchen and grabbed a towel. Wiping the water carefully, she frowned at the slight water stain. "How did that happen?" she wondered aloud.

"Is the vase leaking maybe?" Sam asked, a frown darkening his face.

"I don't think so, but I'll put it in the kitchen, just in case," responded Jessie. "I'm too tired to check it out now."

Sam waited for Jessie to put the vase away. Then she led him up the stairs to the sitting room where everything looked the way Jessie had left it just before she went to bed.

"I guess this was all my imagination," sighed Jessie. "I'm sorry to have troubled you, Sam."

"No trouble at all," Sam replied. "Better safe than sorry. You call any time. Don't take any chances, Jessie."

The serious look on Sam Taylor's face troubled Jessie.

"You do think it was just the house settling, don't you, Sam?"

"I hope so, Jessie. But you looked pretty frightened when I got here, and I don't think you're the type to scare too easily."

"Well, to be honest with you, Sam, I can't shake the feeling that someone was in here. I thought I heard someone on the back porch." Jessie shivered. "But why? Why would anyone want to break into my house? Aside from my antiques, there's nothing else of value here. I don't keep a lot of money in the house."

"I don't know, Jessie," Sam shook his head. "Maybe in the evening you better lock your windows, at least the ones on the ground floor. And don't be afraid to call me." Sam reached for something in his pocket. "Here's my card with my phone number on it. Keep it by the phone. You know I'm just across the street."

"Thanks," said Jessie. "I really appreciate this. Hopefully, this was just another embarrassing moment in the life of Jessie Woods."

Suddenly, a human scream and the fierce barking of a dog erupted outside.

"That's Manny!" exclaimed Sam, running down the stairs. Jessie followed, her heart pounding. Had Manny cornered an intruder?

Sam flung open the front door. Perched precariously atop a porch chair, in a shiny pink sweat suit, a panicked Kay Bantam was frantically waving her arms, trying to shoo the dog away.

"Manny! Down boy," ordered Sam. The dog obeyed and promptly sat down.

"Kay! What are you doing?" exclaimed Jessie, trying not to laugh at the sight of her friend's flailing pink arms.

Sam helped Kay down from the chair.

"I got here as soon as I could!" sputtered Kay. She looked at her friend, choking back laughter. "That's right, laugh all you want! That's the thanks I get for rushing over here to save you from some robber or something." She brushed out the wrinkles in her vivid attire. "Dog nearly scared me half to death and almost ruined my new suit, to boot!" She pushed her big glasses back and sniffed in the direction of the canine.

"Sorry about Manny," said Sam. "But he was sniffing something out before, so I let him out. Thought he might scare out the intruder, if there was one."

"Well," inquired Kay, "what's the verdict? Was there someone lurking about, or what?"

"We're not sure," sighed Jessie. "Nothing seems to have been taken or disturbed."

"Just the same, I told Jessie to be careful," said Sam. "You know, lock the windows at night."

"And I'm staying with you tonight," announced Kay. "You sounded pretty scared over the phone."

"You don't have to do that," protested Jessie. "I'm not a child!"

"I'm here. I'm staying." Kay picked up the overnight bag she had flung aside when fleeing the dog.

"I think it's a great idea," agreed Sam. "I bid you ladies good night. Try to get some sleep."

"Good night," said the women in unison.

Jessie locked the front door and checked on the kitchen. "Want anything to eat?" she asked Kay.

"Hardly," responded Kay. "Let's hit the sack. What time is it, anyway?"

"After one," answered Jessie, checking the blue enamel clock on the wall.

"Oh, boy. Let's go."

Upstairs, Jessie hesitated in front of the guest room.

"Kay, do you mind sleeping in my room with me?" asked Jessie.

"Hey, no problem. You didn't think I was going to sleep all by myself in your guest room, what with all that talk about Mr. Denver and his poor daughter. You know, spooky stuff. And now this tonight. Forget it! I wouldn't sleep alone here if you paid me."

Jessie laughed. "Oh, Kay, you do my heart good. You say the funniest things! Surely you don't believe Camilla's stories, do you?"

"Never mind," sputtered Kay. "Let's get to bed."

Once settled in Jessie's bed, both women lay awake, eyes wide open. The lonely bark of a dog echoed in the distance. The leaves of the very old trees swished with a restless hush, as if remembering times long forgotten by the light of day. Something scampered across the roof.

Kay sat up. "What was that?"

"Probably a squirrel," said Jessie.

"Oh," said Kay. She propped herself up on one elbow. "So. Tell me about Sam. Wasn't it nice having such a handsome, strong, nice man come to the rescue?"

"Oh, Kay, really!" Jessie laughed. "When are you going to give up? Sam and I have agreed to be friends, remember?"

"Don't believe it," huffed Kay. "And what about Henry? He's sweet, and I know he's got a crush on you."

"Kay, aren't you at all sleepy?" Jessie ignored her remarks about Henry.

"Don't try to change the subject," countered the realtor. "It's time you started dating. And to think you've got your pick of two men. Two nice, unattached men. Now, that's a miracle!"

"Forget it, Kay. Not interested. Now, how about I read something to you?" suggested Jessie. "It might help you go to sleep."

"You mean it might shut me up!"

"I'll read you one of Amelia Elizabeth's letters. One of my favorites." Jessie turned on the bedside lamp and picked up the letter she had slipped beneath her Bible.

"Amelia who?"

"Mr. Denver's daughter," answered Jessie.

"Ooh," said Kay. "Read on. This should be fascinating." Kay lay back on her pillow, all ears.

"Let's see, '*Dear Father, Hope all is well. . . .*' " Jessie skimmed the letter. "Ah, here's the part I want to read to you. It's a part where Amelia wrote down what this young girl from Appalachia told her about her home in the mountains."

"Read on, McDuff," commanded Kay.

> *There is a girl I know by the name of Rosemary. There isn't a body as happy as she when she goes walking on her mountains. And it feels like they are hers, whenever she's there, smelling the sweet evergreen and the wild-flowers. Their perfume hovers in the air like a mourning dove fixing to light on the branches of a grand oak. And that old oak stands there, quiet, like the young Shawnee who stood by it when it was just a sapling, bending in the wind.*
>
> *Rosemary doesn't have a care when she's up there in the woods. When she reaches the ridge where a body can see clear across the valley, the sight steals her breath away. Especially in the fall, when all the yellows and oranges and reds shout so loud and fine it makes the joy well up and spill out of her eyes. It's then and there she knows exactly that God must be a mountain man.*

Jessie lay back and held the precious letter to her breast. "Well, Kay, wasn't that just beautiful?"

Kay's answer was the rhythmic breathing of one fast asleep.

"Oh," said the disappointed reader. "Good night, Kay."

She placed the letter under her Bible and then hesitated, touching her hand to the soft leather of the book. Stories flashed through her mind of the many people who met with God in a place of mountains. Abraham, Moses. She remembered the verses about Jesus often withdrawing to the mountains to commune with His Father. Tears formed, sliding quietly down the widow's face. A hunger stirred within her. A yearning she had not felt in years.

She turned off the light. *Maybe Lorena is right,* she thought.

Maybe I have turned my back on You, Lord. Maybe I should talk to someone about this.

Her eyes grew heavy with sleep. She succumbed, and in her dreams she chased after Rosemary on windswept mountains.

Chapter 13

When Henry pulled away the last piece of wall, Jessie eagerly stepped through the opening into the room. Everything inside was enveloped in a thick covering of dust. The furniture stood silently in a gray haze of forgotten time. Only one piece was covered with a sheet. Henry, Sam, and Kay stood respectfully in the hallway, letting Jessie explore the room by herself.

"Wow!" exclaimed Jessie. "This is wild. It looks as if Mr. Denver kept everything just like it was when his daughter left it. It doesn't look as if any of the furniture was removed."

A light flashed from the hall. Kay was snapping pictures of the room. "If you want to leave everything in its original state, you have to record where it is now. After all, when you start cleaning and restoring, the stuff's bound to be moved."

"You're a genius," laughed Jessie.

"I'm impressed," added Sam.

Jessie continued her investigation of the room. She pulled up the shade covering the window. A four-poster bed stood out from the wall, its faded, rose-colored canopy drooping downward like a ragged crown. A lace throw atop the bed's quilt crumbled between Jessie's fingers. On the night stand stood a lamp with a frosty white, glass globe.

"Hepplewhite," breathed Kay.

"What?" chorused Henry, Sam, and Jessie.

"I'd gander a flock of geese that the furniture is Hepplewhite," explained Kay in hushed tones. "Produced in the latter part of the eighteenth century. It's lovely. It's worth a fortune. See the oval-backed chair in the corner over there? Typical Hepplewhite."

Jessie turned to face her audience. "Come on in, you guys," she said. "This room is beautiful!"

Sam, Henry, and Kay walked through the opening and joined Jessie.

"I wonder why Mr. Denver didn't cover everything with sheets?" asked Jessie aloud.

"Maybe at the time he didn't care," responded Sam. "Just wanted to close up the room and try to forget."

"Well, he cared enough about one thing," commented Kay, pointing at the gray, covered mound beneath the window. "How about it, Jess? Let's see what it was."

Jessie walked over to the window, and she grabbed the sheet with both hands. It was heavy with dust. "Ugh." She pulled off the covering. There stood an exquisite writing desk whose smooth wood was rich with color.

"Probably mahogany with a satinwood veneer," Kay guessed, standing next to her friend. "Lovely."

A small stack of cream-colored paper impressed with a D on the top lay neatly on the desk. Next to it was a fountain pen. Kay busily recorded the desk on film. Jessie reached for the pen, then stopped herself. "Think I'll just leave it for now," she said. She wanted to come back by herself and explore the contents of the desk. *Maybe that's the pen she used to write her letters or poetry,* she thought to herself.

"Nice fireplace," observed Henry from the other side of the room. "Not sure you could use it now, but the carving in the woodwork is wonderful."

Jessie joined him at the fireplace. "This is beautiful," she whispered. She stood next to Henry, suddenly aware of the quiet strength of his presence. There was a sense of comfort in it that she could not explain. She felt herself blush.

The snapping and whirring of Kay's camera broke the awkward silence. "This is fantastic!" the realtor exclaimed. "You could totally restore this room to its original state. See the wallpaper? Faded, yes, but not completely! I have an artist friend who could decipher the pattern and recreate the paper for you! We could get Martha to take a look at the bedclothes. She's a whiz at sewing. I'm sure Henry could help retrofit the fixtures for electricity. This could be absolutely fabulous!"

"Sounds expensive," muttered Jessie.

"And look at this marvelous antique rug. Perhaps it could be carefully cleaned and restored. This has real possibilities, Jessie Woods. Why, it would be like a little museum. You could frame the letters and—"

"And charge admittance," snorted Sam.

Jessie laughed. "Kay, you really need to calm down." Jessie turned toward Sam. He was staring at the fireplace. "You've been awfully quiet, Sam. Kay's ideas making your head spin?"

Sam stood back from the fireplace. "Something's missing," he said. "See the blank space above the mantel? My guess is that there was a painting hung there." He pointed to the wall. "See? If you look real close, you can see a faint outline. Must have been a fairly nice-sized painting."

Jessie now stood between Henry and Sam. As they all peered up at the wall, Jessie was painfully aware of both men. She sensed such goodness and kindness in them both. *Calm down, Jess,* she said to herself. *Are you going out of your mind? Steady, girl, steady. Must be a lack of sleep,* she decided. *That's it. I'm tired and feeling emotional.*

Kay pushed her way through the threesome and snapped several photos of the fireplace and blank wall. "This is so thrilling! Don't you think so?" She looked at the two men and her friend stuck uneasily in between. She winked at Jessie. "So thrilling?"

Jessie quickly turned away and strode over to a bureau that stood in another corner of the room. On top of the piece of furniture was a small grouping of pictures. One picture was a daguerreotype; it appeared to be a picture of a very beautiful woman. Jessie reached for it. Kay screeched a resounding "No!" as she rushed over and photographed the bureau. "Don't touch anything until I'm done with the whole room. Okay," she said, walking away from the bureau, "you can touch the picture now. It's a daguerreotype, you know."

Jessie gently picked up the picture. Henry joined her. He handed her a handkerchief. She carefully wiped the dust off the glass.

"She's beautiful," whispered Jessie. The woman in the picture wore a sweeping gown covered with lace. Her hair was swept back with coils of braids about the nape of her neck. Over her ears hung small ringlets. Her eyes were lit with clarity and sweetness.

"Maybe it's Amelia's mother," Jessie pondered aloud. "Too bad she died so early. I've read about her in the letters. Look at those eyes!"

"Yes," said Henry, studying the picture and the woman holding the picture. "She's beautiful."

"I'm ready for lunch," groaned Sam. "I've had enough of the past for today. Can we please go out and grab some lunch? I vote for Cherry's. How does that sound?" Sam walked out of the room. "Anybody coming?" he called over his shoulder.

"I vote yes," chirped Kay. "This is the last of the pictures." She circled the room, snapping away with her camera. "Done!" she cried, taking one last picture of a small corner table. "Let's go!"

Jessie reluctantly restored the daguerreotype to the bureau. "All right," she agreed, eyeing the other photographs on the bureau. "I suppose the rest can await my scrutiny."

"It is lunch time," said Henry, looking at his watch. "Just let me get my tools and put them in the truck. I'll come back later and clean up this mess," he volunteered. There was plaster and chunks of wood scattered in the hallway. "Don't trip," he cautioned Jessie. He reached out his hand to her. She took hold and made her way gingerly through the debris.

At the touch of Jessie's hand, Henry panicked and tripped over his tools. He fell headlong into a pile of wood scraps and plaster. Jessie lost her balance and joined him on the floor. The plaster flew up and engulfed them in a dusty whiteness.

Kay stood in the opening of the wall, unattended. "What am I? Chopped liver?"

Sam heard the commotion and returned to the scene. "What's this?" One look at the two blushing ghosts on the floor and the disgruntled realtor sent the pastor into spasms of laughter. Henry apologized, over and over again. He got up and offered Jessie his hand again, but by now his hands were so sweaty that he lost his grip and down plopped Jessie again.

"Oh, no," apologized Henry. "I'm so sorry, Mrs. Woods. I can't believe it. I'm so—"

"Allow me to intervene before you both hurt yourselves," interrupted Sam. He reached down and helped the fallen woman to her feet.

"Really, Mrs. Woods, I am so sorry. I'm such a lunkhead!" said Henry.

"Jessie," consoled the woman. "My name is Jessie."

"And I'm Kay Bantam," announced the forgotten friend. "Could we please get this entourage on the road?"

Sam laughed and offered Kay his hand. They successfully maneuvered the hazardous hallway. The group descended the stairs, Henry apologizing all the way, Jessie accepting, and Sam laughing 'til the tears came. Kay brought up the rear, muttering about the injustice of it all.

At the diner, the four sat at a booth by a window that looked out onto the street. Jessie and Henry had managed to remove most of the plaster dust from their clothes and hair.

"I don't know, Jess. You've gotten awfully gray in the last few minutes. You ought to think about coloring your hair," Kay suggested with a giggle.

"Very funny," responded Jessie. "Let's order. I'm starved!"

"That's a good sign," said Sam, half under his breath.

Jessie frowned at the Reverend Taylor. She gave him a you'd-better-mind-your-own-business look.

The waitress came, brought them water, and took their orders. She studied Jessie for a moment. "You're the woman who bought the old Denver place, aren't you?"

"Why, yes, I am," Jessie replied.

"Sarah Temple, meet Jessie Woods," said Sam. "Jessie, this is Sarah, the best waitress this side of the Mississippi."

The waitress blushed and picked up the menus. "Oh, Reverend Taylor, you're embarrassing me!"

"Now, Sarah, you know it's true," Sam waved his hand. "I'll let you in on a top secret." He leaned toward his companions for effect. "Sarah makes the best chocolate milkshakes in the world!"

Sarah laughed and stuck her pen behind her ear. "Pshaw. I'll be right back with your orders." She turned to go and then stopped. "Did you open the secret room today?" she asked Jessie Woods.

Jessie choked on the water she was drinking.

"Yes, we're working on it," volunteered Kay. "It's really exciting; we found—"

Kay felt a pain in her leg. "Youch!" she yelped.

"What's the matter?" Henry asked.

Jessie glared at her friend.

"A sharp pain," snorted Kay, "that flares up now and again."

The waitress left with their orders.

"What's the matter, Jess? What did you kick me for?"

Jessie ignored Kay's question. "How did she know about the room? Does the whole town know my business?"

Sam laughed. "Of course the whole town knows. We're small, remember? This is Carlisle, not the Big Apple. We're more like the Small Pear."

"And here comes one of the local fruits now," said Kay under her breath.

Henry tried not to laugh. They looked out the window and saw Mary Benson walking briskly down the street. She caught sight of Sam Taylor in the window of the diner, and her demeanor changed from a brisk walk to a saucy sashay.

Sam dropped his head into his hands. "Oh, no," he groaned. "Somebody help."

"Samuel Taylor," whispered Jessie. "Is that any way for a reverend to talk?"

Henry just laughed and slapped his friend on the back.

"Leave her to me," said Kay matter-of-factly. "I'll handle this."

Sam looked up at Kay and groaned again. "Somebody help me."

Chapter 14

Hello, Sam," cooed Mary as she entered the diner and approached the foursome. "How are you today?"

"Just fine, Mary," responded Sam. "And how are you? Busy today at the boutique?"

"Busy as usual." The woman heaved a grand sigh. "You know how everyone simply adores our clothes and accessories."

"Yes, they certainly do," Kay piped up. "The clothes are simply fantabulous. I adore the new skirts and blouses you have in stock. The colors are so bold and bodacious. They simply scream fashion." Kay fingered her blouse. It was silk, covered with sunflowers on a cream-colored background. "Take this blouse, for instance. It's positively drenched with color."

"It screams something, all right," agreed Jessie. "But what is it screaming? Fashion? Or look out for the revenge of the killer sunflowers?" Jessie laughed. "I know it makes me want to scream."

Henry choked then covered his face with his napkin.

Kay huffed. "You just don't appreciate art, Jessie Woods. Clothes can be a work of art. You know, like Rembrandt."

"Or Picasso," suggested Jessie, holding back the laughter.

Henry looked at Kay. During her intense discourse on fashion, her big maroon glasses had slipped, and now they hung crooked on her nose. Thoughts of Picasso overwhelmed Henry, and he could not help himself. He let it go with a yelp, and the tears rolled down his cheeks. Sam gave him a chiding look.

"Well, I can see at least you appreciate fine clothes," sniffed Mary to the realtor. "There are so few who do."

"Yes," agreed Kay, "so few. But you know, I must say the prices are a bit high."

"They have to be," answered Mary. "Exclusive fashion demands a high price. It's not for everyone." She cast a glance at Jessie. "I've never seen you there," she said, as if giving an example.

Jessie smiled graciously. "I'm not one for high fashion."

"I've noticed," responded Mary sweetly. She turned her attention to the pastor. "What time is the fellowship tomorrow night?"

"Seven o'clock at the parsonage," Sam replied. "And you are all welcome to come," he said, looking at all his companions.

"I'll be there," sang Mary as she walked away. "Have to get back to the store. Bye, Sam."

Sam gave everyone his do-not-say-a-word look. Kay glared at Jessie and Henry. "I hope you two enjoyed yourselves," she said. Henry and Jessie mumbled halfhearted apologies.

"I couldn't help it," said Jessie. "I mean really, Kay. You know how I feel about your taste in clothes."

"I know," giggled Kay. "The same way I feel about yours: one word."

"Gag!" the two friends chorused.

The waitress came with their food, and they set about to enjoy lunch. Several minutes passed as the group concentrated on the delicious food. They did not notice a man approach and stand quietly behind their table.

"Hello, everyone," the man spoke.

Jessie jumped and spilled her water. A startled Kay dropped her fork. It flipped off her plate, sending a green spray of salad flying into Henry's face.

"Herb!" exclaimed Sam.

"Didn't hear me coming, did you!" said Herb Stamping, his voice glowing with triumph.

"You could choke a person doing that," cried Kay.

"And look at this mess!" said Sam, sopping up the water from Jessie's glass.

"Oh, I'm sorry," apologized the postal worker. "You two certainly are a bit jumpy, aren't you? Is everything all right?" he asked, his voice mounting with excitement. "Hey, did you find something unusual in the secret room? What happened?"

Jessie rolled her eyes. "I don't believe this," she said under her breath.

"No, nothing unusual," said Sam. "Just furniture."

Herb looked furtively around the diner, then leaned over the table. "You had better be careful, Mrs. Woods," he said darkly, with a knowing look.

Jessie felt a shiver run up her spine. In the excitement of opening the room, she had forgotten the night of the possible intruder. "Why do you say that, Mr. Stamping?" she asked, trying to sound unconcerned.

"Let's just say there may be someone besides yourself interested in that secret room," he whispered.

"Yeah, like every citizen in Carlisle," sighed Jessie, pouring herself more water.

"Now, Herb," spoke Sam, "where did you get that idea?"

"I wonder," snorted Henry.

Herb ignored Henry. "A very reliable source, I must say."

"Ruby Clearwater?" asked Sam. "Have you been talking to Ruby?"

A faint blush appeared on the man's pale cheeks. His pointy chin jutted out defensively. "Yes, I've spoken to Ruby."

Sam smiled. "Now, Herb, what's our Ruby up to this time?"

Herb relaxed and stuck his hands in his pockets. He glanced at Jessie Woods. "Well," he began, "Ruby says there's someone very interested in the Denver house. She says—"

"Now, Herb, who in this town isn't interested in the Denver house? After all, everyone's heard about the legend of the gold." He gave Herb a look. "Let's not spook Mrs. Woods with any of Ruby's stories."

"Now, Sam," interjected Jessie, "I'd like to hear what the man has to say."

"Me, too," said Kay. "Tell us everything you know! This is turning into a real mystery!"

Herb looked at the expectant women and the frowning men. He cleared his throat. "Ruby says there's a writer in town who's been researching the Denver family."

"So, what's so weird about that?" asked Sam. "The man's a writer. Nothing mysterious about that."

"As a matter of fact," continued Herb, "I happen to know the man is working on a novel about a small town."

"A novel," said Henry. "Case closed."

"Oh," said Jessie.

"But Ruby doesn't like the looks of him," Herb volunteered, ignoring Sam for the moment. "Says he doesn't look like a writer."

Sam laughed. "Just like Irving, remember? The CIA man."

"Well, I must admit, she certainly was wrong that time," chortled Herb.

"Let me explain," said Sam, noting the puzzled looks on the women's faces. "Ruby Clearwater has a very active imagination. She's very creative. In fact, she heads up the drama group in our church. Does a great job. Anyway, she has a way of suspecting strangers who come to town. Thought Irving Winters was with the CIA."

"At any rate, I still say Mrs. Woods should be careful," Herb insisted. "You never know."

"Thank you, Mr. Stamping," said Jessie. "I appreciate your concern."

"All right then," nodded Herb, feeling his point had been made, his mission accomplished. "Good day."

"Interesting," hummed Kay.

"Makes me nervous," said Jessie, poking at her pasta salad with her fork. "What if—"

"Forget about it," suggested Sam. "Those sounds you heard the other night were probably a combination of the wind and the creaky old house."

"Probably," agreed Kay. "Although I must say it's a bit disappointing. After all, between Camilla's stories, Ruby's innuendoes, and Jessie's imagina—"

"I happen to think it was not my imagination!" interrupted Jessie, her voice trembling with emotion. She fished money out of her purse and slapped it on the table. "That should more than cover my lunch. I'm going home to my creaky old house!"

Henry, Sam, and Kay watched as Jessie stomped out of the diner, leaving them there with their mouths hanging open.

"Oops," said Sam. "Guess I shouldn't have said 'creaky old house' to her."

"Double oops," agreed Kay. "She really was frightened the other night. Whether it was her imagination or not, she's still upset about it. Guess I would be, too, living alone in that big old place."

"I'm going to clean up the mess over there," said Henry curtly.

He paid for his lunch and left.

"What's eating him?" Kay asked Sam. "What's going on?"

Sam shook his head and took a sip of his now-cold coffee. "Well, it's my guess that Henry is quite taken with Mrs. Woods."

"And you? What about you?" pressed Kay. "If you haven't noticed, Reverend Taylor, I'm pretty straightforward about things. I call 'em like I see 'em. And it seems to me that Samuel Taylor is quite taken with Jessie Woods, as well. What gives?"

Sam rubbed his hand over his face. His gray-blue eyes glistened with warmth. "You are an interesting woman, Kay. I like your candor, and you're obviously a good, loyal friend to Jessie. Have you ever considered becoming a Christian?"

Kay adjusted her big glasses. "Don't change the subject," she said. "If you must know, I have been thinking about this Christian stuff. Since my divorce, I've come to the conclusion there must be more to life than emotional pain. But we'll talk about that another time. Right now, we're talking about you."

Sam's handsome face lit up with a smile. "Now there's a refreshing occurrence! A pastor being treated like a regular human being with regular human-being needs! Bravo, Ms. Bantam. It will be a pleasure having you for a sister in Christ."

Kay laughed. "You certainly have a way with making grand pronouncements about other people, don't you! First it was your proposal to Jess, now you're telling me I'll surely become a Christian."

"Some things I just know that I know."

"All right, Mr. Know-it-all. What do you know about Jessie, Henry, and you? Spill it," demanded Kay.

"What about you?" countered the pastor. "What do you see?"

"Henry is a great guy. But I think he's just infatuated with Jessie. She's beautiful and kind. He's probably never married, and now here comes Jess. She's swept him off his feet."

Sam laughed. "I don't know. You could say that about me, Kay. I've never married. Jessie is beautiful and kind. Maybe she's swept me off my feet. Maybe it's just infatuation with me, too. Henry and I have been friends for years. He's a great guy." His voice was warm with affection. "I would never stand in the way of either one's happiness."

"Bravo," said Kay. "That's real love. Don't you see? You really do love her. And what about all that stuff you said about God showing you things? Didn't you say that sometimes you just know that you know?"

"Yes, I said that," Sam conceded, "but I've lived long enough to know sometimes I'm wrong about things. I guess my point is that the Lord has His own way of doing things. I don't want to get in the way. He makes all things beautiful in His time," Sam said, paraphrasing Ecclesiastes 3:11.

"All right," said Kay. "You certainly know more about God than I do. And I'm willing to learn. But I will say this: Don't be afraid to speak your mind to Jessie Woods."

"All right," agreed Sam. "Hey, why don't you come to fellowship Sunday night? We're meeting together to discuss the Gospel. There will be both Christians and unbelievers present. It should be interesting."

"I'll be there," replied Kay. "I don't know why, but I find myself being drawn to Christianity. Jessie has tried for years to convert me, but I would never listen. Now, it's different."

"He makes all things beautiful in His time," repeated Sam.

"Could it really happen for me?" asked Kay wistfully.

"All you have to do is say yes," explained Sam. "Say yes to Him."

"I'll take those words home with me, Reverend Taylor," responded Kay. She shook his hand. "Thanks for listening."

"Thank you!" said Sam. "It's been a very refreshing conversation."

Chapter 15

Jessie's hands trembled as she tried to unlock the front door to her home. She turned as she heard the sound of a vehicle in the driveway. It was Henry's red truck.

"Wait, Jessie," Henry called, jumping out of the truck. "I want to talk to you."

Jessie unlocked the door and motioned for Henry to come in. She walked down the hall to the kitchen. "How about a cup of tea?" she asked.

"No, thank you," answered Henry. "I'm fine."

She put the kettle on and sat down at the table. Henry joined her. Jessie fingered the warm grain of the oval oak table. There were a few scattered scars and watermarks from three generations of use. Jessie knew every marking.

"This was my grandmother's table," she said. "There are many fine memories surrounding this lovely wood."

Henry nodded. The stillness in the room was awkward for the two. The only sound was the humming of the teakettle on the electric range. The humming swelled to a whistle. Jessie poured the water into a mug, the teabag bloating and bobbing in the hot water. Jessie and Henry studied it as though it were the most fascinating thing in the world. Anything to avoid eye contact.

Finally, Henry spoke. "I'm sorry about today's conversation at the diner. I know you're still upset about the other night. Sam told me all about it."

"You mean the night I heard crazy sounds in this creaky old house?" said Jessie sarcastically.

"Come on, Jessie," spoke Henry softly. "You know Sam didn't mean anything by it." Henry looked earnestly into Jessie's eyes. "I happen to know Sam cares a great deal about you. He's probably trying to keep things light to keep you from worrying too much about it."

The concern in the man's voice warmed Jessie's heart, pulling at her emotions. Once again the sight of Henry's engaging green eyes swept Jessie into a whirl of feelings she could not decipher. Henry reached across the table and shyly rested his hand over Jessie's.

"I'm worried about you, Jessie. You seem to be struggling with a lot of mixed emotions. I know about your husband. I'm sorry you had to go through that. But I think maybe the Lord is trying to draw you into a new time in your life." He cleared his throat. "I think you need to get out more and fellowship."

Jessie smiled. "And with whom do you suggest I fellowship?"

Henry blushed, pulled his hand away, and promptly knocked Jessie's mug of tea over with a bang.

"Oh, no!" cried Henry. He jumped up and looked around the room for a solution. Spying a sponge on the windowsill above the sink, he grabbed it. His hand caught on the curtain and down it came, rod and all.

"Oh, no!" repeated Henry. "Now look what I've done!"

Jessie valiantly tried not to laugh. She pulled a couple of paper towels from the rack and sopped up the splattered tea.

"I'm sorry, Jessie. I'm afraid I'm just a klutz with delicate things. I can build houses and repair just about anything, but when it comes to stuff like this, I. . ."

Jessie laid her hand on Henry's shoulder. "It's okay, Henry Lewis. No one said you had to be perfect."

Henry hesitated only for a moment. Then he drew Jessie into his strong arms and held her close. She trembled in his arms. Then, to her utter surprise, she began to weep and the tension of the last few days dissolved in a flow of tears. When at last she stopped, Henry gently lifted her head by the chin and kissed her. The sweetness of his kiss was almost more than Jessie could bear.

"Excuse me!" Kay's voice erupted from the doorway to the hall. "I came to see if you were all right, Jess. I let myself in. Sorry about that." Kay adjusted her glasses and inspected the twosome. "I'd say everything is under control, I guess." Her eyes sparkled with glee.

Startled, Henry and Jessie pulled apart from each other.

"Kay!" gasped Jessie. "Did you have to—"

"Sorry," responded her friend. "I didn't mean to interrupt." She folded her arms. "Carry on," she grinned.

Jessie picked up the sponge and threw it at her. Henry stuffed his hands in his pockets. "I guess I'll be going upstairs now to clean up the mess." He hurried past Kay.

"Kay Bantam, I ought to murderize you!" whispered Jessie. "I can't believe you just waltzed right in and—"

"You can't believe it?" hissed Kay. "I can't believe what I just saw! Jessie Woods, Henry Lewis was kissing you!"

Jessie leaned against the sink to steady herself. "I know it, Sherlock." She stopped. "I can't believe it myself."

"Well, what are you going to do about it?" demanded Kay.

"Shh," hushed Jessie. "What do you mean, what am I going to do about it? I don't even know what it means. Now, let's discuss this later, if you please."

"How was it?" Kay asked, her voice squeaking with delight.

"Oh, Kay, calm down. We're not in high school anymore. We're two grown-up, reasonable people. Now, calm down."

"Oh, I'm not the one who needs to calm down," smiled Kay. "Go take a look in the hall mirror, Miss Red-Cheeks-All-Aglow-and-Eyes-Sparkling."

Jessie hurried down the hall. She peered at herself in the mirror that hung over her flower table. The woman looking back at her did, indeed, have a flush to her cheeks. Jessie raised her hand to her face.

"Oh, Kay," she whispered, "what am I going to do?"

"Nothing," Kay whispered back. "Just go with the flow and stop thinking so hard. Maybe God is trying to tell you something."

The doorbell chimed. "That'll be Sam," said Kay. "This is great, isn't it?"

Kay pulled open the door and in strode the pastor. Jessie stood helplessly rooted to the floor. Sam stopped and searched her face for understanding. Something in her eyes made him unsure of himself.

"I'm sorry about what I said," he spoke haltingly. "About the creaky old house. It's a nice house, really. I like it. I didn't mean to sound like I didn't like it. I like old houses. They're nice, in a homey sort of way. I—"

"You're babbling," Kay interjected. "Talk about me babbling when I'm nervous! You're as bad as I am. I bet this is the first time in your life you've ever babbled. I'd say—"

"Kay, you're not going to say anything," said Jessie. "Please!" She turned to Sam. "It's okay, Sam. Apology accepted. I think I was just stressed out from the whole thing."

"You look fine now," commented Sam.

"Oh, she's really fine," drawled Kay. "Super fine."

Jessie threw a glare at her friend.

"I thought I'd help Henry clean up," volunteered the pastor. "Sometimes two work better than one."

"I'd say," laughed Kay.

Sam retreated up the stairs. Jessie listened as he greeted his friend. The two men proceeded to make quick work of the hall and room. Jessie walked Kay out to the front porch, and she shut the door after them.

"I'll see you later," said Kay. "I've got to show a house at two-thirty. Nice one, over on Larchmont."

"Good," responded Jessie. "Keep yourself busy and out of my hair."

"You'll have to face it, sooner or later," cautioned Kay.

"Face what?" Jessie was afraid to ask.

"You've got two men up there who are obviously interested in you, to put it mildly. And you're going to have to choose. I should have such a problem."

"Kay Bantam, I think you're exaggerating. Anyway, I'm not going to think about that right now."

"You'll think about it tomorrow, right, Scarlett?" Kay laughed.

"Shoo," exclaimed Jessie. "Go to work. I'll see you tomorrow. I'm taking my own car to church tomorrow. I promised Lorena I'd give her a ride to her church.

I'll meet you at First Baptist."

"Same pew, same time." Kay smiled. "I'm really starting to like church, Jess. I think all your prayers are starting to work."

"Oh, Kay." Jessie reached for her friend and gave her a hug. "That's wonderful!"

"Bye."

Jessie watched her friend in the sunflowered blouse hurry to her sporty car and drive away. She whispered a prayer for her. A feeling of conviction shot through her. "I'm sorry, Lord," she whispered as Kay's car disappeared down the street. "It's been a long time since I prayed for anyone."

She sat down on one of the white wicker chairs on the porch. The afternoon sun was weaving gold in the branches of the trees. The old rosebushes in the front brimmed with color, rich red against green foliage. Two little girls across the street were giggling. They played make-believe with their beloved dolls. The scattered chirps of birds sprinkled the air with music. From somewhere a boy's voice called for his companion to hurry up and throw the ball. "Come on!" he called, his voice young and clear. The sights and music of the day felt fresh and new to Jessie Woods.

"It's like I'm waking up from a long sleep," mused Jessie. She closed her eyes. The sounds and smells of Lark Avenue filled her senses.

When she opened her eyes, she could see Tom, standing at the bottom of the stone steps. He was smiling up at her. His face radiated with happiness.

"Tom!" Jessie tried to call out to him. "What are you doing here?" The words stuck in her throat.

Tom did not say a word but waved his hand and walked away.

"Tom!" Jessie tried to call to him but could not. She struggled to get out of the chair.

"Jessie! Jessie, wake up!" a voice pierced the haze.

Jessie managed to open her eyes. Lorena was standing over her.

"You fell asleep, my dear. I think you were dreaming."

Jessie looked up into Lorena's kind face. "Yes, I guess I just dozed off."

"I brought you over some fried chicken and biscuits. I know you've been busy with the house and all." She handed Jessie a large basket covered with white linen napkins.

"Oh, this is wonderful!" exclaimed Jessie. "Come on in and see the secret room. I know you'll appreciate it."

Lorena's face lit up. "I would love to see it! This is so exciting. I feel like a schoolgirl on the first day of school."

Jessie brought Lorena inside.

"Don't come up yet!" Henry's voice boomed from upstairs. "Bags of plaster coming down."

Jessie led Lorena into the living room, and they watched as Sam and Henry hauled the bags down the stairs and out the front doorway.

"How nice that Sam and Henry could help you," smiled Lorena. "They certainly are gentlemen."

Jessie smiled, and her eyebrows went up. "They certainly are." Her voice betrayed her nervousness.

Lorena patted Jessie's hand. "This is good, my dear, very good. Everything will turn out just the way the Lord has planned it to be."

"Hi, Lorena. Nice to see you." Sam stood in the doorway. "We're done. We did the best we could, but there's still a film of plaster dust all over. Henry's dumping the last bag in the truck. We're leaving now."

Jessie and Lorena followed Sam out the door. Both men were covered with dust. Henry put the last of his tools into the back of his truck, then he wiped his hands on his pants. "When you figure out how you want to do the wall, let me know," said Henry. "I'll have it fixed up in no time." He smiled. "Nice to see you, Lorena." He nodded to Jessie's neighbor. "It's a beautiful day." He grinned and climbed into his truck.

Sam rolled his eyes. "Beautiful!" he muttered, climbing in next to Henry. "See you tomorrow, ladies!" he said aloud.

"Bye, Pastor Taylor! Bye, Henry!" called Lorena.

Jessie waved. Her heart soared for reasons not yet clear to her.

At last life was awakening within her. Someone was calling her name, and she was beginning to hear His voice more clearly.

"I must say Henry Lewis looks as though he's kind of glowing, wouldn't you say, Jessie?" said Lorena thoughtfully. "Wonder what happened to him?"

Jessie just smiled and led her new friend up the stairs to the secret room.

Chapter 16

After Lorena's tour of the secret room, Jessie was left alone with her thoughts. She sat on the bottom of the stairs in the foyer as the events of the day played out in her mind. It had been an incredible day: Amelia's wonderful room, the diner episode, and especially Henry. . .Henry and Jessie in the kitchen. Her cheeks reddened at the thought of his kiss.

"I can't believe it happened," she said aloud, directing her words to Joseph, the little Scottish terrier statue. She had placed it in the foyer next to the door leading into the living room; a red-and-green plaid ribbon graced his neck. "After all, it's been years since. . . ," her voice trailed away. Images of the dream of Tom on the front porch flickered in her mind.

"Whoa. Maybe that dream means something. Sometimes God speaks to people in dreams, doesn't He, Joseph?" She smiled. "Cute. I'm talking to a statue about dreams!"

Jessie made up her mind to make an appointment with Sam. She felt he had showed himself to be a good friend. Her observations of him as a pastor revealed a man trusted and beloved by his congregation. She knew he had the reputation of being an excellent counselor.

"Well, what have I got to lose?" she asked herself. "He seems to be able to read me like a book. I'll just call him and tell him I need to talk."

She ran up the stairs to her bedroom. The sun was in the process of setting, and its retreating light colored her room with a hazy yellow. Her white eyelet comforter and the wing chair were bathed in pale amber. She walked over to the old print, hanging next to one of the windows. It was a painting of a young girl, sitting at a wishing well. One hand held a clutch of wildflowers, the other rested softly on the edge of the well. Her blue eyes looked with longing beyond the wishing well to a green hill rising faintly in the distance.

"And what are you longing for, little one?" she whispered to the painting.

Sam's card lay on her bedstand where she had put it the night of the big scare. She sat on her bed, picked up the phone, and dialed his number.

"Sam Taylor," his voice answered.

"Sam? This is Jessie."

"Jessie. What are you. . .I mean hello. How are you?" Sam sounded flummoxed.

"Fine, Sam," replied Jessie. "I'm calling to make an appointment with you for a counseling session."

"Oh." Sam sounded disappointed.

"I know the Lord has been working on my heart. Between you, Lorena, and everything else, I'm starting to realize there are some wrongs that need to be made right."

"That's wonderful," Sam responded. "How about Monday at eleven o'clock? Usually my secretary makes the appointments, so you'll have to call to confirm. She's in at nine-thirty. Give her a buzz then to be sure. I tend to forget who's scheduled when, but I would love to see you."

"Sam, it's for counseling. . .not a date," chided Jessie.

"Aw, Jess," drawled Sam, laughing. "But seriously, I think this is great. I've known since I first saw you that you were a time bomb just waiting to go off. I've been praying—"

"Time bomb!" an indignant Jessie exploded. "I resent that statement. I may have a problem, but I certainly am not a basket case about to go off the deep end into a blubbering oblivion. Of all the terrible, low-blow, rotten things to say. You—"

"Jessie," Sam's voice was soft, "calm down."

"I am calm," Jessie hissed into the receiver. "Cool as a cucumber."

"Right," said Sam. "I'll see you tomorrow at church, okay? I'm sorry you're upset—"

"Oh, yes, there's the classic male apology. 'I'm sorry you're upset,' which really means you're not sorry at all. You're putting all the blame on me. After all, you didn't say anything wrong, right? I'm the one that got upset over nothing, right?"

"Jessie, I'm sorry. We'll talk about this on Monday."

"Fat chance!" rebuffed Jessie. "You can forget about my appointment. I wouldn't go to you for counsel if you were the last silver-haired, blue-eyed pastor on this planet!" With that, she banged down the receiver.

Sam sat at the other end of the line, the receiver dangling in his hand. A smile spread slowly across his face. He leaned back in his swivel desk chair and let out a laugh.

" 'Silver-haired, blue-eyed pastor!' She noticed. I think she likes me!"

Jessie sat, shaking, on her bed. "The nerve of that guy," she huffed. She looked down at her trembling hands. "Oh, Lord," she sighed, the anger diffusing. "I guess I really do need some help, after all."

⚭

The next morning at church Jessie again found herself sitting behind little Madeline.

"Mornin', Mrs. Woods," chirped the girl, her blond curls bobbing up and down. "How are you?"

"I'm fine, Madeline. I'm surprised you remembered my name," said Jessie. "You must have a very good memory."

"Yup," replied the child with great satisfaction. "I gots a good rememberer. My dad says I take after Mommy. He says Mommy never forgets nothing, even stuff that happened lots of time ago. Says she's worse than an elephant. Elephants never forget, you know," Madeline explained.

Jessie nodded. "Yes, that's true."

Madeline scrutinized Jessie's face. "Are you all right?" she demanded. "You look kind of pinched."

"My, my," responded Jessie with a smile, "but whatever do you mean?"

Madeline curled her little hands over the top of the pew. "Oh, you know. Like you been crying or you haven't cried enough. My mommy says it's good to let out your tears 'cause otherwise they get stuck. Are your tears stuck, Mrs. Woods? My big brother says if you don't cry, someday your head might explode. He's ten. He knows everything. He can spit farther than Sonny Templeton any day. But my gramma says the tears fall back inside your heart, and your heart gets hard and busts into a million pieces, and then you haven't got any heart anymore." She stopped, out of breath. She looked at Jessie. "Well?"

Jessie placed her hand gently on Madeline's. "I think maybe they're a little stuck," she whispered.

Madeline's forehead puckered. "Then I shall pray to Jesus. He is the best tear unstucker there is. Our pastor man always says Jesus can get that stuff out if we let Him. I guess you have to use a pitcher or a cup or something because you have to pour out your heart to Him. That's for the tears, you know. Do you have a pitcher for your tears, Mrs. Woods?"

"I think so," said Jessie. "I'll check when I get home."

The organ began to sing. Madeline smiled at Jessie, turned around, and plopped back down on her seat, practically disappearing from sight. Jessie looked down at the bulletin in her lap. She shook her head in disbelief. On it was a picture of a brook, flowing rapidly over rocks on a gleaming green hillside. Psalm 62:8 was emblazoned across the top: "Trust in him at all times, O people; pour out your hearts to him, for God is our refuge."

"Oh, thank You, Lord," she whispered. "You are really calling me to Yourself."

After the service, Jessie shook Sam's hand on her way out. "I'm sorry," she said softly.

"That's okay," said Sam. "See you tonight?"

"Yes," replied Jessie. "We'll be there."

∞

While church was in session at First Baptist of Carlisle, a painter's truck appeared at 16 Lark Avenue. Spencer Hart got out of his truck and walked around to the side of the house. After making sure there were no neighbors outside, he hurried onto the back porch. The window was open. He smiled and let himself in.

"You don't have much time, Hart, so you better make it quick," he said to himself.

He climbed the stairs and headed for the secret room. He cursed when he saw the furniture was still covered with dust. "Can't touch anything. Just have to look."

Spencer carefully inspected the bureau, the vanity, and the writing desk. The large, marble-topped vanity caught his attention. He made a mental note of its construction and design. Kneeling down, he scrutinized the base of the piece. A wry smile slowly spread across his stubbled face. Checking his watch, he hurried out of the room and out of the house.

"I'll be back," he said under his breath, "and it'll be pay-dirt time!"

∞

Kay parked her car in Jessie's driveway. Her head was topped with a large-brimmed red hat. The red-and-white pantsuit she wore was accessorized with a fire-engine red purse and matching shoes. Jessie's eyes widened with amazement.

"Not a word," warned Kay.

Together they walked across the street to Reverend Taylor's home. Already there were several cars parked in his driveway and on the street. Jessie noticed Henry's truck.

"This ought to be good," said Kay gleefully. "I love discussions. I hope there's an even spread of disbelievers, believers, and undecideds. It would make for an invigorating conversation. Absolutely salubrious."

Jessie eyed her companion. "Been reading *Reader's Digest* again, Kay?"

"Healthy, good for you. Salubrious. Discussion is good for the soul."

"Oh, boy," said Jessie. "That's all I need. Another heated discussion."

Kay stopped her friend on the sidewalk. "Heated discussion? Hey, who have you been having heated discussions with, Jessie? Come on, tell me all the juicy details. Let me guess. Sam Taylor. He's getting under your skin, isn't he?"

"Well, we've had our moments," was all Jessie would say.

"And what about your moments with a certain Henry Lewis? And I see his truck. He's here tonight. Although I'm sure I didn't notice you noticing a certain red vehicle."

"Oh, Kay, hush before someone hears you. Let's go." She pulled her friend up the walk to Sam's front door.

The door was opened at their knock by none other than the smiling Mary Benson. Her smile quickly faded when she saw the two women standing at the door. Jessie and Kay smiled, said hello, and glided past her into the living room.

"Well, hello there," Martha's voice sounded from the other side of the room. "Welcome!"

Chairs were arranged casually about the large room. Jessie recognized a few people from church; the rest were strangers to her.

"Have a seat," ordered Martha, smiling. "Over here on the couch."

Jessie and Kay obeyed. The kitchen door swung open and in marched Sam and Henry, armed with trays of drinks.

"Hello, ladies." Sam smiled at Jessie and Kay. Henry almost tripped when he saw Jessie.

"Henry!" exclaimed Sam. "Careful!"

Sam laid down his tray on one of the coffee tables and then relieved Henry of his tray. "This is Martha's fruit punch," he announced grandly. "Everyone in Carlisle knows Martha makes the best punch in town. And only I know the secret ingredient, right, Martha?"

"Oh, go on," blushed Martha. "I'll go get the rest of the snacks. Dig in, folks." She bustled into the kitchen.

Sam had everyone introduce themselves. There was quite an assortment of people and a general air of anticipation.

"For those of you who are here for the first time, this is our third meeting," said Sam. "So far it has been a successful experiment, wouldn't you say, Jim?"

The professor from a nearby college nodded. "It's been fun. I quite enjoy it. So far, we've managed to discuss the issue of faith without losing our dignity or our tempers."

Everyone laughed. "That's right," said George, owner of the gas station at the end of town. "It's been good."

Sam beamed. "Tonight our topic is the temptation of Christ."

"You mean the temptation in the wilderness?" asked Herb Stamping.

"No, I mean His temptation at Gethsemane. The greatest temptation Christ ever faced. . .the temptation not to die." Sam proceeded to read the account from Matthew, chapter 26.

Everyone listened attentively. Sam finished reading. "Why was Christ overwhelmed with sorrow? Why did He ask His Father to find another way to atone for the people?"

"Because He was a man," someone replied firmly. "No human wants to die, particularly a horrible, painful death. Jesus was a man, wasn't He?"

"Yes, but He was. . .is God, too," piped up Martha as she walked by bearing a tray of cheese and crackers. "Fully God and fully man," she quoted, placing down her tray.

"If you believe that," said a tall man with dark brown glasses.

"Bob Gadry, I used to wipe your nose when you were knee-high to a grasshopper. Your momma—and we were best friends, you know—didn't raise you to be an atheist!"

"Now, Martha," chided Sam, "let the man speak. We're here to listen to one another, remember?"

"That's okay, Sam," laughed Mr. Gadry. "Martha is a born boss. She can't help it."

Martha smiled and vainly tried to reach over and cuff the young man. He eluded her.

"All right, what about it?" asked Sam. "Why did Christ ask to be released from His Father's plan?"

"I think it's because as a man or human, we all are afraid to lose control over our lives, our bodies. Suffering and death are no easy doors to walk through," said Jessie softly. "He knew there would be great agony in bearing the sins of the world. You'll notice He says 'Abba.' He didn't want to be separated from His Father."

Jessie's words pulled everyone's attention to her side of the room.

"It's an amazing thing, really," spoke the professor. "In John 14:31, just before His arrest, Jesus states that 'the world must learn that I love the Father and that I do exactly what my Father has commanded Me.' And the very thing that would demonstrate it was to willingly be separated from Him for the sake of others. Amazing. Sort of boggles the mind, doesn't it?"

"He would have to be God to do such a thing," said Henry quietly.

"God and man," echoed Sam. "It is what sets Christianity apart from every other religion in the world."

"Love is willing to sacrifice its own desire so that someone else can benefit," said Bob Gadry. "I don't know too many people in our society who would jump right in and do that. This sounds kind of unrealistic to me. After all, this is the 'Me First' generation, isn't it?"

"Now that's a little too cynical, even for me!" scoffed Kay. "There are plenty of stories out there about people who risk their lives for others. How about yesterday's paper? That man who jumped in the river to save that little girl? Just jumped right in, grabbed her, and pulled her to safety. Forgetting he couldn't swim in the first place? How about that? That's a sacrifice."

"Yes," conceded Gadry. "It's honorable. But people do those things at the spur of the moment. This thing Jesus did was a plan. He knew all about it from the beginning. He lived with the knowledge of it every day. And He still went through with it!" Gadry shook his head in disbelief. "I don't know of anyone who'd be able to do that. . .be born to die."

"That's just it!" chirped a triumphant Martha. "Not any man could. Except for Jesus."

"The God/Man," said Sam.

"Touché!" smiled the professor.

"Youch," Bob winced. "You got me that time."

Everyone laughed.

"Time for cake and ice cream!" announced Martha. "Come on, Mary, and help me in the kitchen."

"This is very interesting," commented Kay. "This group certainly has a lot to talk about."

"And some of us talk more than others," laughed the professor. He slapped Henry on the back. "You're a regular chatterbox, as usual."

"Thanks for noticing, Jim," smiled Henry. "I yam what I yam."

Everyone groaned.

"Henry may not say much," said Sam, "but when he does, it usually hits the nail on the head."

"Very apropos for a carpenter man," laughed Bob.

"Oh, please," moaned Kay. "You guys should stick to discussion. Your jokes are terrible. They are a veritable despoliation of humor."

"What?" everyone chorused.

Jessie laughed. "I think it means your jokes are bad."

"Why, thank you," grinned Sam. "I've never been so elegantly insulted in my life."

Martha and Mary brought out trays laden with pieces of chocolate cake topped with vanilla ice cream. Mary made sure she was the one to give a piece to Sam. "Here you are, Sam," she purred sweetly. "Enjoy."

Kay jabbed Jessie in the side. Jess ignored her friend and turned her attention to the cake. She was trying hard to keep from looking in the direction of Henry Lewis.

Chapter 17

Jessie sat outside Sam Taylor's office, fidgeting with her purse. Sam's secretary, a tall, thin woman, glanced over her glasses at the waiting woman. Jessie raised her brows, a faint smile tugging briefly at her lips.

"Reverend Taylor will be with you momentarily, Mrs. Woods," she said. "He's running late this morning. He tends to get so involved in counseling that he invariably forgets to look at his watch."

Jessie smiled. "That's all right. I can wait."

The secretary nodded. "You bought the Denver house, didn't you?" she asked. "How is it coming along? I expect it needed a lot of work?"

"Oh, yes," replied Jessie. "It certainly did. The inside is almost all done now. The next project is the roof and painting the exterior."

"It's a lovely old home," said the secretary. "I love older homes. They have such character. And the Denver house has not only character, but a bit of mystery, as well, so I've heard."

Jessie laughed. "Yes, there are rumors to that effect. The Denvers were an interesting family."

"Would it be forward of me to ask you about the secret room I've heard so much about?"

"There's really not much to tell, Mrs. . . ," spoke Jessie.

"Miss Silvers," the woman answered. "Annie Silvers. I'm a friend of Ruby Clearwater's."

"Oh," responded Jessie. *Here we go again,* she thought. *More ears for more news about the mysterious Denver house.* "Actually, Miss Silvers, it's just a lovely room that had been boarded up by a grieving father. I don't think there's much more to it than that."

Miss Silvers pressed her lips into a thin, faint pink line. "That's not what I heard," she said.

I bet, thought Jessie. She was about to reply when Sam's door flew open. An elderly woman, clutching a gray poodle, walked out first, followed by the pastor.

"Nice to see you again, Mrs. Rockwell. Say hello to Bud for me."

"I will," the woman replied. "Thank you for your time, Pastor."

Sam turned his attention to Jessie. "Come on in, Mrs. Woods," he said. "Sorry to keep you waiting. Annie says I ought to have a giant clock with a buzzer put on my wall to keep me on schedule."

The secretary rolled her eyes and returned to her typewriter.

Sam's office was a comfortable size. His mahogany desk was large and cluttered. Two overstuffed chairs stood in front of the desk. He motioned to Jessie to sit down.

"Nice chairs," she noted. "Very comfortable."

"I want people to feel comfortable when they come here. So many times they are suffering through something. I figure at least the chairs shouldn't cause any pain."

Jessie smiled. "You're a thoughtful man," she said.

Sam blushed. "Thanks," he said. "Now, let's talk about you."

Jessie placed her purse on the floor and folded her hands. "First, I'd like to apologize for losing my temper over the phone. It was wrong of me to take my emotions out on you."

"Forget it," replied Sam. "I know I have. Now, tell me what's going on inside your heart. What have you been thinking about, and what has the Lord been saying to you?"

"Wow," said Jessie. "You don't waste any time on chitchat, do you?"

"Don't have time," laughed Sam. "Miss Silvers sees to that."

Jessie smiled. "Well, I must say that there's a certain little girl in church who's been prying into my private affairs."

"You must mean Madeline. She's a real corker. She can read a person like a book and then won't hesitate to express an opinion."

"She's very perceptive and adorable, besides," agreed Jessie.

"And?"

"And she got me to thinking about my feelings being bottled up inside. Obviously they've been spilling over a bit, lately. You can attest to that, Sam." Jessie sighed. "It was a big move for me, coming to Carlisle. I knew I was in a sense trying to put the past behind me and move on. Unfortunately, the memories and emotions moved with me." Her eyes watered. "It's like I can never move on. And now I don't know if I want to." She cleared her throat and looked right at Sam. She decided she was going to tell him everything. It just did not matter anymore. Her heart needed to be laid bare to someone. And who better than the pastor? "And on top of all that and in spite of my missing Tom, now new feelings are sneaking up on me. Feelings that are upsetting to me."

Sam shifted in his chair. "What kind of feelings?" *Remain calm, Taylor,* he commanded himself. *You're here to listen and be objective.*

"I'm not sure. Maybe it's just infatuation; I don't know," muttered Jessie. "I think I may be infatuated with Henry. When I'm with him, something happens to me. I can't think straight."

Sam sighed. "Well, Henry is a fine man."

Jessie smiled at Sam. "Sam, I learned a long time ago to be frank with people, not beat around the bush or cover things over. You have already expressed your interest in me, right? Remember the proposal?"

Sam blushed. "How could I forget?"

"And according to Kay, it's as plain as the nose on your face that both you and Henry are interested in me. I think you are both wonderful, and I enjoy your company. But I'm finding this a bit overwhelming and confusing. I can't think straight."

Sam sat back. He studied Jessie's face. "I know this is kind of a strange situation. You've come to me for counsel, and yet I'm part of the problem. But I assure you, I will be as objective as I can in all of this. I'll be frank, too. We're not teenagers, right?" Sam took a deep breath. "I admit it was probably foolish to propose to you the way I did. I admit I care about you and would like to get to know you better. And yes, I have hopes about marriage, but it's too soon for any of this to take place. And I promise you this: I am here to help you. I will not take advantage of your confusion to achieve something for myself. You have far more important issues to deal with."

"Thank you, Sam," said Jessie. "I believe you. . .and I trust you." Jessie leaned forward in her chair. "But how can you talk about marriage like that? We hardly know each other."

"Ever heard of love at first sight?" stammered Sam.

"Yes, but I don't believe in it. That's what fairy tales are made of."

"What about Tom? How did you meet him?"

"Well, I met him at a rally at the college," she replied. "He was serving punch and talking to everybody." Her mind turned back the years to that moment. "When I saw him, something pulled at my heart and—"

"Aha!" exclaimed Sam. "So it was love at first sight."

"Well, no," sputtered Jessie. "I didn't even meet him that day. It was later on, when we found ourselves in the same class. We became friends, and the rest is history."

"I rest my case," said Sam with a smug look on his face.

Jessie sat back. "Well, I suppose."

"Now, tell me more about those bottled-up feelings you were talking about before. And about your relationship with the Lord."

"I still miss Tom. I cry now and again; I feel down. But now it's more than just missing him. I realize I am empty inside, kind of deadened to life in general. I do what I have to do and that's it."

"What about your relationship with the Lord?" asked Sam. "How do you perceive that?"

Jessie frowned. "I don't know. I never stopped going to church, and I read my Bible every day. But Lorena says I'm going through the motions."

"Lorena is a very wise woman," Sam said softly.

Jessie's face reddened. "Look, I didn't turn away from the Lord after Tom died. I hung in there. I'm still hanging in there. I told you, I go to church, I read my Bible, I. . ." Weary tears began to flow down Jessie's cheeks. "What more does He want?"

Sam sat silently and watched Jessie cry. It tore at his heart and took all of his strength of will not to rush to her and take her in his arms.

"Jessie, all He wants from you is for you to let Him love you. Maybe you blamed Him for taking Tom. We all get angry with God. And maybe you think you didn't turn away from the Lord, but perhaps in your heart you did."

Jessie's eyes widened as the realization hit her. Sam continued. "You're so polite, Jess. Maybe that's what you've been doing, between God and you. Going to church, reading the Word, praying now and again. All this time you've been polite. He doesn't want polite; He wants truth and honesty. He wants you to pour out your heart to Him and then trust Him with your feelings. You have to know that your life is still in His hands. No matter what happens, He can be trusted."

"I don't know if I can do this," cried Jessie.

"Remember when I said you are one who doesn't scare easily? Well, there is one thing I know that scares the daylights out of you. You're afraid of loving anyone again. And maybe for good reason."

Jessie began to cry again, but Sam pressed on.

"You're afraid to love anyone again for fear you'll lose that person, too, like you lost Tom. But you can't stop living, Jess. Dying is a part of life. In fact we all have to die to ourselves if we really want to follow Christ. Dying to self means giving up our wills, our wants, and pursuing only His. It means giving up control. I haven't yet met a person who faced this crisis decision with ease. It's a tough one. Jesus Himself wrestled with it. But He decided to go His Father's way, all the way. And you and I know what came of His decision. Resurrection, life. New life, a new beginning for all of us.

"Go back to the beginning, Jessie. Go back to when you first met the Lord and gave your life to Him."

Jessie looked into Sam's earnest face. "What do you mean?"

"Remember what it was like when you first walked with the Lord?"

Jessie sat back for a moment. Her thoughts returned to the day when the Lord swept her off her feet. It was at a tent meeting, and a group of young people were singing about Jesus. Their music was sweet and powerful. She practically ran to the altar to pray. After that, every day seemed to be guided by His hand. She knew then that her life was in God's almighty, all-loving hands. He guided her through college, to Tom, to a career.

She drew in a quick breath. "I remember," she whispered. "I trusted the Lord for everything! I saw His hand in everything. I was His child."

"You still are!" exclaimed Sam. "Yes, you've been through a time of suffering that was a shock to you. But your life is still in His hands. He can still be trusted. Choose to love again," pleaded Sam. "Choose life. Choose Him. Remember what you said at the discussion group? How we need to give up control of our lives? You've taken back control, convinced yourself you can protect yourself better than God can. Go back to the garden, Jess."

Jessie's heart pounded with expectation. She knew what needed to be done. She stood up. "I need to go home now," she announced to Sam. "I need to be alone with Him." She trembled with expectation.

Sam jumped up and joined her on the other side of the desk. "I am so happy for you. I knew you would return to your first love." He smiled at her. "I'll be praying. And remember, once you get back to where you belong with the Lord, the other things in your life, your other feelings, will be directed in the way the Lord ordains them to be. You know what I mean?"

Jessie nodded.

Suddenly, Miss Silvers burst into the room. "Jack Smith just called. He found Lorena on the floor in her kitchen. He called for the ambulance, and they rushed her over to Tompkins General. You'd better hurry!"

"Oh, no!" cried Jessie.

Sam placed his hands on Jessie's shoulders. "Don't worry about Lorena. She's a strong woman. You go home and do what you've got to do. I'll let you know what's happening at the hospital."

Jessie looked into Sam's eyes and the reassurance written there calmed her heart. "Okay, Sam," she said softly. "You better run now."

"I'll talk to you later," he promised.

Sam grabbed his keys and rushed out. Jessie followed him out and watched him drive away in his blue sedan.

"Be with Lorena, Lord," Jessie whispered a prayer. "Let her be all right."

⦿

Jessie returned home and headed straight for her bedroom. Kneeling at her bed, she let the tears flow freely. "Oh, Lord," she whispered. "It's been so long since I really reached out for You. I never realized until now that I've been angry with You. It's been such a long time since I called You Father." She lifted her face toward heaven. "Oh, Father, I just want to be with You again. Please forgive me. I need You."

Jessie trembled in awe as a sweeping sense of love and acceptance flowed over and through her. The Presence of the Lord was overwhelmingly sweet and compassionate. It took her breath away. The story of the prodigal son passed through her mind. In a flash she understood that although she had rejected Him, the Lord had never rejected her. He had been waiting and watching for her all this time.

Light from the afternoon sun beamed through the lace curtains and fell with a dazzling brightness onto the white quilt. Jessie reached over and placed her hands in the pool of light on the bed. It felt warm and comforting.

"What a beautiful day," she said aloud. "Thank You, Lord."

Jessie's eyes fell on the Bible sitting on her nightstand. She got up from the floor and picked up the book. Seating herself on the bed, she flipped through the pages until she found Luke 15 and the passage she was looking for. Through tears of joy, she read it aloud:

" 'But while he was still a long way off, his father saw him and was filled with compassion for him; he ran to his son, threw his arms around him and kissed him.' "

She closed the Bible and hugged it close to her heart.

"Thank You for waiting for me, Father. Thank You for watching for me."

Jessie stood up and walked over to her dresser. She picked up a picture of Tom. He was smiling that crooked smile of his that Jessie had loved so dearly.

"Thank You for Tom," she whispered. "He was a wonderful friend and husband. I don't understand why he had to go, but our life together was in Your hands. And now I need to trust You for tomorrow."

She kissed his picture, as if to say good-bye. Suddenly she remembered the dream she'd had when she'd fallen asleep on the porch. A shiver of excitement ran down her spine. "Oh, Lord, maybe You were trying to tell me something!" She retraced the dream in her mind. She remembered Tom was smiling and full of happiness.

"And then he waved and walked away," Jessie said aloud. "I understand! Of course! Tom is with You, Lord. He's absolutely joyful and content. And that's where he's supposed to be."

The tears flowed again, but Jessie did not care. In her heart she said good-bye to her husband. With a great sigh of relief, she finally knew that all was well with Tom and with her. Her grief and anger had blocked her from understanding all this before. Now she knew deep inside that Tom was in God's hands. And so was Jessie Woods.

Chapter 18

Lorena smiled up at Jessie, her face pale against the hospital pillow. "My dear, how kind of you to come and see me," she said, her blue eyes bright despite her weakened state. "Don't know why they're making such a fuss. After all, it was just a little spell. I've had them before."

Jessie leaned over and kissed her neighbor gently on the cheek. "I've brought you these," Jessie said, laying a bouquet of pink roses and white carnations on the bed beside the elderly patient.

"Oh, they're perfectly lovely!" exclaimed Lorena. "You are such a dear." With trembling hands, she picked up the flowers and inhaled their sweet fragrance. "Reminds me of home," she sighed. "Wish I were there right now." She frowned. "The doctor says I have to stay here for a few days. 'For observation,' he says. Observation, my eye. I'll bet you anything that nosey doctor just wants to run some needless tests to keep the nurses busy around here."

"Now, Lorena, you behave," Marion, a nurse, chided as she entered the room. "You know Dr. Freeman only wants what's best for you." The nurse expertly adjusted Lorena's pillows and checked her pulse. "You know you're his favorite patient."

A faint blush of pink appeared on Lorena's pale cheeks. "Yes, I guess you could say that. And he sure enjoys my apple pies. Says I'm the only one in Carlisle who can bake a proper apple pie. Imagine that."

Jessie laughed. "I'd have to agree with Dr. Freeman. Your apple pie is absolutely delicious."

"There you have it," declared the nurse. "Your pie gets first prize. Now promise me you'll behave and stop fussing."

"Oh, all right, Marion. No more complaining."

"Is it all right if I stay for awhile?" Jessie asked the nurse.

"Yes, that would be fine," Marion replied. "It will do her some good to have the company. Just don't talk about politics. You're liable to get her all riled up."

Jessie laughed. "Okay. I promise."

"I'll get a vase for your flowers," added Marion. "Aren't they lovely!" Then she left the room.

Jessie sat down in the chair next to Lorena's bed. Her eyes twinkled with excitement. "I've got a surprise for you, Lorena."

"Oh?" said Lorena. "What could it be? The flowers are enough. And just your being here is present enough for me. What else do you have up your sleeve, Jessie Woods?"

Jessie reached carefully into her oversized leather purse and gently pulled out a thick envelope. "It's a letter," said Jessie.

"A letter," said Lorena, a puzzled look on her face.

"It's a letter from—"

"Don't tell me," whispered Lorena excitedly. "It's from Amelia Elizabeth to her father!"

"Yes," laughed Jessie. "I thought you might like to hear it. It's very interesting. Amelia wrote such wonderful letters."

Lorena pulled up the sheet on her bed and folded her hands. "I'm ready." Her eyes sparkled. "This is so exciting."

"Oh, dear," said Jessie with a frown. "I hope this isn't going to be too much for you today. Maybe I should ask the nurse."

"No!" grunted Lorena. "This will do me good. Save me from being bored to death. Besides, the doctor didn't say I couldn't have visitors. So read, my dear. I can hardly wait."

Jessie sat back in the chair and unfolded the letter.

"It's dated October 25, 1885," Jessie announced.

"Imagine that," sighed Lorena. "My mother was born in 1885."

Jessie continued.

Dear Father,

I hope you've been taking your medicine. Sophie writes that you are a terribly stubborn patient. You really are driving her to distraction. Please do as the doctor orders. You are worrying me!

I've so much to tell you I don't know where to begin. As you know, last weekend I was allowed to go on a short trip with Miss Bristol and Rosemary. We traveled by coach to a little village in the foothills of the Catskills. Miss Bristol has a sister who lives in Cadosia. She and her husband own a lovely farm. They have six children, all of them towheads! They were quite a lively crew, especially for me. The children couldn't quite grasp the fact that I have no siblings. One little fellow by the name of Quentin offered to be my little brother. "Any times you might need a little brother. You know, if there's a bug or frog or somethin' in your room that needs takin' out," he explained. When the others heard of Quentin's offer, they all at once began to quarrel over who would make the best sister or brother. Their mother finally put an end to the riot by announcing they could all be my sisters and brothers. A loud cheering ensued. Honestly, they are all so sweet.

Miss Bristol, Rosemary, and I took several hikes into the hills to study the flora and fauna. I was amazed at their depth of knowledge of all the plants. (I felt like quite the dullard. After all, Father, you can barely remember the name of the yellow flowers that bloom in the front yard every spring. Daffodils, my dear! I am certainly my father's daughter.) Did you know that the Indians used skunk cabbage to cure headaches? They would bind the leaves together and crush them. The odor of the crushed leaves was then inhaled to cure the headache. Maybe I should bring some of the smelly stuff home for you!

On Sunday afternoon I was able to steal away for a few minutes and be alone. I wanted to climb to the top of the hill and savor the beauty of this valley. The surrounding hills were so bright with color, it was astounding. The light from the afternoon sun inflamed the oranges and yellows to a brilliant intensity. Glorious!

From up on the hill, there is a wonderful view of the valley. I could see the road stretching along, dusty and brown. I looked toward the east, the direction of home and school. Sometimes there is a turning in my heart whenever I see a road heading out to a place where I have never been. I suppose the wanderlust that resides in your heart has begun to stir in mine! Really, Father, you have been so many places! I have always envied you that. I cherish my memories of time well-spent with Mother as she and I awaited your return from your latest trip. We played games, had teas, and chased the kittens around the house. It was wonderful! One time we pretended we were going on a trip. We pushed the parlor furniture together to make a boat and away we went to India, the Orient, Europe. All the places you have been. I remember catching Mother with an odd look on her face. Even for one so young, I knew she was longing to be with you, and longing to see the sights you were seeing.

I have never understood why you never let Mother accompany you on your trips. Nurse would have taken fine care of me. But maybe Mother didn't want to leave me. At any rate, I think you were just afraid something would happen to her if she traveled with you. Isn't that so, Father? Am I prying? I can see your face now, turning red, and you puffing away furiously at your pipe. "Amelia Elizabeth, you are talking too much. Don't they teach you manners at that school of yours?"

Miss Charter would laugh at that statement. She provides training for behavior, but she is far more interested in producing women of "Christian excellence," as she is always saying. You and I both know that the Charter School is not a finishing school in the ordinary sense. Miss Charter expects the best of us in every way, and she manages to get it too. I think it's her genuine love for us that does it. She really believes in us. It's not just a job for her; it's a mission. She says the Lord gave her this school and she wants to run it His way. I'm surprised you chose Charter, Father, with Miss

Charter's faith being so vibrant and relevant. You were never a churchgoer, after all. I guess you saw what everyone else sees in the school. It has excellent academics and a true spirit of working for a common goal.

I must say I thought the Bible studies here would be a chore to endure. But they are not! Miss Charter and Miss Bristol talk about the Bible as if they are personally acquainted with its Author! It makes me wonder about God more and more. Suppose He is real and wants us to know Him the way Miss Charter says He does? We must discuss this at Thanksgiving. Tell Sophie I expect all the trimmings—especially her pumpkin pie with plenty of whipped cream. I can hardly wait to be home!

Rosemary is soaking up literature like a dry sponge. Lately, I've been reading her Shakespearean sonnets. Her favorite so far is Sonnet Twenty-nine. She can't believe he could know how she feels. Sometimes ("when I feel small," she says), when she wishes she were someone else or somewhere else, all she has to do is think of her mother. "My mother's love is so sweet and hopeful, like the snowdrop blossom that pokes its head out of the ground, even before all the snow is gone. And I wouldn't trade that for no man's treasure."

I've enclosed a copy of the sonnet for you to read and study. Thought you might enjoy it.

Your loving daughter,
Amelia Elizabeth

Jessie looked over at Lorena. The patient's face glowed with satisfaction.

"That was wonderful!" beamed Lorena. "Fascinating. Do you have all her letters?"

"As far as I know," responded Jessie. "I have one whole box full of letters. I haven't read them all yet."

"It's just like reading a story. You must tell me what happens. Maybe you could read me some more of those letters, if you don't mind. I mean if you could take the time. I know you've been busy with the house."

"I'd be happy to read to you," said Jessie. "It's nice to share the letters with someone who appreciates them as much as I do."

"Do you have the copy of the sonnet there?" asked Lorena.

"Yes. It was tucked inside the envelope. Would you like me to read it to you?" Lorena nodded. Jessie read the poem.

"That is lovely. Read the last few lines for me again, will you?" Jessie nodded.

"Yet in these thoughts myself almost despising,
    Haply I think on thee, and then my state,

Like to the lark at break of day arising
> From sullen earth, sings hymns at heaven's gate;
For thy sweet love rememb'red such wealth brings
> That then I scorn to change my state with kings."

" 'Thy sweet love remembred.' I like that," sighed Lorena. "Sometimes we get overwhelmed with the circumstances of our lives and get to feeling so low. We see other people who seem to have it all together all of the time, and we wish we were like them. But then we see or remember the love of our dear ones, and we are content. Love is such a comfort. Even if the loved one has gone on before us. Even the memory of a true love can bring comfort. I often think of my dear husband. How he loved me! I miss him, of course, and that can be hard sometimes. But remembering his love for me brings a smile to my face. Isn't that so, Jessie?"

Lorena looked at her visitor to see what effect her words were having. Jessie's face was glowing, even as the tears rolled down her cheeks.

"Why, Jessie, my dear, what is it?" whispered Lorena. "I thought you looked different when you walked in here. You looked peaceful in your face. I'll be honest with you. It's the first time I've seen peace in your eyes. What's happened?"

"I finally let go of Tom," Jessie whispered, her eyes glittering with tears of relief. "It's true. The Lord helped me to see that Tom is fine. He's with Jesus." She cleared her throat. "I went to see Sam. He showed me that I have been angry at the Lord all this time. I needed to be reconciled with the Lord. Go back to my first love."

"Trust Him again," smiled Lorena.

Jessie took Lorena's hand. "Yes, trust Him again. With my whole life and all my thoughts and feelings."

"That's wonderful, Jessie. It's an answer to my prayers! Isn't God good?"

"He sure is!" a deep voice agreed heartily. It was Sam. He strode into the room and bestowed the bedstand with a vase of flowers. "The nurse ordered me to deliver these to you. And I brought you this." He handed her a box of candy. "Chocolate-covered almonds. Your favorite. I presume the flowers are from Mrs. Woods?"

"You presume correctly," laughed Lorena. "Aren't they lovely?"

"Almost as lovely as the one who brought them." Sam smiled.

"Oh, my," said Lorena.

Jessie smirked. "Thank you, Sam, for the compliment. You are so charming."

"I aim to please," said Sam. "Now tell me, how are you ladies doing?"

"Fine," said Lorena. "We are fine, aren't we, Jessie?"

"Oh, yes," beamed Jessie. "Couldn't be finer."

Sam smiled. "That's wonderful. Has the doctor been in yet this afternoon?"

"No, not since you were both here this morning. He wants to keep me here for a few days," Lorena murmured. "Can't you talk him into letting me go home tomorrow? I feel fine."

"Lorena Smith! You know I can't do that. Dr. Freeman doesn't like lay-people like me telling him how to carry out his practice. I think I'll stick to sermons, thank you very much."

Jessie looked over at Lorena. "You look a little tired, Lorena. I think I've worn you out. We'd better go and let you rest."

"All right, my dear," sighed Lorena. "I guess I could use a little nap. But do come again. I've so enjoyed our visit. And bring another letter."

"I will," Jessie promised. She leaned over and kissed the elderly woman gently on the forehead.

"Wait for me, will you, Jessie?" asked Sam. "I want to say a prayer with Lorena. I'll be right out."

"Okay," said Jessie. She caught Lorena's eye. The older woman winked. Jessie blushed and hurried out of the room.

A few minutes later Sam joined her in the hospital parking lot. "Thanks for waiting," said Sam, out of breath from hurrying down the hallway of the hospital.

"No problem," responded Jessie.

"I just wanted to hear from your own lips what your peaceful face is telling me."

"I feel alive again," whispered Jessie. "It's as if I've been in a troubled sleep for a long time and I've finally awakened. I can't begin to tell you how wonderful it is!"

Sam let out a whoop. "Thank You, Lord!" he exclaimed. "I am so happy for you."

Jessie looked into Sam's eyes. "I want to thank you for your honesty. You told me the truth, however painful it was for me at first. Your diagnosis of my soul was very accurate," she said warmly. "Thank you, Reverend Taylor."

"Please," Sam spoke quietly, "just call me Sam."

Jessie stood for a moment studying Sam's face. She could see love and compassion in his eyes. She felt something in her own heart, but she was not sure what it was.

"I thought I'd have you and Henry and Kay over for dinner this week," she said hastily. "Why don't you come over on Thursday. You don't have any meetings that day, do you?"

"No, that would be fine. I'd be happy to attend," replied Sam formally. "Can I bring anything? It'll be your first social gathering at your new home, won't it? It should be special."

"Hey, you're right," laughed Jessie. "With all the excitement going on around here, I haven't invited anyone over yet. How very rude of me."

"I wouldn't say rude, Jessie," chided Sam. "You've had a lot on your mind lately."

Jessie smiled. "You're right about that. And I'm afraid my friends have felt the brunt of my mixed-up emotions. Well, I promise to make it up to you all.

How's five-thirty on Thursday for you?"

"That's fine," nodded Sam. "There's no deacon meeting this week. Barring any emergencies, Thursday is free and clear."

"Okay," said Jessie, "I'll see you then."

"See you then." Sam turned to head for his car.

Jessie called out to him, a note of concern in her voice. "Sam?"

Sam turned around to face her. "What is it, Jessie?"

"About Lorena," she spoke earnestly. "How is she, really? Have you spoken to her doctor?"

Sam stuck his hands in his pockets. "A couple of years ago, Lorena suffered a heart attack. It was pretty bad, but she bounced back in an amazing way. Even had the doctors baffled. But Dr. Freeman said her heart was weakened by the attack. This latest 'spell' she had was just another episode related to her heart. The doctor says her weakened heart may give her trouble from time to time. Her blood pressure drops; she passes out. There's not too much we can do about it. That's why someone's always over there checking on her."

Jessie sucked in her breath. "I hope nothing happens to her. I'm just getting to know her, and she's been such a help to me. She really knows the Lord, doesn't she?"

"You can say that again," said Sam. "She's been walking with the Lord for over fifty years, and you can tell it hasn't become a rote religion with her, not by a long shot. Lorena knows His voice and can read a person's heart like you and I would read the newspaper. She's an amazing woman, serving an amazing God."

"I'm glad to know her," sighed Jessie. She looked into Sam's eyes. "The Lord has been merciful to me, Sam. He's given me true friends at a time in my life when I needed them most. I could have made some pretty terrible decisions if God hadn't intervened. I know others who have gone off the deep end of bitterness and have left God and everyone else behind, only to find themselves at a very lonely dead end. I'm grateful, Sam."

Sam tried to still the pounding of his heart for the woman who stood before him. "We'll always be here for you, Jess, as best we can." He cleared his throat. "You know the Lord is faithful to never let us go. He'd pursue us to the ends of the earth."

Jessie's eyes filled with tears. She reached out for Sam and gave him a hug. Sam hugged her back and released her from his arms. She smiled and left him standing in the parking lot. He watched her drive away, his thoughts racing to keep up with the beating of his heart.

Chapter 19

That'll be sixty-nine dollars and fifty-two cents," the cashier drawled. Her pink smock clashed noisily with her curly red hair. "Paper or plastic?"

"Paper, please," answered Jessie.

"Having a party?" asked the girl, eyeing the steak and fresh vegetables.

"As a matter of fact, yes," responded Jessie. "Just a small one."

The girl snapped her gum. "That's nice. You ought to go over to Hansen's Bakery and pick up one of his gourmet chocolate cakes. He's got one called 'Double Chocolate Delight.' It's out of this world."

"That's a great idea. Thanks," said Jessie.

While the girl packed Jessie's groceries, Jessie glanced at the tabloid newspapers next to the cash register. " 'Chihuahua abducted by aliens! Returns with two heads! Scientists baffled!' " Jessie laughed out loud. "That is unbelievable," she said.

"That's nothing," said the cashier. "Last week they had a story about a woman who was raised by giant spiders. Had a picture of her climbing walls, literally." She snapped her gum. "Now that's funny."

Jessie laughed. She fished in her purse for her wallet. A strange scuffing sound reached her ears, and she turned to look. Behind her was a man with a lame foot.

"Ridiculous what people will believe, isn't it?" said the man. He laughed a low, contemptuous laugh.

Jessie turned to reply and looked straight into the face of Spencer Hart, who grinned at her as he said, "Crazy world!"

"Yes," said Jessie. Something in the man's eyes made Jessie feel nervous. She counted out her money and handed it to the cashier. "Thank you."

Jessie put the bags into her cart and pushed it out the doorway of the supermarket. The left front wheel of the cart turned inward, and Jessie came to a halt in the middle of the parking lot. Step, scrape; step, scrape. The peculiar sound reached her ears again. The man had followed her out of the store. Jessie pushed harder at the cart. It moved with a jerk. She hurried toward her car.

"Calm down, Jessie Woods," she muttered to herself. "What is the matter with you?" Jessie turned to look, and she saw the man walking out of the parking lot. She groped for her car keys at the bottom of her purse. With her hands shaking, Jessie unlocked the door and began to laugh. "This is ridiculous!" she said aloud. "You'd think I was getting paranoid or something. Wait till Kay hears about this!"

Jessie drove to the bakery and picked up one of Hansen's chocolate cakes. Conveniently located next door was the flower shop, and she ran in and purchased a bouquet of wildflowers.

Once inside her home, Jessie made preparations for her dinner party. She surveyed the dining room and living room. Everything was in place except for a couple of boxes that needed to be put away. A thin film of dust lay silently on the living room furniture. Jessie reached over toward the cherry lamp table near the window. She ran her finger through the dust.

"That stubborn plaster dust," she sighed. "Will it ever go away?" She retreated to the kitchen and grabbed her dust cloth and vacuum cleaner from the utility closet. In an hour she had succeeded in getting rid of the dust. "For the time being," she muttered. Her eyes fell on the two boxes near the door of the living room. "You are going up to the attic," she announced.

She picked up one of the boxes and hauled it out of the living room. Stopping at the foot of the stairs, she nodded a hello to Joseph. The little sentinel stood faithfully, guarding the grandfather clock. His plaid ribbon bow had slipped to the side, giving him a jaunty look. "You are adorable," complimented Jessie. She steadied her grip on the box and started up the stairs. The box was heavy with books she never intended to read but did not have the heart to throw away. *After all, I might need them sometime,* Jessie had reasoned. Tom used to call her a packrat. She smiled. "Some habits die hard," she said to herself.

Leaning the box against the wall, Jessie pulled open the attic door with her free hand. She flipped on the light switch. The bare bulb greeted her with a pale glow at the top of the stairs. "Here we come," she groaned. She heaved the box up and climbed the narrow steps.

At the top of the stairs she dropped the box onto the floor with a thud. Catching her breath, she looked around the open room for a suitable space for her books. She found an empty spot in a far corner.

"Perfect," she said aloud, and she pushed the box over to the corner. Shoving it back as far as she could, her eyes fell on something tall and flat leaning up against the wall. It was covered with a faded piece of green canvas.

"Wonder what that is," she muttered under her breath. She reached over and carefully pulled the mystery package away from the wall. The thin rope holding the canvas together pulled away easily. Underneath the canvas, a soft, cream-colored sheet created another layer of protection. Jessie unwrapped the sheet. Underneath was another sheet. Beneath the additional covering, she discovered a painting.

What she saw took her breath away. She was eye to eye with a beautiful young woman. The young woman's soft brown eyes held the look of an educated, sweet, young lady. Her features were petite, her brown hair caught up in a soft chignon. She wore a white dress, its collar sweeping up to her delicate chin.

"Amelia Elizabeth," breathed Jessie. "It must be you!"

Jessie stared at the portrait. It was magnificent. The young woman seemed alive, her smile slightly turned to reveal a trace of mischievousness. One arm lay across her lap, while the other trailed gracefully over the chair's arm, resting lightly on—

"Joseph!" exclaimed an excited Jessie Woods. "It's Joseph! She had a dog, a black Scotty. The Professor! You must be the dog who dug up the neighbor's flowers!"

Jessie crowed gleefully with excitement. "This is fantastic!"

She picked up the painting and carried it down the stairs to Amelia's room. She hesitated at the door. The room was still covered with dust. Jessie had not been able to bring herself even to disturb the dust. Reading Amelia's letters made her feel as if she knew Carlton Denver and his entire household. She felt as though she had invaded his privacy by opening up his daughter's room.

"Come on, Jessie," she scolded herself. "You're being too dramatic. The man's gone. This is a lovely painting and a lovely room. It should be restored. A life and love like theirs should be celebrated, not mourned."

Jessie smiled at the words that had just come out of her own mouth. "I certainly didn't think that way a week ago. Lord, You truly are a healer of broken hearts!"

As best she could, Jessie held the painting up near the space over the fireplace. "I'd say it's a perfect fit." She lowered the painting and carried it into the little sitting room. Propping it up on the love seat, Jessie stepped back to get a better look.

The gold-leaf frame was carved with tiny leaves interwoven with delicate flowers. A thin rim of gold inside the frame bordered the edge of the painting, accentuating the browns and golds in the portrait itself. The background was a likeness of pale green wallpaper, strewn lightly with flecks of gold. The gold of the frame and background emphasized the golden locket that the young woman wore around her neck. But everything in the painting was subordinate and complimentary to the subject. Amelia's lovely face was the focal point of the work. Her intelligent eyes glittered with energy, her smile shy but lively. She looked as though she were about to say something funny or sweet or thoughtful.

"I never knew you, Amelia Elizabeth Denver, but I'd say whoever painted you certainly captured your lively spirit." Jessie shook her head. "No wonder your father had this painting removed. It's so lifelike, so real. It must have hurt him to see you this way after—"

The doorbell chimed.

"It's me—Kay," a voice called into the house. "I'm letting myself in." Kay walked into the foyer. "Hello, Joseph. Where's Jess?" Kay stopped in front of the mirror. "Look at me. She's got me talking to that dog statue, too." She adjusted her glasses. "Where are you, Jess?"

"Up here in the sitting room," answered the lady of the house. "Come on up. You've got to see this!"

"Just a sec," responded Kay. "I brought some cheese and crackers. Let me stick the cheese in the fridge." She hurried down the hallway and put it away. "I'm coming."

Kay rushed up the stairs. "What's all the excitement? You sound—" She stopped in midsentence at the sight of the painting. For a few seconds, Kay was speechless.

"Now this is a momentous occasion," grinned Jessie. "Kay Bantam, speechless? This should go down in the record books."

"Thanks," smirked Kay. She peered at the painting. "This is absolutely gorgeous! Understated, yet lifelike. Exquisite! It must be Emily Ann, right?"

"Amelia Elizabeth," corrected Jessie. "Isn't she beautiful?"

"This is amazing. And look!" squealed Kay. "There's Joseph! She must have had a real Scotty."

"The Professor," corrected Jessie. "I believe she called her dog The Professor. She mentions him in her letters."

"Where'd you find it?"

"In the attic," answered Jessie.

"This is great," breathed Kay. "It puts some real meat and bones on the Denver house mystery. Who knows? Maybe there's more to find! Fantastic! Wait till the guys see this!" Kay straightened her plum-colored blazer and yellow satin blouse. A chunky necklace with large purple and yellow beads completed the ensemble.

"Kay. Purple and yellow?" groaned Jessie.

"Isn't it wild? I love it. It's so bold."

"Bold is the word. You have boldly gone where no one in his right mind has ever gone before. Have you been over to the boutique again?" asked Jessie.

"Of course," responded Kay. "Where else would I find such stunning fashions?"

Jessie steered her friend out of the room. "Let's go set the table. I got so involved with the painting I forgot I was having company."

Kay set the table in the dining room while Jessie started the cooking. The singing of the doorbell signaled another arrival.

"I'll get it," called Kay.

She opened the door. Sam Taylor stood smiling, flowers in hand.

"Welcome, Reverend Taylor," Kay said with a grin. "Jess! It's Sam!" she yelled in the direction of the kitchen. "Nice touch," she whispered to Sam, pointing to the pink roses.

"Bring him back here," answered Jessie. "I'm up to my elbows in vegetables." Kay escorted Sam to the kitchen.

"Hi, Sam," said Jessie cheerfully. "Wait until you see what I found in the attic. It's fantastic."

Sam handed the flowers to the hostess. "Congratulations on your lovely home," he said grandly.

Jessie breathed in the fragrance of the roses. "These are beautiful. Thanks, Sam," Jessie said. She took the flowers and disappeared into the dining room.

"Something smells good," commented Sam.

"Rice pilaf is my guess," said Kay. "She makes a mean rice pilaf."

Jessie returned to the kitchen. "Sam, are you any good at grilling steaks?"

"I think I can manage it," answered Sam. "How does everyone like their steaks?"

"Shouldn't we wait for Henry?" asked Jessie.

"I know what he likes," responded Sam. "Now, what about you two?"

"Medium well," replied Kay.

"Medium rare," said Jessie.

"You mean rare, don't you, Dear?" said Kay. She looked at Sam over her glasses. "Jessie used to like her steaks so rare they could still moo and sing the 'Yellow Rose of Texas'!"

"Medium rare is fine," said Jessie. "Kay exaggerates and is rather poetic. A deadly combination, don't you think?"

Sam laughed. The doorbell chimed again.

"That'll be Henry," said Kay, heading out of the kitchen. "I'll get it. Just call me Butler Bantam."

Kay opened the door and choked back the laughter. Henry stood at the door, a bouquet of flowers in his arms.

"Speaking of yellow roses," muttered Kay. "One of you could have at least brought candy!" She laughed at Henry's puzzled look. "Come on in, Mr. Lewis. Reverend Taylor's already here. He's in the kitchen. Right this way, Sir."

Jessie looked up from the stove in time to see Henry enter with his yellow roses.

"It's Henry," announced Kay. "He brought flowers."

Jessie gave Kay a stifling look. "Welcome, Henry. Yellow roses! These are wonderful," she thanked him. "So glad you could come."

"Glad to be here," said Henry. He looked around the kitchen; his eyes met Jessie's eyes. He blushed as he remembered the last time he stood in her kitchen. "Where's Sam?"

"He's out in the back, figuring out my grill," explained Jessie. "We're having steaks. You want to give him a hand?"

Henry nodded and walked through the back porch to the yard. Kay watched him go.

"Well, isn't this interesting," she laughed. "Look at you, woman."

"What?" said Jessie.

"You're standing there, holding onto a bunch of yellow roses for dear life.

Get a grip, girl." She reached for the bouquet. "Give them to me before you choke them to death. Where are the vases?"

"In the dining room," answered Jessie. "In the china closet."

"Found 'em," called Kay from the other room. "Which vase? The white or the crystal?"

"The white," said Jessie.

Kay brought out the vase and filled it with water. She cut off the ends of the stems under running water and arranged the bouquet in the vase.

"Nice," she said aloud. "Now where shall I put them? You're running out of room in the dining room. The place is bursting with flowers."

"Kay, honestly, will you stop joking around," whispered Jessie. "This is terrible. What am I going to do?"

"Do about what?" asked Kay innocently. "So two guys brought you flowers. Is that a crime?"

Henry reappeared at the back door. "Sam wants to know when you want the steaks put on."

Jessie followed Henry out to the yard. The late-day sun cast parting shots of light through the trees and onto the grass. The crickets were already starting up their song.

"You can start the steaks now," said Jessie.

Sam saluted and twirled the spatula in the air. "At your service!"

"It's a beautiful day, isn't it?" she said, sitting down in one of the lawn chairs.

"Perfect," said Sam.

"Absolutely fragrant," chimed in Kay, with a wink. She sat down in a chair next to Jessie.

"I think it's going to rain," said Henry at which point everyone stopped and looked at him.

"I mean later," he said. "It's supposed to rain later. You can tell when the wind blows back the leaves a certain way."

"Oh," said Jessie and Kay together.

"So, Jessie, what's the big discovery you were telling me about?" asked Sam.

"A discovery?" queried Henry.

"Ooh, it is fantastic," said Kay, pushing her glasses back in place.

"Let's show them after dinner," suggested Jessie. "Keep them in suspense."

"Yipee," said Sam with a smirk. "I love surprises."

"Oh, Sam, can't you humor us a little?" Jessie chided.

"All right," he laughed. "How about you, Henry? Can you wait until after dinner?"

"If I must," he sighed with a grin.

Everyone laughed. A squirrel in a nearby maple jabbered at the four humans down below. The trees flung out shadows that danced with the fading sunlight.

Robins called to each other in the twilight breeze. Jessie hugged herself.

"Isn't it a beautiful day?" she repeated. "I better get back to my rice and veggies," she said and then disappeared into the house.

"What's gotten into her?" asked Kay. "She definitely looks different. I can't quite put my finger on it."

"Yeah," said Henry. "She seems, well, peaceful, you know?"

"That's it," agreed Kay. "She doesn't seem troubled and tied up in a ball like she used to. Wonder what happened?"

"Why don't you ask her?" said Sam, deftly flipping a steak. "I'm sure she'll tell you."

Kay turned to look at Sam. "You know something. Spill the beans."

"Come on, Sam," said Henry. "Tell us what happened."

"No way," said Sam. "You ask her yourselves. I'm not saying a word." He flipped the other steak. "These are almost done. Will one of you inform the hostess, please?"

"I'll go," volunteered Henry. "Relax, Kay."

"Relax, Kay, my foot. You're going in there to find out, aren't you?" demanded Kay. "I say we wait and ask her over dinner. That way we can all hear it, hot off the press."

"Okay," agreed Henry.

"That's real nice of you two, but would you mind telling her about the steaks right now?" said an exasperated Sam. "I don't want to overdo them."

"Right, Chief," said Henry. "I'm on my way."

Henry bounded up the back porch steps and disappeared.

Kay glanced over at Sam. "Small world, isn't it?" she said. "Getting smaller and more crowded by the minute, wouldn't you say, Reverend Taylor?"

"Kay Bantam, you are too much," smiled Sam. "Don't you worry about a thing. If there's one thing I know, it's this as stated in Psalm 33: 'The plans of the Lord stand firm forever, the purposes of his heart through all generations.' The Lord's will be done."

"Amen to that," said Kay, smiling.

Chapter 20

For several moments, the only sound to be heard in the dining room of 16 Lark Avenue was the clinking of silver against china. The delicious food was thoroughly enjoyed by the four friends. Finally, Kay looked up from her plate, and she fastened her eyes on Jessie.

"So," said Kay, as nonchalantly as she could, "what's new with you, Jess?"

"Me?" said Jessie. "Why do you ask?"

Kay took a sip of her lemon seltzer water. "Well, for one thing, you look different. And for another thing, I actually heard you singing in the kitchen not ten minutes ago. I do believe that's the first time I've heard you sing since. . .well, it's been a long time."

Jessie blushed. "Well, it's kind of personal. And it just happened so I haven't really been able to think about anything else."

"You're acting like you're engaged or something!" suggested Kay.

"What?" Henry said, almost choking on his water.

"I said Jessie's acting like she's—"

"I'm sure we all heard you, Kay," Sam interrupted. "Jessie, I think you'd better explain before Henry has a stroke."

"It's kind of personal," began Jessie again. "But with the help of Sam and Lorena, I realized that my relationship with the Lord needed to be restored. I've been angry with God all this time, since Tom died. Angry and scared, I guess."

"But you never stopped going to church and stuff like that, did you?" asked a puzzled Kay. "You didn't give up your Christianity."

"I was going through the motions," explained Jessie. "Through my own anger and bitterness, I lost my love for the Lord. And you know what happens when one person loses their love for the other. You may keep walking with the person, but you stop really talking. And eventually there's no relationship at all. If that keeps up, then ultimately the person walks away."

"And the one who still loves is left standing there. . .alone," Kay said softly, her voice tinged with sadness.

Jessie looked at her friend. "But my story doesn't end there," she continued. "I turned back to the Lord. And I found out He'd been waiting for me all this time. He wasn't angry or condemning. He can only look at me with love in His eyes. His love and grace washed over me. I'm alive again. I can trust Him again." Her eyes filled with tears of joy. "And I let go of Tom. I finally let him go."

"Isn't that great?" exclaimed Sam.

"That's wonderful," said Henry.

"Wonderful," choked Kay. She bolted from the table in a flurry of tears.

Astonished at Kay's reaction, Jessie hurried out after her. She found Kay on the back porch, sobbing. Jessie put her arms around her and guided her into a chair. "What's the matter, Kay?" Jessie asked, her voice warm with concern. "Did I say something to upset you?"

"Y—y—yes," stuttered Kay. "When you said the thing about two people walking together until one loses his love for the other. That's what happened to me and Tony. He stopped loving me, Jess. We stopped talking, and the next thing I knew, he was out the door. And I'm left standing. . .all alone. Still loving him. It's not fair, Jessie," she wept. "I think divorce is worse than someone's dying. At least you know Tom died loving you. I know Tony is alive and well and not loving me. He doesn't care. He's gone on with his own life, his own plans." Her shoulders shook with another sob. "I don't know what to do. I'm so tired of being alone. I'm tired of hurting on the inside."

Jessie held Kay's hand. She waited for Kay to stop crying before she spoke again. "Kay," said Jessie softly, "I know Someone who can take the sting out of that loneliness. The Lord loves you, Kay. And what He did for me, He can do for you. There's nothing too hard for Him. He's been waiting for you, Kay."

Kay lifted her head. "What do I need to do?"

"Just say yes to Him," urged Jessie. "Ask Him to forgive your sins and make you His daughter. The blood of Jesus sets us free from sin. Sin separates us from God. Jesus made a way for us to be reconciled to Him."

"Reconciled," Kay repeated the word. "That's what I wanted for Tony and me. I tried so hard, but he wouldn't respond."

"Well, the Lord is ready to reconcile you to Himself. And our relationship with Him lasts forever. It's not like our earthly relationships. Those can change or be terminated, one way or another. But the Lord will never change or leave us. And He can always be trusted. I've finally realized that. I can trust Him no matter what has happened or no matter what tomorrow brings. My life is in His hands."

"I want that, too," said Kay, wiping her tears on the sleeve of her blazer. "I want to know Him like you do."

Jessie threw her arms around her friend. They prayed together, and within the confines of the screened-in porch, the miracle of salvation unfolded. The two friends started laughing and crying at the same time.

A tentative knock drew their attention to the back door. Sam stood in the doorway. "Is everything all right?" he asked.

"Everything is great!" said Jessie.

"Stupendous!" laughed Kay.

Henry followed Sam onto the porch. He held out his two hands, full of napkins. "I thought you might need these," he said.

Jessie and Kay gratefully accepted the offering. With a loud honk, Kay blew her nose. Jessie started laughing again and could not stop. Kay explained to the men what had just transpired.

Sam and Henry grinned at each other and slapped each other on the back. "Wow. This is really something," said Sam. "The Lord is amazing. His timing is impeccable."

"It's a miracle," said Kay. "I feel so quiet on the inside and so loved. For the first time in my life, I feel safe. . .really safe."

"Let's go inside and have dessert," suggested Jessie. "I've got a cake from the bakery that's supposed to be out of this world."

Jessie directed the group into the dining room. "I'll be right back," she said.

Sam and Henry listened as Kay bubbled over with joy. Suddenly, Jessie entered the room, holding the cake. It was brimming with candlelight; Jessie had covered the cake with candles. Sam started to laugh. He nodded at Jessie and began to sing. Henry and Jessie joined in.

"Happy birthday to you, happy birthday to you, happy birthday, dear Kay, happy birthday to you!"

Kay looked in wonderment at her friends. "What are you doing?" she asked.

"Today is your birthday, Kay," beamed Sam. "Today you were born into the kingdom of God. Today you have become a child of God."

Kay clapped her hands together. She pushed up her glasses and took a deep breath. Out went the candles.

Everyone laughed and applauded.

"You don't need to make a wish," commented Henry. "We don't need wishes. We've got a Bible full of promises from a God who keeps each and every one."

"Well said, Henry," smiled Sam.

After dessert the party retired to the living room. While the sun disappeared behind the hills surrounding Carlisle, the four friends discussed the amazing grace of God. Kay was loaded with questions. Sam, Henry, and Jessie tried to keep up with her.

"This is so exciting," Kay gushed. "And to think it happened here in this wonderful old house."

"Hey, speaking of houses, what's the surprise you were going to show Henry and me?" asked Sam. "I presume it has something to do with the saga of the Denver household?"

"As a matter of fact it does," sniffed Jessie. "But you sound as though you've had enough of the mysterious Denvers."

"Well," smiled Sam, "if one more person comes up to me to ask about the secret room, I think I'll—"

"Maybe you'd rather not see the surprise," countered Jessie.

"I'd like to see it," volunteered Henry.

Sam rolled his eyes. "Since when have you been interested in history, Henry? Seems to me it was your worst subject in high school."

Henry's cheeks reddened. "That was a long time ago."

"Sam, what's the matter with you? Stop teasing Henry," scolded Jessie.

"Oh, come on, you guys," said Kay. "Let's go. You'll love it. It's really quite exquisite."

Jessie flipped the light at the foot of the stairs, and her guests followed her up to the sitting room. Amelia's portrait greeted them from the love seat.

Sam let out a low whistle. "That is some painting!" he said. "Is that Denver's daughter?"

"That's her," nodded Jessie. "Amelia Elizabeth Denver. Isn't she lovely?"

Henry leaned over to examine the frame. "Nice work," he observed. "Gilt on wood. And look at the fine, detailed carving."

Kay nodded vigorously. "That is a primo example of fine portraiture. Mark my words, that was not painted by some traveling salesman. That is the work of a master." Kay pulled off her glasses and wiped them clean. "Jessie, this house is a gold mine," she said, restoring her glasses to her face. "Keep your eyes open. I wouldn't be surprised if there is gold hidden away somewhere within these walls. Denver must have been rolling in it."

"That must be what was hanging over the fireplace in her room, right?" asked Sam.

"I think so," replied Jessie. "After I get the room cleaned up, I'm going to restore the painting to its rightful place."

Sam looked at his watch. "Ten o'clock. It's getting late. I'd better be going. I've got a full day tomorrow."

"The time went so fast," Kay exclaimed. "So much has happened."

"You can say that again," agreed Jessie. "It has been a wonderful day."

They descended the stairs and congregated in the foyer.

"Hey, that looks like the dog in the painting," said Henry, pointing at Joseph.

"Well, what do you know," said Sam. "Where'd you find that, Jessie?"

"In the basement," she said. "Isn't it adorable?"

"Adorable," said Sam. "Well, Jessie, thank you for a lovely meal. And God bless you, Kay. Welcome to the family. This is great! Church will be different for you now; you watch and see. The worship and the Word will come alive for you." He shook Henry's hand. "I'll see you Saturday. What time are we supposed to be at the McPhersons'?"

"One o'clock," said Henry.

"See you there." Sam saluted and disappeared out the door. "By the way, Jessie," he called over his shoulder, "good news. Lorena's coming home from the hospital tomorrow."

"Oh, I'm so glad," exclaimed Jessie. "Thanks for the news, Sam. Good night."

Kay retrieved her purse from the living room. She kissed her friend good night. "Thanks for everything, Jess." Kay smiled, tears in her eyes. "I can hardly wait to get home and have a talk with my Father. Bye, guys," she said to Henry and Jessie.

Henry and Jessie stood on the porch and watched Kay drive away. The soothing whisper of leaves, stirred by the night winds, surrounded the house. Suddenly, a splatter of rain filled the air.

"Told you," grinned Henry. "There's the rain."

Jessie laughed and hurried inside. "Come on, before you get wet."

"You don't mind if I stay awhile longer?" asked Henry.

"Of course not," Jessie responded. "How about a cup of tea?"

"I think I'd better not," said Henry. "I don't want to make another mess. Remember what happened the last time we had tea?"

Jessie nodded. "I remember," she said softly. "Maybe we should talk about it tonight."

Henry followed Jessie into the living room. Jessie stopped and listened to the rain. It was falling steadily.

"You know what I would like right now?" she asked Henry.

"What's that?"

"A fire in the fireplace. I know it's crazy in the middle of July, but I'm in the mood."

"Well, fair lady, your wish is my command," said Henry gallantly. "Do you have firewood, M'lady?"

"Actually, I think I do. There's a box beneath the porch."

"I'll find it," said Henry. "I'll make the fire while you put your tea on."

"You'll need a flashlight," she said, walking to the kitchen through the dining room. She grabbed the yellow flashlight plugged into the wall of the kitchen. "Here you go."

"Thanks," Henry smiled.

Jessie busied herself in the kitchen while Henry looked for the wood. Her hands trembled as she prepared the tea. She stopped and held her hands against her cheeks. "I'm shaking. What is the matter with me?" she said to herself. "Why am I so nervous? Am I scared? Excited?"

Jessie listened to the sounds Henry made while on his search. The hatch under the porch creaked as he pulled it open. He dragged out the box and carried it up the back steps. With a loud thump Henry dropped the box onto the floor of the back porch.

"Found it!" Henry called to her.

Jessie opened the door for him. He carried in an armload of wood.

"There's a nice log here and some kindling," he announced. "How about you bring me some newspaper and we'll get this thing started?"

Jessie brought Henry the paper. He knelt down in front of the fireplace, and Jessie sat on the couch and watched him. In a matter of minutes, a lively fire was blazing.

Henry stood up. "There you go," he said.

"Thanks," said Jessie. "It's perfect."

The man stood awkwardly for a moment in front of the fireplace. Jessie closed her eyes. She soaked in the sounds of the pelting summer rain and the crackle of the fire. "Listen to that, Henry," she said. "Isn't it wonderful?" She opened her eyes to look at him.

He smiled. "Yes, it is wonderful." Henry cleared his throat. "Jessie, I hope you weren't. . .I mean the last time I was here, you know what happened. I hope you don't. . ."

Jessie stood up and joined Henry in front of the fire.

"Henry, I'm not sure what happened. Are you?" she said quietly. Jessie stared into the fire. She was afraid to look into Henry's eyes.

"I'm not sure," said Henry. He watched her watch the fire. The glow of the flames shone in her eyes, and her face was flushed. He took a deep breath. "All I know is I can't stop thinking about you, Jessie." He ran his hand through his hair. "I know you've been through a lot and you probably don't want to get involved with anyone. I'm not real good with words. I don't know if. . .well, do you think. . . ?" He stumbled for the right thing to say.

Jessie turned her gaze away from the fire. She looked into Henry's gentle eyes. She searched his face and found compassion there.

"Henry, I don't know if I'm ready for a relationship. So much has happened. Sam said that things would become clearer once I was back with the Lord."

"Sam's right," said Henry, looking into Jessie's deep brown eyes.

"I'm scared," whispered Jessie.

Henry reached out and pulled Jessie into his arms. He held her close. This time it was Henry who was trembling. He hid his face in her hair. When he pulled himself away, his face was wet with tears.

She reached up and touched his face. "What's this?" she asked.

Henry took her hand. "I feel so much for you. . .well, it kind of hurts. Like an ache in my heart. I don't know what to say or what to do."

Jessie squeezed his hand. "Well, maybe we should just take it slow, okay?"

Henry turned and flopped down onto the couch. "Take it slow," he repeated. "I don't know if I can. Being with you makes my head spin. I don't know what to do or say." He threw his arms up in exasperation, promptly knocking the lamp next to the couch onto the floor.

"Oh, man!" Henry scoffed at himself. "I don't believe this."

Jessie laughed and knelt down to pick it up. The bulb was broken. "Henry, you are a walking disaster. It's a good thing you're not like this on the job!"

"No one would hire me," sighed Henry.

Jessie stood and leaned against the mantel as she studied the fire. It was dying down, the flames fluttering lower and lower. The yellow-orange embers pulsated with heat and color. Henry watched her from the sofa.

"What about you, Jessie?" he asked. "What do you. . .I mean do you have. . . do you feel anything?"

Jessie hugged herself. "I have such a peace about things, now that I've come home to the Lord. I feel like life is opening up to me again. I know the Lord has new things planned for me. I know—"

"Jessie, how do you feel about me?" Henry interrupted her. His voice was taut with emotion.

She turned to face him. Tears sprang into her eyes. "Henry Lewis," was all she could say.

Henry jumped up and drew Jessie into his arms. He kissed her. She felt his heart in his kiss. All she could do was cry. He held her while the rain tapped on the windows and poured refreshment onto the land.

"Jessie, why are you crying?" Henry searched her face. "You're always crying. It makes me nervous."

"Why are you always knocking things over?" asked Jessie. "That makes me nervous. Especially considering all the antiques I have."

They laughed together. Jessie rested her head on Henry's chest and hugged him close. "This has been a perfect day," she whispered.

"Yes, it has," agreed Henry. "Perfect. I hope you. . .well, I think we should. . . do you—"

"Shh," hushed Jessie. "We'll talk more tomorrow. For now, let's just listen to the rain."

Chapter 21

After Henry left, Jessie busied herself in the kitchen. She looked up from the sink when the clock on the mantel in the dining room chimed twelve. "Better go to bed," she said to herself. "Tomorrow morning I tackle the dust in the secret room. And then shopping with Kay."

She stopped in the foyer to look at the clock. The slender, arrow-shaped hands were frozen at twelve. The painting of the glowing moon had risen to its place above the numbers. Jessie patted the side of the clock. "Wonderful old clock," she said aloud. "I'll look into getting you running again."

Once in bed, Jessie lay awake thinking about Kay and Henry. She whispered a prayer of thanks for her friend's salvation. Finally! After all these years. She smiled in the darkness. And Henry. He was so sweet and strong. "Give me wisdom, Lord," she prayed. "I don't want to rush into anything. Everything seems so new to me. Guide me, Lord. Let me be rooted and grounded in Your love."

While her thoughts faded into sleep, two dark figures in black rain gear hurried through the rain and into Jessie's backyard. One led the way up the back steps. He pulled at the screen door.

"It's locked," he sputtered. He pulled a utility knife from his pocket and deftly sliced an opening in the screen. A flash of lightning momentarily lit up the yard.

"Hurry up!" hissed the accomplice. "Before someone sees us."

Spencer Hart reached in and unlatched the door. They hurried into the porch and crouched down. "Stay down while I check the window."

The young woman nodded. He walked toward the window and almost tripped on something. "What. . . ?" He turned on his penlight. "Box of firewood," he mumbled. "What kind of a nut uses firewood in the middle of July?"

"Who cares!" the woman whispered. "Turn that light off!"

Spencer turned off the flashlight. He tried the window, cursing under his breath. "Locked. I'll have to go in through the cellar."

He hurried out the door and into the rain. Feeling his way in the dark, he unlatched the small door under the porch. He pulled it open and crawled underneath. Flipping on his small flashlight, he made his way through the dirt and old paint cans to the window.

"There you are," the man cooed to the small, dust-encrusted window. "Come to poppa." He jammed his knife between the window and its frame and easily jiggled the window open. "You gotta love the old wood and rusty hinges of yesteryear." He laughed to himself.

Spencer shone his light into the darkened cellar. "Piece of cake," he whispered. He lowered himself into the cellar, steadying his balance on the stone floor. Quietly he ascended the narrow basement steps. At the top, he stopped and listened, pulling the cellar door open slowly.

All was quiet within the house. In the dark, he crept across the kitchen floor and unlocked the back door. "Stacy!" he whispered. "All clear."

The young woman entered the kitchen. She had taken off her rain gear and had left it on the porch. Spencer shone his light on her while she adjusted her flowing white dress and checked her hair.

"Perfect!" whispered Spencer. "Have you got the candle?"

Stacy held up a slender taper in a candlestick.

"Okay. Now, before you make your move, wait until I get up the stairs and am hidden. And remember to leave time to listen for any movement in the bedroom. If I'm right, she'll come out to investigate the noise."

"And if you're wrong?"

"Plan B. It's messier, but one way or another we'll get her out of the way." Spencer stopped and listened. Except for the storm outside, the house was silent. "Let's go."

Stacy followed Spencer down the hallway to the foyer. Her eyes were accustomed to the dark, and she watched him disappear slowly and carefully up the stairs.

"How he can manage that with his bad foot is a wonder to me," she said to herself.

Stacy waited for a moment until she was sure all was quiet and her partner was safely hidden away. Suddenly, the clock chimed, and she almost dropped the candle.

"Why didn't he tell me about that clock?" she whispered. "I could've had a heart attack!"

She pulled a book of matches from the pocket of her dress. Striking one match, she suddenly illumined the dark in a flash of blue and yellow. She lit the candle and stationed herself at the foot of the stairs.

"Fa–ther," she called out in a thin, singsong voice. "Fa–ther."

Jessie Woods stirred in her sleep.

"Fa–ther."

Jessie opened her eyes. "What was that?" she said to herself. Rain pelted the window and a peal of thunder droned faintly in the stormy night sky.

"I thought I heard something," Jessie mumbled to herself. "Sounded like a voice."

"Fa-ther," the voice cried louder.

The eerie wail hit Jessie's ears like a thunderbolt, and she sat upright in her bed. "What was that?" Her heart started pounding in her chest. She fumbled for the phone.

The woman at the foot of the stairs stepped over the threshold into the living room. She stood inside the door, just out of sight.

Then she mimicked the sound of a yowling cat.

"Oh, brother," sighed Jessie with relief. "It's just a cat. Kay would have loved that. Me, calling her in the middle of the night, because of a stray cat."

The cat sounded again, faintly.

"Strange," wondered Jessie. "Sounds like it's in the house. How did that happen?"

Jessie got out of bed and pulled on her robe. She flipped on the lamp on her bedstand, and the flowered white globe bombarded Jessie's eyes with light. She stepped into the hallway.

She was about to flip the light switch at the top of the stairs, when the woman in the living room reappeared at the foot of the stairs. She held her candle up, letting the glow of light fall on her face.

"Fa–ther," she called, looking up the stairs at Jessie.

Jessie froze. Camilla's stories about the sad Denvers flashed crazily in her mind.

"Amelia?" Jessie's voice cracked in terror, and her eyes widened at the spectacle standing at the foot of her stairs. Fear swept through her body, her knees buckling beneath her.

Suddenly she heard a muffled sound from behind. Step, scrape; step, scrape. But before Jessie could turn around, she felt a forceful push. Down the stairs she plummeted, headfirst. The floor came up hard against her head.

"Well, what did you do that for?" demanded Stacy. "I thought you were going to grab her from behind and gag her."

"I tripped," hissed Spencer. "Cursed foot scuffed on the carpet. Never mind that. Is she out cold?"

Stacy blew out her candle and pulled a small flashlight from her pocket. She bent over and aimed her light at Jessie.

"Out cold," she nodded. "Good work, Hart. Hey, you don't think she's dead, do you?" Stacy recoiled from the prone body. "I won't have anything to do with murder."

"Be quiet," ordered Spencer. He made his way down the stairs and checked for a pulse. "She's alive. Let's tie her up and gag her in case she comes to."

He pulled some rope and a piece of cloth from the back of his pants. The two proceeded to expertly secure their victim.

"All right now," Spencer spoke quietly. "We go up to the room and see what we can find. If I'm right, in five minutes we'll be filthy rich!"

The two conspirators hustled up the stairs. Using the briefest amount of light, Spencer led his partner to the secret room. He stopped at the door to the sitting room.

"Get a load of this," he whispered. He flashed his light on the painting of Amelia Elizabeth.

"Spooky." Stacy stared at the painting.

"Told ya. You're a dead ringer," huffed Spencer.

"Don't use the word *dead*, okay?" said Stacy. "I've heard those stories about these people. It's creepy. What if—"

"Don't be ridiculous! It's a lot of small-town nonsense. Now, come on. I want to get the gold and get out."

They entered the secret room. Spencer headed for the marble-topped dresser. He pulled a piece of paper out of his pocket. The mirror reflected the two as they hovered over the note.

"See?" said Spencer.

"It says don't sleep in the moonlight. And get a load of this!"

He knelt down and pointed his light at the base of the dresser. Carved exquisitely along the front was a row of moons, several crescents on either side of a round, full moon.

"You know I'm familiar with antiques and this particular piece looks as though it has a false front. They were sometimes built with secret drawers."

"Spare me the history lesson and get on with it," spat Stacy. "We haven't got all night."

"All right, all right," he said. "Get down here and hold your light on the base."

Spencer felt along the sides of the base. Finding nothing, he slid his fingers along the bottom. Near the left corner, his hands found a small lever and a spring. "Bingo!" he said and pushed the lever. With a slight twang, the spring loosened, and the base creaked forward. He pulled on it.

"Stuck," he sputtered. "Hasn't been opened in ninety years."

"Pull harder," demanded Stacy.

He pulled and strained at the drawer. Finally, it opened with a painful grating sound of wood on wood.

"Would you look at that!" exclaimed Stacy.

Nestled in the bottom of the drawer was a large rectangular box, encrusted with gold carving and precious jewels.

"Get the key! Get the key!" squealed Stacy.

Spencer fumbled in his pocket for the key. It was an exact replica of the key that Kay Bantam had found in the attic. He pulled the box out of the drawer and eyed the lock on the front of it.

"I don't know," he breathed. "This key looks kind of big for this lock."

"Just try it!" hissed Stacy. "If it doesn't work, we'll just take the box back to the motel and bust it open."

Spencer pushed the key into the lock. "Too big," he said.

Stacy grabbed Spencer's arm. "I think I heard something."

The two froze. "I don't hear anything," he said. "Maybe that Woods dame is coming to. Don't worry, she's not going anywhere. Let's check the drawer again."

They leaned over the drawer and shone both their lights inside.

There was a pile of white silk handkerchiefs edged in green with the letter D embroidered on the corners. A small stack of letters tied in a pink ribbon lay in one corner of the drawer. In the back of the drawer, Spencer spied a tiny, satin pouch. He pulled it out and pulled open the drawstrings.

"Bingo!" he said. "Another key!"

Stacy grabbed the key and thrust it into the golden box. The top flipped open easily.

"What. . . ?" Hart grabbed at the pile of papers that lay inside the box. "There's nothing in here but a bunch of measly papers! It can't be!" He dumped the papers out in a frenzy. "It has to be here. The gold has to be here!"

"Freeze!" A voice shrieked from the direction of the door. A bright light blinded the two intruders.

"Who—"

"Never mind," the voice continued. "Just stay right where you are."

Spencer squinted to see past the light. "Who's there?" he demanded, straining to recognize the voice. "I've heard that voice before. Who—"

"Just stay where you are," the voice croaked.

"Herb Stamping? The guy from the post office?" Spencer smirked and let go a low laugh. He took a step toward the man holding the light.

"I warn you," said Herb, his hand beginning to shake. "My partner has gone for help. The police will be here any minute."

Spencer rushed at Herb. Downstairs, the front door opened with a bang. "Go get him, Manny," Sam ordered.

Manny rushed up the stairs in time to let out a loud bark and furious growl at the intruders. Stacy started screaming. Herb pulled away from Spencer. "Good boy. Good boy, Manny," said a relieved Herb.

Sam flipped on the lights and bounded up the stairs. He found Herb, standing in the doorway behind Manny, pointing his large flashlight as though it were a gun.

"Don't let that dog bite me," Spencer trembled. "I hate dogs. Get him away from me."

"You idiot," snorted Stacy.

Sam ignored the two. "Herb, you can put your weapon down now." Herb reluctantly lowered his oversized flashlight.

A siren wailed to a halt in front of 16 Lark Avenue.

"The police are here," said Sam. "Ruby's checking on Jess; she called an ambulance." His voice strained with anger. "She better be all right."

Jessie was attempting to sit up when the police and paramedics rushed through the front doorway.

"What happened?" she moaned, rubbing her head. "I think I'm going to throw up."

"Now you just sit still," clucked Ruby. "You had a nasty fall. These people are here to help you."

The paramedics examined Jessie. "We're going to put you on the stretcher, Ma'am," one man explained. "You've probably suffered a concussion. They'll need to check you out at the hospital."

"Fine," mumbled Jessie.

Sam hurried down the stairs just as they carried Jessie out. "Is she all right?" Sam asked Ruby.

"Concussion," said Ruby crisply. "They suspect a concussion. She'll be fine. Good thing Herb and I arrived when we did."

Sam looked at Ruby. "You certainly are dressed for the part."

Ruby was wearing black slacks, a black turtleneck, and a black cap. Her cheeks were darkened with charcoal.

"A concerned citizen's got to do what a concerned citizen's got to do!" she sniffed.

The police descended the stairs with the two intruders in tow. Herb, also dressed in black, bustled behind them, giving a blow-by-blow description of what had transpired. One officer remained behind to investigate the scene.

Kay and Henry both arrived in front of Jessie's house just as the ambulance pulled away. Henry pulled open his car door and called to Sam on the front porch. "Jessie?" he yelled, pointing at the ambulance.

"Yes," responded Sam. He headed for the truck to explain, but Henry took off, tires squealing.

Kay hopped out of her car. "What is going on? Where's Jessie?"

"They've taken her to the hospital," Sam said.

"What—"

"She'll be fine," explained Sam. "She bumped her head when she fell down the stairs."

"She was pushed," announced Herb Stamping. Ruby stood beside him, nodding her head.

"More than likely she was pushed down those stairs," agreed Ruby.

"Pushed?" squeaked Kay. "Pushed by whom?"

"Never mind," said Sam. "Let's get over to the hospital before Henry tears the place apart. I'll drive, if you don't mind." He looked at Kay. She appeared to be shaken.

"No problem," she said. "We can take my car."

Sam turned to say thank you to Herb and Ruby, but they were already climbing into Herb's car. They sped off in the direction of the hospital.

"Oh, boy," said Sam. "Looks like Sherlock and Watson will be waiting for us. That's all Jessie needs, an entire committee to greet her at the hospital."

Kay laughed. "I remember the last welcoming committee that graced Jessie's doorstep."

"Here we go again!" sighed Sam. "I'm just glad she's okay."

∞

At the hospital, they found Henry pacing the waiting room. Herb and Ruby stood together, watching him walk back and forth. Ruby gave Herb a knowing look; they both nodded.

"Henry," said Sam as he entered the room. "Calm down, old buddy. She's going to be fine, I'm sure."

"She's in getting an X-ray," Henry said, his voice hoarse. "What happened, Sam?"

"We'll be glad to tell you what happened," volunteered Ruby. "We know all about it."

"Shouldn't you be down at the police station, talking to the chief?" asked Sam.

"He said to come down later," said Ruby.

"I already told them some of it," said a proud Herb.

"Just tell us what happened," demanded Kay. She looked at Ruby and Herb. "And why are you two in that kind of get-up?"

"All right, Ms. Bantam," nodded Ruby. "You poor dear. After all, Mrs. Woods is your best friend."

"Mrs. Clearwater!" Kay cried. "Get on with it!"

"Well," began the librarian, "it all started when I first saw this man—"

"Spencer Hart," interjected Herb.

"I saw him at my library. He was supposedly doing research on the Denver family to help him with the writing of a novel."

"He told me he was writing a novel about a small town," added Herb. "Of course, I never really believed that."

Ruby glared at her friend. "Anyway, I knew he was up to something. And I knew he had an accomplice. This young woman with long brown hair used to meet him in the library. I figured what he was really interested in was the gold rumored to be hidden in the Denver house."

"That's ridiculous," scoffed Sam. "Who would actually believe that nonsense?"

"Well, Spencer Hart took it all in, hook, line, and sinker," announced Herb. "And then Ruby overheard—"

"And then yesterday I heard Hart tell that woman of his that tonight was the night." Ruby laughed and twirled the chain holding her glasses. "You'd be surprised at the things you can hear through the bookshelves at the library. Why, Reverend Sam, it would curl your hair."

"No, thanks," winced Sam.

"So, I called Herb," continued Mrs. Clearwater.

"Why didn't you call the police or at least Sam?" demanded Henry.

"Are you kidding?" scoffed Ruby. "Nobody believes me about this kind of thing! Remember the Irving incident? Nobody would believe me."

Sam swallowed a smile. "She's got you there, Henry."

"So Herb and I devised a plan. Around midnight we drove to Maple Avenue, over to Lorena's house. We knew Lorena wasn't home and that her house is right behind Mrs. Woods's house. We hid behind the bushes."

"We had a clear view of the house," said Herb dramatically. "Even in the dark, it's not so hard to see over there. Between the lightning and the rain and the thunder, there we were, hiding out, watching the house like a couple of hawks just waiting to make our move."

"Well, finally, at about one o'clock, we saw something," said Ruby. "We saw a flicker of light on the back porch. We waited for awhile. Then we made our move."

"We ran to the porch," continued Herb. "Ruby waited for me while I sneaked inside the house. I can walk as quietly as a cheetah stalking its prey. I could hear voices upstairs. To my horror, I almost tripped on Mrs. Woods! Then I hurried back to tell Ruby."

"I ran over to tell Reverend Taylor to call the police," beamed Ruby, "and the rest is history!"

"Wow!" gasped Kay. "Talk about horripilation! I'm covered with it." The men turned and gave Kay quizzical looks. Ruby nodded. "Gooseflesh," explained the librarian. "She's got goose bumps from the telling of this awful story."

Henry ran his hand through his hair as he resumed his pacing. "Poor Jessie," he said with a low voice. "She must have been frightened to death. I've got to see her."

At that moment, a doctor entered the room. "I presume you all are here for Mrs. Woods?" he asked with a kindly voice.

"Yes," said Henry. "How is she?"

"Mrs. Woods'll be fine," said the doctor. "She had quite a fall. Lucky she didn't break any bones. However, she does have a concussion. We'll be keeping her overnight to monitor her." The doctor eyed everyone in the group. "Two of you may see her now. She's fully conscious." He looked at Herb and Ruby. "You two look like you have a story to tell."

"Got a minute?" asked Herb. "We'll tell you all about it. It may help you with your patient, after all. She was probably pushed down those stairs, you know."

Sam pushed Henry to the door. "You and Kay go on in. I'll see her later."

A nurse led Kay and Henry away. Sam leaned against the wall. The light of understanding concerning Jessica Woods and Henry Lewis was dawning on him. As the breaking news story babbled in the background, Sam whispered a prayer for his friends. An unexplainable but familiar peace began to sweep surely through him, pushing the ache right out of his heart.

Chapter 22

J essie!" Henry rushed through the door. "Are you okay?" His green eyes were flooded with concern.

Jessie looked into his face, and her eyes watered with the relief at seeing his loving face. She smiled through her tears. "I'm fine. Just a little woozy from all the excitement."

"Jessie Woods, don't you ever do this to me again!" Kay reprimanded her friend. "Scaring me half to death. I can't believe what happened! Ruby and Herb were telling us—"

"Ruby and Herb?" said Jessie with a questioning look. She reached for a tissue on the bedstand and wiped her tears. "What do Ruby Clearwater and Herbert Stamping have to do with all this?" She gingerly touched her head; a bruise was already forming across her forehead.

"Never mind," said Henry quietly. "We'll tell you all about it tomorrow, when you're feeling better."

"No, please," insisted Jessie as she sat up in the bed. "Tell me what happened. I don't want to wait until tomorrow. The last thing I remember is hearing a voice calling, 'Fa-ther,' and then I saw this figure at the bottom of the stairs. It looked just like Amelia Elizabeth Denver. I was terrified. And then I felt something push me and down the stairs I went."

Henry's jaw tightened as Jessie spoke about being pushed. "Kay, give her a brief synopsis," he said. "Brief."

"Right-o," responded Kay. "It's like this: Some guy named Spencer Somebody and his sidekick broke into your house to look for the Denver gold. They must have cooked up a scheme to frighten and subdue you to buy time for the search." Kay pushed her glasses up the bridge of her shiny nose. "Look at this. I'm sweating like a pig in August. Anyway, Ruby and Herbert suspected these guys of dirty play and followed them into your house. They surprised the intruders and went to Sam's for help."

Jessie sat back in the bed. "I don't believe it. This is incredible. You should have seen that woman. I was so scared, but my mind was telling me it couldn't be real. Then I thought maybe I was dreaming or something." Jessie shivered as she spoke.

Henry reached over and covered her hands with his own. "It's okay, Jess. The Lord was looking out for you. I never thought I'd ever say this, but thank goodness

119

for Ruby's suspicious mind!"

Jessie slowly shook her head. "I just don't believe it. How could anyone actually plan all that, just for some imaginary gold?"

"Now, hey, wait a minute," Kay protested. "I for one think there is every possibility that there is gold hidden in that house. Mark my words."

"Now, Kay, I think Jessie's had enough talk of hidden gold," said Henry. "We better let her rest now."

"Did you say Sam was there tonight?" asked Jessie. "Where is he?"

"He's in the waiting room," replied Henry. "I'll go get him." He smiled at Jessie, his eyes warm with love. "I'll see you tomorrow."

Kay leaned over and kissed her friend good night. "I'll be over tomorrow. Then we'll see how things are over at the house."

"Okay. Thanks, Kay. I love you," said Jessie.

"Love you, too, my dear. Even though you put about a zillion new gray hairs in my head. I'm going to have to go to Evie's and get myself rejuvenated!"

Jessie laughed. Sam passed Kay in the doorway. "Glad to see you laughing," said Sam warmly. "How does the patient feel?"

"The patient has a terrible headache, but that's privileged information," smiled Jessie.

"Thank the Lord! He is faithful, isn't He?" said Sam. "He never sleeps."

"You can say that again," sighed Jessie. She looked into Sam's eyes. "They said you were there?"

"Yes," responded Sam. "Ruby came and pounded on my door. When I opened it, she commanded me to call the police. Said there was a 1031 at Jessie Woods's house."

"A 1031?"

"A burglary in progress. That Ruby is something else. And you should have seen her and Herb. They were dressed totally in black, with charcoal smeared on their faces. They looked like two lost crows."

Jessie laughed and grimaced at the same time. "Don't make me laugh," she groaned. "It hurts!"

"Sorry," said Sam. "Let me pray with you, and then I'll get out of the way. They're going to put you in a room upstairs."

"Thanks for being there, Sam," said Jessie.

"What are friends for?" smiled Sam. He squeezed her hand. "Let's pray and then off I go."

He prayed for a speedy recovery, and together Jessie and Sam thanked the Lord for His deliverance. Fran, the nurse, entered as they spoke the amen.

"Okay, Reverend Taylor, it's time to move the patient," announced Fran.

"All right, Fran, I was just leaving," responded Sam. "I'll see you tomorrow, Jess."

Jessie watched Sam leave, and she sensed something different about him. It seemed to her that there was a peace in his face that she had not seen before. "He's usually kind of uptight whenever he's with me," she said to herself. "I wonder what's happened."

The nurse transported her patient to a room on the second floor.

Jessie fell asleep thanking the Lord that she was alive and well.

∞

"Good morning, my dear," a cheery voice called out to Jessie.

"Lorena!" exclaimed Jessie. "You're up and about! How are you feeling?"

Lorena patted Jessie on the cheek. "The question is, how are you? I heard the dreadful story from one of the nurses. You must have been so frightened!"

"It was awful," agreed Jessie. "But now it seems almost like a dream."

"And to think Ruby Clearwater and Herb Stamping hid in my yard!" beamed Lorena. "I'm so glad they were there to help you."

"Me, too," nodded Jessie. "I'll be sure to thank them for their detective work."

"The Lord works in mysterious ways," laughed Lorena. "We all thought Ruby's skills were limited to the drama club at church. Were we ever wrong!"

"Let's hope she can retire now," said Jessie. "I have a feeling the police are going to ask her to leave the police work to them."

"I imagine so," said Lorena. "It's the Lord's mercy that things didn't turn out worse. But enough about that. I have some good news. I'm going home today, too! You and I will be back in our homes in an hour."

Jessie got up out of her bed and gave Lorena a hug. "I'm so glad! I saw Dr. Freeman this morning. He said you were doing quite well."

"Quite well for an old lady, I'm sure he's thinking." Lorena's eyes twinkled. "I happen to know I'm not an old lady. I've just changed my style a little."

Jessie laughed. "I hope I'm half as vibrant as you when I'm your age."

"The secret is to trust the Lord with yesterday, today, and tomorrow. He's the Alpha and the Omega, the Beginning and the End. He can handle it!"

Lorena's words matched the brightness of the morning sun flooding into Jessie's hospital room. Trust took on a whole new meaning for Jessie as she realized more and more that the Lord had surely watched over her the night before.

Kay arrived in a burst of color to pick up her friend at the hospital.

"Kay!" Jessie squinted. "That outfit's hurting my eyes. Can't you put it out?"

"I shall choose to disregard the insult on account of your weakened condition," spouted Kay. Kay adjusted her canary yellow hat and smoothed the pantlegs of her canary yellow jumpsuit. "Let's go."

The nurse pushed Jessie's wheelchair to the front door of the hospital and the automatic doors opened with a swoosh. Jessie, smiling, walked out to Kay's car, and she looked around the parking lot.

"Looking for someone?" Kay asked sweetly.

"Well, I was hoping Henry had come with you, if you must know," replied

Jessie, opening the front door to Kay's car.

"I must know," said Kay. "I always know. Henry couldn't come. Said he had something he had to do this morning."

"Oh," said Jessie, disappointment in her voice.

Kay rolled her eyes and turned the key in the ignition. "Let's go home, Juliet."

When Kay pulled into the driveway, Jessie gasped. The front porch was overflowing with flowers and balloons.

"What. . . ? Kay, you rascal! That is so beautiful!"

"Don't you rascal me," said Kay. "Unfortunately, I can't take the credit for this buena vista."

The front door flew open, and Henry strode out toward the car. He opened Jessie's door and helped her out. "Welcome home, M'lady!" he said grandly.

"Henry! Did you do all this?" Jessie stared at the bounty of color brimming over the railings of the porch.

"He's guilty, as charged," said Kay, slamming her door with zest. "Isn't this absolutely fantastic?"

"Henry!" scolded Jessie. "This must have cost you a fortune. All these fresh, lovely flowers. I've never seen anything like it!"

"Never?" asked Henry shyly.

"Never," responded Jessie.

"Wait'll you see inside," said Kay.

"Inside?" said Jessie incredulously.

Henry took Jessie by the hand and led her into the house. There she saw flowers overflowing the table in the foyer and baskets of flowers on the floor. A tour through the living room and dining room revealed more of the same. The fragrances and colors overwhelmed Jessie with joy.

"This is wonderful," she whispered. "To tell you the truth, I thought I might be afraid to come back here. But this has made all the difference! This is a lovely home, it's my home, and I'm not going to let the enemy steal it from me!"

"Here, here," a voice echoed from the kitchen.

"Sam?" Jessie walked through the kitchen doorway to see Sam Taylor, busy over the stove, chef hat and all. "I am preparing a feast fit for a queen."

"I'd settle for lunch," said Kay. "I'm starved. All this cops and robbers and flowers stuff can really make a person hungry."

Sam laughed. "It's almost ready." He wiped his hands on his white, bibbed apron. He took Jessie's hand and kissed it with dramatic ceremony. "Welcome back to your castle, Jessie. We are all glad the dark night is over."

Jessie looked at each of her friends. Her shoulders began to shake as the tears flowed from her eyes. She stood in the middle of her kitchen weeping. "The dark night is over," she said through her tears. "But not just last night. My long night of mourning and anger and emptiness is over. The Lord has restored my life to me."

Sam nodded at Henry, and Henry wrapped his arms around Jessie and held her close. "There you go, crying again," he whispered. He let her cry, while Kay and Sam looked on. When the tears subsided, he took his hand and gently lifted her face to his.

"Should we be leaving?" Kay whispered urgently to Sam.

Sam shook his head. "Shh. Listen."

"Jessie Woods," said Henry, trembling, "you don't have to answer me now or tomorrow or even next year. You can take your time. I will wait for you for as long as it takes." Henry took a deep breath. "Will you marry me, Jessie?"

Kay covered her mouth to keep herself from screaming. Sam was grinning from ear to ear, his eyes sparkling with delight. Jessie, amazed, gazed into Henry's eyes.

Sam signaled to Kay. "Now we can go," he whispered.

"Just when it's getting good," Kay protested under her breath.

Kay and Sam went to the front porch and sat on the steps.

"I can't believe what has happened around here," said Kay. "My head is whirling."

"There's never been a dull moment since Jessie moved into the neighborhood," said Sam, grinning.

Kay studied Sam's face. "So, spill the beans. What happened to you and your marriage proposal? Henry's great, and they obviously are in love with each other. What about you?"

Sam pulled a flower from a nearby basket. "Well, the Lord showed me that I jumped the gun with my feelings for Jess. I know now that she's not the one the Lord has for me. We're more like sister and brother; you know what I mean? When I saw Henry at the hospital, that clinched it for me. The look of agony in his face over Jessie's predicament was heartwrenching. I knew then that he loves her with all his heart. I let it go. If the Lord has someone for me, He will bring us together. And you know what? When I let it go, the Lord gave me such a peace. I can't explain it."

"I know what you mean," said Kay, pushing up her glasses. "About the peace, I mean. You just can't explain it. Isn't it great that I can say I know what you mean and actually mean it? You know what I mean?"

Sam pushed back against the step and laughed out loud. "Kay Bantam, you are going to truly be an asset to the body of Christ."

∞

Back in the kitchen, Henry Lewis waited for Jessie's answer to his question.

"Henry Lewis, is this a conspiracy?" asked Jessie, smiling.

"Well, sort of," admitted Henry. "I asked Kay and Sam to be here. Moral support, you know. I'm not real good at, well, you know I find it hard to—"

"I understand, Henry," said Jessie.

"So what do you—"

"Yes, Henry, I will marry you. When—"

Henry ran his hand through his hair and shoved the other hand into his pocket. "Yes?" he whispered, his voice intense with excitement and joy.

"Wait a second, calm down," said Jessie. "Let me finish. I said yes, when we're ready," she answered. "So much has happened, and I think we need some time to get to know each other."

"I feel like I've known you all my life," protested Henry. "Let's get married tomorrow. I know a good preacher man."

"Henry! Let's take it a little slow, okay? I think the Lord will honor that."

"But you did say yes?"

Jessie nodded, her eyes shining. The joy of the Lord flooded her soul. She knew this was the path the Lord was choosing for her. "When the Lord says we're ready, we'll do it."

Chapter 23

Henry let Jessie go, and then he rushed out of the kitchen. "I've got to tell Sam!" he said over his shoulder.

Jessie stood alone in the center of the kitchen. "It's customary for the guy to kiss the girl after he's proposed," she called out after him.

"I'll be right back!" exclaimed Henry.

A big bang resounded in the foyer. "Oh, man," Jessie heard Henry moan.

Jessie hurried to the foyer. Kay and Sam flew through the front door. "What now?" cried Kay.

A sheepish Henry sat on the hardwood floor, rubbing his elbow.

"I tripped on a basket and sort of banged into the grandfather clock. I'm sorry, Jessie. I think I broke it."

"Henry, that doesn't matter," said Jessie. "Are you all right?"

"I'm fine, but look at the clock. I broke the front of the base."

"Broke it, my eye," gasped Kay. She knelt down by the clock. "Well, I'll be. It's a false front! Look!"

"What are you talking about?" said Sam.

All four adults gathered, on their knees, around the clock. The front panel of the base had come off, revealing a small door with a brass keyhole.

"The key in the box!" exclaimed Jessie. "Do you think—"

"Where is it?" squealed Kay, jumping to her feet.

"Upstairs," said Jessie. "In the sitting room on the lampstand."

Kay ran up the stairs and found the box with the brass key inside.

"Hello, Amelia, you beautiful girl, you," Kay said gleefully to the painting. She rushed out the door. "I've got it!"

Kay handed Jessie the key.

"I can't do it. I'm too nervous," Jessie said. She was about to hand the key to Henry, but he vigorously shook his head.

"I'm not touching it," he said. "I've done enough."

"You do it, Sam," suggested Jessie.

"All right, you guys, move back and let the calm, cool, and collected Sam Taylor unlock the mystery of the Denver house. I bet it's just the inner workings of the clock."

"Pastors aren't supposed to bet," scoffed Kay. "Just open it, will you? The suspense is killing me."

Sam slipped the key into the lock. It turned with a click, and the door popped open. On two shelves were neatly stacked ingots of pure gold and a small sack of coins.

Kay screamed. Jessie scooted back against the bottom stairs, her face pale. Henry was speechless.

"I don't believe it!" said Sam in amazement. "The stories were true. There's got to be several thousand dollars in gold in there."

"What's that piece of paper on the top there?" asked Kay, peering into the secret compartment.

"Paper?" said Jessie, perking up. "What is it?"

Sam reached in and carefully extracted the paper. "Looks like a letter, maybe two. I'm not sure. There are two pages and a small envelope."

"A letter?" yelped Jessie and Kay in unison. "Read it, Sam."

"Okay, ladies, calm down," said Sam, unfolding the letter.

"Calm? Who can be calm?" sputtered the realtor. She pulled off her glasses and wiped the lenses on the corner of her brilliant yellow jacket. "Calm, nothing. My lenses are fogged."

"Okay," said Sam, clearing his throat. "Here goes: 'My dear Amelia—' "

"Amelia!" interrupted Jessie. "You mean it's a letter written to Amelia? From her father?"

Sam read the name at the bottom. "Yes, that's what it appears to be."

"Read it already," huffed Kay.

My dear Amelia,

There has not been a day when I have not thought of you since I received the news of your death. No one knows the agony I have suffered over the loss of you. But something wonderful has happened, and I felt I should at least write it down. Sharing it in a letter seemed to be the best way for me to pour out my heart. You used to write such delightful letters when you were away at school. I have treasured every epistle you ever sent me.

First, I wish to apologize for not being the best father for you. I often wish that I had spent more time with both you and your mother. It was my firm belief that my first duty was to provide for you both financially. That is important, but I must admit that I enjoyed the adventure and the challenge of business here and abroad. I could have been home more often than I was. That regret has pierced my heart many times. Forgive me, my dear daughter.

Secondly, I must beg your forgiveness for discouraging you from pursuing the Christian faith. From the time you were very little, you used to ask questions about God and the Bible. I would brush away all questions in an effort to shield you from what I thought was nothing more than an emotional antidote for life's ills. I had no use for religion in any form.

How this has all changed! The last letter I received from you opened my eyes. You said that the dear old missionary who attended to you during your illness spoke of Jesus as though He were right there with her. There was no anguish in your letter, only a vivid hope that I knew was no feverish prattle. I know my little girl. You were never one to give up or try to escape life's trials. And now you have discovered the truth. As you said in your letter: "There is a God, and His name is Jesus."

I can't describe the peace that came when I knelt at my bedside and cried out to Him. I thought I would lose my mind if He wouldn't answer. But answer He did. His Presence showered me with a singular love that I had never before experienced. I have much to be thankful for now.

I have enclosed your last letter with mine. The Lord used the words you wrote to turn me to His unfathomable love in Christ. Reverend Thompson says he would like to publish it in the Baptist Herald *and perhaps make a tract out of our testimony. I think it is a wonderful idea. He suggests that I write it all out for him. I shall put it in a safe place until I am well enough to undertake the project. The doctor says I must rest. He says my heart is in a weakened state.*

When I am stronger, I am going to open your room again and let in the light of day. It was foolish of me, I know. I even had Sophie wrap your portrait and put it up in the attic. I was blind with grief. Grief can drain all reason from a man.

The monies I have hidden in the house I will retrieve and distribute as the Lord leads. I have already given a good portion of it to Miss Bristol for her school for underprivileged girls. It's a grand idea. You would smile to know that when she completes her studies, your Rosemary will be a teacher at the new school.

I love you, Amelia Elizabeth. From my heart I say thank you for sharing your faith with me. We are the last of the Denvers, you and I. I am glad we have been found in Christ. I will see you in glory. With all my love,

Your father,
Carlton Denver

Sam looked up from the letter. Henry, Jessie, and Kay looked up at him. He opened the smaller envelope and pulled out and read the enclosed note.

Dear Father,

Miss Bristol is writing this for me. I'm afraid I haven't the strength to do it myself. Miss Bristol has been so good to me on this trip. I'm glad I came. I know you didn't want me to go. Now I feel a sadness that I probably won't see you again. That is hard to tell you, but you always taught me to be straightforward and honest about all things. My heart is broken over the thought of what you must be feeling now. There is not time for you to come to me. But, Father, you must know that this trip has proved to have a divine purpose.

A dear old missionary woman named Matty Grady has been caring for me in my illness. She speaks to me often of Jesus, as though He were her best friend. Her words softened my heart, and I began to hunger for Him myself. I certainly disdained the idea of a deathbed faith. I wanted my faith to be real and based on truth. I asked Matty to pray for me. When she did, something strange and wonderful happened. It felt as though a band that was wrapped tightly around my heart was loosened and fell off. Now when she reads me the Scriptures, the words are a like a letter to me, a letter from my heavenly Father.

Please consider praying to Jesus, Father. He is the answer to all our questions and heartaches. There is a God, and His name is Jesus!

Matty is the most humble, loving person I have met. You can imagine the kind of care she has to give me, with this miserable dysentery and malaria. Matty never complains and takes care of me with such gentleness and respect. Sometimes, it feels as though her hands are the hands of Christ. Please don't think me mad, but once I turned my head upon my pillow to look at Matty and instead I saw Jesus Himself stooping over to tend me.

Won't Miss Charter be pleased to hear of my faith? I can still hear her voice, reading the Scriptures to us. I used to think she was sweet but eccentric when it came to her faith. Now, all her words ring true in my heart. This has been an amazing journey. I confess I am eager to get on with it now. This morning Matty read Psalm twenty-seven to me. I leave you with this thought: "One thing have I desired of the Lord, that will I seek after; that I may dwell in the house of the Lord all the days of my life, to behold the beauty of the Lord, and to inquire in his temple." (KJV)

Give all my love to Sophie. Take care of The Professor for me. I love you, Father, and miss you terribly.

Your loving daughter,
Amelia Elizabeth

Sam folded the letters and handed them to Jessie. "That is some story," he said, his voice cracking with emotion. "Denver must have died before he was able to open up Amelia's room or write the testimony. But we can write it up now. It can still be used for the sake of the gospel."

Jessie nodded, the tears flowing down her face. Kay hid herself behind her handkerchief. She blew her nose, producing a loud honk.

Henry got up from the floor. "This has been some day," he said.

"I think you better take it easy now, Jess. Let's have lunch, okay?"

Everyone agreed, and they gathered in the kitchen. Sam heated up his famous quiche and produced a fresh salad from the refrigerator.

"I want to go upstairs after lunch," said Jessie. "I want to make sure everything is accounted for."

"The police checked everything out," reported Sam. "But they had to take the box for evidence."

"Box? What box?" asked Jessie.

"Hart and his accomplice found a gold box hidden in the marble-topped dresser. It was filled with papers, apparently poetry."

"That must be Amelia's poetry!" exclaimed Jessie. "Now there's a treasure. I can't wait to get it all back."

"Speaking of treasure," said Kay, "what are you going to do with all that gold?"

"Well, off the top of my head, I'll do some research and see if there's a missionary school or something like it that could use some help."

"Great idea," echoed Sam.

"You're wonderful," said Henry. He reached for Jessie's hand and knocked over her glass of water. "Oops," he winced.

"If you plan on marrying this man, Jessie, I think you better take out some more insurance," laughed Sam, sopping up the mess with a napkin.

"Hey," exclaimed Kay as she pushed up her glasses, "in all the hubbub I forgot about the proposal. What's the verdict?"

"She said yes," said Henry, his face glowing with happiness. "But she says we have to wait and take our time."

Kay let out a scream and hugged Jessie around the neck. "I am so happy for you. I can be your maid of honor, and Sam can do the wedding. If Sam does the wedding, it will be Taylor-made, you know."

Everyone groaned. "If only there were a cure for Kay Bantam's sense of humor," sighed Jessie.

"So, I may get to marry you after all." Sam grinned across the table at Jessie.

"Say what?" Jessie shot back, laughing.

"If I 'do the wedding,' I'll marry you. . .to Henry," Sam explained, a satisfied smile settling on his face. "God bless and keep you always, Jessie."

"Thanks for all your help, Sam," responded Jessie. "I owe you a lot."

"No, the Lord is the One," smiled Sam. "He is the Almighty God!"

Kay got up from the table. "I'll clean this kitchen up. Why don't you go lie down or something, Jess?"

"Yes, and I've got to be going," said Sam. "I've got some afternoon appointments to tend to. I'll see you guys later."

"You're a good reverend," Jessie called after him.

"Thanks!" Sam called back.

Jessie and Henry walked back to the clock. Jessie put the letters back and locked the cabinet, then she pushed the front panel back on.

"Sorry about that," said Henry.

"Don't be sorry. Look at what you uncovered! This has been a wonderful day."

"I've got another surprise for you," said Henry. "It's out back."

"What else could you possibly—"

"You'll see," he said.

Henry took her hand and led her out the front door. Jessie's heart sang with the warmth and security that she felt at his touch.

In the backyard, sitting on the grass, was a large, open box. Henry picked up what was inside the box and placed it in Jessie's arms.

"The Professor!" exclaimed Jessie. "What an adorable puppy!"

The little black Scottish terrier nestled in Jessie's arms. It looked up at her with a twinkle in its eye. "I'll call you Little Professor," she said to the puppy, "after a fine dog who lived here many years ago."

Jessie laughed, closed her eyes, and raised her face to the warm afternoon sun. "The Lord's compassion is new every morning," she spoke with joy.

Henry laughed and put his strong arms around Jessie. They stood for a long time, soaking in the brightness of their new, God-given day.

KJERSTI HOFF BAEZ
Kjersti makes her home with her family in New York. In addition to romance writing, Kjersti also writes children's books.

Santanoni Sunrise

Claire M. Coughlin and Hope Irvin Marston

Dedication

*To my friend and fellow writer, Hope,
who taught me the meaning of persistence* (from Claire).

To Gary Provost, mentor and teacher par excellence (from Hope).

Preface

The construction of enormous estates built in the rustic "Adirondack style" was once a pastime of the wealthiest families in northeast America. These estates, built from the late nineteenth century until the start of World War I, came to be known as "great camps." Today only thirty-five camps remain, among them, Camp Santanoni.

Camp Santanoni occupies 12,500 acres in the town of Newcomb, New York, just south of the Adirondack High Peaks. When we visited Camp Santanoni on an outing with the Adirondack Mountain Club, we were impressed by the grandeur of the main lodge but appalled at the physical condition of that magnificent structure and the other buildings on the estate. After learning the history of the camp, however, we understood why it was in such a state of disrepair.

Our plans to save Santanoni grew out of our discussions with two Camp Santanoni supporters, Dr. Howard Kirschenbaum and Dr. Harvey H. Kaiser. We are indebted to them for sharing their expertise. *Santanoni Sunrise* is an entirely fictitious attempt to create interest and raise support for the preservation of this great camp.

Further information on efforts to preserve Camp Santanoni for the enjoyment and education of future generations can be obtained from the following source:

> Friends of Camp Santanoni
> P.O. Box 113
> Newcomb, NY 12852
> (518) 582-5472

Chapter 1

Rosy tints of dawn ribboned into strawberry rays as the autumn sun ascended over Santanoni Preserve. Alyce stirred in her sleeping bag, but she did not open her eyes. When she awakened several hours later, the sun was shining in her face. She had pitched her tent where she could enjoy the sunrise, and then she had slept through it. She yawned, stretched her slender, lithe legs, and opened one eye to peer at her watch.

"My goodness! Is it really nine o'clock?" That's what she liked about coming to Santanoni. She could relax. She had been coming to this remote preserve for several years, and each time here in the Adirondack wilderness, she renewed her physical and emotional strength. Whenever she needed time to think, she and Max, her affectionate old brindled boxer, would desert Syracuse for a few days of roughing it at the great camp. Though threatened by decay and destruction, this former summer estate with its elegantly proportioned lodge had become a sanctuary to her.

Her previous trips had been escape weekends when the responsibilities of nursing became too heavy. She liked being a private duty nurse, but she knew when it was time to back off for a few days of personal renewal.

But this trip was different: She had been given a mammoth assignment, and she didn't know how to handle it. Camping here beside Newcomb Lake usually renewed her weary mind. This time she hoped it would ease her puzzlement.

She yawned again as she stretched her five-foot frame. Max was nowhere in sight. Not willing to waste such a gorgeous morning sleeping, he was off in the woods creating his own excitement. Alyce vaguely remembered unleashing him when he nudged her in the wee hours of the morning. She had no fear of his running away. He would return once he had made his morning forays.

Her reverie was interrupted by excited yips. Max had probably found a scampering squirrel or a frisky rabbit. Max chased most anything that moved.

"Well, I guess I'd better get out of this sack," she said to the woodland creatures as she shook out her chestnut tresses. It was time for breakfast. Max wouldn't stay away when he smelled her coffee. Coffee meant chow would soon be ready.

She inched her way out of her sleeping bag like a beautiful swallowtail emerging from a chrysalis. After slipping her tiny feet into faded blue Nikes, she walked over to the water's edge to wash her face. Peering at herself in the crystal clear lake water, sparkling dark eyes smiled back at her through mahogany lashes. Her parents must have had those same chocolate brown eyes, she reflected absently. She wished she could remember her mom and dad.

The cold water heightened the dusty rose in her cheeks as it trickled down her short, straight nose. Her lips were full and rounded over perfectly shaped teeth that gleamed as white as the snowy clouds drifting overhead. Though she had recently celebrated her thirtieth birthday, the vision in the lake was one of youthful exuberance, yet at the same time a face endowed with quiet determination, the natural result of having to make important decisions alone.

The sun's rays danced over her dark hair revealing lustrous strands of gold. Though she had hastily tied it in a ponytail before she emerged from her sleeping bag, some escaping wisps charmingly framed her oval face.

Back at her campsite, she pulled out her Peak One stove, pumped it to pressurize the fuel, and lighted it. Next she put water on to boil. She would have enjoyed building her own campfire. She liked the sound of crackling logs and the fragrance of wood smoke, but fires in the forests were dangerous. The stove was faster, and it didn't weigh that much.

Coffee first. At home she preferred herbal tea, but coffee tasted good in the fresh air. Then oatmeal. Quick and easy.

Alyce hummed a few bars from her favorite old song, "Liebestraum," as she untied the ropes that secured her food in a tree. She had hung it high to avoid attracting any marauding animal during the night while she and Max slept. A nocturnal visitor would no doubt awaken Max, but protecting her food might prove difficult for him, especially if a black bear wandered into the camp.

When the water began to boil, she poured out enough for her coffee; then she added the oatmeal to the pan. While it was simmering, she fixed Max's chow. Having returned from his foraging, he wolfed it down and then was off on another excursion.

Suddenly her calm breakfast mood was shattered by a harsh bellow somewhere behind her in the woods.

"Where in thunder did you come from? You shouldn't be running loose in the woods!"

Alyce sucked in her breath. Her body tensed as she heard Max growl. "Max, come!" She whistled for her dog. Her heart thudded in her head as she waited for the inevitable confrontation.

Max bounded into the campsite with the hair on his back standing straight up. He planted himself in front of her. A slow rumble emanated from his throat. Behind him strode a strapping six-foot-tall hiker, a beardless Paul Bunyan with blazing brown eyes.

"Is this your dog?"

A tremor ran through Alyce when she saw the rippling muscles straining against his shirt and the fire in his eyes. Her pulse quickened. She hoped he didn't sense the fear he had kindled in her heart. He was not someone she'd easily forget.

"Y–y–yes," she stammered.

Max growled again. His protectiveness gave Alyce a scrap of courage. Who was this gruff stranger?

"I'm sorry if he was disturbing you." She didn't feel apologetic, and she refused to be intimidated by this crude woodsman. Though her heart was hammering in her head, she spoke with a controlled voice.

"Listen, whoever you are, you're on my land! I do not allow dogs to run loose on my property." He paused as if he weren't sure what to say next. "Now what are you doing here anyway?"

Alyce contemplated him as he stood above her like a towering spruce. His muscular arms were bare below mile-wide shoulders. But muscle or no muscle, what right had he to challenge her presence?

"Your land? This land belongs to all of us. There's no sign posted saying dogs must be leashed!" She was surprised at her own boldness, but she kept it concealed from him. "It's really none of your business what I am doing here, but since you asked so politely, I'll tell you anyway. I'm camping out!" She returned his stony gaze.

His brown eyes like bayonets seemed to pierce her heart, but somehow she found her voice. Alyce wasn't finished.

"Now, who are you, not that it really matters, and what right have you to disturb us?"

The two stood glowering at one another like eight-year-old ruffians ready to trade punches: the petite brunette with hands on slender hips and the tall, sinewy stranger with furrowed brow and smoldering eyes.

For a few tense seconds their eyes locked. The stranger riveted his gaze on her face. Then ever so slowly he scrutinized her from her ponytail to her faded Nikes and back to her ponytail that rocked gently as she confronted him.

His scathing gaze made her skin prickle. Her cheeks flushed. She felt a tingling in the pit of her stomach. Something about the stranger looked familiar. Was it the dimple on his chin? There was a sensuality about his face that caused her heart to continue its frenzied beating. Nevertheless, his size and demeanor were not to be trifled with. She was glad Max was with her.

Having unnerved her with his impudent assessment, the muscles of his jaw and his face softened. The anger began to fade from his dark eyes like mist dispelled by early morning sunrise.

Alyce studied his face as much as her discomfiture allowed. She wondered why it angered him to find Max and her camping by the lake. Something in those penetrating eyes roused her compassion while making her skin prickle. She sensed he was battling a major problem, and she wanted to help him. Max had stopped growling, but he still stood on guard between them.

"You're right, Ma'am." His voice came from a long way off. "I guess this land does belong to everyone. . .now." He gazed out over the lake and then continued. "And, no, there are no posted signs about dogs. I can see you're camping. My apologies."

He went on. "To answer your questions, I'm just walking around m–m–y. . . the estate here." His facial expression had changed from anger to something Alyce could not fathom.

Since he was acting a bit more civilized, Alyce's heart softened. "Do you suppose we could start this conversation again, like civilized human beings? I'm about to make another cup of coffee. Would you care to join me?"

There was an elemental ruggedness about him that suggested he belonged in the outdoors. Yet his skin was light as if he'd spent too many days inside. His dark eyes were a shade lighter than her own, while the set of his jaw suggested a stubborn streak.

She wondered why he looked so unhappy. Whatever had triggered his outburst, he seemed harmless. Besides, how could she ignore anyone so ruggedly handsome? Not that she was interested. She neither wanted nor needed a romance in her busy life. Still, it wouldn't hurt to be friendly. Whoever this wild creature was, he needed a friend.

The intruder paused before responding. "That's very kind of you, especially after I just bit your head off."

The hint of a smile lifted the corners of his mouth. Alyce smiled in return as she tried to ignore the trickle of interest stirring within her. It was a feeling that she had not experienced since the death of her husband, Randy. Surprised by her uncontrollable response to him, she averted her eyes.

"I could use another cup of coffee. However," he continued with a sidelong glance at Max, "I'm not sure your dog shares your forgiving spirit."

Alyce glanced down at Max, still standing between them like an armed sentinel, eyes focused warily on the man. His protective rumblings continued. She gave him a pat.

"It's okay, Max." As she spoke to him, the dog relaxed and settled himself at her feet. When she scratched his ears, his stubby tail gave a tentative wag.

The stranger knelt on one knee and held out his hand, palm upward, to Max. "Good boy, Max. Sorry I disturbed you, old fellow. Let's be friends." He talked softly to the boxer.

Alyce smiled at the contrast between this conversation and his earlier harshness when he had discovered Max loose in the woods. *Well*, she thought, *he knows how to greet a strange dog. He can't be all bad.*

Max evaluated the stranger with his big brown eyes. He sniffed his way toward him, stretching and retreating like a canine rubberband. Gingerly he touched him. The man talked soothingly to him. When Max licked his hand, he stroked him under the chin and behind the ears. Max's stubby tail began to twitch in acquiescence.

Alyce watched the two get acquainted. Max was a good judge of character. He would sense any hidden aggression. If he trusted this man, then she could trust him, too. Still, she wasn't completely comfortable. Where did he come from, and why did he object to their camping on Santanoni Preserve?

The stranger surveyed the neat and orderly campsite while he waited for his coffee. Alyce's two-man tent was anchored properly. She had dug a small ditch around it in case of rain. Her food hung high in a tree. His attention was drawn back to his trim hostess. *I bet she doesn't weigh a hundred pounds,* he mused, *and she's not bad looking, either.*

Alyce handed him his coffee and invited him to sit on a log nearby. Max settled down between them.

"I'm Alyce Anderson," she said. She smiled at him, trying to ignore the sheer attractiveness of a handsome man in faded blue jeans. She hoped she wasn't blushing.

Silence. Then he cleared his throat and spoke. "I'm pleased to meet you, Alyce. I'm, uh, uh, my name is Bill, uh, Bill Morgan."

Alyce couldn't help but wonder why he hesitated when telling his name. Reasoning that it wasn't going to hurt to share a cup of coffee with him, she sat down with her cup.

After a few sips Alyce asked, "Did you camp overnight? I didn't see your name in the logbook when we came in yesterday."

All hikers were asked to register in the logbook kept in a small covered cabinet at the trailhead. Such information as your name, the number in your party, your destination, and the date was needed to justify expenditures in maintaining the trails.

"No." The frown between his eyes seemed to indicate irritation at her question. There was a long pause before he spoke again. "I'm just in for the day. Do you and Max come here often?" He gave his attention to the dog.

"We try to come up two or three times a year. I love it here. It's peaceful, and the air is fresh. Besides, the buildings intrigue me. I knew the last owners of Santanoni. That's how I started coming here."

Bill coughed as he steadied his shaking coffee cup with both hands. "You knew the last owners of Santanoni?"

"Oh, yes." A smile worked its way across her face as she remembered the Hayeses. "I was Will Hayes's nurse for awhile."

"Oh, so you're a nurse? Where do you work?"

"I used to be at Upstate Medical Center in Syracuse. Now I do private duty."

"You say Will Hayes was your patient?"

"Yes. And what a good patient he was. Such a kind man. When he was well enough to leave the hospital, his wife, Nellie, asked me to come work for them. She was so tiny she couldn't lift Will by herself."

"Why did, mmm, you said her name was Nellie? Why did Nellie have to lift him? Why couldn't he lift himself?"

"Mr. Hayes had suffered several strokes. How fortunate he was to have Nellie to love him and care for him." She paused, reflecting on the beautiful relationship Will and Nellie Hayes had shared. *How wonderful to be so much in love after years and years of marriage,* she thought sadly. For them marriage had been for keeps. They were friends as well as lovers.

Bill's blank expression was a mockery of his true feelings. He had returned to Santanoni to be reconciled with Will and Nellie, and he was shocked to learn they weren't there. The condition of his former home was appalling, but he was more concerned with the whereabouts of his parents.

He studied Alyce's countenance as she spoke. Her bright eyes sparkled with animation as she related her tale. Her manner was frank, yet there was no indication she was reaching out to him in anything more than a gesture of friendliness. Now she was telling him Will Hayes had been an invalid.

"What happened to the Hayeses? Are they still living in Syracuse?"

Alyce shook her head. "No, I'm afraid not. You see, Will died six months after he was released from the hospital." She paused, remembering the couple who had treated her as their daughter. Will's obviously paternal gestures made her only love him more.

"What about Mrs. Hayes?" The words tumbled out. Too loud. "Is she still in Syracuse?"

Alyce thought it was strange that this man should ask about Mrs. Hayes: Nellie Hayes's death had brought her to Santanoni this weekend.

"Mrs. Hayes passed away two years ago last month." Alyce's eyes glistened with unshed tears.

There was a pregnant silence between them. Then the newcomer spoke again. "You loved the Hayeses, didn't you?"

Alyce nodded as she contemplated her coffee. "I gave up my job at Upstate to care for Will."

"What about Will's family? Couldn't they have helped him?"

Alyce frowned and sighed. Since the man seemed genuinely interested, he might as well know the whole story. "The Hayeses had three children. Their son and daughter were early teenagers when another son was born. They named him Jimmy. They looked upon him as a special blessing from the Lord.

"One day when he was only eight, Jimmy wandered away from the lodge. When he didn't return, the largest manhunt in the history of the Adirondacks was launched. Hundreds of people searched for him."

Alyce concentrated on recalling the events Nellie Hayes had shared with her.

"They combed one hundred square miles for six weeks without finding a trace of the child. A couple dozen mountain rescue specialists from California came to help as well as crews from the army and the marines. Even the Green Berets helped in the search." She shook her head. "They just couldn't find the little guy."

Bill swallowed often as Alyce recounted the familiar details of the search for his little brother.

"A few years later the older children left Santanoni because of some family disagreements. Neither ever contacted Will or Nellie. What a pity. The Hayeses were beautiful people, and they missed their children terribly. After so much heartache at the camp, they moved out and returned to Syracuse."

Bill stared at Alyce as she recited his family's history.

"Will and Nellie were so lonely when I met them. Nellie told me she felt as if all three of their children had died. Will insisted that she get rid of all their pictures. After he passed away, Nellie showed me a photo she had kept. She cried when she got it out of the drawer."

Bill blinked several times. He hoped Alyce didn't notice.

"A few years after the Hayeses left Santanoni, the camp was sold to the New York Nature Conservancy. Later it was purchased by the State of New York. I met Will and Nellie about four years ago. I was just out of training."

At the mention of the estate being sold, Bill gulped. His hands shook, and he nearly dropped his cup.

Alyce paused. Perhaps she had talked too much. Well, she couldn't take back her words. Besides, there was no need for her to do that. Whoever this man was, he was not only a good listener, he was also the most handsome man she had met since her husband's death. She brushed an errant curl from her face and winced as a pang of regret over what might have been flitted through her mind.

"Now that I've told you my story, how about yours?" Her eyebrows arched expectantly.

Bill hesitated. He was drawn to this attractive woman, but he was driven by a deeper desire to find out about his family. His eyes darkened when he finally spoke.

"There's really not much to tell." He seemed to be measuring his words against some invisible quota that had been meted out to him. "I've been working for the government in Europe for some time. I just came back a few weeks ago." After a momentary lapse, he asked, "What did you say happened to Mrs. Hayes?"

"Oh. Maybe I didn't tell you. Nothing traumatic. She just lost her desire to live after Will died."

"I see. Well, I really must be going." He handed her his empty cup. "Thanks for the coffee." The corners of his mouth twitched briefly upward. "How long are you and Max staying at Santanoni?"

"Just a couple of days. I have to be back for work Monday evening."

He looked at her as if he were seeing her for the first time. "I'll be in the area a few more days myself. I'm staying at the Antlers Lodge. Would you let me treat you to dinner before you go back to Syracuse? To make up for my rudeness?"

Alyce's eyes darkened as she tucked in her chin. "Apologies accepted. You need do nothing more." Her response was cool and impersonal. She had answered all of his questions, in excruciating detail, she feared. When she had asked him about himself, he was quick to change the subject.

"Please?" His voice was soft and gentle, almost pleading. "I'm really sorry I shouted at you."

His deep-set dark eyes begged forgiveness. "Can't you stop at the Antlers on your way home? We could have dinner, a lunch, or whatever you wish. Please give me a chance to make amends."

Alyce deliberated. She wished she had never gotten involved with this puzzling intruder. On the other hand, what did it matter? Evident in those dark eyes was a raw hurt, a pain not caused, she knew, by her presence at Santanoni. Anyway, she'd be needing a good meal before she drove home. Maybe she could find out what his problem was.

"Well, I suppose we could stop." She brushed some stray wisps of hair away from her face as she pondered the invitation. She felt a bit apprehensive, but she didn't know why. Was it because there was something familiar about his face? She wished she knew.

"All right. Max and I will stop around one on Monday. It will have to be a quick lunch, though, as I have to get back to my patient."

Bill's lips moved in a semblance of a smile. "Thanks, Alyce. It was a pleasure meeting you. I'll see you Monday. So long, Max."

Alyce watched him as he walked away, his broad shoulders finally disappearing into the woods.

As she cleared away the breakfast trappings, she replayed the morning's encounter. The thought of seeing Bill Morgan on Monday was intriguing, but today she had a problem to solve. She hoped being at Santanoni as the broken bits of summer scattered into the shorter days of autumn would provide the stimulus she needed. Sometimes she wished life would offer her fewer challenges, and today was one of those times. She stowed away her food, whistled for Max, and headed down to the water. A long walk around the lake should give her time to think.

Chapter 2

Alyce glanced heavenward, noting that the early morning clouds had drifted out of sight. The Lord had given her a perfect day for a hike. As she scanned the skies, her mind drifted back to the summer she met Randy Anderson. It was the summer after her junior year in high school when she was working at the Frosty Shoppe on the edge of Amber Lake.

Randy and his twin brother, Rodney, were hiking and camping in the Catskill Mountains. This would be their last summer together before their senior year at Albany State. One sticky July afternoon they stopped for a milkshake on their way back to their campsite, and Alyce came to the carryout window to take their orders.

"May I help you, please?" Her innocent smile masked her rapidly beating heart as she stared into identical sets of the most beautiful, bottomless blue eyes she had ever seen.

Two endearing smiles greeted her in return. "Oh, yes. You certainly may," Randy responded with a wink at his brother. His bright eyes sparkled as he gave their orders.

Throughout that summer the twins came often to the Frosty Shoppe. Although they were four years older than Alyce, they developed a close friendship with her. They became the brothers Alyce never had.

Alyce enjoyed the time she could spend with the twins, but something special was growing between her and Randy. In addition to those compelling blue eyes set in such a handsome face, Alyce was captivated by Randy's zest for the out-of-doors. Here was a man she'd like to depend on, someone to love her and care for her the rest of her days.

When the twins returned to school in Albany, Randy took Alyce's heart with him. Letters from Albany came frequently to Amber Lake that fall, and whenever he could arrange it, Randy came to visit Alyce on weekends. On Valentine's Day weekend, he asked her to marry him. A few weeks later he presented her with a dainty solitaire diamond ring. They were married a month after her high school graduation.

Alyce smiled as she recalled her wedding day. Now she had a family of her own! How proud she was of her handsome new husband and his look-alike brother.

Rodney had teased her, "It's a good thing Randy saw you first." His eyes twinkled in merriment. "Otherwise you would be marrying me today."

Alyce glanced at her husband. She wondered what Rodney meant. Randy placed a protective arm around her and glared at his brother with feigned anger. "Tough luck, brother!" he said as he drew Alyce closer to himself.

Rodney kissed her gently on the cheek. "Welcome to our family, Alyce. I'm glad to have you as my new sister."

Alyce blushed. She knew both men loved her, but Randy's love was that priceless love of a man for his wife. Not only did she have a wonderful husband, but she also had a terrific brother-in-law. This was the happiest day of her life.

Rodney's words echoed in her ears as she thought about him. Four years later a speedboat driven by a drug-crazed teenager had rammed into Rodney's eighteen-foot *Windrose*. Randy had been thrown from the boat upon impact and had drowned; Rodney had succumbed while attempting to rescue Randy and Alyce's three-year-old daughter, Maria. Upon her release from the hospital, Alyce learned Rodney had named her as his sole beneficiary. She grieved for him as much as for Randy and Maria.

After their marriage Randy had insisted that she not work outside the home. "I want you to be waiting for me when I get home from work each day," he told her. When Alyce knew for certain she was carrying his child, she told him. He swung her into his arms and twirled her around the living room.

They could scarcely wait for their baby to be born. The empty nursery began to fill with stuffed animals brought home by a happy father. Little Maria was born on their first wedding anniversary. She had her father's dark hair and the same deep blue eyes. Their joy as husband and wife was complete.

Alyce's thoughts were momentarily swept aside as she took in the glorious day. The trees were already sporting their fall wardrobes. Velvety greens transformed themselves into shimmering yellows and gold, with just a tinge of orange and crimson thrown in. Heralding the arrival of fall, the Creator was wielding with flourish His giant paintbrush.

"Chick-a-dee-dee-dee!" Breaking the natural silence of the forest, a pair of cheerful little black-capped birds chattered loudly as they flitted from tree to tree. A noisy red squirrel squabbled with his neighbors, and a blue jay announced his position in an old elm to her left. Alyce studied him for a few moments. Then she walked on through the flowering goldenrod and the New York asters gracing her path amid the abundant seedpods of the summer blooms.

There was so much to enjoy on this trail, but she needed to concentrate on her current problem. She had been asked to do the impossible: to find a way to stop the deterioration of this great camp, Camp Santanoni, and to restore it to its original splendor.

Even if she could figure out a plan, it would be so costly, who could afford to carry it out? Only God in heaven knew how the great camp could be saved. Thus far He hadn't chosen to reveal His plans to any mortal being. One thing was certain. She could always hear Him speak more clearly at Santanoni. She had come asking Him for wisdom, and she intended to be tuned in to whatever He answered.

The pungent dry leaves crackled underfoot as she and Max skirted ancient trees that had been hurled headlong across her path by long-forgotten winds. Near the campsite the walking was easy, but Alyce knew that would change shortly. She didn't mind. She and Max had made this trip before.

As she scuffled along through the multicolored carpet of leaves, the autumn sun warmed her back, and the crisp air put a spring into her step. Her six months' stay in the mountains of Switzerland had shown her that God could restore and renew her broken heart.

As she ambled along the shoreline of Lake Newcomb, her mind wandered back to Randy and Maria. How happy they had been as a family. A smile hovered at the corners of her mouth as she recalled the fun they had camping together.

Her reminiscing was interrupted by a rustling in the leaves. She glanced down to find a pair of chipmunks scampering over a rotten log, their cheek pouches bulging with seeds. They stopped to *churr* at her. She *churred* back with her best chipmunk imitation. Then they were off to stow away their loot with Max hot on their trail. It didn't take long for them to disappear and for Max to return to continue his journey with his mistress.

"You silly dog. You know you can't catch a chipmunk." She stooped down and gave him a pat on the favorite spot on his head.

Maria had loved little creatures in the woods, especially chipmunks. Maybe that was because Randy had bought her a soft cuddly one three months before she was born.

A gentle splash caught her attention and diverted her thoughts. She glanced at the lake but saw nothing. She scanned the water carefully. She guessed who it was playing games with her. Then she saw him halfway across the lake. What looked like a periscope appeared first, followed by a spotted body as the magnificent loon surfaced. Alyce wondered to herself if he would dive again. She knew he would come up quietly where she least expected to see him.

As she watched, the loon began to sink like a submarine, disappearing without a sound. This fellow seemed to be watching something. Instead of submerging himself completely, he lowered only his body and kept his watchful eyes just below the surface. Alyce contemplated the beautiful creature a few minutes and then trudged on.

She considered Nellie Hayes's will. She knew little about inheritances and estates, yet Nellie had requested that she settle her estate in the absence of her estranged children.

Alyce felt a twinge in her heart. She had loved Will and Nellie Hayes. She couldn't imagine why their children had deserted them. She would have given anything to have Randy and Maria back. Although years had passed since their deaths, the memories of the traumatic experience were etched on her heart.

A soft breeze ruffled her ponytail as she walked along. A widow at twenty-one, at first she had clung to her memories of the happy days with her husband and their little daughter. It was her faith in the Lord's ability to supply her needs that enabled her to work through the initial shock. Then came a period of frantic activity that she embraced to keep her mind occupied. When she hit rock bottom, her cousin Barbara convinced her to go to L'Abri.

"You need to put some distance between yourself and the unpleasant memories," she said.

Alyce spent six months at L'Abri in the Swiss Alps. Surrounded by people who loved her and encouraged her, she learned to live again. Her new friends demanded nothing of her. They were ready to listen or to talk whenever she needed someone near. She spent her mornings helping with the routine work. In the afternoons she roamed about, letting the rhythms of God's nature in the rugged Alps minister to her.

As she wandered about the chalet day after day, the grief she carried began to dissipate. When she contemplated the majestic mountain paradise in which she found herself, she felt a calmness in her soul that had fled when Randy and Maria died. She sensed the orderliness of things as God had created them. The Creator of such natural beauty and order could bring peace back into her life, too.

When Alyce left L'Abri, it was with gratitude to those who had helped her. Difficult experiences happened to everyone. She would accept hers and move on. Coupled with acceptance was the realization that she could capture the joy that surrounded her. She would be grateful for the love of friends and take comfort in the kindness of strangers. She would forgive the injustices in the world as well as the people responsible for them. And that included the young man who had snuffed out the lives of those she had loved most. With that forgiveness came healing.

Alyce decided to become a nurse. She would spend her time tending the hurts of others. She returned home and applied for admittance to the fall class at Upstate Medical Center in Syracuse.

The next few years were busy ones. She applied herself diligently to her studies. She accepted every opportunity afforded her to work in the hospital. At her graduation ceremony she was awarded the highest academic honors, and shortly afterward, the director of nurses at Upstate asked her to work at the hospital.

Alyce met the Hayeses during her first year at the hospital. From their first meeting they filled a void in her life. A compassionate woman by nature, Alyce developed a special fondness for Will and Nellie Hayes. Perhaps it was an innate ability of each to realize the other bore emotional scars that were too painful to be touched.

Her deepening love for them made her think about the parents she had never known. She was grateful to her aunt who had taken her in and raised her when her mother died during childbirth, but she missed having a mother of her own.

Alyce was delighted when after three months Will recovered enough to go home. His doctor told him he could leave the hospital in another week if he secured a nurse to care for him at home. Alyce hoped they would find a nurse who would be extra kind to Will. Being incapacitated was a traumatic expedience, and Will deserved kindness.

Alyce was pleased when the Hayeses asked her to leave the hospital to become Will's private nurse. Private duty nursing would give her more control over her life. She could decide when and where she would work. Besides, if she could make life more bearable for Will, she would do it.

The friendship between Alyce and the Hayes family deepened as the days went by. Nellie liked to talk with her. Now that she worked for them exclusively, they shared many hours together. They discussed most everything, but each respected the other's right not to divulge more than she wished, though each sensed the other was harboring painful memories.

Alyce cared for Will at home for six months until one spring morning when he did not wake up. She stayed with Nellie until she had settled matters relating to her husband's death, and then she found another patient.

Several months after Alyce had left the Hayeses, Nellie called to ask her to come see her. She greeted Alyce with a warm embrace. There was a mist in her eyes as she poured them each a cup of tea.

"Thank you so much for coming today. And thank you again for being so kind to Will. He loved you as much as he ever loved his own daughter, you know. And I love you just as much, Alyce."

"I'm glad you called. I'm delighted to see you again. How are you doing? Is there something I can do for you?"

Nellie smiled. "Yes, there is. . . . I do hope you won't feel I'm imposing when I ask."

"Nellie, you know there isn't anything I wouldn't do for you," Alyce protested. "What do you need?"

Nellie regarded her thoughtfully. "I don't want to sound morbid, but I'm really looking forward to going to heaven to be with Will. I don't know when the Lord will take me, but I hope it will be soon." Her face glowed as if she were seeing herself with Will, standing in the presence of Almighty God.

She continued. "I need to make some revisions in my will—concerning my property in the Adirondacks. Can you contact my lawyer and set up an appointment at a time you'll be free to take me? I hate to bother you, but since I don't drive, I would really appreciate it."

Alyce remembered how much Nellie hated taxicabs. She'd be glad to oblige her friend.

"Will and I once owned one of the great camps in the Adirondacks," she said. She began to smile as she continued. "It's called Santanoni. That's an Indian word for Saint Anthony. It's a beautiful place. . . ." She paused, envisioning the home she hadn't seen in years.

"We purchased Santanoni at an auction about thirty years ago. The estate covers 12,500 acres. There are two beautiful lakes there, Newcomb Lake and Moose Pond. At one time they were full of speckled trout." Her face contorted. "I suppose the trout are gone now," she said.

"Because of the acid rain?" asked Alyce. She and Nellie had had many discussions about the environment. Since Nellie didn't drive, she seldom left home. But she was an avid reader, and her mind was keen. She kept abreast of current affairs.

Nellie nodded. "Let me tell you about Santanoni. There are two mountains nearby, Moose and Baldwin. They're not tall enough to belong to the prestigious 46ers, but they are great for bushwacking." Her eyes twinkled at some memory. "Will and I loved to hike those mountains. We spent days tramping about just enjoying the mountains. . .and each other. . . ." Her voice trailed off into the air.

Alyce wanted to learn more about Santanoni. She and Randy had enjoyed camping in the Catskills, but she didn't know anything about Adirondack camping.

"Santanoni sounds like a lovely place. Did you have a log cabin in the center of that big estate?"

Nellie chortled. "A cabin? Well, I'd hardly call it that, though it was built with fifteen hundred logs. There was a main lodge in the center of a cluster of buildings. It had six sprawling buildings under one roof. The buildings were tied together with a system of porches. We had eighteen bedrooms in our lodge."

Alyce's eyes widened as Nellie described Camp Santanoni. This was no ordinary little mountain retreat.

"The lodge was flanked by a lovely artist's studio. And there was a boathouse, too."

Alyce tried to picture Santanoni as Nellie described it to her. "It sounds like a marvelous place," she said. "I'd love to see it."

"There's no reason why you can't," said Nellie. Her voice had gained its former determination. She went on to describe two other clusters of buildings: the gatehouse complex in the hamlet of Newcomb and the farm complex about a mile north of the gatehouse on the trail to Newcomb Lake.

Without telling her why, Nellie said she and Will had sold the estate. "We had a tragedy in our family, Alyce. . . ." She grimaced. "Actually it was the first of several tragedies. That's what brought on Will's first stroke, I think. We couldn't go back to Santanoni after so much heartache. We decided to sell the estate and try to forget the unhappiness we experienced when we lived there."

Alyce listened intently as Nellie spoke of things she had kept hidden in the recesses of her heart.

"Once we moved out of Santanoni, we never went back. We read in the newspaper that the Conservancy Committee resold Santanoni a year later to the State of New York. It became part of the great Adirondack Forest Preserve. Once it became part of the preserve, it was opened up to hikers and campers. I don't know what it is like now." She gave a long, pensive sigh. "I hope someone is taking good care of it. I'm sorry the Nature Conservancy didn't keep it."

"Why, Nellie? To keep the public out?"

"Oh, no, Alyce. Quite to the contrary. Once Santanoni became part of the Adirondack Park, the 'Forever Wild' clause prevented the state from maintaining or using the camp. I shudder to think what the camp must look like now. It hurts to think of those grand structures standing there deteriorating through mandated neglect."

Alyce sensed the pain these remembrances were eliciting for Nellie. She loved her. She wanted to assuage that heartache if she could. Suddenly she had an idea.

"Nellie," she asked, "would you like me to take you to Santanoni?" She wasn't sure just when she could do that, but somehow, for Nellie's sake, she'd do it. Besides, she'd like to see the camp, too.

Nellie's eyes brimmed with tears as she took Alyce's hand and gently squeezed it. "Oh, you dear, dear girl. Thank you for your offer, but I could never go back to Santanoni. . .except in my memories. I wouldn't go now that Will is gone. Besides, I couldn't go. It's a five-mile hike into the camp. You can't drive into Santanoni Preserve. Motorized vehicles are not permitted there."

She looked at Alyce. "I have my memories. Some good. And some not so pleasant. That's sufficient. Now if you'll arrange for me to see my lawyer, I shall be grateful."

Alyce arose. She gave Nellie a hug and left, a woman on a mission. First she would arrange for Nellie to visit her lawyer. Then she would check her own schedule. She intended to see Santanoni Preserve for herself.

Chapter 3

Alyce delighted in the late summer flowers blooming along the lakeshore. The lavender wild asters. The yellow goldenrod. The white Queen Anne's lace. Though their colors were fading, their beauty lingered to be enjoyed briefly before the onslaught of winter changed the landscape to a dull grayish brown.

As she meandered along deep in thought, Alyce glanced down. The sandy beach was imprinted with delicate Vs, sure proof that deer had left the cover of the deep woods to venture down to the shore to drink. They could do that safely now that most people had gone from the lake.

A slapping in the water diverted Alyce's attention, and she glanced up in time to see a beaver. Max heard him, too, but he never pursued animals in the water.

Alyce smiled at the sight of another wild animal. How she wished she could see one of the lynxes that had been released in the Adirondacks the past spring. She'd love it if one of their summer kittens should wander down from Baldwin Mountain in search of adventure. But that was expecting too much.

The animals, she knew, had already recognized that change was in the air and were preparing for it. Likewise, people needed to accept changes in their lives. She walked on, continuing her thoughtful journey.

She had taken Nellie to see her lawyer. Then, without telling Nellie, she had taken her first free weekend to go to Santanoni. She had little difficulty finding the trailhead once she got to Newcomb. The five-mile hike into the camp was a delight, but she was unprepared for the dilapidated buildings. Her heart sank at the sight of the once magnificent lodge standing like a weary vagrant on a deserted street corner, its shadowy veranda now the property of barn swallows.

As she picked her way through the fragrant balsam and Lapland rosebay threatening to hide the stone steps leading down to the lake, Alyce knew she must never tell Nellie what she had discovered. Her heart would break at the thought of her beautiful home in such a neglected state.

The next time she could get away, she went to the village authorities in Newcomb to find out why the great camp was not being cared for. The Newcomb postmistress was the first to tell her about the disappearance of the Hayes's son, the first tragedy.

Alyce's heart ached for the Hayeses. Their grief had been so deep that even years later they still could not talk about it with her. She had never told them about Randy, Maria, and Rodney.

Nellie never discussed the disagreements that caused her children to leave home. Alyce wondered what had been such a big issue that they could not resolve it. The tragedies in her own life had taught her that we should cling to our families for as long as we have them.

After Nellie's death, Alyce cared for a number of patients. Though her insurance money from Randy and Rodney had left her financially independent, she continued working. She liked private duty nursing because she could choose her patients and her schedule was flexible.

Two years later she received a letter postmarked Newcomb. She inspected the envelope. Although she had returned to Santanoni to hike a number of times, she had never met anyone in Newcomb except the postmistress. She glanced at the return address.

An attorney's office? She knew no attorney in Newcomb. She ripped the letter open and scanned it hastily. She blinked, sat up straighter, and read the letter again. The letter simply stated that she, Alyce Anderson, R.N., of Syracuse, New York, had been named the executor of the will of Nellie Hayes. Would she, as soon as possible, make an appointment to meet with the lawyer to expedite the conditions of the will?

She had called the attorney, a Mr. Roberts, but his secretary was unwilling to discuss the matter over the phone. It was mid-August before she was able to get away. Her plan was to drive up in the morning, meet the attorney in the late afternoon, spend one night in Newcomb, and return the following morning.

Alyce paused to scan the lake. She was hoping to see more loons. The babies would be a couple of months old now and no longer chicks but large grayish birds that looked out of place behind their speckled parents. Instantly she pictured Maria, jumping up and down when she saw a loon chick riding piggyback on his mother's back.

Randy had explained to her that the little loons could become watersoaked if they stayed in the water too long. When they rode on their parent's back, they were safe from large fish and snapping turtles that would have gobbled them up for lunch. The whole family had been excited the day they saw two chicks riding on their mother's back.

There would be no hitchhikers this late in the fall. If they tried it, the chicks would swamp the parent and find themselves back in the water. Though she looked carefully, Alyce saw nothing on the lake other than an occasional fish jumping. She trekked on.

By now she was replaying her visit to the attorney's office. She parked her car in front of the library and walked across the street to a modest white ranch-style home with green trim. A neatly lettered sign on the front lawn, surrounded by brown and yellow chrysanthemums, declared the law practice of one Robert D. Roberts.

Soft chimes from the doorbell drifted out from the open window. The door was opened promptly by a petite, blue-eyed blond.

"Hello! Please come in. You must be Ms. Anderson. I was just leaving."

Before Alyce could say more than "Good afternoon," the woman was out the door and halfway down the sidewalk. Alyce looked around. She found herself in a well-appointed, cozy sitting room. Its accents of yellow, green, and orange reflected good taste as well as warmth.

Suddenly but unobtrusively a man of medium height and build appeared. His charcoal pin-striped suit, immaculate white shirt, and green and maroon tie were worn with the casual style of a man whose life is in order.

"Good afternoon," he said, extending his hand. "I'm Rob Roberts." His lips curved, and a smile crinkled his eyes. "You must be Alyce Anderson."

"I'm pleased to meet you, Mr. Roberts. Yes, I'm Ms. Anderson."

They shook hands and he gestured toward a chair. "As you can see, I have my office in my home. I hope you'll feel comfortable here." He seated himself behind his desk. "My secretary will be back momentarily. May I offer you something to drink? You must be tired after your long drive from Syracuse. Coffee? Iced tea? A ginger ale? Or perhaps you'd prefer something a bit stronger?"

Alyce winced. His familiarity sent her adrenaline coursing through her body. "No, thank you." She didn't meant to sound so curt. "Frankly, I'd like to get down to business right away if we may." She was coloring her words with neutral shades.

"Certainly, Ms. Anderson." He had picked up her signal. He offered her a weak smile and reached for a folder on the corner of his desk.

At least he has the decency not to call me by my first name, Alyce mused. She felt uncomfortable.

"As my secretary informed you, you have been named the executor as well as a beneficiary in Mrs. Hayes's will." He retrieved his glasses from his pocket, put them on, and opened the folder. "Mrs. Hayes was my client when I lived in Syracuse a few years ago," he said. He handed Alyce a document. "Here is a copy of the will."

Alyce scanned the lengthy document and handed it back to the lawyer. "Mr. Roberts, this will states that the inheritance shall go to the Hayeses' children, William and Elisabeth. They are the heirs, not I. The estate belongs to them."

The attorney smiled and shook his head. "No, Ms. Anderson. If you read more carefully, you'll see that the children have forfeited their inheritance. The will states that if they do not try to contact their parents within two years of Mrs. Hayes's death, they will lose their rights as heirs. The estate becomes yours to settle. Twenty-five thousand dollars goes to you personally. The remainder, about one hundred thousand dollars, is to be used for the preservation of Camp Santanoni."

The attorney sensed that Alyce was having difficulty grasping the enormity of the inheritance. He continued. "I haven't seen Santanoni, but I would be delighted if you would permit me to take you there." It was a statement, not a question.

"That will not be necessary," Alyce said, rising from her chair. "I've been there a number of times. Thank you for the appointment, Mr. Roberts." She extended her hand, not because she wanted to, but because courtesy dictated that she do so. As he took her hand in both of his, she felt red color creeping up her neck.

"Please call me Rob. It was a pleasure to serve you. Do let me know if there is anything else I might do for you. I'm at your service." He did not release her hand as he smiled directly into her eyes.

Alyce disengaged herself from his grasp, embarrassed by his unprofessional conduct. "Thank you, Mr. Rob. . .uh, Rob. . . ."

She was freed from the lawyer's attentions by the ringing of the phone. Since his secretary was out, he had no choice but to answer it himself. As he did so, Alyce made her escape, her face flushed with displeasure.

Safely seated in her red Escort, she rested her head on the steering wheel. Nellie's will was a surprise, and that lawyer was too friendly. She shook a thick swatch of brown hair off her shoulder and tried to clear her head. A slow smile etched its path across her face. Then she began to laugh. The idea was ludicrous. Why would Nellie Hayes leave twenty-five thousand dollars to her? And how could she ever carry out Nellie's wishes for Santanoni?

She thought about her relationship with Will and Nellie. They never flaunted their wealth, though she knew they were people of means. They lived in the valley in a home filled with fine furniture. Not everyone could afford a private nurse. Still, the value of their estate boggled her mind. She needed to find a place to think. She turned the key in the ignition and headed back to the room she had secured at the Antlers.

Back in her room she read the will again and again. She wondered what had happened to the Hayeses' children. Even when writing the will, Nellie had hoped they would return. She had given them two years to show up, and they hadn't come.

Alyce spent a restless night, her brain operating in overdrive. What she needed was a day at Santanoni, but she had to be back by six to relieve a nurse now on duty for her.

She got up at sunrise, packed her few possessions in her overnighter, paid for her lodging, and headed back to Syracuse. She would eat breakfast en route. Perhaps she'd be able to formulate a plan on her long drive home.

She was committed to caring for Mrs. Martinez through Labor Day weekend. The first weekend after Labor Day she and Max could go to Santanoni for three days. That should give her enough time to come up with a solution. Besides, Max would love three days at the camp.

By now Alyce and Max were three-quarters of the way around the lake. *Okay, Alyce,* she chided herself. *You've spent all of this time looking back. Now you must move ahead. Just what are you going to do about Santanoni?*

For the hundredth time she contemplated the provisions of the will. Nellie was asking her to take the bulk of the estate to preserve Santanoni. That meant finding a means that met the conditions of the "Forever Wild" clause. Nellie had told her it was assumed that Santanoni came under that clause that doomed it to destruction by natural forces. But what if that assumption were wrong?

She had prayed asking the Lord to give her wisdom to know what to do. Now a plan was forming in her mind. When she and Max got back to Syracuse, she would contact her friend Joe Heisler, a state senator in Albany. Joe could find out what she needed to know about Santanoni. He might have some suggestions on how the money could be used to stop the deterioration.

For one thing, the lodge roof needed to be fixed immediately. Anyone could see that. Some of the smaller buildings were beyond repair, but not the magnificent lodge. The gatehouse was in pretty good shape. So was the milkhouse. But the others. . . Preserving Santanoni would require the expertise of a restoration architect. She was sure of that.

She would find a way to do it for Will and Nellie. . .and for Randy and Maria and Rodney. A restored Santanoni would be her monument to the five people she had loved and had lost.

She had been so engrossed in her thoughts, she didn't realize they were almost back to their campsite. Max had tired of his forays. He was nearly twelve now, after all, and his weary legs had dictated he stay beside her for the last mile.

Alyce had a late lunch and then headed down to the beach. The warm afternoon sun would be pleasant. She was relieved that she had reached some conclusions. She stretched out on the beach, and soon she and Max were fast asleep. They missed a pair of majestic loons paddling by, their still earthbound chicks in tow.

Chapter 4

Instead of heading back to the main lodge, Bill bushwhacked his way through the brush to the deserted studio. A wan smile crossed his face. So Will and Nellie were dead. Will and Nellie, not Mom and Dad. He had started calling his parents by their first names in his early teens. A form of rebellion maybe, but the names had stuck. Well, one more regret to add to his growing list.

He had made three trips into the camp since his return from Europe, each more painful than the previous one. He was aggrieved to see the devastation of what had been such a well-kept estate. A lump was forming in his throat, and no matter how often he swallowed, it wouldn't go away. He eased himself down on the steps of the abandoned studio.

His thoughts drifted back over the years to his heated discussions with his father. Unlike his father and grandfather, he had never been interested in stocks and bonds or other financial dealings. They had made good investments, and as a result, they lived well. Thus when Camp Santanoni came up for sale, they had the cash to buy it. They wanted Bill to follow in their footsteps. To carry out their plans. To pursue their dreams.

But Bill was interested in buildings, not bonds. He wanted to design and create out of wood and stone. For a time he thought he'd become a carpenter. As he grew older, he developed an appreciation for the fine buildings at Santanoni. Maybe he would become an architect.

He was fascinated by the huge lodge. Whoever had built it had been a master builder. At one time he and his sister decided they would count the black logs to see if there really were fifteen hundred in the building. They gave up soon, but Bill continued to admire the sound construction and the seeming indestructibility of the sprawling building.

As a child he played with his father's prize Jerseys in the meadow or the barn. When he tired of that, he walked across the road to watch the men working in the milkhouse. As he grew older, he learned to appreciate the beautiful studio, the little cottage with its cathedral window overlooking the lake and the mountains. The studio was also his sister's favorite hideaway, and the two of them spent hours there playing together. Afterward Bill would head back to his room in the lodge and reconstruct the building on paper.

His infatuation with architecture continued into high school, that is, until he developed an interest in girls and sports. He still dabbled with his designs of miniature buildings, however, and he kept abreast of the financial world, mostly to please his family.

When he registered for his freshman year in college, he chose a career in liberal arts. Because his mother was French Canadian, Bill had been brought up speaking two languages. When a certain Puerto Rican beauty sent his pulse rate skyward, he decided first to study Spanish, and then to follow her major, political science. By and by the lovely young woman went her way, but Bill was hooked on the machinations of politics throughout history.

When his parents cut off his financial aid following a bitter dispute concerning his future, his grandmother Willa, for whom he was named, came to his rescue. She paid his tuition and gave him a monthly allowance that permitted him to continue his studies at New York University.

Things seemed to go well for him after he received his degree. He became an aide in the office of a senator, and eventually he applied for a position in the diplomatic corps. Empowered by his quick grasp of foreign languages, his photographic mind, and his winsome personality, he quickly rose through the ranks. But there was an emptiness in his life that he couldn't satisfy. Although he dated some pleasant women, he did not meet anyone he wanted to marry.

Ever since he had arrived in Europe he had kept journals, and the thought had been growing in his mind for some time that what he had written was marketable. Maybe it was time to go home, back to Santanoni, to make peace with Will and Nellie. There, in the quietness of the great camp, he could edit his journals for publication.

What fools we were, he lamented, thinking of both his sister and himself. *Why did I wait so long to come back?* The lump in his throat was growing. *How am I ever going to explain everything to Bette?* He didn't even know where his sister lived. How much grief had he caused his parents? He sank to the steps. The tears he'd not yet been able to shed finally were released. He'd been a rotten son and a lousy brother. If only he could start his life all over again. . .

He sat on the steps a long time reviewing his life and regretting his failures. Finally he made his way back to his rented Lincoln Continental parked beside the red Escort. Now he knew who owned that car. She had fooled him. He had assumed Max was her male companion when he saw the names in the logbook. He frowned and shook his head. He unlocked his car and slid behind the wheel. The five-mile hike back from the lodge had done little to lift his burden of discouragement and frustration.

His troubles buzzed through his aching head like bees swarming in May. He continued to berate himself silently. *You come home to find campers are enjoying your family's estate. The buildings you loved are inhabited by spiders and mice. A stranger tells you your parents have died heartbroken and your home has been sold to the State of New York.*

He shuddered as he thought about the "Forever Wild" clause. It would tie the estate into legal knots that only a Houdini could untangle. *I'm glad I didn't give that woman my full name,* he mused, but he was having second thoughts. *I didn't really lie about my name. I just didn't tell her the whole truth.* But deep inside he knew better. He scowled as he turned the key in the ignition and backed out of the parking lot.

∞

Alyce glanced around the campsite. She wanted to make certain she was leaving nothing behind except her footprints. "If you carry it in, carry it out." That was the motto of every bona fide lover of the wilderness, and she subscribed to it.

She took one last look at the lake. She wanted to remember it as she had seen it at the break of dawn when the mist was gently rising. She was disappointed that no loons had awakened her with their eerie yodels during the predawn hours. Still, the quiet beauty of that September morning had refreshed her. She was leaving Santanoni renewed in spirit.

She gave Max a pat. "Okay, ol' pal. It's time for your load." The dog pranced about while she adjusted the straps on his backpack that fitted over his muscular back like miniature saddlebags. His stubby tail twitched. He carried his little load as though he enjoyed it.

"There you are, Max. Now just give me a minute to get into mine."

She set her pack on a stump and stooped down to ease into it. No newcomer to a backpack, she had learned to carry only necessities when she and Randy backpacked into the Catskills. Squaring her shoulders, she shifted her pack, adjusted the straps, and picked up "Wally," her walnut walking stick.

"Okay, Max. We're off."

It was almost one o'clock when Alyce parked her Escort wagon in the lot behind Antlers Inn. Max roused himself, hoping to be let out.

"No, Max. Stay! Sorry, but you can't come this time." Retrieving her lipstick from her purse, she passed the carnation pink tube over her mouth. She anchored her ponytail with a pink bandana and tucked her checkered shirt into her jeans. She tried to brush aside what she was feeling about Bill Morgan. So what if he's got magnificent muscles and an impregnable wall for a chest? Without intending to do so, she was giving her heart a little slack.

She rolled down the windows so the boxer would have plenty of air, gave him an affectionate pat on the head, and slipped out of the car. The butterflies in her stomach began a delicate ballet. She took three deep breaths and walked into the inn.

Bill was sitting at a corner table by the window having an animated chat with the waitress who was obviously enjoying her attractive guest. The rich outlines of his shoulders strained against the blue plaid fabric of his flannel shirt while wisps of curly brown hair crept out from under his collar. Draped across his shoulders was an azure blue V-necked sweater. He took a casual sip of iced tea as he listened to the waitress.

Something about those rugged features looked familiar. Mahogany eyes. Aquiline nose. Firm and sensual lips. Teeth white and even. Chin dimpled and determined. A wan shaft of sunlight struck his thick, dark hair, making it gleam like burnished gold. Where had she seen this man before?

She reminded herself that she wasn't looking for romantic involvement. Randy was the first and only man in her life, and after his death she thought she wouldn't exist without him. Now she suffered only occasional bouts of loneliness, usually late at night. She never considered loving another man. Now Bill unconsciously was reminding her how empty her nights had been since Randy's death.

As she entered the dining room, Bill dismissed the waitress with a polite but firm, "Excuse me, please," and rose to greet her.

"Hello, Bill." There was more warmth in her voice than she intended. "It's nice to see you again." The waitress melted away, her face reflecting envy.

"Hello, Alyce." He gave her a gentle smile that sent her pulse racing. "I was afraid you wouldn't come." His dark eyes softened as they looked into her face. "I can see why you wear pink."

"Thanks. You don't look too bad yourself. I love your sweater. Is it handknit?"

"Yes, it is. I bought it in Switzerland last winter."

"Oh, you've been to Switzerland, too?" Alyce chided herself silently at the obvious redundancy of that statement.

Sensing her embarrassment, Bill went on. "How was your weekend at Santanoni? Did you come upon any more bullies?"

Why did he change the subject? she wondered, slightly irritated. *Why won't he talk about himself?* "Max and I had a great time." Her voice held a slight edge as she spoke. She took a deep breath. "And how about you?" She didn't intend to pry, but she was curious to know why he was staying at the Antlers.

A slight hesitation shaded his eyes. "Oh, I haven't done much since Saturday." He paused like a chess player weighing his next move. Then he continued. "I have some business in Syracuse that I must tend to in a week or so."

"You do?" Alyce wished she hadn't sounded so enthusiastic. *What would he think?*

Her quick response was not wasted on Bill. His deep brown eyes gleamed. "Could we get together when I'm in your fair city?"

"I guess so." It was Alyce's turn to be surprised. Why would he want to see her again? Not that she minded.

The waitress returned to take their orders. Their lunches were served promptly, and they chatted amiably over their egg salad sandwiches. Each one carefully avoided anything too personal.

Alyce related some of her camping experiences with Max. Bill spoke of having some business dealings in Syracuse, but he did not elaborate despite Alyce's subtle probing. His brief, vague comments annoyed Alyce.

"Do you go to Syracuse often?" She hoped her tone sounded impersonal.

"No." His tone implied that she should not ask anything more. But she did not give up easily.

"How long do you plan to be in Syracuse this time?"

"I'm not sure, Alyce."

She tried switching topics. "How long were you in Switzerland?"

He hesitated before responding. Looking into her eyes, he said softly, "For about six months. But let's not talk about me. I'd rather talk about you." He disarmed her again with his smile.

Lunch soon ended, and it was time for them to go their separate ways. Alyce had a long drive ahead of her. As she rose from the table, her arm brushed her glass, spilling the water. She grabbed her napkin to catch it before it drenched Bill. Since he had risen with her, little splashed on him.

"Ooooooooh!" Alyce was mortified. "I'm so sorry. Are you all wet?"

Bill chuckled. "Now that's what I call a personal question." His dark eyes danced, but he added gently, "Relax, Alyce. It was an accident." He was sorry he had teased her.

The waitress came to their rescue. They thanked her with a generous tip and left the dining room together with Bill's arm gently encircling her waist.

"I'd better say good-bye to Max," he said. "I'd like to stay on friendly terms with him."

He patted Max. "So long, boy. See you again sometime, I hope." Max rolled his dark eyes at him, licked his hand, and wagged his tail.

"I'll call you when I get to Syracuse." It was a promise gently spoken. Not trusting herself to respond verbally, Alyce smiled and nodded.

She put the car in reverse and slowly backed out of the parking lot. She studied him a moment through her rearview mirror, then she pulled onto the highway and headed west to Syracuse.

Chapter 5

The phone jangled impatiently as Alyce shuffled her bag of groceries so she could unlock the door. Why did that lock always stick when she was in a hurry? She tried it a second time. The lock wouldn't budge. Finally the door swung open, but by the time she picked up the receiver, the caller had hung up.

Who was calling at that hour? Someone who knew her schedule well, or a stranger taking a chance that she would be home for the dinner hour? She hoped it was Bill Morgan. He had said he would call.

She deposited her groceries on the kitchen counter and dialed her landlord's number. Mr. Jameson promised he'd stop by the next day and fix the lock. He could fix anything. Whenever he came to Alyce's apartment, Sarah, his vivacious wife, came along.

"I don't trust him out alone," she said with a wink at Alyce the first time they came. However, it was soon apparent that the love between the two was on a firm foundation. Sarah came because she was hungry for "woman talk." While her husband tended to whatever needed fixing, she and Alyce visited over a pot of herbal tea.

Alyce was the Jamesons' favorite tenant. She had occupied one of their apartments ever since coming to Syracuse to begin her nursing training. They admired her spunk and went out of their way to encourage her in any way they could. Alyce knew the lock would be fixed by the time she got home the next day.

She eyed the kitchen clock as she put away her groceries and fed Max. She wondered again if Bill had tried to call. She hummed a snappy tune as she fixed herself a light supper.

Her patient had needed so much attention that day that she scarcely had time to catch her breath. After a brief debate with herself, she opted for a quick shower instead of a relaxing soak in the tub. She didn't want to miss another call.

She threw on an old sweatsuit and toweled her hair, finally brushing it back into a ponytail. Suddenly the doorbell rang. She slipped her damp feet into black slippers and hurried to the front door.

A smile lit her eyes as she looked through the peephole. Flinging open the door, she greeted her old friend Joe Heisler. "What a nice surprise!" Joe clasped her in a warm embrace.

"Hello, Alyce. I hope you don't mind an unannounced caller. I was in the neighborhood and thought I'd stop and answer your questions in person." His eyes reflected admiration as he released her. "I tried to call you earlier, but I didn't catch you in."

"Well, come on in. May I fix you a cup of coffee?"

"That would hit the spot. Thanks."

Alyce plugged in the coffee pot and got out two cups. She didn't like coffee in the evening, but she remembered that Joe did.

"How are things at the Statehouse? Are you as busy as ever in Albany?"

"Now that's an understatement, Alyce. We're trying to get things sewed up so we can go home for Christmas recess." A smile edged up the corners of his mouth as he thought about his work. He had represented his legislative district well for six years, due primarily to the personal interest he took in each one of his constituents. His visit to Alyce's home was typical of his homespun style.

He looked at Alyce with questioning eyes. "How are things with you, Alyce? Is everything all right? Are you happy?"

Alyce knew his questions were prompted by a genuine interest in her welfare. After the death of her husband, he had hoped for a deeper relationship, but when he realized she wasn't interested, gentleman that he was, he backed off.

Alyce had followed his legislative career through the media. He had a reputation for honesty and integrity. When she returned from her weekend at Santanoni, she had written him to find out how to carry out the wishes of Nellie Hayes. She was pleased with his prompt response.

"Max and I are doing all right," she said, studying her hands. "I get lonesome sometimes, but we make out okay. Right now I'm so concerned about Santanoni and Mrs. Hayes's will, I spend most of my waking hours wondering how to proceed."

She didn't mention the part Bill Morgan was playing in her drama. Her agitated emotional state was in large part due to him.

Joe glanced at his watch. "I will come right to the point. I'm sorry, but I have an appointment at eight, and I won't be back in Syracuse for two months."

His deep blue eyes sparkled as he surveyed her again from ponytail to slippers. She sensed his quickening pulse, and she felt her own breath quicken and her cheeks flush. She needed to divert his attention and fast. "What did you find out? Is Santanoni doomed to destruction because of the 'Forever Wild' clause?"

A slight frown darkened Joe's countenance before he responded. "Not really, though for a time it was assumed that it came under those restrictions. You can thank our governor for signing a bill to save historic structures in the forest preserve like Santanoni. The law requires that an advisory committee inventory such structures. That law also allows the state to maintain places like that great camp."

Alyce interrupted. "Then we don't have to worry. If the law says it can be maintained, we just need to find the financial resources to maintain it!"

"Wait just one minute. Have you any idea how much it would cost to restore those buildings? They've been sitting there decaying for twenty years. Besides that, the new law may be challenged as unconstitutional by environmental groups."

Alyce frowned and sighed. Nothing was ever easy in this world. "Tell me, Joe, do you honestly think there is a way to save Santanoni?"

It was Joe's turn to sigh. He captured her eyes with his, and she felt the color rising once again in her cheeks. She instinctively lowered her thick brown lashes. She wished he wouldn't look at her that way.

After what seemed like an eternity, he asked, "How important is it to save Santanoni? How hard are you willing to work? Do you have the time and the patience to work through the legalities? And once the legal hurdles are overcome, what about the finances? Do you have some rich uncle with treasure-laden ships ready to dock at your port?"

Alyce knew that Joe was only helping her see that she was contemplating a gargantuan task. She wasn't a quitter, but she wasn't indefatigable, either.

Joe continued. "I'm not trying to discourage you." He smiled again. "I just want to make sure you understand the obstacles in your path."

He hesitated a moment and then spoke as though he were weighing each word before letting it escape. "I doubt that you or any other woman could accomplish such a task alone. If you would like me to work side by side with you, I could. . . ."

Alyce cut off his words with a nod. She knew what Joe was hoping for, but she wasn't interested in that kind of partnership. "Thanks, Joe. I'll find a way to save Santanoni. I appreciate your taking time to help me understand the obstacles in my path."

Joe glanced at his watch again. "There are a few more things you should know; then I must be going." He settled back into his chair and continued. "I don't know what your plans are for Santanoni, but you need to have something definite in mind. Legally the camp can't be leased for private enterprise. That would certainly be challenged. It's possible that it could become a center for interpreting the Forest Preserve to the public."

Alyce readjusted her cushion as Joe explained.

"Maybe it could become a hostel for campers and hikers. It could offer a crackling fire, a warm meal, and a dry bed. Or perhaps educational programs could be presented there for the public."

"Could it be leased to a private group like the Adirondack Mountain Club for a wilderness lodge?"

"That, too, might be possible. The big problem is that no one, or no organization, has the funds to restore Santanoni." He paused absently, running his hand through his hair.

"There is an encouraging note to all this. The lodge and supporting structures at Newcomb Lake have been reviewed by the State Historical Preservation officer. So have the old farm site and the gatehouse. All three have been declared eligible for inclusion in the National Register of Historic Places. The gatehouse has been selected to become a tourist information center. Thanks to our governor, God bless him, it has been singled out for immediate financing. Keep a close watch on what happens with the other buildings at Santanoni."

He rose, picked up his coffee cup, and took it to the kitchen. "I really must be going, Alyce. Thanks for the coffee."

"You're welcome. You've been a big help." She smiled her thanks and then laughed. "I'll remember you when you're up for reelection."

"If the matter should come to a referendum, and that's entirely possible, you can count on my support." He brushed her check with his warm lips and headed for the door. At that precise moment, the doorbell rang. He turned to Alyce. "Expecting someone?"

Alyce shook her head and opened the door.

"Hello, Alyce. I hope you don't mind my dropping in. . . ."

Bill Morgan's chin dropped when he saw Alyce was not alone. "I'm sorry, I didn't realize you had company." His tone was relatively civil, but his mahogany eyes were blazing.

"Not at all. I was just leaving." Joe turned to Alyce. She merely stared, tongue-tied. "I'll be seeing you."

Alyce watched him go down the steps. She had appreciated his coming, but now she was stalling for time. She didn't want to face Bill. The fire in his eyes had not been fueled by brotherly love.

Slowly she turned around. Bill was staring at her trying to draw a response. His dark eyes seemed to probe her very soul. A suffocating sensation tightened her throat. She wanted to explain that Joe was a friend of the family, but it was too late now. As uncomfortable as she felt, she was also excited. She dropped her eyes to avoid his stare. "Come in," she said. "I'll get you a cup of coffee." With that she escaped to the kitchen.

Chapter 6

Alyce leaned against the refrigerator door. What else could happen tonight? She glanced at her reflection in the coffee pot and sighed. If she could have her way, she'd never go back into the living room. She didn't want to face those smoldering eyes.

She shrugged her shoulders and poured two cups of coffee. She didn't want another cup. She knew already she'd be awake half the night, but she needed something to do with her hands. She moistened her dry lips, swallowed, and picked up the coffee.

When she returned to the living room, Bill was sprawled on her velour sofa staring at the photo on the television set. It was a family photo of her with Randy and Maria on Rodney's Windrose when Maria was two years old. As she watched, he slowly lifted himself from the sofa, walked over, and picked up the picture. He studied it a few moments. Gently he returned the photo to its place.

He looked up to see Alyce, and slowly he advanced toward her. Then a finger under her chin gently tilted her face upward. He traced the smooth line of her jaw, and their eyes met tentatively over the coffee.

In place of the anger she had anticipated, she saw compassion in Bill's eyes. She swallowed to relieve the tightness in her throat.

"I brought you a cup of coffee." She gestured toward the sofa. "Please, won't you sit down?" She eased herself onto the sofa and gestured to the cushion beside her. A fleeting smile touched the corners of his mouth.

"I really am glad to see you. . . ." She hoped he couldn't hear her heart hammering in her head.

He seated himself to her right. His slender fingers wrapped around the cup as he lifted it to his lips. She was pleased he was not wearing a wedding band. She hadn't thought about that before.

"How have you been? And how's my friend Max?"

"Oh, we're fine. How have you been? Is your business in Syracuse completed?"

"No, it isn't." He continued. "I stopped to ask if you would have dinner with me tomorrow evening." He studied her face. "But perhaps you have other plans."

Alyce caught the inference and hesitated before responding. She didn't want him to know how eager she was to be with him. "Well," she responded as though she wasn't quite sure she could manage it, "let me check my calendar."

She retrieved her datebook from her purse and studied it carefully. "Yes, I'm free tomorrow evening." She didn't tell him, but if she hadn't been, she would have moved mountains to become so. "What time did you have in mind?"

"Suppose I pick you up about seven. I was afraid you might not be free on such short notice." He glanced at his watch. "I must be going. I have some work to finish tonight. I'll see you tomorrow evening."

At the door Bill turned to face her, and his dark, thoughtful eyes looked straight into hers. She was unnerved by the tenderness reflected in them, and her heart leaped. He dipped his head, and Alyce knew then that he was going to kiss her. His mouth caressed her lips lightly. "Good night, Alyce."

As Alyce closed the door, her knees felt like she had climbed Mount Marcy. She unplugged the coffee pot in the kitchen and then gave Max a good night pat and floated into her bedroom.

The next day Alyce had difficulty thinking about her patient, but fortunately Mrs. Spellman slept a lot. *What will I wear? Should I try something a bit more sophisticated with my hair than my ponytail? I don't want Bill to think I'm a country bumpkin.*

She shook her head. "Keep your mind on your work," she scolded herself out loud. "You're thirty, not thirteen! This is just a friendly dinner date. Nothing more." But while common sense said one thing, her heart was thumping out a different message.

It was nearly six when she got home from work the next day. She fed Max and let him out for a run in his yard. When she stepped into the shower, she still hadn't decided what to wear. Alyce didn't own many clothes. She wore her uniforms to work and spent her weekends in jeans and pullovers. The only time she dressed up was for church.

She decided on her favorite suit, a gentle Ming plaid with a knife-pleated skirt and a fitted jacket. Though many women had to stay away from pleats, her petite figure made them flattering. The fitted jacket accented her graceful curves, and the delicate Irish lace on the collar and cuffs of her matching blouse added just the right touch. Alyce felt good when she wore this suit. Ming green was her color.

She wore her black pumps that matched her leather clutch bag. Golden hoop earrings and matching twin bracelets completed her ensemble.

Bill arrived a few minutes before seven, but she was ready. He greeted her with a smile that was warm enough almost to make her forget the coat. "I don't believe this. A woman ready on time. Are you for real?"

It was Alyce's turn to laugh. "Yes, indeed. Very real. It goes with my upbringing. My aunt insisted on punctuality."

"Your aunt?"

"Yes. Aunt May. My mother died when I was born. My dad never came back from Europe. He was in the army, a career man. My uncle Patrick was killed in the same freak accident with my father. So my mother's sister took me in. She had a five-year-old daughter at that time. Aunt May reared the two of us alone.

She treated me just like she treated Barbara. We didn't have much money, but we were happy."

Alyce continued her explanation as she got her Harris tweed overcoat from the hall closet. "We had enough money for food and clothing and things like that, but not for luxuries. Aunt May gave us love and understanding in place of the things that money could have bought. I appreciate that now."

The lines of concentration deepened on Bill's brow as he listened to her story. Alyce smiled at the handsomely attired man who had come to take her to dinner. *The perfect executive,* she thought, as she appraised his impeccable three-piece suit and tastefully patterned tie. Bill opened the door, and then a firm masculine arm curved around her waist as he guided her to his car.

A myriad of dangerous thoughts fluttered through Alyce's mind. Bill's gentle gestures reminded her of Randy. She had loved him with all her heart, but she had ceased wearing her emotional pain like a cement shroud.

"I've made reservations at Sylvia's. I hope that you approve," he said, interrupting her reverie. "I'm sorry I didn't think to ask if you had a favorite restaurant."

"Sylvia's will be fine." Dollar signs flashed before her eyes. She had lived in Syracuse for a number of years, but she had never eaten at Sylvia's. Whenever she had occasion to dine out, it was at a more conservative establishment.

The dining room of Sylvia's was ornate, with huge crystal chandeliers and cozy tables spread with snowy white linen. Candles glowed softly from their black wrought-iron holders. Soft dinner music, which Alyce recognized as one of her favorite symphonies from Tchaikovsky, added an elegant but soothing touch.

This was not the atmosphere in which Alyce routinely lived her life, but tonight she felt both comfortable and special. A few female heads looked wistfully at Bill and enviously at her. She ignored the smiles of appreciation that were aimed in her direction.

Alyce appreciated the meticulously dressed waiter with his crisp red bow tie who led them to their table. He exuded efficiency as he filled their water glasses. They had been seated no more than a minute when an attractive cocktail waitress materialized at their side. With her red and white miniskirt uniform, black braid, and black net stockings, she was dressed to please the male diners.

"Good evening. My name is Diane. I'm your cocktail waitress this evening. May I bring you a drink before dinner?"

Alyce declined politely, and so did Bill. Hiding her disappointment behind a painted smile, the waitress excused herself.

Bill looked at Alyce. "Are you a teetotaler?"

Alyce nodded. "I don't need what drinks have to offer. How about you?"

"I wasn't always, but I've become one. I admire people who don't drink and who don't make a big issue about their abstinence."

At that point Philip arrived at their table. He bid them good evening and presented them menus. "I recommend our beef bourguignon this evening," he said. "I'll be back to take your orders once you have had time to make your selections."

Alyce chose chicken cordon bleu while Bill opted for a rare prime rib. After their order was taken, there was a brief silence as if each were weighing his words before beginning a conversation. Bill smiled at Alyce, totally unaware of how he was unsettling her equilibrium with his glance.

The conversation drifted to likes and dislikes in food, clothing, books, and hobbies. In no time at all the waiter returned with their salads and rolls. They were discussing their interests in sports when he arrived with their entrees. A half-hour later, they were still chatting easily.

They had almost finished dinner when a stranger, short and balding, stopped at their table.

"If it isn't Bill. . ."

Before he could finish his greeting, he was interrupted by Bill's enthusiastic response. "Hey! What do you say, Paul?"

"Well, hello, old buddy! How are you? When did you get back to the States? And what are you doing in Syracuse?"

The men shook hands vigorously, the newcomer grinning with pleasure at having discovered an old friend.

"I'm fine, Paul. It sure is great to see you again. I've been home for about a month now." Bill then introduced him to Alyce, and they shook hands.

"Well, Bill, I don't want to interrupt. It was nice to see you. Give me a call. I'm living in Syracuse now. Have my own business, and business is pretty good. Look me up, okay? We'll get together for old times' sake. Nice to have met you, Ms. Anderson." He tipped an imaginary hat and rejoined his friends.

Bill glanced at Alyce and realized that she had finished her dinner. Philip headed toward their table.

"Would you like dessert, Alyce?"

"No, thanks. I couldn't possibly eat another bite." She returned his smile.

Bill signaled for the check and signed it. In no time at all they arrived back at Alyce's apartment. Bill guided her to her door with a gentle hand on her back.

"Would you like to come in?"

Bill paused as though the question stymied him. "I'd enjoy that very much, but I'd better say no. I have a busy schedule tomorrow. There's some paperwork I must get done tonight."

"I understand. I've had a lovely time. The dinner was delicious."

"I've had a good time, too. Could I see you again soon?"

"That would be nice."

The brief conversation brought them to the door. Bill's fingers traced the delicate line of her chin as he had done in her apartment. Their eyes met in the semidarkness as his fingers curved around the back of her neck and drew her to his chest. He lowered his attention to her softly parted lips. His kiss was gentle. Raising his mouth from hers, he gazed into her eyes. "Good night, Alyce. . . I'll call you."

Alyce watched until the car door slammed behind him. His kiss had sent another stunning reminder of what she had been missing for nine years.

She put her purse on her bed and took off her coat. Then she turned on the light and looked at herself in the mirror. Slowly she touched her lips with her fingers. Not since Randy's death had she been kissed like that.

She wrapped her arms about herself and closed her eyes. Bill had stirred something in her that she had bound up years ago. For years she had existed, even happily at times, without romantic attachments. Now she was struggling against a desire so pure and natural she was unnerved. She hadn't been looking for male companionship, but Bill Morgan had come barging into her life anyway. How she hoped he would stay.

∞

Back at his hotel room Bill removed his tie, kicked off his shoes, and made himself comfortable at his desk. He needed to make some corrections on his manuscript before he met with his editor the next day. He stared at the papers, but his mind refused to focus on the lines needing his attention. He got up, got a drink of water, and tried again. It was no use. He wandered over to the window and looked out at the street lights. He could not get Alyce off his mind.

He thought about their first meeting at Santanoni, and then when he had decided to cultivate her friendship to learn more about his family. Since Will and Nellie were dead, what could she tell him that really mattered? He had no need to continue seeing her, except that he felt drawn to her like a black labrador drawn to water.

What an impression he must have made on her with his bullying questions the first time they met! At first he considered her too feisty, but as he got to know her, he respected her spunk. She had been honest and open with him since the day they met. He wished he had treated her the same way. Though she looked like a fragile china doll, he sensed she would not break easily. He'd hate to oppose her on a matter she felt was important. He knew she would fight for her principles.

Well, Bill. . .the roving bachelor, eh? You could have had any woman you wanted while you floated around Europe. Now you come home to untold disappointment. You fall for a squatter on your land. Correction! Your former land! Sure she's attractive, intelligent, and honest. Are you really ready to settle down? And what about Santanoni? What are you going to do about your old home?

He inhaled deeply and sighed with remorse. He had hoped to see a lawyer while in Syracuse, but thus far his time had been eaten up with his publisher. His mind reeled with his problems, but his heart kept returning to Alyce.

Her responses to his touch and to his kiss told him she found him desirable. But how desirable would he be when she found out he had lied about his name? He shuddered, thinking of how close Paul had come to revealing the truth. Maybe it would have been better if he had not interrupted him. That might have given him an opportunity to explain to Alyce. But what explanation could he give for such inane behavior?

A dull ache was spreading across Bill's forehead. He had made a mess of things, and he needed to get some sleep. As he turned out the light and eased himself into bed, one thought consumed him. Soon. . .very soon. . .he would tell Alyce.

Chapter 7

Alyce had lots of time to think as she drove to Newcomb. Despite her attempts at putting everything in its proper perspective, her thoughts centered on Bill Morgan. What an enigma he had become to her. Something about him was familiar, but she knew she hadn't met him before. Why was he angry when he met her and Max at Santanoni? Why did he ignore her after their pleasant dinner date?

"I'll call you. . . ." His words still echoed in her ears. But he hadn't called. By now he must be back in Newcomb. She wondered what he was doing. She shrugged her shoulders as she parked her Escort in front of the office of Robert D. Roberts.

After Joe Heisler's visit, she decided she needed a lawyer to investigate some of Joe's suggestions for saving Santanoni. She could find a lawyer in Syracuse, but since Roberts lived in the Adirondacks, he was more apt to be tuned in to the regulations of the Adirondack Park Agency. Robert Roberts had left no doubt in her mind that he would enjoy helping her. She would try to forget Bill Morgan and get on with saving Santanoni.

The attorney's young secretary greeted her. "Come right in, Ms. Anderson. Mr. Roberts is expecting you." She flashed Alyce a welcoming smile that quieted the butterflies in her stomach momentarily. But it was obvious that she had a consuming interest in what would transpire between Alyce and her boss.

Robert Roberts rose to greet her. "How do you do, Ms. Anderson? I'm glad to see you again." There was an awkward pause. Then he took her hand. "I'm glad I can serve you once more."

"How do you do? I appreciate your arranging our meeting at this hour. I hope it didn't inconvenience you too much."

"Not at all. Do have a seat, and we'll get to work." He gestured to a Chippendale chair opposite his oak desk. "I've done some research on the great camps, and I've come up with a suggestion. It's an encouraging note that the gatehouse at Santanoni has been selected as a Tourist Information Center. At least the governor is on your side."

Alyce settled back into her chair. She needed the help of more than the governor. She hoped she'd get some workable suggestions from Robert Roberts.

The attorney's steely blue eyes swept over Alyce as he began his explanation. "Here is my suggestion. I believe it will be acceptable to the state legislature, and I think it handles the Adirondack Park Agency's 'Forever Wild' clause in a satisfactory manner. Listen carefully and then tell me what you think about my plan.

"I suggest you form a nonprofit foundation for Santanoni. The members of the foundation would provide the initial funds to begin the restoration of the camp. They would submit a proposal to the state for a management agreement."

Alyce interrupted. "Excuse me, but is a management agreement the same as a lease?"

"No, it isn't. According to the 'Forever Wild' clause, a lease would be unconstitutional. If the legislature accepts your proposal, then it will likely have to come before the voters for their approval."

Alyce nodded. Joe had mentioned a referendum.

Mr. Roberts continued. "We have no way of knowing how the public will vote in a referendum. We can be optimistic, though. A few years back the people of New York State voted an overwhelming approval when the fate of Camp Sagamore was in the balance."

He paused again. "You know, Ms. Anderson, it's a strange situation. We feel we know what is best for our own property. Yet the whole state gets to decide what we can do with it. I'm not sure I agree with that policy. What gives me the right to decide what folks anywhere else should do with their public lands?"

Alyce pondered his question. "That's the way it is, isn't it? People who want to come here for a vacation don't want us to do anything to disrupt their fun. They don't see the situation as we do, do they? I wonder how those people would like it if we in the Adirondacks told them how to handle their property in Manhattan or their condominiums in Coral Gables?"

"I hear what you are saying, Ms. Anderson. We have to accept things as they are at the present. I would suggest you find some people who share your interest in the great camp and who are financially able to assist in this project."

"Do you have any idea how much money we'd have to come up with initially?"

"Yes, I do. I'd say you'd need a minimum of $500,000. It will probably take twice that amount to restore Santanoni, but if you have half of the money up front, that would be a good start. If you had a five-member foundation, each would need to give $100,000. If I recall correctly, you have that much from the Hayes estate. If you had another $100,000 of your own, you would have two votes which would give you control over the foundation."

Alyce coughed at the thought of having another $100,000 at her immediate disposal.

"If the foundation came up with $500,000, the funds could be invested immediately so they could draw interest while you await legislative approval. Meanwhile you could advertise your goals and solicit funds from the public."

Alyce settled more comfortably into her chair. Asking Robert Roberts for help seemed to have been a smart move on her part. She listened as he continued his explanation.

"The foundation would have to restore Santanoni at its own expense. Once the restoration was completed and the camp was able to turn a profit, it would be good for public relations to contribute a percentage of that profit to the Adirondack Park Agency, or some other group working to preserve the Adirondack Mountains."

Alyce was forming a plan in her mind. "Of course we would respect the wilderness character of the surrounding Forest Preserve, and we'd be careful to observe the state regulations. We'd continue to restrict access to the camp. Visitors would have to hike into the camp or travel on horseback."

"Good thinking on your part. What you're suggesting would be essential to any proposal you make. Now let's think about the buildings. I'd suggest restoring the lodge first to make it available to those who like to explore the Adirondacks. I mean hikers, skiers, and hunters."

"And fishermen, horseback riders, architectural buffs, and nature lovers," Alyce added.

The attorney continued. "You might offer tours, light meals, and simple overnight accommodations at reasonable rates. To avoid overuse, you could insist that those coming to Santanoni register in advance."

Alyce had another idea. "Perhaps the foundation could offer a program of nature interpretation to complement what is offered at the interpretative center at the gatehouse."

It was Roberts's turn to smile. "You have some good ideas, too. You should be able to find others who care enough to give their financial support to save Santanoni. I believe the state will listen to a foundation that is holding $500,000 in its hands. One of the reasons Santanoni has fallen into such disrepair has been the lack of funds. The state sold Topridge when it couldn't afford to keep it. If we show how we can save Santanoni without disturbing the environment, we should be able to save it, too."

Alyce's brow furrowed, but she was encouraged by what the attorney was saying. The bottom line was the financial arrangements. "I don't know four people who know about Santanoni, to say nothing of their being willing to part with that amount of cash to secure its future."

"At the risk of being presumptuous, I have begun to seek out some interested parties for you. I felt if you trusted me as your attorney, you would not object."

"Not at all. I want to carry out the wishes of Will and Nellie Hayes. I'd like to restore Santanoni for them." She was pensive, and Roberts hesitated to interrupt her thoughts.

After a brief silence she asked, "Did you find anyone who was interested in the kind of partnership you are suggesting?"

"As a matter of fact I did. I have two prospects." He looked at her directly. "If you would permit me to do so, I would like to become one of the members of the foundation. Not just to prove I think the idea is sound, but because I care about Santanoni, too."

Alyce bristled inwardly at his suggestion.

"Though I'm a newcomer to the Adirondacks, relatively speaking, I'm at home in the mountains. After practicing law in Syracuse for five years, I had my fill of city life. I wanted to return to a less populated area. That's one reason why I established my office here in Newcomb."

He went on to explain how he had grown up in the Blue Ridge Mountains of Virginia. "After you came to see me that first time, I hiked in to the Santanoni Preserve. I'm not sure what I was expecting, but I was appalled when I saw that magnificent lodge deteriorating like a long-neglected castle. To let that building fall down would be a crime. If it goes, it will take with it a piece of our Adirondack heritage."

As he spoke, Alyce could see his deep appreciation for Santanoni. Since he had suggested the criteria for membership in the foundation, he must have the financial resources required. Yet in the back of her mind, she remembered their first meeting. Was he offering his help because he was interested in Santanoni? Or was he only interested in her?

"I appreciate your offer, Mr. Roberts. Please give me some time to think about it." *And some way to politely tell you no,* she wanted to add.

"That's fine with me. If you decide to include me in the foundation, you'll need to get another lawyer to handle the establishment of the foundation. If you wish, I could suggest someone. But perhaps you'd rather handle that yourself."

Alyce appreciated his frankness. She pondered his offer, but she would not be hasty in her decision. After a few minutes, her eyes brightened. "You said you had two possibilities? Who is the other?"

"Again at the risk of being presumptuous, I took the liberty of talking with an acquaintance who, unlike me, is a native of this area. Assuming you would be spending the night at the Antlers, I arranged dinner for the three of us this evening at the inn. Our reservations are for six-thirty."

He studied her face to see if she were angry. Ever so slowly a smile made its way through her mask of uncertainty. Robert Roberts was being helpful; she'd consider his true motives later. Today he had kept his place. She would trust him through dinner.

"My thanks again. Of course I'm staying at the Antlers." She chuckled. It was not only a comfortable inn, it was the only lodging in Newcomb.

At precisely six-thirty Alyce left her room for the dining room. She hadn't had time to think about their afternoon meeting, but she'd consider Roberts's suggestions on her drive back to Syracuse. She was toying with the idea of getting up early so she could hike into Santanoni at dawn. She'd have time to do that and still not be too late getting home if she didn't linger long at the camp. She wished she had brought Max along with her.

As she scanned the dining room for Roberts, a gasp escaped her lips. Sitting with his back to the door, his broad shoulders visible above the chair back, a man was deep in conversation with her attorney. She strode into the dining room and came face to face with Bill Morgan.

Chapter 8

A tumble of muddled thoughts and feelings assailed Alyce as she tried to force her confused emotions into order. What was Bill Morgan doing here? She took a deep breath, but still she could not get her tongue to move. The two men rose to greet her, Robert Roberts exuding his usual charm and Bill wearing a look of utter astonishment.

For a few moments Bill and Alyce contemplated each other, their bemused eyes locked in silence. The attorney, sensing something was going on to which he was not privy, glanced nervously from one to the other. Unable to comprehend the situation or to endure the silence, he yanked at his tie and asked, "Have you two already met?"

Not trusting herself to speak, Alyce gestured to Bill. Bill turned from Alyce to face Robert Roberts. During that brief moment the puzzlement in his eyes turned to anger. Alyce could not help but recall the way his dark eyes had blazed when they had met at Santanoni and when he had found Joe Heisler at her apartment.

Alyce watched his lips tighten. A flush of fury darkened his face. She prayed that anger would never again be unleashed against her. She was glad she was neither the cause nor the target of his rage.

"Yes, Rob, Alyce and I have met. I wish you'd not been so secretive about this meeting." He spoke through clenched teeth, and there was a chill in his voice as he addressed the lawyer, his words landing like hailstones on a tin roof. "You could have saved us both some embarrassment."

He turned back to Alyce. "Please sit down, Alyce. I apologize for what has happened. There are a few details about this meeting that I had not been told."

Discovering Alyce's direct involvement in the future of Santanoni had caught Bill off guard. He gave her a sidelong glance and tried to disguise his annoyance at the revelation, but his vexation was obvious. *Well*, he mused, *Ms. Anderson doesn't reveal the whole truth, either*. There was much more he needed to learn about this enigmatic nurse from Syracuse.

The tense situation was eased momentarily by the waitress coming to take their orders. As she departed for the kitchen, Bill turned again to Alyce.

"Please believe me, I had no idea I would be meeting you here this evening. I assure you it's a pleasure." He paused. "I owe you an explanation for not calling before I left Syracuse, but that's a matter for us to discuss at another time and place."

Alyce attempted a smile. She would be civil though she, too, was angry at Roberts. Why didn't he tell her he had talked with Bill about the foundation plans? Just what was Bill's interest in Santanoni? She knew so little about him. Since Robert Roberts had invited him to consider becoming part of the foundation to save Santanoni, he must have money. Paupers didn't drive Lincolns.

If only she hadn't allowed herself to become interested in him. She didn't know how or where it had happened, but she had to admit she had fallen in love with Bill. In many ways he was a stranger, but one with very endearing ways. Well, she would let Roberts take charge of this meeting. He had arranged it. She would listen and try to be rational, but it would be hard with Bill Morgan sitting beside her.

Robert Roberts cleared his throat and fumbled again with his tie. He glanced from Alyce to Bill as he spoke. "Well, I guess I've made a first-class faux pas this time. I apologize to both of you."

Alyce couldn't remain mute all evening. True, he had not handled this situation well, but what was done was done. He couldn't start the evening all over again.

"I forgive you. We all err sometimes." She sounded more magnanimous than she felt.

"That goes for me, too." Bill's voice was firm, but it had lost its angry edge.

"I hope I haven't spoiled your dinner. Perhaps we can discuss my proposal after we have eaten."

Before they could answer, the waitress returned with their rolls and salads. Bothered by the unanswered questions that swirled about her, Alyce picked at her food. What interested Bill so much about Santanoni? Robert Roberts had referred to him as a native of the area, but that's all she had learned about him from the attorney.

She knew Bill had been in Europe for several years. He had some kind of business to attend to in Syracuse. He knew how to befriend a dog. He seemed at home in the woods.

The conversation was light as they ate their dinners. Over coffee the attorney cleared his throat to signal the start of the business at hand.

"Ms. Anderson, with your permission, I'd like to tell Bill about my suggestion for a foundation to save Santanoni." He looked at her, seeking her approval, and she knew he was sincere in asking. Not having any reason to refuse other than the peculiar way he had arranged the dinner meeting, she nodded affirmatively.

Robert Roberts sighed, took a deep breath, and began to explain his plan to Bill. As he made his suggestions, the lines of concentration deepened along Bill's brow and under his eyes.

"So I think such a foundation would be acceptable to the Adirondack Park Agency and to the state of New York. I am excited about the possibilities, and I've told Ms. Anderson I'd like to be one of the five members." He glanced at

Alyce as he concluded his explanation.

Bill looked at Alyce with questioning eyes before he responded. Though he could see determination and strength reflected in her face, he could not discern her reaction to the possibility of his becoming a part of the foundation. When he spoke, his voice was firm and final.

"Well, Rob, I must say you have done your homework." He turned to Alyce. His voice was calm, his gaze steady. "Since you two have already discussed this plan, I presume you find it acceptable." He spoke in such a way that she could agree or disagree without giving offense.

Alyce nodded her assent. The thought of having Bill as part of the foundation was causing her pulse to race. She'd have to be dead to ignore the excitement that was growing within her as she considered the prospect of having him working by her side to carry out the wishes of Nellie Hayes.

She was glad that Bill was interested in Santanoni, glad that this meeting had been arranged. But could she act rationally with him so close? It wouldn't do to let him know how she felt about him. He had promised to call her but he had broken his promise. Could he be depended on now? The way her heart was pounding, she knew she'd give him another chance.

Finally she gained her voice. "The plan sounds workable to me. I have explained to Mr. Roberts that I do not know others who would be interested in this kind of an investment." She swallowed. "I appreciate the interest both of you have shown in Santanoni. At this point I don't understand why either of you should care so much about the camp, but I'm glad that you do."

She glanced from Bill to Robert Roberts. "Will you please give me time to think about this? I don't make hasty decisions. I need to look for other interested parties should I decide the three of us could work together." She knew she wanted Bill as part of the group. She wasn't so sure about Robert Roberts.

"That's fine with me. It's your ball game." Bill looked at her as if he were analyzing her reaction. "I spent a lot of time at Santanoni when I was a kid. I'd like to help restore the camp to the way I remember it." As he spoke, his eyes clouded. He blinked and turned away.

"I agree, Ms. Anderson." Roberts smiled at her. "Do you think a month would be sufficient time for you to make up your mind? We don't mean to rush you, but Santanoni can't wait. The deterioration goes on. If you accept us as partners, remember you'll need to find another lawyer. The sooner you set your plans in motion, the better it will be for the camp."

"I understand that. A month is enough time." She looked at Bill, his expression unreadable. "I'll let you know my decision within thirty days. Thank you for dinner. Now if you will excuse me, I'd like to go to my room." She nodded at both men as they rose from the table.

Alyce felt wrapped in an invisible warmth as she left the dining room. Once in her room she replayed the latest events in her real-life drama. Not in her wildest imaginings did she expect to have dinner with Bill Morgan tonight. She had hoped she might see him again, though she had no idea how that would happen.

Her head was so full of new considerations she felt it would burst. There was one place she knew she could go to sort things out: Sunrise would find her hiking into Santanoni Preserve. She didn't understand fully, but she knew God spoke to her most clearly in the out-of-doors. She slipped into her nightgown and settled herself under the homey patchwork quilt, closing her eyes on a world of intriguing possibilities.

The earliest rays of dawn were chasing away the darkness when Alyce signed the camper's register at the gatehouse. She missed Max, but this would not be a leisurely hike. She must be on her way back to Syracuse by one o'clock. If she walked briskly, she'd be able to spend an hour at the lodge.

The dry leaves crunched under her feet as she set her face toward Santanoni. She had made it a habit to keep her daypack in the trunk, and today she was glad she had. She knew the importance of taking sufficient water on every hike, and she also tucked in an orange she had saved from breakfast.

The chipmunks were still racing through the forest, and at one point she startled a partridge. The poor bird gave a frightened squawk and disappeared into the thicket.

Alyce hiked up the gentle incline that led directly to Santanoni's impressive lodge and sat down on the steps to see what was going on out on the lake. She wished she had her binoculars.

She had been sitting there for perhaps twenty minutes when she heard someone whistling. Then she heard footsteps on the porch of the lodge around the corner from where she sat. Whoever was coming wasn't trying to be quiet. If Max were with her, she'd feel a lot more comfortable about being alone—and vulnerable—five miles into the wilderness.

She got up and headed in the direction of the footsteps. They echoed louder as the intruder walked from one section of the labyrinthine porch toward the place where she had been sitting. She rounded the corner at her usual speedy clip and collided with a familiar six-foot frame.

The collision startled her, but Bill steadied her and then maintained his gentle but firm grip on her arm. Ever so slowly he drew her to his steely chest, and she thrilled to the rippling of his arm muscles as he held her to him. The movement of his breathing sent electrifying vibrations through her as he searched her eyes for an affirmative response. Her heart fluttered wildly in her throat.

"I'm so glad I've found you here," he murmured into her hair. His breath was warm and moist, and her heart raced. Instinctively she wound her arms around his neck. Standing on tiptoe, she touched her lips to his. His response was gentle, and his lips were warm and sweet.

Aware of his strength and the warmth of his flesh, Alyce felt a tingling in the pit of her stomach. She knew she must disengage herself, and so gently she placed her hands on his cheeks and pulled away from him.

"Why did you come looking for me? How did you know I was here?"

Bill took her by the hand and led her to the steps where they could sit together. "I took a chance, and I'm so glad I did. I have a lot of explaining to do. First, there's the matter of the phone call. I. . ."

Alyce laid a gentle hand over his lips. "Tell me some other time, okay? I have to leave soon. Can we just sit and enjoy this lovely spot together until then?"

Bill nodded. "Fair enough," he said. They sat in silence for a few moments. Then Bill spoke again. "Alyce, will you come back to Santanoni for me? I have commitments that will keep me here for the next six weeks. I can't come to see you. Please come to me."

Alyce did not trust her voice. Bill did care about her. That was all that mattered. Her mind was racing as fast as her heart. At that moment she would have climbed Mount Marcy in her bare feet if he had asked her to do it for him.

"Will you come back and have Thanksgiving dinner with me? I don't have any family here. It would mean a lot to me. You could stay at the Antlers, and we could come back to Santanoni. I could show you around."

Alyce's voice was soft when she responded. "I would enjoy that very much."

His dark eyes glistened. "I promise I won't badger you about your decision concerning the foundation or its members. But if you should decide to count me in, maybe we could begin to make some plans together."

Alyce nodded and then glanced at her watch. "I'm sorry, but I must head back to the gatehouse. Thanks. . .for coming to look for me."

It was Bill's turn to smile. "I assure you, Madam, it was my pleasure. May I walk back with you?"

Alyce flashed him her warmest smile as she took his hand.

Chapter 9

Alyce was not able to leave Syracuse as early as she had hoped. It was one-thirty when she finally headed east to Newcomb. Bill wasn't expecting her until the next day, so that was no problem. She put a cassette into the player, allowed herself the luxury of a long sigh, and settled back into her seat. The gentle strains of "Liebestraum" would quiet her heart before she had traveled too many miles. She was grateful for a good weather report. She didn't like driving on slippery roads, and New York weather in late November was unpredictable.

Snow had begun to fall in big fluffy flakes when she arrived at the Antlers Inn. "I hope there's a room available tonight," she muttered to herself. "Why didn't I take time to make a reservation? Serves me right if I have to sleep in my car." Suddenly the snow didn't look so lovely.

Fortunately there was one room available. Glancing at her watch, she decided she had better have dinner right away. The Antlers Inn was located in a remote section of the Adirondacks and, consequently, did not draw the kind of clientele that dined fashionably late. She would unpack after she had eaten. She looked forward to a relaxing evening, something that her work schedule of late had not allowed. She pulled the door shut behind her, stuffed her key into her jeans pocket, and headed downstairs.

She chose a table in the rear of the cozy dining room with a good view of the doorway. She enjoyed watching diners come and go. Her waitress was soon at her table to remove the extra place setting. Alyce picked up the menu and scanned it.

She was about to place her order when some other guests arrived for dinner. She glanced toward the entrance and felt her heart race. Coming through the doorway was Bill Morgan looking as handsome as ever in a blue turtleneck and navy trousers. Reluctantly Alyce tore her gaze from his face only to note that clinging to his arm was a gorgeous blond. Not one hair was out of place in her stylish French twist. Her black, long-sleeved dress was simple in design and moved in a fluid motion with her slender body. Despite the woman's natural beauty and style, her countenance was grave, her features drawn.

The color drained from Alyce's face as she stared at the couple. Her stomach slowly tied itself into a hard knot, and she had difficulty breathing.

"Ma'am? Are you all right? Excuse me, Ma'am, are you okay?" The young waitress put a gentle hand on Alyce's shoulder.

The concern on the young woman's face was the catalyst Alyce needed to cushion her shock. She shuddered. "I'm so sorry to have frightened you. I'm okay. Just tired, I guess." She tried to smile to put the waitress at ease.

"I'll have a tuna on rye, toasted, please, and a cup of black coffee." Alyce hated tuna fish, and she didn't like coffee at night, but that was the first thing that came to mind. She didn't want the waitress hovering over her.

As she gazed at Bill's companion, she had a sneaking suspicion that that woman, whoever she was, would look regal in a potato sack. It was time she reexamined her relationship with Bill Morgan. Was she interested in him only as a member of the Foundation to Save Santanoni? It was easy to say that. Before she succumbed to another tender moment with him, Alyce decided she should know what she wanted, from him and for herself. She should also make sure that they shared the same spiritual foundation; she had allowed her emotions free rein for too long.

Alyce's frenzied thoughts were interrupted by the waitress returning with her sandwich. "May I get you anything else, Ma'am?"

Alyce shook her head, and the waitress disappeared into the kitchen. She stared at the sandwich and then made a halfhearted attempt to eat it but gave up after two tries. It tasted like fishy cardboard.

"Please, Lord, don't let Bill see me here," she prayed with her eyes open.

She glanced down, suddenly appalled at her attire. Faded corduroy jeans, her favorite flannel shirt, and her old Nikes were far from haute couture. She had intended to change for dinner when she arrived at the inn. What a day this had turned out to be. *The sooner this day is over, the better,* she surmised, but first she had to decide what she was going to do about tomorrow.

She swallowed a few sips of her coffee and requested her check. Her scarcely touched sandwich did not go unnoticed.

"I'm sorry you didn't enjoy your sandwich. Was there something wrong with it?"

"Oh, no," Alyce responded through a pasted-on smile. "I guess I just wasn't hungry. But I'll make up for it at dinner tomorrow."

"Great! You'll love our Thanksgiving feast. My name is Babs. I'm working this entire weekend, so I'll see you at breakfast." She looked at Alyce to make certain she was all right. "I hope you rest well."

One glance at Bill assured her he was giving his friend 110 percent of his attention. Not wanting Babs to feel she was at fault for the uneaten sandwich, Alyce left a generous tip. Now for her escape. She tiptoed to the door. Two more steps and she would be out of sight and into the hallway.

Her heart thumped like a metronome gone berserk. For some insane reason she turned around. As she did, Bill looked away from his stunning companion and straight at her. She knew she should flee the dining room, but her sneakers felt nailed to the floor.

Bill turned back to his companion and said something. Then he rose and came toward her. He greeted her with a quick, warm embrace.

"Alyce, I wasn't expecting you until tomorrow. When did you arrive?"

Alyce tried to stay calm. It was obvious he hadn't been expecting her. She glanced at Bill and then at his companion.

"Hello, Bill." Her voice was weak and uncontrolled. She hoped he couldn't see how close she was to tears. "I arrived a short time ago. I left Syracuse later than I had planned." She was mumbling as she edged toward the exit.

Bill put a staying hand on her arm as he sensed she was leaving. "Please, don't go. There's someone I want you to meet." He gently propelled her toward his table.

Short of creating an ugly scene, she could do nothing but accept his invitation to meet his friend. She thought of thirty-nine places she would rather be at that very moment.

Bill made the formal introductions. "I'd like you to meet my sister, Bette Montgomery."

Alyce retrieved her false smile and pasted it on again. "How do you do, Bette? I'm pleased to meet you." She hoped she sounded sincere. She wondered how much longer her legs would hold her up.

Bette extended her hand. It was a friendly gesture on her part, but something was clearly awry. Alyce's nursing instincts detected tension in her grasp.

"Won't you join us for a cup of coffee?" It was Bill's invitation.

Alyce hesitated, but Bill pulled a chair out for her anyway.

"This is my lucky day. I don't deserve having the two most beautiful women in the world sitting at my table." Bill beamed his disarming smile, first at Alyce, and then at his sister. "What a great Thanksgiving celebration this is going to be!"

Alyce toyed with her napkin. She was having trouble finding her tongue. She'd better find it soon before Bill's sister decided she was incapable of rational speech. Bette spoke again.

"Bill has told me all about you. I was looking forward to meeting you tomorrow at dinner." Her voice was soft and controlled. "I'm glad you arrived safely."

Feeling like one of Cinderella's stepsisters, Alyce smiled weakly. She was tired, and now she felt chagrin at the false conclusions she had drawn about Bill. She was also more puzzled about Bill's past.

"Thank you, but I'd rather forget the coffee. It's been a traumatic day. I'm sure you'll find my company more acceptable after I've had a good night's rest. I'll see you at dinner tomorrow."

As she delivered her speech, Alyce tried to get used to the idea that Bill had a sister. What other secrets was he harboring?

At this point she didn't know, and she was too tired to care. She looked at Bill and then at Bette. "Please excuse me. It was nice meeting you, Bette." She gave Bill a lingering, enigmatic look and left the dining room.

Chapter 10

B ill studied his coffee cup after Alyce left their table. Bette watched him for a few moments before she spoke. "You're in love with her, aren't you?" Bill nodded. "Yes," he said, "but there are complications in our relationship."

Bette smiled knowingly. Her own ill-fated marriage had been destined for disaster. At sixteen she had eloped with her high school art teacher.

"Do you want to talk about them?" She and Bill had shared their troubles when they were growing up. Maybe they could recapture some of that warmth that had bound them together when they had quarreled with their parents.

Bill nodded again and sighed. "Let's go back to your room." He hoped he could find the right words when he got there. Once ensconced in her comfortable quarters, Bette wasted no time.

"Okay, big brother, do you want to tell me what's wrong?"

Bill smiled. It was ironic that Bette was taking the lead in the conversation. "I didn't tell her I had a sister, Bette."

"So? What does that matter? It's obvious she's interested in you. Why else would she come to Newcomb for Thanksgiving dinner? There certainly are more interesting places to enjoy a holiday."

"It's not just about you. There's something else I haven't told Alyce. Something important." Bill shut his eyes momentarily as if by doing so he could shut out his problems. "Alyce is more than a passing fancy. I'd like to marry her."

"Have you asked her to marry you?"

"No. . . ."

"Come on, Bill. Why not? You've always gone after whatever you wanted."

Bill knew she was alluding to the quarrel that had erupted between him and their father when Bill left for college. He never saw his father again. Bill was wiser now. His problem had been the impatience of youth while his father's had been grief at the disappearance of his younger son.

Bill grinned at his sister. "I haven't changed. But things get so complicated. You see, Alyce is interested in Santanoni."

"So? Why is that a problem? Aren't you interested in our home anymore?"

Bill gulped at her comment. "Of course I am. That's what brought me back from Europe. I wanted to settle down, to spend my time writing. I've got enough ideas to keep me writing for the rest of my life. I came home to reconcile my differences with Will and Nellie. I'd hoped to find you again, and then

I looked forward to spending my days writing at Santanoni."

"What's stopping you?"

Bill felt his heart leap into his throat as Bette eyed him carefully. He turned to face her, glad that she was sitting down. She looked so pale. He didn't know where to begin. He couldn't keep his voice from trembling. Growing up at Santanoni, the two of them had been inseparable; Bill had grown to realize only recently how much he loved her. It must have broken her heart to be left behind when he left for college. Now he had to tell her about their parents.

"Bette," he said gently, "Will and Nellie are dead. They died in Syracuse a couple of years ago."

As painful and difficult as it was for them both, Bill continued. He wasn't sure he'd be able to begin again if he stopped. "After we left home, they sold Santanoni. It now belongs to the State of New York, as part of the Adirondack Park."

When he mentioned the sale of the property, Bette gasped. Though she regretted her estrangement from her parents, she accepted their deaths as inevitable. But to lose Santanoni was too much. During the years since her marriage ended, she had become a fashion designer and a good one, too. Along with her talent, she had developed an unshakable professional exterior even when she was being torn to shreds inside. She could usually hide her feelings, but now she trembled like a leaf in a March wind.

Bill continued. "Except for a few minor donations here and there, the bulk of Will and Nellie's estate was bequeathed to the nurse who took care of them during their final years. She's supposed to find a way to restore the camp."

Bette detected a dramatic change in Bill's tone when he mentioned the nurse who was named the beneficiary of the estate.

"The nurse is trying to establish a foundation to save Santanoni," he continued. "I feel so bad that I came back from Europe too late to make peace with Will and Nellie. Why can't we see things more clearly when we are young? We could avoid so much heartache."

Bette did not answer Bill's rhetorical question. She had come home to rest at Santanoni—the doctor had ordered it—and now the one stable thing she had counted on, her old home in the woods, had been yanked away during her absence. She said nothing as she stared into Bill's eyes.

Bill was frightened. Why couldn't he have found a better way to tell her? But even as he chided himself, he knew there was no easy way. Bette was here. She needed to know the truth. *Dear God,* he prayed silently, *don't let the pain be more than she can bear. She's all the family I have left.*

"Bette, are you okay?" He knelt beside her and grasped her hands. At first she said nothing. He took his handkerchief and wiped the tiny rivulets trailing down her cheeks.

Bette's shoulders began to shake as she gave way to sobbing. "I'm too late, Bill. . . ." Her mascara was now streaked across her once lovely face. "Too late. . . too late. God knows I loved Will and Nellie, but they didn't know it." She looked at her brother. "Oh, Bill, I'm too late."

Bill held her until her sobs subsided. He searched for words to comfort her. It was too late for them to mend the relationship with their parents. But they were young, and Santanoni was still there. They could do something about the home they had loved and had lost.

"We'll find a way to save the camp. Perhaps we could become part of the Foundation to Save Santanoni."

Bette looked at her brother, and a tentative smile threatened to ease concern on her face. Once they had done everything together. Maybe they could make up for the years they had been separated.

The two sat immersed in their private thoughts for some time. Then Bette remembered they had been talking about Bill's relationship with Alyce. She hoped he'd find a wife and have a happy marriage.

She had arrived only a few hours earlier. They had twenty years of catching up to do. Bill told her where he'd been, about his travels throughout Europe, and about his writing career. He explained that his latest manuscript was in his publisher's hands in Syracuse. He talked about his return to Newcomb.

Then he told Bette about his trip to Santanoni when he discovered backpackers camping in the preserve. "I met Nellie's beneficiary camping on the lake shore," he said. When he mentioned the beneficiary, his tone softened.

After he finished his monologue, Bette had many questions and Bill answered each as best he could. When she probed deeper about the beneficiary, however, he began to choose his words carefully.

Bette was angry that some gold-digging nurse would be named in her parents' will. She knew she and Bill were undeserving, but to leave it all to a stranger? She wanted to know more about this woman.

"What's this nurse like?"

Bill inhaled deeply before replying. "Well, she's a woodswoman. She loves backpacking and camping. She comes up to Santanoni from Syracuse a couple of weekends each year with Max."

"Who's Max? Her husband?" She hoped her brother hadn't fallen in love with another man's wife. He certainly sounded interested in her.

Bill chuckled at her question. "Max is her boxer dog!"

Bette laughed at that. Then she grew silent. "Bill?" Her tone jerked him to attention. "Is my hideaway still there?"

Bill smiled in relief. For once he could give an answer that wouldn't upset her. "Yes, Bette. The studio is still there guarding your section of the lake."

He waited a few minutes for Bette to come back to him. Then he went on.

"Well, since I've told you this much, I might as well confess the rest of it. I seem to have backed myself into a corner." He swallowed and then continued. Maybe he'd feel better after he told her. Perhaps she could help him out of his dilemma.

"When I first met Alyce, I didn't tell her my name."

"What difference does that make?"

"It makes a big difference. I mean I didn't tell her my real name."

"Come on, Bill. Who did you say you were? Paul Newman?"

"Bette, it's not funny. I told her my name was William Morgan."

Bette rolled her eyes heavenward. "I'm afraid I don't understand your problem. I thought that was your name!"

Bill was becoming annoyed with Bette. He was in no mood for jokes. He'd try once more to explain. They were both tired, and this day had had a full measure of emotional shocks. "She thinks my name is William Morgan. She doesn't know I'm William Morgan Hayes."

Bill could see that Bette didn't consider that a major problem. He went on. "I don't know why I said my name was Bill Morgan. I certainly didn't expect to see her again so it didn't matter who I said I was. I never dreamed I would fall in love with her."

Bette's big blue eyes bored through him like an auger digging post holes. She was beginning to get the picture, but it wasn't quite in focus. She couldn't believe her brother had lied about his name, but that was his problem. Now he was telling her he was in love with two women.

"Let me sort this out, Bill." Bette began to pace back and forth as she eyed him squarely. She could see that he had more than a passing interest in Alyce Anderson. "I find it hard to believe that you deliberately lied about your name. You'd better get that straightened out fast! But take it from me, you're going to get into big trouble courting two women at the same time."

It was Bill's turn to be surprised. "Two women? I have enough complications with one."

Bette's brow furrowed. "Tell me, who do you love? That gold-digging nurse or Alyce Anderson?"

Bill looked at her bemused. Suddenly it all made sense. He threw back his head and roared with laughter. "Bette," he said, as he tried to gain control of himself, "don't make my life more complicated than it already is. Your 'gold-digging' nurse is Alyce Anderson."

Chapter 11

The Thanksgiving dinner at the Antlers Inn was a traditional one served family style. Some of the guests had elected to dress up, while others donned more casual garb. Bill wore his well-cut navy suit. Bette was attired in one of her own creations, a dark brown cashmere dress with a sweetheart neckline. Alyce wore her azure blue dress with the pleated skirt and the long fitted bodice. Her tiny waist was encircled in a filigree gold belt with tiny tassels.

Bill's eyes sparkled as she approached the dinner table. The three were soon so deep in conversation that they were scarcely aware of the festive food. Bill listened intently as Bette and Alyce got acquainted. All too soon they were finishing their after-dinner coffee.

The conversation had been light and pleasant. Bette turned to Alyce and asked, "Wouldn't it be fun to hike into Santanoni tomorrow morning? The snow isn't too deep. What do you say?"

Alyce liked that idea. "I've never been to Santanoni when there was snow on the ground. That sounds like fun. What you do think, Bill?" As she posed the question, her pulse began to flutter. Although she gave Bette an encouraging smile, inside she wished the two of them could make the trip without Bette.

Alyce's wish was not to be granted. The next morning the three of them enjoyed an early breakfast and arrived at the camp by nine.

"I'll sign us in," said Alyce as she headed for the registration box. Despite the stubby pencil, which, like all trailhead pencils, needed sharpening, Alyce's handwriting was delicate and precise. She closed the log book and glanced at Bette and Bill. Bette was frowning. Then Bill spoke softly to her, and she looked at him and nodded. With Bill in the lead, the three of them headed down the snow-covered trail toward the old lodge.

At first sight of the main grounds, Bette uttered a moan. The light snowfall did not hide the overgrown lawn, rotted out buildings, or broken windows. She hastened to the old lodge and peered inside. A steady drip was falling on the buckled hardwood floors as snow melted through the roof.

"Would you like to go inside?" Bill asked as he extricated a key from his pocket.

Alyce's eyebrows shot upward. "Where did you get a key?"

There was a slight hesitation before Bill answered. "You know how it is. You just have to know the right people." He tried to laugh the matter off, but Alyce wasn't smiling. Bill fumbled for a better explanation. "Remember, I grew up around here. I know someone who has a key."

Alyce's brow furrowed as if to question Bill's answer, but she trooped obediently into the lodge behind Bette.

Despite the years of neglect, the interior of the first floor was amazingly well preserved, and the paneled hallway going up to the second story was in perfect condition. The gigantic stone fireplace stood like a lovely monolith dividing the living room from the dining room. Looking out the front windows, they could see the silent lake, and beyond it, the majestic snow-capped mountain.

Alyce was awed by her surroundings. She couldn't believe she was actually inside the lodge. As she turned to express her thanks to Bill, she noticed Bette gently rubbing her hand over the windowsill, almost like a caress.

After they had explored the main lodge, they headed down to the studio on the shore of Lake Newcomb. Part of the roof had caved in and some windows had been boarded up. When she saw the broken cathedral window, Bette burst into tears.

Bill put his arm around her and drew her close as they walked back to the main lodge and then down to the boathouse. They spent about an hour checking the various states of decay of other buildings. By now the sun had disappeared. Bill suggested it might be wise to head back to Newcomb. "We could be in for some foul weather. Since none of us is dressed for that, we'd better start back."

Though they agreed with him, Bette seemed reluctant to leave. Alyce noticed how often she and Bill had made comments about certain buildings, trees, and even the beach. They seemed very knowledgeable about Santanoni.

They exchanged few words on the hike back to the parking lot. The visit to the great camp had left them in a somber mood. When they reached their car, Bill spoke first.

"It's been a long time since breakfast. Let's go back and get something to eat."

As they drove back to the Antlers, Alyce mentally replayed their outing at Santanoni. Robert Roberts had told her Bill was a native of the area, so he and Bette would know about the camp. But Bette seemed interested in every nook and cranny of the lodge. She had lingered long after the others were ready to leave. Why was she so upset when they visited the studio?

Furthermore, Bill seemed to be paying more attention to his sister than to her. Alyce might as well stop thinking about the attraction she felt for him and get on with saving Santanoni. At least she would give it her best shot.

The three talked about Santanoni over their late lunch. Alyce commented with a sigh, "It's really a shame to see such a beautiful estate falling apart. Every time I go there, I consider how it could be fixed up if one had unlimited resources."

She paused. "I wish I could find a couple of people who were interested in joining our Foundation to Save Santanoni." She looked at Bill, who had just exchanged a furtive glance with Bette.

"I haven't told you, Bill, but I accept your offer to become a part of that group." Alyce hesitated, watching his reaction. Seeing his pleasure at her announcement, she continued. "I'm not comfortable working with Robert Roberts, though. I'm sorry. I know he's your friend, but I feel uneasy around him."

Again she looked at Bill to gauge his response. "Do you suppose we could find a lawyer in Syracuse to handle this foundation idea? I know we'd need to find three others to work with us, and maybe that's asking for the impossible." She hoped she hadn't offended Bill, but she felt the need for complete honesty. As she spoke, Bette nudged Bill with her elbow.

An awkward silence followed, and then Bill cleared his throat. "I have a friend in Syracuse named Peter Brown who specializes in estates. He's part of a team of lawyers. They're former classmates of mine. If you wish, I could ask him to look into this matter for you."

He spoke hesitantly as he looked at Alyce. "Perhaps you should meet Peter and see what legal advice he has to offer."

Bette smiled at Bill's suggestion, but he was waiting for Alyce's response.

"I'd be grateful if you would do that. It's hard for me to know where to turn in legal matters." Randy had always taken care of those things. She thought of how efficient he had been, a trait she admired in a man.

Alyce turned to Bette and Bill. "You know, the Hayeses had a son and a daughter. I wonder what happened to them. They would be so sad to see Santanoni now." She looked down at her hands and then went on. "Well, maybe they wouldn't care. They didn't care much about their parents."

As Alyce voiced her speculations, Bette's eyes brimmed with tears, and her lips trembled. Bill diverted Alyce's attention away from her.

"You know the saying, 'Where there's a will, there's a way.' I've always found that to be true. Do you want me to talk with Roberts? I can explain the situation to him in an inoffensive way. He's embarrassed about this whole matter anyway."

"Thank you, Bill, I'd appreciate that." Alyce felt relieved to have that matter settled. She hadn't figured out how to tell the attorney herself, and now she wouldn't have to. *Thank You, Lord. Again You've answered before I asked,* she prayed silently.

"Consider it done," said Bill with an air of efficiency.

Bette had remained silent during this discussion, but when Bill spoke, her eyes widened, and a warning cloud settled over her features. She opened her mouth as if to comment, but Bill was not finished.

"Bette and I spent a lot of time at Santanoni when we were kids. We know the grounds well."

Alyce stared at him. Why was he telling her this now? Was it because she had told him she wanted him to be a part of the Foundation to Save Santanoni? What else did he know that he hadn't revealed? She made a herculean effort to keep her voice from reflecting her inner turmoil.

Without emotion she asked, "And did you know the Hayeses?"

Sensing the drama that was unfolding, Bette put a gentle but shaky hand on Alyce's arm. Before Bill could respond, she said softly, "Yes, Alyce, we knew them well." She glanced at her brother. "I'm surprised Bill hasn't told you that. So much has happened since we left the Newcomb area. It's been nearly twenty years since we have seen each other. We're both dealing with some weighty emotional trauma."

Looking directly into Alyce's eyes, Bette asked, "Will you let me be the third member of your team to save Santanoni? The camp is the one tie I have with my childhood. I don't want to let it slip away like so many other things."

Visions of the well-dressed princess paraded before Alyce's eyes. Bette's clothes reflected good taste and financial resources, and Bette herself was obviously interested in the camp. If Alyce accepted Bette's offer, she'd need to find only two more benefactors for Santanoni. She smiled at Bette.

"I will give that some thought. Thanks for offering."

Bette nodded as Alyce folded her napkin and left the table.

Alyce had to return to Syracuse Sunday afternoon. The three of them attended worship services at the little village chapel in the morning and then had dinner together at the Antlers. That morning before church, the question of Bill's faith had again surfaced in Alyce's mind. Although she and Bill would need to share their Christian testimony in greater depth, she had sensed a sincere desire in Bill as he listened intently to the minister's sermon and held her hand during the congregational prayer.

After four days together Bette and Alyce had become friends. Still, the only part of her life that Bette had shared centered on her activities as one of California's hardest-working fashion designers.

"Living on the edge of physical and mental exhaustion hasn't been fun," Bette admitted, "but in a way I'm glad. If I hadn't worked myself into such a state, I would never have come home. My doctor insisted I take six weeks off and do nothing. 'Forget Fashion World and your boutiques for awhile,' he commanded. At first I ignored him. Then through a strange series of coincidences, I found out my brother was coming home from Europe. I sent him a message through some former friends still living in Newcomb. Bill responded by asking me to meet him here at Santanoni."

She looked at Bill. "I'm sorry that I didn't answer the letter you wrote me several years ago. I was glad to hear from you. I guess it shows how much I needed a rest. Last Monday I knew I had to come back here. I was fortunate to get a plane reservation to Albany on such short notice. Someone's cancellation became my blessing." She looked at Alyce. "I'm glad I decided to come home."

"I'm glad you did, too, Bette." Then she added as though it were an afterthought, "I was quite surprised to learn Bill had a sister." She paused, looking at Bill. "Your brother will never be accused of talking too much."

With a furtive glance Bette telephoned an urgent message to Bill. For the sake of his future relationship with Alyce, she hoped he wouldn't ignore it.

Bill began to speak, but it wasn't the confession Bette hoped he'd make. "This time I do have something to say. I plan to come to Syracuse the middle of next month. My publisher expects the press sheets for my new book to be run by then." He addressed Alyce. "May I call you when I get there?"

His question reminded both of them of another time when he had promised to call, and Alyce winced at the memory. *So he's a writer,* Alyce mused. *I never suspected that. I was beginning to think he was involved in some sort of undercover work.*

"May I, Alyce?"

She tried to remember his question. Oh, yes. He was coming to Syracuse again, and he wanted to call her. She was glad he didn't know how disappointed she was when he didn't call that first time. She had kept her heartache a secret.

"I'll be glad to hear from you when you come to Syracuse, Bill." *Please do call me this time.* She turned to Bette. "Can you come, too?"

"We'll see. I'm supposed to be here to rest." She cast a knowing glance at her brother. "Maybe Bill has secrets to share with you. I fear I've been as useful as a toothache this weekend."

"Don't feel that way. Please come if you can." She turned to Bill. "Do you think you'll have time to look up Peter Brown while you're in Syracuse? It would be easier for me if the business of saving Santanoni could be carried out in Syracuse rather than in Newcomb."

"Consider it done, but I don't intend this trip to be all business. After I see my publisher, we could go out to dinner and then to the Ice Follies. How does that sound?"

Alyce's eyes brightened. Skating had been one of her favorite winter diversions, but she had little time for it anymore. "That sounds lovely."

She looked at her wristwatch and gathered her purse and coat. After giving Bette an affectionate embrace she said, "Take care, Bette, and please come to Syracuse with Bill."

"Perhaps," said Bette. "Drive carefully."

Bill carried Alyce's bag to the car and placed it in the trunk. Then he drew her to him. "Thank you for coming," he whispered, his voice almost lost in her hair. "You don't know how much this meant to me. One day I'll have a lot of explanations for you." He lowered his head and kissed her with lips soft and gentle as the snowflakes that were beginning to fall.

Alyce wound her arms around the warm chest inside his jacket. She could hear his heart beating as they embraced. She would have stayed there forever, but the falling snow brought her back to reality. "I've had a wonderful time," she said as she released her lips from his.

"I'll see you soon, Alyce."

Bill opened her door, and she slid in. As he watched her back out of the parking lot and head west, he knew he could not live without her. He would never be content until he had asked her to marry him. Not even another blizzard like the one in '77 would keep him from seeing her in December in Syracuse.

Alyce was thankful the snowfall was light as she drove home. She wanted to think about her weekend with Bill, and she couldn't do that if the driving were hazardous.

The time they had spent together had made her painfully aware of how lonely she was. She could handle the days. But how nice it would be to have someone to love and to come home to each night.

Visions of Bill invaded her thoughts. She remembered every detail of his clothing. No matter what he wore, it enhanced his near perfect physique. She wondered what it would be like to be held in his arms every night. For the first time—without feeling the least bit disloyal to Randy and Maria—she pondered a future with a new husband.

Chapter 12

Bill lost no time in contacting Peter Brown once he had settled his business with his publisher. Peter's specialty was legacies, state-owned properties, and the like. He agreed to contact the Adirondack Park Agency to discuss the tentative plans that had been made for the Foundation to Save Santanoni. Then he suggested Bill contact the legal offices of Barkley, Cole, and Murray.

His stint as administrative assistant to a U.S. senator gained Bill a listening ear from a team of attorneys whose expertise could move mountains. It wouldn't hurt the cause of Santanoni that these men had connections in the governor's mansion.

Bill deplored using friends to accomplish personal goals, but with Santanoni at stake, he'd draw on whatever resources he needed. Barkley, Cole, and Murray were located in downtown Syracuse, not far from the company that was publishing his book.

Bill left the law office with a spring in his step and his fingers crossed. Now for a call to one lovely lady. He had something on his mind to share with Alyce, and it was not just his success at the law office. But first he must settle the matter he had been avoiding for too long. He must tell Alyce his full name.

When Alyce arrived home from work, there was a letter in her mailbox. Eagerly she tore open the envelope.

> *Dear Alyce,*
>   *I'm so sorry I missed you. Our meeting with Peter Brown is set for next Friday morning at nine a.m. I'll call you tonight for confirmation.*
>
> > *Love,*
> > *Bill*

Alyce grinned. Bill hadn't wasted any time. She had kept a light work schedule so she could concentrate on Santanoni. However, when a nursing friend came down with a serious virus, she agreed to work in her place for three nights. Now she was sorry, but she always kept her promises.

Bill called around seven and explained where the law office was located. He wouldn't be coming to Syracuse until late Thursday. He would meet her at the attorney's office Friday morning. His call was brief and businesslike, and Alyce was dismayed by his impersonal tone.

To Alyce the days crept by like a snail in reverse. Friday finally arrived and Alyce arrived a few minutes early at the law office. The receptionist, a chic, middle-aged woman, smiled as she gave her name. "Go right in, Ms. Anderson. Everyone else has arrived." The warm smile she flashed at Alyce failed to quiet the butterfly ballet in her stomach. Being with Bill and saving Santanoni was too much at one time.

The men rose as Alyce walked into the inner office. Bill's broad smile set her heart racing even faster. Bette hugged her. After he introduced her to Peter Brown, Bill motioned for her to sit at his right. She felt like she'd just stepped off a roller coaster.

Peter took charge of the conversation. "Now that we're all here, let's get right to work. I have given your project top priority since Bill contacted me. Both Bill and I have had consultations with Barkley, Cole, and Murray. Your suggestion for the Foundation to Save Santanoni seems to be a viable one. We think the foundation idea will be acceptable to the New York State legislature, and it does not seem to go against the 'Forever Wild' policy of the Adirondack Park Agency."

Alyce relaxed a bit. She liked the way Peter spoke with authority; gratefulness surged through her as she considered Bill's role in securing his help with the Santanoni project.

"I've drawn up copies of the proposal for each of you." He paused to distribute them. "Look carefully at the fine points. See if I have interpreted your wishes accurately. After you have read the proposal, we'll discuss each point." He sat down to await their responses.

Alyce scanned her copy and then went back to the beginning to read it carefully. Legalese was hard for her to interpret, and the phrasing intimidated her. The proposal seemed sound to her, however, and it was drawn up according to the suggestions made by Robert D. Roberts.

When everyone had finished reading, Peter Brown answered questions and clarified points. Alyce then raised the issue of two more members for the foundation.

"At this time," she said, "I don't have any possibilities. I'll have to beat the bushes looking for them. I'll do that now that our proposal appears acceptable."

Peter spoke again. "I've taken quite a personal interest in this effort to save Camp Santanoni. After Bill explained the situation to me, I drove up to Newcomb. Bill took me into the preserve. I experienced the same gut-wrenching feelings as you when I saw what was happening to that magnificent lodge. I'd like to join your foundation, but it would be unethical to handle the legalities and be part of the group, too. I'll content myself with helping save Santanoni by being your attorney."

No one commented so he began again. "It's important to move quickly. Surmising that you might not know where to find two other members for your foundation, I took the liberty of making some inquiries. I have two business associates who are interested in joining your Foundation to Save Santanoni. May I suggest Roger Murray and Charlie Cole of Barkley, Cole, and Murray?

"Roger is familiar with the Santanoni Preserve, and he has the legal expertise to find solutions to whatever problems we may encounter. Charlie is an outdoorsman and a preservationist. He loves the Adirondacks and spends as much time up there as he can."

Bill and Bette deferred to Alyce. She looked from one to the other. "I'm willing to accept them on your recommendation if it's okay with Bette and Bill." They nodded affirmatively. Alyce was relieved.

Having settled the important matter of personnel, and seeing nothing wrong with the basic tenets of the proposal, Bill suggested they take the weekend to think about the whole matter.

Peter stood up and offered his hand to all. "I would be pleased if we could do that and meet Monday to sign the papers. I'll contact Roger and Charlie. I'm leaving a week from today for a vacation in the Bahamas. It would be good if we had this proposition ready to submit before I depart."

As they left the law office, Bill suggested the three meet for dinner that evening. "We need to talk about Santanoni. Why not do it over a delicious meal?"

"Oh, Bill, I can't," Bette spoke first. "I've already made some plans to have dinner with the manager of Giselle's Boutique."

Bill looked at Alyce.

"I can't make it, either, Bill. I'm covering for a sick friend."

"How about tomorrow then? Could we eat early so we have time to talk? Then we could get tickets to the Ice Follies."

"I'm really sorry, but I've promised to work the next three nights for Peggy."

Bill would not give up. "Then when can we get together? It's important that we discuss this proposal before we sign the papers." He knew it was also important that he discuss something else with Alyce before Monday.

"How about Sunday? We could go to church, and then you could come to my apartment for brunch."

Bill and Bette exchanged glances. Although Bill had committed his life to Jesus Christ in recent years, he wasn't sure about Bette. Growing up, they were not accustomed to attending church services, except perhaps on holidays. Bill was quite sure that the Thanksgiving Sunday they had gone to church with Alyce was the first time in many years that Bette had entered a church for worship. He didn't want to coerce Bette; still, there was no time like the present to be a Christian witness.

"Why not?" It was Bill who had asked the question. "What time shall we pick you up?"

Alyce drove home, gave Max a bit of attention, and had a nap. She would be working from eleven to seven. When she had that shift, she napped a few hours so she would arrive fresh at her patient's home. She'd enjoy thinking about Bill and the future of Santanoni as she took care of Peggy's patient. The one advantage of night shifts was that often the patient slept, and she had to do nothing more than be there.

Following the morning worship at Alyce's church, a brunch of fruit, rolls, and cheese was both attractive and tasty. Alyce reflected that the minister's sermon topic, based on the grace of God as reflected by the gift of His Son, was no more a coincidence than her first encounter with Bill Morgan. She was sure both were destined by God.

They ate leisurely as they discussed the Foundation to Save Santanoni. Alyce gazed often at Bill. There was so much she admired about him in both his personality and his appearance. The flip side, she determined, was that he didn't seem interested in a permanent relationship.

As he discussed Santanoni, Alyce studied his face. It was animated as always when he talked about the camp, but today he seemed distracted. He had something on his mind that he wasn't sharing. She wished they could be alone, but the afternoon passed quickly, and Bill and Bette left about five.

Maybe she was reading more into their relationship than she should. She hated the thought that Bill might feel Santanoni was more important than her. Things should never take priority over people. She'd have her nap, take care of her patient, and see Bill and Bette at the lawyer's office in the morning.

Bill and Bette had agreed to meet Alyce in the front lobby of the attorney's building at a little before nine. Alyce arrived first, her petite figure encased in a black wool coat. A kelly green scarf about her neck matched her beret and gloves. She stamped the snow from her leather boots. It had been snowing since the previous evening, and high boots were in order.

A taxi arrived shortly and deposited a glamorous Bette, clad in a dark brown mink with matching hat. Alyce's heart did a triple beat when Bill appeared from nowhere. The gray lamb's wool collar of his coat complemented nicely his dark hair with its hint of silvery temple "wings." She wondered if he had any idea how his presence excited her. Bette and Bill spotted Alyce at the same time. They smiled and walked over to join her.

"Hi, Alyce. You look stunning. That green does wonderful things for your eyes."

"Thanks, Bette. You look quite elegant yourself."

Bill paused a moment before asking, with a twinkle in his eye, "And what about me?"

"You look great, too." Her casual tone aside, Alyce meant it from the bottom of her heart. The three chuckled as they headed for the elevator.

Once inside Peter Brown's office, they were introduced to Roger Murray and Charlie Cole. Alyce assessed them quietly. Both exuded three qualities she appreciated: confidence, efficiency, and self-control.

Roger spoke first. "I am delighted to become a member of your foundation," he said. "Thank you for accepting me. I'll do my best not to disappoint you. I hope my background will be an asset to your group. Permit me to elaborate on my interest in Santanoni."

He settled back into his chair and surveyed the group before speaking. "The Adirondacks are my second home. I go up there to camp and hike as often as I can get away. I've observed the gradual deterioration of Camp Santanoni, and it has disturbed me. I've wished there were something I could do to stop it. When Pete called to tell me about your plans, I told him how interested I was in the project. I was pleased when he asked me to join the Foundation to Save Santanoni."

"Thank you, Roger. We're in complete agreement that you should be the fourth member of our group." Bill nodded toward Peter. "Your friend recommends you very highly."

Charlie Cole explained his interest in Santanoni. Alyce could see he'd be an asset to their foundation. The others gave their approval as well.

Peter then handed each a copy of the proposal. "I want you to read your copy again. There's nothing here that wasn't in the copies I gave you last week. I just want to be sure you know what you're agreeing to. We're tackling Goliath, and we need to be fully armed. It's going to take all of your energies and then some to rescue Santanoni."

Alyce wanted to concentrate on the document, but with Bill so near it was hard to focus on the paper in front of her. The fragrance of his citrus aftershave was wreaking havoc with her senses.

"If you have questions, now's the time to get answers before you sign the document. Once you have signed it, my secretary will get the proposal into the hands of the state legislature."

Alyce steeled herself against the distracting emotions she was experiencing and began to read each word. She was relieved to have four investors who were willing to help her carry out the wishes of Nellie Hayes. The burden would be much lighter when it was carried by ten hands instead of two.

The names of the five members were listed alphabetically at the end of the document:

Alyce Miller Anderson
Charles Edward Cole
William Morgan Hayes
Elisabeth Hayes Montgomery
Roger Lee Murray

Alyce nodded her head to register her approval of the document. She was about to express her thanks to Peter Brown when suddenly she realized what she had read. Her eyes opened wide, and she gasped.

She shot a look at Bill and another at Bette. She didn't want to admit what she was seeing. Bill heard her gasp and turned to face her. He was about to speak when she blurted, "William Morgan Hayes!"

Bette leaped to her feet, her face ashen. She flashed an I-warned-you-what-might-happen look at her big brother.

"And you! Elisabeth Hayes Montgomery!" Alyce's voice shook. It took every ounce of reserve she had to keep from bursting into tears. "I thought you were my friends. That you loved Santanoni. That you wanted to stop the ruin as much as I. You pretended to be my friends to get Santanoni back!" She was almost shrieking.

"Well, friends, it was a nice try but it won't work. You had Santanoni once, but you didn't appreciate it. Your parents died praying for your return. You gave Santanoni up, now don't try to steal it from me. I won't let you have it." Her face was flushed. Her voice cracked, and her tirade ended in sobs.

She threw her copy of the proposal on Peter Brown's desk, snatched her coat from the rack, and bolted out the door. Bill was right behind her.

"Alyce! Alyce! Please come back. Let me explain. You've misjudged us."

By the time Bill made it to the elevator, the door was closing in his face. His sister had warned him. Now he had not only lost his opportunity to help restore his old home, but he had lost the only woman he'd ever loved. He shuffled back to the law office. How would he ever explain this?

When he returned to the office, Bette was leaving. She was too angry with Bill to feel sorry for him. Peter and Roger were staring at her.

"Don't look at me that way. Big brother can tell you what a fool he has made of himself in more ways than one! Now I'm going to try to undo some of the damage he's done."

Her eyes hurled more daggers in Bill's direction as she faced him briefly before running to the elevator.

Alyce unlocked her car door with trembling hands. Once inside, her seatbelt wouldn't fasten. She was crying so hard, she couldn't see to put the key into the ignition. As she glanced into her rearview mirror, she spotted Bette charging out of the building.

Bette glanced from left to right trying to find her. Alyce eased her car out of her parking place and was swallowed up by the midmorning traffic. She was glad she didn't have to go to work. Her emotions were shattered and right now she couldn't bear to see or talk to anyone. She drove straight home, staggered into her apartment, and slumped into the nearest chair. Though she was still wearing her coat, she was shivering.

Sensing his mistress's distress, Max tried to nuzzle her face, but it was buried under her arm, and she pushed him away. How could she have been such a fool?

After all these years, she should have learned to follow her instincts. Now she knew why Bill looked so familiar. His father had the same brown eyes and a dimpled chin. No wonder Bill knew so much about Santanoni. It was his home.

The one she had trusted had deceived her. She could forgive most wrongs, but she valued truth and honesty. Being the victim of outright deception threw her into a panic.

Her thoughts were interrupted by the phone, but she let it ring. After at least a dozen rings, her head ached from the incessant jangling. In her frustration she grabbed a nearby pillow and threw it at the phone. Finally she got up and removed her coat. She put her hat and scarf away and pondered her next move. There was no use lying down. She wouldn't be able to relax enough to sleep.

She was removing her boots when the doorbell rang. All she asked was to be left alone with her throbbing head and her broken heart. The bell stopped ringing only to be replaced by loud knocking. Alyce did not move.

"Please open the door, Alyce. It's Bette. I must know if you're all right. Just let me see that you are, and I promise not to stay."

Realizing she'd get no peace until she did, Alyce opened the door slowly. "I'm okay, Bette," she lied. Her voice broke.

Bette hugged her, and both women cried together. "Alyce, please give me a chance to explain. I know we have hurt you deeply, and I regret that. If we could have foreseen what was going to happen, we would have handled things differently. You must hate us both, and with just cause. But there is an explanation."

Alyce stared at her. She did not trust her voice.

Bette pleaded, "Please let me come back tomorrow evening. I'll tell you exactly how this terrible misunderstanding began. Please, Alyce. . . ?"

"I don't ever want to see Bill Morgan again. . .or even talk to him." She could not restrain the sobs that shook her shoulders.

Chapter 13

At seven on the dot the doorbell rang. Alyce, clad in a mint paisley lounging robe, faced Bette in her beautiful mink. Bette's swollen eyes and pale cheeks revealed she had not had an easy day, either. With forced politeness, Alyce invited her in.

She took her coat and hung it on a padded hanger in the hall closet. Running her hand over the coat's sumptuous lapels, Alyce thought this was the most gorgeous fur she had ever seen, and Bette had the figure and the finesse to do it justice.

"I've made a pot of herbal tea. Or would you prefer coffee?"

"Tea will be fine, thanks. It was kind of you to let me come. I'm not here to plead my brother's case. I'm here strictly on my own. I know we have hurt you badly."

Alyce listened without comment.

"I'm sorry for that," Bette continued. "I appreciate you as a friend. In California in my circle of friends, or perhaps I should say acquaintances, there are few genuine friendships. The glitter, the glamour, the smiles, they may be broad, but they are only a quarter-inch deep. You're different, Alyce. You're honest and sincere." Still Alyce said nothing, and Bette took a deep breath.

"It was a shock to come home and find out my parents were deceased. I was overcome with guilt and remorse. Many years ago, against my parents' wishes, I eloped with my high school art teacher. What I thought was love was mere infatuation. My marriage was a horrible mistake."

She frowned as though she were looking through the wrong end of a telescope and was not able to see what she wanted. Finally she went on.

"It took me five years to admit that my husband had married me because of my artistic talent and my family's money. I loved him from the start, and I still love him despite what he did to me. In time he began to abuse me physically. Whatever artistic ability I had was slowly being stifled. I knew I had to get away from him."

She shook her head as if to shake away the unpleasantness of her foolish marriage.

"When I left my husband, I had no money and no place to go. I got a job in a small boutique as a salesperson. The pay was minimal, and I struggled to pay my bills. I had always been interested in fashion, and secretly I began to design clothing for our customers. I was in my dream world. Sometimes I prepared entire wardrobes on paper for the wealthy women who came to the boutique. Of course, they never saw my work."

She stopped for a sip of tea. Alyce sat in stony silence.

She had little interest in Bette's narrative of her personal misfortunes. She wanted to know why Bill had lied about his name.

Bette set her cup down and resumed her narrative.

"One day my boss came to my apartment. He had never been there before, and I was unprepared for guests. He saw my designs strewn about the living room. He praised them and chided me for keeping my talent a secret. He asked to see other things I had designed. After I showed him my notebook, he insisted on sending me to the Venus School of Design so I could develop my talent. When he decided to retire, he sold me his shop at a ridiculously low price. He said it was a gift in appreciation for my hard work for him and his satisfied customers.

"As time went on, I was able to open shops in three more cities. Then about three months ago, I collapsed at an opening in Honolulu. My doctor ordered me to take time off and to do absolutely nothing for six weeks."

Alyce wondered why she was telling her all of this. It wouldn't change her mind about Bill.

"Having worked fourteen- to sixteen-hour days for years, I found that was a hard prescription. In addition to that my doctor warned me to give up smoking. I had been a chain smoker for years. Bill and I never kept in touch except on our birthdays, which happened to be the same day. Bill is one year older than I. Somehow we lost contact with each other until an acquaintance of mine returned from Europe, having met Bill in Paris. I tracked him down and found out he was going home to Santanoni. . .to see Will and Nellie and to make amends for the years of neglect. Once he had made the decision to return, he couldn't wait to go home."

At the mention of Bill's name, Alyce perked up.

"From the time we became teenagers we called our folks Will and Nellie. Chalk that up to those crazy teen years. Bill asked me to meet him in Newcomb at Thanksgiving so we could go home together. I was busy with my boutiques so I ignored his request. Then when my doctor threatened me with what lay ahead if I continued at my present breakneck pace, I decided to come home."

Alyce was sitting erect now. Thus far the picture Bette had painted did not reveal any sinister secrets that would incriminate Bill or her. They seemed like typical teens with the usual parental clashes. But then she hadn't had time to think about what Nellie had told her about her children. She needed to piece that together with what Bette was saying. Maybe she would find some clues to the present state of events.

"My brother and I both realized, too late unfortunately, that we had been foolish in leaving home against our parents' wishes. We also sorely regretted our stubborn refusals to go back."

Alyce warmed their cups, and Bette smiled her thanks. "You're a good listener, Alyce. There is a bit more I need to tell you. Bill met me at the airport in Albany the day before Thanksgiving. We arrived in Newcomb in late afternoon. Seeing how distraught I was, he insisted I have a nap before we talked. Then he met me for dinner. After our meal together, we went back to my room. Bill told me that Will and Nellie were gone and that Santanoni had been sold to the state of New York."

Alyce flinched at the mention of that evening at the Antlers.

"My muddled mind was having such a time comprehending everything I was finding out. Bill tried to console me while also telling me that an attractive nurse from Syracuse had been named executor of Nellie's will. I was angry when he told me about you. I couldn't believe that your befriending my parents was due to nothing but innate kindness on your part. Forgive me, Alyce, but I've lived in the world of dog-eat-dog for a long time. I judged you to have ulterior motives. I was so bitter. I should have been grateful that someone provided Will and Nellie some happiness in their twilight years.

"As Bill talked, I sensed his feelings for you were deep. When I quizzed him, he told me there was a big problem in your relationship, namely that he had not told you who he was. I knew right then he was in trouble. I should have insisted that he get that straightened out. Bill and I were close when we were growing up. I knew that deception would prove disastrous."

As truthful as she believed Bette to be, Alyce flinched at Bill's dishonesty.

"Bill couldn't. . .perhaps because there wasn't any reason he should have lied. True, he was upset when he came home and found Santanoni frequented by hikers and in sad disrepair. Maybe that initial shock caused him to speak so hastily."

Alyce wanted to find some rationale for Bill's behavior so she could forgive him. What would have happened if Bill had told her who he was when they first met? Would that have made any difference in their relationship?

"Alyce, have you ever said something absolutely idiotic and then realized that as soon as the words left your mouth? I think Bill shocked himself. Once he said he was Bill Morgan, he didn't know why he had said it or what to do about it. So he did nothing. That doesn't excuse him, but I think that's what happened."

Alyce thought about that first encounter with Bill. She remembered how he had yelled at Max and at her, too. She recalled how tight-lipped he had been about himself after she had rambled on about her life. She had been annoyed with his silence. Now she was beginning to understand. If she could understand, maybe she could forgive him. She remembered assessing him as a wild man in need of a friend.

"I could see how you felt about him. I knew there would be a day of reckoning.

I almost told you a couple of times myself. But that would have been interfering with Bill's affairs. I have learned not to be a meddler."

Bette grimaced as though in pain. "I realize now I'm just as guilty as Bill. I'm here to beg your forgiveness for the part I played in this deception. You have every right to be angry with me. I deserve it. Yet, I felt you deserved an explanation."

Bette had hoped for some kind of response from Alyce, any sign that would show she understood. Getting none, she tried once more to make her position clear without defending her brother.

"I'd still like to be a part of the Foundation to Save Santanoni, if you will let me. If you can't forgive me, let me make my contribution as a memorial to Will and Nellie. I owe them so much. I know you love Santanoni as much as Bill and I. Keeping our identities secret was not a calculated move to reclaim Santanoni, though it looks like that. We surrendered our inheritance when we left home many years ago. Can't we work together for the sake of the camp? We need each other."

She hesitated. Then she made one final plea. "Alyce, life doesn't always treat us kindly or fairly. We have to grab happiness wherever it can be found. I know you love Bill even though he has hurt you. I loved my husband, too. . . ."

Bette's eyes swelled with tears, and Alyce found herself overcome with emotion as well.

"Bill loves you, Alyce. This is the first time in his life he has been in love. If you can't forgive him right now, will you try to keep your feelings for him separate from your concern for Santanoni? Take as much time as you need to sort out your feelings, but please reconsider the foundation plans. I have to return to California soon. I want to go back knowing there's an active war being waged to save my former home."

Bette rose from her chair and took her cup to the kitchen. She would not stay longer. Alyce got her coat and helped her put it on, and together they walked to the door. Bette turned and hugged her. "Thanks for letting me come, Alyce, and thanks for listening."

Alyce nodded and then asked, "Will you stop again before you return to California?"

"Of course I will."

With that she was gone.

Chapter 14

Wednesday afternoon Alyce took Max for a long walk. The snow had melted, and the sidewalks were clear. Since her meeting with Bette, Alyce had put her mind in neutral and kept it there. That was easier than dealing with Bill's lie about his name. She still saw it as an attempt to regain Santanoni. Had she been able to think more rationally, she could have seen the fallacy in her reasoning. She was no threat to Bill when he found her camping on the Santanoni Preserve.

She had scarcely returned to her apartment when the phone rang. Alyce glanced at the clock. It was four-fifteen, a strange time for her to be getting a call. Maybe Peggy needed her again. Sometimes those sneaking viruses lasted longer than usual. She hoped for Peggy's sake that was not the case.

After she answered there was a pause and then a deep, soft voice spoke. "Alyce?" Another pause. "Please don't hang up on me."

Alyce's heart thumped in her throat. She was torn between tears of anger and disbelief. It was she who spoke first, but only a monosyllable. "Yes. . . ."

"I wanted to talk to you sooner, to come to you, to apologize for not telling you the truth. I couldn't come. I kept telling myself if I were in your shoes, I would never want to hear from me again."

Bill's words trickled over her like soap bubbles, tickling her emotions.

"You know I love you. I can't throw away those feelings. I believe you love me, too. Remember how you suggested we start our first conversation over again after I barked at you and Max in the woods? Alyce, can't we make another start? I will never deceive you again, so help me, God."

He waited for her answer. The only sound he heard was her soft breath. She was trying to sort out her feelings. Finally she managed a brief sigh.

"What do you expect me to do? Forget the past? That's impossible. Honesty is important to me."

Bill spoke with measured words, and his tone held none of the arrogance she recalled from their first meeting. "I hear you, Alyce. Please don't hate me. Will you try to forgive me? I admit I deceived you, and how I regret that. Please try to understand that it was not an attempt to get Santanoni away from you. Alyce, when I met you and Max at Santanoni, I didn't know you had any direct interest in Santanoni other than as a delightful spot for camping out."

Alyce hadn't considered that.

Bill continued. "What can I do to convince you of my sincerity? I've tried to see things from your perspective. You are more important to me than Santanoni. I need your forgiveness. Please give me another chance."

Alyce's mind was in too much turmoil for her to speak.

"I must leave Syracuse for a few months, but I can't go without making peace with you."

She wanted to accept his olive branch, but his next comment clipped the thin bough of trust she was hanging on to.

"Of course I still care about Santanoni. I hope you are mature enough to see the necessity of signing the proposal so we can get it to Albany by the time the state legislature convenes again."

Alyce felt a stab in the pit of her stomach. Bill was still speaking. "I know you want to see the camp restored in memory of Will and Nellie. Can't you set your personal feelings aside so we can get on with saving Santanoni?"

His words rained on her ears like an icy shower. She had the urge to hang up on him, but she knew he would call again. Her head was aching. She might as well hear him out. She hoped he would be quick about it.

Bill's voice was gentle now. "Someday I'll find a way to prove to you my sincerity." He paused. "I'm leaving soon for California, and after that I may return to Europe. I'm starting a new book, and I need to clear my head."

Still Alyce said nothing.

"You can contact me through Peter Brown's office. Pete will always be able to reach me. Please, Alyce, think about what I've said."

She had to say something to end Bill's monologue. "I'll think about it," she said in a voice devoid of emotion.

"There's one more thing. Please keep in touch with Bette. She needs you. I love you, Alyce." The line went dead.

Alyce stared at the receiver in her hand and carefully put it back in its cradle. She certainly would think. She'd think about a way to erase Bill Morgan Hayes from her life. Once she succeeded at that, she would have to come up with someone else to help her save Santanoni.

Max was sitting by his dish waiting for his supper. Stooping down, she gave him a hug as the tears began to roll down her cheeks. Max was all she had to love, and there was not a deceptive bone in his body.

Chapter 15

Alyce sat in her lonely apartment on Christmas Eve, a cup of tea in her hands, staring at the small Christmas tree in the corner of her living room. Even Max had deserted her for his favorite spot near the heating vent in the kitchen. She had not heard from Bill, but then she didn't expect to. Why should he call? She was the one who had closed the door on their relationship.

After much painful deliberation, she had signed the papers forming the Foundation to Save Santanoni. She would keep the Santanoni issue separate from her relationship with Bill as Bette had suggested. She owed that much to Will and Nellie. Deep down, though, she was doing it for Bill as well.

Life is fleeting and earth's pleasures are not eternal, she reflected, and personal relationships are important. Bill had strained their relationship severely. She knew that. So did he. Could they still be friends? *If we can still be friends,* Alyce thought, *perhaps in time we can become more than friends.*

There on that night set aside to honor God's gift to the world of the Greatest Friend one could ever have, a tiny seed of hope was planted in Alyce's heart. She knelt beside her chair and prayed softly to her heavenly Father.

"Dear God, please forgive me for the times I've sinned against You. Help me to forgive Bill. Lord, You know I love him. I want to forgive him. But, God, it still hurts so much. With Your help, I'll forgive him and forget the pain I suffered. Thank You, Lord, for forgiving me when I sin against You. In Jesus' name."

A gentle nudge from a cold nose awakened Alyce. She found herself still kneeling by her chair. Max needed to go out. She got up and stretched. She was surprised to see she had been asleep for forty minutes. She arose unaware that the Lord was gently binding up her wounds.

While Max was out, she thought about Bette. After some gentle persuasion on Bette's part, they had had lunch together before Bette returned to California. True to her word, there was no mention of Bill or his whereabouts. A few days ago Bette had sent her a beautiful Christmas card. The message was so personal Bette could have composed it herself.

Alyce's thoughts turned again to Bill. *I wonder where he is tonight. I wonder if he is happy. Is he remembering this is the anniversary of Christ's birth? Does he know Jesus? If he doesn't know You, Lord, please, help him to see You in my life. I wonder if he is alone.* She grimaced at the thought of his being with someone else.

A tiny tear crept out of one dark eye and made its way down her cheek.

Before long another joined it. She thought she wanted to be alone. Now she regretted that decision. She wiped the tears, picked up her tea cup, and headed for the kitchen.

When the doorbell rang, she glanced at the clock. It was eight-thirty. She wasn't expecting anyone. She looked out the window. A floral delivery van was parked in her driveway. She opened the door.

"Good evening, Ma'am. Are you Ms. Alyce Anderson?"

She nodded.

"A Christmas Eve delivery for you. I'm sorry to be so late, I hope you don't mind." He handed her a large box.

After she thanked him and gave him a generous tip, he bounded down the steps and almost fell as he hit the thin layer of ice that had formed at the bottom. He hopped into his van, slammed the door, and zoomed down the street looking for his next customer. Alyce shook her head and smiled at his youthful exuberance.

She was surprised at the size of the box as she carefully removed the green bow and ribbon and lifted the lid. Inside were two dozen red roses, cradled in baby's breath and greenery. She counted them again as she delicately removed each one from the box to find the card.

Inside a red envelope was the computer-generated message, "Please give me a second chance. Love, Bill."

∞

Knowing that holidays could be especially hard for Alyce, Bette called on Christmas morning and launched into a lengthy conversation.

When Alyce told her about the lovely flowers from Bill, Bette had little response. They talked of unimportant things until they said their good-byes. Bette's gentle reminder that Alyce should follow her heart did not fall on deaf ears.

Blustery snowfalls followed Christmas into the new year and then continued to frustrate many a plan as the Syracuse area was blanketed with three feet of snow straight off Lake Ontario.

"It's what we get when the lake doesn't freeze," Alyce reminded her patient. "We've had a warm winter thus far. We're going to keep getting those lake effect storms until Lake Ontario freezes over."

February arrived and so did Valentine's Day. On that day Alyce received more red roses along with a huge box of chocolates. There were two notes with the gifts. The note with the flowers said simply, "I love you, Alyce. Bill." The other note read, "To the sweetest woman in the world."

Alyce was delighted with the gifts, but what she wanted most was to speak to Bill. Bette had sent her a funny valentine, and she had called again. She talked of many things, but she never mentioned Bill. Alyce was too proud to ask about him.

March came roaring in and gradually the weather warmed, the pussy willows budded, and people began to smile. Alyce had maintained a busy work schedule, devoting her pent-up passion to her patients. Her heartache over Bill no longer gnawed at her inner being. She still thought about him, but the bitterness was gone. She simply longed to see him. Peter Brown had called several times to let her know how things were proceeding with the Foundation to Save Santanoni, but he, too, avoided any reference to Bill.

Bette continued to contact her by letter and by phone. They discussed Santanoni and the fact that so far the legislature had not considered their proposal. They both wished they could oil the slow-moving wheels of government.

Alyce ached to know where Bill was and what he was doing. She didn't know how to interpret his gifts since he never called. Unfortunately for both of them, their stubborn pride was keeping them apart. No matter how much Alyce longed to hear from him, she could not bring herself to ask Bette or Peter where he was. Would she ever conquer her foolish pride?

Chapter 16

For most of March Alyce continued working days instead of nights. She enjoyed her evenings at home as her mind needed time to be at ease. She read or napped, or thought about the past and wondered about the future. Two questions kept popping into her mind. Would the state legislature accept their proposal for a Foundation to Save Santanoni? Would she ever see Bill Hayes again?

She was beginning to read the *Post Standard* when the phone jangled. As it was St. Patrick's Day and she was feeling a bit impish, she answered in her best imitation brogue.

"Sure, and I'll be wishin' you a good evenin' and a happy St. Paddy's Day."

There was silence on the line while the caller caught his breath. "I beg your pardon. I must have dialed the wrong number. Please excuse me."

Alyce drew in her breath as she heard the click on the other end. If she lived to be 238, she would recognize that voice. It was Bill, and she, trying to be cute, had made him hang up. Her heart was thumping. Her mouth went dry. She swallowed again and again, and tears coursed down her cheeks. She had hoped and prayed he'd call. Would he try again?

Her answer came shortly. *Brrrring! Brrrring!*

Now she was giggling through her tears. She let it ring a third time before she answered.

"Hello. . . ?"

"Hello, Alyce. This is Bill. Happy St. Patrick's Day."

"Hi, Bill." She felt tongue-tied.

"How are you?"

"Fine." Why couldn't she utter more than one syllable at a time?

"Uh. . .I've missed you. . . I need. . . I want to see you again, Alyce."

She wished her heart would stop hammering in her head. She wanted to get her tongue in gear, but it wouldn't budge. She'd better at least thank him for the flowers. She had been bothered by not knowing how to do that when they first arrived. The seconds ticked by.

"I flew into Hancock Field last night. I'm only here for one day. I called Pete Brown. He has some news about the foundation." He hesitated a moment.

"Alyce, would you be willing to meet with the foundation members at

Santanoni during Easter weekend? We need to discuss some specific plans. Perhaps by then the state legislature will have considered our proposal."

She checked the calendar hanging next to the phone. Finally she found her voice. She hoped it didn't register what she was feeling inside.

"Yes, I can be there. I'll be glad to come." Then she added after a short pause, "I'm glad you called. Thank you for the lovely roses. I had no way to let you know how much I appreciated them."

"The pleasure was mine. I'm glad you liked them. Thanks for being willing to come to Newcomb. Would you like for me to make a reservation for you at the Antlers?"

"That would be nice. I'm scheduled to work on Maundy Thursday evening. I'll catch some sleep in the morning. I should arrive in time for dinner on Good Friday." As she mentioned dinner, she remembered other dinners at the Antlers. For such an insignificant little inn, it was playing a major role in her life.

"I'll take care of it for you. Good-bye until Easter."

Alyce was crushed. Bill had sounded so glad to hear her voice, but then the conversation was all business. After three months all he had said was that he was glad she liked the roses. He was in Syracuse, and he had made no effort to see her. Had the separation convinced him he could live without her? Had he erased her from the secret part of his heart?

She did know that hearing Bill's voice after all those weeks of silence had sent her heart soaring. How she hoped that, somewhere up there in the clouds, his heart would come floating by.

∞

"Good afternoon, Mr. Hayes. It's nice to have you back with us. Will you be staying long?" Matt Flack, a tall, thin man with inquisitive black eyes and a shock of gray hair, extended his hand with enthusiasm.

"About a week this time, Matt," Bill replied as he signed the guest register at the Antlers. "Ms. Anderson, Charlie Cole, Roger Murray, and my sister, Bette, will be arriving later this afternoon."

Matt scanned his register. "Oh, yes. We have their reservations, Mr. Hayes."

"Please call me Bill."

"Okay, Bill. I see you're driving an Audi this time instead of your Lincoln."

Bill smiled inwardly. Matt didn't miss much that was going on around the Antlers. "That was a rental car. Since I intend to stay stateside, I bought my own wheels."

Matt paused and then brought up the subject that was uppermost in his mind whenever he saw Bill. "I have never forgotten what happened to your brother, Jimmy. I'm sorry he was never found. This whole community grieved over his disappearance. How we wished we could have found him."

"Everyone tried to find him, Matt. I wonder if he is alive somewhere still."

Matt had elicited some painful memories that Bill wasn't anxious to rekindle. He had no desire to discuss the matter with him. His brother's disappearance had produced a chain of painful events that he wished had never happened. He couldn't change the past, but he could concentrate on building a better, happier future.

"Are you planning to make Santanoni your home?" Bill's eyebrows arched at Matt's question.

Before he could answer, Matt went on. "You know how things are in a small town like Newcomb. News travels fast."

"And so do rumors," Bill said under his breath.

"The older folks in town have all been to Santanoni. They talk about how things used to be. As soon as they heard you and your sister were back in the area, there was an upsurge of interest in the camp."

"Hold on a minute, Matt. I'm afraid you are getting carried away with your speculations. Santanoni no longer belongs to our family. It's part of the Adirondack Park." He explained how the Foundation to Save Santanoni had been organized and that they were waiting for movement from Albany. They couldn't proceed with plans for preservation or restoration without official approval.

"Once we secure the blessing of the state legislature, we can move full steam ahead. Of course our first priority will be to put an end to the deterioration. Then we can think of restoration. It's an expensive proposition. We're going to need help from every possible source we can find. We're hoping you local folks will want to help, too."

"You can count on us! The restoration of Santanoni would be a plus for us all." He looked at Bill as if he had just received a divine revelation. "You know you've already increased my business. A number of former residents have heard the rumors and have come back to catch up on the gossip. Those who don't have family in the area stay at the Antlers and pump me for details." His voice reflected his pleasure in reaping the benefits of Bill's plans.

Since people were asking questions, it seemed to Bill a good time to spread some truth to accompany the rumors. "What we have in mind for Santanoni is somewhat like what Howie Kirschenbaum did for Sagamore Camp. We hope we can have as good a program at Santanoni, though we don't plan to duplicate what's already being offered to the public at Raquette Lake."

Since Matt expressed so much interest, Bill went over the tentative pains. The next time someone asked what was going on at Santanoni, he'd have lots to tell. Bill knew this was good publicity for the foundation. The more people knew about their plans, the more apt they would be to help bring them to fruition.

They shook hands, and Bill picked up his bag. He needed to get to his room and get settled before the others arrived.

"Thanks for sharing your plans, Bill. I wish you the best of luck in seeing them realized. We're happy to have you home again. Let us know how we can help, from fund-raising to elbow grease. I can post notices on my walls anytime, and most of the town folks will read them."

∞

As he unpacked his belongings, Bill thought that this weekend was off to a good start. That boded well for the next few days. Now if only he could regain the ground he had lost with Alyce. He'd lived through four months of agony when he didn't have the nerve to contact her. How he hoped she had been able to forgive him. He whistled to himself as he hung up his jacket.

There was something about her personality that made Alyce Anderson special and different from other women he had dated. He was first aware of it that Thanksgiving Sunday when he had gone to church with her. Was it her high-minded principles. . .or the light that shone from her eyes when she smiled at him? Suddenly he realized what he perhaps had known from the moment he met her: Alyce was a Christian. As a new believer, and because of his peripatetic wanderings, Bill hadn't had much chance to meet unattached Christian women.

Bill dropped to his knees by the bed and buried his head in his hands. "Dear Lord," he prayed, "thank You for bringing me back home again, and thank You most of all for leading me to Alyce. Now I know for sure that she is a gift from You. Please direct my words so that in time she will forgive me, if this is Your will. I ask this in Jesus' name. Amen."

Chapter 17

No sunshine heralded the day as the foundation members squeezed into Charlie Cole's four-wheel drive and headed toward the Santanoni gatehouse. The soggy morning was the fallout from a twelve-hour rainfall. They were in for a muddy hike. Undaunted, they had come equipped with notepads, levels, measures, and protective raingear. Only after they determined how extensive the deterioration was to the buildings could they begin to estimate the costs for restoring and preserving the great camp.

The five had enjoyed a pre-Easter supper together at the Antlers. The cook, having been made privy to their plans for the following day, packed them a lunch, and they found it waiting for them along with thermoses of coffee and tea at the front desk when they left the inn that morning. The only complaint came from Bill, the most seasoned hiker in the lot, who wished the abundant provisions had not been stowed away in a large picnic basket.

They parked at the gatehouse and each collected his personal possessions. "I wish I had my backpack with me," said Bill.

Charlie eyed the lunch and then spoke up. "I think the old pack I used to take fishing is under the seat. I'm not sure what it smells like, but a little fish odor might be easier to carry than a picnic basket." He poked around under the seat until he found it.

Alyce signed them in at the register. It was such a natural thing for her to do, but she missed having Max with her. They had not gone far when a raccoon ran across their path. "Too bad you didn't bring Max with you, Alyce. He'd have warned us that we had company."

Bill's comment was music to her ears. She smiled as she explained to Charlie and Roger that Max was her boxer dog as well as her camping companion. Everyone laughed, and the trip began on a light-hearted note despite the soggy weather.

Alyce was thinking her own thoughts as they sloshed along. They weren't about Max, as much as he would have enjoyed being there with them. She was telling herself she had been right in forgiving Bill. She remembered the passage she had read in her Bible the previous night, the one in which Jesus had told a crowd of accusers that the one who was without sin should cast the first stone. One by one the men slipped away. When the last accuser had fled and Jesus was alone with the woman, He offered her forgiveness. "Go and leave your life of sin," He said.

Alyce knew at that moment she had forgiven Bill. His reason for lying about his name was no longer important. Together they would restore Santanoni. It would be a memorial to loved ones from their past as well as a monument to their future.

Then a cloud of doubt hovered over her. She had forgiven Bill, but he had not made any direct moves to renew their relationship. After his four months' absence, his contact with her had been strictly a business arrangement. That thought disturbed her as she tramped along behind him on the muddy path. She'd better not let him know how much she cared about him. She was still trying to figure out why he left the area so abruptly last December.

By the time they reached the lodge, the sky was clearing. Bill suggested they enjoy their lunch first since it was nearly noon, and then they could work uninterrupted until they finished. They sat on the lodge steps overlooking Newcomb Lake and feasted on the bountiful provisions.

As the sun broke through the clouds, they headed down to the boathouse. The studio would be next on their agenda, and if time permitted, they would take a look at the lodge. They knew they would need the services of a restoration architect, but they wanted a rough idea of the extent of the damage before they approached someone with the job.

Bette volunteered to be the scribe. Alyce would hold the tape as Bill took measurements to see how much the building's foundation had settled. Meantime Charlie and Roger would check the windows to see what they needed. Alyce was delighted to be paired with Bill. She wondered whose idea that was.

Bill was smiling as he handed her the tape. Did his hand linger a moment longer than necessary as she took it from him?

Part of the floor inside the boathouse was rotted away. Bill glanced up at the roof. Rain and melting snow had leaked through. The roof was in bad shape.

Charlie and Roger found three of the windows needed new glazing, and one of the sills needed to be replaced. One pane was missing and the opening had been boarded up. Boarded-up windows bothered Alyce. They seemed like someone who used to care didn't anymore. Was that how Bill felt about her?

The large doors that opened to allow the small boats to be loaded and unloaded were in good shape. The cables that operated them were rusty, but a good cleaning and oiling would make a big difference.

"I think we'd better take a look at the roof next," Bill said.

Not having a ladder available, Bill scaled the blue spruce that grew flush with the right side of the building. He was careful to choose thick, strong branches that would not be harmed by his weight. Gingerly he picked his way across the sloping roof that was covered with a thick layer of soggy leaves and pine needles. He placed each foot carefully, testing every spot before letting his weight rest on it. His rubber boots gave him sure footing, but there was no way of knowing the condition of the roof under the debris.

As Bill picked his way across, he examined the edge and then worked his way up to the top. The heavy build-up of pine needles had weakened the roof. He tried shoving them off with his feet as he crept along.

Bette cautioned him, "Be careful, Bill. We don't want to carry you back to the gatehouse."

Her words were lost as the roof under Bill gave way. An ominous sound of splintering wood was followed by Bill's cry. There was a sickening thud and then silence.

Bill lay on his left side on the floor of the boathouse. Alyce reached him first. She knelt beside him and unbuttoned his shirt to feel his carotid pulse in his neck. Even as she checked his pulse, she prayed his injuries were not serious.

Dear God, she prayed silently, *I pray he hasn't broken his neck or injured his spinal cord. I love him so much, and I've never told him I forgive him. Maybe I'll never have the chance. Please, God, help him. Even if he must be paralyzed, don't take him away from me. I'll take care of him no matter what condition he is in.*

Her nursing skills in full play, she felt his pulse, faint as it was. She was determined not to cry.

"We need to get him on his back, Charlie. I'll steady his head and neck. Lift him as gently as you can."

Together they straightened him out on Bette's raincoat. Bill moaned. His eyelids fluttered. "My arm feels like an elephant sat on it." His voice was faint.

Alyce could see his arm was broken. When she touched it just below the elbow, he groaned again. It was already beginning to swell.

"Try to lie still, Bill. I need to see where else you're hurt."

Pain blotted out the gentle probing of Alyce's hands. Having determined there were no more serious injuries, Alyce asked Bill to try to stand. With Charlie and Roger on either side of him, he was able to get to his feet. Gingerly he took a few steps. Though shaken and weak, he seemed to be all right except for his arm.

Alyce removed his jacket from his swollen arm and wrapped it around his shoulder. She didn't want him to get chilled. She looked around. "We need something for a sling until we can get you to the emergency room."

Bette offered the warm scarf she had been wearing. Using the scarf and the strap from Charlie's fishing pack, Alyce fashioned a sling to hold the broken arm in place. Her hands trembled as she secured Bill's injured arm in the makeshift sling. She must not let him know how badly his fall frightened her.

"We'll get you to the hospital as quickly as we can, Bill." She winced as she thought of the five miles that separated them from their vehicle. It would be a long walk, and there was nothing she could give Bill for the pain. She offered him a weak smile. "Do you think you can make it?" Charlie and Roger were supporting him as he struggled to the door of the boathouse.

Bill grimaced with each step. He looked at his companions. "Looks like I'll have to, doesn't it? I'd freeze to death if I stayed here."

A prayer of thanksgiving winged its way heavenward as Alyce and Bette watched the three men make their way out the door. The restoration of Santanoni would have to wait a little longer.

Meantime Bette and Alyce picked up Charlie's pack and the other things the group had brought with them. Most everything fit into the empty pack. It was inconvenient not having the strap, but they would take turns carrying it back to the gatehouse.

When they had gone about halfway, Charlie ran ahead to get the vehicle. "I'll have it warm, and I'll see if I can't drive in as far as the barn. I can turn around there. That'll save Bill some walking."

Alyce handed the fishing pack to Bette and took Charlie's place at Bill's side. She hoped he couldn't feel her racing heart as she encircled him with her right arm and continued to lift him to the Lord in prayer.

Black clouds were again forming overhead. Bette watched them scud across the sky. She frowned. Then she voiced what each one had been thinking. "I hope it holds off until we get Bill safely inside."

"It will!" Alyce's tone was determined.

When the barn was in sight, they cheered when they saw Charlie waiting for them. Carefully Alyce and Roger eased Bill into the back seat. Alyce climbed in and sat beside him, willing him to bear the pain until they could get him relief.

As they headed back to the gatehouse, she laid her hand on his head and whispered, "I'm sorry we don't have anything for the pain, Bill." She would gladly have borne it for him had there been a way. Bill understood. He took her hand and gave it a feeble squeeze. Then he closed his eyes and gritted his teeth.

Alyce remained with Bill as his arm was X-rayed and set in a cast. The attending doctor administered a strong painkiller. Bill was insistent that he not be admitted to the hospital. The doctor acquiesced when he learned Alyce was a nurse. However, he warned Bill of the consequences of not taking it easy until the arm as well as the rest of his bruised body had healed.

Alyce put her arm around Bill's waist to steady him as they left the emergency room. He responded by squeezing her gently with his uninjured hand. She gazed up at him and met a weak smile.

"Alyce, I love you with all of my heart. I know I could never get along without you. Today proved it. Will you marry me?"

The relief of Bill's being able to go home and then the suddenness of his proposal left Alyce speechless. Did she hear him correctly? Or was she dreaming? She was used to patients being so grateful that they made rash promises as soon as they began to feel better. Bill didn't know what he was asking. She didn't know whether to laugh or to cry. By the time they reached the waiting room, she was doing both, and she had not answered Bill's question. Her friends welcomed them with applause.

No one had much to say as they drove back to the Antlers. Bill dozed, thanks to the sedative he had been given. Alyce was enduring almost as much mental turmoil as Bill was suffering physically as she wrestled with his proposal. As much as she wanted to believe he meant it, she attributed the question to his accident and his being overwrought.

She bowed her head and prayed silently. *Lord, thank You that Bill did not break his neck in the accident. Thank You for helping us get him to the hospital. Please heal his bruises and his broken arm. Lord, You know I love him. I don't know if he loves me. Please, God, help me know what I should do.*

Chapter 18

Bill and Bette had to return to California by the end of the week, and Alyce volunteered to drive them to Hancock Field. Once again she found herself battling inner turmoil as Bill sat beside her enroute to the airport. Did he really want to marry her? She wanted to believe he did, but she was afraid to. She wished she could put her finger on the cause for her doubts. She had been in love with him for a long time, and the months he was away had been painful for her.

Bill would be expecting an answer before he left the airport. She had to tell him something. *Please, God, help me know what I should say,* she sent heavenward desperately.

She had seen Bill only once since his accident, and that had been in the presence of others. His searching eyes pleaded for a positive response at that meeting, but she was not able to give it to him. They would soon be parting. Did she or didn't she trust Bill Hayes?

At the airport Alyce was surprised to see that Charlie Cole had come to say good-bye. She made a mental note that Bette, on the other hand, seemed unusually pleased to see him.

When their flight to San Francisco was announced, Alyce hugged Bette and urged her to write as soon as she got home.

"Do us both a big favor and marry my brother," Bette whispered as they embraced. "He's too miserable to function without you. Alyce, you are the first woman he has ever wanted to marry."

"Don't rush me, Bette. Try those designer wedding gowns on your California brides until I make up my mind."

Then Bill was holding her, and the world around her disappeared. He gazed into her eyes seeking an answer. "Will you, Alyce?"

She looked long into those intense dark eyes, but she didn't speak. Bill's farewell kiss left no doubt in her mind that he wanted her and needed her.

"I'll wait as long as I have to," he whispered. "I love you with all of my heart."

He released her and joined Bette at the boarding gate. Alyce stayed on the observation deck until their plane was airborne and then out of sight.

As Alyce drove back to her apartment, she pondered her indecision. She didn't enjoy fighting invisible dragons. She was reminded of some verses of Scripture from a sermon she had heard on the radio. "Dear Lord, You have told us that if any man lacks wisdom, let him ask of God who giveth to all men liberally.

Well, I'm asking, Lord, because that's what I need. Wisdom."

She thought about Gideon, a Bible character with whom she could surely identify. The Lord had reduced his mighty army to three hundred and then told him to go fight. Gideon wanted proof of the Lord's presence. So he tested Him twice. Each time, the Lord honored his test. Gideon went forth with his little army and his trust in the Lord, and he gained a great victory.

It was time to ask the Lord for His direct intervention in her life. "Father in heaven," she prayed, "I need Your assurance just as Gideon did. You know I love Bill. He says he loves me, and I believe him. Yet I have doubts about marrying him. Father, please remove my doubts. Make something happen to show me that Bill and I are to marry. Or," she hesitated a few seconds, "show me clearly that we should not. In Jesus' name."

∞

The legislative hearings were set for the first of June, and the Santanoni proposal was on the agenda. Senator McKunckle had informed the attorney's office all was in order for the presentation. He would ask for approval of Phase I. That would provide for the formation of a nonprofit foundation to restore the existing buildings and manage them exclusively for educational and recreational purposes. Any changes in the policies governing the Adirondack Park had to be approved by two consecutive legislative assemblies. After that the proposal would be submitted to the voting public.

Peter Brown was delighted, and he quickly relayed the news to each of the members of the proposed foundation. Roger was the last member he called. It took several days to reach him. Finally he was able to speak to him and tell him what was happening in Albany. He waited for Roger's response, expecting him to be as enthusiastic as the others.

"I hate to tell you this, Pete, but I have a big problem," Roger said tentatively when he finally got through to Pete. "That's why I've been away. I'll spare you the nasty details, but I'm going to have to withdraw from the foundation before we get started. I'm sorry, but the funds I was counting on to invest in this camp did not materialize."

Pete's mind was racing ahead. Where could they find a replacement in such a short time?

"I'm terribly embarrassed about the situation, but I can't come up with $100,000. My heart is with you and your plans for Santanoni, but you need cash that I can't provide."

"Roger, I'm sorry, too. I'll explain the situation to the others. They'll be disappointed, of course, but I'm sure they'll understand. Let me know if your situation changes."

Pete dictated letters to the others explaining the latest snag in their plans. He would wait for suggestions for a replacement for Roger. He hoped they'd be able to find someone by the time the legislative hearings began. If approval were granted to form the foundation, they could speed up their plans.

When Bill received word of Roger's financial dilemma, he sent a telegram to Pete telling him to proceed with the plans. He would provide the $100,000 they were expecting from Roger.

A week later when Bette called Alyce to discuss the upcoming hearings, Alyce commented, "I'm glad we're finally going to get a hearing, but I'm worried about a replacement for Roger."

"Don't worry, Alyce. With four of us looking, we should find somebody in due time."

"But what's due time? If we get legislative approval and don't have our replacement, we'll be $100,000 short. What's that going to tell those lawmakers?"

"That's no problem. When Bill heard about Roger's pulling out, he wired Pete telling him he would put in the extra $100,000."

Alyce couldn't believe it. Or rather, she didn't want to believe what Bette was saying. By adding that money, Bill and Bette controlled three-fifths of the foundation.

"Alyce? Alyce? Are you still there?"

"I'm here, Bette. Thanks for calling." With slow, deliberate movements, she put the phone back into its cradle and burst into tears. *Well, Lord, I guess I have my answer.* It wasn't the one she wanted, but she would accept it.

Alyce stared into space. Bill had acted without consulting her and that hurt. But it bothered her more to learn that he was so wealthy he could fling down another $100,000. That he had concealed his wealth was disturbing. She was not a rich woman, and she didn't want to be one.

"Lord, I asked You for a sign. I hoped it was Your will for me to marry Bill. I can't marry someone I don't trust." She blew her nose and continued her prayer. "Lord, You know how much I hurt. Please take away the pain. Help me give Bill the gift of forgiveness. I know You have a plan for my life and for his life, too. Show me the plans You have for me, and I'll follow them. That's the only way I'll find peace."

After thrashing her way through a long night, Alyce got up early and composed her long overdue letter to Bill.

> *Dear Bill,*
> *I'm sorry. My answer is no.*
>> *Alyce*

Two could be as silent as one, she reasoned, as she sealed the envelope with trembling hands. Later that day she made a quick decision to attend a conference in Atlanta. Spring would already have arrived there, and she'd enjoy the flowers.

The conference would last three days. Then she'd take two more days to enjoy the sights.

By the time Bill received her note, she would be winging her way south. Since Bill wouldn't know where she was, he couldn't call to demand an explanation. She grimaced. She knew the time would come when she'd have to explain, but she refused to think about that now.

∞

Alyce returned home refreshed. Springtime in Atlanta was beautiful, and the conference had proved stimulating. She could go on without Bill. In time she'd look back on their relationship as another one of those experiences that made life interesting. She'd bury herself in her work again. There were countless hurting people who needed love and attention, and she'd give it to them.

She had been home only three hours when she received a frenzied call from Bette.

"Alyce, what in the world is going on between you and Bill? We're both frantic. We've been trying to reach you ever since Bill got your letter. Are you ill? Ever since you wrote, Bill has been behaving like a madman."

Alyce knew exactly what Bette meant. Hadn't she witnessed that behavior the first time she and Bill met? It was no concern of hers how he was acting. She would be kind to Bette because she liked her, but that would not change her relationship with him.

"I'm sorry, Bette, but Bill and I no longer have a relationship. How he acts is no concern of mine."

"What are you talking about? I thought you two were about to announce your engagement."

"I'm afraid not, not now or any other time." It was hard for Alyce to get those words out. Each one was painful, but they needed to be uttered. Speaking them out loud seemed to finalize her decision.

There was a pause as Bette absorbed what Alyce had said. "You aren't going to marry my brother?" The way she asked it brought Alyce to the brink of tears.

"No, I'm not," she responded with a quiver in her voice.

"Alyce, please tell me why. Forgive me for prying, but you're so suited to each other. You both know what you want, and you're both fighters. Bill wouldn't give me your reason for rejecting him. He went storming off to Brussels saying he had business to attend to, and he didn't know when he'd get back. I know you both. Neither one of you will be happy without the other. What is this foolishness anyway?"

Alyce was annoyed. She liked Bette, but this matter was between her and Bill. She didn't feel she needed to explain. "Look, Bette. Bill didn't give you any reason because I didn't give him one. If he wants to pursue the matter, that's his privilege. I'm sorry, but I don't wish to discuss it now. Thank you for calling. I hope you and I can still be friends."

Later that evening as Alyce prepared for bed the phone rang again. She glanced at the clock, wondering who would be calling at that hour. She had scarcely said hello when Bill interrupted her.

"Alyce, what on earth is going on? Are you ill? Your letter was so curt. What do you mean your answer is no? You can't tell me you don't love me. Why are you refusing me? I love you, and I know you love me. I saw it in your eyes. I felt it when I held you in my arms. What has happened?"

With tears cascading down her cheeks, she opened her mouth three times before words would come. Her heart was in her throat. She felt her breath being squeezed from her lungs. "I didn't think I owed you an explanation, Bill. You haven't been too free about giving explanations to me."

"What on earth are you talking about?" He felt her sigh and sensed her anguish all the way to Brussels.

"I'm talking about your latest covert activity," she said through clenched teeth. "You might have consulted me before adding more of your abundant wealth to the Foundation to Save Santanoni. It is my project, or did you forget that?"

"Oh, Alyce. Is that the problem? My dear, you don't understand. I had to put the money up front so we could keep moving. Once we have a replacement for Roger, I'll withdraw it. It wouldn't have been right for me to let our plans flounder while we search for a new member. Santanoni is too important to all of us for that. It was my way of helping."

"I agree, Bill. It would help a lot to have three-fifths of the foundation's funds provided by the Hayeses. It would be convenient to have three-fifths of the votes when issues come up, wouldn't it?"

Bill's mind was racing as he tried to see things from Alyce's perspective.

"Bill, if and when I marry again, it will be to someone whom I trust completely. Marriage must be based on openness and trust between husband and wife."

Bill's frustration was reaching the danger point. "Alyce, I promised you I would never deceive you again. I've kept that promise. I love you. I want you. I need you. If I have to give up my interest in Santanoni to prove my love for you, I'm willing to do that."

He paused for a quick breath.

"I'm flying home to San Francisco on Monday. I'll be there for three weeks. Please reconsider. You can call me at Bette's house. If I don't hear from you, I promise I'll get out of your life. I'll withdraw my interest in Santanoni and turn the whole thing over to you and Pete and Bette."

Alyce blanched at Bill's ultimatum. She didn't know how to respond.

"There's nothing more I can say. I love you enough to respect your wishes. If you close the door on me this time, I won't knock again. Good night, Darling."

There was a soft click and then silence.

Chapter 19

The days dragged by, and the nights plodded along behind them. Alyce was oblivious to her surroundings. No matter how busy she kept herself in the daytime, she couldn't get a good night's rest. Whenever she closed her eyes, she envisioned Bill, phone in hand, issuing his ultimatum. *If you close the door on me this time, I won't knock again.* Over and over the words echoed through her head until she wanted to scream.

When she got that scene out of her mind, others took its place. Dinner at Sylvia's. Their surprise meeting with Robert Roberts. Bill finding her at Santanoni. And most frightening, Bill's fall at the boathouse. Her heart beat faster as she relived that accident. The possibility that Bill had been seriously injured had made her realize how much she loved him.

After tossing and turning for hours, Alyce got up and made a cup of herbal tea. She patted Max when he came into the kitchen to keep her company. "Oh, Max, whatever am I going to do?"

Max focused his liquid brown eyes on her as if to say, "Don't worry. Things will turn out all right."

She set her cup on the table. Her eyes filled with tears remembering her gift of red roses. It had been two weeks since Bill had called from Brussels. Her time was running out.

During her restless nights she had replayed his final words over and over in her mind. *I had to put the money up front so we could keep moving while we find a replacement for Roger. . . . It wouldn't have been right to let our plans flounder. . . . Santanoni is too important for that. . . . If I do not hear from you, I'll get out of your life. . . . I love you too much to ignore your wishes.*

"Lord, what am I going to do?"

She picked up her Bible and began to turn pages. When she was troubled, she found comfort in leafing through the Scriptures and reading those passages she had underlined. If she read long enough, she usually found a verse or two that helped her with her current crisis.

The Lord God said, "It is not good for the man to be alone. I will make a helper suitable for him.". . . So the Lord God caused the man to fall into a deep sleep; and while he was sleeping, he took one of the man's ribs and closed up the place with flesh. Then the Lord God made a woman from the rib he had taken out of the man, and he brought her to the man. . . . For this reason a man will leave his father and mother and be united to his wife, and they will become one flesh (Genesis 2:18, 21–22, 24).

Alyce read the passage a second time. God did not intend for man to live alone. Could it be He did not intend for her or for Bill Hayes to live alone? The last time she and Bill had attended church, hadn't she been positive he shared her faith? Had God been preparing them for each other?

She recalled Bill's conversation once more, his determination to find out why she had refused him, his explanation which she now realized was sensible. She had been concerned with having to tell the state legislators they had lost a member of their proposed foundation along with $100,000 in support. Instead of being infuriated, she should have been grateful that Bill had the foresight to see the money needed to be available at once. Again she had jumped to a false conclusion.

Her mind continued its racing, but things were making sense. There was one more obstacle. Bill was a rich man. He had grown up surrounded by wealth, and now in his own business and his writing, he had continued to be successful. A lack of funds would never be a problem for him. Alyce was reared in a frugal household. Would her thrifty ways embarrass him? Would he be ashamed of her as he got to know her better?

She picked up her Bible again. She was grateful that her aunt had raised her in a Christian home. She turned to the thirteenth chapter of 1 Corinthians, the love chapter, and scanned it. She had parts of it memorized, so it didn't take long to find the verses she was looking for. "Love is patient. . . . It is not self-seeking. . . it keeps no record of wrongs."

"Forgive me, Lord," she prayed. "I've been keeping a record that needs to be erased. Teach me to forgive even as You have forgiven me."

She read on. "Love never fails." That was the assurance she needed. She knew she loved Bill despite the real and imaginary hurts she had experienced. Though she didn't always understand him, she loved him and she knew he loved her. . .so much that he would stay away if that's what she wanted. She could entrust her future to him.

She glanced at the clock, calculated what time it would be in San Francisco, and picked up the phone. She couldn't wait another minute before calling Bill. Her hand trembled as she dialed Bette's number.

"Hello?" Bette peered at the clock on her nightstand. Who on earth was calling her at that frightful hour?

"Bette, this is Alyce." Bette would not have recognized the soft, restrained voice.

"Alyce! How are you? Is something wrong?"

"Nothing's wrong. Well, yes, lots of things are wrong. I mean. . . . Oh, please let me talk with Bill."

Bette smiled. She hoped the call meant Alyce had had a change of heart. "Just a minute. I'll go wake him up."

The past few days Bill had tried to ignore her whenever possible or offered curt replies to the few questions she asked. Bette knew what was bothering him, and she had tried to be patient. She hoped Alyce's call would return him to civility. At least it was a move in the right direction.

There was a fumbling of the phone, and then Bill spoke.

"Alyce. I was beginning to lose hope."

Tears were streaming down her cheeks. She knew what she was doing was right, yet she struggled for words. "Oh, Bill. I've been so miserable without you. I need to see you, to talk with you, to let you hold me in your arms."

Bill felt he should pinch himself to make sure this conversation was really taking place. "Darling, do you really mean that?"

"Yes, oh, yes, I do. I haven't been able to sleep for days. I'm so sorry I misjudged you. You love me. You've done what you could to prove your love. You gave more than your share to keep the Santanoni proposal intact, and I criticized you for that. I've wronged you. I'm so sorry. Please forgive me."

"Of course I forgive you. You've just made me the happiest man in the state of California! How I wish I could be there to hold you and to kiss away those tears."

"I'm sorry I hurt you. Please come to Syracuse."

"Darling, I'd be there tonight if it were possible, but it's not. I have several commitments here for the next few weeks." He held the phone in one hand and rummaged for his pocket calendar. "How about spending the Fourth of July weekend with me at Santanoni? We could return to the Antlers and take day trips backpacking into the camp." He found himself chuckling. "You could even bring Max."

Alyce was feeling light-headed. "We'd both enjoy that! Bill, I'm sorry that I called you at such a ridiculous hour. Once I made up my mind it was the thing to do, I couldn't wait another minute. Please forgive me."

Bill laughed. "Promise me you'll never change. I love you, Darling. I'm glad you called. I'll see you soon. We have a lot to talk about."

Alyce sighed with pleasure and relief as she hung up the phone. She gave Max a hug and danced into her bedroom. In her dreams she and Bill strolled arm in arm through the restored lodge at Santanoni.

∞

Alyce and Max arrived at the gatehouse shortly before noon. Bill had left a note for her at the trailhead to meet him farther down the trail. He had signed it, "I love you, Bill."

As she signed the trail register, she smiled with anticipation. This time she didn't have to sign Max's name. She had another protector awaiting her.

Alyce was too excited to appreciate the early spring flowers as she hurried along. She did not have long to wait. As she rounded the bend near the barn, she saw Bill standing beside the old milkhouse. His back was toward the path as he appraised the structure, so he did not see her approaching. She could scarcely contain herself. Soon she would be in his arms. *How I love him!* she thought ecstatically. *How good God is to bring us together.*

Max spied his old friend and scampered to him with his stubby tail twitching wildly. Bill turned to face her, and Alyce paused, drinking him in. They looked long at each other, and then Bill smiled and held out his arms to receive her.

They clung to each other as if their clinging would erase all the hurt and misunderstanding, all that would ever come between them. Bill kissed away her tears as he hugged her to his chest. He knew they were tears of joy, and they mingled with his own.

Finally he released her. "Let's walk down by the lake, and we can talk there."

They hiked hand in hand to the lodge, stopping often to embrace in the warm sun. "I just can't hold you enough," Bill whispered in her ear.

While Max made his usual investigations, they walked down to the beach and sat in the sun. Bill drew Alyce to him. "I want you to know something I should have told you months before. A short time ago I dedicated my life to the Lord. You have always been so forthcoming about your faith, and I, well, I'm just starting to feel confident about expressing myself. I do know that the Lord has brought us together, and together we can. . ." He paused and cupped his hands around her face. "Alyce, do you still want to marry me?"

"Yes!" she whispered. She had never been more sure in her life. Together they would create a Christian home, and together their marriage would be forever sustained by the Lord.

Bill hugged her again. He reached into his pocket and pulled out a small gold box. He opened it and removed a one-carat diamond solitaire ring and slipped it on her finger.

As Alyce stared at the ring, tears welled up in her eyes. "Thank you, Darling," she whispered. "I will treasure it forever."

"I think it's time we made some wedding plans, don't you?"

Alyce nodded. "Since it all began right here, wouldn't it be nice to be married at the lodge? Maybe someday we could make Santanoni our home."

"Home for me will always be wherever you are, but I like the idea of being married here. Max can come to the wedding!"

They laughed and hugged, and then Bill reached into his pocket again. "I have something else for you." He handed her a sealed letter. It was addressed to the Foundation to Save Santanoni; the return address was the New York State

Senate.

"Pete forwarded the letter to me at the Antlers. I wanted us to open it together."

Alyce looked into his eyes as she took the letter. With trembling hands she ran her forefinger under the seal and then removed the contents. Her eyes opened wider as she scanned the page, then she threw her arms around him. "Oh, Bill! Listen to this!"

CLAIRE M. COUGHLIN and **HOPE IRVIN MARSTON**
Claire and Hope wrote this inspirational romance to draw attention to Camp Santanoni, an Adirondack Great Camp in New York State's Forest Preserve. Since the publication of *Santanoni Sunrise* in 1994, the camp has been designated a National Historic Landmark. Considerable progress has been made toward restoring the camp during the past few years thanks to the efforts of the Town of Newcomb, the Friends of Santanoni Camp, and funding from public and private organizations and individuals.

A Touching Performance

Ginger O'Neil

Chapter 1

A grotesque, mangled face flashed onto the thirty-nine-inch screen. Black strings of hair framed the mask, with blood from scalp wounds pooling around still-staring eyes before streaking down into the contorted mouth of the victim.

Twenty-seven-year-old Claire Rossiter allowed herself only a fleeting glance. A reluctant and bewildered participant in the proceedings, she squirmed in her chair to the left of the eight other witnesses in the Fulton Falls courtroom.

She'd seen accident victims on the television news often enough, but never had she beheld a visage so disfigured as the one before her now.

On the witness stand a nervous, elderly man answered the endless questions of a persistent prosecutor.

That witness actually had seen the accident happen. Claire had not.

How foolish it seemed to have to report to a hearing in this backwater village when she hardly qualified as a witness at all—her car was the ninth in the ten-car chain of minor collisions resulting from the fatal crash.

The only pertinent information she could provide dealt with weather and the road condition. She hadn't a shred of evidence suggesting that the death of the female victim resulted from a hit-and-run, or that it was purposeful killing inflicted with Mafia-style malicious intent. Malicious intent?

How could it be? she thought to herself as she clenched and unclenched her fingers. What kind of human being would create such carnage intentionally and then drive away?

Never, as far back as Claire could remember, had "malicious intent" been part of her world, a world dominated by music—both in childhood under the guidance of doting parents and teachers and in her late teens and early twenties as she performed in concerts organized by supportive conductors and agents.

Astonishing success had recently arrived for Claire after she won the celebrated East Coast Schumann Piano competition. However, to her great dismay, that award, plus the ten-city concert tour it guaranteed, had come six years too late for her adorable papa to share. He'd gone—almost eagerly, it had seemed—to a heavenly reunion with his wife, Claire's whisper-soft mother whom he'd lost fifteen years earlier.

A sense of obligation to the litigants forced Claire to steal another glimpse at the video that was grinding out ever more hideous angles of the corpse.

Death here screamed out at her with sickening viciousness, whereas death in her own family had been nothing more than quiet relinquishment—Mozart melodies in church escorting a soul to eternity.

She ran her long fingers through scales and cadences on the arm of her chair until, quite accidentally, her fifth finger tapped a C-sharp onto the arm of the woman next to her. Claire offered a sheepish, "Oh, I'm so sorry."

The highly rouged, red-haired woman smiled back. "No problem." With a shrug of a shoulder she whispered a husky "This is the pits."

The heady perfume of the woman's bouffant hair assailed Claire, who seldom used hair spray—or any cosmetics at all. Most of the time, a puff or two of face powder on her cheeks and the application of a lustrous, rose-colored lipstick was enough.

Claire knew she didn't need much in the way of artificial enhancement. Over the years, her appearance had seemed to please the most critical audiences, both those attending her performances and those among her closest associates at State University, where she taught.

Her long, lean bone structure of face and body appeared fragile. "A deception," her teacher in Switzerland had declared. Madame Bouchard had compared Claire to a stained-glass window. "Exquisitely lucent, yet skillfully crafted to withstand stress."

She smiled, remembering.

Interrupting the attorney in midsentence, the judge pounded his gavel, announcing a fifteen-minute recess, the first of the morning. According to the printed schedule, Claire noted that she'd be the next witness to be called. A good thing; she definitely had to get to New York by midafternoon for a few hours of practice.

The lawyers had rescheduled her. They knew about her well-publicized recital the next evening at Lincoln Center.

"Boy, could I go for a strong cappuccino," announced the red-haired woman, her chair squeaking as she stood up. "How 'bout you, Dearie?"

Claire offered the woman a relieved grin. "That sounds ideal right now."

"There's a snack bar downstairs," added the woman. "Why don't we check it out?"

"Great." Claire thrust legal papers into her briefcase on top of her music, picked up her purse, and followed the woman out of the courtroom.

Because the mobbed snack bar had only a few tables, most of the patrons drank their coffee and munched bagels standing up, shoulder to shoulder. A shelf by the doorway held a pile of miscellaneous briefcases and portfolios. Claire put hers there and lined up for coffee with the other woman.

She scanned the packed room. All manner of conversations buffeted her ears. To her right, a group of women were denouncing a sex-education course being taught at the local high school. To her left, two farmers were discussing the best feed for hogs. And in the background she could hear voices debating a zoning ordinance dealing with a sanitary landfill.

It had been a long time since she'd considered the necessity for sanitary landfills—or high school sex education. Maybe that wasn't a good thing. Living in an ivory tower of music had its drawbacks.

Standing above his companions in a group near the tables was a tall man who appeared as out of place in the surroundings as she assumed herself to be. *He's more suited to a tennis court than a courthouse*, Claire told herself, pleased with her private play on words.

What is the exact color of his hair? Claire pondered. She decided it was a toss-up between corn silk and Dijon mustard. An unlikely combination, yes. But on him it looked tremendous.

Because his hair had a casual going-every-which-way-at-once style, at first glance someone might think he'd let a frivolous girlfriend go at it with a pair of rusty scissors, but Claire knew otherwise. That effect—tousled and carefree—required the hands of a skilled stylist who knew what he was doing.

Errant strands, permitting no semblance of a part, went into free-fall across the young man's high, bronzed forehead; at the moment, his eyes were squinting in merriment over some comment made by one of the four men standing with him.

The "What'll it be, ladies?" from across the counter prompted Claire to place her order.

Fortunately, a table became vacant almost immediately. The redhead maneuvered through the crowd to grab it.

"This coffee's a lifesaver," said the woman. "I had to get off work to come up here today. Boy, that kills. I'm a waitress in the city, see. I lose a couple hundred bucks in tips on days off."

"It's been inconvenient for me, too," Claire added, finding the woman's conversation a refreshing change from the deliberations in the courtroom.

"What kind of work do you do?"

"Most of the time, I teach," Claire answered, realizing she might make the woman uncomfortable if she admitted she was a concert pianist, her teaching duties secondary in importance.

Even as she tried to be cordial with her companion, Claire couldn't prevent her eyes from analyzing the tall blond man. The chest-high part of his tan suit, which was about all she could see, was well tailored. A striped tie lay loose below his collar, establishing an understated flair, almost as if he'd put it on, already knotted, over his head.

He stood tall with his hands behind his back, like members of the British royal family. His companions, none quite so smartly turned out or as young as he, were all prosperously clothed gentlemen. Though they did most of the talking, the tall man seemed to be the leader of the group—not due to his height, but, rather, because he had the demeanor of one who was in charge.

"What do you teach?" the redhead asked.

Trying desperately to be polite to the woman, Claire smiled as she replied, "Piano and keyboard at the state university."

"Well, whadda you know! Say, we have a terrific piano player where I work. He can play anything. My favorite's 'Come Back to Sorrento.' Can you play that?"

Claire grinned good-naturedly. "Yes, I've run through that a few times."

To Claire's delight, the tall man's group was being pushed closer to the table where she and the redhead sat.

Claire studied the sharply delineated jaw of the blond man. His chin barely missed being too long; it had been clipped by nature just in time. But "nature," or what more accurately should be described as the Divine Sculptor, had bestowed on him full, expressive lips, which he now pressed tightly together as he listened to the other men.

She figured he must be about thirty-eight. And she was willing to bet he boasted a Dutch or Nordic heritage.

"You're so pretty," the redhead stated. "You should play in a club yourself. You've got gorgeous black hair. I bet you can twist it up real elegant-like."

Claire nodded, shifting so she could see the woman and the tall blond man at the same time. "Sometimes I do wear a chignon," she offered.

"Hey, put a little more eye shadow on and find yourself a slinky gown. You'd be a sensation. This piano player at our place could get you into a club in the city. He knows everybody."

Claire laughed. "I might consider it."

"If you get sick of teachin', come on in. You meet swell people in restaurants and clubs. I like my work a lot. The hours aren't bad and. . ."

The woman's comments now competed with the conversation of the blond man's group—that group discussing prisoners and paroles, subjects both startling and fascinating to Claire.

"Zimblatz deserves to be paroled," said a squat man in a brown suit. "I'm not going to stand here and let you convince me otherwise, Nick. Everettsville's bursting at its seams. Even with the new facility, you're going to be crowded. Zimblatz has played by the rules for fifteen years. He deserves his walking papers."

"I'm sorry, Ed, I don't agree," replied the tall man, shaking his head, a look of regret on his face. Claire was delighted with the name Nick. She decided it suited him perfectly.

"Granted, Frankie Zimblatz has been an industrious mechanic over the years," the Nick-guy continued. "He's kept the engine purring on my chariot; I can't fault him on that score."

"So, Nick, that proves he's responsible," said another man in the group.

"His record looks pretty good on the surface," Nick said, shrugging a shoulder and lowering his head to one side, causing strands of hair to fall a different way. "It's been a year since he's been involved with drugs or had a fight, but there are things that don't get entered on the record. His expression, his way of looking at you, tells me he doesn't have his life together yet."

Nick paused. The other men appeared impatient as they waited for him to continue.

Despite his opposition to the prisoner's parole, there didn't appear to be any severity in his startlingly blue eyes, recessed under soft, straw-colored brows.

The red-haired woman cleared her throat. ". . .So you can see how great it is where I work. It kills me to lose all those tips."

Claire feigned interest, barely hearing what the woman was saying as she tried to juggle the two conversations, the woman's job losing ground to the Zimblatz parole.

"I've seen Zimblatz's hostility a thousand times in other men," Nick continued, "and it always tells me they're not ready. Zimblatz hasn't worked things out inside, down in his spirit, where it counts. I know this sounds unscientific, but—"

"Unscientific! It's downright medieval, and you know it," countered the man in the brown suit. "What kind of malarkey are you handing us, Nick? Who among us ever has everything worked out down inside 'where it counts,' as you say. Do you?"

"I like to think so, yes. But it didn't come easy."

"No, I guess not," the man responded, rubbing his chin, "especially in your case. But some of us, for whatever reason, don't share your belief in things of the spirit—things like God or eternal life or whatever. I don't happen to think a man has to nail himself to a cross or declare himself saved over a loudspeaker to be given a parole."

Nick responded quickly, with some irritation, "Ed, you know me well enough to realize I never let a prisoner's religion or lack of same influence my recommendations to a parole board. I've been scrupulous about this."

He lowered his eyelids reflectively as he continued. "But I'll readily admit I think these guys under my charge would benefit enormously if God became a part of their lives."

Claire was struck by the intensity of his words as he went on. "To go back out on the streets after ten, twenty years behind bars and face the complexities and prejudices of an unsympathetic environment is a monumental task. Without God as the sidelines coach, it's virtually a no-win situation. But never have I required religious allegiance in a parole approval."

"He's right," a man with a black mustache stated in acquiescence. "We've all dealt with Nick enough to know that's true."

"Thanks, Len." Nick's mouth formed a smile. "In Frankie Zimblatz's case

I'm doing society and Frankie a favor keeping him incarcerated."

"You're still a sadist in my book," the brown-suited man chortled. "If you had your way, you'd turn thumbscrews and go back to the lockstep."

"Give me a break," Nick said with a scowl, retaining the telltale smile lines in his cheeks. "Ed, I've recommended plenty of paroles for you these past four years since I've been at Everettsville. Only last month I pushed hard for the release of Sam Baker and Clyde Randolph, hardly saints in either case. I'm just telling you, your buddy Zimblatz isn't going to make it. He has three murders to his credit. Would you like to make it four? If you and the board release him, it's your ball game entirely. I won't sign an endorsement."

One of the men offered to get coffee for the others. Nick said a barely audible, "No, thanks." Claire noted he was the only one in the group who didn't already have a cup or a snack in his hand.

He's a health freak, Claire thought. No caffeine and no cholesterol.

The red-haired woman cleared her throat. ". . .So you see how great it is where I work. Drop in sometime. It's the Ravenna Lounge off Washington Square. Just ask for me—Emma. I'll see that you get yourself a thick Omaha steak."

"I'm sure you would, ah, er, Emma," Claire managed with a smile, wondering if the tall blond man would ever blow his healthy regimen and order himself a thick Omaha steak in the woman's bistro.

"Those inmates must hate your guts," said the mustached man. "Nick, there's probably a contract out on you."

"I'm sure there's more than one," Nick replied, amusement fading slowly from his smile.

Contracts?

Claire shuddered at the very word, all lightheartedness vanishing from her thoughts. Nick-the-warden had just admitted there likely were contracts out on him, apparently not at all unusual in his line of work.

"Actually," said the man named Ed, "it amazes me, Len, but Nick has an excellent rapport with most of the inmates at Everettsville."

"Except at parole time," joked Len.

"Yeah, except at parole time," echoed the other.

Claire was startled to see the red-haired woman getting up to go.

". . .So, really," said the woman, who had continued her conversation unheeded, "I think it's time for us to get back."

"You're right," replied a startled Claire, looking at her watch. She was reluctant to leave because she'd developed a deep curiosity about the fate of the unfortunate Zimblatz.

More than that, she was captivated by this Nick person, who apparently held some sort of major position in a penitentiary.

He didn't fit the picture she would draw of a prison warden, not that she'd spent an inordinate amount of time over the years trying to envision such a person. In every respect, the man appeared too East Hampton sophisticated for a role of that type.

She couldn't imagine him ever shouting at squads of men, ordering them over catwalks or back into cages.

But more than anything else, his Christian witness astonished her. It seemed inconsistent, somehow, for this tennis-buff kind of man to acknowledge so confidently his dependence on God.

Claire considered herself a responsible Christian, often accompanying choruses and performances in churches of many denominations, as well as her own. On Sundays she regularly attended church services. But her day-to-day prayer time had become slipshod. It had been ages since she'd prayed for God's direction in her life.

As a child, she'd prayed every night with her father. Before bedtime there'd be a story, usually in French, and then a little chat, also in French, with le Pere éternel.

But as she grew beyond childhood, piano practice had taken up more and more time. Talking to "the Eternal Father" had been relegated to the background of her life. After her father's death, she'd let her daily prayer time slip away with him.

In more recent years, she'd more or less assumed ministers and the university philosophy department were handling things like that for her. Music was enough for her to handle. More than enough. Mastery of any one field didn't permit spreading oneself too thin.

Yet there were moments in music—such as after the sustained echoes of a perfect cadenza in Franck or the interlacing of a Bach fugue—when she was transcended to an all-encompassing ecstasy that couldn't be explained by harmony, the science of acoustics, or just her basic love of music.

There'd been that afternoon last year in Westminster Abbey when she'd heard the Laudamus Te of Haydn's Lord Nelson Mass. That simple, yet so ethereal, selection had stunned her with its majesty. She'd left the abbey shaken by what could only be described as the awesome presence of God, a God who needed more of her than she was giving Him.

In a similar way, Nick's strong statements had unnerved her. She hadn't expected to be so emotionally stirred in this environment.

The red-haired woman headed into the group of corrections personnel. "How's about letting us get outta here, fellas?" she quipped as she edged her way around the man named Ed.

Feeling like a quarterback following a center tackle, Claire stayed close to the other woman. "Excuse us," she mumbled to the men, unable to prevent her eyes from searching out the expression of the rivetingly handsome Nick.

His eyes, like chips from a blue glacier, returned her glance in a way that forced her knees to buckle a little, hampering maneuverability for a second.

"Show your manners, men; let the ladies through," Nick announced with exaggerated command, as he stepped back into the crowd of farmers behind him. "Although we don't show much prison know-how, allowing two such gorgeous creatures to escape so easily," he added.

He permitted a smirk to take over his puckish lips.

Claire couldn't help but laughingly reply in a similar dramatic tone as she shouldered a path to the door. "Thank you, kind sirs, for providing us safe passage."

He's probably married, with at least five children and a harried wife, she thought as she picked up her briefcase from the shelf. Maybe his wife and children march lockstep to their beds. She snickered as she contemplated this scene.

Buoyed into a more cheerful frame of mind by the roguish Nick, she headed back to the courtroom.

But, she reminded herself, Nick was roguish only up to a point. His comments and mannerisms indicated he was well aware of the power he wielded over prisoners and their paroles. He was anything but frivolous in his approach to his job.

With his drollery, his captivating eyes, and his expressive lips, Nick dominated her mind as she stepped into her place next to the other witnesses.

How she wished she'd been able to listen to him longer. His conversation certainly had more going for it than the dismal dirge of the accident hearing. In fact, his conversation was more interesting than most she was a party to back at the university.

She and the redhead had no more than gotten comfortable in their seats when the judge announced the lawyers had come to a settlement in the case. The remaining witnesses wouldn't be needed. He thanked them and told them they were free to leave.

Claire looked at her watch. Only 11:37. She'd have plenty of practice time that afternoon, after all.

She turned to the red-haired woman, and they both shook their heads.

"That beats all," said the waitress. "I take this whole crummy day to drive up here, and they never even ask me to get up on the stand. Man, this has been murder! I bet you're as mad as I am."

"It's exasperating, but chalk it up as an experience. For me, it's been an education," Claire admitted.

"For me, it's been a bummer," stormed the woman. "So, see you around. Remember now, the Ravenna Lounge. If you ever need a job, come on in."

"Thank you," said Claire, touched by the woman's sincere concern. "You never know. Right now things are going pretty well for me. But if I do need a job I'll look you up."

"Right. So long." The red-haired woman pushed her chair back and strutted from the room.

Claire got up slowly. For the waitress, this day had been a "bummer." By all accounts, it should have been a bummer for her, as well. But it hadn't been. Listening to Nick talk with his colleagues about paroles had made it more than worth the inconvenience.

As she started down the path toward her car, she weighed Nick's comments. There was something so steadfast and rock-bottom-reliable about Nick's manner that she was convinced his actions would never be frivolous or petty.

It made her feel secure and almost cozy as she drove down the highway to the city, knowing that a man named Nick carefully screened the prisoners he released back into society.

Chapter 2

Claire took no time for lunch when she got to New York, but went directly to Lincoln Center for her practice session.

Tossing off her jacket, she spun through a series of arpeggios and exercises. To her disappointment, the third-octave G had poor action. She'd have to mention that to the tuner in the morning.

She flipped open her briefcase to check the time the tuner was expected. To her bewilderment, her briefcase held nothing familiar. No jottings about the accident. No subpoena. No folder of music. No program. Nothing of hers.

Who was playing tricks on her?

Closing the case, she examined the cover. It looked exactly like hers. The handles were the same. But it wasn't hers! The black leather had a slightly different grain.

There were black initials near the handle—N.S.V. Immediately her mind registered N for Nick. Might this briefcase belong to the attractive warden of Everettsville Prison? It might very well, she reasoned, because the mix-up could only have happened in the snack bar at the courthouse. She'd grabbed the wrong case from the shelf.

"Good grief," she groaned. "If this is his briefcase, I've done a terrible thing to that guy."

Once again she opened the briefcase. It was imperative she find out for sure who the owner was. She'd have to phone the courthouse right away—try to get in touch with the owner before he or she left for the day. Whoever it was had already been without notes now for most of the afternoon.

Her own inconvenience paled in comparison. She didn't really need her music; she'd had everything committed to memory for months. Only the program and some memos would have come in handy. But it was discomforting to realize she'd inconvenienced someone else to the extent that crucial decisions might have been made haphazardly—in situations like that of the prisoner Zimblatz.

What a careless, stupid thing she'd done.

She thumbed through the brochures and magazines that lay in the briefcase. They all dealt with prisons. There was a pamphlet on juvenile recidivism, a manual on penal codes, several corrections periodicals. She felt almost criminal herself, pawing through someone else's material. But it was necessary. Unless she found a name written somewhere, she couldn't be sure the briefcase belonged to Nick.

Maybe it was the property of a person named Nelson, Neil—even Nancy or. . .

Then she saw it. The full name and address on a magazine. And it was Nick—Nicklaus S. Van Vierssen. How many Nicks in a rural courthouse would have a briefcase filled with material on prisons and penology? It had to be the tall blond man.

Nicklaus Van Vierssen. So very Dutch. It was the ideal name for him. She could almost see him standing on a sluice gate, wearing a white cable-knit sweater, and looking out over a canal, his hair whipped into a frenzy by a North Sea blast.

But she mustn't squander time in daydreams. She had to phone the courthouse right away and report what had happened.

As soon as possible, she had to drive back to Fulton Falls with the briefcase. Dinner with Henri would have to be canceled.

Removing her cell phone from her purse, she located the number for the county clerk's office in Fulton Falls. That would do. They could locate Nick Van Vierssen, if he hadn't gone home. But certainly if he had gone, he'd have left word with someone that his briefcase was missing.

Thank heaven her recital wasn't scheduled for that evening. But she'd still have to phone Henri and tell him she couldn't make their dinner engagement. Or maybe Henri would drive up with her. . . .

"County clerk's office," answered a female voice.

"This is Claire-Therese Rossiter, and I'm calling from the city," she said, trying to compose her unsteady voice. "I have the most absurd problem. When I was in Fulton Falls today for a hearing, I accidentally picked up the wrong briefcase. It was a foolish mistake, and I'm so embarrassed. Anyway, I have in my possession the papers of a man named Van Vierssen."

"Oh, yes, Nick Van Vierssen from the prison."

"That's the man, yes. Is there any way you could locate Mr. Van Vierssen and have him call me back? He must be greatly distressed by this."

"I can try."

"Oh, please do. Have him call my cell phone," she said, giving the woman her number. "If he's gone for the day, would you be kind enough to phone the prison and leave a message for him? I'll be at the Embassy Hotel after seven this evening, but he can still reach me by cell phone."

"All right. The Embassy Hotel after seven. I'll see that he gets your message."

"Thank you so much."

The woman clicked off. Claire plopped down in an overstuffed chair backstage. If she started practicing again, she might not hear the phone. And if Nick Van Vierssen was still in the courthouse, he would call as soon as he got the message. She'd already caused the man a great deal of frustration; he didn't need extra rings of a phone. She had difficulty deciding just what she would say to him when he finally did call. She had no way of knowing how he'd react.

Because he dealt with legal matters, it wouldn't surprise her if he were less than civil over the phone, despite his easygoing manner in the courthouse snack bar.

As the minutes moved along, however, her dread became pleasant anticipation. It would be sort of a thrill to have him talk to her—even if he were angry.

When the phone rang, she bolted up and quickly answered it.

"Mr. Van Vierssen?" she asked.

"Yes. Is this Ms. Rossiter?"

She had difficulty controlling her quavering lips to say "Yes."

"I hear you have a briefcase that belongs to me."

His voice sounded just as free from anxiety as it had during the discussion with the men at the courthouse. For this she was supremely thankful.

"I do have it," she stumbled along, insecure, as she pictured the impressive face that went with the Nick-voice. "Please forgive me. I must have grabbed it by mistake in the snack bar."

"That's what happened, I'm sure."

"What inconvenience I've caused you. How did you ever get through your meetings?"

"Oh, I recited the Gettysburg Address a few times and then leaped boldly into Henry the Fifth's Agincourt appeal to his troops. I managed to hold my own in one session with my oratory."

Because she had studied him so thoroughly in the snack bar, she could imagine him thrusting his lower lip up over the upper after making such a droll comment, his eyes alert for the expected playful response.

Chuckling, she offered, "Seriously, it had to have been awkward. I hope I wasn't responsible for some poor prisoner missing out on his parole."

He laughed heartily with a strong baritone resonance. "No, nothing quite that world-shattering."

She recalled the way his lips separated when he laughed, erasing any tension others might have with him. By that laugh she knew he wasn't too out of sorts with her.

"I only had one meeting this afternoon," he added. "I could have used some of my notes, but they weren't absolutely necessary. If the papers had been confidential, I wouldn't have left the briefcase unlocked and on that shelf. So you see, you worried needlessly. However, tomorrow it would help if I had the pamphlets."

"Of course. I'm going to drive to Fulton Falls as soon as we hang up. I realize the courthouse will be closed, but just tell me where I can meet you, and I'll be there."

"You won't have to do that. I'm going to be in the city tomorrow. My meeting's at eleven. I could pick up my papers before that meeting."

"Are you sure? I really don't mind driving up tonight."

"No, no. I'm serious. It's no problem. You're staying at the Embassy Hotel, right?"

"Yes, but I plan to be here at Lincoln Center's Tully Hall at nine and remain here throughout the day."

"You're going to be at the auditorium all day tomorrow?"

"Yes, I'll be practicing. I have a recital tomorrow night."

"Really! You're a soloist of some sort?"

"I'm a pianist."

"Outstanding," he replied enthusiastically. "All right, then. I'll stop by at the auditorium around nine-thirty. . .with your briefcase in tow. It was the only one left in the snack bar, so I figured someone had taken mine by mistake. Like you, I took the liberty of opening it to determine its owner."

"Oh? Of course," she mumbled, trying to picture the attractive warden going through the music in her briefcase. Had she left anything there that might prove embarrassing to her? No, not that she could recall.

"Fortunately, I didn't have to look far," he continued. "There was a letter on top with an address to a Ms. Rossiter at the university, plus a subpoena with your name on it."

As he continued, he made no mention of the interchange he had had with her when she and the waitress had exited the snack bar. He apparently didn't connect her voice with that incident.

"I phoned the university and left word with them," he explained. "So I was expecting your call—but not from the city. It works out much better for me this way."

"I'm relieved about that."

"You'll have your music or whatever you need in the morning. No later than ten o'clock."

"Actually, I have everything down for the recital. There's no rush."

"If you don't mind my asking, what are you performing?"

"Bach, Haydn, a jazz variation, some Liszt. Do you like Liszt?"

"Yes, he's one of my favorites. Are you playing any Rachmaninoff?"

"Not this time."

"Too bad. If I were a pianist I'd always play something by Rachmaninoff."

"I bet you'd be sensational," she commented, recalling his height, which would suggest he'd have hands with great power and reach. "You'd give me a lot of competition."

"Er, no, I don't think so," he said in a hesitant way that rather puzzled her, but only in passing.

"You just have your hands full taking care of prisoners," she said with a coy impudence.

"That's about it, yes. So, until tomorrow then, don't practice too hard, Ms.

Rossiter—Ms. Claire-Therese Rossiter, is that right?"

"Yes, that's what it says on subpoenas and programs because I'm Swiss-French, from Montreux. Some folks still address me by the whole hyphenated mouthful, but I've been known to answer to Claire all by itself just as readily."

"Well, then, Claire, don't wear yourself out practicing. Save some steam for the recital."

"I'll try to."

After he clicked off, she attempted to return to the piano and the Haydn that needed extra work because of the sluggish G, but her mind wouldn't focus on the job at hand.

Nicklaus Van Vierssen played havoc with her thoughts. The low resonance of his voice seemed far more melodious and tantalizing than the theme from Haydn.

He hadn't been angry at all. Not pompous, condescending, or even annoyed. Just pleasantly congenial, if unpredictable, with a comfortable, security-blanket kind of ease, allowing her to relax in his presence.

Perhaps his children didn't walk lockstep to their bedrooms, after all.

Perhaps he had no children.

Oh, no, he'd have to have children. That whimsical hair almost cried out to be rumpled by a youngster. Those Arctic eyes—perceptive, yes, but so tenderly welcoming—those superbly crafted facial features—all needed to be passed on to another generation of Dutchmen. He would most definitely have to have children.

But maybe he didn't. Maybe he didn't even have a wife.

That was definitely wishful thinking; of course he had a wife. How long would a striking Siegfried like that go without a wife? Undoubtedly he'd be married to an exotic blond mannequin.

Claire tried to dismiss him from her mind. After all, the episode was over—or would be the next morning. Nicklaus Van Vierssen would bow out of her life and return to his prison world.

∞

Dinner with Henri Poncelet didn't have to be canceled after all. Claire was glad. She always looked forward to being with Henri.

He was almost the caricature of a Frenchman. Claire delighted in his overly dramatic Continental mannerisms—effusive compliments, gallant kissing of hands, flamboyant dressing.

Her delight, however, did not extend to his cavalier attitude about marriage—getting married one day, divorced virtually the next. Nevertheless, following her father's tolerant acceptance of Henri's shortcomings, she valued his friendship as a business adviser.

A partner with her father in an importing business for nearly twenty years, Henri was almost a family member, the only "uncle" she would ever know.

Four months of the year he and his daughter Yolande lived in Paris, the remainder of the time in the States. Whenever they found themselves in the same city, Claire and Henri would meet for dinner. He made Herculean efforts to attend her recitals.

∞

Claire opened the door of her hotel room to receive Henri, and he swooped in, kissing not only her hand but both cheeks as well. "Claire-Therese, how is it possible for an already magnificent woman to grow more enticing by the day? *Mais oui*, it is true. Your hair looks regal in a chignon."

Henri had grown a goatee that made him look more the *bon vivant* than on his previous visit. She suspected he'd also dyed his hair, because she didn't see a strand of his former premature gray lurking anywhere.

"So, are you ready for tomorrow?" he asked. "You've planned an ambitious program."

"I know. The Liszt is strenuous, and I'm a bit edgy about the Haydn. All in all, I think the selections will go well."

"Wasn't that Bach selection one of your father's favorites?"

"It was." Tears still beaded in her eyes when she thought of her darling papa. He'd been so devoted to her, spending a fortune for the best piano coaches in Paris and New York. After her mother's death, he'd never remarried. Claire became the center of his world.

"So, how was the trip down from the university?" he asked, adjusting his jacket collar. "Wasn't this the day you were to report for that hearing? What are you snickering about?"

"Something amusing occurred."

"I can't imagine anything amusing about a collision hearing."

"I made a careless mistake, Henri," she replied, proceeding to relate the details of the briefcase episode.

"What a dilemma for the wretched fellow," he responded in a tone that asked for further details.

"He was extremely civil."

"I would have been furious. Without a briefcase or my laptop, I'm helpless."

"You would have thrown a Napoleonic fit. Well, anyway, this man didn't. Actually, I half expected him to because he has a high-pressure job. He's a prison warden."

"A what?" asked Henri, his eyes wide with curiosity.

"A warden—or something like that—at a place called Everettsville."

"You're not serious?"

"I am. He's an intriguing guy." She ran her palm slowly across the right side of her swept-back hair. "On the surface he's the embodiment of carefree GQ. But beneath this exterior, through his conversation with associates he conveyed intense dedication to his work. His demeanor didn't match his job."

Henri studied her for a few moments, his voice becoming grave. "Everettsville's a massive, forbidding place. You've never heard of it?"

"No, never."

"It's on Route 54, beyond the reservoir, just off the thruway. Maximum security. They had a riot there ten years ago. A guard and five or six prisoners were killed."

She shook her head in denial. Although she knew Everettsville would be an unpleasant place to work, she'd hardly thought of it as hazardous to the point of massacre. "How cheerful. Now let's talk about the rack and guillotine for a few more jollies."

"All I'm saying is that it's a grim place for anyone to work. The man you're meeting tomorrow must be a gutsy individual."

A shiver raced down her spine, anxiety taking over as she weighed the circumstances surrounding the charming young warden.

In an effort to restore a more upbeat tone for the evening, she quipped, "So I'm relieved we're not going to Everettsville for dinner tonight. The bread and water up there isn't served nearly as elegantly as ours will be tonight at the Chalet Royal."

Henri chuckled and patted her hand affectionately. "Indeed not, *chérie*. I have reservations for nine o'clock. And they're preparing your favorite—Ris de Veau."

Chapter 3

The next morning, as Claire ran through her scales, she knew the tuner had done his job well—the piano responded perfectly.

It wasn't until she got to the fermata near the end of the Bach that she realized someone else was in the auditorium. She stopped abruptly.

Peering out across the dark seats, she called, "Mr. Van Vierssen—is that you?"

"Yes, good morning," a louder version of the snack bar voice replied from the blackened theater. "Please, don't stop. Johann Sebastian would have a fit. It's savagery to chop that fugue off and let it hang there incomplete. Go on; finish it."

Smiling with pleasure and impressed by his recognition of the composer, she dashed off the remainder of the piece with a lighthearted flourish.

"Marvelous," he called, as he came down the aisle. *"Encore,"* he said from just below the stage.

She laughed. "Oh, how I wish Cahill of the Times were as easy to please as you."

She hurried over to the edge of the stage. Bending down on one knee, she squinted into the concert hall. She could see him now, standing in the aisle, ramrod stiff, his hands in the pockets of sand-colored trousers, topped by an olive jacket and an open-collared green and yellow plaid shirt. A stunning outfit—an arresting complement to his blond hair.

She was glad she'd worn slacks. It was easy to sit down on the edge of the stage.

"Your briefcase is there in the first row," she said, nearly tongue-tied; she was nervous about carrying on a one-on-one conversation with the Nick of the snack bar.

"I saw it, so I put yours there, too." He moved closer and spoke from only a few feet below her.

"I'm sorry about what happened," she said. "I'd like to think there's some way I could repay you for this inconvenience."

He grinned widely, his head cocked to one side, but he remained very straight, his hands still in his pockets.

"There's no need to be too hard on yourself, but if you do feel a twinge of guilt, you could erase most of it by letting me stay for awhile to listen to you practice."

"I'm flattered."

"You deserve to be. I had no idea when I talked to you on the phone that you were so accomplished and well-known. After I hung up, I dug out the theater section of the Times, where I found quite a blurb on Claire-Therese Rossiter. This is no small event tonight. And the passage you just raced through proves without a doubt that you're worthy of the glowing Times critique."

"This has been a good year. I've been lucky."

"Luck doesn't produce that level of Bach. I'd say you most certainly have a God-given talent, but there have been thirty hours a day of practice, too, I'll bet."

"Some days it seems like thirty hours."

"The article said you're a professor at State."

"An assistant professor."

"When you spoke to me in the courthouse snack bar, I would have sworn you were no older than a college student."

"You remember me," she responded with delight.

"When I walked in here, I recognized you immediately. You and another woman had to body-wrestle me and my friends to exit, if I recall correctly."

Claire decided a few words of explanation were necessary. "She was a fellow witness on an accident case."

"I figured as much. She hardly came across as your mom. Courtrooms have a way of bringing all sorts of folks together."

Like you and me, she was tempted to say.

"Anyway," he went on, "I said to myself, that beautiful young woman I'm about to talk with can't possibly be the pianist written up in the Times."

"If you were up here on the stage, you'd see beauty in short supply—gigantic calluses on my fingers; short, ugly, unpolished nails; wrinkles around my eyes from lack of sleep. . ."

"I saw no wrinkles in the snack bar, and that was at close range."

"That snack bar had a way of crowding out even the wrinkles," she said, laughing.

He laughed, too. A warm laugh. How easy he was to talk to. She felt as comfortable with him as she assumed his associates from the courthouse had been.

"I trust you've made some CDs," he said as his laughter subsided.

"I'm going to have a studio session on this tour. The CD will be released in October."

"Please write and tell me the release date, so I can buy one."

"Don't be silly. I wouldn't let you buy one. I'll send you one. Let me get my notepad." She scurried back to the piano for her pad and pencil so she could write down his address.

"It isn't necessary to feel obligated to me at all," he called over to her. "I'll be happy to go to a music store and—"

"Nonsense. I wouldn't hear of it." She scampered back to the edge of the stage and poised herself with a pad and pencil. "Where shall I send the CD?"

"You don't need to write anything down. Just mail it to Everettsville Prison with the same zip code as your subpoena. My title is deputy superintendent, security, but with or without my august title, I'll get it."

"You want me to send it to the prison?" she asked in a startled voice. "Not to a home address?"

"I live at the prison."

Her eyes widened in surprise. "You live there?"

"Yes, I have quarters on the grounds."

"Oh—well, er, I see. Okay, I'll send it out to you there. Fine. And if you care to attend tonight's concert—I mean, if you'd really like to come, I can leave a ticket at the box office."

"That would be great. I'd love to come. However, early in the evening, I'm tied up; I couldn't get here much before nine." He lowered his head in thought. "But perhaps I could catch your finale or an encore." He smiled back up at her. "I'd like to come to at least part of the program."

"Marvelous. Why don't I leave several tickets and you can bring your wife, or. . ."

"One ticket will be adequate. Ah. . ." He paused, his discerning eyes suggesting he saw through her. "I don't have a wife. And I'll be so rushed getting here, it'll be best I come alone without friend or, er, coworker. So one ticket will be fine. Thank you."

He wasn't married. She was inordinately pleased by this revelation—more pleased, she knew, than she had a right to be. Common sense told her this terrific human being wasn't waiting around for her to bring arpeggios into his life.

"I'm glad you're coming," she continued. "I better be asked for an encore."

"You will be," he said decisively. "Anyway, I've kept you from your practicing much too long. Why don't I just sit here for a short while and let you continue?"

"Actually, I had better put my fingers through their paces."

"Right." His voice took on an authoritative, Beethoven severity. "Back to vork, Fräulein."

She giggled as she rendered him a theatrical cringe.

Her mood hardly seemed serious enough for practice. But discipline won out. Once she stretched her fingers a few times, she was ready to tackle Liszt.

The music had an exciting new pizzazz. Startled, she realized that having Nick Van Vierssen in the audience was not only relaxing, but thrilling. To a degree, it was as it used to be when her father had listened to her. Nick's presence brought her to new heights of performance.

As she neared the Liszt finale, she recalled that she hadn't invited Nick to the reception planned for her at the Fontaine-bleau Club after the performance.

She played the final chord and glanced out at the seats. Radiant, she waited for a comment or applause.

But there was neither. She walked over to the edge of the stage. Nick had gone. She wondered why his sudden absence gave her such a sense of emptiness.

The audience that evening proved to be remarkably large—especially for a new artist. Claire was pleased with the enthusiastic response she received after the first half of her program.

During intermission, she made a special point to check her hair and makeup, a good bit more makeup than she usually wore. Emma, the waitress, would have applauded her effort. Because Nick would be there for the final numbers, she wanted him to be captivated, not only by her music, but also by her appearance.

How immature I'm being, she tried to tell herself. Men had come and gone in her life—dozens. Charming professors, such as Dr. Ernst Griesing, whom she'd worshiped in Salzburg. And fellow faculty members—Gerry Hawlin and Bill Lansing.

But never had she met a man like Nick, who devoted himself to something so startlingly dangerous and out of the spotlight as handling prisoners. What had prompted this sophisticated young man to closet himself in a penitentiary far away from the mainstream of civilization?

As she went out onto the stage for the second half of her program, she wasn't thinking about critics in the audience. She knew she'd be playing only for Nick.

Yet maybe that was why the Liszt went so well. Even by her own standards, it was a sensation. The audience went wild with applause.

Her jazz variations on a spiritual were successful also. But it was the Liszt with its sudden fortissimo explosions that took the house down. The audience called her back for three encores.

Well-wishers jammed the dressing room. Henri held her hand fawningly. Others embraced her. There were flowers everywhere. And people everywhere. Noise, confusion, festive chaos.

Even so, her eyes moved in wayward fashion, scanning the crowd for Nick.

As she hugged Elaine Adinolfi and later Bernadine Krueger, she peered over their shoulders to see if Nick had arrived.

Finally he was there—standing by the door, pillar-tall in a dark, conservative, well-tailored pin-striped suit that blended astonishingly well with his still undisciplined hair and loose tie. Some men had the capacity to carry off any combination of clothing and hair—Nick certainly was one of them.

In black suede gloves he held an enormous bouquet, a veritable garden of plum-colored roses.

"Excuse me, Bernadine," she sputtered, "there's a person I must greet. Pardon me a moment. . . ."

Weaving through the crowd, she noticed out of the corner of her eye that Henri was watching her intently.

"Nick," she called. It surprised her that she could call out his first name so readily after knowing him only one day. His smile indicated he was pleased she had.

"Claire, it was staggering," he responded with an exuberance that seemed mixed with an embarrassed shyness she hadn't expected.

"When did you arrive?" she asked.

"During the last movement of Haydn. Superlative. Then the Liszt—unreal. Were some of those stretches tenths?"

"Yes."

"I would have been bowled over by your performance tonight even if I'd never met you." He paused, his mouth twisting with an obvious lack of confidence, as if he were searching for the right words.

When he did speak, it was as if he had spent years in preparation for that speech, his lips barely enunciating the soft-spoken words. "The fact that I had met you, that I knew what a delightful person you are—well, that made the experience an event of major importance for me. But it wasn't only the music that was worthy of raves, Claire-Therese Rossiter. Your gown is elegant. You are supremely elegant, and then some."

He handed her the roses. "Careful now, don't let the thorns damage those splendid fingers."

"Thank you so much, Nick," she murmured, tearing her eyes away from his to look at the roses. "They're gorgeous. The edges are almost translucent—like amethysts. They must have been frightfully expensive."

"Mmmm, yes, somewhat. But how often do I have the opportunity to purchase flowers for a famous pianist? Women like you don't meander into a man's life every day of the week."

"Nick, I don't deserve any kind of gift after the anxiety I put you through about the briefcase."

"Hey, wait a minute. I'm glad you swiped the briefcase. It was a fortunate misadventure."

She brought the roses up to her face and all but kissed them. Then she remembered the reception. "Oh, Nick, we're all going to a party at the Fontaine-bleau Club in a few minutes. You'll join us, of course. . . ."

"I'm sorry, Claire. I'd like to but. . ."

How could he possibly turn down her invitation? He had no plans for the evening, or he wouldn't have attended the concert. Did he think he'd be a fish out of water?

Nonsense. He'd be a desirable asset to any gathering, no matter how mundane or upscale. Everyone would adore him. Even the discriminating Bernadine Krueger.

Henri would relish a few words with him about Everettsville.

"Oh, you must come with us," she insisted with a vehemence that surprised her. "Most of my friends have never encountered a man who does something as outlandish as you do for a living."

He laughed, but his laugh now had a hollow ring that made her uneasy. "I'm really sorry. Some other time." He stepped back out into the hallway. "I have to drive back to Everettsville tonight."

Staring at him in disbelief, Claire persisted, displaying uncustomary urgency. "An hour or two can't make a difference, Nick. Certainly you're not declining because we've just met one another and you don't know my friends. You'll be very welcome—you know that, don't you?"

"Actually, I do know that, Claire."

"You wouldn't be an outsider; I wouldn't let you be."

"I'm sure you wouldn't. In fact, I can't imagine any situation where you wouldn't try very hard to make me comfortable."

"Then, why not come? The Fontaine-bleau Club is north of here, almost on your way. Come along with us for an hour or so. Have something to eat before your drive back."

"Claire, I can't swing it tonight," he said unconvincingly, as he became engulfed by the hallway crowd.

She attempted to follow. "I'll see you again, won't I, Nick?"

"I'm sure," he said, his arm up, his gloved hand offering a little wave. "I'll be looking for your CD in the mail. Bye now, Claire."

To her chagrin, Elaine Adinolfi got between them, making it impossible for Claire to return his wave.

"The aspic will be melty if we don't get up to the Fontaine-bleau soon," said Elaine. "It's a gloppy mess whenever we're late—oh, my, aren't those the loveliest roses?"

"Yes, aren't they?" replied Claire, studying them with a twinge of sadness.

"Rare indeed," added Henri, approaching them both. "And who might that gentleman have been, Claire? I've never seen him before."

"He's—he's the prison warden."

"You don't mean it," said Henri with a questioning turn of his mouth. "Interesting."

"A prison warden?" asked Elaine. "What's a prison warden doing here?"

"Oh, he's an old friend of Claire's," said Henri with a wink. "Her Chopin's hot stuff in the 'big house.' "

Claire tried to dismiss the subject with a polite chuckle.

But it wasn't quite so easy to dismiss Nick from her mind. He had made a great effort to get to her performance. His glance had all but screamed out his desire to be with her.

She was sure something unpleasant prevented him from accepting her invitation to the reception—an event that turned out to be the last word in elegance.

Hordes of prominent people attended. All were pleased that the evening had been a financial, as well as an artistic, success. She glowed as she mingled with her many friends and wealthy sponsors.

From the roof garden, the city lights spread to the horizon. This was a day she had looked forward to for so long.

It would have been ideal if Nick had come. Why did his absence cause her such unhappiness? Wasn't it foolish to dwell on him at all, someone she'd known for only a couple of hours?

Nevertheless, despite being in the company of the city's most aristocratic people, she missed him. He was the most fascinating man she'd ever met.

Later, as she went to bed, the last things she gazed at were the plum-colored roses in the vase by the dresser. She refused to believe Nick hadn't been attracted to her—that he wasn't thinking of her, as well—even though he'd chosen not to attend the reception in her honor.

Chapter 4

With the exception of Philadelphia, the recitals in September went well. In Cincinnati, she experienced a singular event: perfection. She took bows to thunderous applause with a standing ovation from the jubilant crowd in the municipal recital hall.

How she wished Nick had been in Cincinnati.

To her dismay, however, she experienced emotional letdown in the days that followed Cincinnati. How could she ever put on a performance like that again? Claire was confronted by the worst kind of competition possible—herself! Herself, under ideal conditions.

In her final two programs, she played well—the audience was more than pleased. But when she returned to the university campus October 11, she felt exhausted in spirit as well as in body.

The following weekend, she didn't go to the piano at all. Instead, she sat for hours in her living room, studying the antics of her cat, a stray ragamuffin that she'd christened Galuppi after an insignificant Baroque composer, Baldassare Galuppi.

A student had cared for Galuppi during her concert tour, but the little creature had missed Claire. He was underfoot or sitting by her side constantly. One Sunday afternoon she found herself with Galuppi on her blue modular sofa, just staring at the grand piano.

As Claire scrutinized the room, she became aware of how spartan her home was. It looked more like a music store than a home—her impressive Steinway grand dominated the center of the living room, with electronic keyboards and a spinet against the walls on either side of the fireplace. "Nick would be horrified that a female could live in such a cell," she sputtered to Galuppi. "This place looks worse than a prison. Even the prisoner Zimblatz probably has pictures or something on the walls."

She had nothing.

Nick wouldn't be impressed with the place, she decided. But why should she care what Nick might think? She would never see him again. He'd made that obvious when he refused her invitation to the reception at the Fontaine-bleau Club.

Why should Nick Van Vierssen need her or her Fontaine-bleau Club? As if there weren't mobs of other events and people in his life, including, more than likely, an attractive, churchgoing girlfriend who was more "Christian" than Claire had the right to call herself.

What made her think a Nick-type guy would attach much significance to his buying roses and expressing appreciation for her music?

But she'd had enough experience with men to know they didn't buy exceptional bouquets like his merely as a backstage compliment. Nick Van Vierssen had thought through that purchase carefully, wanting his backstage flowers to be uniquely lovely.

So, she convinced herself, it was in the realm of possibility he might come to State sometime and look her up. If he did, he would see her miserable hovel.

The next day, she went into town and bought some things to brighten up her abode—two framed Picasso prints, a rather intricate macramé wall hanging, a hand-carved chess set with stand, and two handsome Peruvian pillows.

On her way home, she passed a flower shop, in the window of which she spied an outlandish plant with gigantic plum-colored flowers—not nearly so exquisite as the roses Nick had given her, but almost the exact same shade. He would think the plant gauche.

It was gauche. But it would look amusing and cheerful in her bay window. She absolutely had to have it.

And it did cheer the room up enormously. Galuppi liked playing games with its enormous leaves.

∞

On Friday Claire received a phone call from the recording company, saying her tapes and CDs were available. They were to be distributed through the company's sales outlets immediately.

"As we told you," said the shipping clerk, "we're sending twenty to those friends of yours on the list you provided. Do you have any deletions or additions to that list?"

"No, I don't think so."

"The packaging's terrific, with a folded poster of you, Ms. Rossiter. A dandy shot. You don't find many classical pianists who are so good-looking. I'm even going to give a listen to your CD, and I don't usually dig that kind of music."

She chuckled at the candor of the clerk.

In a matter of days, Nick would be getting his CD. Maybe he'd phone to tell her he'd received it. She hoped he would. What a delight it would be to hear his voice again.

She had no trouble convincing herself it would be appropriate to write him to tell him to expect the CD. He wouldn't find such a letter out of order—a nice, friendly, casual letter.

She decided writing it personally on attractive stationery would be better than punching it out on a computer. But once she took pen in hand, she found she had difficulty putting appropriate thoughts on paper. Stating her true feelings was out of the question. To do less was maddening.

She tore up several attempts before she finally wrote a note that set the proper tone:

Dear Nick,

The recording company informed me that my CD is being released. They're sending one to you. Despite the fact that Rachmaninoff wasn't on my original program, I managed to polish up a brief prelude and squeeze it in—yes, just for you.

My tour was satisfying, if exhausting, and I'm back at the university, teaching.

I hope I don't have to commit a heinous crime to see you again. If you're in the vicinity of State, drop by. I'll treat you to cheese fondue—the only thing, sorry to say, that I cook with finesse.

The roses lasted well over a week. Luckily, I was able to purchase an enormous Papa-Bear plant with blossoms of the same plum shade. I didn't want to exist in an amethyst-free environment after having the roses with me so long.

So, if you ever happen to be looking for my house on Regent Street, keep your eyes peeled for a plum-colored jungle in a bay window—that will be "me."

Most sincerely,
Claire

Nick's reply came a week later. It was in a plain, unadorned envelope with no special markings. Like the envelope, the letter was printed on a computer.

Dear Claire,

How sensational to receive your CD and charming letter. I've played the selections continuously. You're as good as Andre Watts!

I was thrilled with the Rachmaninoff that you included to please me. It's marvelous, the conclusion exceptionally brilliant. I'm in awe of your skill and accomplishment.

The promo shot of you that came with the CD couldn't be better. It vividly illustrates how magnificent you looked the night I met you backstage after your concert, many weeks ago now. An exciting event for both of us.

I wish you continued success in your endeavors. Be sure to set aside some time for your own compositions; you should be chugging away at more of those jazz variations.

Warmest regards,
Nicklaus Van Vierssen

And that was all. No suggestion they see one another again. No request that she write back. And even the hastily scrawled scratch-marks he passed off as a signature were his full, formal name, not just "Nick."

Why? The mood of the letter was completely informal. So upbeat. It didn't match the signature at all.

She considered phoning him. They could chat, and she could feel him out.

But she didn't have the courage to call. Her pride, her honest appreciation of her own worth, wouldn't allow her to beg attention from a man.

That evening she spent two hours playing Rachmaninoff, Galuppi resting under the grand and enjoying the vibrations while purring with satisfaction. She glanced over at the plum-colored plant.

"What did I say or do that turned him off?" she asked herself, recalling his obvious pleasure when he gave her the roses backstage.

But confounding her was the way he had melted into the crowd after refusing her invitation to the Fontaine-bleau Club—with a look on his face that seemed to say, "I want to go with you, but. . ."

Like a seacoast mist, the crowd had enveloped him, shrouding his reason for keeping his distance.

∞

It was Tuesday, and an astonished Claire had just read in the faculty newsletter—in an obscure article—that there was to be a seminar on prison reform in mid-November. It would be sponsored by the sociology department. Among the four guest speakers would be Nicklaus Van Vierssen, "the chief of security at Everettsville Prison."

She couldn't believe her eyes. Nick was scheduled to be on campus in a matter of weeks. He hadn't even mentioned this fact in his letter.

"He's going to surprise me," she mumbled halfheartedly. But the newsletter shook in her hand. Anger, frustration, or some indefinable emotion was taking hold of her.

"He doesn't have to make any big project out of this," she stormed aloud. "No major commitments whatsoever. He can be engaged, going into a monastery, or simply dead-set against marriage. But does that mean he can't call me to say hello? And tell me he's coming to this campus so I can make changes in my schedule to take in his presentation? Why wouldn't he want me there? What possible reason is there for this unexplainable behavior?"

Of one thing she was confident: He had no Freudian quirks. There were no psychotic aberrations, or he'd never have been hired to fill the job at Everettsville.

His demeanor was assertive, forthright, and masculine. When he looked into her eyes that night of the recital there had been desire for her. He had responded to her signals.

Then why? Why wouldn't he tell her he was coming to State?

Claire knew she could never keep herself away from that seminar. Curiosity, if nothing else, would force her to be present. She had to see Nick again, listen to his presentation, and find an opportunity to learn why he had behaved so strangely.

Her schedule showed a minor conflict on the Saturday morning of the seminar. Irene Dabrovsky was having a recording session for a Beethoven competition. The studio had already been reserved.

Irene had worked much too hard to be without Claire's guidance and assistance. There was no way to get out of that commitment.

But, Claire figured, the recording session would be over by eleven, which would give her time to hear part of the summations and see Nick during the lunch break.

According to the newsletter, the afternoon had been set up by the sociology department for student conferences with the guest lecturers. However, there would be a second open session at seven in the evening.

A wind ensemble concert was on her calendar for that evening. All music department personnel were expected to attend. But it wasn't obligatory. She could miss the concert without too much censure from her department chairman.

The Monday before the seminar, she phoned the sociology department to get more details.

"Jim Gleason here," said the exuberant voice of the young chairman of sociology.

"Hello, Jim, this is Claire Rossiter."

"Claire! No fooling? What a surprise. To what do I owe this charming interruption to an otherwise tedious day?"

"I noticed you're having a seminar Saturday—on prisons. Well. . .er, I wanted to get more information because, quite frankly, I'd like to attend."

"Is this for real? I think you must have the wrong idea. We're not going to be discussing your kind of keys. No B-flat or F-sharp minor or anything like that. Just large, unwieldy things that clank and unlock clammy dungeons and snake pits."

She smiled, imagining Jim's merry eyes as he said these words. He was a great guy, an asset to any gathering. With Peg, his wife, he was a conspicuous sight on campus, the couple forever followed by dozens of children—not just their own, surely, but whole neighborhoods'. The Gleasons, who attended her church, could be counted on to provide games and guitar-accompanied skits for Sunday school outings.

Frequently she saw Jim tossing baseballs to kids on the lawn behind Old Main or driving into a fast-food parking lot in his SUV. Always he had a big wave for her.

"I'm serious," she replied. "I want to attend because—um, you see, I have a friend who's a warden of a prison."

"Where? At the Bastille?"

"No, sorry. Anyway, I was wondering if any of the men on your panel have written articles or books that I might look over."

"They all have. You don't think I'd bring any second-rate Charlies up here to talk to my troops, not to the campus where we have such a celebrated pianist as Claire-Therese Rossiter on the faculty of music."

She grinned. "You're impossible."

"Impossible, am I? In my book, you're celebrated, Lady. Tell you what: I'll run off some articles that I think are of interest and send them over to you."

"That would be fine. Thanks so much."

"Claire, by the way, if you're coming, why don't you give us a little rendition on the eighty-eight of 'Jailhouse Rock' as a curtain-raiser?"

"What would you say if I said, 'Okay, I will'?"

He snickered. "Hey, I'll accept that offer. Peg and I are having an open house at our place after the evening session. You can play 'Jailhouse Rock' there for the edification of our guests. How's that?

"Seriously," he continued, "how 'bout coming to the party? A couple of those speakers are single. They wouldn't mind looking at the likes of you over the cheese dip. What do you say? Since you like prisons, you might enjoy the informal conversation. I'm sure it'll cover such scintillating topics as 'How I spread-eagled Pretty Boy Maloney'—that sort of thing. Shall I tell Peg you'll be there?"

She had to let Jim ramble on because she honestly didn't know how to reply to his invitation. Thoughts raced through her mind. Would Nick want her there? If she could only know if he wanted her there—or even wanted to see her at all—then she would be able to give Jim an answer.

"Claire, are you still with me?" asked Jim.

"Yes—yes, Jim, I'm still here. About Saturday night, I'm not sure. I can't say right now. There's a departmental concert that night. The wind ensemble—"

"The what?"

"The wind ensemble."

"Why, it's my patriotic duty to rescue you from an evening like that. You get yourself to my place. We'll be expecting you."

"Jim, I'm not sure."

"You be there—ya hear? I'll get those articles to you tomorrow morning."

⚭

The next day Claire set aside her whole lunch hour to read the articles Jim had sent over.

She had to devour Nick's first. Taken from a national magazine, it was written for the general public in a concise and readable fashion.

To her chagrin, a biography had been torn away. This exasperated her because she yearned to know more about Nick—his early life, where he'd gone to college, why he'd chosen a career in corrections, how he'd experienced such a close bond with God. A biographical sketch might even have given her a clue as to why he behaved so unpredictably with her.

But there was a picture of him. She studied it for a long time. His eyes seemed to be accusing her, telling her it was wrong to possess him, even a picture of him. Yet the picture was precious to her. At least a representation of Nick could remain in her life.

In the article, he wrote: "As deputy superintendent in charge of security, I'm responsible for keeping order and preventing escapes, riots, and personal injury. My background in engineering as well as corrections allows me to keep abreast of state-of-the-art technology to ascertain the most efficient and economical ways to confine men securely. The expenditures for more attractive and more open facilities must be carefully weighed to evaluate the degree to which they will improve the rehabilitation and safety of prisoners, and, I might add, the safety of the corrections staff who must keep them incarcerated."

The article went on to describe revolutionary new prisons in Chicago and Los Angeles. Apparently, an equally new complex was being constructed at Everettsville.

"We mustn't expect miracles from ferroconcrete, plastic, and electronics," the article concluded. "New prisons will not eliminate the need for competent, dedicated corrections personnel. But when cutting-edge technology can assist these officers to better care for the inmate population, then we heartily support it."

There was no attempt in the article to come off as a uniquely qualified specialist. Or a martyr. It was just a straightforward evaluation of the innovations of penitentiaries around the country, Everettsville in particular.

She looked again at his picture. For no good or sensible reason, she felt optimistic that her encounter with him on Saturday would not be unpleasant and would provide a few answers to the multitudes of questions she wanted to ask him.

In all of her instructions and practicing sessions Thursday and Friday, concentration was all but impossible. She spent both evenings on her blue modular sofa, petting Galuppi and thinking out a strategy for greeting Nick if he should phone.

But he didn't phone. Even on Friday night there was no phone call.

It infuriated her to know he must be somewhere in town—maybe at Jim's, right in town within walking distance—and he didn't phone.

She had dressed in a vibrant red "tres chic" jumpsuit, in case he stopped by. But by ten o'clock she knew he had no intention of doing that. She put her head down on the sofa, tears forming in her eyes, her spirit in an emotional chasm between anger and disappointment.

Chapter 5

Thankfully, on Saturday Irene Dabrovsky was so well prepared for the recording session that Claire was able to get away by ten-thirty.

She grabbed her coat and all but ran to the Student Union. The conference room was packed, every seat taken. A large crowd stood near the entrance as well.

Someone was already speaking. It sounded like Nick, but the amplification distorted the voice, so Claire couldn't be sure.

She craned her neck to see who it was. A man ahead of her moved sufficiently to the left so that she could view the dais.

Yes, it was Nick—standing behind the big, old maple lectern. The ceiling lights of the auditorium seemed to be panning his hair for gold, highlighting shades of lemon only to move on to bronze. He had made a trip to his barber-stylist, she noted, because the strands on his forehead were both shorter and less wayward than at the recital.

She was queasy at the sight of him, wanting to rush up there to make her presence known.

It was a question/answer period. A gangly student had arisen to challenge Nick on some point he'd made. "You're not too optimistic about the new prisons," the student retorted with condescension.

"Optimistic in what way?" Nick asked.

"Well, you seem to think prisoners won't be reformed no matter what kind of place they're in."

"When it comes to the type of inmates I work with at Everettsville, I'm not convinced a high-tech building will work miracles in the rate of recidivism. That doesn't mean we shouldn't avail ourselves of new materials and make a prison as pleasant as possible."

Nick leaned over the lectern and looked at the student. "The laminated polycarbonate windows, for example, are an improvement over bars. As I mentioned earlier, electronic impulses penetrate these windows, telling us instantly of an impending escape. We have closed-circuit surveillance in all corridors. So we're able to minimize the number of guards needed in direct-contact situations. Anytime I can relieve an officer of duty in a contact situation, I'm overjoyed, but—"

The student interrupted. "Most prisoners have had a rough life. A decent environment might help them turn themselves around."

Nick didn't answer right away. Yet he didn't appear ill-at-ease. He seemed to have no nervous mannerisms—no tapping on the lectern, no rubbing of his chin. The only animated part of his body remained his expressive face—now deadly serious, with no trace of a smile.

"Keep in mind that Everettsville houses violent men. I agree; most come from unhealthy environments. But not necessarily a ghetto."

"What are you getting at?" the student pursued with a sarcastic edge to his voice.

Nick went on. "Many inmates at Everettsville cruised in the jet set before their convictions. If we replaced steel bars with cocktail bars or a gym with parallel bars, most of our best efforts would be a comedown for them."

He paused for a brief grin. "A lot have been fat cats. They've had custom sports cars and stayed in the best resorts. In some cases they owned the resorts. Physical plants, alone, won't work miracles."

A young woman a few rows to Claire's left leaped to her feet, her hand pummeling the air to be recognized.

Nick acknowledged her. "Yes, Miss?"

"In old prisons human beings were caged animals. Most criminals may never have known love even if they owned posh resorts."

Nick's expression showed he liked the girl's spunk.

"We probably don't dispense enough loving-kindness. Basic sympathy often wears thin," he said, somewhat tongue in cheek, standing tall once again.

"Several years ago we built an outside visiting area—new picnic tables, baseball diamond, playground equipment for children, the works. We open this area several times a week. But every time—without exception—we have contraband brought into the prison. Policing the area's not easy."

Claire listened with rapt attention, recalling the comments of Nick's friends in the courthouse snack bar. They had thought Nick tough. He was talking tough now.

"Nearly every prisoner at Everettsville strategizes to get contraband into the prison—crack, heroin, liquor—items that threaten security and can be used for services rendered within the walls. We find heroin in heels of women's shoes, crack carried in balloons in the mouth, liquor in resoldered orange juice cans. Many inmates control empires of crime on the outside, people ready to do their bidding. What would occur, I ask you, if someone got explosives into the compound?"

Explosives!

Claire's eyes scrunched up in disbelief. Everettsville could conceivably be a war zone. Why did Nick choose to live there?

"Also, don't forget," he went on, "we can be sued if inmates are abused or become infected with AIDS."

A wide grin broke across Nick's face. "All's not lost, however, even at

Everettsville. I'll have positive things to say in my presentation tonight. It's time for your next speaker, though, my friend Arnold Saxby. He's an expert on juvenile facilities, where a swimming pool and chocolate shakes can make a difference."

As he concluded, Nick received enthusiastic applause from the students, many of whom stood up directly in front of Claire. She couldn't see the dais at all.

When the applause died down, she heard someone introducing Arnold Saxby. The students took their seats. Claire got a glimpse of the new speaker, also a young man, with an oversized beard and more laid-back clothing than Nick's. His talk began with lighthearted lampooning of Nick's reputed severity.

She couldn't see Nick, but she could hear his laughter. It was evident from Arnold Saxby's comments that he and Nick had been sparring partners before.

Claire found it almost impossible to concentrate on the Saxby presentation, though. All she could think of was Nick, sitting up there beyond view in the same room as she.

Twenty minutes later, when the session was over, the students mobbed the dais to speak to the participants. A photographer snapped pictures. There was the usual din of an assembly dispersing.

She spied Jim Gleason. He seemed to be studying her as he sauntered over, a questioning smirk on his mischievous round face.

"So, Claire, you have a friend who's a warden. That friend couldn't be one of my guest speakers, by any chance?"

Embarrassed, she sputtered, "Are you suggesting that—"

"That you showed particular interest in one of them? Yes. I was watching you as Nick Van Vierssen was speaking. You were on tiptoes the whole time."

She'd have to admit the obvious. "Okay, I'm acquainted with Nick. We met in Fulton Falls several months ago under wild circumstances. I walked off with his briefcase by accident."

"Did he plop you in solitary?"

"He was pretty decent about the whole thing. Anyway, it was the beginning of—well, a friendship of sorts. I had never met a corrections officer and considered Nick a rather remarkable person."

Jim's expression became more sober. "Nick's only a little short of awesome."

"Awesome, you say. That's a pretty heady evaluation."

"He's the big man in our lives, Peg's and mine. We're pleased to admit he's nearly one of the family."

"Really—does he come here often?"

"No, he has a difficult time breaking out of that loony bin he inhabits. We see him only a few times a year. Sometimes we ski together. He's a great skier—even does some jumping. But most of the time when we get together we can only fit in a few games of Ping-Pong."

She glanced toward the dais at Nick, who was still surrounded by the crowd.

It was fun studying him from afar—learning new insights into his character. She imagined him wearing ski goggles, swooshing down a slope at sixty miles an hour, then soaring through the air after taking off from a ski jump.

"Watching him play Ping-Pong is something else again," Jim went on. "He always draws a crowd. Surprisingly, crowds don't bother him."

She smiled and turned back to Jim, picking up the thread of the conversation.

"He draws a crowd, hmmm? For Ping-Pong? He doesn't look like the type who'd be playing Ping-Pong seriously. Skiing, yes; sailing, definitely. But Ping-Pong? No. So you're not in his league in the art of table tennis. Does Nick beat you all the time?"

Jim's eyes glinted accusingly, which disarmed her. "He doesn't beat me all the time. No," he said hesitatingly.

She was bewildered by Jim's obvious discomfort.

Finally, Jim finished his statement, "But Nick's some kind of fierce for a guy with no hands."

She laughed politely.

Jim actually glared at her, seething with what appeared to her to be a hard-to-control rage.

Flustered by his behavior, she stammered. "Forgive me, Jim; I'm not up on table tennis jargon." Why was he staring at her so menacingly? "A guy with no hands—I don't understand what that expression means," she continued, bewildered.

Jim's fury subsided. His eyelids appeared weighted by sadness. "Claire, I thought you said you knew Nick!" he said slowly. "When I said he had no hands, I meant just that—he has no hands. He's an amputee."

The blood rushed in a torrent from her head to her feet. She felt faint as she stared at Jim. He seemed to be fading. She groped for him and then grabbed his arm, trembling violently.

"No hands. That's not true. I've seen Nick numerous times—on three occasions. . . ."

"It is true, Claire. I can't imagine how you could have seen him on even one occasion and not known. He rarely—if ever—conceals the fact."

"Nooooo," she groaned, shaking her head in firm denial. She turned to the dais where Nick was smiling with the other men for pictures. "Not Nick. Not that man up there. I know it's not true. He gave me flowers after my concert—using his hands. At least one of them. He waved good-bye to me. I tell you, Jim, I saw his hands that night of my recital. He had on black gloves and. . ."

"Did you touch either of his hands, Claire? Did he touch you with one?" Jim asked, his demeanor now filled only with compassion.

She suppressed a scream with her fists. "Oh, God, oh, my dear God," she gulped out, making a genuine attempt at prayer, seeking strength from a long-neglected Lord. "You mean that hand that waved to me was. . . ?"

"An artificial hand—a prosthesis—probably operated by an electronic device. Nick has many different prostheses." Jim touched her shoulder. "Claire, I'm sorry I had to be the one to tell you. And in such a crude and unfeeling fashion."

"I've got to get out of here," she managed, through jaws that seemed to be locking. "I've—oh, Jim, please get me out of here. I can't let Nick see me. Help me out of here before I become ill and create a scene."

Putting his arm around her, Jim led her down the corridor to an unused office. Then he closed the door and assisted her into a chair.

"Let me get you some ice water, you poor kid."

She shook her head. Ice water wouldn't do the trick. "Just sit with me," she implored while she tried to let the reality sink in.

"For a few minutes, Claire, but I have to get back to those guys and escort them to lunch."

"To lunch?" she stammered. How under the sun could a man with no hands eat lunch? How could he play Ping-Pong? Or ski? Or handle all the myriad activities of life?

"Let me get this straight, Jim. Right now, Nick has artificial electronic fingers on both hands. They look like flesh and blood fingers, but. . ."

Jim pulled a chair from behind a desk and sat down next to her. "That's not exactly true, Claire. Today Nick has the ersatz hand on one arm, and on the other he's using metal Greifer pincers."

"Pincers?" Her eyes were wild. Nick was using metal pincers?

Jim gripped her hand tightly. "Claire, this is an awful blow to you, but I assure you Nick is not to be pitied. He's adjusted to this handicap. So has everyone who knows him. When our family thinks of Nick, we just associate the Greifers with him as you would a pair of eyeglasses with someone else."

"You don't honestly believe Nick thinks of those metal things the way you and I might think of a pair of glasses?"

"Actually, I do. What's more to the point, you must try to look at them that way."

"I could never do that!" She got up and went over to the window, leaned on the sill, and began to sob convulsively. She couldn't control the painful wrenching in her stomach.

"So," she moaned, "this is the awful secret. This is why Nick didn't tell me he was coming here. It had nothing to do with how he felt about me. He just didn't want me to know he was an, an. . ."

"Ordinarily he's very candid about his handicap, Claire. He's a man of enormous spiritual depth. In fact, he told me once he thinks his handicap has made it possible for him to have a ministry to prisoners. An encounter with some handicapped kid somewhere prompted him to pursue this mission he believes he has. He gives lots of talks in rehab centers—works with kids who've lost limbs.

His handicap is not something he usually hides."

"I tell you, Jim, he tried to hide it from me. Perhaps because I'm a pianist."

"Possibly. He may have thought you'd be uncomfortable playing in front of him."

"And he would have been correct." She turned to face Jim. "I will never play for him again. Oh, Jim, you don't know how grossly I behaved. I sent him a CD of my music. I remember even asking him if he played the piano. What must he have thought?"

"I'm sure he enjoyed your CD. He's a connoisseur of classical music. All kinds of music, for that matter."

She tried to sort through the words she'd spoken to Nick during their moments together. How many inappropriate things had she said to him in her ignorance? So delightful was his manner and repartee, so pleasant were the words they'd exchanged, she had trouble recalling statements she'd made that might have been painful for him.

She decided to force her mind onto another track. "How did it happen, Jim? Was he born. . . ?"

"He was a midshipman at Annapolis—a junior, I think."

"A midshipman; yes, he fits the part."

It was easy to picture him in his whites at the Naval Academy, a bright future lying ahead of him.

Jim continued. "He was on a training cruise. A defective weapon exploded; a petty officer and another midshipman were killed. There was a fire and—"

"Oh, no." She closed her eyes, the tears flowing, her head throbbing. How tragic. Such a young man. . .his life just beginning. "Those first few weeks and months must have been. . ."

"Horrendous. Yes."

She began to shake once again. Jim moved over to her and held her arms tightly.

"Did you know him then?" she stammered, as the shaking began to abate.

Jim released her slowly. "No, I met him in grad school. We had a sociology course together. Peg and I were going through a bad time, and I felt myself a martyr. Then I ran smack into this no-handed so-and-so who seemed to have things all straightened out for himself."

Jim walked away from her. He scratched the side of his face as he added, "I wanted to know what his secret was. When he told me it was simply because he'd become a Christian, I didn't believe him."

"It couldn't be that simple."

"He just said that he'd become convinced Jesus Christ planned his agenda with good things in mind. As the weeks became months and I studied this incredible guy—his fortitude, his optimism, his sense of humor and consideration for others, his indomitable faith in God—I knew I had to check into the Jesus angle further. Peg and I did, and hey, the Holy Spirit brought a million blessings into our lives. They've never stopped coming."

"I see." Her throat seemed constricted, her thoughts so clouded she wasn't able to give her full attention to Jim. She was in no mood, anyway, for a Sunday school lesson.

She sat down on the corner of the desk. "How could God have any kind of purpose in crippling a great guy like Nick?" She sputtered, "That kind of thinking is beyond me."

"It's not up to us to understand everything, Claire, though Nick could provide a more satisfactory answer to your question than I can."

She inhaled deeply and stared up at the ceiling. "You've got to get back to your guests, Jim," she went on, shaking her head. "Nick and the others must have their lunch."

"I hate to leave you like this."

"I'll manage. Go on, Jim."

"I'm not sure you're all right alone."

She rubbed a knuckle back and forth across her forehead. A hysterical laugh came forth. "How does anyone become 'all right' again after learning something like this about a person who, who. . ."

She waved her palm in a signal for him to leave. "Just go now, Jim. Honestly, I'll pull myself together and get home okay."

Jim went to the door. "Claire, why don't I tell Nick you're here and that you know everything. He'd put your mind at ease with a few good jokes. . . ."

Her eyes all but jumped out of their sockets. "Don't you dare tell him I'm here. Don't tell him anything about what happened to me. I simply couldn't face him now. I'm not sure I can ever see him, with his metal pincers for. . ."

She went over to Jim and grabbed his arm. "Promise me you won't tell him."

"Claire, tonight—you'll come to my home to the open house?"

She'd forgotten about the open house. "There's no way, Jim," she said, shaking her head. "I'm sorry."

He stared at her several minutes, his eyes filled with both sympathy and regret. "Nick needs someone so much in his life, if only to date on occasion. He deserves a break, Claire. Please come this evening."

"Impossible. I've just been torn in two by this disclosure, and you're asking me to rally and go to a party."

"How will you feel tomorrow, Claire, if you don't speak to Nick all weekend and he leaves never knowing you're aware of his handicap? Even if there's no big romance between you two, apparently a friendship has evolved. Are you going to sabotage that friendship because the guy has prostheses instead of hands? How will you be able to. . . ?"

"Stop it! Stop it right now, Jim," she stormed. "The scenario goes this way, remember? He didn't tell me he was coming here. He didn't want to see me."

"Come now, Claire. You know better than that. You've nailed the reason he didn't want to see you. That reason doesn't exist anymore."

Jim was correct. She hated to admit it, but she would indeed despise herself in the weeks to come if she didn't speak to Nick.

"Forgive me," she apologized, closing her eyes to Jim's scrutiny. "I shouldn't be angry with you. You're right. I should take the initiative and do something. But frankly, I don't know how I can get through an evening with him. I respect and admire him so much—he's so self-assured and dynamic. I mustn't weep in his presence."

"Why don't you see how things look this evening? As a professional performer, you've been in many tense situations before and come out fine. So this is a performance of a different kind. Give it a try." He opened the door. "I'll see you later, I hope. Listen to that crowd, Claire. There's still a big group down there. And Nick's having such a great time with those kids."

She bit her lip and nodded.

"He'll put you at ease, Claire. He's had this handicap so long that he's a veteran at making people comfortable with it. Try to come tonight." He winked at her as he closed the door behind him.

But after Jim left, she wept herself into exhaustion. Only when she was sure not a soul remained in the hallway did she sneak out and leave by a back exit.

Once home, she cried out to the walls, "Darling Nick, what frustration I've caused you, pounding away at tenths in Liszt, adding to your discomfort."

Pictures emerged again in her mind—of Nick as a midshipman, trim in those whites. So physically perfect, with dozens of girlfriends, surely. Then to have such an accident—the gross mutilation, the helplessness, the months of rehab. She shuddered, thinking of the embarrassment of having to wear metal contraptions and having people stare. It was so unspeakably unfair, so grim.

There was a maternal impulse that urged her to run to him wherever he was and to hug him away from curious hordes.

Yet at the same time, deep down in the recesses of her mind was another little voice that told her to flee from any further encounter with him while there was still a chance.

Most considerately, he hadn't contacted her so she would not have to experience his disfigurement. She must have been in his thoughts when he arrived on campus.

If she didn't attend the party—if she left well enough alone—she probably would never see him again, a detestable outcome based solely on her cowardice.

She realized she had to force herself to go to Jim's open house. However, she'd have to convince Nick she'd known all along that he was an amputee; he must never learn about the afternoon scene.

But how could she fool a man who analyzed facial expressions with such skill?

She'd have to be more successful than Zimblatz had been. It would be the performance of her lifetime, and she'd deserve more than a Schumann Medal if she pulled it off.

Chapter 6

As she dressed for the evening programs, Claire's thoughts centered on the complications Nick must have, doing even the most basic things. How could he knot a tie? Buckle a belt? Put on socks? How, with such an appalling handicap, did he manage those things?

And a million others.

She drew her hair up into the chignon and put on simple gold earrings. It was, she decided, imperative that she stuff her purse with tissue—in case she fell apart and had to rush to an adjacent room to weep, all over again. She tossed on her charcoal coat and, with hesitancy, pulled fur-lined gloves from her pockets. It was chilly, and she needed them.

Nick would never need gloves.

As at the earlier session, there was a large crowd in the auditorium. She sat on the left side of the hall—in the middle of a row, to be as inconspicuous as possible.

Arnold Saxby was the first onto the dais behind Jim Gleason. Nick held the door for the two older speakers with what would have to be the plastic hand prosthesis. As they went past, he apparently said something amusing, because they both began to laugh uproariously.

Then as the three approached, she saw it—attached to his right arm was the prosthesis with the mechanical pincers. What had Jim called it? A Griffin? No, a Greifer. With it, Nick was holding his familiar briefcase.

It obviously was a routine thing for him. He really was an amputee. And shock above all shocks, he did accept that fact. Yet to her, this was all too new to accept. It was like a masquerade, as if someone were attempting that old pirate trick—any moment he'd drop the pincers to the floor and the normal hand would come out of his sleeve. Ta da! He would then wave to the crowd, trick completed.

But no such magic was forthcoming.

The dais was arranged informally with five chairs around a conference table. Microphones had been set up for each speaker.

Nick sat on the end closest to her, but faced the right side of the hall.

In stupefied horror, she studied him. With the prostheses he opened the briefcase and painstakingly extracted his papers. For sure, he deserved more applause than she did performing Bach fugues. The hours of practice that must have gone into such an achievement staggered her mind. If she'd thought of him as remarkable in the Fulton Falls courthouse, her admiration had increased a hundredfold.

When finally he rested his arm on the table, the prostheses were hidden from view, and Claire was able to give her attention to the rest of his person. He wore a preppie Harris tweed jacket, his conventional loose-collared shirt, and a rust-colored tie. His trousers were a dark reddish-brown. With sadness she noted that his well-polished brown loafers had no laces to tie.

As before, his blond hair couldn't escape the ceiling lights of the auditorium.

Jim made the introduction, announcing the evening's topic: the future of prisons in the United States. As he opened the floor to the first man, Samuel Schwartz, his eyes picked her up in the audience. A smile came to his lips. She returned a halfhearted nod.

Samuel Schwartz and the second speaker discussed, with equal pessimism, the lack of success they'd had with innovative policies. By contrast, Arnold Saxby, who followed, lauded the efforts made at his detention center.

Nick was last. He glanced out over the audience for several moments before he spoke. Then he began with a startling statement: "Well, how does it feel to be in prison?"

The crowd snickered. A few students made disparaging remarks about the university.

"All of you should know what it's like," Nick continued, "because you're all incarcerated, after all—in prisons of your own creation, or society's."

Some of the students leaned forward in their chairs.

"Mature people know that for a society to function smoothly, individuals must accept certain forms of enslavement, putting handcuffs and fetters on their behavior. Whenever we make a commitment to somebody or something—husband or wife, children, a job, an education, faith in God—we relinquish freedom to do and say whatever we'd like, whenever we'd like. Each one of you has had to do that most of your life, or you wouldn't be in this university or in this room. I wouldn't, either."

He glanced toward Claire's side of the room, so she slunk down in her chair. His eyes missed her.

"We're childish," he continued, "to the degree that we're unable to manacle our hostilities and demands, or to the extent we deprive others of their rights and privileges.

"Once in awhile, however, even the most mature adult acts in a childish manner. I do myself, often. Sometimes, with my handicap, I try the impossible, and it boomerangs."

He was actually talking about his handicap, Claire realized. How could he call attention to something so horrible?

He now rested both prostheses on the table, in plain sight of the audience.

"Once, a few years ago," he began again, "when I first began wearing artificial hand machinery, I played soccer with some neighborhood kids.

"The prostheses I had at that time were sharp. I accidentally fell over one of the youngsters, ripping open the child's leg. He had to have twenty stitches in that leg. I had no business doing such a stupid thing. My actions resulted in unnecessary misery for another individual. It seemed important to me to show those kids I could play soccer—and that I wasn't totally helpless.

"But I shouldn't have done it. Because I was going through an elementary phase of rehabilitation, I wasn't aware of the damage that could be inflicted by my mechanical fingers. I haven't given up soccer entirely, but when I do play, I don't have the freedom to go all out for the win."

A girl in front of Claire whispered to a companion, "That's a phony hand on his left arm, too. Doesn't that give you chills?"

Claire pressed her fingers hard against her eyes, the girl's words reverberating through her brain. She swallowed several times before looking back up at Nick.

"Most of the inmates in my prison are infantile, with little self-control and little recognition of someone else's needs or emotions."

He proceeded to discuss, in the nomenclature of sociology, specific case histories from his experience, of egocentric immaturity that resulted in violence.

"Regrettably, as long as inflamed or disturbed citizens commit mayhem in our communities, penitentiaries will be needed. But I firmly believe that, in the future, we won't need so many of them as we have now."

None of the other men had expressed this opinion. Claire was surprised Nick did. He went on to describe the progress made in counseling, reading instruction, job training, prisoner rehab, and limited access to guns.

"Also, in the next decade," he announced, "medicine will win victories in treating brain injuries, birth defects, malnutrition, alcoholism, and drug addiction."

His tone became pensive. "Modern technology has allowed us to place human beings into compounds of isolation, with supervision now possible from safe distances—well-insulated cubicles down the hall, or even down the hill.

"Meals can be dispensed through machines similar to the ones here on campus in dorms. Some of this food may be better fare than what you have dished out in the university dining hall."

He grinned at the groans this remark generated. But the students quieted down quickly as he continued. "Machines are cost-effective. But isn't it pathetic when an inmate survives in a moonscape world alone, or one shared only by individuals just as unprincipled as himself?"

He paused, his head bent down. When he raised it, his eyes seemed to peer over and out beyond the students. Deep in thought, he proceeded. "I hope the inmate of the future will come to appreciate the few decent individuals who bother to enter his world—be they counselors, chaplains, teachers, medics, or even dour-faced superintendents of security like myself. If he doesn't, insanity, more than likely, will be the alternative."

Nick's voice echoed through a quiet room where no coughs or scraping of chairs could be heard at all.

"No, physical plants will not do the job of caring for prisoners adequately," he said. "People, with God's guidance, always must be in the forefront of appropriate incarceration policy. Corrections personnel must never allow themselves to be so hardened by the very real violence of the surroundings that they forget that some noble men and women have been unjustly imprisoned over the centuries—Gandhi, Joan of Arc, Martin Luther King, Jesus Christ, to name a few. Nobility of character can and often does exist in bondage and chains—even today.

"In summation, as we go about the very necessary task of shutting men and women away from society, we must be careful we don't shut them off from the pathway that leads to their own soul and the destiny possible for that soul."

He ended his statement in a subdued tone. For a second or two there was no response.

Then wild applause erupted.

Hands went up all over the room—healthy, strong young hands, Claire noted. What did Nick think when he saw so many hands raised up before him? His face betrayed no distress.

Afterward, the students thronged the dais. Nick was explaining something to a muscular African-American student as Claire headed into the crowded aisle.

It would be better, she reasoned, if she just spoke to Nick before he saw her, because surely he wouldn't be comfortable knowing she'd held back, gawking at close range. It'd be better to rush right up. That's what she would do if she'd known all along he was an amputee.

She raised her chin, bit her lip just once, and then found some deep reservoir of strength that propelled her forward. She went up the steps onto the dais.

In that instant, Nick glanced her way. She waved, then hurried right up to him. "Your presentation was superb. Where do we line up to vote for you for president, Mr. Van Vierssen?"

He walked around the table and came forward eagerly, his eyes warmly receptive. "Claire, what a nice surprise," he said. "Do you mean to tell me you sat through this whole spiel?"

"Every minute of it." She tried to concentrate on his eyes and avoid looking at the Greifer prosthesis. "And I'm more impressed with you, Sir, than you ever could have been with me."

She was relieved he didn't offer the Greifer to shake, or touch her in any way with either prosthesis.

"Impossible."

"Not really, because you'd been to concerts, whereas I had never explored the

275

complexities of prison wardening. To learn there are men like you on this planet, delivering speeches with such expertise and élan—well, that impresses me no end."

"Thank you, Maestra," he said with a grin.

She hesitated before blurting out the obvious. "Why didn't you tell me you were coming up to State? Or shouldn't I ask?"

He tilted his head in a paternal manner. "You shouldn't ask."

"I spent two rather miserable evenings trying to come up with a reason why you hadn't mentioned the conference in your letter. I couldn't remember doing or saying anything obnoxious to you. Was there something I did or said or wrote that—"

"No, no. Don't consider such things."

"It's put me in an awkward spot, Nick, because when Jim Gleason learned I wanted to attend the seminar, he invited me to his open house, and frankly, I didn't know how to reply."

"Claire," he replied slowly, his eyes narrowing in thought, "I nearly phoned you. One night soon after I received your CD, I lifted the phone to do just that. I desperately wanted to talk to you."

He spoke hesitantly, as if he wasn't sure how to proceed. He folded his arms across his chest in a way that caused a barely discernible clink—something other than flesh against flesh.

Then, slowly, he moved those arms behind his back, out of sight.

"After a great deal of soul-searching," he continued, "I decided I better not call. I figured that, as a pianist, if you learned I was an amputee, it would make you uneasy in my presence—much more so than it would most people. That's the reason I didn't phone or drop by your house when I arrived on campus this trip. It's that simple. You mustn't think you said or did anything thoughtless or rude. Quite the contrary. But you fooled me; I worked overtime trying to conceal my handicap from you. I was sure you didn't know about it."

She paused a second. His candor and deep eye contact disarmed her. Nevertheless, she felt satisfied with her performance. She had succeeded in deceiving him up to that point. "Well, I do—I do know. I've known a long time."

"You knew in the city? The night of the recital?"

"I suspected from the first," she offered. "Anyway, didn't you think that I'd learn about it when you came here for the conference?"

"I didn't know what I was going to do if you saw me here. On this enormous campus, I figured there was a good chance you wouldn't be aware of the events scheduled by the sociology department. But I obviously was off base on all counts. Things have turned out perfectly."

His cerulean eyes were penetrating hers like X-rays. Knowing of his strong Christian convictions, she felt particularly sinful, resorting to falsehood. But she could see, by the relaxed lines of his mouth, that he was happy it had turned out the way it did.

"So you knew about my disability all along," he said, "and it doesn't matter that much. Is that right?"

"Of course it matters," she replied cautiously, with a bit more confidence. "I guess it's my opinion that any guy who can control stockades full of rapacious prisoners has everything together, ah, hands or no hands."

"Not quite everything together, Claire, but—"

"Hey, you two," called Jim, coming toward them. "We're all going on over to the house now. Are you ready to join us?"

"Yes, I think we are," said Nick, accepting the invitation for her. "I'm so pleased to see Claire, Jim. Did she tell you how we met?"

"Yes—unreal! What I want to know, Nick, old buddy, is how you could have encountered such a magnificent female and avoided locking her up in a tower for safekeeping."

"That entered my mind," replied Nick, his chin crinkling in an amused manner.

"I've got to run on ahead to check on the others," Jim added as he backed toward a side door. "Peg's going to be furious that we're late."

He hurried out the door to the coatroom.

The students had gone. Claire and Nick were alone.

With the metal prosthesis, Nick picked up the briefcase in a casual way. But it took heroic self-control on Claire's part to conceal her revulsion. For a second, she steadied herself against the table.

As they headed for the coatroom, she racked her brain to come up with nonsense chatter to relax herself.

"Careful, Nick. I could end up stealing that briefcase again if you don't watch out. This time I might blackmail you."

"And what nefarious terms would you demand for its safe return?" he asked, his eyes glinting in fabricated terror.

He put his "hand" prosthesis against her back as they walked through the open doorway into the coatroom. It was comforting to have his arm there—more comfortable than she'd thought it would be with the artificial hand.

"Oh, I might blackmail you by demanding a ski trip to Vail."

"So, Jim told you I ski," he responded, putting down his briefcase and taking his coat, a well-tailored camel's hair, from a coatrack. She couldn't decide whether to help him or not. In those few moments of indecision, he had thrown the coat around himself and was getting into it, awkwardly for sure, but with his own inimitable savoir-faire.

"Jim said you're a sensational skier," she commented, slipping into her own coat.

"Hardly sensational," he said as they went out the side door of the building. "Suffice it to say, I manage to get to the bottom of the mountain most of the time."

277

They descended the steps, his artificial hand now resting gently on her shoulder. It was a brisk evening, an apple-pie moon emerging over the trees. She was ecstatic to be sharing it with this marvelous man, whose friendship she now valued more than a Telemann fugue or a Beethoven sonata. And for a musician, that was dangerously close to adoration.

"Have you ever skied?" he asked.

"Everyone who's ever lived in Switzerland skis—at least a little bit."

"And you lived in Switzerland?"

"Yes, when I was a youngster. Eventually my music took precedence over skiing, and just about everything else."

"It would have to. Downhill skiing would be too hazardous for you now. If you broke your wrist, you wouldn't be able to honor your contracts. And that would be little short of a disaster."

It was beyond comprehension that they could be talking about broken wrists and piano recitals with such nonchalance. She managed to continue with an almost incoherent, "Yes, I'm sure it would."

"You'll have to stick to watching characters like me out there on the runs. It's no catastrophe if I break my shoulder or arm. I can still function with a cast— at least for a few weeks. I've done such a job on this old body that a broken arm isn't going to be the end of the world. But for you, it'd be a different story entirely. Why don't you blackmail me with something else?"

"All right, but I'd still love to see you outfitted for the slopes, goggles and all. Jim says you even do some jumping."

He laughed. "If the visibility's about five hundred miles. Jim's house is down this street to the right."

"I have a vague idea where it is. I've seen him pulling in and out of the driveway. He always waves."

"I'm sure he does. So, how's the semester going for you? Will your recitals cut into your teaching heavily?"

"No. The only remaining performances are at the beginning of the second semester in January. I'm playing the Schumann A-Minor in Nashville and New Orleans."

"That means a lot of work."

"A busy Christmas vacation, yes."

"No time for caroling. . .or sitting on Santa's knees," he stated bewitchingly.

She laughed. "Actually, I'll be relieved when this season's over. It's been too demanding, though there were highlights. Cincinnati was close to perfection. I was able to perform everything just the way I had always dreamed I could. . . . Oh, I shouldn't go on like this. It's so silly to. . ."

"No, no, I want to hear all about it. But I warn you, you're never going to convince me that anything you played in Cincinnati could top the selections

I heard that night in New York.

"Everything was better—better, in fact, than on your CD."

As the wind picked up, he pressed his prosthesis against her shoulder and brought her closer. Once again, she was struck by the fact that she'd been rambling on about her keyboard accomplishments, and for several moments she'd all but forgotten that Nick was without hands.

Yet even being aware of this, she found herself as eager to share her experiences and thoughts with him as she'd been that afternoon at the Lincoln Center. *Why is that?* she wondered.

Immediately she answered her own question—Nick came back with caring, appropriate statements that proved his interest. Somehow, she felt compelled to confide her anxieties about her performances following Cincinnati. "The devastating thing is that I'll never have a recital like Cincinnati again."

"Nonsense, of course you will."

"I really doubt it. A 'Cincinnati' comes along very seldom in a career—sometimes only once. Sometimes never. And, Nick, the frustrations of pitting oneself against that one great performance are maddening. The practice needed to reach that pinnacle a second time looms oppressively on the horizon."

He patted her shoulder. "Don't be discouraged by things like that, Claire. Your performance in any city will be a winner. I can see, though, that we both could write books about frustrations, couldn't we?"

He coughed before continuing. "How many hundreds of 'one more times' have we faced, conquering some infinitesimal detail? But because we've been willing to go the distance that hundredth time, we've had successes in ways we never would have thought possible. That's a blessing. It toughens us for that next 'one more time' we may well face tomorrow—if things run true to form."

"Or the 'one more time' we might face tonight?" she found herself asking.

"Possibly even the 'one more time' we could face tonight, yes," he added in a tone of gentle reassurance.

Chapter 7

They crossed the street in front of Jim's house. The door was open, and music, blending with laughter and conversation, floated out invitingly into the night air. Claire could see Jim's silhouette in the doorway.

Jim called out to them. "Get in here, you two. I was ready to send out the gendarmes."

He took Nick's briefcase, helped them remove their coats, and led them to the living room, where a group of about thirty people were enjoying each other's company.

Peg approached with a tray of stuffed popovers.

"How did it go, Nick?" she asked in the concerned voice of someone who knew him like family.

"Fair enough, Peg," he answered. "We didn't have to use bullhorns to get attention as we do sometimes in the prison yard, so that was encouraging. Peg, you know Claire, I'm sure."

"Of course. I'm so glad you could come, Claire. Would either of you care for an hors d'oeuvre? My pièce de résistance—popovers with shrimp."

Claire took one. "They look scrumptious."

"Nick?" Peg offered.

"I'd rather not, thanks," he said, almost as an aside, denoting an understanding between them.

"Oh, Nick, I forgot," said Peg in painful embarrassment. "These kinds of things are so—oh, I'm so sorry. Forgive me. There's roast beef, ham, plates and forks, and a lot of other things on the table. . . ."

"I don't need anything right now, Peg," he said, waving his simulated hand with an easy air. "And don't think any more about it, please. I'll get some ham later."

Claire felt a shudder surge through her. She tried frantically to hide it. The popovers, stuffed to overflowing with shrimp, were undoubtedly too gooey for Nick to manage well.

For a few moments, amid the pleasant din of the crowd, she'd forgotten again about Nick's horrible disability. But he could never forget. For him it was always there.

In her distress, she could barely chew the popover. Fortunately, Peg was still talking to Nick. They didn't notice her discomfort.

"How 'bout a glass of punch?" asked Peg.

"Wonderful," Nick replied enthusiastically. "Claire, would you care for punch?"

She nodded and was able to add a mumbled "Yes, thanks," as she swallowed the last of the popover.

Peg directed them to a table in the library.

It was a convivial crowd, a large number of the guests young marrieds who traveled the byways of the campus with a retinue of children and bouncy dogs. They were eager to talk with Nick and appeared overjoyed to have Claire in their midst.

Here and there were maverick personalities like Tina Gutierrez from the Spanish department, who chattered up a storm with the folks around her. Excited about meeting Nick, Tina introduced him to her boyfriend, a state policeman who had escorted prisoners to Everettsville several times.

Guest lecturers Schwartz and Fillmore had brought their wives along on the trip. Mrs. Schwartz, a smartly dressed woman, outgoing and assertive, seemed particularly excited to learn Claire was from Switzerland.

"Don't you just love the Meinholtz Emporium in Berne?" she asked.

Claire had to confess that she wasn't familiar with the Meinholtz Emporium.

Arnold Saxby had been to Claire's recital in September. He admitted he was flabbergasted to see her at the party, incredulous that she had "condescended" to participate in such a "mundane" gathering.

He managed to get her alone in a corner of the dining room.

"How could a sophisticated woman like you be interested in prisons?" he asked.

"I wasn't—until I met Nick."

"Oh, yes, of course. . .you and Nick are friends."

"Actually, we've known each other only a short time."

"Doesn't it give Nick some qualms to be friends with a girl who has such accomplished—"

"Fingers?"

"Yeah."

How could she get through this evening, Claire wondered, if she had to respond to questions as penetrating as this one? What did she really know about Nick and his qualms? Or about Nick in any regard?

Frantic words tumbled from her mouth. She hoped they made sense. "If he had qualms about me, he'd also have qualms about friends who are baseball players or surgeons. If he hadn't conquered his, er, qualms—he wouldn't have any friends at all."

Arnold raised his eyebrows and nodded. "I'm sure you're right. And he has legions of friends. Was he at your recital in New York, too?"

"Yes."

"Your performance was incredible. Pardon me for asking, but you and Nick—surely, you and Nick aren't. . .serious, are you?"

Another powerhouse question.

Serious? What kind of relationship did she have with Nick? She couldn't answer that question for herself, let alone for Arnold Saxby.

Might she become serious with Nick someday? Her gaze sped across the dining room to the library, where he was standing so tall and self-possessed in a group with Tina Gutierrez; he was still very much the Annapolis midshipman.

"Well, what about it?" Arnold continued, pressing a bit too hard.

She paused, trying to pry an intelligent response from her brain. "Nick and I do have mutual interests, but—"

"It'd be tough to plan much of a future with him," Arnold commented. "I mean. . .his handicap's a big thing to overcome."

"It would be, yes."

"In addition, he's got this hang-up about a God-mandated commitment to inmates. Nothing more seems to be on his agenda. Nick's a great guy; no question about that. I wish him the best. But, frankly, if I were a woman, I'd keep my distance."

She nodded, knowing that keeping her distance from Nick was exactly what she had wanted to do earlier that day.

"Anyway," he went on, "if things don't work out with you and Nick, and you're still turned on by jailers, why don't you look me up?" He handed her his card.

With a half-smile, she thanked him and put his card in her skirt pocket.

"I never thought I'd actually envy Nick Van Vierssen," said Arnold, "but right now I sure do. You are a desirable woman."

She touched his arm kindly. Then, realizing she now needed the safe harbor of Nick's presence, she moved toward the library. In addition, a jealousy had crept in as she watched Nick with Tina and the others. She was missing everything he was saying. And because her own time with him was so valuable, she resented others monopolizing him.

Even from the dining room she could hear Tina gushing about something. "That's amazing," she was spouting in her high-spirited voice.

As she moved closer, Claire noticed, to her horror, that Nick was removing his jacket so Tina could examine the artificial hand attached to his left arm. Apparently not embarrassed, he pushed up his sleeve to show her where some sort of battery was located.

Claire pressed a knuckle hard against her teeth. Tina infuriated her—such a nosy and insensitive woman, pestering Nick about the workings of that grotesque device. How could Tina touch it without recoiling?

Appalled with herself, Claire realized that she, too, was curious. She wanted to know how Nick's prostheses worked, but it jarred her to observe Tina's ease and open curiosity with Nick's accouterments.

Claire studied the demonstration from a few feet away, unobserved by Nick. "There are small myoelectric signals in the muscles of my arms, Tina," Nick was explaining, "that control the opening and closing of my apparatus. They're pretty weak, for sure. But powered by a small battery here on my arm, this mechanism can pick up these signals on the skin surface and amplify them several hundred thousand times, causing a type of muscle interaction that allows the artificial hand or the prehensile Greifer to move like a normal hand. Well, almost. . ."

He lowered his head a bit before adding, "but not quite."

"That's phenomenal," Tina exclaimed as the rest of the group watched intently.

"The simulated hand looks a lot better, right? But I don't have the dexterity with that which I have with the Greifer." He was now demonstrating the prosthesis on his right hand. "Here you can see the movements more clearly."

Tina was handling the prosthesis. "What a remarkable invention," she commented.

"It's done wonders for me," he continued. "But often I have to revert to a hooklike unit at the prison, where appearance is less important than functionality. I seldom use the simulated hand while on duty."

Claire felt an arm around her waist. She turned and looked into Jim's comforting countenance.

"Do you think you should be watching this?" he whispered.

She began to shake, but his arm held her steady. "I think it's something I have to do, Jim," she replied, her mouth barely shaping the words. "I'll have to try to be more like Tina if I'm to. . ."

"Give me a break. The day you behave like Tina, I'll personally give you a sound thrashing," he said playfully.

"She's not upset at all. Oh, Jim, how can Nick demonstrate those awful things?"

"He knows people have a natural curiosity, so he doesn't mind demonstrating his equipment. After a time, these demonstrations won't upset you, either."

She shook her head doubtfully.

"Be patient with yourself. This has been a rough day. You sure came through tonight, Claire—Nick's happy you're here. From the look of things, I think more than a briefcase passed between the two of you."

They moved nearer Nick. With the help of the state trooper, he had put on his jacket and was taking a slow sip of punch, the demonstration over.

Tina was talking to someone else as Nick polished off the rest of his punch. But she abruptly turned back to him. "Man," she blurted, "how long did it take you to learn how to do that, Nick—to drink from a punch cup?"

He shrugged his shoulder and answered her in the same patient fashion. "I can't say, Tina. You learn a lot of things simultaneously. I suppose it took a half hour, after months of exercise and practicing with basics. I can't say for sure."

As he spoke, he turned his head a little to the side and noticed Claire. "Oh, there you are, Claire. I wondered what had happened to you."

With soothing eye contact, Claire conveyed a compassion she thought Nick needed after the performance he'd just given.

"Tina," he continued, "like myself, Claire's an old hand at practice that achieves what seems to be the impossible. I bet once in awhile she's had to practice three or four weeks on two pages of a Bach fugue. You might say Claire and I represent the poles of manual dexterity. For her it's an accomplishment to play the presto section in that fugue. For me, it's picking up a punch cup. Most of the rest of you fall somewhere between the two of us."

The seconds that followed these words were awkward—nobody appeared to know how to reply to such a profound remark. Even Tina appeared at a loss for words. But Nick had spoken with no perceivable bitterness.

Claire found herself grabbing his right arm, clasping it tightly for strength, feeling the taut biceps below his shoulder. She knew she had to speak—to rescue him and the others from the stalled conversation.

"Nick may fall short of my mark in manual dexterity," she managed, "but he can outski most of us. On those slopes his legs more than make up for his manual deficiency."

"No fooling," said Craig, an instructor from the physics department. "Now you're talking my language."

"He's even done some jumping," Claire added.

"Wait a minute. Hold everything." Shaking his head, Nick grinned at Craig. "With my disability, I can only tackle the most innocent trails. No slalom. But yes, I do jump, though I probably shouldn't. It's kamikaze-time when I take off."

"I tried jumping once, Van Vierssen," said Craig. "It scared the pants off me."

Nick laughed. "It's supposed to. But after you get the hang of it, it's not that hard. Downhill can be just as dangerous."

Craig wanted to know where Nick skied. They compared notes, then decided they'd have to plan a trip together. "Be sure to wear suspenders for your pants," Nick joked.

The party didn't wind down till nearly one o'clock. After the others had left, Nick volunteered his and Claire's services to help the Gleasons pick up. Then he offered to escort Claire home.

Jim walked out to the porch with them. He patted Claire on the shoulder. "It was great you could make it, Claire. Stop in again—and soon."

"I will, Jim, and. . .thanks—thanks for inviting me." She spoke the words slowly, hoping Jim would read into them the deep appreciation she had for his encouragement throughout the traumatic hours of the most soul-searching day of her life.

Though the air was a bit colder than it had been when they'd come from the Student Union, it was still comfortable enough for Claire to take pleasure in the short stroll.

"It may be a bit too windy to cross the parade grounds," she said. "Do you mind if we go down Chestnut Street and around?"

"That's fine," Nick replied. "I marched across enough windy parade grounds and football fields when I was at the Naval Academy to last me a lifetime."

She wasn't prepared for this reference to his naval career because of the reason it had been cut short. A garbled reply was all she could come up with as they started up the sidewalk.

"Oh, I guess you didn't know I went to Annapolis?"

"Ah—er, yes, Jim told me."

"I thought he probably had."

She hoped he wouldn't pursue this subject. She had prepared no script for discussing the trauma he'd experienced during this phase of his life.

But he went on with no hesitation whatsoever. "It was the third summer I was a midshipman that I sustained the injury that took my hands. So parade grounds don't conjure up many happy memories, Claire."

"I can see why," she gulped, deciding to change the subject immediately. "Nice party, wasn't it?"

"Yes. I'm glad you were there. Peg and Jim are terrific people, and so are their kids. Do you know their children?"

"No, I really don't."

"They were farmed out tonight, with neighbors. But you'll have to meet them. Todd's the best swimmer—he's won a lot of ribbons."

"They have three children, right?"

"Yes, but Jim told me tonight that Peg's expecting another."

"That'll be a houseful. How will they ever manage?"

Nick shook his head. "I haven't the foggiest idea. They both come from large families, though. I guess that prepares a couple for an onslaught of little ones. I'm an only child myself. What about you, Claire?"

"I'm an 'only,' too. My parents were middle-aged when they married—my mother was a petite Swiss woman, delicate like a Spanish figurine. She died when I was five, so I have only sketchy memories of her; none of them suggest she was ever frazzled with the care of an infant."

"But she was. And from my observation, her efforts paid off in great style."

Claire laughed. "Thank you. Nevertheless, the fact remains, I have a hard time envisioning my mother as anything but dreamlike. Papa idolized her. He never fully coped with her death. I'm sure he was anxious to join her when he died six years ago."

Nick looked down at her, his eyes in the light of a street lamp projecting deep sadness. "It must be lonely for you sometimes."

"Sometimes, yes. But I have cousins in Boston who are considerate and kind. And, of course, I have Henri Poncelet and his daughter."

"Who exactly are those folks?"

"My dearest friends—more family than friends." Claire indicated a turn away from the parade grounds. "Henri was my father's business partner, but also my 'little uncle.' Before Papa died, he made sure Henri would see to my welfare. Anyway, the Poncelets spoil me fiercely, phoning often, even from Paris.

"Actually, I don't know what I'd do without them. Henri's fanatically French. A lady's man of the first order, so his marriages never last. As a Christian, Papa didn't approve of Henri's cavalier attitude toward marriage. I don't, either, but Henri's a good man and tremendously happy."

Nick gave her a questioning look. "Is he? I doubt it. His life sounds like a dismal merry-go-round."

She went on to tell him about some of Henri's outlandish women. "Babette was my favorite. She made mouthwatering crepes."

"Do you think Henri married her just for her crepes?" Nick asked mischievously.

"She did have other notable qualities." Claire chuckled, picturing the statuesque Babette. "However, those qualities, even with the crepes, didn't fill the bill. Henri divorced her three years ago."

"It's sad he's never found a lasting relationship. I'm sure he experiences few days of real contentment, despite outward appearances."

They walked on in silence for a few moments, both inhabiting their own thoughts, with Claire focusing on the contrast between Henri and Nick.

Despite their differences, they were exceptional men. She admired them both. She knew they would enjoy each other's company if they ever met.

But Henri didn't have Nick's indomitable fortitude. She had the feeling a handicap like Nick's would have prompted her French uncle to commit suicide.

She scuffed the leaves as they walked, making a scrunching, swishing sound on the sidewalk. Nick kicked up a few also, and they laughed as the leaves took flight into the swirling wind.

She bent down to pick some up, but they were brittle and decaying.

"None of the leaves this late in the year are worth keeping," she commented.

"They've had their day," he responded. "It's on to the next season. I, for one, am looking forward to winter. Time to get out my skis. We can't dwell on the broken leaves of autumn, Claire. You just grind them up and send them on their way."

There were a hundred ways to interpret Nick's words.

What was behind these comments about discarded leaves? Because he was such a new acquaintance, and because he lived with such a horrendous disability, Claire simply didn't have sufficient insight to understand his references to discarded leaves—or anything else.

Chapter 8

Turn left here," Claire said, directing Nick onto Regent Street. "My house is halfway down the block, the one with the light peeking through the wisteria bush. I'll bet you don't have a wisteria bobbing about outside your window at Everettsville."

"I don't have a bush or tree within a hundred yards of my window," he replied with humorous emphasis. "But, Claire, my apartment is hardly a cell, even though my address is the prison. I have a nice place, actually."

"No bars on your doors or carbo-whatever windows with electrical impulses to prevent your escape?"

He chuckled a reply. "No. Nothing like that."

"Do all the superintendents live on the grounds?"

"I'm the only one who does. My boss and the rest of the senior staff are married and live in Fulton Falls or Ridglea."

"And you wouldn't rather live in town, too, Nick? Doesn't it get depressing being at the prison all the time?"

"Now and then it does, yes. But I get away, often—to Canada skiing, sometimes to Norfolk to visit my parents, and to assorted locales on lecture tours, like this one. Once in awhile I even sneak down to the city and take in a piano recital or two."

The droll tone implied a smile, but it was too dark away from a streetlight for her to notice. His tone became more serious as he went on.

"You have to understand, though, Claire, that living at the prison has advantages for me—advantages over living in town. Every now and then I can't manage something without assistance—a knot or a latch, for example, or something dumb like that. When that happens, I can call the officer at the desk. He'll send someone over—to give me a hand, literally."

Fortunately, darkness under the trees prevented Nick from noticing the startled pain in her eyes. The details he was relating slashed her mind like so many machetes. Would she ever accept the fact that Nick Van Vierssen—strong, confident, brilliant, sophisticated Nick—was handicapped?

He had accepted this fact, but could she? How many months or years would it take for her to adjust to the fact that this super guy had to live in a place as grim as a prison so he could call upon someone to help him if he couldn't untie a knot?

Unaware of her discomfort, he continued. "I have personnel to clean up the place—to make my bed and do some of those other pesky details. So, you see, my life's pretty soft, after all. I'll bet you had no idea how posh it was to live in a prison."

"No, I never knew it could be so. . .so, ah, comfortable," she replied, amazed she was able to answer him at all.

"I have a closet-sized kitchen, a disorderly bedroom, and a living room knee-deep in books. I have a fine stereo system, a necessity because I receive CDs in the mail now and then from celebrated musicians."

He was in such a good mood, she found her own spirits beginning to perk up. She responded cheerfully, "Well, aren't you the lucky bum?"

"I'd say so. One of my friends is so famous, she has write-ups regularly in the Times." He looped his arm through hers and pulled her toward him playfully with the artificial hand, as they turned into her walkway by the wisteria bush.

"You're coming in, aren't you?" she said persuasively, convinced he would.

"I don't think I better, Claire. Do you have any idea how late it is?"

"Who looks at the time? I'm going to have a cup of hot chocolate—top quality, right from Bern. Besides, aren't you just dying to see my plum-colored plant?"

He laughed in resignation. "As a matter of fact, yes, I am. Okay. Hot chocolate would be great."

Unlocking the door that opened into the living room, she turned on a light on a side table.

"Why, this is a great place, Claire. The modular sofa's right out of Rodeo Drive. Nothing that elegant graces my apartment at Everettsville."

"It's the most expensive thing I ever bought."

He swung off his coat and tossed it over the banister.

"Let me hang that up for you."

"Oh, no. Don't bother." He scanned the room and then burst into laughter. "So there's the plant! I don't believe it. Even Luther Burbank would rave over that specimen."

"Isn't it monstrous?" She tossed her own coat over the sofa. "I'm sure it's some sort of mongrel with the ability to devour me. Who knows?"

"I wouldn't like that to happen," he replied with a theatrical scowl, "although I'm sure even the plant must think of you as a choice morsel." He folded his arms and studied the room further. "You play a little chess, I see."

"Rather poorly. Do you play?"

"I used to be pretty fair, but not many men at Everettsville play chess. Poker is more their speed. . . . Ah, and look at that grand piano—it's magnificent."

"My papa bought it for me when I was thirteen."

"Your father was very supportive, then, of your career?"

"Oh, yes. He was a darling. You and he would have hit it off well. Everyone loved my father—goatherds near our home in Montreux, businessmen in New York where we had an apartment. Papa had genuine respect for everyone. Like you do, Nick."

"Like me?" His eyes narrowed in puzzlement. He wrinkled amused lips as he reached over and put his arm on her shoulder. "Some of the inmates don't think I have much empathy at all, Claire. But thanks for the compliment. I'm honored to be compared to your father."

"He was a Christian, too, as you are," she added. "I liked the way he prayed with me when I was a child. God seemed very close in those days."

"Not in these days?"

"Well, not exactly. Although I get to church most Sundays, I've been short-changing God when it comes to private prayer. Asking God's guidance in my pursuits doesn't pull the weight that it should."

She paused, expecting him to jump right into a Christian platitude, but he didn't. He merely allowed his glance to rest softly on hers, waiting for her to continue. Awkwardly, she headed for the kitchen. "Let me see about getting that cocoa going."

"Good."

She put milk into a saucepan and turned on the stove, while Nick removed mugs from a mug tree. For too long, her eyes concentrated on what he was doing, executed with jerky arm and shoulder movements. She knew he detected her discomfort, but he said nothing.

He suddenly looked startled. Claire noticed the cat had brushed through his legs. "Galuppi's playing London Bridge with you," she remarked, glad to have a cause for a chuckle.

He smiled when he saw it was a cat. He bent down on one knee to stroke Galuppi. "I really like cats, Claire; we have something in common—claws."

Claire all but dropped the chocolate tin she was holding. She recalled he had mentioned a hook prosthesis in his talk that day. Trembling, she set the tin down on the counter. Unable to utter a word, barely able to breathe, she smothered a gasp that almost escaped her chest.

Not at all ill-at-ease, Nick seemed to be getting a kick out of the cat. "How did you choose the name Galuppi?"

She took a deep breath, able to reply, "Baldasare Galuppi was a talented eighteenth-century composer who's pretty much ignored today. The name's always amused me. When this stray feline appeared on the scene, I named him Galuppi after that composer."

He stroked the cat with the Greifer. "It's a sensational name."

"Galuppi likes you. That's unusual. He's a terrible snob."

"Well, I like Galuppi," he said, getting back up on his feet.

She forced a sparkle of sorts into her voice. "Galuppi's had to adjust to a legion of cat sitters. As you know, I'm out of town a lot. Next summer, I'll be in Paris for three months."

"With Henri and—ah, Yolande?"

"Yes."

"You prefer Europe to the States, don't you?"

"Only because my closest friends live in Paris and Switzerland. I haven't many close friends here."

"That surprises me. You're so lovely." He studied her face. "In your dressing room that night at Lincoln Center, you were surrounded by friends, all basking in your success. I just assumed your life was one soiree after another."

He continued, almost sadly. "But I should have remembered, skilled artists like you can't indulge in many soirees. You probably don't have time away from practice for chess, dancing, or much fun at all."

"That's about it. Even on vacation, a day without practice is costly." She poured the cocoa into the mugs.

"Today you were derelict in your duties, spending a good share of it listening to four jokers rant and rave about lockups."

"Yes, but I'm not a bit sorry."

He put a spoon in his mug and lifted it from the counter with both prostheses. So much maneuvering was involved, Claire's uneasiness returned as she watched him. However, he appeared oblivious to this as they went into the living room.

"Don't you yearn sometimes for a release from all the pressure?" he asked. "You're too young to live as a hermit, practicing all the time. I'll wager there are erudite history professors and virile football coaches clamoring at your door while you're practicing all those hundreds of hours. In fact, I bet you had to cancel a date to attend the seminar and party."

He put the mug on the coffee table and sat down on the sofa.

"Actually," she said, sitting next to him, "I hardly sequester myself, Nick. I date often—on weekends—as much as I care to right now."

"Good. I'm relieved to know you're in circulation. I must tell Jim to keep an eye on you."

He bent over and took a spoonful of cocoa. "This is good chocolate, Claire. Anyway, as I was saying, Jim better check on you. Music's a noble art, but all of us need an occasional change of pace in our routine, commitment or no commitment."

The joy of relaxing with him had swiftly returned, despite the pain she experienced as she observed his difficulty in drinking from the mug. She was drawn to him by a kind of magnetism. She found she was temporarily able to put his disability aside as they chatted.

"So that's why you ski?"

"Yes—and I like to travel, too. I've been to Paris myself."

"You're the sly one. Why didn't you say so earlier?"

"No reason to."

"Don't you love it?"

"Somewhat, but I prefer Salzburg and Innsbruck."

"Because of the ski slopes?"

"I suppose."

"You'd love Paris, too, if I took you around—showed you the delicious nooks and crannies and introduced you to my friends."

"I'd like to think that would make a difference."

"You belong in Europe, Nick, striding up the Place Ven-dome, or perusing the stock reports over a drink in a café near the Bois. You're so out of place at a prison. How can you stand it?"

"The same way you can stand practicing for hours at your piano. We've found jobs that consume us, Claire, and we're fortunate to have those jobs—at least I certainly am. I'm not so comfortable in the cafés in Paris as I am in Everettsville. For me, new situations are often frustrating, always embarrassing, and sometimes downright unsafe. I enjoy traveling; don't get me wrong. But it's important for me to have my prison. It's there where I make a difference, and it's there where I'm needed. That's my calling. God wants me there."

"You sincerely believe that?"

"Yes, I do," he answered with conviction.

"God might want you to try something special next summer, though. He might want you to share the sights with me in Paris, now that we've become friends."

He paused before he answered her. "Claire, it's risky for us to think of each other as friends."

"It is? Riskier for us than the rest of mankind?"

"Yes, much more so. We're hardly similar to the rest of mankind. You're a recognized performing artist. I have a debilitating handicap and a job with a great deal of responsibility. We're not careless, frivolous individuals. Perhaps that's why we find each other's company so enjoyable. We've touched each other profoundly, haven't we?"

He cleared his throat as if he were attempting to find the exact words to express his thoughts. "Even the word *touch* has an awesome meaning for us. Touch is taken for granted by most people—but never by you, and most definitely never by me. Claire, it's something both of us weave our dreams around. But we're locked into demanding roles, and without them we'd be lost—bereft of purpose. If we neglected our careers we couldn't live with the guilt, or the—"

"But, Nick, couldn't you and I have these same careers and also find time for a now-and-then type of friendship? You said everyone needs an escape."

She clutched his upper right arm, where she knew he would feel the power of her grip. How marvelous it felt to press her fingers into that muscular arm. "Come to Paris next summer, Nick. Visit us in Paris—Henri, Yolande, and me. We'll see that you have all the comforts of. . .ah. . .of prison. And I'll learn how to fix escargot."

He took a deep breath. "I'll consider it, Claire. That's the best I can say."

She forced a smile.

He stood and let her hand slip away. "Claire, it's after two. Hadn't we better say good night?"

"I hate to."

"I know. But you'll be tired tomorrow—not up to the eight hours of practice your schedule calls for."

"I haven't even thought of my schedule tonight."

"But you must. And tomorrow I have to drive back to Everettsville."

He picked up his coat from the banister and maneuvered into it. Though it took great restraint, she refrained from assisting him.

"I'll see you tomorrow before you go, surely," she said.

"No, I don't think so. I'm getting an early start so that I can relieve another guy at one o'clock. I gave my word—he's going to a family reunion."

With great effort, he attempted to open the door. Then he turned to her. "Knowing you has been a fine experience for me, Claire." He put both prostheses around her back. Then he leaned over and kissed her forehead.

Her head fell between the lapels of his overcoat and jacket and rested on his chest, her face enveloped by a musky aftershave. She could almost feel his skin through his shirt.

"You've given me a wonderful evening, Honey," he whispered softly down to her. "And I appreciate it—especially because I know how difficult it was for you."

She pulled away in surprise. "It wasn't difficult at all. I loved being with you—every second."

"It was difficult because—ah—because you didn't know before today that I was an amputee, did you?"

She staggered back, but he kept her from falling, and as he did, she felt a hard metal prosthesis against her back. He grimaced, knowing it had caught her off guard.

"Jim should never have told you," she said angrily. "It was wrong and cruel of him to—"

"Jim didn't tell me. But I knew. . ."

"All evening. . .you knew?"

"Yes. There was no way you could have found out in the city. You obviously didn't know at the recital. And there were things tonight that gave you away. But Claire, you're a stoic, heroic, and thoughtful person—without exception, the most accomplished and astonishing woman I've ever known."

The tears she had tried so hard to control now cascaded from her eyes. "I was sure I'd fooled you. Oh, Nick, I was so sure. This afternoon when I found out. . .it was. . .it was just so devastating for me. I didn't want to lie to you, but I felt I had to. It was all I could do to go to Jim's open house. Nick, I've never faced anything so. . ."

"Don't cry—please. The evening's been such a winner. But it was important that I tell you I knew—things should be out in the open between us, Claire. Besides, I had to express how profoundly moved I've been this evening by your restraint and your most successful attempt to make me feel comfortable. You've been extremely considerate of my feelings. That means a lot to me. Thank you so much."

Impulse got the better of her. She pulled his face down to hers, and pressed her cheek against his. "Nick, don't just walk away again as you did in the city. Please don't. Your being an amputee doesn't matter a bit. Consider a little escape kind of friendship with me. Nothing more. Call me next week. . . ." The tears flowed down both her cheeks.

He held her tight. Then his lips found hers. And they were experienced lips, lips that had kissed women passionately before. If not recently, at one time, certainly. In his kiss there was desperate urgency that gripped her whole being. He released her slowly, kissing her hair in a gesture of farewell.

"You'll call, Nick? And come back soon?" she pleaded, almost in a gasp, still breathing heavily from the overwhelming pressure of his lips.

He answered only with a few slow nods. Then he was out the door and down the path.

He waved as he crossed the street into the wind. The gusts had picked up velocity and swirled bitingly against her face, forcing her to close the door.

Something extraordinary had happened to both of them, she knew. His kiss had made that obvious. Yet he was not coming back. He wouldn't return, she was sure, despite the powerful attraction they shared. She knew he would be steeling himself against this love he had not bargained for, a love that had popped into his monastic life like a jack-in-the-box.

And it had been the same for her. She hadn't expected anything like this to show up on her packed agenda.

Yet, here indeed was a man to whom she could commit for a lifetime.

Was the "Pere éternel," the "Eternal Father," whom Nick honored so completely, working behind the scenes, calling such strange plays as briefcase exchanges for Nick and herself?

It seemed that might be true.

She fell back against the wall, pressing her fingers to her eyes. "Oh, God, on the chance that You're out there listening, I appeal to You. You know how much that sensational man deserves joy and happiness in his life. I pray—yes, Lord, I do pray—that if You've chosen me to be the agent of his happiness, You will show me how to bring it about."

She brushed her hair back from her face, her tears drying salty against her cheeks, as she remembered to add, "in Jesus' name."

Chapter 9

At first, Claire had clung to a glimmer of hope that Nick would drop her a line. But that glimmer faded as the days marched drearily onward.

Jim and Peg had become close friends of Claire since their party in the fall. Claire loved their darling children and enjoyed picking out Christmas gifts for them.

On New Year's Day she stopped by the Gleasons' for a brief visit. The children eagerly showed her their presents, many still under the tree. Claire felt an anguished joy handling the gifts that had come from Nick—adorable puppets for the girls and a spaceship for Todd. As Claire fondled these toys, it was as if a bit of Nick were with her, sharing the holiday spirit.

She'd sent him a card. It had taken her hours to find one, yet it barely skimmed the surface of her feelings. When she tried to add a personal message, she couldn't think of anything appropriate to say.

It was excruciating to know that, even though Nick had displayed incredibly deep feelings for her, she would not see him again. The leaves of their moments together had become brittle, only to be pulverized and tossed into the swirling wind of memory.

His card to her had arrived in mid-December, the day after she'd sent hers, so she realized with some satisfaction that his card was not a response to the one she had sent. It was a well-designed card featuring the three wise kings; it was simply signed "Nick."

The only thing she could hang onto was the fact that the "k" in his name had an excessively long tail, as if he hadn't wanted to lift the pen from the paper, that he, too, had wanted to write something more, but couldn't.

When she got on the plane to fly south for her two concerts, she felt no enthusiasm whatsoever. Her brilliant career had become merely a job.

❧

The morning after her return to campus, as Claire headed across the parade grounds, she heard Jim Gleason's voice ringing out from the steps of the arts building. It lifted her spirits, and she managed a smile and a wave.

He hurried down to her. "Wait a minute," he called, explaining he'd seen her from his office window. He was without a jacket, rubbing his arms in the chilly morning air. "I tried to get you on the phone—the baby came early this morning."

"Oh, Jim, I'm so glad. Tell me, was the sonogram accurate? Was it a boy?"

"Oh, yes, a hearty boy. His name's Josh. Peg's fine. She'll be home tomorrow."

"So soon?"

"They don't pamper mothers in hospitals anymore. It's in and out, so they can return to the spinning wheel and butter churn where they belong."

Claire laughed. "I'll get over to the house soon to see Peg and Josh. Is there anything I can do? I've been rather a fair-weather friend, but maybe I can make up for lost time. The past few weeks have been so. . ."

"You look ragged out, Claire. Are you well?"

"I'll make it."

"You should have devoured more grits down South. Survival in the bayous requires the consumption of a platter of grits and chitlins every morning."

"Now he tells me. In any event, I'm sure I'll outlive you—especially if you stay out in your shirtsleeves."

He rubbed his arms more vigorously. "Could you step into the building for a minute? There's something I want to discuss with you."

"It's like this. . . ," he said with some embarrassment as they sat down in his office. "Nick phoned last week—about a possible field trip for my students through the new building at Everettsville. I thought it only fair to tell you—in case you'd like to go along."

"That's considerate of you, Jim," she answered slowly, her feelings halfway between jubilation and grave apprehension. "Did Nick invite me?"

"No—no, he didn't. And it's stupid, because he's crazy about you. He always asks what you're doing when he calls. This time was no exception. He was hoping all was going well with your concert tour."

"But he didn't ask me to join the field trip?"

"No."

"And you didn't tell him you were thinking of asking me?"

"I didn't, no, because—"

"Jim, I couldn't just breeze down there without telling him."

"No, you can't. It's not permitted, in fact. I have to fax the names ahead of time so they can run security checks." Jim shook his head. "I just thought, once Nick sees you again, he'll realize what a bozo he is. If he doesn't want you there— well, once he gets the list, he can phone us and say so. That's the way I see it. Do you think you'd like to go?"

She interlaced her fingers tightly before replying. "I'd give anything to see him again. You know that. When is this field trip scheduled?"

"March 26. It's a Saturday."

"I'm free that weekend, so, ah—do you need an extra car?"

"We might. Yes, I think we will." He folded his arms and stared into her eyes. "Claire, this whole Nick thing is so rough on you. I wish I could. . ."

"Yes, it's rough. But I make sure I'm terribly busy. In June I'm going to Paris.

Maybe I can get myself back on keel over there. It doesn't make much sense for a man to affect me as Nick has. I barely know the guy."

"Sometimes that's the way it happens, though. You meet someone and life does an about-face."

"Apparently, that's what did happen to me." She paused in thought for a moment, then added, "Jim, do you think Nick's handicap is so devastating that he and I couldn't get around it somehow, at least as friends?"

"Frankly, it's not within my power to understand his situation, even though he's discussed it with me a good bit," Jim said, tapping his mouse pad. "But more and more lately, a vivid and most unpleasant scene comes to mind. I walked in on Nick once when he didn't have his prostheses on. He was getting out of bed in a hotel room when I popped in. His door was open, and. . ."

"And?"

"It shook me up. I've got to admit, it did shake me up."

"So we're not dealing with a pair of glasses here, after all, are we? And we never were."

"No, we're not, Claire. I played things down to help Nick have fun the night of the open house, having no idea how much you cared for him. Since that night, Peg and I have considered you as a good friend, too. Your feelings matter to us as much as Nick's."

Jim got up and put a hand on her shoulder. "Peg and I have prayed about your situation because seeing this relationship between the two of you fizzle saddens us—especially when you're both so miserable alone. For my money, that briefcase episode was arranged by the Holy Spirit to bring together two remarkable human beings."

"I'd love to believe that, Jim. It's a big step for me to embrace a faith that accepts God working in one's life, but I'm reading the Bible regularly, trying to take that step. I'll try to convince myself this excursion to Everettsville is part of God's plan."

"Let's just declare it is, and let God take it from there, while we. . ."

The buzzer for class muffled Jim's words.

"I have to run, Claire," he declared. "I'll give you a call when we have all the details firmed up about the field trip."

"Fine. And, Jim, I'll stop over in a few days to see Peg."

He squeezed her arm gently as they walked toward the door. "Wait 'til you get a load of that baby. A real winner. The spittin' image of the old man."

Claire grinned as she watched Jim bound down the stairs to class.

∽

A few weeks later, Jim phoned. "All systems are go, Claire. You're on the list—signed, sealed, and approved. The letter came from Nick's office, so he must have seen your name."

"You're sure, now?"

"Yup—you're on board, Lady. And by the way, we can use your car if the offer still holds."

"It does."

"Good. Front of Old Main—nine o'clock—and wear something subdued, like cotton baseball sweats. There are guidelines here: no peekaboo nylon thingie. All females are to be swaddled in flannel like they've spent the winter in bed with the croup. That's the mandate from your sanctimonious friend, Van Vierssen."

She giggled. "Nick's not quite that sanctimonious. Seriously, what should I wear?"

"The actual guidelines are as follows: 'Improperly clothed females will be prevented from touring the grounds.'"

Despite her mixed feelings about the pending excursion, she had to burst out laughing. "I'll scrounge up a potato sack somewhere."

"Perfect," he chortled.

⸙

The day of the outing, she settled on a denim skirt and a beige sweater set. Rather than putting her hair up in a chignon, she allowed it to fall softly to her shoulders so she'd more readily blend in with the students. She splashed on only a hint of cologne.

She pulled up into the caravan in front of Old Main at eight-thirty, and the four waiting students piled in.

For awhile she chatted with them. But as they got closer to Everettsville, she became more detached. None of the kids seemed to share her anxiety about visiting a maximum security prison.

From the bluff of a hill, she got her first view of the compound. Though illuminated by the brilliant shafts of a warm sun, the buildings below remained cold, almost menacing. It was a vast reservation, as large as the university. Patrol towers erupted from numerous corners of the dozen or so three-story-tall peripheral buildings.

Two rows of high fencing topped with twisted loops of razor wire—which resembled, in supreme irony, a Slinky toy—snaked around the vast compound, up beyond a knoll to a far horizon. Inside the fencing, nearest the highway, stood a sizable new building of gray concrete.

But even with its spanking new walls and roof, it looked austere against the stark landscape, bereft of foliage so early in the spring. What few trees there were on the grounds looked pathetic in their leafless state.

It was inconceivable to Claire that Nick could inhabit such a place. Nicks of the world belonged at Wimbledon or Hilton Head for Renaissance Weekend, consorting with the jet set, not here on this remote hillside, behind barbed wire, in the company of felons.

Jim led the group—which numbered about forty individuals—into a small building on the edge of the lot. Holding the door for them, he followed Claire and the students into the reception room: a nondescript place with brown plastic furniture and a utilitarian, amber-colored carpet.

Jim spoke with a female receptionist, and she picked up a phone to punch a number.

"Mr. Van Vierssen will be here in a few minutes," Jim announced to the students as he took a pile of papers from the counter. "I'm passing around some instruction sheets for you to read—and heed. Everything written here must be followed to the letter. Such tours as this are rare. Your safety depends on the respect you pay to the instructions on these sheets."

The papers were passed throughout the group, and Claire glanced at the outline in a cursory manner. How could she concentrate on printed matter when in the next instant Nick would walk through the double doors by the counter?

Faintly she heard an outer door bang shut. Then the doors in front of them swung open automatically. There he was—the tall, commanding presence of him! The Nick of her every waking thought.

To her regret, the dim lights of the room showed no particular interest in highlighting his goldenrod hair, which seemed more carefully combed than at the university. His cheeks had no crinkles of merriment by the eyes. His mouth formed no smile.

Beneath the familiar olive green jacket he'd had on that morning at Lincoln Center, he now wore a stiffly starched white shirt and an austere, striped tie.

On his left arm he had the Greifer prosthesis, on his right, the sharper, claw-like hook he'd mentioned in his talk at the sociology seminar. Claire decided no one would ever wear something so gross unless efficiency—or safety—demanded it.

But the effect was hideous. Nevertheless, the students seemed electrified by his presence. Nobody spoke or moved.

His eyes looked particularly weary as they scanned the room until they found her. Then they paused. Effort twisted his mouth into a bittersweet smile. She found it difficult to respond with a smile of her own. But one did come forth. And she waved her hand a trifle, glad she could at least do that.

He was followed into the room by four men in black trousers and maroon blazers, a uniform of sorts.

When he addressed the students, there was none of the relaxed levity he had displayed at the university.

"We're pleased you have an interest in our new facility. It's state of the art, and we're eager to move in after the dedication ceremonies tomorrow."

Gingerly he slid one of the papers from the pile on the counter, manipulating it from one prosthesis to the other. Claire gritted her teeth watching the operation, recognizing how difficult it was for him to grasp something as thin as a sheet of paper.

"You have one of these, I trust. I'm going to insist you follow everything scrupulously. This is not a safe place for any of you, least of all you young women."

He allowed one corner of his mouth to relax. "As the instructions state, you're to refrain from conversing with inmates as you walk about. Later in the day you'll have an opportunity to talk with a group of them in our conference room. You can ask questions freely at that time."

He put the Greifer into the crook of his elbow and the hook from his other arm against his chin. "At no time will you be permitted to wander off on your own. Under no circumstances will you accept from or give to an inmate anything at all—not anything! Such action will be justification for your immediate removal from the grounds."

Claire saw that his eyes remained focused on her for the few seconds needed to complete his instructions. "Because I have a meeting, I'll be unable to escort you around this morning. But after lunch I'll join you in the conference room."

He turned to the men next to him. "These men will be your guides. Mr. Dudley, Mr. Thompson, Mr. Renzi, and Mr. Henson. All are knowledgeable about the entire complex here at Everettsville. Gentlemen, they're all yours."

Mr. Henson stepped forward and announced the procedures for entering through the sally port, instructing them to leave valuables at the desk. "Each of you individually will go through a metal detector, be photographed, and frisked—er, checked over."

He blushed slightly, then continued, "It's only a superficial check. We'll assemble in the yard beyond the far door."

As the students lined up by the sally port, Jim spoke to Nick in muted tones. He put his hand on Nick's arm, said something calming, and they both began to chuckle, after which Jim went on to the sally port.

Nick edged through the crowd toward Claire.

"It's good to see you again," he said, mowing down her composure with his powerful blue eyes, causing a shiver to permeate her entire body. "But this wasn't wise, for many reasons."

She surveyed his face, trying to commit to memory every detail. "It was, ah, too great an opportunity for me to miss, Nick. Jim thought I'd like to check out the prison—and you. Since you didn't phone him when you saw my name on the list, he figured you didn't mind my being part of the group. Was he right?"

"Contrary to my better judgment, Claire, I did want to see you again. Very much." He hesitated, then added, "You look pale. Galuppi can't be taking very good care of you."

With these words the crow's-feet began to crinkle, and the familiar smile returned to his lips.

"This modern generation of cats has no responsibility at all," she replied, glad he was relaxed enough to discuss Galuppi.

"You've been overdoing, I'm sure, with the concerts in Tennessee and New Orleans."

"I'm glad the tour's over."

"The Schumann Concerto—no problems?"

"No, the orchestras were superb, Nick. You'd have loved the conductor in New Orleans. He was the wildest gnome of a man."

"Is there any chance of my getting another CD? Of that performance?"

"It'll be in the mail Monday."

"Great. Jim said you've been back since last month."

"I returned the same day the Gleasons' baby made his appearance."

He grinned as he asked, "Have you seen little Josh?"

"Yes, often. He's darling. It's been far too long since I've been close to an infant, and, well, he's precious—for me a precious novelty."

"I'll have to get up there and look him over."

"You must, yes, and. . ." Suddenly she could no longer look up at him because it upset her so.

"And what?" he asked, raising her chin with his Greifer, forcing her to face him.

"I just wanted to say that if you come up—well, I'm living in the same old place."

He nodded several times, his grin fading. "That's good to know."

She tossed her head a little and changed the subject. "I see most of my group has gone on—I'd better get up there and follow them."

She started toward the sally port, and he followed.

Abruptly, he put his Greifer under her arm and drew her back. "Claire," he said, his eyes riveted on hers, "you're much too attractive for a hole like this. Please be careful. Use extreme caution as you tour the grounds."

"Don't worry about me, Nick. I've hiked through the Red Light district of Paris and the docks in London. I won't swish my skirt an inch or bat an eye."

"To those men in the cell blocks, you and the other girls are just so many. . ." He mumbled syllables of words she couldn't quite decipher but only guess at.

As she looked into his eyes, she wondered if he was reading her thoughts, which kept pummeling her brain with the question: *And, Nick, what am I to you?*

"Claire," he added, reluctantly letting her go, "don't lower your guard, not for a second. Understand?"

"I understand," she replied, continuing on to the sally port.

Chapter 10

The group toured the new unit first. Designed to accommodate several hundred men, the facility featured windows free of bars and steel mesh on the doors. Claire remembered the windows could electronically register attempted escapes. The cells, though small, had nicely painted walls, with furnishings of attractive, durable plastic.

"Hey," said one of the girls as they left the new complex, "those rooms are better than mine at Grainger Hall. I think I'll move down here. My plaid curtains would look great in that pad we just saw."

"But not your teddy bear," chided a quarterback called Bif.

The old cell blocks, however, were another story entirely. Mr. Henson informed the students that, because of the overcrowded conditions, these buildings would continue to be used even after the new complex was opened. Cell block C looked like a scene out of an old flick, the central exercise area echoing shouts, catcalls, and some obnoxious obscenities from the cells above. Because prisoners had to be locked in their cells when visitors toured, rattling of bars and the banging of metal exacerbated the noise level into a cacophony that jangled the nerves.

Surveillance monitors hung from the ceilings of each room and hallway. Uniformed guards, a few of them women, roamed the halls watchfully at frequent intervals.

The halls seemed to go on forever. The din hammered into Claire's skull until she trembled, realizing only too well that unhealthy overcrowding existed throughout the complex. Claire sensed the walls were advancing in on her, as the woods of Birnam had moved on Macbeth—threatening walls that promised a horrible form of annihilation.

She simply couldn't drum up the compassion for the inmates she would have expected from herself. How could Nick endure the place—its omnipresent threshold of danger, the undercurrents of resentment, the whole edgy environment?

Under Henson's direction, the group moved on to a main dining room, a library, and classrooms, one equipped with computers. Although the general order when visitors roamed the halls kept inmates in their cells, a dozen worked at these computers behind locked doors. Claire noted that the two that did glance up and look at them through the thick-paned window had menacing, superior, most unwelcoming glances.

The last building on the agenda contained a power plant, boiler room, and laundry. The prisoners here seemed to be conscientious older men employed in purposeful pursuits. Instead of the orange jumpsuits worn by the other inmates, these men had on slate-gray work shirts and pants.

Only one inmate was in the laundry, an unimpressive, overweight, and sullen individual of about fifty, his stomach bulging over his belt. He bore a resemblance to many stagehands Claire had met on her tours—uncommunicative men generally, but up to their tasks and cooperative if you approached them without condescension.

Henson answered questions as they continued on. Claire paused a moment. Something had gotten into her eye. Standing behind the group, she rubbed her eyelid to generate tears to wash out the speck.

"Here's a clean towel you can use to get that out, Lady," said the laundryman.

"Oh, thank you so much," she replied, "that's kind of you." She pulled up her eyelid and gently wiped across the cornea. "I think that did the trick." She started away quickly to catch up with her group, which was already exiting at the far end of the hall.

Suddenly she was yanked backward, down onto the stone floor. One massive hand dragged her by her arm into the laundry room, while the other clamped her mouth shut. She could neither scream nor bite the laundryman's massive hand.

The rough stone floor lacerated her hips and legs as he pulled her along. Her hips and legs burned with excruciating pain. The man hauled her into a storage room and pulled the door closed behind him. She let out a piercing scream as he threw her head down hard against the cement floor, stunning her into a semiconsciousness that made the room spin.

With beastlike groans, the man pushed a massive metal shelf against the door.

Her next scream was muffled by a piece of sheeting he tied brutally across her nose and mouth. Everything was done so quickly, Claire had no time to plan a strategy of resistance. The gag muffled all Claire's screams into choking whispers. It was so difficult to breathe, she couldn't think of anything else. To breathe became all-important.

The man stretched her arms up over her head, tying her wrists together with cord in a savage manner that tore the skin of her wrists, exposing nerve endings that pulsated with agony.

She tried to twist herself free, to bite away at the gag that was cutting viciously now on the right side of her jaw. With almost satanic glee, the man punched her across her face.

Oh, Lord Jesus, please come to my rescue. Forgive my indifference to You in the past. I beg You, help me. Carbon dioxide seemed to be about to explode her brain.

The man bent over her with eager, half-starved, craven eyes as he pressed his knees down hard against her hips and thighs. In lustful frenzy, he tore her skirt in two.

Death—her death at the hands of a madman—was imminent. Within moments, his crime would be discovered, and he'd face the severest of sentences. He must realize that. *God—oh, God, come quickly.*

What a fool she'd been—disregarding the basic rules—those simple rules Nick wanted her to be so mindful of. Here she was, seconds from death in this remote storeroom—only a few hundred yards from. . . .

From approaching voices, accompanied by hurried stomping through the laundry. What seemed to be Nick's voice shouted above the rest, "Claire! Claire, can you hear me? We'll have you out of there in a minute."

The laundryman's mouth twisted in anger; his eyes bugged out with rage.

God had heard her. A miracle was on the other side of the door. Fiercely she tried to hold out against death, the carbon dioxide ballooning in her head, her chest falling in a desperate effort to exhale.

Above the hubbub beyond the door, she could hear Nick command Henson to take the students upstairs out of the area. A pounding like a battering ram forced the door open. Metal shelving clattered to the floor.

Nick was without his jacket, his short-sleeved shirt exposing the prostheses' cuffs attached on his lower arms. Prying the man away from her with both prostheses, he hurled him against the wall. The man screamed in pain, throwing a fist at Nick, but Nick deflected the blow with the left prosthesis.

"Porter, nobody in this place swings at Van Vierssen," one of the guards intoned in a low, steady voice as he handcuffed the laundryman, ". . .because if he swings back—and don't for one minute think he won't—his hook could take an eye of yours with it."

The other guard dove to the floor to assist Nick in loosening Claire's gag. With the release of the first knot, she began to expel the carbon dioxide that had mushroomed in her head. She gulped the air. By the narrowest of margins she'd averted death. She was going to live. A prayer of thanksgiving filled her soul. *Thank You, Lord,* her brain kept repeating over and over—but her lips proved immobile.

"Do you want him in F-10?" asked the guard with the prisoner.

"That's best," Nick replied from his position on the floor. "I can manage here now, Drake," he said to the man who'd removed her gag.

"Are you sure?"

"Yes, I can handle everything with Ms. Rossiter. Just take care of Porter. Get him out of here. I'll be up later. And, thanks. I mean, this time we were winners. I appreciate it."

The guards pushed the prisoner ahead of them out of the room. Nick, his face glistening with perspiration, yanked away the remaining cord. His hook prosthesis scratched her, but she didn't mind.

He draped a sheet across her body. "Thank God, oh, thank God," he said in a barely audible moan. "You were on that tour with Henson only a few minutes before I realized I had to come down and be with you."

She wanted to tell him a million things—to apologize in some way for her reckless behavior. But her voice came in croaks and gasps. "Nick—I–I. . ." Her pummeled jaw and torn mouth had difficulty forming the words. "Sorry—"

"Claire, don't try to talk," he said. "Just relax, as best you can. I was out of my mind not to take you around myself right from the start."

Her jaw throbbed, her lips burned from the abrasive gag. "It was. . .all my. . . f-fault. My eye—he gave me. . .towel."

"Please don't talk, Claire. Your mouth is so badly bruised. Your cheeks are bleeding." He pressed a facecloth against her lips, then brushed her hair from her face. "I'll call the ambulance crew immediately. We have our own service in the prison, so it'll be only a few minutes, and they'll have you on your way to the hospital in Fulton Falls."

"Nick, no. No hospital."

"Of course you'll go. It's important we get X-rays of your jaw and wrists and get those wounds cleaned up. I want Doc Bremmer to check you over. It's mainly your face and hands, isn't it?" he asked, hesitantly, biting his upper lip. "Porter never managed to. . ."

"Rape me?" she whispered. "No."

He sighed, his relief obvious, as he tapped buttons on the telecommunication unit that hung from his belt. "Sam, Van Vierssen here. We're going to have to have a stretcher in G-20. I'm with Ms. Rossiter now, in the laundry storage room. Phone the hospital and have Dr. Bremmer on duty in emergency. I'll stay here till the orderlies move her out. Yes, she looks good, all things considered. Oh, and Sam, send someone up to that professor. . .Jim Gleason in D-3. Tell him Claire is okay. Right. Just tell him she's going to be fine. Got that? Thanks."

He pressed off the unit. "Things'll be looking up soon, Claire."

"Sorry." She couldn't stop crying. "Didn't mean to disobey. I didn't tease—"

"Oh, Honey, I know you didn't! You didn't do anything wrong!"

"He looked so innocent."

"Innocent? Oh, Claire, Porter was a professional hit man. Very innocent guy!" He raked the Greifer gently through her hair.

She shuddered with this disclosure. A hit man—no stranger to murder. "It was such a close call. Nick, I. . .I prayed."

"That makes two of us. God spared us a hideous 'might have been,' though this whole episode was bad enough.

"From the moment your group went through that sally port, I had misgivings. What madness to let you out of my sight in this place. I arrived at G-20 just as

Henson started looking for you. The students tried to assure Henson and me that you were just back around the corner and everything would be okay, but Henson and I knew better. You 'free world' people have no idea what inmates are capable of."

He sat back against a concrete pillar, raised one knee, and leaned his elbow on it. "Praise God, the guard came with equipment to ram through the door quickly."

He closed his eyes for a second. "I've seen some bad sights, Claire, and the nightmares that ran through my mind as we barreled into that door. . .well, all I can say is, I was actually relieved your situation wasn't worse."

He coughed nervously as his eyes sought hers again. "What a miracle to see you alive."

The poignancy of the moment was shattered by new voices in the laundry room. Two white-suited orderlies, carrying a stretcher, entered the storeroom. "Watch her wrists and jaw," Nick advised.

"Will do," said one of the attendants. "I'm sorry, Miss; you're obviously hurtin' plenty," he said as he and the other attendant lifted her onto the stretcher. "We can't give you an injection for pain before Dr. Bremmer checks you over."

She was forced to grit her teeth to suppress a moan; the agony was so intense. They strapped a blanket over her.

"Claire, I can't ride to the hospital with you," said Nick, the crow's-feet around his eyes deepening, "because I'm not allowed to leave the compound until I get in a replacement. Also, I have to go up and have a little chat with that. . ." He got to his feet and wiped his own forehead with a towel. ". . .with Porter. I'll have to write up a report. I may have to call his lawyer. We wouldn't want to deny Porter his legal rights, now, would we?"

He shook his head disgustedly as he went on. "But Doc Bremmer'll be at the hospital, Claire. He's a surgeon—top-notch—and a friend of mine. He'll take good care of you."

"Nick, I'm so, so sorry."

"Claire, things like this occur here almost every day. It's exceptional for me only because it happened to you, to an incredible and decent person like you. Please don't chastise yourself. You had a real problem, and Porter took advantage of it. Right now we just have to get you comfortable and have you checked over. I'll get over to the hospital as soon as I can, and I'll have Jim stop to see you before he goes back to the campus."

"Nick, I. . ." She wanted so much to say "I love you," but the attendants were watching. She couldn't embarrass Nick in front of them.

They carried her out of the laundry room and down unpeopled corridors, doors electronically unlocking and locking behind them as they went along. Finally, they came to the entrance where the ambulance waited. No prisoners were around—just one guard, the two orderlies, and Nick.

The orderlies lifted her up into the ambulance. One of them climbed in with her. The other closed the door behind him. They then drove out of a gate and headed for the hospital, without the aid of sirens.

Chapter 11

X-rays and a thorough examination by Dr. Bremmer showed mainly abrasions, cuts, and a seriously injured jaw and neck. "Tomorrow you'll be feeling better, but your face will be discolored. I regret having to tell you I'm holding off prescribing pain medication now because you may have suffered a mild concussion. We're going to keep you overnight for observation.

"Van Vierssen's coming in soon to check on you. Sister, you sure had him scared," he said, forming a teasing grin. "He's usually a cool cat about things up at that fun house of his. But this time, Lady, he—well, he was majorly upset. He asked several times about your hands. You're a pianist, right?"

She managed a weak "Yes."

"Your wrists are raw right now. But no great harm done. The ointment we put on should ease some of the sting. After head trauma like you've experienced, a patient often becomes drowsy even without heavy-duty pills or injections for pain. Don't be surprised if you fall asleep." Before he left her room, he and a nurse placed a foam collar around her neck to keep her head immobile. The collar and hand ointment, plus ice packs, gave her enough relief to doze off.

Later, she saw Jim standing by her bed, his face tense. She couldn't make out exactly what he said—something about the students driving her car back to the campus.

When she awoke, it was evening. Out of the corner of her eye, she could see Nick silhouetted by the sun, a few shocks of his hair reflecting the last rays of the day. He had changed into chino pants and a navy, wide-necked, short-sleeved yachting shirt—the prostheses' cuffs conspicuously attached to his arms. However, the hook prosthesis was gone, replaced by the synthetic hand on his left arm. His jacket lay across the adjustable table.

She spoke, calling to him in a faraway voice that required little movement of mouth and jaw. He hurried to her bed and peered down at her with anxious eyes. "Welcome back to planet earth, Darlin'." He shook his head and scowled. "I bet there isn't an inch of your body that doesn't hurt."

"Talking hurts. It hurts a lot, Nick—to talk."

"I'll do the talking for both of us. What good news, though. No broken bones and apparently no serious concussion."

Nick grinned now, the creases around his eyes crinkling in "up" fashion. "Don't worry about anything, Claire. Medical care here is all covered. And if you wish to press charges in the days ahead, you'll certainly be. . ."

"I don't think I'll have any reason to do that."

"You might down the road. In any case, you'll have to write up a report for our files—but not today. Today you're going to concentrate on getting better and trying to erase trauma from your mind."

She nodded as much as pain or the collar would allow. "Nick, I prayed. In that storage closet, I did pray. And God answered my prayer. I'm relieved to be alive and able to spend time here with you. Did you talk to Porter?"

He rubbed the back of the artificial hand along his chin. "Yes."

"He's a disturbed man, obviously. What will happen to him?"

"Wednesday he'll be shipped to another prison. With luck, he may end up in some rose-colored playground supervised by Arnie Saxby." He manipulated his Greifer several times seemingly to relieve tension as he continued, "Saxby can put him out to pasture. Just so long as he stays away from me. When something hits 'home' like this, Claire, a corrections officer can't be expected to work with that prisoner again. I'd assume it's like a doctor not delivering his own baby. Objectivity ceases."

Had she heard him right? Had he said "hit home"? Was he talking about a husband-wife relationship? It sounded that way. Immobile as her neck was, her spirit was doing cartwheels. Her magnificent Nick of the courthouse, Nick of the plum-colored roses stood next to her, speaking to her as if she were his wife.

"Anyway," Nick went on, "it's in circumstances like this, Claire, where God's purposes seem so unclear. We keep asking why. When trauma's fresh, we have to hold onto faith that, in the big scheme of things, God does work for good with those He loves."

He blanketed her with a tender glance. "Claire, we turn to the story of Job. Where were any of us, when God created the behemoth? So how can we grasp the way we fit into His scheme of things?"

How can we indeed? Claire asked herself. She wasn't noticing Greifers any-more. Nick's fathomless eyes, his strong face, his caring smile so dominated his person that prostheses faded into the background.

"Try not to be too upset, Nick," she managed, though her mouth moved painfully as she spoke the words. "I don't need behemoths. Being with you is proof enough that God's out there, planning good things for me. Dr. Bremmer says I'll be fine by the end of the week. Since I have no recitals pending, perhaps I can take the time to compose more jazz variations."

"Hey, that's the way to go," he replied with enthusiasm. "Or, why don't you take a stab at a musical? Since you love France, set the scene in the French Revolution. Turn out something on Dickens's *A Tale of Two Cities*—Madame De Farge knitting at the guillotine. She'd be a contralto, I think, don't you?"

"Absolutely."

"Or you could tackle *The Three Musketeers*. Something Debussyish for Porthos would be catchy."

She could hardly control a belly laugh at this absurd suggestion. Debussy's wistful melodies could never set the scene for the burly Porthos. "Please don't kid around like that, Nick. Laughing smarts!"

"I'm sorry. But I'm only half joking. You could manage an operetta or a musical comedy, no trouble at all."

His prostheses rested on the bed rail, and he leaned down over her, his face so temptingly close that she craved his lips. Ironically, she was now the handicapped one. Her arms and her hands were the limbs that lay helpless, too weak to bring his head to hers. On impulse, she found herself saying, "Nick, I'm not so bruised that I wouldn't welcome a kiss."

"Claire, I can't do that—your cheeks and mouth are much too sore for. . ."

"Just a fifty-cent kiss—on my forehead."

He did nothing for a few seconds. Then he lowered the bed railing and brought his face to hers. Putting his right arm carefully under her head, he kissed her first in feather-duster fashion on her lips, then more firmly on her cheek and more firmly still on her forehead.

Slowly he pulled away from her, and she looked up at him. "We simply must never lose each other again," she whispered.

His mouth had formed an ethereal smile, the type one might receive from a cloistered Trappist monk on the other side of a monastery gate. *Yet,* she tried to tell herself, *no gates could ever come between us after the experience of this day*.

A nurse barged into the room. "Excuse me, but it's eight-thirty—time for visitors to depart. Oh, wait a minute, Dr. Bremmer has given you permission, Mr. Van Vierssen, to stay through the night with this patient, hasn't he?"

Nick nodded. "Yes, he has."

Claire looked up in surprise. "Is that correct? You're staying throughout the whole night, Nick?"

"Um-hum, yes, the whole night." He went over to the nurse. "Our patient hasn't had anything since breakfast. I think she could go for some liquid refreshment besides water."

The nurse looked at her chart once again. "Dr. Bremmer wants her to lay low on intake because of the possible concussion."

"I realize that," Nick replied, "but couldn't she have a small juice or soda?"

The woman smiled. "I'm sure we can get something to tide her over."

Once the nurse had left the room, Claire spoke out in a startled voice. "Nick, how can you plan to stay here all night when you need your rest to cope with the governor's reception tomorrow?"

"Claire, I've slept in enough uncomfortable positions in my life to know I'll get sufficient rest in that chair by the window. . .for the governor or anyone who happens by. Even wild horses ridden by the governor won't deter me from my vigil here with you tonight. If I hadn't been so neglectful of you earlier today, the ordeal with Porter would never have happened."

"Actually," she said somewhat sheepishly, "I'm awfully glad you're going to be here. I'm feeling a bit trembly, I admit."

"I'm sure you are."

"But I'm not sleepy."

"I'll sit beside you and keep you entertained."

Nick was well into reminiscing about an experience he'd had at a church camp when he was interrupted by the nurse's arrival with two milk shakes. "One's for you, Mr. Van Vierssen," she announced with a big grin. "Dr. Bremmer thought you needed a treat yourself."

Nick laughed as he got up to assist the nurse in arranging the bed and table so Claire could drink from the straw.

"Dr. Bremmer also phoned the desk just to check on you. Because you're signed in for the night, you're not to leave the hospital until three P.M. tomorrow. Dr. Bremmer also added an emphatic message for you, Mr. Van Vierssen: If you spend the night here, you're to behave yourself as a gentleman, under the staff's strictest supervision."

Nick shook his head as he winked at Claire and took a sip of his milk shake. "Tell Doc Bremmer I'm promising nothing."

"I'll convey your message." The nurse giggled as she headed for the door. "If the milk shake doesn't give you grief, Ms. Rossiter, I'll return with ibuprofen in an hour."

"I bet you're glad to get that news, Claire," Nick said. "At ten o'clock I'm going to tuck you in and insist we both call it a day and try to get some sleep."

∞

Claire woke up with the sun sending shafts of light across the floor. To her dismay, when she called to Nick, he didn't answer. He wasn't there. Her dismay, however, was short-lived. Nick, with a trace of light-colored whiskers, bustled into the room with the morning nurse, who carried a breakfast tray—only soft cream cereal, orange juice, and coffee, but a breakfast, nevertheless.

"Do you think you can manage breakfast okay by yourself, Claire?" Nick asked after the nurse had gone.

"Yes." *As little of it as I'll take. My neck and head hurt more today than yesterday— but I'm not about to tell him that.*

"I'm going to have to leave in a few minutes," Nick reminded her. "There's the governor, as you know, who's probably assembling his white-gloved troops for the afternoon inspection of my august institution."

"May I suggest you shave before you meet the governor," she offered as she took a sip of coffee.

311

"Do you really think I have to?" He scowled petulantly.

"I do, yes," she said with mock severity.

"All right. I'll take care of that to please you and the governor. There are a few logistical details I have to sort out with you before we head back to your campus this evening. You'll need to have something to wear. Tell me your dress size so I can go into Ridglea later this morning to get you a suitable exit ensemble."

"But, Nick, is that really necessary?"

"I insist, sweet maiden." He looked quickly at his watch. "Okay, since I have to add shaving to my agenda, I better get going. Quick now, tell me the size I should ask for at the dress shop in Ridglea."

"I can't let you do this for me, Nick, I. . ."

"And how, in your condition, are you going to stop me? Behave yourself and tell me your size."

"You've got to let me reimburse you."

His mouth pursed in disgust, as he took an exasperated deep breath. "Woman, how do I tolerate this nonsense of yours? If you don't tell me your size, I'll ask the nurses—or I'll guess. And if I do that, you may end up with an atrocious tent. It'll be your own fault."

She snickered as she replied, "I wear size eight tall."

"Eight tall it is."

"You are, without a doubt, the most impossibly forceful, dear, and outrageous tyrant I've ever run across."

"That's my job description, Honey." He leaned down over her breakfast tray, wiped her chin with a napkin, and gave her a good-bye kiss. "The nurses tell me they'll have you ready to depart the premises at six. I'll see that the store delivers your new outfit in plenty of time for you to get yourself into it for your journey."

∞

By noon Claire realized the throbbing in her jaw and neck had abated considerably. No question, the ibuprofen helped a great deal. After assisting her with a shower, an aide put her in a clean gown and robe, affixed the foam collar around her neck, and told her she was free to walk about the hospital.

Looking at herself in the bathroom mirror, Claire was horrified. Her face was swollen and grotesque. Dark blue-black discoloration permeated her entire left cheek, down through her neck. Her left eye was bloodshot. A large area of her lips was scabbing up. "I'm a monster!"

However, walking about the pleasant little hospital facility buoyed her spirits. From a sunroom she looked out onto a garden where a few purple-veined crocuses strained their heads to speak to the sun.

No one would ever guess that a few miles over the hills in the distance, Everettsville prison covered a barren valley. It would be a nice day for the governor's reception. She could picture Nick greeting the contingent from the capital. He'd be dressed in an exceedingly well-tailored suit, maybe the one he'd worn to her recital. Like everyone else, the governor would be impressed by him. Then, if the pattern held true, he'd be uncomfortable noticing Nick's disability. . .but with lighthearted remarks, Nick would put him at ease, and the moment would be quickly behind them.

Nick's handicap wasn't something that had a long-term effect on people's relationships with him. Claire was convinced it would no longer be a factor in the relationship she had with him, either.

At one Nick's package arrived from the dress shop. Folded carefully in layers of tissue paper were chic delphinium blue slacks, an exquisite silk blouse of the same shade, along with a matching faux-suede jacket. Without a doubt, it was one of the loveliest ensembles Claire had ever seen. At the bottom of the box, in a discreet bag, lay packaged undergarments next to a blue voile scarf. In the folds of the scarf was a typed note. "For the veiled look, in case you're sensitive about your rainbow-hued face en route. Nick."

She grinned as she read this. Yes, it would indeed be a good idea to have a scarf handy to tie loosely around her face, especially if they stopped anywhere and got out of the car.

Chapter 12

It was well past six before Nick got to the hospital. Claire sat in the hospital foyer, dressed in her new outfit. An aide had attractively fixed her hair.

He helped her up. "That outfit's ideal for you," he exclaimed, delight evident on his face. "I'll have to admit, it's the perfect shade for you under the present circumstance because there's no doubt about it; your face really is blue, Cindy Sue."

"You're mean," she snapped. "Generous to a fault, a man of exceptionally good taste, and very irresistible—but still mean."

Fortunately, the pain in her mouth and jaw had abated sufficiently for her to put her arms around his waist and give him a tiny hug.

He whispered in her ear, "Actually, Honey, you look one hundred percent better today. With your hair curled forward like that, most of the bruised area's covered." He backed away slowly and looked her up and down. "You're a stunning woman, Claire, bluebird jaw and all. I'm glad you've shed the foam collar, but you may want to use it in the car."

"I'll try going without it for awhile."

"Be sure to have it handy, just in case."

She picked up a plastic bag from the floor. "It's right here."

Claire could almost feel all the eyes in the foyer gazing at them. Gossip being what it is, she suspected everyone knew about her monstrous ordeal at the prison.

Virtually everyone in the hospital knew Nick, who at that moment was a splendid sight to behold. No question about it—he had come directly from the dinner for the governor. Although he wasn't wearing the sophisticated pinstripe he'd worn at her concert, the suit he was wearing was a standout. . .steel gray with a subtle sheen, radiating power, class, and authority. Above suit and tie, Claire noticed, was his normally closely shaven face—the face she dearly loved.

He took the bag from her and led her out to his car, an understated late-model silver sports coupe with sunroof. Claire wasn't prepared, however, for custom-made pressure-panels on doors so Nick could open them. Nor was she ready for knobs on the steering wheel.

Sadly, she had to admit to herself, she'd failed to conquer all the queasiness about his handicap over the last few monumentally transforming hours. Out here in the big, wide world were circumstances she hadn't bargained for—cars, for example, that had adjustments so Nick could cope.

He was wearing both Greifers—because, she supposed, he needed as much dexterity as possible, driving the highway and caring for her.

Once satisfied she was comfortable, he went around and got into his side of the car. They were soon on the highway, winding into hills north of town with which Nick obviously had great familiarity. It was a warm evening, warm enough to keep the sunroof slightly open. As they headed onto the thruway and increased their speed, the breeze carried with it the fragrance of newly turned earth and awakened wildflowers.

Nick turned on a CD. "If you'd rather listen to Beethoven," he commented after a minute or two of light rock, "I think the Eighth Symphony's in that case there."

"No, the CD that's playing is pleasant. I don't often relax listening to Beethoven because I'm always analyzing it—anticipating the orchestral techniques in the development."

He laughed. "I'm that way watching prison shows on TV. Always studying the procedures portrayed. When you know too much about a subject, the errors in script or performance bombard you. You can't take your shoes off, sit back, and just enjoy it."

"I'd like to see you with your shoes off—just relaxing some evening, watching TV."

She noticed him inhale deeply between tightened lips. She'd accidentally stumbled on a subject—whatever it might be—that upset him.

"What I mean is," she explained, trying to extricate herself, "you're nearly always dressed up—ready to give a speech, or coming from a governor's reception. Like tonight, for example, even though you've loosened your tie, you look a bit uptight and formal in that sensational suit. I hope you don't think you have to dress up all the time with me, Nick. As it turns out, I've hardly ever seen you without a jacket—in casual attire, like on Saturday afternoon."

"And was it shocking to you?" he replied much too seriously.

"You mean because. . ."

"Because you could see where the prostheses join my arms?"

"No, because I'd seen that before. At Jim's party."

"Claire," he said with a determination she found unsettling, "relaxing for me often means taking off one or both of my prostheses. That kind of relaxation you wouldn't want to see."

"Silly. I can't imagine not wanting to see you any way at all, with or without your prostheses."

Staring straight ahead, he spoke in barely audible tones, "When I'm alone in my room with all this equipment off—nobody sees me like that."

A chill came over her. She touched his arm, soothingly. "Nick, I'm sorry I've upset you. Let's change the subject. Have you talked with Jim since he's been back?"

He continued to look out over the wheel but followed her suggestion to direct the conversation elsewhere. "Yes, I phoned him earlier today. I told him I was driving you back home and that you'd need a student to give you some assistance for a few days. I know Peg can't be of much help because she's so busy with the baby. But surely someone can get over to help you out."

"Oh, I can always call Irene Dabrovsky. I'm feeling so much better, Nick, that—"

"Be sure to call Irene, Claire—or someone. You aren't supposed to get those wrists wet. And I know you'll be on the pain medication for a few more days. Jim said he had called your department. They're assigning a grad student to teach your lessons."

"I'm glad that's taken care of."

"Jim and Peg wanted us to stop for dinner tonight, but I told them we'd eat on the way. There's an Italian restaurant up the road. Maybe you could manage a sip or two of minestrone—or possibly some manicotti."

He turned his head for a second and tossed her the hint of a smile.

"I'll give manicotti a try," she replied.

They drove on in silence for awhile, Nick seeming to concentrate on thoughts he didn't wish to share with her.

"Did Jim say the students enjoyed their outing at the prison?" she asked, tongue in cheek, breaking the silence.

"We sure gave them something to write home about, didn't we?" She was relieved to see a bit of merriment had returned to his face. "I hope we scared some of those girls out of a career in penology—at least in an institution like Everettsville."

"With proper training they might prove themselves valuable in time, Nick."

"I suppose. I'm still disturbed by women personnel in a male institution. And it's even getting legally tougher and tougher to make any judgment calls about where we place them."

What was on his mind? She was certain there was more to this conversation than was evident on the surface. "Some of the women must be effective in these jobs, though," she offered.

"Yes, some. A few spiritual souls who dress in a subdued fashion and aren't so well-endowed by nature that they immediately direct the men's attention to those endowments. But take yourself, Claire. How could you ever look unattractive enough to divert a man's attention from your alluring womanhood? It couldn't be done.

"By way of example, a year ago an attractive young woman came in to teach ceramics. A jealous inmate put a contract out on her husband, hiring an accomplice on the outside to murder him on his way to work. His altruistic-but-naive wife had a breakdown that required hospitalization."

Claire shuddered. The men in the Fulton Falls courthouse had discussed contracts on Nick himself.

Hesitantly she asked, "Nick, have there been—I mean, have you had any contracts put out on you?"

"A few. Quite awhile ago, actually."

"And that doesn't terrify you? What I'm trying to say. . ."

"At first, it did. But the Lord has brought me through so many skirmishes, like the one we both faced with Porter, that I have to turn to Psalm 18 and believe He rescues me from violent enemies. Also, I'm convinced that it helps to be an amputee."

The darkness of Nick's mood was intensified by the blackness of the interstate as the car plunged through the night.

"What are you trying to tell me, Nick?"

"Merely that I think the inmates don't look upon me as someone to envy."

Nick's honest evaluation of his circumstances bombarded her senses once again. Few people would envy him. Arnold Saxby had told her he didn't.

The governor probably hadn't, either.

As the road veered off to the right, she noticed a lighted exit sign over the highway in the distance, backed by the neon lights of a rest stop. Nick took that exit.

"I'm sure they feel I've already had a contract done on me," Nick continued, "and that hasn't made me grovel. A future contract, short of death, wouldn't do the job for them anyway. The restaurant's just ahead; it's a good one, with high, dark booths that conceal hooks and jaws and anything that might happen to give you embarrassment."

The small-town diner was crowded and poorly lighted. Nick directed her to a corner booth.

"What can I get you, Warden?" asked the waitress, who recognized Nick.

Claire wondered what the woman thought, seeing Nick, a prison official, escorting a woman with a highly battered face.

Not so battered, fortunately, that she couldn't eat manicotti.

At first, it upset her to notice the difficulty Nick had with his utensils. But because he didn't seem unduly embarrassed, after a few moments she was able to overlook his awkwardness enough to enjoy her meal.

The main thrust of the conversation was Nick's insistence she direct her talents into composing a musical. Such a project wasn't pie-in-the-sky fantasy, as far as he was concerned.

"Claire, you should focus on a project like that over the next few months, 'til your wrists heal," Nick said with fervor. "Forget everything else."

It jarred her a bit the way he stressed "everything else" with that faraway look in his blue eyes.

"It's something to think about," she answered, knowing full well that both of them were skirting the subject that filled their minds—namely, their personal lives and their destiny together, if any.

Once they were back in the car, Nick continued to avoid these issues by talking about prisoners he'd dealt with over the years.

"But, Nick, how on earth did you ever get into corrections in the first place?" she asked.

"My career choice was made when, in a rehab hospital, I became friends with a kid of about thirteen named Rick, who was crippled in both legs—and blind. It seems Rick's uncle had appeared from out of the blue and had sent Rick into the streets to peddle drugs. The poor kid misplaced a package of heroin, and his uncle became enraged. He pummeled the youngster with fists and crowbar, crippling and blinding Rick for life."

Claire cringed. "A monster, a madman something like, er—like Porter?"

Taking a deep breath, Nick spoke in a voice both deliberate and soft. "Not exactly. A shade worse, I'd say, because this man was deranged by drugs. But, like Porter, he was a convicted murderer. He had escaped from a penitentiary, so you could say a careless prison staff was responsible for Rick's misery. When I learned this, I was so livid I wanted to phone the White House, or the FBI, or someone on the boy's behalf.

"I didn't, of course. At the time I could barely use a telephone. But I started reading everything I could on the subject of penology, convinced that this was to be my ministry. In time, I enrolled in a university program in corrections in California. It's been my commitment ever since, Claire, to spare a few other kids a fate like Rick's."

"I bet your family was less than overjoyed about your career choice. Ten to one they tried to get you to change your mind."

He rubbed his chin as he nodded. "Ah, yes. They made every effort to talk me out of penology. My dad even tried to convince me I'd never be hired because I wouldn't be able to fire a gun. But I fooled him and rigged up a pistol I could handle. Then I badgered some people in high places to give me a chance. My dad was a vice admiral in the navy before he retired, so he has a few friends who pull weight in Washington. That didn't hurt my chances. But what it basically came down to is, there was a shortage of personnel in a facility near Hartford, so I got the job."

Hartford—she'd performed in Hartford once. Playing her concert there, she'd given nary a thought to prisons.

"So that goes to show you, Claire," he declared, "that once the Lord taps you on the shoulder for something, He also gives you the persistence and the imagination—and the opportunities—to follow through with it. But you're right; it didn't thrill my folks. They'd have preferred my going into my dad's business."

Curious, Claire commented, "I gather that resembles in no way, shape, or form a penitentiary."

He chuckled. "Not hardly. He runs a marina and mast and rigging outfit down near Norfolk. For centuries, the Van Vierssens have been men who went down to sea in ships."

"Operating sailboats on the Chesapeake sounds sensational to me. How could you refuse such a—"

"Oh, Claire, that would be the worst place for me. When I'm down there, I can take a motorboat out for a spin. That's done simply by turning a key. But working with masts and ropes would be out of the question for someone with my disability. In my dad's company, I'd be no more than an overprotected office drone."

They'd arrived at the campus, and he was driving around the parade grounds to Regent Street. "When all is said and done, I've found an important job in which I excel. I've found my own little corner of the universe where I can perform a service.

"Also," he said, enunciating each word much too carefully, "I'm in a field where being single is a distinct advantage. So that's important, too."

"But, Nick," she choked out after a split second of shocked silence, "you don't expect to be single all your life. Not anymore. Not after. . ."

He stared intently at the street ahead and moistened his lips several times before he spoke.

"I'm never going to get married, Claire; marriage can't be a part of my world. It's something a guy like me couldn't cope with. I'm sorry, but I just couldn't share my private pain with a woman I loved."

She was aghast at the finality with which he said these words—so stupefied, she couldn't answer him.

He pulled into her driveway behind her hatchback, which had been parked there by the students Saturday night. Switching off the engine, he turned to her.

"Claire, you're not well enough to discuss anything heavy tonight. It's unfortunate that the subject of marriage came up. But, since it did, I must convey to you right now the realities of my life, and why marriage is out for me."

She grasped his arm. "Nick, you can't possibly mean that after all we've been through this weekend, there's no future for us—none at all."

"You've got to be brave for both of us," he appealed. "Let me help you out of the car. I'll fix you some tea, coffee, cocoa, whatever, and make you comfortable so you can get some sleep."

He was leaning away, sliding out of the car. "We'll talk it over inside," he said. He went around and opened her door. "Come on, now, up you go. You'll understand better after I've explained things to you."

"I'll never understand," she stammered as she stepped out of the car. He pulled her toward him, his face a breath away from hers.

"My darling Claire, sometimes we have to face up to tragedy head-on, with squared shoulders and no emotion whatsoever. The Lord does expect this now and then. Isaiah tells us that the direction we might like to go isn't necessarily the way the Lord would want us to go. He often has a higher way. Frequently, it's tough for us to accept that higher way. Years ago I had to face up to this handicap of mine. Tonight I'm going to have to help you face up to it, too."

"Nick, I have faced up to it," she cried, allowing her shoulder to fall under his muscular arm, as he walked her to the door. "I've come such a long way these past few months. Seeing you with a serious disability saddens me, yes. I think it's dreadful, but our not being together would be more dreadful. I can't bear the thought of that anymore."

"Let's have your key so we can go inside," he stated. "We can't stand out here indefinitely. You need to lie down."

She fumbled in her purse for the key. Shaking, she inserted it into the lock. With both prostheses, plus her weak assistance, Nick pushed open the door.

Chapter 13

Once inside, Claire clutched Nick's arms tightly, despite throbbing pain coursing through her arms and jaw, making her eyes water.

"Nick, I will not accept this. You're indispensable in my life now. I'm sure you care for me as well. That's what's destroying me—knowing that you care for me but won't admit it. Jesus personifies compassion and gentle kindness. He couldn't possibly expect us to go our separate ways."

Nick took a deep breath but said nothing, letting her continue. "I'm not as familiar with Scripture passages as you are, but I've felt from the moment I first met you that there was more than coincidence in all of this. It was a manifestation of divine direction. We have to see each other again—and often—if for no other reason than that we are God-anointed best friends. You have become"—she pulled away and glanced up at him—"my dearest friend."

He shook his head several times. "Claire, I can't see you again. We're already well beyond friendship. We've reached a point of agony. Certainly I have. Going on like this will bring me to marriage or madness, or should I say marriage and madness. Marriage is out of the question because insanity is something I know the Lord doesn't want."

"Nick, why is marriage so out of the question? I have no intention of wrenching you away from your ministry to prisoners. Couldn't we, as married people, come up with some satisfactory arrangement? If you worried about my safety near the prison, I could continue living here—keeping my own name—and we could be together on weekends. Or I could live in the city. It's only a short sprint from Everettsville. We'd have an unlisted phone number. . . ."

"Claire, stop all this nonsense."

With needlelike pain racing down her arms, she had to let go of him. Her legs could barely hold her up.

Nick caught her to prevent her from falling. Steadying her with his strong right arm, he helped her to the sofa in the living room.

He knelt down next to her on one knee. "You're exhausted, Claire. Why, oh, why must we torture ourselves talking about marriage when it can never happen for us?"

Frantic pleading poured from her lips. "For me, it's got to happen. God respects the kind of love I have for you, Nick. How can you toss me aside? You love me! Don't try to tell me otherwise. I know you do."

"That's not the major thing to consider. . . ."

"It is for me. Frankly, I'd just like to hear you tell me, yes or no: Are you in love with me?"

Nick put an elbow on the edge of the couch and allowed his head to fall down on the prosthesis. His voice was barely audible. "Claire, of course I'm in love with you. A man would have to be blind, deaf, and demented not to love you. I'm so crazy about you, I can't even keep my thoughts straight anymore."

"So, if you love me, what kind of gamble is there?" She sat up and wove her fingers through a strand of his exquisite hair. "We can go on much as we've been doing in our careers. We have incomes satisfactory to keep us solvent. We're both Christians, and I'd so enjoy your teaching me more about God. Nick, I understand and accept your handicap completely, and. . ."

Extricating himself from her touch, he stood up and moved away from her, then abruptly turned back. "Claire, that's precisely the problem. You do not understand my handicap completely. You could never accept it." His beautiful lips enunciated these words softly but with a terrifying insistence.

"What absurdity! I hardly think about your prostheses or your limitations anymore," she replied, her voice, as well as her entire body, trembling out of control. "I was attracted to you before I knew you had any handicap. I've accepted the fact that you have one. I could manage as your wife very well."

He walked slowly over to the fireplace. Putting both his arms down on the mantel, he rested his head on his arms for several minutes. Then he raised it slowly.

"So you think you know me, Claire," he said, his face now addressing the bricks of the chimney. "Would it surprise you to know that at this moment I'm a most unrighteous individual? I'm identifying with Porter—Porter, that murderous goon who nearly killed you in the storage room. And you know what? I'm as miserable a slob as he is. I desperately, frantically want to make love to you. Right now, I'm envious of that punk."

He attempted a halfhearted, almost sardonic smile. "I'm jealous of him and all the other Porters of the world who have the capacity to touch you—to finger your beautiful face and caress your body."

He pounded one of his prostheses down on the mantel with a violent thud. "I'm so torn up inside with desire for you that I'm close to the brink myself."

She wanted to scream her outrage. But the screams caught in her throat, a throat paralyzed in incredulity, causing those screams to emerge as gasps.

"I'm every bit as big a ghoul as the Porters of that hole of a prison, Claire," Nick continued. "The only difference is that I'm locked in a different kind of prison—with a life sentence and no key—so even if I wear a five-hundred-dollar suit, speak more coherently than Porter, and beg God to forgive me, I'm no better than he is. I want you the same way he did—maybe more."

"Nick," she finally hurled back at him, "what you're saying is outrageous.

You're nothing like Porter."

Tears surged from her eyes. She hurried to him and leaned full against his back, her face now pulsing with pain against the arch of his spine. "How could you think such hideous thoughts? Is it wrong to admit that you're a human being? Did God create you to be an emotionless automaton? So you have machine fingers; does that mean you're to replace a sensitive and loving spirit with some sort of machine there, as well?"

Her words stumbled forth between sobs. "Loving me is not a mortal sin, Nick. It's natural. It's wonderful. I want you to desire me. And I want to return your love. Furthermore, I'm confident we can make it. Why don't you at least let us give it a try?"

"No! We can't, Claire. We can't!" he shouted. It frightened her to hear him shout. "That's exactly what we cannot do—give it a try."

He turned to her, his lips tight, obviously attempting to keep his emotions in check. In a more controlled voice he went on. "That's the reason it won't work, don't you see, Darling? Because it would be an experiment, an experiment filled with appalling embarrassment and frustration for us both. In a lab, if an experiment fails, the scientist starts over again with clean vials, discarding the original contents. And you could do that! You could go back to your millionaire backers and your friends on campus, chalking up our marriage as an experiment that just didn't happen to work out. Isn't that true?"

For a second or two she was tongue-tied by the savage scrutiny of his eyes. It was not an idle accusation he was making. He really believed there was truth in those odious words.

"I resent that," she seethed. "It would not be just an experiment. Granted, I've been a lapsed Christian, but I would not take the vows of matrimony lightly. I'd never think of marriage to you as a mere experiment."

"It would have to be, Claire, because there are so many things you don't know about and probably couldn't live with. What I'm trying to say is that you could survive a divorce or an annulment. But I couldn't."

His voice had become distant and introspective. "I think you should be sitting down. You aren't strong enough to stand for so long."

He put an arm around her waist and propelled her back to the sofa. "I want you to lie still and let me try to explain as honestly and candidly as I can the complications of this situation."

The weight of disillusionment more than the pain in her face caused her to slump onto the sofa. Her jaw throbbed unmercifully as she lowered it against a pillow he had positioned there.

"Why don't you let me get you a cup of tea?" he asked.

She shook her head.

"Coffee?"

"Nothing."

He slid to the floor and sat catty-corner to her, his back against the side unit of the sofa, one of his knees raised. He looked up at her and continued. "Claire, you may think I'm being exceedingly selfish about all this, that I'm not thinking about you. Trust me when I say that I am. Some of my friends in various hospitals were married—several of them fathers of young children. I saw whole families dissolve over handicaps like mine—in most cases, they weren't even as debilitating as mine. I saw men of brilliant mind and supreme courage crumple into madness. In fact, I'm one of the fortunate ones. Do you believe that? It's true; I am.

"I often think the fact that I'd been at the Naval Academy was the main reason I made it. That sounds ridiculous in light of the fact that if I hadn't gone to Annapolis, the accident wouldn't have happened at all. Ironically, though, the training I had there made the difference in my recovery."

He stretched his arms up behind him along the edge of the cushions. "You see, I had to stand in formation and put up with little annoyances like a mosquito on my forehead—or an unbearable itch on my arm. That discipline, being able to endure tactile irritation without flinching, got me through the early weeks after the accident. Navy discipline, superb help from my parents, chaplain Buck Wilson with a faith that moved mountains, and a terrific hospital staff kept me on keel. So I'm in pretty good shape, all things considered."

"Nick, I think you'd have come through successfully no matter where you went to school or who was at your bedside," she stammered. "You're the most mature human being I've ever met."

"Oh, darling Claire, you can't imagine what it's been like. I haven't always been mature. Oh, man," he groaned, "many days I–I—well, I can only say I was anything but mature."

Inhaling deeply, he leaned his head back against the sofa seat and stared at the ceiling. "You can't begin to comprehend my limitations—just from what you've observed when we've been together. Even in that laundry room, when you saw I couldn't untie the gag quickly enough and had to let Drake do it, that's just the tip of the iceberg. Beneath this facade of conventional exterior, Claire, is the most barbarous of creatures. If you could see me in the privacy of my shower—after I've removed these plastic cuffs, fixtures, and batteries—if you could witness the helplessness of your beloved, you'd be wretched and overcome with revulsion."

"Stop it!" she stormed at him, rising to reach down and press her hand firmly on his knee. "I won't let you go on castigating yourself like that. It's fruitless, and it takes us nowhere."

"Hear me out, Claire, just hear me out, because you won't understand fully unless I tell you these things. You could never fathom how helpless I am."

Galuppi had come in and jumped up on Nick's lap. Looking down at the cat, Nick began stroking him slowly. "I'm what is known in medical circles as a wrist and below-elbow bilateral amputee," he continued. "That's basically what I amount to in clinical terms. And you should know those terms.

"Because I was a decent enough athlete as a youngster, I have well-developed muscles that respond favorably to state-of-the-art devices that can perform a motion that brings two or three surfaces in opposition, allowing for grasp of objects. Easy? Automatic? No, it's difficult in the extreme, requiring effort and great concentration that I often wish I could ignore once in awhile.

"I was lucky to have had superlative surgery, but besides the normal phantom pain, which can be excruciating, I have an unusual problem: sensitive skin. My stumps often become tingly. I get severe prickly aggravation, even swelling. On hot days I can develop irritation, itching, and occasionally a rash—a bit like you might if you were to wear plastic gloves night and day. When that happens, I desperately look forward to the hour when I can return to my quarters, remove one or both of these prostheses, and finally put my stumps on a horizontal surface—preferably my bed—and cool off."

She stared down at him, feeling ill. Why was he talking about such things as "stumps," a term so gross that hearing it prompted waves of nausea to well up in her stomach?

He went on. "I have a wand that I can manipulate with my teeth—or my stumps together, if I want to turn pages of a book, or turn on the television, or make a phone call. A pencil with an eraser can be effective also. I can put the wand or pencil in the crook of my elbow and function somewhat.

"But neither of these things can open doors, so I live in constant dread of fire. Even with my prostheses on, I'm in mortal fear of fire. Occasionally I have nightmares about it. I pray the Lord will one day release me from this fear, but He hasn't yet. I never close my door or window tightly, if I can help it."

Trembling with this revelation, Claire realized she had not envisioned these horrors. Suppressed sobs escaped her chest.

But Nick's modulated voice drove onward. "An amputee learns over many months that if he's going to make it, he has to start compensating for the loss of his hands with toes, teeth, chin—you name it. I'm sure it will come as a surprise to you to learn that I'm remarkably dexterous with my toes. The truth is, I can sign my name with my toes as well as I can with my Greifer. Most people are revolted by this accomplishment, so I don't mention it often."

He paused. Gradually his head turned to her. He sighed in despair before proceeding. "Perhaps you have some curiosity as to how I get dressed or put on these mechanical hands. It's truly a sight to behold. My gyrations and contortions with arms, knees, and chin are not a pretty sight. My mother saw me getting into my paraphernalia once, Claire, and fainted; a rescue squad had to come to the house. How do you think it feels to see someone I love collapse at the sight of me getting ready for my day's occupation?"

His eyes pierced hers. However, there was no sign of anger present in eyes or in tone of voice, just an eerie persistence.

"There are even more unsavory situations that I won't go into, but I think you get the drift. How long after a wedding do you think you could endure witnessing my existence? A week? A month, maybe? Perhaps a year, with God's help. But that would be pushing it, don't you suppose?

"And, as I said before, once we split up, you could make a promising future for yourself—you know you could. You could return to Henri in Paris, and he'd welcome you with open arms—open arms ending in fingers of flesh. But what would that do to me? My psychological survival would be at stake."

Ignorant of the tension of the moment, Galuppi slept, purring on Nick's lap. "St. Paul tells us, Claire, in his first letter to the Corinthians, that love doesn't insist on its own way. Any love we have for each other cannot insist on its own way. The prison community depends on me. God depends on me to do His work there. Furthermore, I can't present to my father and mother in their senior years a son who is mad as well as mutilated. Marriage is not in the Lord's plan for me, despite your thoughts to the contrary. To become involved with you is to destroy myself."

He raised his arm and rested it gently on her legs. "Tell me, how could I let you go if you were my wife? If I had kissed you as passionately, albeit clumsily, as I desire to, and we had consummated our love? How could I face your looks of pity, the moisture welling in your eyes day in and day out? Or the clenched teeth as you went about 'seeing things through.' It's tough enough to see my parents responding this way when I visit them. But every day, with you as my wife. . .well, it would be impossible. And when you finally decided you had to leave, I could not survive it. It will be hard enough to survive today—or this week."

He pressed a prosthesis against one eye for a few seconds, then let it slam down to the floor by his side. Claire's whole body shook, and she felt tears spilling from her eyes.

"Claire, Porter's savage attack on you all but did me in emotionally. Yes, it's going to be no small task to recover from this week. My existence up to now has been plodding along, better than I ever expected it would. I contribute significantly in my field. The Lord has worked through me to salvage many lives. Like St. Paul, with his thorn in the flesh, I witness victories. Can any of us hope for much more than that, in Christ's name? I don't think we can."

"Nick, I. . . ," she began, but found she was unable to formulate any sensible reply. Her lips were limp. Nick's words had left her spirit limp, as well.

"Look at yourself," he said with the hint of a smile, in an attempt at cheerfulness. "The mishap that befell you won't affect your performances in the long run. You'll have recitals galore. What's more, you're going to turn your attention to composing, allowing the Holy Spirit to inspire you to write music that may well edify thousands."

But she was unable to think of herself or her future. The sting of his statements about his tragic existence had seared her brain, prompting reevaluation. She had wormed her way into the life of a noble human being whose private world was a living nightmare.

She had tempted him most sinfully. The fact that she'd pushed him, a man she idolized, to this unhappy point made her feel cheap, almost sadistic, and full of remorse.

If she really loved him—and she did, in a way she never could have believed possible to love any man—she would have to allow him to return to the impenetrable cocoon he'd woven for himself.

Shamefully, she recognized that her love for Nick, for far too long, had indeed been insisting on its own way.

Slowly, she slid down onto the floor next to him, picked up Galuppi, and laid the cat on the rug. Unfathomable, undefinable emotion directed her fingers to trace the indentations of his cheek.

The words came slowly. "My dearest, dearest Nick. I never could have known—I had no idea, honestly. I regret so deeply that I've brought you to the point where you felt you had to disclose all these painful things to me. I've been selfish and cruel—but not intentionally. Nick, you have to believe I never meant to be cruel."

"You don't have to tell me that, Claire."

"How wrong I've been from the start—beginning with the briefcase incident. Despite my best efforts, I've brought you nothing since we met but frustration, expense, inconvenience, and anguish."

"That isn't true at all. You've brought me joy, a type of joy I hadn't experienced since—since I was a kid, I guess. To have been acquainted with someone as adorable, talented, and fascinating as you, Claire, and as perceptive and decent—well, our time together has provided me with great pleasure. And fun! I'm thrilled that you love me, and I'd marry you in an instant if things were different. No Henri or wealthy impresario or any three-hundred-pound wrestling coach here at State would stand in my way."

"Nick, I'd give my life, I really would—I'd give up my music, everything—if I could wipe away the frustrations of your life. I'd gladly open your doors and windows and put out the fearful fires. . . ."

He pressed his arm closely around her, his biceps taut and firm, and so comforting. "I appreciate those words, Claire." He tousled her hair. "Now I'm going to go out into that kitchen of yours and rustle up some soup, coffee, lemonade, or something."

He got up, and she did, too, though her head ached as she did so.

"No, Nick—I'm going to do that. There's chocolate cake and ice cream in the freezer, and I have some rather exotic spiced tea and—"

"My limitations do not include getting ice cream or cake from the freezer or fixing a cup of tea. Claire, don't you believe I can do these things for you?"

"Of course I believe you can. I know you can. You can do almost everything. But tonight I want to do this myself because I'd like things to be special. Besides, there's something else I want you to do. Select a CD of mellow music and play it for us. We'll eat right in here."

"I'd rather you just relax on the sofa and let me—"

"I have a Belgian lace cloth for this side table. It'll be elegant. Then after we've eaten, Nick, I'm going to take my medication; I'm getting pain in my jaw—it's becoming severe."

"That's because you're overdoing. You've been through a lot of trauma, and you should be resting."

"Not right now, because I want to plan a tiny party for us. Listen to me carefully. After we've eaten, as I said, I'm going to take my medication, and you're going to hold me in your arms—those strong muscles of yours are going to hold me until. . ."

He was looking down at her with questioning but patient eyes. "I've discussed all this so thoroughly, Claire. This is not the way to go."

"I want your arms around me, Nick," she went on determinedly. "I'll behave myself like a good little girl—no flirtations, no teasing, no come-ons. I'll let the medication take effect, and I'll fall asleep. I'll fall peacefully to sleep in your arms." She began to find the words difficult to say. "And, Nick, when I wake up, you'll be gone. Sometime in the night you'll get up and leave. Because. . .because, my dearest, if there's one pain I can't bear, it's seeing you walk out of my life again."

He bit his upper lip. Then he rubbed his forehead with his forearm. "All right," he said, lowering his arm, "if that's what you want."

"It's the only way I can let you go—for good. And, Nick, I promise, I really do, not to bounce my way into your world again." She trembled with the awful chill of these words. "I'll never storm your private barricades."

"Claire. . ."

"You can send me all the forms I have to sign regarding Porter—I'll sign them and send them right back. And if I ever need to get in touch with you for any reason, I'll do it through Jim. Should our paths cross, you have my word I won't lose my cool or embarrass you. Now I'm going to get our snack ready." She attempted to generate a sprightly air. "Act the DJ, please, and select a CD from the stereo cabinet."

He pulled her to him, turning her head to his. He leaned down and kissed her hair. Then he rested his head against hers and spoke softly into her ear, "Darling Claire, my sweet love, I'll do exactly as you wish. But I want you to know, as you fall asleep tonight, that in my thoughts I'll be holding you as my own, all of my life."

Chapter 14

Claire's June 6 arrival in Paris for her annual eight weeks with Henri and Yolande failed to raise her spirits sufficiently for her to recover from the trauma of losing Nick. She hadn't spent more than a few days with them before Henri disclosed his alarm about her appearance and lack of enthusiasm.

"You're not well, Claire-Therese. Yolande and I will have to outdo ourselves to put that sparkle back in your eyes. There's a Cezanne exhibit at the Louvre, a recital at Sacre Coeur, a—"

"Oh, Henri, I'm not up to all that. I've barely unpacked."

From the living room window, the tip of the Eiffel Tower reflected the setting sun over neighborhood rooftops. Below, on the street heading toward the Bois, autos scurried in and out of lanes, honking a welcome to the tantalizing Paris evening.

Claire's thoughts slipped back to Nick. What time would it be at Everettsville right now? Two o'clock, she calculated.

She pictured him walking through the new complex and down the catwalks of the old. In Paris, purple twilight descended on well-dressed people, a great contrast to the characters who walked past Nick in those awful cell blocks.

"Chérie, you are ill," Henri remarked. "You should see a doctor."

She shook her head, "No, I don't need a doctor." Tears she couldn't control beaded in her eyes as she turned around to face her kind family friend.

His expression told her he'd stumbled on the truth.

"You're in love, aren't you," he said.

She took several deep breaths to gain composure. "It was nothing more than a mere interlude."

He walked over to her and touched her eyes with his handkerchief. "Interludes do not create such havoc in the eyes of the accomplished Claire-Therese Rossiter, eyes I've observed since you were a child. Wouldn't it help to talk about it? Perhaps there is some way I can help."

"Talking is therapeutic, yes, but in this case, so difficult."

Henri guided her into a chair. Sitting on the adjacent couch, he listened attentively as she described her friendship with Nick.

At the mention of Nick being an amputee, Henri's eyes widened in shock. "An amputee. How did this happen?"

"An explosion while he was a student at Annapolis," Claire explained. "He

329

refuses to consider marriage at all—and it's destroying me. I love him so much." The sobs surged up from her chest and soon convulsed her.

"*Ma petite amie*—how sad for you, for him as well.

"Where did you encounter this man? Is he a fellow professor? He can't be a musician, or. . ."

He paused, his eyes narrowing. "Wait a minute. Last fall, at your first recital of the season—at Lincoln Center. That good-looking prison warden came backstage with sumptuous roses—the warden whose briefcase you swiped by mistake. I remember that you were euphoric when you saw him. But he isn't an amputee— or is he?"

She tossed her head back and looked at the ceiling. "Yes, he's the guy."

"Oh, how tragic. He's a fine-looking chap—such a strong face. What a calamity. But, Claire-Therese, exceptional men and women often find solutions for the impossible. If there's some way I can help you and your noble friend, the warden. . ."

"My sweet Henri. . ." With tenderness she clasped his hand tightly. "There's no way—we can only hurt him further. Although he loves me, he believes we shouldn't see each other again. I reluctantly agreed. That's why I need a change of scenery so much this summer—my visit here and, next week, a few hours in Switzerland with Madame Bouchard, my childhood teacher."

"Personally, I don't think that you should traipse off to Montreux—by train alone. I'm worried about you, now more than ever, with this unhappy experience weighing on your spirit. I'd be glad to drive—"

"Henri, I'll manage fine. Besides, it's only for a couple of days. Then I'll be back here in Paris once again for almost two months before I head home to the States."

∞

Friday, as the train drew near Montreux, the familiar mountains appeared like roly-poly circus bears cavorting one on top of the other. They generated in her the joyful anticipation she needed to lighten her spirit.

Once in the city itself, she sat beside the lake to soak up the fairy-tale view. Across the iridescent water stood Byron's Castle of Chillon, famous as a prison for a family of patriots.

Unlike Everettsville, this prison stood surrounded by alpine magnificence.

Yet, inside this idyllic castle, Claire knew, lay dark dungeons more depressing than anything at Everettsville. Nick would find the castle's cells professionally intriguing.

She longed to share the castle with Nick, as well as picturesque Montreux. All of it, the quaint awninged buildings and the welcoming cafes and shops.

After settling in at the hotel, she went downstairs and asked the concierge to arrange for a car rental the next day to drive to Madame Bouchard's well-known school.

To her surprise, the concierge informed her the school didn't exist any longer. Instead, it had become a retreat center. She handed Claire a brochure that described the center, established by Madame Bouchard with assistance from such individuals as the nationally famous Austrian mezzo-soprano Gretl Schutt and shipping tycoon Giovanni Cambini.

That evening, when she phoned Henri to report that all was well, she couldn't control her excitement about visiting the center. "It's a Christian community, Henri—ecumenical, from what I gather—and well-known among the intelligentsia on the Continent."

"Claire, please change your mind," he implored. "Your Madame Bouchard's at least eighty. Her mind may be failing."

A grin engulfed Claire's face. "I sincerely doubt it. Under the circumstances, I want to see her more than ever."

"Claire-Therese, may I remind you, you're already on the downswing into melancholy about this amputee you're in love with. Do you think it sensible to waste time listening to a senile old woman ruminate in a smelly cloister about heaven and angels? You better get out of there and on the train back. . ."

"Not a chance," she declared. "I'm off to heaven and angels."

⁓

What an excursion into nostalgia for Claire to drive up the familiar mountain highway to the old school. At every turn in the road, a pine tree or rock formation joined the wind in calling out hello. The mountains hugged her to them. Chalets curtsied in recognition.

Her meeting with Madame Bouchard exceeded all expectations. The frail, white-haired teacher hugged her with arms that yet had youthful strength as she ushered Claire into the familiar library.

"Claire-Therese, I was delirious with excitement when you called from Montreux to tell me you were coming to see me." She spoke in French, as did Claire. "A treat—a blessing—to enrich my day."

She pelted Claire with kisses as she continued, "I'm so eager to talk to you, and to hear you play for me. It has been too many years since I've seen you."

Nothing had changed since Claire's graduation. Every piece of furniture, including the ornate upright piano, was in the same place.

"So, what will it be? Mozart? Chopin?" asked the woman.

Claire raised her hands in obedient acquiescence. "Mozart? How will Mozart do?"

"Wonderfully."

Claire sat on the leather tufted bench and began a rondo that readily came to mind. Her mentor leaned against the side of the upright, her eyes bathing Claire with affection.

After the last note was played, Claire could see tears in those eyes.

"Claire-Therese, oh, my dear child, that was sublime," she crooned. "You are every bit as accomplished as the reports. Play something else, please."

"Only one more selection. There's so much to talk about. So many things for you to tell me. I must spend time listening to you."

The woman shrugged her shoulders and nodded yes.

Claire began the downward passages of a Bartok favorite, a vigorous, showy piece that she knew would satisfy as a finale.

With the last resounding chord echoing through the room, she rose from the bench and embraced the old teacher, who was visibly shaken by the power of the music.

They moved to two needlepoint chairs and sat down side by side.

"Now tell me, why did you give up the school?" Claire asked.

The woman described how individuals throughout Europe had felt the need to establish a center where they could join together in prayer for discernment—discernment to ameliorate the traumas of a hostile and chaotic world.

Madame Bouchard took a moment to squeeze Claire's hand in sweet friendship. "Too long we've neglected examining the Lord's purposes," she declared. "And our planet is in peril because of this neglect. People are crying out for altruistic role models who can help them find solutions for inequality and injustice.

"James 1:17 says: 'Every good and perfect gift is from above, coming down from the Father of the heavenly lights. . . .' Think of that—every good gift, such as your enormous musical ability."

Fingering back a wide swath through her short, uncoiffed white hair, Madame Bouchard proceeded, "The retreat program here was rather like a thunderbolt from the Holy Spirit that touched many individuals at the same time. Together, we turned this spot into an ecumenical Christian community. Oh, the blessings the Lord Jesus has showered on us. Each day we witness manifestations of His love. Like your coming into my life once again."

Claire looked back up into her teacher's face, which reflected a radiance that defied description.

Getting up from the chair, Claire walked to the west window, which framed splendor unsurpassed anywhere else on earth. Instead of feeling intimidated by the grandeur of the landscape, so illustrating God's mighty handiwork, she was overwhelmed by a realization of her value in God's eyes.

"Nick," she spoke softly to herself. "Oh, my precious Nick, is this it? Is the Lord really knocking at the door of my life to come in? Oh, I want You to do so, dear Lord Jesus. Forgive me for my neglect of You and for my selfish offenses. I need Your grace in my life."

A serenity settled upon Claire, promising a mystical bond between Nick and herself—and God—that oceans, mountains, and walls could never sever, no matter where her steps would take her in the future.

Blinking away tears of joy, she turned back to Madame Bouchard.

"You are one of us in the Spirit, I think," the woman said, "anointed by the Holy Counselor."

Claire smiled a yes, the tears flowing copiously. It was beyond words, this experience.

∞

Dinner in the community was simple fare, served buffet style to about fifty men and women in the large dining room. All appeared comfortable with the routine of the community, enthusiastically committed to its overriding policy—namely, that five weeks of every year be tithed to God, ideally one week in prayer at Montreux and four in "foot washing" service to the poor or infirm.

An Italian banker at her table had worked as a laborer building septic tanks in Sicily. One of the writers had manned a London ghetto youth center.

"This way of life is not for everyone," said the banker, Signor Alessandro Galdieri, "but for us, it is the answer. We have been richly endowed, most of us, with families, money, and skills. But God calls us to assist the less fortunate. Our community here helps us focus on the area that commitment will take."

After dinner, as they headed for a chapel service, Signor Galdieri took her aside. "Even tonight, your being here, Ms. Rossiter, is in the nature of a spectacular blessing. At least, I think it may be. Following a phone call this very afternoon, I find myself in need of a musician."

"Surely not this musician," Claire replied, amusement in her eyes.

Signor Galdieri shrugged his shoulder, a beguiling smile on his face. "Quite possibly. I back a ballet company in Torino, which will be touring the United States next spring—it's opening in Houston. A protégé of mine, a highly skilled young ballerina of exceptional promise, was collaborating with an elderly composer on the subject of the poem 'Pippa Passes' by Robert Browning.

"If you recall, the poem deals with the little Italian factory girl whose cheerfulness alters the lives of many prominent citizens of Asolo."

"I do remember a bit about that poem, yes. It's a gem."

"The theme's especially engaging for this troupe because it employs an Italian subject immortalized by Browning, who made his home in Florence. I received word earlier today that the composer has suffered a stroke and cannot continue work on the ballet. Your success on the concert stage is well-known. And your comment over dinner that you have quite a few weeks yet of vacation leads me to wonder if you aren't the one the Lord has selected to help us out. We must go into production and rehearsal in two weeks' time."

Claire was prepared to give Alessandro Galdieri her customary expression of gentle dismissal, followed by the words, "I'm sorry, but. . ." Then she checked herself. This was the very thing Nick thought she should be doing. If he were there, he'd be pushing her to accept the commission.

Her hesitancy caused the gentleman to speak further. "I know you will want to pray about this."

He paused and took a card from his wallet. Handing it to her, he continued. "I find myself in such a corner right now, I am behaving more impulsively than manners would dictate. The score is almost finished—only a *pas de deux* is yet to be written, plus, perhaps, some polishing needed on the whole." His sentences spilled out, his eagerness to have her aboard anything but subtle. "Naturally, you and the original composer would be listed as collaborators on the score."

"As a matter of fact, Signor Galdieri," she responded, "I have done some accompanying for the dance, so I do have an understanding of the type of music you need. But you're right when you say I must think about it—er, pray about it, if you will. Yes, I do need to do some praying. I'll give you my answer tomorrow morning."

When she phoned Henri the next day, she told him she had accepted an astonishing offer from a Signor Galdieri of Turin.

His reaction surprised her. "Alessandro Galdieri's one of the most influential men in the Po Valley, and you're telling me he was up on the mountaintop praying?"

"Yes, he's one of the many luminaries up there."

"Praying?"

"Yes, praying. Actually, Signor Galdieri believed I was the answer to his prayer."

"This is all very bewildering to me. But all I can say, Claire-Therese, is if this ballet comes off to rave reviews in Houston, I myself may fall on my knees." She could hear him chortling as he said this.

"Consider it done," she laughed back. With prayer, she now knew, even Henri on his knees might become a reality.

Chapter 15

Within days of the mountaintop meeting with Signor Galdieri, Claire found herself ensconced in a spacious apartment in Turin. The ballet production staff had provided her with a computer and a fine grand piano—the piano not only necessary for composing ballet music, but also for the practice required for her fall tour.

"Nick would never believe these palatial quarters," she gasped when she first beheld her surroundings. "A prison cell it is not."

In the ensuing weeks, collaboration with the ballerina Gina Vitale and the ailing composer, Guido Fardisi, proved to be virtually trouble free.

Watching Gina execute steps to the music left Claire incredulous, overcome with the realization that the fine performance unfolding before her was the result of her efforts—hers, Guido's, Gina's—and the Lord's.

And Nick's as well. At Madame Bouchard's she had almost sensed him prompting the yes she gave to Signor Galdieri.

Prayer indeed had caused this startling adventure to happen. Each day she asked the Holy Spirit to breathe His song into the music. To her surprise, melody upon melody, cadence upon cadence came from within and made their way to her fingers, the piano, and eventually to the computer.

Rehearsal went on even as final drafts were being sent for copyright and print-outs. Claire found herself caught up in the ebullience of the dedicated troupe, hardly willing to call it quits even when sessions continued well past midnight.

Signor Galdieri was jubilant, more than ever convinced God had sent Claire to him. He agreed with Gina that when the ballet was finally staged in Houston the results would be "dazzling."

Dazzling! Could a ballet she had helped compose actually be dazzling? It seemed that might be so.

"Next summer," Signor Galdieri proposed, "we shall want you back with us again, my dear young friend, for a work based on the life of St. Francis. With much symbolism—dancers as birds, animals, and the like. Over the winter you will put down all the tunes that pop into your head. Fax them on to me. I foresee for you, sweet lady, a most remarkable career."

Already plans were made for Claire's trip to Houston in May for the opening night, a gala Henri and Yolande planned to attend. Jim and Peg might be there, too. But not Nick.

She debated about contacting him in what certainly had to be an exceptional occurrence. But with misgiving, she decided no; it was up to Jim and Peg to tell him about the ballet opening.

After the show's video became available, she'd give Jim an extra one to send to Nick.

She'd do that. But nothing more.

∞

Because of the extended weeks in Turin, Claire returned to the States facing a ferocious schedule. She had no regrets—the experience had proved to be exhilarating. But the project had forced her to squeeze a week of business into an afternoon.

The morning she landed, after the flight from Paris, she took a cab from the airport shuttle drop-off in the city to meet with her agent. There were loose ends about the fall tour—papers to sign, dates to be double-checked.

As the taxi snaked through the city traffic, she had time to lean back and assess the life-transforming weeks she'd just spent in Turin.

Sitting in the cab, Claire tried to organize her thoughts. There would be no lessons. Not 'til spring semester because the concert tour was so ambitious. Seven, eight hours of practice a day would be minimum to hone the Chopin E Minor Concerto—plus several encore selections—by October.

On October 11 she'd travel to Milwaukee for three days' rehearsal with the Great Lakes Philharmonic, which would make the tour with her.

The six weeks ahead would be devoted to lonely practice once again, with no hope of ever duplicating that tour de force in Cincinnati.

How much more enjoyable it would be to remain in Turin, watching the ballet evolve into a polished, professional production. Or even just to return to the campus and take things easy for a month, rusticating on Regent Street with Galuppi, possibly experimenting with new musical ideas that even now arabesqued through her brain.

For weeks the ballet had been pleasurably enervating, erasing thoughts of Nick much of the time—or at least blurring them. Blurring them was more accurate. They were still there.

Returning to New York brought them painfully into focus.

Just a dozen or so blocks ahead was good old Lincoln Center. She could almost hear Nick's voice repeating that phone conversation with his ridiculous comment about reciting the Gettysburg Address in one meeting. She smiled painfully.

Had she loved him then? Or had she even loved him at the courthouse, listening to his evaluation of Zimblatz?

Had she ever not loved Nick? That was more to the point. And would there be a time in the uncharted future when she'd stop loving him?

The cab wove through the financial district, traffic all but impassable during lunch hour, jaywalkers darting in front of the cars at every stoplight.

She could take no time for lunch. As soon as she finished with her agent, she'd get her car at the garage leased by Henri's company. Then on up the thruway to campus and home.

Tomorrow—and all the tomorrows in the foreseeable future—would be devoted to nothing but practice, with interruption only for prayer. Prayer had now become an essential part of her day.

Even her visits with Jim and Peg would have to be infrequent. She'd get over to see them with the little remembrances she'd brought from Europe, yes, but evenings at Gleasons' could not be a regular part of her weekly calendar.

By January this tour would be behind her. Never again would she plan something so arduous and all-consuming. After it was over, she'd direct her musical energies into teaching and composition.

While the traffic halted at an unfamiliar intersection, Claire noticed to her right a maze of high rises that appeared to be a hospital center. Which one? she asked herself.

Then she saw the sign. Davis Memorial.

Davis Memorial? She'd read about Davis Memorial in a recent news magazine. World-famous, Davis Memorial Hospital was noted for orthopedics, including artificial limb rehab. Why hadn't she ever seen it before?

The answer was simple. Before she'd met Nick, orthopedic hospitals had held no interest for her.

In that complex right now there would be patients like Nick, adjusting to the trauma of amputation—young men, women, kids even, whose whole future seemed bleak.

As the cabby stopped for a traffic light, Claire had the overwhelming urge to get out and go into that hospital. Was that why the light seemed to take so long to change? Was the Holy Spirit telling her to go in there *now?*

No, she decided. The day was much too busy as it was.

And what would she do if she did go in? Stare with curious eyes at those disabled individuals, only adding to their discomfort, as she had to Nick's? Without skills or training, what could she do to ease their adjustments to life?

Still the inner voice seemed to be telling her she could learn. But learn what?

Learn everything! How a prosthesis was affixed to the arm, plus the rudimentary steps an amputee would take in manipulating the prosthesis. She would observe the frustrations that would occur—and how to help a patient handle them. She could learn a thousand things.

Why did she desperately want to learn these things if she had no intention of seeing Nick again or meeting up with guys like him? Ah, but her subconscious still clung to straws that cruelly suggested a future encounter with him.

She mustn't permit such thoughts to take hold. Unless—and this might well be true—unless knowing Nick could be a springboard to working with other kids and grown-ups who needed encouragement, hope, and discovery of the purpose God had for their lives.

There must be a program at Davis Memorial for volunteers, the inner voice continued.

"I'm sorry, Lord, it just isn't on my agenda for today," she whispered. "Next year I might be able to fit it in." Yes, next year she could give it a whirl.

With the light green, the cab surged forward and headed northwest to the theater district, leaving Davis Memorial behind.

∞

Her agent, Stan Frolich, was on the phone when she stepped into his office. He smiled sheepishly, indicating she should take a seat. As he talked to the other party, his smile turned into a grimace. Putting his hand over the receiver, he mouthed a comment, "I've got some lousy news that's not going to make your day."

Finally hanging up the phone with an exasperated good-bye, he turned to her. "Today I'm on the ropes. That call's from a violinist who just broke his arm. Playing croquet! He's scheduled for five recitals in New England, starting in three weeks. Isn't that beautiful!"

"Poor guy," Claire responded.

"Yeah. How 'bout poor me? Okay, now we turn to your tour." He zipped through his computer to her readout and then thumbed through a pile of folders, pulling out hers. He slammed it on the desk in disgust. "You won't believe this, Ms. Rossiter. The orchestra scheduled for your tour has gone on strike."

Claire sat forward, her eyes wide. "Has what?"

"Two days ago the Great Lakes Philharmonic went on strike. No rehearsals—nothing. The orchestra's canceling the tour."

"Can they do that?"

"They've done it! Somewhere there's fine print about union benefits that aren't being honored. Lawyers have been called in. I only have to pick up the pieces with the cities on the tour and unruffle their feathers."

Claire began to snicker. Then that snicker became a full-fledged, shoulder-shaking laugh. "This is unreal."

She slapped a palm against her forehead and leaned back in her chair.

A bewildered Stan Frolich stammered, "It's shattering for you, Ms. Rossiter, I know that. You were counting on this tour. I'm sorry for you, I really am—but, bu—why under the sun are you laughing?"

"Because it had to happen. This concert tour was never meant to be. I have better things to do."

"No, wait a minute, Ms. Rossiter, we have no intention of leaving you dangling. One of the other orchestras we're considering might be able to include you. We can get you work—it's just going to take some juggling."

She sat up and tried to manage a serious demeanor. "Do I have to perform somewhere to fulfill my contract? I mean, legally, is it possible to just not perform anywhere at all?"

"Under these circumstances, yup, since you didn't initiate the action—you're within your rights to do that. In fact, you'll be paid a fee of five thousand dollars sitting at home doing zilch. But you'll want exposure somewhere. You're just getting things off the ground professionally. And you're good."

"Five thousand dollars would take care of me fine for several months. Stan, over the summer I became involved in composing ballet music. It's been lucrative as well as satisfying. Also I'll be back teaching at State in January, so money isn't tight right now. In addition, something else has come up—nothing to do with music—that I'd like to explore."

"You mean you're not about to sue me?"

"Hardly. Accept this for what it's worth; God doesn't want me to go on this tour. He wants me to channel my energies into something else for a few months. Let me make a suggestion."

"I'm all ears."

"Are the violinist's recitals in major concert halls?"

"No. Mainly at universities and art museums, but well-respected places on the recital circuit."

"Fine. I could easily handle them. And I won't accept another penny beyond the five thousand you're giving me."

"I couldn't let you do that. The violinist was going to get. . ."

"Sure, you could. I have to practice every day, anyway, to keep up my dexterity. So, I'll resurrect some of my old standbys. What can an audience expect from a substitute?"

Stan eyed her for a moment. Then his face broke into a canvas of smiles. "I don't know about God having something else for you to do—but I know this much, you've been a boon and a blessing to me today. I dreaded facing you. And look how it's turned out. Yeah, I could use you for those recitals. Boy, could I."

She grabbed her purse and stood up. "Stan, just fax me the details about the recitals. I'll keep in touch. But right now, you'll have to excuse me if I run." She reached for his hand.

He stood and shook hers. "Run, Lady, run. You have yourself a deal. And—er, boatloads of thanks."

⋘⋙

Tension, confusion about where she would go and to whom she would speak, bombarded Claire as she entered the spacious lobby of Davis Memorial Hospital. A receptionist informed her a nurse-administrator named Sandra Hunt headed the staff on the floor dealing with amputation. She directed her to the elevator which would take her to that floor.

Though professional in appearance and demeanor, Sandra Hunt received her warmly. Claire felt at ease telling her about her association with the university, the cancellation of her concert tour, and explaining her reasons for wanting to volunteer at Davis. "A very dear friend is a bilateral amputee. I'd like to think my volunteering here would be a tribute to him. Since my fall tour just got canceled a few moments ago, I have all this extra time this fall. What better way to spend it than to help you out here at Davis?"

Nearly as an aside, Claire mentioned her ballet project.

Sandra Hunt shook her head in amazement. "You've written a ballet? That's amazing."

"I've collaborated on one, yes."

"On this floor, Ms. Rossiter—er, Claire, we don't take hands for granted. I'm moved by the fact that your capable fingers will be available to assist others to achieve manual dexterity. That means so much to me."

As she got up to leave, Claire handed Sandra Hunt her card. "I absolutely mustn't keep you any longer, Mrs. Hunt. Let me give you my card so you can reach me."

The woman walked around the desk and held Claire's fingers, almost reverently. "I'll be calling you soon—in a day or so."

Claire weighed the comment she was about to make, then boldly aired it. "It just dawned on me, you may know my friend—well, anyway, my wonderful amputee friend, Nick Van Vierssen."

Sandra Hunt's eyes lit up. "I do know him. Actually, I've only met him at a conference we had last year. I'm sure he doesn't remember me. Why, he's a charming man, so well-adjusted to his handicap."

"Not really all that well-adjusted, Mrs. Hunt. At least when it comes to marriage. Although he's admitted he loves me, he doesn't believe I could cope with his disability if we were married. We've decided not to see one another."

"I'm sorry to hear that. He's a fine and capable man. But now that I've met you, I'd say you are equally fine and capable."

"He told me I'd be appalled by his private life."

"I'm not that sure you would be, but Mr. Van Vierssen would know what would be best for him."

"Second best might be helping the folks on this floor. . .giving them confidence that they can reach for much more in this world than they expected they could when their disability first occurred."

Sandra Hunt squeezed Claire's hand as they walked to the elevator. "A noble idea. I'll feel privileged to help you in this effort."

∞

Sandra Hunt was as good as her word, phoning Claire within the week. Outfitted with appropriate slacks and tops—and substantial shoes, Claire reported for duty at Davis Memorial on September 10.

Chapter 16

The first week at Davis, Claire wondered, as a new Christian, if she'd misread God's directing her into this volunteer venture after all. Initially, she was assigned to a practical nurse who supervised temperature-taking, baths, and basic patient needs. Simple tasks under normal circumstances, but when done with amputees, Claire found the exercise emotionally draining.

Viewing for the first time the severed stumps—their discolorations along surgical closures—left her limp. Several times she was forced to leave a patient's room and go out into the hall to fight back tears.

The idyllic mountains of Montreux seemed so far away. Not infrequently, God seemed far away as well. In these moments when her faith foundered, she turned to the psalmist's words: "Show me your ways, O Lord; teach me your paths."

Adding to her anxiety was the realization that Nick must have gone through the agony of phantom pain in addition to the helplessness resulting from his lost hands. So preoccupied was she about what Nick must have gone through, she couldn't get to sleep many nights.

By the end of the second week on duty, however, activities that weakened her the first few days became more or less routine. Still Claire knew she had yet to face the ultimate test: Unlike Nick, none of the patients she helped had lost both hands. Sandra Hunt assured her such a patient would appear on the scene eventually.

Ed Lytton was that patient.

He had been brought in by helicopter from upstate, a victim of a collapsed roof in an auto body shop. "Lytton's case is far from pleasant, Claire," said Sandra Hunt. "But I think you're ready to face it."

"Yes, Sandra, I'm ready," Claire insisted, her conviction shrouded in misgivings. "This is why I came to Davis in the first place."

"It's unlikely the emotional makeup of this man will be anything like that of your friend, Mr. Van Vierssen," cautioned Sandra.

"I understand that."

Sandra grasped her arm firmly. "He was airlifted here because he's made little progress and. . ."

Her words were blotted out by a bellowing voice from the room where they were heading. "Isn't there anyone—anyone at all out there—who can get in here and scratch my shoulder?" This was followed by an almost inhuman, primordial sound.

Sandra steadied Claire and gave her an encouraging smile as they entered the darkened room. Once her eyes became accustomed to the darkness, Claire witnessed the helpless man. He was lying flat on the bed, the prostheses already attached to his arms like tree limbs on a snowy field.

His head tossed spasmodically from side to side, the mouth clenched. The compassion that welled up in her throat made it impossible for Claire to say hello—cheerful or otherwise—to the man. Easy banter seemed to be out of place—almost sadistic. Yet it was this very approach that Sandra employed.

"Mr. Lytton," she said, "what a great day. Ms. Rossiter and I will remove your equipment. Then, you're going to trot yourself into that bathroom to shower yourself into respectability."

"Respectability? That's some kind of a joke, Lady," he shouted at her. "Just scratch my back and get lost. I don't care if I rot to death."

"Well, I regret to tell you rotting to death isn't permitted. The Board of Health opposed that unanimously several decades ago," Sandra replied in a no-nonsense manner, opening the blinds and turning on the light. "We must protect our licensing. So right now the schedule says shower."

The man sputtered through grinding teeth as Sandra and Claire began removing the right Greifer. "In a week or so," said Sandra, "you'll be putting these on and taking them off by yourself. You'll be able to take showers by yourself whenever you wish."

"There's no way I'll be able to do that, and you know it," he answered bitterly.

"Oh, you'll be able to do all those things in a breeze, mark my word. Our shower stalls have nifty foot pedals rigged to the shower head—one to deliver sudsy flow, clear water from the other—just like a car wash. You'll have no trouble at all."

Claire stared at the man who lay before her, his torso now bared—the prostheses removed. Although his stumps were healing, there were still angry red lines where the staples had been. It was impossible to see anything of Nick in the man lying there. He certainly didn't possess Nick's handsome face with its infectious grin. Or Nick's stunning eyes, so often overflowing with merriment.

She couldn't imagine Nick's torso resembling Ed Lytton's sweat-soaked body that lay on the rumpled sheets.

As she looked at the man, all Claire could think of were scenes from movies about the Inquisition where a man was being stretched on the rack. She almost felt like a torturer, ready to turn the wheel that would take the victim over the edge into screaming insanity.

The helplessness and despair of this man overwhelmed Claire. She wanted to just hold Ed Lytton in her arms and rock him, as a mother would a newborn.

Sandra kept up a persistent patter, bringing Ed up on his feet and directing him to the shower. "I can't stand up and walk in there," he stormed. "I can't dangle these—these. . ."

" 'Stumps' is a word you'll have to get used to, Ed," said Sandra.

"All right. I can't dangle these stumps. It hurts like mad. I tell you I can't walk in there." He added a stream of obscenities.

"In and out—just in and out. It'll give you such a boost," prodded Sandra.

In an overpowering instant, as Ed Lytton made his way to the shower, Claire saw the depth of Nick's private purgatory portrayed in graphic outline. That back and those shoulders could have been Nick's. The abbreviated, so unevenly severed handless arms—the male figure before her that stood so barbarously incomplete— was the Nick she had never seen.

Violent nausea churned up from her stomach. It took several deep breaths to attempt to keep it at bay.

"Sandra. . . ," she mumbled, "I–I have to leave. I. . ."

"Buzz for another nurse," mouthed Sandra. "I can manage until she arrives."

Claire rang the buzzer twice and then slipped from the room as decorously as possible. Once in the hall, she ran to the ladies' room. "Lord, I'm not strong enough," she groaned. "I came here with pure intent, wanting to give these individuals a reason for living. But I can't rise above my love for Nick. Seeing the state Ed Lytton's in has destroyed my objectivity. I want so desperately to talk to Nick. . .to hold him to me, and to. . .Lord, I want to love him. In the deepest recesses of my being, I feel that all I'm doing here is to learn how to live with Nick, and I'm ashamed of that selfishness.

"Help me return to my original purpose in coming here. . .to provide assistance to any amputee, here or anywhere else. Help me to make the Ed Lyttons my priority, not Nick. Hard as it is for me to believe, I do think You—and Nick—would want me to do that. Help me honor my commitment to stay here until December and do my best."

                ∞

Despite great misgivings, she discovered as November approached that she could provide care plus encouragement to Ed Lytton. Taking cues from Sandra Hunt, she supervised and assisted him in putting on prostheses, using a spoon and fork to feed himself, and even playing cards with the help of a card tray.

Soon Ed could handle many activities well. He could turn on the television, thumb through the pages of a book, play electronic games—scribble his name. In their conversations, Claire often made reference to her friend who was also an amputee, yet able to ski, play table tennis, and hold a responsible position in a prison.

Frequently Ed asked her to read the Bible to him. He was particularly interested in the story of the man with the withered arm. "But I can't be healed like that," he said. "Do you expect me to believe God's going to paste my hands back on?"

"Isn't that really what He has done, Ed?" she replied with words that didn't seem to originate with herself. "Those prostheses are hands He has pasted back on. He's expecting you to learn to use the new hands He's given you—perhaps for a task you've never imagined for yourself."

Two other similar amputees became patients in late November. Jake, a sixty-year-old auto mechanic, was a tough fellow, a bachelor, whose sense of humor heroically got him through the first few days. Even though much of his conversation was crude, Claire admired his stoicism. But one remark he made proved unsettling to Claire. Over a game of electronic baseball, he said, "I'm sure glad I'm not married to a doll as pretty as you. I'd be bananas in a month. Not to have fingers to touch a wife like you would be some kind of torture, Sweetheart."

Her relationship with Sam, the other amputee, was equally jarring. So distraught was his wife over her husband's condition, she moaned, "What a cross to bear. I can't live with this situation. Sam used to be such a dynamic man. Coaching little league. Repairing things around the house. Now he's helpless and can't do anything."

Lunch with Sam's therapist further undermined Claire's optimism. "Forever and a day, spouses give amputees a bad time," she declared.

"Always?" asked Claire, trying to hide her emotions. Apparently Sandra Hunt hadn't told the staff about Nick and herself.

"Ninety-five percent of the time," added the therapist. "They complain too much or wait on their husbands hand and foot, so guys like Sam never gain sufficient skill with their prostheses to return to meaningful work. Some never keep up with their therapy. They give up totally."

Claire attempted a weak smile, her mood anything but cheerful.

∞

Only a few more days remained for Claire at Davis once the Christmas season arrived. In the new year the second semester would begin at State. She would resume a full schedule of lessons, and her volunteer stint would be over.

On December 17 the staff took her out to a surprise luncheon, presenting her with a charming plaque. Ed Lytton joined the celebration. His words of gratitude for her assistance over some "rough days" touched her immensely. He had turned his life over to Christ, he'd announced. Everyone at the dinner commented on his newborn optimism and self-assurance.

With reluctance and sadness, she approached Sandra Hunt's office on her last day to say good-bye. Sandra embraced her warmly. "Your stint here comes to a close, Claire. But our friendship will continue."

"I'm only sorry I can't help you on a regular basis next semester, Sandra. My training here has been worthwhile, not only for me but for others, too, apparently."

"You'll be back to see us often, I hope. You and Mr. Van Vierssen."

Claire took Sandra's hand as they walked to the elevator.

"You're an individual who well deserves the exciting future that lies ahead for you." Not sure how she would respond to Sandra about the future, she let the nurse go on. "You have the success in your music to look forward to, as well as your reunion with that superb man you love. I do hope I'll at least receive an announcement of your wedding."

The elevator opened and they got on. Fortunately, they were alone. Claire turned to her friend. "Sandra, I don't know how to say this to you—but, ah, I've decided it is wisest to honor my promise not to get in touch with Nick Van Vierssen."

Dropping her hand from Claire's grasp, Sandra looked at her incredulously. "You can't mean that. How can you deny that fine man a chance to know what you've done?"

"I've grown much wiser these past few months."

"Have you? You'd call this decision a wise one? What happened to the Holy Spirit's propelling you to this hospital?"

"I misread God's direction for me, that's all. He did have a plan, yes. He wanted to prove to me that Nick does know best. A satisfactory marriage is all but impossible for the men I've met here. I made a promise to Nick. I'm sticking to it."

The elevator opened. Taking Claire's arm firmly, Sandra directed her into an empty lounge adjacent to the lobby, forcing her to sit down on a sofa. "You've been strongly influenced by a very negative individual—someone on my staff?"

"Not entirely."

"I think you have, Claire. It's my opinion that my conclusions have as much if not more merit than those of anyone in this hospital. I'll readily admit that I have seen unsavory consequences of amputation. Suicides, insanity, divorce—you name it. But I've also seen men and women go out of here to live useful lives. I've seen some marriages work, sometimes better than they ever did before."

Sandra began to talk faster and in a more vehement tone. "Last year a farmer with several young children went back to his family and made an excellent adjustment to both family and farm. He and his wife were tremendous people. But so are you, Claire, and from my observation of Mr. Van Vierssen at that conference, so is he."

"He's tremendous, all right, Sandra. But you can't compare his situation with that farmer's. The farmer was already married. Nick would prefer to live his life alone. Keep this in mind as you. . ."

"Let me finish," Sandra interrupted with great urgency. "Just bear with me, and let me finish. There's no way in the world you can convince me Mr. Van Vierssen is content without you. I'm sure he's agonizingly lonely. What young buck wouldn't be, after being in your company?

"Certainly you and he will have frustrations, yes, but you are both mature enough to cope with them, especially now that you've experienced so much here."

"Sandra, we'll face hurdles not covered here."

"Of course you will. But amputees aren't the only folks to have hurdles in a marriage. Everyone has a handicap of some sort—physical, emotional, educational, spiritual. Married couples must have the patience to alleviate the pain caused by these disabilities.

"If God hadn't given me my Bob," Sandra continued, "who has a few annoying emotional handicaps of his own—if I didn't have him and my two daughters to go home to, I couldn't do this job. Please reconsider your decision. At least give Mr. Van Vierssen himself the opportunity to reevaluate the situation in light of your efforts here. Give him that Christmas gift he so deserves."

Claire shook her head. "No, Sandra, I'm not going to do that. You're correct when you said I do have a plateful of exciting projects ahead. And I want you to know that the time I've spent here has been valuable to me. I wouldn't have missed it for the world."

"I'm heartbroken," said the woman. "I'm truly heartbroken about this."

"Please don't be, Sandra. With the Lord's help, I'll sever Nick from my life and adjust to my amputation from him, just as he and the patients here have had to adjust to theirs."

Claire got up from the sofa. From her purse she gave Sandra a tiny gift wrapped in green Christmas foil. Then she reached over and kissed her. "Thank you so much, Sandra—for teaching me how to assist amputees, and for giving me enough of an insider's view of their complicated world—so that finally I can let Nick go."

Chapter 17

It was fortunate Claire had curtailed her activities at Davis when she did. On December 24 a five-inch snowfall made the driving hazardous.

Falling snow had enveloped the campus in a womb of white. With the students absent now for the holidays, an almost celestial quiet pervaded the ivory world beyond Claire's window.

She'd temporarily replaced the plum-colored plant with a good-sized crèche containing hand-carved figures purchased in Zurich many years ago.

On Saturday she had attended a faculty dinner with Pete Crane from the physics department. So far the holiday season had been enjoyable.

Fortunately, there weren't many things on the agenda for the day. She could concentrate on a run-through of *Messiah,* which she would accompany for Holy Redeemer Church at four o'clock, after which there was to be a reception at the dean's.

Tomorrow she'd be with Jim and Peg and their adorable children for Christmas dinner.

She strolled into the living room, her coral lounging robe swishing across the carpet. It was a lounging robe kind of morning. She scanned the cards on the mantel, many of them from students who'd achieved success in the world of music. It made her seem almost ancient to know that Billy Ramirez had joined the music faculty at UCLA, Doreen Tremont was touring in Brazil, and Deke Leavitt had his own jazz band in Miami.

Although it was nonsense to think of herself as middle-aged at twenty-eight, she did feel too elder-statespersonish for comfort.

Behind a tiny, tempting gift from the Poncelets, there was a card from Arnold Saxby, of all people, and one from Sandra Hunt and the Davis staff, flanked by poignant notes from Madame Bouchard and the ballet company.

Then there was Nick's card, even though she hadn't sent him one. Each time she passed the mantel, she had to pick it up to look at that distinctive signature with its long tail on the "k" that said so much. It was easy now, since her tenure at Davis, to picture him penning his name. She knew only too well how long it had taken him to learn to do it so skillfully with phony fingers. Or toes.

He had added a few scrawled words in pen. "Terrific news about the ballet. I'm thrilled for you."

Jim had told her he'd mentioned it to Nick.

Putting the card back on the mantel with the others, she went to the piano and let her fingers meander for a few thoughtful moments. There was no great need to open the music for *Messiah*. She knew it well, but the choir director had noted a few special phrasings and crescendos. She opened to that masterful selection "For Unto Us," astounded, as always, by Handel's sublime genius, now more than ever thrilled by the message so eloquently conveyed. "Unto us a child is born." The Savior Child she now welcomed so fervently into her being.

Envisioning that Child in a stable, she thought about little Josh Gleason, so precious to his family. She wondered if she would have a child someday.

Even though she knew she would never marry Nick, she doubted she would ever care to bear anyone else a son.

Oh, what a boy Nick would have, with Nick's calm and empathetic authority mixed at all the right moments with relaxed levity. As she played the music, she yearned to meet that son—his son—their son.

Or a daughter. Nick's daughter would be kind, regal, and sensible. She well might have long, sun-speckled cascades of lovely hair—and maybe elegant sapphire eyes.

Claire ached to see these children.

The finale of the piece, with the four-voice parts building to that magnificent unison, illustrated majestically the power of the greatest Child who had ever lived—Jesus, the Son of God, the Messiah foreseen by Isaiah the prophet.

The music left her awed and breathless.

A sudden strong breeze across her back proved she was no longer alone. She mustn't have closed the door tightly when she went to bed.

Tensely, she realized someone else was in the room. The wind from the opened front door caused a shiver to ripple down her spine. She was afraid to turn around.

Slowly, she pivoted.

Standing by the stairs near the front door was. . .Nick!

Her eyes must be tricking her. It had to be a figment of her imagination.

No, it was the real McCoy—Nick in the flesh, wearing his fine camel's-hair overcoat with the collar turned up, separating strands of the snow-sprinkled shock of windblown hair that framed his face, now ruddy-red from the snow and the blustery wind.

This time. . .oh, this time it had to be forever. He was smiling as if it were. His mouth was relaxed, his arms open to her.

She leaped from the bench, lifted the skirt of her robe, and ran into his arms. His crushing embrace told her all she needed to know. He had come to tell her he wanted to share her life as her husband.

He raised her face to his and kissed her, not with an anxious frenzy as he had before, but with the confident lips of a man who'd finally arrived home after a long journey.

He pulled away slightly.

"Nick, no," she cried. "Oh, my darling, don't let go of me yet. I've waited much too long for you to. . ."

"Let me at least take off my coat," he said with amusement in his eyes. "Will you permit me, please, to do that, you incorrigible, unpredictable little minx, you?"

"Just do it quickly."

He tossed the coat over the banister. Under a black, bulky knit sweater, she could see just the open collar of a red candy-striped shirt at his neck as she fell back against his chest again.

His lips found her cheeks, then her eyes, her hair. . .her lips.

"Not a trace of black and blue or green anywhere, is there?" he noted, laughing.

"No."

"No pain in the old jaw?"

"None."

"You're the most captivating woman. Has anyone besides Henri and a hundred newspaper critics ever told you that?"

"Does it matter if they have? When I hear it from you, that's all that counts. Nick, being with me this time means. . . ?"

"Means I'm going to marry you, yes. And, Claire, I'm going to make it all work out for us or die trying."

Putting his arm around her shoulder, he directed her into the living room. "What a beautiful crèche, Claire," he said, moving to the bay window to inspect it. "But you didn't throw out the plum-colored plant, I hope."

"Oh, never—it's in my bedroom. I'll never part with it. Can I get you something? A cup of coffee? Waffles? I can whip up waffles in. . ."

"The coffee'll be fine, but not just yet."

His arm still resting on her shoulder, he leaned against the window frame. She traced the lines of his face with the care she'd used handling the crèche figures.

"My darling, seeing you is a miracle," she said. "Thank God. . . . Oh, thank You, God. Nick, why did you change your mind?"

She moved back a few steps and studied his sensitive eyes, now filled with dancing glimmers of light that played affectionate games with her.

"You were right all along, Claire. God absolutely does want us together. He went so far as to send an angelic emissary into my life who related the most far-fetched story—about an individual who rearranged her schedule to work with amputees. By any chance, do you happen to know that saga, Claire?"

He fixed his eyes on hers, and their souls touched.

"Jim must have been that emissary," she responded. "But how did he ever find out about Davis? I didn't let anyone on campus know about my work there."

Nick shook his head. "It wasn't Jim, but I'm glad it was someone. If I hadn't found out. . .Claire, it's horrifying to think I might never have found out! Is it possible you weren't going to tell me?"

"I'd made a promise to you, Nick. I decided to live up to that promise."

"But when you went to work at Davis, your intention was to let me know eventually?"

"Yes."

"And you felt God had directed you in that venture?"

"Yes."

"Then you changed your mind."

"I figured you'd been wise all along. So many of those patients did have wives who couldn't manage to—"

"But they didn't have you. I should have known with a woman like you, nothing is quite by the book. Anyone who plays Liszt as you do can accomplish anything."

"Right!" she said with dramatic bravado. "Now, you cruel ogre, tell me how you found out my secret. I bet you went to a conference and someone from Davis was there who happened to mention my name and. . ."

"No, there wasn't any conference." He paused, scowling dramatically. "This is a spellbinding story, but taxing on an empty stomach. Why don't you fix me that coffee so I'll be fortified and not apt to miss any of the juicy details?"

"You're a tease," she spouted in a scolding tone. "But in this case I'll be glad to oblige." She moved toward the kitchen. "Waffles, too?"

"No, just coffee—and maybe a piece of toast," he said, following her.

"The coffee's still hot," she said, feeling the pot on the coffee-maker. She poured a cup. "Cream and sugar?"

"Cream. I'll get it." He opened the refrigerator and took out the carton. Carefully he poured the cream. Instead of pity, she now looked upon this feat with a clinical awe. He was such a champ using his prostheses, she almost shouted out a hearty bravo.

She tossed slices of bread into the toaster.

From under the table, Galuppi came slinking out. He trotted up to Nick, nuzzling his leg.

"Galuppi, you remember me," Nick said, getting down on one knee and stroking the cat. "And you're glad to see me, too—what a nice welcome." He glanced up at Claire, caressing her with that look.

She still couldn't believe he was here in the kitchen with her.

Nick lifted the cat's mouth up to his ear.

"Galuppi tells me you didn't miss me at all," he joked. "You were too busy entertaining the men of the math department, romping most precipitously through logarithms and complex variables."

"Galuppi's a notorious liar," she retorted with a smirk.

He dropped the cat gently, and they took the coffee and toast into the living room.

"Now, no more stalling," she said, curling up next to him on the sofa. "Who told you about my work at Davis?"

"A wise individual named—Sandra Hunt!"

Claire stared at Nick in total surprise, as he smugly munched a piece of toast. "That's impossible. Sandra Hunt's a professional to the nth degree. She'd never. . ."

"Well, in this instance, I'm afraid she did. She thought this situation called for action on her part. Let me recap," he continued. "I was in my office yesterday morning, working on a report, when I got a call from a woman who sounded terribly ill-at-ease. When she said she was on staff at Davis, I figured she wanted me to give a talk or a demonstration, and I was prepared to say no. We've been so busy with hearings in Washington lately, I didn't feel up to adding an extra speaking engagement to the calendar."

He took Claire's hand in his Greifer, seeming to know it wouldn't upset her any longer. "The report I was writing took precedence over her call, I'm afraid, so I gave her only half an ear. During the conversation, I kept scanning my report and running some figures through my calculator. Then I heard her say something like, 'and this lovely girl is Claire Rossiter, a friend of yours.'"

He took several sips of coffee before he went on. "I bolted up in my chair, completely nonplused, and barked at that poor woman, 'Claire Rossiter? Hold everything. Repeat that story again, please.'

"The woman sounded relieved to know I was at least interested, so she continued, much more confidently, to tell me how reluctant she'd been to phone, and that she hoped I'd forgive her for interfering in my private life. She'd never done anything like this before, she admitted. I assured her I was keenly interested in all the accomplishments of the celebrated Ms. Rossiter."

He paused a minute, shaking his head as his eyes searched the depths of hers. "But, darling Claire, I wasn't prepared for the disclosures she presented. I'm glad no one else was in my office at the time, because I lost control of myself. I covered the receiver and broke down right there."

"Nick, oh, my dearest—it was uncanny that I came upon Davis. When I saw the place, I knew I had to go in there. It was imperative that I learn, that I observe firsthand what you've been through."

"I've been pigheaded, Claire. A pietistic idiot, never imagining any woman, least of all a talented person like you, could ever be in love with me enough to accept my limitations over the long haul."

Tenderly he raked a prosthesis through her hair. "Selfishly, I let my own pride interfere with a relationship that was orchestrated from the beginning by the Lord. Yesterday, when I realized how I'd hurt you by never comprehending the depth of your love, I was so ashamed. I've been a selfish, egotistical fool."

"Nick, you could never be selfish and egotistical."

"I have been, Claire, with you. Mrs. Hunt told me how you'd worked tirelessly on that floor, consoling families, feeding men and women—and doing a dozen other unpleasant tasks I can picture only too clearly."

He bit his lip in thought, then continued. "She told me you planned to tell me about your work 'through a friend.' Jim, I trust. Then, out of the blue, you changed your mind. She said she pleaded with you to reconsider. After many sleepless nights, she decided I should know. I assured her I certainly should know. In fact, I told her my gratitude knew no bounds. She'd provided me with a future on planet earth I'd thought was well beyond my uniquely limited grasp. I promised her I'd thank her properly by taking her to dinner at the Gentilhomme Restaurant in the city—the sky's the limit—truffles, caviar, the works."

"Will I be included in that festive event?"

He wrinkled up his nose, as if he'd think about that. "Hmm, maybe, if I don't have you scrubbing floors eight hours a day to make my Dutch household spotless. I don't want to over-truffle you like Henri has."

She wrinkled her nose as well. "Thanks a lot."

He laughed heartily. "You'll be there."

"I'll give Sandra a piece of my mind, that appalling, dear, thoughtful, sensational woman." Tears flowed down Claire's cheeks—tears so expressive of her joy that she didn't want to wipe them away.

"As soon as Mrs. Hunt got off the phone," Nick continued, "I called the superintendent and told him I had to have three days off."

"Three days? We have three days together?"

"Yes."

"And the superintendent didn't mind?"

"He was so impressed by what you'd done at Davis, he ordered me to take off this morning. He said he'd see that all sally ports were covered, even if he had to work two shifts and have his family eat Christmas dinner in a prison mess hall. I didn't argue with him—just packed my bags early this morning and left before dawn. In fact, I got here at nine o'clock and waited around until I thought it was a decent enough hour to come to your door."

"Oh, no—you mean there were extra minutes we could have spent together?"

"A few."

"We can't waste any more minutes like that, my dearest."

He shook his head a few times. "No, we can't."

"Three whole days—it's heaven, or almost. But, Nick, there are complications today." She got up and walked to the piano to get a program. "I have a service this afternoon. The folks at Holy Redeemer Church are singing *Messiah*. I'm the accompanist—they really need me."

She smiled with a trace of affected pain as she handed him the program.

He scanned it quickly but returned his eyes to her. "I'd love to attend *Messiah* on Christmas Eve. If you're the accompanist, it will be even more enjoyable."

"There's a reception at the dean's at seven. I should stop in for a minute or two."

"I'd like to meet the dean. In fact, I brought along my gray suit just for such an occasion."

She took a Greifer in both her hands. "Perfect. I can't wait for everyone to meet you—I'm so proud of you and the type of work you do. I love you so. Tomorrow I've planned to go to Jim and Peg's for dinner."

"Sensational. I don't think they'll mind at all if we celebrate our engagement with them."

"Jim will go into shock."

"He will, won't he?"

She became serious for a second. "But your parents, Nick; don't you usually celebrate part of Christmas week with them?"

"Not always, no. Besides, I phoned them last night. They were ecstatic at hearing my news. My mother whispered a reverent 'Hallelujah!' when I told her I was going to propose to the most magnificent girl on earth—someone famous, with a pair of hands that would more than compensate for mine in a marriage."

She smiled down at him. "Next year we'll give them a grandchild," she murmured, barely audibly.

But he'd heard her. "Wait a minute now. That's rushing things a bit, isn't it? You don't want to have morning sickness for the opening of that ballet in Houston."

This made her chuckle. "Well, no, I guess that would be bad planning. But I'm not going to let ballets stand in my way forever. I'm getting very old, you know."

As if she were a little girl, his strong arms pulled her to him and set her on his lap. He stretched out his legs on the sofa. "Yes, you're edging toward thirty, I bet—a veritable relic. Claire, it's beyond me that we're talking about children—our children. Me, a father to a child of yours! That's a responsibility too awesome to contemplate.

"Darling, coming up the walk this morning, I could hear your brilliant Handel. When I found the door unlocked, I just stepped in to what seemed to me a mirage. There you were, so incredibly lovely, sitting at the piano. I had to pause in wonderment, in acceptance of the fact that that magnificent creature loved me enough to go into hospital rooms and scrub stumps and scratch itches and brush away tears."

Tears were escaping his own eyes. "I've learned a mighty lesson these last dozen hours or so. You honestly love this miserable body of mine—a great deal more than I do. What's more, God loves me a lot more than I'd imagined. He's given you to me, to share my life. In His sight I'm pretty valuable, hands or no hands. Correct?"

"You're the most valuable human being alive, as far as I'm concerned."

"And that leads into what marriage is all about, Claire. Last night I reexamined Ephesians 5:28. Husbands should love their wives as their own bodies. It's a holy act to love you, to the best of my ability. But I have to love myself in the process."

She nodded.

"Claire, your foot-washing service to those patients at Davis was done for me, so I hope I'll have the good sense to rejoice on those occasions, which will certainly come up in our marriage, when I may have to ask you to undo a belt, or open a door—in other words, when I let you love me."

He squeezed her closer to him. "I'll tell you this: When I walked into this house and saw you over there, knowing how you feel about me, well, if I had had fingers at that moment, I'd have snapped them in front of my face several times to see if I were asleep or awake."

Her giggle became a laugh. Startled, she knew maturity was in that laugh. "Nick, did you notice? I laughed at that remark! I burst into laughter when you said that."

"So?"

"That's it—it's being able to empathize with you about this handicap of yours. It's being able to laugh or cry with you, free from hang-ups or facades."

He raised interested eyebrows as she went on. "A year ago I wouldn't have been able to laugh with you over a comment like that. And now I think it's funny. You meant it to be funny, so immediately I accepted it that way. Working at Davis did make a difference."

"Yes, it would have to, I'd say."

"And in Montreux—oh, my darling, at my old school, the Holy Spirit took hold of me and turned my life around."

"I sensed that He must have introduced Himself to you somewhere."

"So I have to take you to Montreux, Nick. You'll have to meet Madame Bouchard and all the others."

"I'd like that. There's a world of wonderful things we'll do together."

"Signor Galdieri wants me back in Turin next August to work on another ballet, but I'll tell him I can't manage—"

"Whoa, take it easy. Why wouldn't you go to Turin? We'll work out something. It'll be tough for me, but I could let you go off for several weeks alone—then I'll join you for a few weeks."

"I'm overcome by all this, Nick. Two weeks with you in Turin would be. . ." She groped for words. None seemed appropriate.

"But don't misunderstand me, Claire," he said in a slow, droll manner that suggested a lurking punch line, "I'm not allowing you to be out of my sight for very long. And never forget, Lady, when you marry a prison warden, you're shackled for good."

"No parole?" she asked, attempting to keep a straight face.

"From me? A parole? Not on your life!"

GINGER O'NEIL

Ginger is thrilled with the publication of her first novel. She lives in Texas with her retired air force lieutenant colonel husband. They have six grown children and several grandchildren. Music and writing have played a large part in her life, so she has combined those loves in *A Touching Performance*.

The Quiet Heart

Ellyn Sanna

Chapter 1

Her new home looked nothing like she had expected. Dorrie Carpenter sat in her car staring at the sagging line of the roof, at the unpainted clapboards. The tiny house stood alone on the empty country road, surrounded by a grove of oak trees; it looked quiet and unused. Dorrie rolled down her window, trying to catch the sound of a neighbor's lawn mower or a child's voice calling, but the only noise was the wind whispering in the oak leaves overhead.

The stillness rang in her ears. For the last eight hours, during the long drive from her parents' home in southern Pennsylvania, she had traveled in a steady stream of song and prayer, listening to tapes and talking out loud to God. "The other drivers will think you're a crazy woman if they see you talking to the air," she had told herself, but she'd been too excited to care. She was on her way to her new job in upstate New York, and she knew a whole new life was waiting for her.

Clem, her roommate from college, had found this house for the two of them to rent. Clem had already begun her nursing job at the town clinic, and Dorrie soon would be starting her first teaching position at a nearby Christian children's home. Dorrie felt as though she had been buzzing in circles, whirling with excitement for weeks, as she had gotten ready for the trip here.

And now here she was at last. She opened her car door and stood up, stretching her long arms and legs. The quiet seemed to settle over her like a blanket. She shifted her shoulders and frowned, longing for a sound to break the stillness.

"You don't like it. I can see it on your face."

She whirled toward the voice. Clem stood at the edge of the field beyond the oak trees, her arms full of goldenrod and purple asters. Beneath her short, yellow curls, her small, round face was rosy and full of dimples, and Dorrie smiled, thinking she looked like a child in some old-fashioned illustration.

"It's just so quiet here," Dorrie said. "I'm used to the city, remember? And I *was* wondering if that roof will keep out the rain. Not to mention the wind and snow." She laughed and ran to hug Clem. "I'm so glad to see you—I don't care what the house looks like. I know it was all we could afford. And like I told Mom, now that we're sharing a house, we'll soon be saving a bundle just on our long-distance phone bill. No more two-hour phone calls every time you and Mason have a fight." Clem rolled her eyes, and Dorrie laughed. "So come on. Show me the place."

Inside, the house had a bedroom for each of them, with a large kitchen-living room in the middle. A braided rug was on the floor, and patchwork pillows were plumped high on the deep sofa and chairs.

"The truck with your stuff came last night," Clem said, pointing to the sofa and chairs, the round kitchen table that stood in one corner, and a stack of dishes still wrapped in newspapers. "My brother came over last night, and he and Mason lugged everything inside and helped me arrange things. The bedrooms are just alike with the same view, so I didn't think you'd mind not being here to fight with me over who got which. Mason and Liam set up your bed, and they're bringing mine later today."

Clem reached for a glass jar from the cupboard beneath the sink and filled it with water. She pushed the gleaming flowers into it and set it on the center of the table. "There. It's starting to look like home already, don't you think? You'll have to tell your mom how much I appreciate her letting us use your grandmother's old furniture. The place would be pretty empty otherwise."

Dorrie flopped down in one of the overstuffed chairs and looked around. "Where did all the homey touches come from, though?" She looked at the braided rug and hand-sewn pillows, the ruffled curtains and the glowing pictures of English cottages that hung on the walls. "Don't tell me you had all this stuff in your old apartment. My place at graduate school was a veritable hole—dark and dreary with plastic furniture that had belonged to the landlord, and a torn yellow shade over the only window. I kept meaning to make it look nicer, but I was hardly ever there, I was so busy. But this—this is a real home. This is wonderful." She picked up one of the patchwork pillows and hugged it to her.

Clem smiled. "It is nice, isn't it? Despite how it looks from the outside. Gram sewed the pillows and curtains herself. And the pictures are from her attic. She says she remembers them from her mother's house when she was a little girl. Do you like them?"

Dorrie nodded. "They're perfect. And what about the rug? Is that from her, too?"

Clem shook her head. "We have my brother to thank for that. He said it never went with the rest of the stuff in his apartment, and he thought it looked like something we would like."

"That was nice of Liam." Dorrie tried to keep her voice casual. "And it was nice of him to put in a good word for me at the children's home. Who knows if I would have gotten the job there if he hadn't worked there already." She picked up the end of her long red braid and studied it, as though she were searching for split ends. "So how is he these days?"

A shadow flickered across Clem's face. "Liam's all right. So far as I know. It's just—oh, I don't know. The same old thing I used to tell you back in college. He says all the right things—but I always feel his heart isn't really behind his words."

She sat down in the other chair and curled her legs under her. "You know, Dorrie. Growing up with Gram and Grandpop, what with Grandpop being a pastor and all, the church was as much our home as the parsonage. I used to feel I was being soaked with God's presence; it seemed such a constant thing. After Mom and Dad died, that atmosphere of love and prayer healed me. But with Liam it was different, maybe because he was older. I could feel him pulling into this hard, tight shell. The shell was a nice, shiny one, but the real Liam was hidden away inside it. It was like—oh, as though he were learning the language of a foreign country, while shutting out the very heart of that country's culture. He knows the right things to say, but I'm not sure he knows Christ."

Dorrie's hands clenched the soft pillow. Clem's brother Liam was the one subject she and her friend had never agreed on. She forced her hands to relax and said lightly, "Come on, Clem. After spending the summer with my own sister and brother, I know how easy it can be to see your siblings' faults. I'm sure they could see mine as clearly as I did theirs. But that doesn't mean we doubt each other's commitment to Christ. We understand we're still all too human, that God's still working on us."

Clem shook her head. "That's not what I mean about Liam. If anything, he's *too* perfect. Not humble enough, maybe. I never hear him talk about needing God's help with this or that. Oh, I don't know how to make you see." She looked at her friend's face and sighed. "You still feel the same way about him, don't you? That's what worries me."

Dorrie's cheeks burned. She tried to laugh. "I don't know why you should worry. It's not as though he's ever tried to sweep me off my feet."

Clem sighed again and pushed the short yellow curls off her forehead. "Well, I wouldn't mind if he did, you know; if I could be sure things were right between him and God. You two are the people I love most in the world."

"What about Mason?"

Clem blushed. "Him, too, of course. But he is definitely *not* sweeping me off my feet. Here we've been dating three years, ever since our senior year at college, and we're still not engaged. And now—" She looked down at her hands and frowned. "You remember how last summer he visited that friend of his who's a missionary in Colombia? Well, now Mason says he thinks God may be calling him to the mission field, too. He's all excited about translating the Bible into native languages."

"So?" Dorrie looked at Clem's face. "Why should that make you sad? Missionaries get married. And you loved South America that year we went as summer missionaries after our sophomore year. So what's the problem?"

Clem got to her feet. She straightened a picture, pushed the ruffled curtains back from the window. "No problem," she said at last. "Except that he's never even mentioned marriage. I could use my nursing down there. Before Mason even mentioned the mission field, I was wondering if that's where God was leading me. You know me. I love other countries, I love learning new languages, and I love—" She leaned closer to the window, her face hidden.

"And you love Mason," Dorrie finished for her.

Clem laughed, but her voice was muffled, and she kept her face turned away. "Except that he makes me so mad sometimes. But I can't imagine not being with him, not seeing him. I guess I really just wish things could stay the way they are between us. I sense that he's feeling restless—and that scares me." She took a deep breath. "And speaking of which, here he is now." She turned away from the window and ran a quick hand across her eyes. "Liam's truck just turned down our road. The two of them must be here to deliver my bed."

Dorrie's stomach clenched with excitement, and her hand went to her hair. She tried to smooth the wisps that had come loose from her braid. Clem laughed. "You look fine. More than fine. Beautiful, in fact." She followed Dorrie to the door and hugged her quickly. "I'm so glad you're here, Dorrie. Whatever happens with Mason, I know it will be easier now that you're here with me."

Dorrie returned the hug, but her eyes went over Clem's shoulder to the small pickup that bounced up the dirt road to their new home. On the passenger side she could see Mason's square face and short sandy hair, and beyond him— She took a deep breath, trying to still the trembling of her heart.

The truck pulled into their driveway and stopped behind her car. The doors slammed. "Hey, Dorrie, you still driving that heap of junk?" Mason called.

Dorrie grinned and nodded. She looked past Mason and met Liam's blue eyes, as blue as the sky beyond them, she noticed. His dark hair was a little shorter than the last time she had seen him, but it still had the same black gleam as a crow's feathers. He had grown a trim beard that emphasized the line of his jaw, and the hair on his face was a shade lighter, more brown than the hair on his head. She hadn't seen him for more than two years, not since her college graduation, and she felt now that she would never be able to look at him long enough to make up for those long and empty years. Her eyes moved from his face to his muscled shoulders beneath the navy knit shirt he wore, down to his khaki pants, noticing each detail, feeding on the sight of him.

"Hi, Dorrie." At the sound of his voice, her eyes leapt back to his face, and she blushed. He smiled. "I've missed you." Something inside her heart seemed to leap out of place, leaving an empty hole behind. She swallowed hard.

"I've missed you, too," she murmured, hoping he wouldn't hear the quaver in her voice.

She watched while he and Mason unloaded the pieces of Clem's bed frame from the back of the truck. "Just let us get this set up," Mason said over his shoulder, "and then we're taking you two women out for pizza. We figure Dorrie needs to relax after her long drive."

∞

Later, hoping she didn't have tomato sauce on her chin, Dorrie watched Liam as he talked with Mason. She thought his beard made his dark, narrow face look like a French courtier's; she was fascinated by the way his slim fingers moved, folding and unfolding a paper napkin. She smiled dreamily, then caught Clem's frown and dragged her attention back to the conversation.

They were discussing their jobs, she realized. Mason was a youth pastor at the same church that Liam and Clem's grandfather still pastored, while Liam was the athletic director at the Christian children's home where Dorrie would soon be teaching.

"When do you start work, Dorrie?" Mason asked, his mouth full of his fifth slice of pizza.

"Next week."

"We're awfully glad to have you," Liam said. "The children need someone who really knows the Lord."

Dorrie glanced at Clem. *See*, she wanted to say, *how can you say this man isn't right with God?* "I'm excited," she said out loud. "And nervous, too. I did my student teaching back in college, of course, and then I did an internship at a pediatric psychiatric hospital as part of my master's program. But this will be my first experience actually being on my own with a group of kids, responsible for them for an entire day." She met Liam's blue gaze and faltered, shaken by the attentive interest she saw there. "Tell me something about the kids, Liam," she managed to say, glad to have a reason to stop talking and merely watch his face.

Liam shrugged. "They're a needy bunch. Most of them from broken homes. The reason they're at the Home is because they've run into trouble either at home or school—or both. Either the state child protective agency or the local school districts pay for most of their boards and tuitions." His eyes were on the paper napkin between his fingers; he folded it into an accordion, unfolded it, folded it again. "There's about three times as many boys as girls—and they don't have a lot of manners. You'll have your hands full, I have to say, Dorrie." He looked up then into her eyes, and he smiled. "But with the training and experience you've had, I know you can handle them, Dorrie. I have confidence in you. That's why I recommended you so highly to our administration."

Once again, Dorrie felt her face glow.

∞

"What was with you and Liam tonight?" Mason and Liam had gone home, and Dorrie stood in the doorway of the tiny bathroom, watching Clem wash her face. In the mirror, Clem looked at her above the washcloth.

"What do you mean?" Dorrie asked.

"You know." Clem's voice was muffled by the cloth. "All those long, warm gazes the two of you kept exchanging. Is something going on I don't know about?"

"How could something be going on? The only time I've even talked to him in the last two years was when you suggested I call him about the job at the children's home. I never even saw him when I came up for the interview." Dorrie remembered the dark disappointment she had felt, and smiled, knowing now that God had been in control all along. She shrugged her shoulders, trying to hide from Clem the certainty she felt inside. "He was just being friendly."

Clem shook her head. "I've seen that look on Liam's face before." She hung up the washcloth, then turned back to her friend. "Liam's good with women. He likes to make them fall in love with him. But he never gets serious, and the women always get hurt. Believe me, I've seen it happen before." She frowned and shook her head. "Oh, Dorrie, your face is so easy to read. First you were jealous about the other women, and then relieved because I said he never got serious. Well, just be careful with him. I don't want to see you hurt. If he asks you out, pray about it before you say yes. Please. As a favor to me."

"Oh, Clem. You're overreacting."

"I don't think I am. Please, just promise me that you'll pray about it."

Dorrie smiled; she had already prayed about Liam enough that she could truthfully answer, "I promise. But you shouldn't be such a worrywart, you know, Clem. God will take care of me."

Clem looked at her friend and shook her head. "You're always so trusting. And I'm always so cautious, aren't I? What a combination we make." She went into her bedroom. "I don't know about you, but I'm exhausted from all this settling in. We'll talk more tomorrow, okay? Good night, Dorrie. Don't be mad at me about Liam. You know I love you."

Dorrie sighed and went into her own bedroom. She slid sweaters into drawers, hung dresses in the closet, and made up the bed with sheets and blankets. When she was done, she knew she was still filled with too much excited energy to be able to sleep. At college Clem had always been the one in bed by ten, while Dorrie had stayed up late to study or talk with other friends.

Now, the quiet of the little house settled around her, but she was still buzzing with restlessness. She sat for a moment on her bed and tried to pray; around her, the house was absolutely still, a quietness that seemed to be waiting patiently, unchanging in its stillness. She shook her head at her imagination and jumped up to stare out her bedroom window at the moonlit field behind the house. A line of trees edged the back of the field, and behind them, Clem had told her, a river ran. On impulse, Dorrie pulled on her sneakers and slipped out the back door to go exploring.

Though the day had been warm, the cool night air against her face told her summer was nearly over. She pushed her way through the tall grass, soaking her jeans with dew. The tang of goldenrod filled the air and overhead wheeled the silent stars. She tipped her head back to see them. "Alleluia, alleluia," she whispered, then ran as hard and fast as she could to the edge of the field.

On the bank above the river she found a fallen log for a seat and settled herself there above the moonlit water's gleam and ripple. She took a deep breath, trying to relax her muscles and calm her heart.

Instead, she found herself breathing even faster, her arms hugged tight around her knees, while she remembered again every word Liam had spoken, every expression on his face, every look that had passed between them.

She had loved him so long. Back when she and Clem were both freshmen in college, he had seemed so much older, so far beyond her reach, but now the age difference was no longer as important. And Clem was right—something *had* been different tonight, something in the way he had smiled and said her name, the way he had listened when she'd talked, the way he had looked so deeply into her eyes.

Despite Clem's doubts, she had believed for a long time that Liam was the only man she could marry. That belief had kept her from getting serious with any of the other men she had dated, and whenever she had felt discouraged or lonely, she had told herself that, in time, God would work things out. She hugged her knees tighter. This could finally be the time. Maybe God knew she and Liam were ready at last. When she had gotten the job at the children's home and known she would be working with Liam, she had been sure that her dreams would soon come true. God's hand was working; she knew it was.

She leaned back on the log and took another deep breath. Here outside, the night was quiet, just as it had been inside the house, but it was a busy sort of stillness, filled with the chirp of crickets, the gurgle of the river, and the sigh and flutter of the wind in the leaves. "Alleluia," she sang out loud, joining her voice with all the other night voices.

"Alleluia," a strange male voice answered her.

Chapter 2

D orrie froze. "Who's there?"

A dark shape rose from the edge of the river below her, a very large dark shape. She shrank back against her log as the man scrambled up the bank. "Alec MacIntyre," he said and held out his hand. "At your service."

Dorrie looked up into his face. In the moonlight she could see only the slant of dark eyes above high, square cheekbones. Her own face burned; she had thought she was all alone with God, and instead this stranger had been watching and listening. Reluctantly, she took his hand, then jerked away in surprise when he pulled her to her feet.

"Sorry," he said. "I just thought we might be able to see each other better if we were on the same level." But his head was still higher than hers, Dorrie realized. As tall as she was, she wasn't used to tipping her head back to see into someone's face; most of the men she knew were only a few inches taller than she was, but this man towered above her. She took a step backward.

"You must be my new neighbor," he said. "Clem told me you were coming today. My house is farther down the road from yours and Clem's. I'm sorry I startled you. I heard you come, but I didn't want to disturb your solitude. Then when you sang, it echoed my own feelings so well—it's a beautiful night, isn't it?" When she didn't answer, he stepped closer to her and peered into her face. "You are Dorrie, aren't you?"

"Yes." He was so close she could feel his breath on her face. Dorrie took another step backward. "I really have to be getting back, Mr. MacIntyre."

She saw the gleam of his teeth and knew he smiled. He backed away from her and held up his hands. "I've scared you, haven't I? Sorry. My mother always says I'm like a St. Bernard dog, bumbling around, too stupid to know I'm scaring people with my size. I'm safe, honest. What do you think of your new house?"

"It's very nice." She would have liked to say, *You remind me more of some big buzzing insect, flitting from thing to thing, the way you talk,* but she pressed her lips together to keep back the words.

"I live in its twin—except I finally painted mine this summer. You and Clem will have to come over for supper one night. You can meet Esther."

"Your wife?"

He laughed. "My cat. I'm not married."

Dorrie could think of no response, and after a moment the silence made her

366

shift her feet uncomfortably. She glanced up at his face and saw he was looking over her head across the moonlit river. "See the way the moon reflects in the river?" he said. "Like a million tiny lines of light. On nights like this, I can finally start to be quiet."

Not so I've noticed, Dorrie thought. He glanced at her as though he'd heard her thoughts and grinned. "I like to talk. You can probably tell that about me already. The trouble is, I like to think, too, so even when no one is around, all those words just keep pouring out of me. Sometimes I call it prayer—sometimes it *is* prayer—but sometimes all the noise I make keeps me from hearing God's voice. On a night like this, everything's so quiet, I get caught up in the beauty until I forget to make words inside my head. And in the midst of all the stillness and beauty, sometimes God's voice slips through. You know what I mean?"

"I'm not sure." For an instant she felt a flicker of understanding, but then he took another step closer to her. *I wish you would stop looming over me,* she thought. "I've had a long day, Mr. MacIntyre," she said out loud. "It was nice meeting you, but I've really got to get back now. I'm sure we'll run into each other again."

"Oh, we will." She saw his teeth flash again in the moonlight. "You see, I teach at the children's home, too. The grade below yours. Your room will be right down the hall from mine."

❦

"Alec is really very nice," Clem told her the next morning. She set down her coffee cup and giggled. "Although I can see how he must have startled you, rising out of the river bank like that. That's no reason to dislike the poor man, though."

Dorrie took a bite of toast. "I suppose. Something about him set my teeth on edge. He was just so—I don't know—big."

Clem giggled again. "That's certainly a good reason not to like him, Dorrie. How Christian of you."

"Well, he talked a lot, too. As though we'd been friends forever." She laughed sheepishly. "All right. I guess I was just embarrassed. I'll try to keep an open mind the next time I see—"

A loud honk interrupted her. Clem took her coffee cup to the front door and looked out. "I can't believe it. I've seen my brother more in the last two days than I usually do in two months." She turned to look at Dorrie with her eyebrows raised, but Dorrie had already leapt up and dashed to the bathroom mirror. She wiped toast crumbs from her mouth, ran a brush through her long hair, still damp from her morning's shower, and frowned at her blue jeans and old T-shirt.

"You're fine." Clem's voice was dry. "Go see what he wants."

Dorrie touched her wet hair. "Couldn't you talk to him while I blow-dry my hair? He's probably here to see you anyway—"

Clem waved an impatient hand. "I doubt it, Dorrie. Go on. I'll try to mind my own business."

367

Dorrie hesitated in the open door. Overhead, the sun gleamed through the oak leaves, casting a flickering pattern of light and shadow across Liam's face as he leaned out the window of his truck. He smiled. She looked back over her shoulder at Clem, then pulled the door shut behind her. "Hi," she said.

"Hi. I'm on my way to school to check over some new equipment. I thought maybe you'd like to come along. Look over your classroom. Get a feel for the place. I probably should have called, but I just thought of you when I drove by your road. Somehow I couldn't go past without at least stopping to say hello. I won't be offended if you have other plans for your day."

"No." Dorrie shoved her hands in her jeans' pockets to hide their trembling. "No, I'd—" She swallowed hard. "I'd love to go with you." She glanced down at her T-shirt. "Maybe you could give me a minute to change my clothes? I don't think I look very professional."

Liam grinned and shook his head. "You don't look any less professional than I do. See?" He opened the truck door to show her his own jeans and T-shirt. "We won't be seeing any kids. And any other teachers who might come in today will be dressed just as casually. I've even seen Margaret Truesdell—that's our principal, you remember—in jeans during the break between semesters."

Dorrie remembered the dignified gray-haired woman and smiled. Her smile grew into laughter from sheer happiness. "Just let me tell Clem where I'm going."

In the truck she sat on her hands so he wouldn't see the way she shook. She looked out the window and took long, deep breaths to calm herself.

He chuckled. "You look like an eager little kid, Dorrie. Sometimes I have to remind myself that you and Clem are really all grown up now." She glanced at him, and his smile widened. "And quite nicely, I might add. But I can't help but still feel protective. I hope this job doesn't prove to be a disappointment for you."

She kept her eyes on his face. "Why should it? I love working with kids. Being able to do it in a Christian setting sounds perfect."

Liam frowned, his eyes on the road. "These kids are a challenge, Dorrie," he said after a moment. "I don't want to mislead you. I know you'll be wonderful at the job, and I'm more glad than I can say to have you teaching here."

He pulled into the Home's long driveway. At the top of the hill, the brick school sprawled on one side of the road, while on the other a row of white cottages curved down into the woods. A group of children were playing on a playground, and Dorrie caught the shouts of a game being played on the soccer field beside them. Liam parked the car and stared at the boys running back and forth on the grass. He sighed.

"Next week it will be me out there with those boys, blowing my whistle, trying to teach them—" He shook his head. "Sorry, Dorrie. I always dread the end of my vacation. But I don't want to put a wet blanket on your enthusiasm."

Dorrie frowned. "But you do like your job, don't you, Liam? I always imagined it being the perfect spot for you—a place where you'd have room for both your love of God and your love of sports."

She couldn't decide on the meaning of the twist he gave his mouth. He didn't say anything for a moment, just sat very still, while she searched his face with her eyes. "Just don't expect them to be loveable little tykes, Dorrie," he said at last. "Teaching them is a continual power struggle. I get tired of it sometimes." He took a breath and unlatched his door. "Come on. Enough sitting here while I brood. I know Margaret must have taken you on the official tour when she interviewed you, but let me show you around again. Then I'll leave you at your room while I go to the gym."

The building was empty except for a secretary typing in the main office. "Most of the teachers will be in later this week to get their rooms ready," Liam said. "Right now they're still vacationing. The break between the summer term and the fall semester is all too short."

Dorrie followed him down the shadowy halls, trying to memorize the location of library and faculty lounge, science lab and bathrooms. "What do the kids do while school's not in session?"

"The houseparents organize activities for them," Liam answered. "About two thirds of the kids go home, though, during break, depending on the kid and what the situation is like at home." He pushed open a door at the end of the hall. "Here it is, the sixth grade classroom—your room. And here's your class list, already tacked to your bulletin board."

He handed Dorrie the sheet of paper. She glanced at it, then looked around the room. Twelve desks stood in a circle, and bright checked curtains fluttered at the open window. Bookcases sectioned off a corner of the room where bean bag chairs were clustered on a bright rag rug. "I love it. Especially that reading corner."

Liam laughed. "That's one of Margaret's new ideas—but good luck getting the little monsters to sit still long enough to read. They're more likely to use the chairs as tumbling equipment—or the books as missiles. These kids aren't exactly the bookish sort."

Dorrie looked at him. "You're so negative today."

"Not negative. Just honest." His hand touched her cheek. Dorrie froze, forgetting everything but the feel of his fingers against her skin. "I hope you're happy in this classroom, Dorrie." His voice was soft. "I hope the job's everything you want it to be."

He was standing so close to her that she was certain she could feel his warmth, like a blanket she longed to pull around her shoulders. Her breath came faster and faster, and then his hand dropped from her face. He moved away. "I'd rather stay here with you, believe me, but if I can get my work done now, maybe we could go out for lunch?"

"I'd like that," she managed to say.

"Then I'll see you in an hour or two."

After he had left the room, she sank down into one of the bean bag chairs, replaying their conversation in her mind. She put her hand to her face where his fingers had touched her.

At last she remembered the class list in her hand and looked down at it. Eight boys and four girls. She read their names over, imagining their faces, then found her way back to the main office to ask the secretary for their records.

While she was waiting for Mrs. Hutter to pull the folders from the filing cabinet, the door opened behind her. "Why, hello, Dorrie."

Dorrie turned around. "Hello, Mrs. Truesdell." She smiled at the principal, noticing that as Liam had predicted, she was dressed in jeans and a cotton shirt. "I'm about to start getting to know my new students."

Margaret Truesdell smiled. "They're some of my favorite kids." She waited while Dorrie collected the pile of folders and thanked Mrs. Hutter. "I'll walk with you up to your classroom."

They climbed the stairs in silence. Dorrie noticed that the top of Margaret's silver head came only to her shoulder, but the older woman carried herself with such an air of assurance and authority that Dorrie found herself feeling very young beside her.

They reached Dorrie's classroom, and Dorrie dropped the folders on her desk. Margaret walked around the room. "What do you think? Have you noticed anything missing, anything you think you'll need?"

Dorrie shook her head. "Not yet. I really just got here. Liam Adams drove me over." She felt her cheeks grow warm, as though Margaret's cool gray eyes could somehow read that she'd spent her time so far dreaming about Liam. "I haven't had a chance to really look things over yet," she finished, trying to sound composed and professional.

Margaret nodded. She straightened one of the bean bag chairs, then looked over her shoulder at Dorrie. "Did Liam tell you what he thinks of my reading nooks, my newest additions to the rooms?"

Dorrie hesitated. "He was a little pessimistic."

Margaret nodded. "To say the least, I'm sure. I hope you won't let his attitude influence you too much."

"Oh, I think a reading corner is a wonderful idea," Dorrie answered. "If I were a child, I would love to curl up here and read."

Margaret shook her head. "These children won't. Not at first. Liam's absolutely right—they have no idea of the proper use for chairs and books. But my philosophy is, they will never learn different ways if they're not given the opportunity. When I was growing up, reading was the way I escaped, the thing that kept me sane—and one of the main ways that God touched me during those years. Most of these children will eventually have to go back to lives that are far from perfect. Unfortunately, there's nothing we can do to change those lives very much. But we can help them to grow strong—and offer them some escape hatches. Like books. Something besides drugs and sex, the only escapes they usually can find on their own."

Margaret ran her hand through her short gray hair, then turned toward the window. She was silent for a moment. Dorrie looked at the delicate, narrow bones of her face and waited. "Liam may have told you," Margaret said at last, her eyes still focused on the playing field outside the window, "these aren't easy children. They don't open their hearts easily—and because of that you may find it more difficult to open your heart to them." Dorrie made a movement, as though to deny Margaret's words; the older woman glanced at her and smiled. "That may not be the case with you. I remember very clearly your recommendation from your internship supervisor—she said you have a loving heart for wounded children. That's one of the main reasons I hired you. But loving hearts are sometimes easily hurt, and these children are experts at hurting others. They've learned to be that way to protect themselves."

Margaret sighed. She put her hand on Dorrie's arm and looked up into her face. "I'd like to suggest, Dorrie, that you go slowly with these kids. Be patient with them. Be patient with yourself. Keep your heart quiet. Pay close attention to who these children really are, and how it is that God wants to speak to them. Try to let God use you in whatever way He wants. This isn't the sort of job you can come to with your mind on other things. It needs your whole attention."

Her lips curved a little, and she shook her head. "I probably don't make any sense to you right now, do I? You'll have to wait 'til you've been with the kids for awhile. September is always such a hectic month—if I forget to schedule an appointment with you, track me down and make sure we talk again." Her smile widened. "I'm glad you're here, Dorrie."

After she had gone, Dorrie turned to the stack of folders. For the first time since she had been hired for this job, she found herself forgetting about Liam and what working with him could mean for their relationship. Instead, Margaret had helped her to realize the reality of the children she would soon be teaching. "After all, God, I must be here for them, too, not just because of Liam," she said. She worked her way through the twelve folders, filling several sheets of paper with notes and ideas.

The room was very quiet, but she barely noticed. Only once she heard a small rustle from somewhere in the room. She looked up from her paper; *a mouse,* she thought, and imagined a small, bright-eyed creature sharing the quiet with her. "I don't know how you can stand those little things," her mother would always say and shudder, but Dorrie liked mice. She smiled and picked up her pen once more.

At last she stood up and stretched, then went to the shelves that lined one wall to inspect the supplies and textbooks. She leaned back against the shelves and looked around the room, noticing for the first time how still it was.

The sun poured through the windows, laying squares of light across the desks and wooden floor. Faintly, she could hear the shouts from the soccer game, but that was the only noise. For once, she felt comfortable with the quiet, as though something in the room's calm had washed over her busy heart, leaving her cleaner and more peaceful than before.

"I know You're here, God," she said softly. "I can almost feel Your Spirit's breath. Please use me in this room. Let the children see You through me. Help them to learn and grow strong and whole."

She leaned forward and opened a closet door, expecting to find more supplies. Instead, her eyes fell on a nearly life-size drawing of a tiger. A small sound made her eyes drop lower. She froze.

She caught the gleam of glasses. From behind them, a pair of brown and unfriendly eyes stared back at her.

Chapter 3

"You're not a mouse."

The boy's mouth twisted. "Of course not. That time I made that rustling noise, it was because I had to scratch my arm. That was the only time I moved at all, but I figured you heard me. I can sit still for hours usually, but the mosquitoes were wicked last night. We had evening devotions outside. What a stupid idea. If I hadn't been covered with bites, I never would moved at all. You thought I was a mouse? Bet you were scared, weren't you? Did you jump up on top of your desk?"

Dorrie shook her head. "I like mice. Although I suppose I wouldn't want to share my house with them if I could help it."

"Ephesians Cottage had mice this summer. They poisoned them. Do you like my tiger?"

Dorrie looked again at the drawing. "He's beautiful. Where did you get him?"

"I drew him, stupid. I'm pretty good, aren't I? Isn't he awesome?"

"Totally." She smiled at him, but his eyes flicked away from her gaze. "I'm impressed. You're very talented."

He shrugged. "I'm also very intelligent. I'm the smartest kid at the Home. I'm probably smarter than you are. My IQ is 148. So I really don't need a teacher, at least not one like you. It's irrational to make me go to school here."

"So why do you think you're here?"

He shrugged and made a face. "My mom kept locking me out of the trailer. I drive her crazy. She used to hit me with her hairbrush 'til I'd run outside, and then she'd lock the door quick. I got so, though, I'd go outside as soon as she picked up the brush. It was no big deal really. There was a hole underneath the trailer I could crawl into. I used to keep things there, kind of like this closet. But then last winter, one of our nosy neighbors called child protective. A couple of other things happened at school, too."

"Like what?"

He shrugged again. "Oh, this jerk tried to shove me around." He stared up into Dorrie's face. "He was the gym teacher," he said significantly, "just like Mr. Adams. Anyways, I lost my cool. They say I hit him and yelled all sorts of stuff. He shouldn't have touched me, though. They said I was emotionally disturbed. Eventually, I ended up here. I hate this place."

He was still sitting hunched in the dark closet. She could see very little of him except the straight dark hair that fell across his glasses. "Who are you anyway?" she asked.

"Felix."

She picked up her class list and looked down at it. "Felix Jones. Right? I'm Miss Carpenter. You're going to be in my class next week when classes start. What are you doing in my closet?"

"It's not *your* closet."

"All right." She smiled. "What are you doing in *the* closet?"

"What's it look like I'm doing?"

She shrugged. "I don't know. You can't have been doing much of anything. With the door closed, it must be pitch black in here."

"There's a light, stupid. I turned it off when I heard you walking this way. I was hoping you wouldn't see me. People usually only see what they're expecting to see."

"It was kind of hard to miss that tiger," Dorrie said mildly. She noticed then the long string hanging from the bulb in the ceiling and reached out to pull it. With its light, she could see that the walk-in closet was filled with neatly stacked drawing paper, books, boxes of colored pencils, pastels, markers, and watercolor paints. A row of apples was lined up along one shelf, and drawings of animals were taped everywhere. Felix sat on a bean bag chair, his finger in a book. His knees were hunched close to his small shoulders, and his brown eyes glared up at Dorrie.

"I'm small for my age."

Dorrie nodded.

"But I'm smarter than you."

"I remember you mentioned that."

"I'm probably even smarter than—" He broke off, and his gaze shifted beyond Dorrie's face. She saw his face grow tighter. "I'm definitely smarter than *him,*" he finished.

Dorrie turned to find Liam standing behind her. "Look who I found." She moved to let Liam see into the closet.

Liam frowned. "Just what do you think you're doing here, Mr. Jones? Where are you supposed to be?"

Felix got to his feet, his shoulders straight and tense. "I'm *supposed* to be playing some idiotic game, *Mr.* Adams. You'll remember, though, that I don't like games."

Liam shook his head. "I suggest, Mr. Jones, you get back to wherever it is you belong. You know the school building is off-limits when classes aren't in session. I'll speak to your houseparents to make sure you get the proper number of demerits. Which cottage are you in?"

"Why should I tell you?"

Dorrie had never seen Liam's face look so hard. "Because if you waste my time by making me look it up, I'll see that you get double the usual amount of demerits. You won't have to worry about playing stupid games, because you won't be seeing anything except the inside of the detention center."

Felix shrugged. "I like detention. I know someone with your limited mental abilities, Mr. Adams, wouldn't understand—but I like to have uninterrupted time to think. No one bothers me in detention. But if it will make you happier—I live in Corinthians."

Dorrie stepped forward to end the confrontation. "I'll look forward to seeing you next week, Felix."

Felix ducked past her. "Wait just a minute, Mr. Jones," snapped Liam. "You owe me an apology for your rudeness, don't you think?" Before Felix could respond, Liam stepped forward and grabbed a corner of the tiger drawing. "And get your things out of Miss Carpenter's closet."

Dorrie put her hand on Liam's arm. "No, I—"

Before she could say more, Felix sprang between Liam and the drawing, his small face screwed tight. "Don't you touch that!" He knocked Liam's hand away from the drawing.

"Now, see here—"

Dorrie felt the muscles in Liam's arms clench, and she clutched him tighter. "No, Liam," she whispered. "Let it go."

He glanced at her, then shrugged his arm free. "You're coming with me, Mr. Jones. Straight to the detention center."

Felix stood small and straight, his back pressed against his drawing. "I'm not going anywhere. You can't make me." His voice wavered, but his chin came up, and his eyes locked with Liam's.

Dorrie tried to think of a way to end the power struggle, a way that would save face for both Liam and Felix, but her mind was blank.

"Hi, everybody," said a calm voice.

A man leaned against the door frame of her classroom. From his size, she knew who he had to be. She watched Alec MacIntyre's dark eyes move from face to face. "Looks like your hideout was discovered, Felix." He smiled at Dorrie. "I hope you don't mind that I gave Felix permission to use this closet for his things. Privacy's a pretty slim commodity around here."

"You gave him permission?" Liam looked as though he didn't believe it.

Alec nodded. "So long as he checks in with his houseparents whenever he comes here. He needed a safe place for his books and art work."

Liam turned back to Felix. "Why didn't you say so?"

"You didn't ask."

Dorrie heard Liam take a deep breath.

"Sometimes a simple explanation saves everyone a lot of trouble, Felix," Alec said easily. "Come on, why don't we show Miss Carpenter the wall mural you did in my room last year."

Felix's shoulders relaxed. He stepped away from the tiger drawing, then glanced from Liam to Dorrie.

"You're welcome to this space, Felix," Dorrie said. "But maybe we could hang the tiger on the outside of the door instead of inside. That way everybody could appreciate it. If you don't mind."

"No." Felix shook his head and closed the closet door firmly behind him. "The other kids would ruin it." He followed Alec to the door.

"Mr. MacIntyre?" Liam said. Alec looked back over his shoulder. "I'm not very happy with this situation you've set up. Could we talk about it another time?"

Alec shrugged. "At your convenience." His eyes moved to Dorrie. "Coming?"

"Miss Carpenter and I are going out to lunch," Liam said stiffly. "Another time, Mr. MacIntyre."

Dorrie looked from Alec to Liam. She had known last night in the dark that Alec was several inches taller than Liam, but she had not realized how much bigger he was all over. Next to Alec's broad shoulders and lanky arms and legs, Liam's slim frame looked trim and neat. Alec's brown hair curled wildly above the square, prominent bones of his face, while Liam's black head was smooth and narrow. *Like the difference between a well-groomed thoroughbred and some huge farm horse,* Dorrie thought to herself. She saw that Liam's expression was as stiff as his voice had been, and when she turned back to Alec, she hated the small smile on his lips, as though he knew he had been able to handle a situation that had been too much for Liam. She wanted to turn away from Alec MacIntyre; she wanted to go out to lunch with Liam and forget all about him. But something about the set of Felix's small shoulders changed her mind.

"Could you wait just a few minutes?" she asked Liam. "I would like to see Felix's mural."

"Whatever. I'll be in the truck."

Dorrie watched him stride across the room and out the door, hoping his anger would not destroy the new warmth that had been growing between them. She turned to find Alec's eyes on her face.

"We won't take long," he said quietly. "I don't want to interfere with your lunch date."

Felix looked up at her as they walked down the hall to the fifth grade class-room. "You're going out with Mr. *Adams?*"

Dorrie's cheeks grew warm. "We're just having lunch together. He gave me a ride here today."

"Do you *like* him?"

"Yes, I do."

Felix shrugged. "What can you expect from someone who talks to herself?

Your perception of reality is obviously severely distorted."

"What do you mean?" Dorrie smiled.

"I heard you. When I was in the closet. First, you were talking to Mr. Adams. 'Believe me, Dorrie, I'd rather stay here with you.' It made me want to gag. And then after awhile you and Mrs. Truesdell talked. And then I'm sure you were all alone. And I heard you talking."

"Oh." Dorrie laughed. "I think I was talking to God."

Felix's mouth twisted. "Aren't you too old for an imaginary friend? Now, I know you're crazy, talking to someone no one's ever seen."

Alec put his hand on Felix's shoulder. "Look at this," he said to Dorrie, pointing to a mural of the solar system on his classroom wall. "Didn't Felix do a great job? Didn't you tell me, Felix, you used some of Copernicus' drawings when you were doing this?"

"That's right."

"Funny, isn't it, that Copernicus could portray some of the outermost planets when he had never seen them?"

"He could tell they were there by their effect on the planets he could see," Felix said. "Their gravitational pull."

"Maybe one way we can see God is by the way He affects the world around us."

Felix shook his head. "I knew you were working up to one of your bad analogies. Copernicus never *talked* to those planets. The fact that something *may* exist doesn't imply we should pretend to have a personal relationship with it."

"Well, I guess you're right about the analogy not being a very good one. Maybe Miss Carpenter talks to God, though, because the effects of His love in her life are more evident and constant than the gravitational pull of a distant planet."

Felix scowled. "He hasn't been real *or* constant in *my* life."

"You'd be surprised." Alec's voice was gentle. He glanced up at the clock. "Go on with you now, or you'll be late for lunch. I'll see you next week."

After Felix was gone, Alec turned to Dorrie. "He's an interesting kid. And very bright."

"He told me."

Alec laughed. "He would. He's also very wounded. Like most of the kids here. It's hard to believe in God's love when you have doubts about your own mother's love."

Dorrie nodded. She looked at Alec's strong features, surprised by the gentleness she saw there.

"You were good with him," he said, his eyes on her face.

Dorrie looked away. *Thank you for granting me your approval,* she wanted to say, but instead she shrugged. "I like him."

"I'm sorry about the situation that developed over the closet. I got Margaret's approval, but I should have put a memo in all the faculty's boxes. My own closet is chock-full, and I thought I'd have a chance to talk to you about it before you came into school. I never would have set Felix up for a run-in with Liam Adams. If I had thought things through better, I should have realized you and he would be friends, and Liam would be apt to come to your room before classes started. Liam and Felix haven't gotten along since the day Felix got here."

"Felix told me he had a problem with a gym teacher in his old school. Maybe that's why his attitude is bad about Liam."

Alec shrugged. "Maybe."

They were silent for a moment. Again Dorrie was aware of how quiet the school building was, but this time she longed to escape from the silence. She looked past Alec and through the window saw Liam sitting in his truck, his arm resting on the open window while his fingers drummed on the roof top. Alec turned to follow her gaze. "I've held you up, haven't I?" he said. "I'm sorry."

"That's okay." She took a step toward the doorway, longing to hurry outside to Liam, but Alec put his hand on her arm. She looked down at his large fingers, and something like a shudder ran through her body.

"At the risk of sounding as though I have the social skills of Felix Jones," he said, his brown eyes smiling into hers, "I'd like to ask you something."

Dorrie was nearly jiggling with impatience, longing to be gone. "Yes?"

"*Are* you and Liam dating?"

"No." *But I'd like to be,* her heart cried.

"Then would you go to dinner with me tonight?"

Chapter 4

I would never have thought he'd ask me out," Dorrie said to Clem later that afternoon. They sat on their front lawn, fishing leaves out of the blackberries they had just picked.

Clem grinned. "I was hoping you and Alec would hit it off. When is he picking you up?"

"He's not. And we're not. He makes me uncomfortable. Your Gram would probably tell me to pray about my attitude—but I really don't like him very much. So I told him I wanted to spend the evening with you. It's true. I feel like I've hardly seen you yet."

Clem set aside her berry basket. "Well, you're not going to see me tonight. Mason called me at work today. He asked if we could get together tonight. He says he needs to talk to me about something." She leaned back on her hands and frowned. "I'm sorry, Dorrie."

Dorrie popped a berry into her mouth. "That's all right. We'll have lots of time together. Mainly, I just wanted an excuse for not going out with Alec."

"But why? Why don't you like him?"

Dorrie shrugged. "I don't know." She tipped back her head to watch the flicker of oak leaves overhead. "Something about him just rubs me the wrong way. He seems so— I don't know. Smug. Like he knows all the answers."

"I don't think he's like that really. He just likes to talk. You'd like him if you got to know him, I know you would. The two of you have a lot in common; I've thought so ever since I met him."

Dorrie looked at her friend. "Don't you go matchmaking, Clementine Adams. I'm truly not interested. Not in the least."

Clem held up her hands and laughed. "I won't. Promise. But I guess I did hope that—"

"What?"

"Oh, that when you saw Alec and Liam together, you'd see how much more—real, I guess, Alec is than Liam."

Dorrie snorted. "Will you stop that, Clem? Why are you so negative about your own brother? As a matter of fact, when I saw them together, I had the opposite reaction—I thought Liam was the much more attractive of the two. Alec looks like a huge clodhopper next to Liam."

Clem's delicate eyebrows pulled together. "Alec's attractive, Dorrie. But I

wasn't referring to their looks. Alec is always honest and open, whereas Liam—"
She threw up her hands. "You know what I think. Just look at the difference in
the way the two of them handled that boy in your closet. Liam was angry and
rigid, heading for a confrontation—"

"I never said he was perfect," Dorrie interrupted. "So he's having some problems with his job—that doesn't mean I'll stop caring for him. And remember
how you were complaining that Liam seems too perfect, that he never shares his
problems? Well, today he was sharing with me his feelings about his job. I think
he's feeling a little burnt-out. At lunch he even asked me to pray for him. This
job is so right for him—I know God will show him the way to get back his
enthusiasm."

"I'm glad he talked to you like that." Clem smiled at Dorrie, but the two
small lines between her brows told Dorrie she was still worried. Clem picked a
small green worm off a berry and set it carefully on a blade of grass. "I never did
think Liam was particularly well-suited for working with kids."

Dorrie sighed. "Will you listen to yourself? You can't say anything good
about Liam."

Clem looked up from the worm, her blue eyes round and wide. "It's no sin
to be poorly suited for working with kids. Some people are, some people aren't.
You and Mason and Alec happen to be very good at it. I'm not. I don't think
Liam is, either. That has nothing to do with my other worries about him. Except
that I wonder if you even see the real Liam. I worry that you've fallen in love with
a fantasy—your idea of who Liam is instead of who he really is."

Dorrie grabbed her berry basket and got to her feet. "You're wrong, Clem."
The screen door slapped shut behind her.

She poured the berries into a colander and rinsed them under the faucet.
"Shall I make these into a pie?" she asked when Clem had followed her inside.

"That would be wonderful." Clem handed her the other berry basket. She
leaned against the counter beside Dorrie. "I'm sorry," she said after a moment. "I
keep telling myself to mind my own business about you and Liam. My only
excuse this time is that I'm nervous."

Dorrie looked up from the berries. "About what?"

"I'm scared of what Mason wants to say to me tonight. He sounded so serious."

Dorrie dumped the berries into a bowl. She smiled. "Maybe he has something important he wants to ask you."

Clem shook her head. "I don't think so."

Dorrie laughed. "You are such a pessimist, Clemmie. A regular little Eeyore.
Now go on." She gave Clem's arm a push. "Your hands are all scratched and
stained, your lips are purple from sneaking berries when you thought I wasn't
looking, and your hair is full of twigs. Go take a shower and make yourself beautiful. I have a feeling that tonight's the night Mason will finally get up his nerve.

You worry too much. This world is run by a God who loves us, remember?"

"That doesn't mean He gives us nothing but happy endings, though," Clem muttered, but she disappeared into the bathroom and turned on the shower.

∽

Dorrie set the blackberry pie on the counter to cool. With Clem out with Mason, the house was quiet. Once again, the stillness irritated Dorrie. It seemed almost like a hand patiently stretched out, waiting to be held. She shook her head at her fancies and moved restlessly from the living room to her bedroom, then back to the kitchen. She got herself a glass of water, looked in the refrigerator, turned the radio on and then off again.

At last she gathered up her textbooks and teaching ideas, and with her canvas bag full, she went outside and back through the field to the river. For several minutes she worked furiously, but then, her chin in her hand, her eyes on the river's ripple, her mind drifted away from curriculum planning. Instead, it circled around and around the thought of Liam.

"You and Clem tired of each other already?"

Dorrie jumped. Alec MacIntyre was stretched out by the river just below her, his brown corduroy pants and dark green T-shirt blending with the leaves and bark around him. "You again!" She flushed. "Mason wanted to see Clem," she said guiltily.

He lay on his back looking up at her for a moment, perfectly still, his dark eyes watching her, and then he sat up. "You could have called me. Or we could still go get something to eat together. It's not too late, and I for one haven't eaten yet. What about you?"

He climbed up beside her, moving aside an arithmetic book so that he could settle next to her on the fallen log. She wanted to inch farther away from him, but she could feel his eyes on her. She kept her own gaze fixed on the river. "I'm not particularly hungry," she said. Immediately her stomach growled loudly, and her cheeks burned.

He smiled and then said softly, "Something tells me you're not particularly interested in seeing any more of me than you have to."

She couldn't think of an answer. *You don't believe in beating around the bush, do you?* she thought. *If you get the message, then why can't you politely go away?* She felt guilty for her thoughts, but before she could form a courteous response to his words, he said gently, "That's all right. Although I wasn't asking for a lifetime commitment. Just an evening out. A chance to get to know each other better. I guess I've been feeling lonely lately, and when I met you, I thought—" He shrugged his shoulders.

She made herself turn and meet his eyes. "I'm sorry. Maybe it's just that you seem to keep popping up when I'm least prepared." She tried to smile. "Like a jack-in-the-box. At least this time you didn't catch me singing."

His mouth softened. His eyes rested on the river; she glanced down at his large hands lying quietly on his knees, and she thought of the way Liam's hands constantly moved. Liam seemed always driven by a restless energy; she knew he would never be able to sit here like Alec, absolutely still.

"Sometimes," Alec said, his eyes still on the river, "I think God likes to surprise us so that He can show us Himself. We like to figure things out and put God all neat and tidy in a box. Then we can get busy with our lives and forget to pay daily attention to who our God really is. I do it all the time—but then He shows me He's bigger than any box I could ever imagine. He surprises me. Like a jack-in-the-box. That's why I love the unexpected. Like finding you here last night, and then again today. If my heart is quiet enough, if I'm not too busy to even notice, sometimes I catch a brand new glimpse of God's face."

Dorrie frowned. "I'm not sure I know what you mean."

Alec smiled. "You have the most beautiful hair, did you know? When the sun shines on it, it looks just like a flame."

Dorrie felt her face grow warm. She put her hand to her hair, as though to hide it, and looked away from his smiling eyes. *First you babble about God being a jack-in-the-box, and now you try to feed me a line about my hair,* she thought. *Why can't you just leave? Sitting here like this with you, you bother me. You're just too—big.*

"Sorry," he said. "Sometimes I have the bad habit of saying whatever pops into my head." She felt his eyes on her face, but when she finally took her own eyes from the river, he was looking down, studying an ant that was climbing his leg. "Sometimes," he said, "I probably talk too much all together."

Dorrie listened to the ripple of the water and the cawing of a crow. Somehow, the sounds seemed only to add to the quiet, the same way Alec's voice had blended with the stillness. She remembered the busy restaurant Liam had taken her to for lunch, the constant motion of his face and hands as he and she ate and talked, and she wished she could be there again with him, instead of here with Alec. She shifted uncomfortably on the log and searched for something to say. "What did you mean about God surprising us?" she asked at last.

She heard him sigh. "I guess I was thinking about Isaiah 55 where God says, 'For my thoughts are not your thoughts, neither are your ways my ways.' In my mind, I always put that together with what it says in Psalm 46, 'Be still, and know that I am God.' Sometimes I get so impressed with my own ideas that I miss what God really wants for me. My head's too full with my own noisy thinking to catch that 'still small voice.'" He turned his head, and his dark eyes studied her face. "I'm afraid that's what I've been doing with you."

She pulled a blade of grass and began tearing it into tiny pieces. "What do you mean?"

He smiled. "I mean I think you're awfully pretty, Dorrie Carpenter. In fact, I've been thinking of very little else all day long. And now I can see it's time to quiet down my heart so that I can hear God's voice again. Sometimes His surprises don't mean exactly what we'd like them to." He got to his feet. "I'm sorry I intruded on your privacy yet another time." He looked down at her and one corner of his wide mouth turned up. "I guess I'll have to find myself another hideout. Otherwise, every time one of us wants to be alone by the river, we'll find ourselves bumping into each other instead." He touched one finger to the top of her head. "I'll see you later, Dorrie."

Dorrie watched him go, his long legs jumping easily over rocks and fallen logs, until he had disappeared between the trees around the river's bend. She felt the warmth of the evening sun on the top of her head, the same place he'd touched her. She put up her hand as though she could rub the warmth away.

She spread out her work again and tried to concentrate. After a few minutes, she slapped her notebook shut and piled her books back in the bag. *I think you're awfully pretty, Dorrie Carpenter,* she heard his voice say inside her head, and she shook her head impatiently. She got to her feet and made her way back across the field to the house.

When she went in the back door, she was surprised to find Clem scrubbing furiously at the baking dishes Dorrie had left in the sink.

"You're home early," Dorrie said. "How come?"

Two tears dripped off Clem's cheeks into the dishwater. "I can't talk about it right now, Dorrie." Her voice was choked.

Dorrie looked at her bent head, then went to the front door and saw Mason still sitting in his car in the driveway. She looked back at Clem, then softly opened the door and went outside.

"What's going on?" she asked Mason through his open window.

He was slouched down behind the wheel; at her voice, he turned his head, and she barely recognized his face. Mason always smiled, she realized, but now his mouth turned down, and his eyes were blank. He shrugged his shoulders. "I don't know, Dorrie. I don't understand her."

Dorrie made a face. "Come on, Mason. She's not that hard to understand. You two have been going together for years now. The whole world expects you to get married. You can't blame her for thinking about it, too. In fact, I don't think it makes much sense for your relationship to just go on and on like this, unless it's leading somewhere."

"I know." Mason stared straight ahead at the dashboard. "But every time I've tried to talk about the future, Clem's always changed the subject. It's like it scares her. I've applied to a mission board—and I need to tell them whether I'll be married or single. Tonight I had to find out where I stood."

"What are you talking about? Clem's in there crying."

"I know." Mason's voice was husky. "I don't understand what she wants. I asked her to marry me. But she said no."

Chapter 5

H ow could you tell him no?" Dorrie asked. "Here, you've been complaining to me about how Mason never wants to get serious. And now he tells me the same thing—about you! What is it with the two of you?"

Clem leaned her forehead against the kitchen wall. "I know, I know," she said, her voice muffled. "I must be losing my mind. I don't understand myself any better than you do." She raised her tear-streaked face and looked at Dorrie. "I thought I wanted to marry him more than anything else in the world. I really did. But when I heard him asking me, actually saying the words—I don't know. All I could feel was scared. Terrified. Like something wasn't right. I couldn't say yes."

Dorrie put her arm around Clem's shoulders. "But did you have to say no? Poor Mason. He was sitting out there in his car like a dog who had just been kicked. He had tears in his eyes."

Clem gulped back a sob. "I know, I know. That's why I feel so terrible. I know how much I've hurt him."

Dorrie looked at the fresh tears welling in Clem's eyes. "Don't you think it's like you said—you just got scared? It wouldn't hurt you so much to see Mason hurt if you didn't really love him."

"I *know* I love him." Clem pushed away from Dorrie. "That's not the problem. It just doesn't feel right." She grabbed a tissue and blew her nose. "I don't think it can be God's will for us to be together after all."

"Oh, Clemmie. Are you sure?"

Clem sniffed. "I can't talk anymore, Dorrie. Crying always makes me sleepy. I've got to go to bed. Maybe things will make more sense tomorrow."

"I hope so. I'll be praying, Clem."

∞

But the next day and for the remainder of the week, Clem refused to talk about Mason. At church on Sunday, Dorrie saw Mason's gaze go again and again to Clem, but Clem kept her eyes fixed on her grandfather as he preached; her round face was calm and still, but the rosiness was gone from her cheeks.

Dorrie's own eyes were drawn to Liam's narrow, dark face. She watched the earnest way he turned the pages of his Bible, the way his attention never faltered from his grandfather's sermon, and she smiled to herself. *Oh, God,* she prayed silently, *I love him so much.*

Once as she looked across the church, her eye caught Alec MacIntyre's. He looked away quickly, and so did she.

When the last hymn had been sung and Grandpop Adams had pronounced the benediction, Dorrie tried to steer Clem in the direction of Liam and Mason as they stood talking in the vestibule. Clem, however, her small face set, grabbed Dorrie's elbow and pulled her in the opposite direction.

"Hello, Alec." Clem smiled. "I hear you and Dorrie keep stumbling over each other."

Alec put the pile of hymnals he carried in the corner of a pew. "Afraid so." He stretched for another hymnal and did not look at the two girls.

Dorrie pulled surreptitiously at Clem's arm, but Clem ignored her. "You all ready for classes to start tomorrow?" Clem took a step closer to Alec and smiled up at him. "Dorrie's been going into school every day to work in her room. I think she's starting to get a little obsessed. I swear I heard her muttering about bulletin boards in her sleep last night."

"Oh, you did not." Dorrie shook her head at Clem, trying to signal with her eyes her longing to be gone.

"Good morning, Clem, Dorrie." Dorrie turned with relief away from Alec to Clem's grandmother. "I've just invited the boys to dinner. We want you two girls, too, of course." The small, white-haired woman put out her hand and caught Alec's sleeve as he was turning away. "You, too, Alec. We've plenty of food."

Clem's smile had disappeared. "The boys, Gram?"

"Yes, of course, Dear." Her grandmother's eyes had gone beyond Clem, and her voice was absent. "Liam and Mason."

"But, Gram, I can't—"

"Excuse me, Dear, but I have to talk to Mrs. Simpson about the flowers for next week. I'll see you all in about a half hour at the house."

"But—" Clem turned helplessly to Dorrie. "I can't eat dinner with Mason. Not now."

Dorrie grinned. "Serves you right." She looked at Alec as he looked after Gram Adams, his dark eyes unreadable. Dorrie's smile faded, and she added softly, "Not that I'm any happier about this arrangement than you are."

Alec's eyes met hers. He shrugged. "I guess we will all go and have dinner. I think we were just issued our orders."

Dorrie nodded. "Gram Adams is a wonderful cook," she said politely. She looked across the church, and caught Liam's blue gaze. Her smile returned. She could put up with having dinner with Alec MacIntyre as long as Liam would be there, too.

⧆

Dorrie ate her last bite of apple pie and leaned back in her chair. She looked around the Adams' dining room, from the red geraniums on the windowsills to the baskets and copper kettles that lined the shelves. The room, like the rest of the house, was as cozy and welcoming as the English cottages in the prints Gram had given Clem for their new house. Dorrie looked from Grandpop Adams, with his thin white hair and beaklike nose, to Gram, who looked exactly the way Clem would look in another fifty years, from her round, childlike face to her small, practical body. Dorrie smiled, glad that when she and Liam were married, she would belong to Gram and Grandpop, too.

Gram had seated her between Liam and Alec, across from Clem and Mason. Clem had kept her eyes on her plate, never glancing at Mason once during the entire meal, saying very little. Alec was as quiet as Clem, but Liam, Dorrie, and Mason had discussed upcoming church activities with Grandpop Adams. Mason's voice was strained, though, and he kept glancing sideways at Clem, trying to include her in the conversation. She seemed unaware of him, her blue eyes cloudy and preoccupied.

From her end of the table, Gram had been watching them all quietly. "What did you think of the sermon today, Dorrie?" she asked now, a hint of a smile in the round blue eyes that were so much like Clem's.

"I—" Dorrie hesitated; she searched her memory, but she could not call to mind even the text Grandpop had used. "I always love Grandpop's sermons," she said at last.

"How tactful, Dear," Gram murmured, the smile in her eyes growing. She turned to Clem. "What about you, Clem? Did you agree with Grandpop's interpretation of Paul's words?"

Clem's eyes rose from her plate to meet her grandmother's gaze, and her cheeks took on their usual rosiness. "I'll have to think about it."

"Ah." Gram's white head nodded. "How wise of you. Never a good idea to leap to an opinion rashly." Her eyes went next to Alec.

Dorrie saw that he was waiting for Gram's question, his dark eyes gleaming. "And you, Alec? Were you able to form an opinion about the sermon?"

He grinned. "I'm sorry, Mrs. Adams, but I have to be honest—I'm afraid my mind was on other things this morning."

Mason smiled shamefacedly. "Before it's my turn, I'll confess, too, Gram." He shrugged his shoulders and looked around the table. "What a sorry bunch we are. Is that why you insisted we all come to dinner—so you could show us how inattentive we were to God's Word?"

Gram shook her head reproachfully. "Of course not, Mason. That's between you and the Lord. I was just a little amused, watching the four of you. Your minds were so obviously on other things."

Her husband leaned back in his chair and laughed. "Well, at least you children will keep me humble. I looked out at your faces, and I felt proud knowing you were all listening to me so attentively." He reached for his coffee cup and laughed again.

"Poor Grandpop." Liam turned to his grandfather. "Casting your pearls before these swine. I for one can tell you exactly what I thought about your sermon." He grinned at Clem. "I certainly know your text had nothing to do with anything Paul wrote, since it was from the book of Isaiah."

Clem stuck out her tongue at Liam. She pushed back her chair and joined Alec as he collected dirty dishes from the table. "How about if Dorrie and Alec and I do these dishes as our penance?" she said. She gave her grandmother a gentle push. "You go sit in the living room and tell Mason what it was he missed at church today. The rest of us swine will clean up the mess in the kitchen."

Clem kept up a stream of chatter while Alec washed the dishes and she and Dorrie dried. Alec and Dorrie worked silently, answering Clem when she asked a question but never looking at each other. From the corner of her eye, Dorrie was aware of Alec's white sleeves rolled up above his elbows and the dark hairs that grew down his arms and onto his long-fingered hands. Once when she reached for a dish from the hot rinse water, her hand brushed Alec's bare arm; they both pulled away as quickly as if they had been burned.

Clem fell quiet, and for several minutes they worked in silence. Through the door into the dining room, Dorrie could hear Liam and his grandfather discussing the morning's sermon. She listened to the rise and fall of Liam's tenor voice and she smiled, but Clem shook her head and made a face.

"That Liam. Always Mr. Saintly."

"Clem." Dorrie's voice was reproachful.

Alec looked up from the dishwater and turned from Clem's face to Dorrie's, his eyebrows raised.

"Really," Clem asked him, her voice high, "don't you think my brother is a little hard to take sometimes?"

Alec grinned and shook his head. He let out the dishwater and dried his hands. "From Dorrie's expression, I don't think she agrees with you." His eyes were on Dorrie's face, his voice soft. "Do you, Dorrie?"

Dorrie flung her thick braid over her shoulder. She felt her face grow warm, but she kept her voice even. "I think Clem's too hard on her brother. That's all. She always has been. I feel sorry for him." *But why am I trying to deny my feelings for Liam?* she asked herself. *Why not let Alec see how I feel?* She couldn't answer the question she had asked herself; she knew only that she would like to hide as much as she could of herself from Alec's dark gaze. His eyes made her uncomfortable, as though they could see too deeply inside her, deeper than a near stranger had any right to look.

"Poor Liam," Alec said dryly. "He seems to survive, though."

Clem snorted. Dorrie bent to pet Gram's old tabby cat, hiding her face from both of them.

"I'd like to be getting home soon, Dorrie," Clem said.

"In a minute." Dorrie settled crosslegged on the kitchen floor, while the cat climbed into her lap purring. "Nice Samantha," she murmured, stroking the cat. She kept her head bent while Clem left the kitchen to tell her grandparents good-bye. For a moment she could feel Alec's eyes on her, like an itchy spot on the top of her head, but then he, too, followed Clem into the other room. "Pretty kitty," Dorrie crooned, trying to let the peculiar tension she felt flow from her hands as they stroked the limp cat.

"There you are, Dear." Dorrie looked up into Gram's calm eyes. "I hope my teasing didn't make you uncomfortable."

Dorrie shrugged. "A little." Her lip curled. "But I deserved it."

Gram smiled. "I'll tell you a secret. I couldn't have answered any quizzes myself on today's sermon. I confess I was too busy watching Mason watch Clem, and you watch Liam, while Alec watched you. I hadn't realized until today what a complicated web you young people have been busy stringing. All through the service, I was trying to think of ways to help you sort it all out. Perhaps that's why I thought the text was taken from one of Paul's writings. Because eventually the eleventh verse of the fourth chapter of First Thessalonians came into my mind quite clearly: 'Study to be quiet.' I realized then that my planning and scheming, even my praying for what *I* wanted, was like noise coming between me and our Savior's voice."

Dorrie couldn't meet Gram's frank blue gaze.

"I won't say anything more, Dear." Gram's voice was gentle. "I can see I've made you uncomfortable again. I just wanted to let you know I can see what is happening in the hearts of you young people. I won't involve myself—but I shall be quietly praying. . .for all of you." Her small hand patted Dorrie's cheek. "Come. I think the others are ready to say good-bye."

Outside, Clem climbed immediately into Dorrie's car. Dorrie hesitated, watching Liam as he said good-bye to his grandparents in the doorway. She had hoped for some new sign that he was beginning to care for her, but nothing had happened. *Alec's fault,* she thought unreasonably.

Liam came down the steps and turned to Alec. "About that situation the other day, Alec," he said. "I think you handled it all wrong."

Alec had opened his car door, but he turned now to Liam. "Which situation was that?" he asked easily.

Liam's lips pressed together. "The one with Felix Jones in Dorrie's closet. It doesn't make sense to me—giving a kid like that extra privileges unless he's earned them."

Alec looked past Liam's face to Gram's pink roses that climbed the white trestle around the door. "Doesn't God give us good things, things we've done nothing to merit? He gives them to us not because we deserve them, but because He knows they'll help us grow, help us reach our full potential. That's how I felt about

Felix and the closet. For him to be himself, the best, most creative part of Felix Jones, the part God created and longs for him to be, he desperately needs a time and place where he can be alone sometimes. Otherwise, that part of him will die."

Liam shook his head impatiently. "I don't want to get into a spiritual discussion here. I'm talking about a messed up little kid, a delinquent who could do who knows what kind of damage when he's unsupervised like that inside the school building. I'm surprised Margaret and the houseparents would ever agree to such a thing. It just doesn't make sense."

Alec looked at Liam thoughtfully. "I think both Margaret and the Corinthians Cottage houseparents recognized that this privilege is too important to Felix for him to risk losing it by abusing it. If we don't do *something* to nurture the inquisitive, creative side of Felix Jones, then it will wither up and die— and then we *will* be left with just another little delinquent." His gaze shifted to Dorrie. "What do you think, Dorrie? Felix will be in your class now. He's really not my responsibility anymore."

Dorrie hesitated. She looked from Liam's dark, impatient face to Alec's quiet gaze. From inside the car, she heard Clem make a small, disgusted noise, and Dorrie longed to put herself firmly on Liam's side. "I guess I have to agree with you," she said reluctantly to Alec. "It sounds to me as though Felix needs that closet." Her eyes went to Liam. "Though I can understand your position, too, Liam."

Liam shook his head. "You don't know, Dorrie. You haven't worked with these kids yet. You're setting yourself up for problems."

"As I said," Alec said quietly, "it's really not up to me anymore." He slid into his car and shut the door.

Liam waited until Alec had backed out of the driveway. "Anybody want to get together for pizza later?" he asked then. He bent his head to see into Dorrie's car. "Clem? How about it, Mason?"

Dorrie looked hopefully at Clem, but she shook her head violently.

"Another time, Liam," Mason muttered and climbed into his own car.

Liam looked from Mason to Clem, then met Dorrie's eyes and shrugged. He smiled, and she hugged around her the warmth of his gaze.

❧

"What's going on with those two?" he asked Dorrie the next day as they walked into the school together.

Dorrie shook her head. "I'm not sure. I guess Clem just doesn't feel it's God's will for her to marry Mason."

Liam snorted. "What did God do—send her a telegram? I love the way people blame their own decisions on what 'the Lord told them.'"

Dorrie looked at him doubtfully. "But God does show us His will. Don't you believe that?" When he didn't answer, she sighed. "I just hate to see Clem so miserable."

"She'll be all right. She's survived worse things." He held the door open for Dorrie then touched her shoulder. "Good luck today, Dorrie. I hope your first day of classes goes well for you. Remember, be tough with the little monsters."

Dorrie stood in the hallway staring after him as he strode toward the gym. She put her hand to her shoulder, and slowly her frown turned into a smile.

Inside her own classroom, the curtains were drawn. The room was dim and quiet, but from beneath the closet door a line of light shone. She smiled and crossed the room. "Good morning, Felix," she said as she opened the closet door.

He was crouched on the floor, a piece of charcoal in his fingers, the long, gentle face of a giraffe taking shape beneath his hand. He shook back his lank, dark hair and scowled up at her. "Haven't you ever heard of knocking?"

Chapter 6

Y ou're right," Dorrie said. "I should have knocked. Next time I'll remember."
Felix nodded curtly, then went back to his drawing. After a moment,
he looked up at Dorrie again. "Well? Did you want something?"

She smiled. "Not really. Just to say hello. Your drawing is beautiful. How do
you know how to draw a giraffe like that? Without looking at anything, I mean."

He shrugged. "I've been researching giraffes. At the library. Before I draw an
animal, I always find out as much as I can about it, look at as many pictures as I
can." His hand on the paper moved more slowly, and his voice softened.
"Sometimes I try to turn into the animal." He glanced up quickly at Dorrie, then
back to his picture.

Dorrie nodded seriously, knowing he had been afraid she would laugh.
"Would you like to be a giraffe?"

Felix made a face. "They're too stupid. The only reason they don't get eaten
by everyone is that they're so big. They're too gentle. Too quiet."

Dorrie looked up at the picture of the roaring tiger above Felix's head.
"Would you rather be a tiger?"

Felix leaned closer to his drawing. "No one hurts tigers," he said after a
moment. "They eat everyone else, and no one eats them."

Dorrie sank down on her heels in front of the closet. She nodded. "Do you
think you're like a tiger?"

He carefully drew the gentle flare of the giraffe's nostrils. He seemed almost
to have forgotten Dorrie, so absorbed was he in his drawing, and she thought he
would not answer her question. He smudged the charcoal line carefully with his
fingertip, and then at last he said, "I'm too small."

"Too small to hurt others the way a tiger would?"

He nodded.

"But you wish you could?"

He raised his head for an instant and looked at her, his eyes flat and dark.
"Of course. It's only the animals who hurt others who don't get hurt themselves."

Dorrie longed to reach out and put her hand on his small, thin shoulder.
Instead, she said, "I'm not sure it works like that with people. I think maybe the
people who hurt others are the ones who end up hurting themselves most of all."

His dark brows drew together, and he shook his head impatiently. Dorrie
smiled. "Who is it that's hurt you, Felix?" she asked softly.

Again, he was quiet so long she was certain he would not answer. *Too fast, Dorrie, you're pushing him too fast,* she told herself, but then he whispered, so softly she could barely hear him, "My mom."

She did reach her hand toward him then, but he raised his head and scowled at her as though warning her to come no closer. "Everyone," he added in a louder voice. "Kids like to pick on small people."

She nodded. "But think about your mom. Don't you think she hurts, too? If she didn't hurt inside, I bet she wouldn't hurt you. And I bet that after she's hurt you, she hurts inside more than ever."

His frown wrinkled his whole face, like a baby about to cry, and then suddenly he wiped his face smooth and bent once more over his drawing. "What do you know?" he muttered.

"Not much," Dorrie admitted. "But I do know for certain that if your mom wasn't hurt inside herself, she would never hurt you. And the reason I know that, Felix Jones, is because there's no reason in the world why you should be hurt like that. *You* didn't do anything to make your mother hurt you."

"Maybe I was the one who hurt her in the first place." His voice was a whisper again.

Dorrie shook her head. "You didn't, Felix. You're not to blame for your mother being the way she is."

He was drawing the giraffe's spots now, each one different from the one before, the tip of his tongue caught between his teeth. Dorrie waited while the silence grew longer and longer until she realized that as far as he was concerned, the conversation was over. She smiled. "You know what animal you remind me of?"

"What?" He sighed, as though humoring her.

"A snapping turtle. Because you have two ways to protect yourself. You can snap at anyone who comes too close. Or you can pull inside your own little world that you carry around with you—your art."

Felix made a face. He finished the giraffe and then leaned back. "There."

"It's beautiful."

He glanced at her. "You kind of remind me of a giraffe, come to think of it."

"Because I'm tall?"

He nodded. "That—and you're pretty stupid, too." His dark eyes suddenly gleamed, as though he were keeping back a grin.

Dorrie smiled. "Oh yeah?"

"Yeah."

"Well," she said thoughtfully, "you may be right. I think I'm fairly gentle, too. But I'm not particularly quiet."

"No," he sighed, "you talk an awful lot." He looked past her to the clock on the wall, and his face changed, grew hard and tense again. "The others will be here soon."

Almost immediately, Dorrie heard the sound of feet in the hallway. She got to her feet, and Felix scurried to his desk, looking suddenly more like a mouse than anything else. She smiled at him, but he avoided her eyes, and she turned to the doorway to greet the other students.

As they came in, Dorrie tried to match them with their names. The girls came first, and they were easy, since she had only four of them: Tammy, her hair in a greasy ponytail, her head ducked as though she expected a blow; fat little Polly; pretty Kristen with her eyes outlined with mascara; and LaSandra, who thrust her chin forward as though daring the world to do its worst. Dorrie smiled at them, but only Polly smiled back.

She heard a sound like thunder from the hallway then. "Slow down." She recognized Alec's voice. "There's no fire that I know of."

Seven boys burst into her room. "So you're the new teacher," one of them said. "What's your name?"

"Miss Carpenter. Who are you?"

"Kenny." He sat on top of one of the desks, a big boy with a shock of straight blond hair that flopped over his forehead. "What do you think, Lamar?"

Lamar grinned shyly at Dorrie, his teeth white against his dark skin. He took a chair and did not answer Kenny.

"I think she's pretty," said a thin, freckle-faced boy.

"I like your hair," Kristen said. "Do you dye it?"

"Nope," said Dorrie. "It came that way." She caught Felix's dark stare and smiled, but he looked away quickly. She looked around the rest of the circle of students and took a deep breath, feeling as though she was about to plunge into deep water.

"Now that we're all here, let's start the day by talking to God. I'll go first, and then anyone who wants to can go next, and when we're done, I'll finish up." Dorrie closed her eyes.

"Thank You, God, for this classroom." She heard a giggle, but she kept her eyes closed. "Thank You for each one of these students. I know You love them all very much." She waited, but all she heard was more giggles and the shifting of feet. She sighed. "Thank You for being with us today. Help us to see You more clearly. In Your Son's name. Amen."

She opened her eyes and looked around the circle of faces; all were either filled with laughter or carefully blank. "Let's get to know each other a little now. I want each of you to tell me one thing about yourself, and then one thing that you know about the person next to you on the right. I'll go first." She hesitated. "Let's see. One thing about myself. And I don't mean something you can tell just by looking at me, like I have red hair or I'm tall. Let's see." Her eye caught Felix's again, and she smiled. "I've been told recently that I like to talk. I never thought about it before, but I guess that's pretty true. I like to talk to whoever will listen to me. I like to talk even when no one at all will listen to me. Sometimes I talk to God. Sometimes I just talk to myself. I guess it's one of the important ways I handle life—by talking about it."

She turned to Kenny, who sat to her right. "Now, let's see, Kenny. I just met you five minutes ago—but I could tell one thing about you as soon as you came through the door."

Kenny shook back his blond hair. "What's that?"

"You're a leader."

"What's that supposed to mean?"

LaSandra answered before Dorrie could, "It means you're good at bossing people. And she's right about that."

Kenny scowled at LaSandra and then turned to Dorrie, his eyes cold. "Somebody has to tell people what to do. Otherwise nothing happens."

Dorrie smiled. "You're absolutely right. Every group needs a leader. Being a leader is a real gift. It's also a big responsibility. Do you know what I'm talking about?"

Kenny shrugged.

"Well, suppose you got up and jumped out the window, and everyone in the class jumped right after you. That would be an example where a leader didn't use his power responsibly."

Kristen giggled. "Knowing Kenny, he'd be more likely to get up and *break* the window. And then all the boys would jump up and start breaking windows, too."

Dorrie nodded. "That would be another example of a leader not being responsible."

LaSandra stuck her nose in the air. "Well, he's not my leader, that's sure. No white boy tells me what to do."

Kenny's gaze was cold and flat. "Oh, yeah?"

"It's your turn, Kenny," Dorrie said hurriedly. "Tell us something about yourself."

Kenny made a face. "I don't know anything about myself. What you see is what you get."

"What do you like to do?" Dorrie asked. "What are you good at?"

"Uh, I'm good at shooting baskets." He looked around the circle. "I bet I could beat any of you here." He grinned. "This afternoon in the gym. How about it? Who'll take me on?"

"Why don't you discuss that another time," Dorrie said. "Can you tell us something about Jamie there on the right?"

Kenny looked at Jamie. "Uh, he's got curly hair."

"You're right, Kenny, he does have beautiful curly hair." The class giggled at the word beautiful, and Jamie rolled his eyes. "But can you tell us something we can't tell just by looking at Jamie?"

"Sure." Kenny grinned wickedly. "You can't tell it by looking at him, but old

Jamie boy is really *dumb*."

Jamie's face turned red, and Dorrie took a deep breath. "Jamie is *not* dumb. I meant, Kenny, can you tell me something positive about Jamie?"

"You mean something good?"

"That's right."

Kenny looked at Jamie consideringly. "Nope," he said after a moment, "I can't." The class burst into laughter.

Only Felix did not laugh. His face was expressionless, but when he looked at Dorrie, his dark eyes were mocking. Again Dorrie took a breath. "Let's back up a little here. The purpose of this exercise is not to give you a chance to toss around insults. I should have specified from the beginning—I want you to tell me one good thing about yourself, and then one good thing about the person sitting on your right. Jamie, it's your turn."

∞

By the end of the day, Dorrie was exhausted. She slumped against her desk as her students thundered from the room, leaving tipped chairs and scattered papers behind them.

"I like them," she told Clem that night. "I like them a lot. But I had this feeling all day like I was just barely in control. The kind of feeling you have when you're driving on ice. For the time being, everything's going okay. But one wrong move and—" She threw out her hands. "Disaster. It's a scary feeling."

"It was your first day," Clem said absently, as though her mind were on other things. "You'll be more comfortable with them as you get to know each other better."

Dorrie shook her head. "I kept doing stupid things. Setting myself up for situations I should have been able to avoid if I'd just thought things through better." But the last few days, she had been daydreaming about Liam, she knew, more than she had been planning for her students. She frowned. "All day long, at the last minute I'd pull things back together, get them headed back in the right direction."

"Well, that's good then," Clem said, staring at some paperwork she had brought home from the clinic.

"But it's not good, Clem. Don't you see? I don't have enough practice handling a group. My experience has all been one on one, or in small groups of three or four. I feel like a juggler trying to keep too many balls in the air at once. Sooner or later they're all going to fall and scatter all over the place."

Clem looked up from her paper and sighed. "You'll be fine, Dorrie. Just give yourself some time. I'm sure you'll find you have more confidence in yourself every day."

∞

But she didn't. Each day, Dorrie felt her muscles clenching tighter as she drove to work as though they were preparing for a fight. Each day, her class pushed her authority a little further. One day Kenny called Felix an obscene name, loud enough for Dorrie to hear, although she pretended she hadn't. The next day John shot a paper airplane across the room. The following day she caught Kristen and LaSandra giggling and passing notes instead of working on a history project.

Through it all, Felix sat quietly. He seldom said anything to the others, and for the most part, they ignored him. When he looked at Dorrie, she thought he sneered, as though he could see all too clearly the mistakes she was making.

"I'm losing them," Dorrie told Clem as they washed dishes together.

"Don't get discouraged." Clem's eyes were focused on the window, and as usual these days, her voice was preoccupied.

"I guess I just want them to like me. And I get the feeling they think I'm pretty silly."

"Of course they like you." Clem's answer sounded automatic. Dorrie stared at her, frustrated. After a moment, she threw down her dish towel and went outside.

The evening air was sharp with a tang that smelled of fall. The late sunlight gleamed on the goldenrod in the field across the road and made the first scarlet leaves of the sumac turn brilliant. As always, everything was quiet, the only sound the faint whisper as the wind stirred the sunlit weeds. Dorrie flopped her arms in frustration, as though she could drive the quiet away, and then she ran as hard and as fast as she could up the narrow dirt road.

When she could see Alec MacIntyre's small house through the trees, she stopped. She stood for a moment in the center of the road, panting, and then she turned and walked back. Inside the little house she shared with Clem, she knew she would find only more quiet waiting for her.

❧

"How's everything going?" The next morning, Liam came up behind her in the hallway on her way to her classroom. She had barely seen him in the past two weeks, not since the first day of school, and his absence from her life had added to the weight of her discouragement. She smiled at him now as he put a hand on her shoulder and took a step closer. "You look tired. Having problems with the monsters?"

She shook her head. "You shouldn't call them that. It just adds to your negative mind-set, you know." She felt her worries disappear, though, as a glow spread from her shoulder through the rest of her body. "I'm just adjusting to the new routine," she told him. "I'm still not used to my alarm going off at six every morning. I'm glad tomorrow is Saturday so I can finally catch up on my sleep."

"I know what you mean. Listen, I've got to run, but let's get together some time soon, okay?" He squeezed her shoulder and then turned down the hallway before she could answer. She looked after him, still smiling.

"You look like you just saw God Himself," said a small, hard voice behind her.

She spun around and found Felix leaning against the wall within the shadows of a doorwell. "I haven't seen you in your closet lately," she said to him.

He shook his head. "I've been using it after school. I can use it any time that Mr. MacIntyre is in his room, and he usually works late. It's quieter in the afternoons." He frowned at Dorrie as though to let her know she was the one he was avoiding.

Dorrie opened her classroom door. "What have you been working on lately?" she asked mildly.

He glanced up at her. "Last week it was this neat baboon from India. This week it's been field mice."

Dorrie smiled as she opened the curtains. "One of my favorites, remember?"

He shrugged. "I like the way they're put together."

Dorrie nodded. "I think God must have had fun creating the animals."

Felix flung himself into his seat. "Give me a break. Why do you have to make God a part of everything?"

"Because He just *is* a part of everything, I suppose. Come on, think how much fun you have drawing the animals. More than anyone else, God must know what it feels like to be absorbed in creation, the way you are when you're working on a drawing. He must really love you to have made you so much like Himself in that way."

Felix shook his head. "When are you going to leave?"

"You're changing the subject. What do you mean?"

"I mean, when are you going to give up and leave? I give you another month, tops."

"What are you talking about? I'm not going anywhere. My contract is for one school year. And I'm planning on being here next year, too." *Of course, I'll be here,* she thought; *this is where Liam is.*

"You'll never make it that long." He grinned, but the smile did not reach his eyes. "Hey, don't feel bad. Since I've been here, lots of teachers have come and gone. I heard the third grade teacher just quit yesterday—she didn't even make it through two weeks. And Corinthians Cottage has had two new houseparents since I came. I figure not many people are like Mr. MacIntyre." His mouth twisted. "Or like Mr. Adams, either, for that matter." He shook his head at Dorrie. "I can tell. You're one of the ones who'll have enough sense to get out of this place."

Dorrie leaned against her desk and looked at Felix thoughtfully. "It must have been hard having your houseparents leave like that."

Felix shrugged. "Why should I care? They're all the same." He looked straight into Dorrie's face as though daring her to disagree.

"Well," she said lightly, "I'm not going anywhere. I can promise you that."

"You will," he insisted. "We'll make you leave. We're good at getting rid of people."

"No." Dorrie leaned over and put her hand against the side of Felix's dark head. "No one is getting rid of me."

He shook her hand away. She thought she saw as much fear in his eyes as she did anger.

While she stood watching him, wondering what she should say next, she heard Liam's voice in the hall. She spun toward the door, smiling. "Don't forget," he called through the open doorway, "we're getting together soon."

Dorrie turned away from Felix toward her desk. The warmth from Liam's words lasted through the arrival of her other students. She smiled at them, happier than she had felt in days, listened to their chatter, and then called them to begin work on their classroom newspaper.

"Who has a piece of news for us today?"

To her surprise, Felix, who usually never said a word during class, raised his hand. "I do."

"Go on, Felix," she said, pleased he was responding to her at last.

Felix looked around at the other students. "Miss Carpenter is in love with Mr. Adams," he announced. "I saw them kissing this morning in the hallway."

Dorrie felt her face flush. "You did not."

"I did," Felix said calmly.

"That creep?" Kenny got up from his seat and looked Dorrie up and down. "You could do better, Miss Carpenter."

Kristen had taken out a jar of nail polish and was painting her nails. "I think Mr. Adams is cute," she said without looking up.

LaSandra shook her head. "I know his sort. My mama's living with one like him. Smile real nice 'til they get you. Then they beat you bad."

"We're supposed to be working on a newspaper here, people," Dorrie reminded them.

"Who cares? I'm sick of this stupid class newspaper." Kenny gave John a nudge. "Bet you can't beat me arm wrestling." The other boys gathered around as Kenny and John linked hands over John's desk.

"Get back in your seats, please." Dorrie's voice was drowned by cheers from the boys as Kenny pushed over John's arm. "I said, everyone back in their seats." Her voice was louder this time.

One or two glanced at her, but now Lamar and Kenny were wrestling. Tammy joined the group of boys, giggling. Kristen and LaSandra had gone to the window and were leaning out to wave at someone in the soccer field below. Only Felix and little Polly were still in their seats. Dorrie's eyes met Felix's; he grinned, and a wave of anger washed over Dorrie.

"Get back in your seats!" she screamed.

Their heads swiveled to look at her, and they were momentarily quiet. Then they burst into laughter.

"Hey, look, everybody," Kenny shouted, "we're done with the newspaper, and now it's reading time." He went to the reading corner and began tossing books off the shelves. The other boys caught them, then shot them back at Kenny.

Kenny's arm was over his head, ready to throw another book, when he suddenly stood still and lowered his arm. Dorrie saw his eyes shift beyond her to the doorway.

"You having a party in here or what?" asked Alec MacIntyre.

Chapter 7

When the day was finally over and the students had gone back to their cottages for the weekend, Alec MacIntyre came and once more leaned against the doorway of Dorrie's classroom.

"I hope you didn't mind my interrupting like that." Two lines drew his dark brows together. He ducked his head, trying to see into Dorrie's face, but after one quick glance up, Dorrie kept her eyes fixed on the papers spread across her desk. She felt her face grow warm.

"No," she managed to say. "Obviously, I had lost control of the class."

Alec folded his long frame into one of the students' seats. "Want to talk about it?"

Not particularly, she longed to answer. She drew tiny red circles along the margin of her plan book. "I don't seem to be as good at this as I had thought I would be," she said stiffly. "I have no idea how to control them. I don't really even *want* to be 'in control' of them—I just wanted them to like me. But obviously I can't accomplish anything at all without more order. The way things are now, they don't even respect me, let alone like me."

Alec shook his head. "Respect doesn't come easy to these kids. I'm fairly certain they already like you—but respect is another thing altogether for them." He tipped back in the too-small seat. "Do you like them?"

Dorrie looked up for the first time. She nodded. "I love them."

"Then you're not the failure you think you are. More than anything else—more than their need for discipline or learning—these kids need to know they're loved and accepted. That's the only way they're ever going to be able to comprehend a loving God. From talking to the kids, I think they already sense the genuine liking and concern you have for them." His dark eyes met hers, and he smiled. "Next question: do *you* respect *them?*"

"I think so."

Alec nodded. "I could tell from the way you interacted with Felix that day before classes started that you saw him as a person in his own right. These kids aren't objects put here for our pleasure or convenience. Before God, we and our students are equals. Agreed?"

How condescending he is, she thought, but she swallowed her resentment and nodded.

"Then can you respect and love these kids enough to set aside your own selfish need to be liked?"

Dorrie gripped her red pen until her knuckles turned white. "What do you mean?" She saw his eyes drop to her hand, and a small corner of his lip curled; she forced her fingers to relax.

"I'm sorry," he said, his voice suddenly very soft. "Am I being insufferable?"

Their eyes met. Dorrie felt her own face grow hot again, even as she was surprised to see the red that tinged Alec's high cheek bones. "I always say the wrong thing to you in the wrong way, don't I?" He shook his head, then ran a hand through his hair. The thick curls stood on end even after his hand was gone, as though his hair were made of wire. For the first time, she nearly smiled.

She saw his eyes note the change in her expression, and his own face relaxed a little. She shifted in her chair; she had never met anyone so sensitive to each tiny change in her face and muscles, and for a moment she had the sensation of being examined under a microscope.

He cleared his throat. "I've been working here six years now, but when I started, I was just like you. I interacted with the kids the way I would have if they had been people I'd met socially—my main goal was to make them like me. They *did* like me—and for a year or so I was too self-centered to understand that wasn't enough.

"Eventually, it occurred to me that as a follower of Christ, I was also supposed to be an imitator of Christ. Christ didn't come to earth to make people like Him. He wasn't the sort of one-man-show that I had been trying to be. Instead, I think a lot of the time He was quiet, and He listened. When He did speak, He spoke directly to people's needs.

"When I realized that, I saw that I couldn't put myself at the center of my relationship with the kids. I have to put God there instead. When I finally did that, I saw that one of the things these kids desperately need is the security of a sense of order, a system of checks and balances. Most of their home lives have lacked that, so they behave like a ball bouncing wildly back and forth, up and down, trying to see if there are any limits. If we love them and respect them, then I think it's our job to set the limits, the boundary lines of what's acceptable behavior." With one long finger, he traced a name scored into the desk by some past student. "I know you have the school rules posted on the wall like the rest of us—but have you established any classroom rules?"

Dorrie shook her head. Her sense of her own foolishness added to her resentment. *Anyone who can talk as long as he can obviously missed his calling as a minister,* she thought.

Alec's eyes were on his hands, and he seemed unaware of her discomfort. "You might think about coming up with a set of ten or so rules. Do it with the kids. Your job will be to help them keep it short and pertinent. Otherwise, they'll include everything from not wiping your nose on your sleeve to saying, 'Excuse me,' when you burp. And for each rule there should be a consequence that will occur if the rule is broken, as well as if it is followed." He looked up at her. "If you'd like to use a system of tokens and rewards, maybe we could combine our classes on Fridays for some special activity. A movie maybe, or a picnic, or a trip into town. What do you think?"

She swallowed. *I know this; I knew everything he told me. So why wasn't I doing it? Why did I set myself up for this whole depressing situation?* "I—I guess so," she said out loud.

"Believe me, things get a lot simpler when you have a structure to work inside. You're merely enforcing rules they made themselves—and you don't have that uneasy feeling that things are creeping more and more out of hand."

In spite of herself, Dorrie's gaze met his, and she smiled. "I've had that feeling a lot ever since classes started." She set her red pen down on the desk and sighed. "Thanks, Alec," she made herself say. "You've been a big help."

"I'm glad." She felt his eyes resting on her face. "And I'm glad you've finally put down that pen. For awhile there I was afraid you were going to stab me with it."

She grinned but looked away from the smile in his eyes. "I've got to get home." She stood up and reached for her briefcase. Her sleeve brushed the red pen and sent it rolling to the floor; she bent to pick it up at the same time he reached for it. Their arms bumped, and she felt his warmth. Strands of her red hair caught on the wool of his sweater, and she put up her hand to smooth her head as she stood up quickly. She heard his breath catch and glanced down into his face.

"Sorry," he said, but for once he was not looking at her; instead, his lashes lay in dark half-circles against his cheeks. He stood up and put his hands in his pockets. "I'd better be getting home, too."

Dorrie looked after him; in spite of herself, she found herself noticing the breadth of his shoulders beneath his sweater, the length of his legs within the casual corduroys he always wore. She shrugged and turned back to her desk to pack up her briefcase.

∞

As she came out of the school building, she caught a glimpse of Liam's dark head disappearing into his truck. She walked faster, hoping he would at least wave as he pulled out of the parking lot, but by the time she had reached her own car, his truck was gone. She sighed and drove home slowly. For the moment she forgot her class, forgot Alec MacIntyre with his pushy good advice, and thought only of Liam. *Please, God, let something happen between us soon.*

When she pulled into the dirt road, in the distance she could see Clem's car already in their driveway with Mason's car parked behind. She smiled to herself, certain she would find them snuggled on the sofa, their differences resolved.

But when she went through the front door, singing "Amazing Grace" loudly to let them know she was coming, she found Mason standing just inside the door, while Clem leaned against the kitchen counter, her shoulders stiff.

"Oh, come on, you two." Dorrie laughed. "Can't you just kiss and make up?"

"It's not that simple, Dorrie." Clem's voice was small and tight.

Mason threw out his hands helplessly. "I give up. Let me know if you change your mind, Clem. In the meantime, I won't bother you anymore." He glanced at Dorrie. "Nice to see you, Dorrie. I'd better be going, though."

Dorrie waited until the door closed behind him, then turned to Clem. "Come on, Clemmie, can't you see how miserable you're making the both of you? How can this be God's will for you? He wants us to be happy, remember?"

Clem's lips pressed into a tight line. "He wants us to follow Him. To take up our cross and follow Him. I don't think He necessarily said anything about being happy."

"But He did. Remember in John 16—'ask, and you shall receive, that your joy may be full'?"

Clem shook her head. She turned her back to Dorrie and stood staring out the kitchen window. "Grow up, Dorrie." Dorrie had never heard Clem's voice sound so hard. "We don't get all the things we selfishly want. That's not what Christ meant. In fact, more often than not, the thing we think we want most is the very thing God will ask us to give up. I learned that a long time ago when Mom and Dad died. Maybe the joy comes later—but that's different from the selfish happiness that comes from having your own way." She turned around and met Dorrie's gaze, her blue eyes cool and level. "Maybe it's time you thought about that in connection with Liam, Dorrie."

Dorrie stared at her. Suddenly, Clem's eyes softened, then filled with tears. "I'm sorry, Dorrie. Forget I said that. I just need to be alone for awhile."

Dorrie took a step closer to her. "Remember when I first came? You said that whatever happened with Mason, it would be easier because you and I would be together."

Clem brushed her hand across her eyes and nodded.

"Well, don't you think it might help if you just talked about all this with me? You've been shutting yourself off not only from Mason, but from me, too. I feel as confused as he must. It just doesn't make sense to me."

Clem's hands clenched at her sides. "I'm sorry, Dorrie. But this isn't something that it would do any good to talk about. I'm quite certain I can't marry Mason. I'm afraid I'd rather be alone while I learn to deal with that. Please try to understand." Her voice was thick with unshed tears; she rushed across the room and shut her bedroom door behind her.

Dorrie looked after her, then sighed and went to change from her school clothes into jeans and a sweater. When she came out of her room, Clem's door was still closed. As always, the little house was very quiet. Dorrie made a face and went outside to sit beneath the giant oak.

She leaned back against its solid bulk and stretched her legs out in the grass. Two people had told her she was selfish today. A russet oak leaf drifted down into her lap; she ran her finger along its lobes and tried to piece Clem's words together with Alec MacIntyre's. *Am I selfish, God?* Her mind raced in circles from thoughts of her class to Liam and back again, from Alec MacIntyre to Clem and Mason and back once more to Liam. *Liam. . .*

∞

"Dor–riee!" called Clem's voice from the house. "Tele–phone!"

Dorrie scrambled to her feet, her heart suddenly thudding. "It's my mother, right?" she asked Clem as she raced through the door.

Clem made a face and shook her head. She handed Dorrie the telephone.

"Dorrie?" said Liam's voice, and her heart pounded still harder. "I hope I didn't interrupt anything."

"No. No. I was just—I was just outside. Hi, Liam." She felt her mouth stretching into a smile so wide it hurt her cheeks, and she saw Clem roll her eyes before she went back into her room.

"We promised to get together soon, remember?" said Liam's light voice in her ear. "And since it's Friday night, I was wondering if you were doing anything? I know it's the last moment, but I thought maybe we could get something to eat, maybe see a movie. You know—go out on a real date."

Chapter 8

You promised me you'd pray about it before you went out with Liam." Clem's voice was small and hard.

Dorrie whirled away from the telephone, still smiling. "Oh, Clem, can't you see? This *is* an answer to prayer." She hugged Clem's stiff shoulders. "He asked me out! Why, just today, on the way home, I was praying—" She twirled around Clem, feeling as though her every muscle were jingling with joy. Clem looked at her, not smiling. "Come on, Clemmie, please. Be just a little happy for me, can't you? You know this is what I've wanted for years."

"It's just a date, Dorrie. Don't make more out of it than it is."

"You should talk, Clem. You're the one acting as though I've done something dangerous and immense." Dorrie hugged herself. "But in a way you're right. I know it's a beginning. I know it is. I *know* this is God's hand in my life."

"How can you be so sure?"

"I just feel it inside. You know—a kind of certainty." Dorrie stopped twirling and looked at Clem. "I suppose," she said slowly, "the same way you're so sure God *doesn't* want you to marry Mason." For a moment they stared at each other. Then both looked away.

"Oh, come on, Clem. Help me decide what to wear."

∞

Clem refused to help her, but Dorrie finally decided on a dark green crushed velvet top that hung down over black leggings. Her green eyes stared back at her from the mirror, as she gave her red hair one last brush. "Please, God," she whispered, "let him like the way I look."

She heard Liam's truck in the driveway and dashed out of the bathroom. "Bye," she called into Clem's room and ran out the door.

Liam's blue eyes glowed when she slid into the truck beside him. "You look beautiful, Dorrie," he said softly.

Dorrie forced herself to lean back against the seat, to relax her legs, her arms, her hands. "Thank you," she whispered.

"How's my sister?" he asked as he turned the truck around.

Dorrie let out her breath in a sigh. "Gloomy. I've never seen her like this. I don't understand her."

Liam's eyes were steady on the road ahead. "Clem and I have never been the chummy sort of brother and sister," he said after a moment, "but I think I can guess why she's thinking the way she is. Maybe I should talk to her sometime."

Dorrie turned to him. "I wish you would. She's just making herself miserable. And everyone around her, too. I know you could help her."

Liam smiled. "Little Dorrie. You always have such confidence in me."

Dorrie grinned. "I do have confidence in you. But I'm hardly little."

Liam shrugged. "I always see you the way you looked the first time I talked with you. You were so young then, you made me hurt inside." He smiled at her sideways. "All long legs and big eyes, like a fawn or a foal."

Oh, Father, he remembers the first time he talked to me. Dorrie remembered, too; she had fallen in love with him by the end of that first conversation.

Liam shook his head. "I'm afraid your confidence is misplaced this time, though. I'm not very good at counseling people. And Clem's always been the spiritual giant of the family. She probably wouldn't listen to anything I had to say anyway. She knows me too well."

"What do you mean?"

He grimaced. "Oh, Clem's always seen through me pretty well. She probably knows my weaknesses better than I do myself." He glanced at Dorrie. "I bet she's filled you in on them, too, hasn't she?"

Dorrie shifted her legs, stared out the window at the lights of the town they were approaching, and then set her lips firmly. "I don't listen to her."

Liam laughed; Dorrie smiled and turned toward him. "Well, look at the way she's acting now about Mason. I love her dearly—but sometimes her perceptions are obviously—well, warped, I guess."

Liam laughed again. "Meaning, I guess, that on the one hand, my fears about my sister's opinion of me have just been confirmed—but on the other hand, you've relieved me considerably."

Dorrie looked at him shyly. "Why?"

"Because," he answered softly, "what you think about me is important to me, little Dorrie. I think I'd rather you didn't see me too clearly."

Maybe I see you more clearly than anyone else. The words hung on her lips, unsaid. She looked at the side of his dark, bearded face, the straight angles of his jaw and nose, the curve of his small, neat ear, the sleek shine of his hair, and she felt as though she might burst from loving him. He turned his head and smiled at her; the look in his eyes seemed to say he understood what she was still too shy to say out loud.

They ate at a quiet restaurant converted from an old Victorian home. A fire crackled on the hearth next to them, and candles caught the blue lights in Liam's black hair. "You're even prettier in candlelight," he said softly.

Dorrie felt his eyes on her. She looked down at her food and struggled for something intelligent to say. "How is work going for you?" she asked at last.

He reached across the table and lay a finger against her lips. "Shh. Don't mention that place. Not tonight. Tonight is magic."

Her mouth burned where he had touched her. The silence stretched between them, but she no longer minded. Whenever she met his eyes, they seemed full of messages too special for words. *For once,* she thought, *I don't mind the quiet. I can be still with Liam, see that, God? I don't have to talk, and neither does he, not like Alec MacIntyre. That must show that our spirits are close in You, Father, don't You think? I could look at him forever and never notice the quiet at all. Oh, Father, thank You for tonight.*

"What are you thinking?"

"Oh." She lowered her gaze to the cup of tea in her hand. "Nothing much. I was just appreciating the quiet."

"That's something I've always liked about you, Dorrie—your ability to be quiet. I'm never comfortable with people who talk too much. Whenever I'm with someone who chatters, I find myself soon itching to be somewhere else."

She raised her eyes from her teacup. "I talk a lot sometimes, Liam," she had to say. *Are You changing me into a whole new sort of person, Father? Or does Liam see a part of me that even I don't know?*

He smiled. "Dorrie, I've known you for years now, and I've never known you to be anything but quiet and peaceful."

She returned his smile doubtfully. She had always been tongue-tied around him, overwhelmed by her feelings for him; that was the reason for her quietness around him, she knew, but perhaps she could cultivate a new, truer stillness in her soul.

At the movie theater she stared at the flickering screen, but her thoughts circled round and round this new quietness she must learn to develop. *Isn't that what everyone has been saying to me lately, God? Even Alec MacIntyre, hadn't he said something about being still? And so had Gram, and so had Margaret Truesdell. Even the house. Maybe the reason I've been noticing the quiet so much is because You were trying to get a message through to me. You knew what Liam needed, and You were trying to get me ready. I wasn't comfortable with the quiet before, because I didn't understand, but now I do, and oh, God, thank You so much for this night. I'm ready to change in whatever way I need to so that I can be the sort of woman Liam needs.*

She closed her eyes, chattering on and on to God about this new quietness she knew was about to blossom inside her until she felt Liam move beside her. In the darkness, his hand reached toward her. His warm, slender fingers linked with hers, and her thoughts were scattered; for the rest of the evening, the messages from her excited body blocked out all other sound.

∞

"So how was it?" Clem was curled up on the sofa reading when Dorrie came through the door.

"It was wonderful." Dorrie smiled. "Were you waiting up for me, Mother?"

Clem made a face. "Yes, I was. I wanted to talk to you."

Dorrie glanced at Clem's serious eyes, and she sighed. "Couldn't we wait until tomorrow? I already know what you think about your brother, I know you're not happy I went out with him, I know you're not happy about anything right now. But I am. I just want to go to bed and be quiet."

Clem looked at her. "Are you okay? You, Dorrie Carpenter, 'just want to be quiet'? This I thought I'd never hear."

Dorrie looked down at her hand, the hand Liam had held for the remainder of the movie, and smiled. "I'm going to change, Clem, I'm already changing. I'm going to learn to be a quiet person."

Clem snorted, then burst into laughter. "I'll believe that when I see it. Come on, Dorrie, what's brought this on?" She stared at Dorrie's dreamy face, and then she grimaced. "Not Liam. Please tell me you're not going to try to change yourself for Liam."

Dorrie moved around the room, stretching her long legs after sitting still all evening. "Isn't that what people do for the people they love?"

"No. They don't." Clem put her head in her hands. "Honestly, Dorrie, this thing with Liam is getting worse and worse. It's like you're bewitched. You don't see Liam the way he really is. You think you do, but I know you don't. That was bad enough. But now you want to make him see you some way that you're really not. Don't you see, even if you could have a relationship, even if Liam wants that, it wouldn't be *real*?"

Dorrie shook her head. "I don't want to make him *see* me a way that I'm not. I want to *be* the way he needs me to be."

"Oh, please, Dorrie, Liam doesn't need you to be anything. He wants you to fall in love with him, I'll grant you that. I see the way he looks at you, and it's the same old pattern. I've watched him do it ever since he was a teenager. He likes to make girls love him. Maybe it's because he's insecure inside; maybe it comforts the scared little boy who felt abandoned when Mom and Dad died. But whatever the reason, he uses girls to make himself feel good, and then he hurts them. Because I'm warning you, Dorrie, Liam isn't looking for a serious relationship. The sooner he's certain you've fallen for him, the sooner he'll drop you and move on to someone else. That's just the way he is."

"No," Dorrie shouted, suddenly angry, "you're wrong! You're just jealous because you can't let yourself be happy with Mason. You don't believe God wants anyone to be happy." She stared at Clem for a moment longer, her cheeks like fire, and then she flung herself out the door. She ran up the dark road, her feet thudding, her breath loud, filling the still, cold night with her own angry noise.

∞

For the rest of the weekend, Dorrie and Clem were careful and polite with each other. At church on Sunday, Liam sat beside Dorrie, and she missed yet another of

Grandpop Adams' sermons. She felt Clem's level gaze on her as she stood talking with Liam after the service, but she ignored her friend and kept her eyes on Liam. Between the black of his hair and beard, his blue eyes blazed; looking into them, she tried to let him see the new quietness unfolding within her.

"I'll see you tomorrow," he said. She looked after his straight back, then turned to retrieve her Bible from the pew where she had left it. As she reached between the pews, she barely noticed she had brushed against someone until she heard Alec MacIntyre's voice.

"Hello, Dorrie," he said quietly.

"Oh, sorry," she said, "I didn't see you."

He nodded gravely. "I'm easy to miss. It's my petite stature, I suppose."

She smiled reluctantly. "I guess my mind was just on other things."

He nodded. The look on his face made her shift her feet and inch toward the aisle. *But he can't know how I feel about Liam. And I wouldn't care if he did.*

"Was your mind so busy that you missed who came to church with me?"

She looked up at him. "I guess it must have been. Who did you bring to church?"

"The last person you might expect. He called me up this morning, said he wanted to try another church besides the chapel at the Home." Alec grinned. "His exact words actually were, 'I want to see if one is any less stupid than the other.'"

"Not Felix Jones?"

Alec nodded. "He's waiting out in my car."

"I can't believe I didn't see him."

"Like you said, Dorrie, your mind was on other things. I don't think you looked our way once."

Dorrie's cheeks grew warm, but before she could answer, Alec continued, "I'm giving Felix dinner out at my place." He shrugged his shoulders, and she noticed the warm color along the high bones of his cheeks. "He said I should ask you to join us."

She stared at him, forgetting her embarrassment. "Felix said that? I had the impression the last time I saw him Friday that he would just as soon never see me again. He wouldn't even look at me."

"Maybe he's had a change of heart." He smiled. "Come on out to my car. Let's see."

She followed him out of the church to the car that was as small and old as her own. Inside, Felix sat waiting, his fingers tapping on the door. When he saw Dorrie, he scowled and rolled down the window. "Are you going to come?"

Dorrie looked from him to Alec, and then her eyes went back to Felix. She nodded. "I'll come." She turned to Alec. "Clem drove today, and I think she's going to her grandparents' for dinner. You'll have to give me a ride."

He smiled. "I think we can handle that."

Felix made a face. "His back seat is full of cat hairs. I suppose that means we'll all have to sit in the front. But I'm not sitting in the middle. I get claustrophobic."

Dorrie ran to let Clem know where she was going. She ignored the pleased expression on her friend's face and turned back to Alec's car. She took a deep breath and reminded herself she was doing this for the sake of her relationship with Felix, and then she climbed into the middle of the front seat.

They said very little on the short drive back to Alec's house. Alec seemed to be concentrating on the road, while Felix's head was turned toward the side window. Dorrie stared straight ahead feeling smothered. She did not mind the warmth of Felix's small shoulder on her right side, but the heat from Alec's big body on her left annoyed her. She shifted uncomfortably, trying to squeeze closer to Felix.

"Stop squashing me," he said crossly.

"I'm sorry." She turned toward him. "We had a terrible day Friday. I'm glad you wanted me to come today."

His head turned, and his eyes behind their thick lenses glared at her. "Is that what he told you?" He leaned forward so he could see Alec's face, and then he smiled smugly. "I told him to ask you because I like to make life harder for Mr. Adams."

"What do you mean?"

Alec cleared his throat loudly, but Felix's eyes gleamed, and he said, "Both Mr. Adams and Mr. MacIntyre are obviously hot for you. I may be betting on the underdog, but my money's on Mr. MacIntyre."

Chapter 9

That was not a socially appropriate comment." Alec's voice was calm and level. He drove past Dorrie and Clem's house and up the road to his own small house.

Felix smirked. "You can't deny it is true, though, can you, Mr. MacIntyre?"

"That's really not any of your business, Felix," Alec said pleasantly. He parked the car in his driveway. "Come on, you two. I am about to impress you both with my amazing skill in the kitchen."

Dorrie followed Felix out of the car, but she was thinking about Alec's words on Friday, when he had compared the students to bouncing balls looking for their limits. Felix had tried to bounce high and fast, just as he had in her classroom on Friday; Alec, however, had neatly caught the ball and quietly, but firmly, sent it back within its limits. She followed his tall figure up the path through the trees to his house, then hurried to catch up with him. "You handled that well," she murmured as he opened his door.

He glanced at her sideways, and the corner of his mouth curved. "I'm glad you thought so."

As she followed him through the door, she looked at him curiously and saw that the tips of his ears were red. *Can Alec MacIntyre really be attracted to me, God?* She pushed the uncomfortable thought away and bent to pet the ginger cat that was rubbing against her leg. "This must be Esther."

Alec nodded. "That," he said to Felix, pointing to the cat, "is the only woman in my life." He grinned. "For all our sakes, please remember that in the future."

"Sure," Felix muttered. He knelt beside the cat and watched her. "I had a cat once." He held out his hand carefully and let Esther sniff his fingers.

Dorrie looked around the small house, noticing the stacks of books everywhere, then settled on the floor beside Felix. "Mr. MacIntyre seems to use his chairs as receptacles for books. Apparently he hasn't heard of shelves." She smiled at Felix. "What was your cat's name?"

"Sam. He got run over by a car."

Dorrie watched the careful way Felix touched Esther. "I'm sorry."

He shrugged. "Animals are always getting run over at the trailer court where I live. They're so stupid, they sleep in the road. Some guy has too much beer and peels out without looking—" He shrugged again. "I saw a squashed dog one time. You could see its intestines."

Alec pulled a mixing bowl out of the cupboard. "Thank you, Felix," he said over his shoulder, "but descriptions of dead animals are generally also inappropriate topics for polite conversation."

Felix made a face. " 'Inappropriate.' 'Polite.' Who cares? You people need to face the real world."

Alec broke an egg into the bowl. "What exactly is the 'real' world?"

Felix lay on his stomach, his chin on his hands, and stared at Esther. "Come visit my mom at the trailer court. That place is what reality is all about. You guys at the Home, that old guy talking at church today, you're all living in fantasy land."

Alec reached into the refrigerator and brought out a package of chicken cutlets. "There are all kinds of realities, Felix," he said. "With the amount of reading you do, I know you already know there's a whole world outside the trailer court." He began dipping the cutlets into the egg, then rolled them in bread crumbs. "I happen to believe that the things that are most truly 'real' are found in God. A lot of the other stuff, whether you find it at the trailer court or in the politest society in the world, is just lies."

Felix scowled. "That's what I mean—fantasy land. You don't want to accept reality, so you pretend it's not there." He looked up at Alec over his glasses. "Sorry, Mr. MacIntyre, but people out there hurt each other and use each other. That's real life. The trailer court's not pretty, but at least it doesn't pretend life's about some fantasy superhero who runs everything, the way you do."

Dorrie leaned back on her hands and waited while Alec dropped the meat into a hot frying pan. He ran water into a kettle and set it on the stove, and she noticed how calm his face was, how efficient and unhurried his movement around the kitchen. She put her hand on Esther's warm fur, and a strange sort of peace settled over her. *How odd,* she thought, for the quiet calm inside her heart felt unfamiliar and yet comfortable. She closed her eyes, absorbing through her fingers Esther's quiet purr while she listened to Felix's and Alec's voices.

"Christ is bigger than a superhero," Alec was saying now. "Use that marvelous brain we hear so much about and read some of the new physics. Even in the midst of chaos, there's more beauty and order than our small minds ever dreamed." Dorrie heard the clatter of a pan, but she felt the stillness around her absorb the noise, undisturbed.

"And when I said a lot of the other stuff in the world is lies," Alec went on, "I meant it's based on lies." She heard him beat something with a spoon. "For instance, it's a lie that we need anything out there to make us happy and complete, whether it's sex or drugs or money or whatever. We think we do—and that's why we use people, and people end up hurt."

The cat purred; the oven door creaked open and shut; the water in the kettle began to bubble and spatter; Dorrie was almost asleep. "St. Augustine said that all of us strive for unending happiness, but our hearts are restless until they rest in God," Alec said. "T. S. Elliot called God the still point of the turning world. And James in the Bible calls Him the Father of lights, who has no shadow of turning." The refrigerator door opened and closed. "It's that stillness, that security, that we all need. Only when we find it can we truly rest. And that, Felix, in more words than you ever wanted to hear," Dorrie heard the smile in Alec's voice, "is what I believe about reality."

"What about Sleeping Beauty here?" asked Felix. "I bet she thinks she needs Mr. Adams in order to be happy. I see the way she looks at him."

Dorrie opened her eyes, the quietness shattered. She looked up and met Alec's gaze. "We're all still human," he said gently, but something about his voice made her think he was talking about himself more than her. She turned away from the wistfulness in his eyes and looked at Felix.

He was lying on his stomach, nose to nose with Esther, but his dark eyes skewed in her direction. "You going to marry Mr. Adams, Miss Carpenter?"

Dorrie hesitated. She looked at Alec, but his eyes were now on the frying pan, and he did not look up again. She knew he was listening, though, and she found herself reluctant to answer Felix's question. *I am going to marry Liam, aren't I, God?* But of course she could not tell Felix that, when Liam himself did not know it yet. She shifted uncomfortably, feeling her old restlessness come over her. "I don't know," she said at last, reluctantly.

Felix laughed. "She doesn't know. What's that mean?"

Alec turned from the stove. "You don't have to answer him, you know, Dorrie." His dark eyes were clouded, but his voice was gentle. "There's no reason that our students have to know every intimate detail of our personal lives. As I reminded Felix earlier, it's really none of their business." Dorrie heard the message in his voice; she realized she had been thinking of Felix as that social acquaintance whom she wanted to like her, rather than keeping the distance that needed to be between a student and teacher.

Alec grinned and flicked the top of Felix's head with his fingertips. "Sorry, Felix, no matter how much we love you, we're not going to lay out our love lives for you to examine."

The corners of Felix's mouth turned down. "Right. Like you really love me."

Dorrie smiled. "Well, we do."

Felix squirmed. After a moment, though, he looked sideways at her again and grinned evilly. "As much as you love Mr. Adams?"

Dorrie grabbed a book from the nearest stack and leaned over to smack Felix gently on the head with it. "Enough!"

Felix giggled, and for the first time since she'd met him, Dorrie thought he looked like an eleven-year-old boy, his expression no longer hard and guarded.

Alec pulled a loaf of warm bread from the oven. "Here, Dorrie," he said, "make yourself useful and slice this for me. And you, Felix," he reached across the table and pulled a piece of paper and a pencil from beneath another pile of books, "take this and draw me a picture of Esther while we finish getting this meal on the table. Maybe that will occupy that busy little brain of yours long enough to give Dorrie and me some peace." He smiled.

Felix grabbed the paper and pencil and put it on the floor in front of him. He wiggled back away from Esther a few inches, and then, still lying on his stomach, began to sketch the gentle curve of the cat's back. Dorrie watched for a second, then turned to take the bread knife from Alec's hand.

The kitchen work space was small; Dorrie found herself brushing against Alec every time she moved. "Sorry," she muttered when they jumped away after running into each other yet again. *It's no big deal,* she told herself. She felt nervous and on edge, though, and for the first time, she wished she had gone with Clem to her grandparents'. Maybe Liam would have come over, too, and right now she could have been with him, instead of here with this man who was so large she could barely breathe without touching him.

She remembered then the quietness she had felt for a few moments, and she thought smugly, *You're already changing me into the quiet person Liam needs, aren't You, God?* She wished she had been with Liam when she had experienced it, instead of wasting the moment on Alec MacIntyre.

"This is obviously a one-person kitchen," Alec said. He smiled, but his voice was oddly breathless. "Why don't you go sit down? I can manage the rest."

Dorrie moved gratefully away from the kitchen area. "Where do you suggest I sit?" She looked at the dining room table spread with papers and books, all but one of the chairs piled with still more books.

"Improvise," Alec answered.

Dorrie began piling up the books and papers on the table, glancing at the book titles as she did so. Besides several different versions of the Bible, Alec seemed to be reading five novels, two documentaries, three scientific books, an autobiography, a history book, and four inspirational books, all simultaneously.

In spite of herself, Dorrie smiled. She looked at the books thoughtfully, realizing that most of them were either favorites of hers or books she had been wanting to read. "I don't have to ask what you do with your spare time," she said lightly. She took the books off the chairs and stacked them on the floor against the wall.

Alec set a bowl of spaghetti and pesto on the table. "I guess you could say that those are my companions." He nodded toward the stacks of books. "Esther's nice, but she doesn't talk much. Living by myself, my mind tends to get a little hyperactive if I don't have someone else's thoughts and ideas to act as a balance. When I first lived alone, I felt so restless, I thought I'd go crazy. Then I started inviting friends over." He reached for one of the books. "This one's by C. S. Lewis—a very good friend."

Dorrie turned to look at him. He was closer behind her than she had thought, but for once she did not jump away. She found herself looking up into his eyes, absently noticing the way they slanted above his high cheekbones. "Even though I live with Clem," she heard herself say, "sometimes I feel as though I might as well be living alone. Things are a little hard with her right now." She paused, surprised she was telling him this. "The house seems so quiet. I feel like I can't stand it sometimes." She reached for the plates he had set on the counter and began putting them on the table. She glanced up at him quickly. "Usually, I like to read, too. But lately even that seems too quiet. I'm always running out of the house, trying to escape."

He nodded. "I see you on the road sometimes. Running." He moved away, reaching for the glasses from the cupboard. "Learning to be quiet can be uncomfortable," he said over his shoulder. "I think it's because only in stillness can we hear God's voice—and God's voice isn't always a comfortable thing. We're like Jonah, running away, insisting on our own way." He handed her the glasses and took silverware from a drawer. "Must have been awfully quiet inside that whale. No one to talk to, nowhere to run. Jonah had to finally face himself—and God."

He came around the table to set the silverware beside the plates, and Dorrie again pulled back from his closeness. *You're like a whale yourself, Alec MacIntyre— huge and threatening, chasing me down when I just want to escape.* She giggled nervously at her thoughts, then shook her head when Alec looked at her questioningly. *Just leave me alone. Stop following me with your eyes. Stop noticing my every expression, my every thought.* She moved to the other side of the table; she knew he would have noted her movement and probably guessed that she was trying to distance herself from him, but she refused to look at him again.

The awkwardness between them eased when Felix joined them at the table. He waited impatiently while Alec gave thanks for the food, then raised his eyebrows in pretended disbelief as he looked at the plates of food. "Green spaghetti?"

"Pesto," Alec told him.

"Yuck."

"Expand your horizons," Dorrie said. "It's delicious. Everything is." She smiled at Alec, though she avoided meeting his eyes.

Felix took a forkful of spaghetti. "Not bad," he admitted. "Of course anything's better than the slop they feed us over at the Home."

"I think," Alec said, "if I read between the lines, I can interpret that as, 'Thank you for inviting me for dinner, Mr. MacIntyre. I really appreciate the home-cooked meal.' Am I right?"

Felix shrugged, sucking in a long strand of spaghetti. "I guess."

Dorrie found herself exchanging glances with Alec over Felix's head. They smiled, and suddenly the uneasiness inside her relaxed; once again, she felt that odd sense of comfortable peace. "So, Felix," she said, "tell me when you started drawing."

The rest of the meal passed easily. Felix told them stories about life in the trailer court, and Dorrie found herself laughing with Alec until their eyes watered; other times, she felt her eyes burn with unshed tears as she listened to Felix.

When they had finished eating, she and Felix did the dishes. Felix washed and managed to spill quantities of water on the floor, while Esther retreated to the top of the refrigerator to watch. Alec leaned against the kitchen table behind them; Dorrie felt his eyes on her, and now and then she glanced over her shoulder at him and smiled. She could not explain the change in her feelings, as though a door inside her had first opened, then slammed shut, and now stood open again; she only knew that her heart felt quiet and content, as though she were resting close to God.

She and Felix finished the last dish. "How about a game of Monopoly?" Alec asked.

Felix groaned. "I despise Monopoly. It's the most boring game ever invented."

"It's the only game I own, though," Alec answered.

"I know," Dorrie said, "let's play the dictionary game. I know you must have a dictionary somewhere, Alec, and I'm sure Felix will be good at making up definitions." She explained the rules of the game.

Again, Dorrie found herself laughing till tears ran down her cheeks at Felix's and Alec's crazy and creative definitions. She could not remember when she had last felt so relaxed, so simply happy. When Alec announced that the time had come to take Felix back to the Home, she was disappointed to have the afternoon end.

She hesitated in the doorway of Alec's house, giving Esther one last stroke along her back. She felt strangely reluctant to leave, as though she knew the magic spell would end once she left Alec's cluttered little house, and she would be back to being her old restless self; that door inside her would slam shut again, separating her from the warmth she saw in Alec's eyes.

What am I thinking? She backed out of the door quickly. "Did you want your drawing of Esther?" she asked Felix.

He shrugged. "Mr. MacIntyre can have it."

"Thank you, Felix," Alec said. "Maybe I can have it framed."

"Right," Felix said sarcastically.

"Seriously," Alec answered. "It's a very good drawing. It means a lot to me that you gave it to me. I've always wished I could have one of your drawings."

Felix shrugged. He, too, seemed to be changing back into his old self, pulling his defenses tight around him once more.

"Want me to drop you at your house?" Alec asked Dorrie as they walked out to his car.

Dorrie shook her head. "I think I'll walk home." She smiled at Felix. "I'll see you tomorrow, Felix. I enjoyed being with you this afternoon very much." She glanced quickly at Alec. "Thank you for dinner. It was a nice time."

He nodded. "It was." He opened his mouth as though to say something more, then closed it again. "I'll see you" was all he said at last.

Dorrie waved as his car pulled away and then walked slowly home. *I should have been with Liam this afternoon,* she thought, but then she remembered Felix's giggles when he had stumped her at the dictionary game. She smiled.

As she walked along the quiet road, she felt God's presence with her. "Thank You, God," she began, and then found she had no more words, and so she said again, "Thank You." She listened to the small sounds of the wind blowing leaves across the road, a crow cawing in the oak trees overhead, and the crunch of her own feet in the gravel along the shoulder of the road. "Thank You," she whispered once more, and then the door inside her heart swung open wide, welcoming His quiet presence.

∞

Her sense of peace lasted through the evening and was still with her as she drove to the Home the next morning. She was planning how to set up her classroom rules as she swung into the parking lot. "Please help me," she whispered to God and then got out of her car.

She noticed Alec's car in the parking lot, and her step quickened, for she hoped that this morning Felix might be in his closet in her room. She had found herself thinking about him again and again during the night, wishing she could give him a different sort of life than the one he had experienced so far. *He's so smart and funny, so hungry to be loved,* she thought as she went in the school building. *Alec talks to him so easily about You, God. Please give me opportunities to show him Your love, too. What I really wish, God, is that I could take him home and show him what it's like to be loved and secure. If Liam and I get married, then maybe we could adopt. . . .* She remembered the tension between Felix and Liam, and she grimaced. *Well, God, You can work miracles, can't You?* She tried to recapture the quiet sense of God's presence that she had been feeling, but somehow it had evaporated. She climbed the stairs to the second floor, frowning.

"Is there a problem, Dorrie?" Margaret Truesdell stood at the top of the stairwell, looking down at her. "You look like a thundercloud."

Dorrie smiled sheepishly. "No. I was just thinking—" She broke off, unable to explain her thoughts to Margaret. She grabbed hold of an earlier thought. "I've been having some discipline problems with my class, I'm afraid. Alec MacIntyre gave me some suggestions about setting up some classroom rules. I'm planning to do that today."

Margaret walked with her down the hall. "Good. I'm sorry if I haven't been more available to you during these first weeks. Time always slips away from me during the fall—and frankly, I'd heard nothing but good about you, so I assumed you were doing fine on your own." She stopped outside Dorrie's classroom door and turned toward Dorrie. "I'm glad, though, that you've been getting advice from Alec. He's a very fine teacher, gifted, I might even say. I remember that as a new teacher, I found my friendships with more experienced teachers to be invaluable. So I've been glad to hear that you and Alec are getting to know each other."

"Yes. Yes, we are." Dorrie shifted her feet awkwardly. "Of course," she added, "I already knew Liam. He's been teaching longer than Alec." *Why did I have to bring Liam up?* She felt her face grow warm.

Margaret looked at her thoughtfully. "Yes," she said, "that's true. Liam has been teaching longer than Alec. But I—" She shook her head and then she smiled. "Stop down to my office today after school, Dorrie. I'd like to hear how your new rules work out."

Dorrie agreed. She stood in the hall a moment longer after Margaret left. *Why do I feel so unsettled again, God? She didn't mention Liam, and yet I felt as though I had to bring him into the conversation, as though I had to defend him somehow against Alec MacIntyre. Why am I so silly sometimes?* She pushed the heavy hair back from her face, then opened the door of her classroom.

Inside, she was surprised to find Felix already seated at his desk, rather than inside his closet. He was hunched over a paper, his fingers tight on a drawing pencil, but he looked up when she opened the door. He pushed his glasses up his nose. "It's about time. I've been waiting for you."

Dorrie smiled. "I was talking to Mrs. Truesdell. Did you want something?"

Felix nodded. "Could you give me a Bible?"

Chapter 10

"Don't look so pleased," Felix said, shaking his head. "It's not like I asked you to help me convert or something. All I want is a Bible to read. I could ask my houseparents or Mr. MacIntyre, but I figured they'd get too excited. Make too big a deal out of it. So don't you go and do the same thing."

Dorrie walked over to her desk and opened a drawer. "I keep an extra Bible here. You can have it." She leaned to hand it to Felix. "Why did you want it?"

He shrugged. "Just curious. We hear so many sermons in this place, people quoting the Bible left and right. I thought I'd like to be able to check things out for myself. I don't like feeling like everyone has access to a source of possible information that I don't." He stuck his chin out and narrowed his eyes at Dorrie. "Notice I said *possible*. And who knows—maybe everyone's interpreting the whole thing all wrong. Maybe it really says something totally different when you look at the complete context. Know what I mean? I don't like to trust anyone's mind but my own."

Dorrie nodded. "Makes sense to me."

"It does?"

"Sure. No one can tell you what to believe. You have to figure that out for yourself." She turned away to open the curtains so he wouldn't see her smile.

He watched her for a moment. "You're not going to give me some little tract with the twelve steps to salvation or something?"

Dorrie turned around and let him see her smile. "Nope."

Felix shook his head. "I'm surprised." He got up and put the Bible inside the closet with his other books. "Don't tell anyone. Not the other kids."

"How come?"

"They give me a hard enough time without them thinking I'm turning into a religious freak. I can just hear Kenny now."

Dorrie sat down at her desk. "You and Kenny are a lot alike in some ways, you know."

Felix made a face. "We're *nothing* alike. He's a big, stupid jock. All the other guys like him; he's good at all those stupid games Mr. Adams thinks are so important—and I'm little and smart, and none of the guys like me. When I have to be on someone's team, they all groan."

Dorrie nodded. "And I'm sure Kenny's just as envious of your reading and drawing abilities."

Felix scowled. "I'm not envious of him. Who wants to be a big, stupid jock?"

Dorrie shrugged. "See what I mean? You both insult the people you really envy—I think that's called sour grapes. You both like to be in control. You both have a hard time letting people get close to you—and you use your smart mouths to keep people at a distance. And you both have a hard time accepting authority. Don't you?"

Felix looked down at his drawing and erased a line. "Maybe," he said finally. He leaned over his drawing, his tongue between his teeth as he sketched the thick, round lines of a hippopotamus. Dorrie leaned against her desk, watching him. He drew the bristles on the heavy jowls and then looked up at Dorrie. "Things were pretty bad in here on Friday with Kenny and the others, weren't they?"

Dorrie nodded.

"You really lost control, didn't you? Good thing for you that Mr. MacIntyre came along when he did."

Dorrie nodded again.

Felix looked down at his drawing. "I guess I started the whole thing, didn't I?"

Dorrie lifted her shoulders. "You started that particular incident. As Mr. MacIntyre would say, you were a whole lot less than appropriate. But it was coming anyway. Something like it would have happened eventually, whether you started it or not."

"So are you going to let us get away with stuff like that?"

She shook her head.

"Are you going to quit?"

"Nope."

"What are you going to do?"

Dorrie smiled. "Wait and see."

Felix squinted his eyes at her. "I bet you don't know how to be mean. Not mean enough to control us. Unless you've been taking lessons from your precious Mr. Adams. He's plenty mean."

Dorrie opened her mouth and then closed it. She looked out the window. "Like I said, Felix, wait and see."

∞∞

At the end of the day, Dorrie closed her classroom door and went down the stairs to Margaret Truesdell's office. Margaret looked up and smiled when Dorrie came through the door.

"How did it go?"

Dorrie looked around Margaret's office. It was decorated in shades of green, and after her noisy classroom, it seemed to Dorrie as peaceful as a forest. She noticed the threadbare velvet curtains that hung at the windows, the worn velvet chairs that circled Margaret's desk; she sighed. "All right. Nothing miraculous." She smiled ruefully. "I guess I was imagining myself transformed overnight into

420

the perfect teacher. But the atmosphere in my classroom has definitely changed. The kids weren't too happy about it—but I keep telling myself that doesn't matter. I think I'm starting to see the light at the end of the tunnel—or something. I guess what I mean is that at least I know what I'm working toward in my classroom—instead of just wandering aimlessly the way I'd been doing." She dropped into the chair that Margaret pushed toward her. "I never knew teaching would be so hard."

Margaret's gray eyes crinkled. "I've stood in the hallway and observed you several times while you were teaching, Dorrie. You're a natural at it. You just need to get your stride, find your own personal rhythms. Once you do, you'll find you can relax more. But I do agree that teaching can be very difficult, especially if we're emotionally involved with something else. Teaching these particular students seems to demand a sort of emotional concentration."

Dorrie thought of the many times she had been distracted from her class by thoughts of Liam, sometimes even when she was in the midst of teaching. She nodded slowly.

Margaret leaned toward Dorrie and touched her arm. "I thank God that you came to us, Dorrie. Be patient with yourself while you grow. I know God is using you."

∽∞∾

"I thought you had to work tonight," Dorrie said to Clem when she came through the door and found her friend curled up on the sofa.

Clem blew her nose and pulled a quilt around her shoulders. "I was supposed to. But I think I'm coming down with something. The doctor sent me home—said he didn't want me sneezing on all his patients." She wiped her nose again and shivered.

"You sound terrible. Can I get you something?"

Clem shook her head.

"How about some tea?"

Clem smiled weakly. "I don't know why you want to be nice to me when I've been so hard to live with lately."

Dorrie filled the kettle with water. She smiled over her shoulder at Clem. "Because I love you."

Clem's blue eyes glittered with tears. Dorrie put down the tea kettle and went to kneel beside her on the sofa. "Oh, Dorrie," Clem said, leaning her head against Dorrie's shoulder, "I've been feeling so awful inside. So hard. And scared. I know that can't be right. If I was really following God about not marrying Mason, don't you think I'd feel a sense of peace about it?"

Dorrie nodded.

"Well, I don't. I feel awful. Cold and lonely, like everyone I'm close to is getting further and further away. You, Gram and Grandpop, Mason—" She rubbed her eyes with her fists, and Dorrie thought she looked like an unhappy ten year old. "I just don't know what to do. I know I love him, Dorrie. But I *can't* marry him."

Dorrie stroked Clem's rumpled curls. "It's okay," she said gently. "The people who love you haven't gone anywhere—we're all still right here. We can wait while you figure things out. But probably tonight when you feel so sick isn't the right time to be doing any serious thinking. Just rest." Dorrie smiled, and then she repeated Margaret Truesdell's words to her: "Be patient with yourself while you grow." Clem sighed and blew her nose, and Dorrie got up and put the kettle on the stove.

While she waited for the water to boil, she told Clem about her day at school. "I guess I thought the kids would be as excited about making these rules as I was. They weren't." She shook her head. "They're so good at emotional blackmail—you do what I want, and I'll be your friend. At least now I can see what they're doing—thanks to Alec." She poured the hot water over the tea bag and handed the steaming cup to Clem.

"Mmmm." As she drank, Clem smiled her thanks over the cup's rim. "So you admit that Alec's not such a bad guy after all?"

Dorrie shrugged her shoulders. "I admit he's a very good teacher."

"Better than Liam?"

Dorrie's lips tightened. "Liam's having some problems right now with his approach to teaching. That has nothing to do with how I feel about him."

"I understand," Clem said mildly. She sipped her tea in silence while Dorrie began to make supper.

∞

By the end of the week, Clem's cold was even worse. She huddled on the sofa, shivering and sweating by turns, the box of tissues tucked next to her. "I think you have the flu," Dorrie said when she came home from work Friday. She touched Clem's hot head, then went to the refrigerator and poured her a glass of orange juice.

"Thank you, Nurse Carpenter," Clem murmured as she took the glass of juice. "How was work today?"

Dorrie smiled. "Better. Lots better. Things are really starting to settle down. There's a feeling of order to the classroom—and we all seem so much more relaxed. Like we're not all trying to prove something anymore, myself included. For the first time, I feel I can actually concentrate on teaching instead of trying to tiptoe around potential disasters the way I was doing. They were even quiet while I read to them this morning. And during their free time, I found Polly and Lamar in the reading corner—and they were actually reading."

She sighed and settled down in one of the big chairs. "Alec and I are going to have a 'store' together—things the kids can 'buy' with the points they earn for appropriate behavior. And next week whoever has enough points can exchange them for a trip to the roller skating rink. Margaret has approved a bus to take Alec's and my classes."

Clem set the empty glass on the floor beside her. She coughed and pushed her limp curls away from her face. "Sounds good," she said listlessly, and then frowned, as though she were making an effort to concentrate. "A roller skating rink doesn't sound like something your friend Felix will enjoy, though."

Dorrie grinned. "No. Alec and I thought of that. So there will be another after-school trip offered the next day—this one to the art gallery. I'm pretty sure Felix will be the only one interested in that excursion." She stretched her long legs out in front of her, then kicked off her shoes. "I'm looking forward to having some time with Felix. I love all the kids, I really do, but there's something about Felix. I keep wishing I could bring him home and keep him."

The phone rang and Dorrie leapt to answer it. During the week, she had been concentrating so hard on her students that she had barely thought of Liam. On the way home from work, though, she had wondered if she would hear from him over the weekend, and all the while she had been talking with Clem, part of her had been listening for the phone. Her heart pounded now as she picked up the receiver. "Hello?"

"Hi, Dorrie."

Dorrie let out the breath she had been holding. "Hi, Liam." She smiled.

"I know this is last minute again, but every time I've tried to talk to you at school, you seem to be busy with Alec MacIntyre."

"Just school stuff," Dorrie said quickly. "We've been working on a joint behavior management program for our two classes."

"Oh. Well, what I wanted to ask—are you busy tonight? I'd really like to see you."

"I'm not busy—" Dorrie started to say, and then she looked at Clem. "I'm not busy," she repeated, "but your sister is pretty sick. I think she has the flu. I hate to leave her after she's been here alone all day."

Clem made a face and waved her hand at Dorrie. "Go on," she whispered. "I'll be fine."

"Poor Clemmie." Liam hesitated. "I know. Ask her if she wants to go over to Gram's house. That's where she belongs if she's sick. She can lie in bed and be pampered and eat Gram's chicken soup. Gram will love it, and so will Clem. We could drop her over there, and then you and I could go out somewhere."

"Hold on," Dorrie answered. "I'll see what she says."

⚬⚬⚬

"The house is going to seem empty," Dorrie said as she packed a bag for Clem. "I'm going to miss you."

"I don't know why," Clem sniffed. "I've been such a wretch."

Dorrie laughed. "You *are* sick, Clemmie, when you start sounding so pathetic."

She looked out the window. "Here's Liam now. Think you can manage to walk out to the car?"

"I'm not an invalid," Clem said as she tottered toward the door. She leaned against the wall and shut her eyes. "But maybe it would be good for Liam to have to help me out to the car." She took a deep breath and opened her eyes. "You know, teach him to be more sensitive and empathetic. You just go out and tell him his little sister needs him."

Liam's smile was crooked when Dorrie repeated Clem's message. "I bet," he said, but he came out the door a moment later carrying Clem in his arms.

"I can walk," she insisted. "I just wanted to lean on you a little."

"Shut up, Clem," he said. "You weigh about as much as that old cat of Gram's. Besides, I used to carry you around all the time when you were little." He grinned as he put his sister in the truck and tucked a blanket around her. "Don't you remember?"

"Vaguely." Clem moved to the middle of the seat so that Dorrie could climb in beside her. "That was a long time ago."

Liam started the engine. "Before Mom and Dad died."

Dorrie saw Clem's small hands clutch the blanket tighter to her. "Yes."

Liam backed the truck out of their driveway. "You talked to Mason lately, Clem?" he asked as he pulled out onto the dirt road.

"No."

"I didn't think so. I gave him a call before I came over here. Told him you were sick."

Dorrie saw Clem's head turn toward Liam. "Why ever would you go and do a thing like that?"

"I don't know. I guess I thought he'd want to know. So he can pray for you."

"Right." Clem's voice was dry. Her fingers tightened and loosened, tightened and loosened on the blanket. "You know," she said after a moment, "that's really not like you, Liam. If nothing else, you usually mind your own business."

"Usually." Liam's voice was mild. "I guess you could say I'm concerned about you, Clem."

Clem snorted.

"Well, I am. You seem pretty serious about breaking up with Mason. And that would be a really stupid thing to do."

"Yeah?" Clem's voice was tight.

"Yeah. You two are obviously right for each other. I'd hate to see you throw that away just because you're scared."

Clem's hands jerked tight into fists. "What do you know, Liam?"

Liam drove silently for a moment. "I know," he said at last, "that you're scared. I know that it's because of Mom and Dad. I guess—oh, I don't know. I guess you probably think that if you dare get married and be happy, then something will happen to Mason."

"How dare you, Liam," Clem said in a small, hard voice, "how dare you try to analyze me, when—when—" Dorrie heard her swallow hard, as though she were keeping back her words by sheer willpower.

"I know," Liam said quietly, "I know. But maybe that's why I understand." He pulled into the Adams' driveway. "Look, Clem, I know you're sick, and this probably isn't the best time. But I know Mason is going to try to see you tomorrow, and I'd hate to have you turn him away. He's been accepted by the mission board—and one day he may not come back to you again." He turned off the motor, and Dorrie felt him slide his arm around Clem's shoulders. "Believe it or not, Clemmie," he said softly, "I love you." He got out of the truck, then reached back for Clem.

Dorrie followed them inside. She waited while Gram and Grandpop fussed over Clem and then bundled her upstairs to bed. "Get better," she told her friend. She looked down at Clem's small, pale face and saw the sheen of tears in her heavy eyes. "Don't worry about anything; don't think. Just rest. We all love you. I'll see you soon." She closed the bedroom door softly behind her.

Downstairs, Gram pressed her lips together and shook her head. "She hasn't been sleeping well ever since this thing with Mason. I could tell from her eyes. She looked the same way when something was troubling her when she was a child—and then she'd end up sick."

Grandpop put his hand on Gram's shoulder. "Well, she'll get the rest she needs now, with you to coddle her."

"I hope so." Gram shook her head again. "But I can't make her mind rest easy."

"No." Grandpop smiled. "But our Lord can."

Liam cleared his throat. "Dorrie and I are going to get going now."

Grandpop turned his smile on them. "Stay awhile. There's an old John Wayne movie on. Remember how you used to love them when you were a kid, Liam? Gram was just going to make popcorn."

Liam smiled but shook his head. "Another time, Grandpop. Dorrie and I are going to go out to eat now."

Gram looked from Liam to Dorrie. "Have a good time," she said, her eyes resting thoughtfully on Dorrie's face. Dorrie felt herself flush, as though Gram could read her heart better than she could herself. Gram smiled. "We'll see you Sunday, children."

⚭

They went to a dim Italian restaurant, nearly empty because of the late hour. Liam said very little while he ate. Dorrie watched his face, thinking of the love he had shown Clem. Again and again she opened her mouth, about to say something about Clem and Mason, but each time she caught herself in time. Liam needed her to be quiet, she reminded herself. She tried to find the peaceful quietness she had experienced more and more during the past week, but her mind kept working busily, ticking off the many ways she loved Liam, as though she were keeping a score card.

After they had finished eating, he drove her back to her house. "Are you nervous about being alone?" he asked as they sat in the driveway.

Dorrie shook her head. "Not really."

"Want me to come in with you?"

Dorrie looked at him. "For a minute. I could make coffee."

Inside, Liam watched her while she made the coffee. The silence between them made Dorrie uneasy, but she forced herself to ignore it. She smiled at him while the coffee maker began its sighing and dripping. He smiled back.

"You look pretty tonight, little Dorrie."

"Thanks." *Not exactly a conversation opener,* she thought. The coffee finished brewing, and she poured them each a cup.

Liam took his cup and came to stand beside her where she leaned against the kitchen counter. She could feel his warmth very close, his shoulder brushing hers, but she felt tense and on edge. She looked into his face, and at last she could stand the silence no longer. "You were wonderful with Clem," she said softly.

His mouth twisted. "She wasn't exactly receptive to what I had to say. Not that I blame her."

"She's just so sick right now. But I know she'll appreciate what you said when she feels better."

Liam shrugged.

"I never thought before about what you said," Dorrie continued, "about her being afraid to marry Mason because of what happened to your parents. But it makes sense."

Liam sipped his coffee.

"I mean," Dorrie said, "the death of your parents at such a young age had to affect her psychologically. Both of you." She looked again into his face.

He smiled. Then he reached and took the coffee cup from her hand and set it on the counter behind them. "Shh, Dorrie," he said and pulled her into his arms.

Dorrie stood with her face against his beard, feeling awkward and breathless. After a moment, he turned his head and his lips touched hers, gently first and then more deeply.

"Oh, Liam," Dorrie said when at last they drew apart, "I love you so much."

Chapter 11

Liam smiled and drew her close again. "I feel the same, little Dorrie," he whispered as his lips found hers once more.

His kisses grew longer and deeper. At last, Dorrie pushed him away. "You'd better go," she said breathlessly.

"I suppose." His lips curved, while his hand moved up and down her back. "Can I come over tomorrow?"

She nodded. "Maybe we could go for a walk," she said shyly.

"Whatever you want." He pulled her tight against him one more time, and then he said good night.

For a long time after he left, Dorrie stood by the kitchen counter, surrounded by the quiet house. "Liam loves me," she said out loud. "Did you hear that? He said he loves me."

She threw the cold coffee down the drain and rinsed out their cups. Then she got ready for bed, wishing Clem were there to share her happiness. *She wouldn't be happy for me, though,* she reminded herself. *She'd be full of gloom and worry, saying all sorts of negative things about Liam. Better that she's gone tonight so I can enjoy this moment without her nagging.*

She lay in bed staring up at the dark ceiling, going over and over Liam's words, remembering his kisses. *I am happier than I have ever been,* she told herself. The house creaked quietly as it settled for the night; outside an owl hooted. Everything else was still, but in her mind Dorrie thought she heard a whisper, *Who are you trying to convince?* She rolled over restlessly. After a long time, she slept.

∞

"Liam loves me," she said out loud as soon as she opened her eyes the next morning. Somehow, she still couldn't believe that last night had really happened. If Liam loved her, wouldn't she be nearly flying with joy?

She got up and showered. Remembering that he had said he would come over today, she dressed carefully and put on makeup. When she was done, she looked at her reflection thoughtfully. "Maybe you're scared to believe your good fortune," she said. "Maybe you're a little like Clem, afraid to believe that something so good can be true."

She made her bed and picked up her laundry, then moved around the house aimlessly, wiping the already clean table, plumping the patchwork pillows. "I should do some school work," she said and sat down on the sofa. She picked up her plan book, then put it down. She leafed through some of her students' writing, trying to concentrate.

When the knock came at the door, she jumped to her feet. "Oh, Liam—" She swung open the door.

Alec MacIntyre stood on her doorstep, his head ducked to look through the doorway. "Oh, it's you," Dorrie blurted. She stepped back to let him in.

"Were you expecting someone else?" He glanced around the room. "Where's Clem?"

"She has the flu," Dorrie answered. "Liam and I took her to their grandparents' last night."

"Oh." Alec looked at her thoughtfully. "That must have been where you were when I called." He shifted his weight awkwardly; when he looked down, Dorrie found herself noticing the way his lashes lay in a dark fringe against his cheeks.

"Did you want something?" she asked him.

He shrugged his wide shoulders. "Some friends of mine are cleaning out their attic. The kids are off to college now, and there's a bunch of old toys up there. They said we could take anything we wanted for our classroom 'store.'" He glanced at her, then picked up a pillow and turned it round and round in his big hands. "I was just wondering if you wanted to come with me to help sort through the stuff."

"I'd like to." She was surprised to find she meant her words. *I'm excited about working on the store, that's all.* She yawned, sleepy after lying awake the night before; she looked at Alec's bulky sweater and wished she could lean her head, just for a moment, against his chest. *I didn't get enough sleep last night. Either that or I'm losing my mind.* She shook her head firmly. "I can't today, Alec. I'd like to, but I can't."

He looked into her face. "Are you okay? You've got circles under your eyes. And you seem a little—I don't know—different. Soft around the edges or something." He frowned. "Maybe you're coming down with the flu, too."

Dorrie shook her head again. "I'm fine." She had a sudden panicky feeling that Liam would come through the door at any minute. *What would be so bad about that?* she reminded herself. But she wanted Alec gone. She felt herself scowling, wishing suddenly she could take her hands and push him out the door. She imagined the way his sweater would feel beneath her fingers, and she found herself growing warm.

"You're flushed," Alec said, his eyes intent on her face.

"Maybe I *am* getting the flu," she said and turned away from him. "You'd better go before you catch it."

Alec smiled and shook his head. "You must be getting sick. You seem strange, Dorrie. Not like yourself."

I don't feel like myself. What is wrong with me? Liam loves me—and all I can think about is touching Alec MacIntyre. Her face burned even hotter.

She made herself smile. "No, no, really, I'm fine. Just busy." She pointed to her school books spread out on the sofa. "See? I promised myself I would get caught up on my paperwork today. You go and pick out whatever you think we can use. I trust your judgment."

"All right," he said at last, still staring at her. He put his fingers against her face. Dorrie flinched and then stood very still, feeling as though she had been burned. His dark brows pulled together. "You're hot, Dorrie." His eyes met hers, and suddenly he, too, flushed.

No, she wailed inside her head, *you can't be able to read my face that well. You can't know what I was thinking this time. I don't even know what I was thinking, so how can you?* She tore her gaze from his.

She saw his throat move, as though he had swallowed hard. "I'll call you later," he said in a strange, quick voice, "to make sure you're okay. If you're feeling better and you get your work done, maybe you could come up later and help me organize the stuff." He let out his breath in a long sigh and dropped the pillow he still held back on the sofa. He smiled. "I'll even cook you supper, if you want."

Dorrie turned away from the hope in his eyes. "Maybe," she said. "I'll see."

∞

After he had left, she flung herself full-length on the sofa. "What is wrong with me?" she cried to the quiet house. "I *know* I love Liam. I've loved him for years. I know he's the man God wants for me. I believe that. And now Liam finally loves me, too. We'll be married, and we'll have our own little house, and maybe someday Felix will live with us. . . ." She closed her eyes as though she could shut out the thought of Alec. "Maybe Satan is trying to tempt me away from God's plan for me. Maybe that's what's happening." She took long, slow breaths. "But Alec MacIntyre?" Suddenly she giggled and put her hands over her face. "Oh, how can I be tempted by Alec MacIntyre? I don't even *like* him. And I love Liam so much."

She heard the sound of a motor outside in the driveway and jumped back to her feet. She ran her hand over her hair and then across her face, as though she could erase the warmth that still lingered in her skin. "Liam," she said as she opened the door for him, "I'm glad to see you."

He leaned toward her and kissed her lips. "Good morning, little Dorrie. Have you eaten yet?"

She shook her head.

"Want to go get some breakfast? I know this great little diner."

Over breakfast, Dorrie could stand the silence no longer. She found herself chattering about her class, about the new "store," about the planned trips to the skating rink and the art museum. Liam ate his scrambled eggs and said nothing.

When Dorrie at last fell silent, he grinned and lifted an eyebrow at her. "Being alone last night get to you, Dorrie? I don't think I've ever heard you talk so much."

Dorrie flushed and pressed her lips together. "I'm sorry."

"That's okay." He pushed back his plate and drew patterns on his napkin with his fork, and then he shook his head. "But I have to tell you, I hate seeing you so influenced by Alec MacIntyre. I think his approach to the kids is all wrong. Giving them all these special treats—it's like you're bribing them to be good. They're such little manipulators, such users—they'll play the system for all it's worth and take all they can get. What they really need is a good firm hand. Come down on them hard if you have to, and let them know who's boss. A little healthy fear might teach them to have some respect."

Dorrie bit her lip. "I guess that's one approach," she said at last. "But even then I think you need to temper that firm hand with love."

Liam shrugged. Dorrie looked into his face, trying to read what he was feeling, but his blue eyes told her nothing. "Sometimes, Liam," she said slowly, "you seem so angry when I hear you talking with one of the kids. You—" She shook her head, determined to say no more.

He shrugged again and smiled. "Like you said, Dorrie," he said lightly, "we all have our own approach." He picked up the bill and pushed back his chair. "Let's not ruin a beautiful day by talking about the monsters."

He drove her back to her house, and they stood together by his truck, looking up at the blue sky that shone through the russet oak leaves. "What a wonderful day," Dorrie said.

He moved closer to her, so close that his breath stirred the loose hairs around her face. "Let's go inside," he murmured.

She looked quickly into his face and then took a step away from him. "It's too beautiful to be inside," she said and grabbed his hand. "Let's go for a walk."

They walked down to the river hand in hand. *I must be dreaming,* Dorrie thought. *This is one of my daydreams. This can't be real.* She looked sideways at Liam, noticing the way the sun caught the blue lights in his hair; he turned toward her and smiled, and his blue eyes were as clear and bright as the sky above their heads. She shook her head as though to clear her mind. *Why don't I feel happier?*

At the fallen log, they sat down. Liam slid his arm around Dorrie's shoulders and pulled her against him. She closed her eyes, concentrating on the feel of him, the smell of him, but she found herself remembering instead the two times she had seen Alec here by the river.

In the sunlight, your hair looks just like a flame. Isn't that what he had said? She shook her head. *No, I will not think of Alec MacIntyre. I love Liam.* She turned her head and let her lips meet his.

The sound of a stick snapping made her jump and pull away. She opened her eyes. Alec MacIntyre stood below them on the river bank, looking up at them. His eyes were blank, his face as hard as though it were carved of stone.

Chapter 12

I'm sorry," Alec said stiffly. "I didn't mean to interrupt." He looked over their heads at the browning goldenrod behind them. "I called you on the phone." His eyes met Dorrie's quickly, then went back to the goldenrod. "When you didn't answer, I thought you might be down here." His mouth twisted. "Guess I was right."

"Alec—" Dorrie couldn't think of what to say.

He lifted his shoulders. "Sorry I bothered you." His hands in his pockets, he turned away. Dorrie frowned and watched him make his way through the trees until he disappeared.

"He likes you." Liam's voice was oddly gentle. "More than likes you."

Dorrie shook her head. She met Liam's eyes, but she couldn't read the expression she saw there.

Liam looked out over the river. "Actually, you know, you and he would look good together. You probably have a lot in common."

Dorrie grabbed Liam's hand and shook her head. He smiled faintly. "You look scared, little Dorrie."

She looked down at his long, slim fingers, and then she took a deep breath. "It's *you* I love, Liam." She leaned toward him, waiting for his lips to claim hers.

⚭

Liam picked her up for church the next day. Sitting beside him on the pew, she listened to his tenor voice singing the hymns, then watched the sure way he turned the pages of his Bible. He glanced at her and smiled; she returned his smile and never once let her eyes stray across the church to where she knew Alec MacIntyre sat.

After the service, Gram Adams waited for them in the vestibule. "Come to dinner," she said. "Clem's lonely for some company." She turned as Alec came out the door. "You, too, Alec. Won't you have dinner with us?"

"No," he said. "I'm afraid I can't." He did not look at Dorrie. "Thank you for the invitation." He hurried away.

Gram watched him, two lines between her silver brows. She turned back to Dorrie and Liam, and her eyes fell on Liam's hand where it rested on Dorrie's shoulder. The lines between her brows grew deeper.

"We'd love to come," Liam said. "Right, Dorrie?"

She nodded, but she found she couldn't meet Gram's blue eyes.

After dinner, Dorrie went upstairs to spend some time with Clem. "How are you feeling?"

Clem smiled, but her cheeks were still pale. "A little better. I've been missing you—but it seems good to be back in the snug little bed I grew up in. Gram and Grandpop make me feel so safe."

Dorrie settled on the bed beside her. "Did Mason come over yesterday?"

Clem nodded. "But Gram wouldn't let him see me. Bless her. She said I needed to rest—physically and emotionally—before I try to make any more decisions." Clem sighed. "What a relief. I just don't feel up to facing him yet. I'm starting to have doubts about breaking up with him—and yet I still can't say I'll marry him. I just can't." Her hands clenched tight on the blanket.

"Don't think about it right now," Dorrie soothed. "Give yourself time to heal."

Clem's hands loosened. After a moment, she sighed and fell back against the pillow. "What about you? How was your date with Liam?"

"Good." Dorrie picked a loose thread off the coverlet. "We had a nice time." She felt Clem's eyes on her, and she tried to say more, but the words stuck in her throat.

"You look awfully subdued," Clem said at last. "Did something happen?"

Dorrie hesitated. "He said he loves me." She held her breath, waiting for Clem's reaction.

"Do you believe him?" Clem's voice was mild, as though she were merely curious.

"I don't know." Dorrie met her friend's eyes. She took a deep breath. "I guess that's what's bothering me. Here I've wanted him to love me for so long, and now all of a sudden he says he does. It seems too good to be true."

Clem touched Dorrie's hand. "Just be careful, Dorrie."

Dorrie felt better, though, after she had talked to Clem. *After all the things Clem's told me about Liam and women, it's no wonder I feel a little scared*, she told herself that night as she got ready for bed. *That's what's been bothering me, I know it is. It will just take a little time, time for me to know I can really trust him. Right, God?* Suddenly exhausted, she hurried into bed without waiting for an answer.

At school that week, Liam stopped by her classroom at least once a day. His blue eyes would smile into hers, and he would touch her hair or steal a quick kiss. On Tuesday and Wednesday he ate lunch with her, and Dorrie found herself beginning to accept that he really did love her. She smiled and pushed the thought of Alec MacIntyre far to the back of her mind.

She was dreading, though, the trips with Alec and their classes to the skating rink and art museum. She had managed to avoid Alec all week, ducking into her room whenever she heard his voice in the hall. By Thursday, the day of the afterschool outing, she felt sick to her stomach with nervousness. *How can we be comfortable together professionally after what happened?*

To her surprise, though, he acted as though nothing had happened at all. He laughed with the kids and smiled easily at Dorrie as they circled round and round the rink on their skates. With a feeling that felt strangely like disappointment, she decided she had imagined that he was hurt by seeing her with Liam. *I must have imagined that he was attracted to me.* Hesitantly, she returned his smile. She let out her breath in a long sigh.

The next day, he met her at her room for their trip with Felix to the art museum. All of his own students had chosen the trip to the roller skate rink rather than this one, but to their surprise, Lamar had asked to go to the museum. The two boys sat on their desks, waiting for Alec and Dorrie.

"Think we can all fit in my car?" Alec asked.

Felix made a face. "I'm not riding in the back with all those cat hairs."

Alec grinned. "I thought you liked cats."

"I like *cats*. I don't like their unattached hair."

"Why don't we take my car?" Dorrie offered.

The two boys climbed in the back, while Alec sat in the front with her. "I'd sit in the back," he said, "but I don't think there'd be room for my legs."

Dorrie smiled and shook her head. She kept her eyes on the road ahead during the hour ride to the city art museum. Alec talked with the two boys, making them giggle with his stories.

"I was only thirteen, see," he said. "None of the other boys shaved yet. I felt like a freak. And here I was covered with little bits of light green toilet paper where I'd cut myself—and I mean covered with it. I looked like I was molding or something. And who should come to my house selling cookies but Allison Jenkins, the prettiest girl in my class. I took one look at her and—guess what I did?"

Dorrie smiled. She let their voices flow around her, and she found herself relaxing for the first time in what seemed like a long time. *It's because I'm beginning to believe that Liam really does love me,* she thought. *That's why I feel so happy.*

At the art museum Felix was entranced. He stood so long in front of some works that eventually Lamar would grab him by the arm and drag him away.

"Come on, man, what's so fascinating?" Lamar asked. "It's just a picture of some flowers. It's not like it's a naked lady or anything."

Felix shook his head. "Look, look at the way he made this line. See? See the way it makes the flower look like it's moving, like the wind's blowing it. And look at the colors he used. That's something I'm not good at yet. I can get the lines. But I can't get the colors. 'Course, I don't have any oils. Maybe if I did. . . ." He let Lamar pull him to the next painting, still muttering under his breath.

Dorrie smiled. She looked at Alec, wanting to share her pleasure, but his eyes were on the painting. "Nice," he said and followed the two boys away from her.

"Can't I stay here while you go eat?" Felix begged when it was time for them to leave. "This is better than eating."

Alec ruffled his hair. "You do look like you're getting nourishment here that you need more than any Big Mac. But no, you can't stay by yourself. We'll bring you again, though."

Felix scowled. "Sure."

"I promise, Felix," Dorrie said quietly. "We'll get you here again."

But Felix scuffed his feet and would not look at her. At the fast food restaurant he refused to eat his cheeseburger. He used a french fry to draw gremlin faces in his ketchup and hung his head.

Alec talked easily to Lamar, making Dorrie realize how little she had gotten to know the other boy. She listened to them, sipping her soda, while she watched Felix out of the corner of her eye.

Suddenly, he raised his head and stared at her. "So," he said, "looks like I lost my bet."

"What do you mean?" Too late, Dorrie caught the quick shake of Alec's head.

Felix smiled, but his eyes behind their glasses were flat. "You and Mr. Adams. I put my money on Mr. MacIntyre, but it looks like he lost."

Lamar looked from Dorrie to Alec. "You dating Mr. Adams, Miss Carpenter?" he asked curiously.

"That's Miss Carpenter's business," Alec reminded quietly. "Now, who wants dessert?"

Dorrie found her eyes lingering on the strong bones of Alec's face. *He could look frightening,* she thought. *With that face, he could be some long-ago heathen warrior, swooping down to ravage and burn. And yet he's so gentle.* She listened to him laughing with the two boys. *He's so good with them. If only Liam. . .* She sighed. *Dear God, let Liam and Alec become friends. Liam could learn so much from Alec. . . .*

She drove the two boys back to the Home, and then Alec followed her home in his car. All the way, she felt his headlights in her rearview mirror, as though they were his eyes watching her. He honked his horn when she pulled into her driveway, and then she watched his lights disappear over the hill. She went into the empty house, feeling suddenly lonely.

∽∾

The next day Clem came home, still weak but with the roses back in her round cheeks. Dorrie tucked her in on the sofa.

"I'm so glad to have you home. This empty house was starting to drive me nuts."

Clem smiled. "No one to talk to, huh?"

Dorrie grinned. "You know me. I kept right on talking anyways. Nothing stops me. But I was starting to feel like a lunatic when I caught myself talking to a ladybug that was crawling on my window the other day."

Clem laughed. "What happened to this new, quiet Dorrie you were going to change into?"

Dorrie shrugged ruefully. "I guess I gave up on that for the time being. I can only handle so much at once." She looked at Clem. "Of course I still have faith that God will help me become the person Liam needs me to be."

"And vice versa?"

"What do you mean?"

"Is God going to change Liam into the person you need him to be, too?"

Dorrie hesitated. "Well, isn't that the way it works? I mean, look at how perfectly Gram and Grandpop fit together, like two halves of a whole. They can't have started out that way, can they?"

Clem smiled. "No. You should hear Gram tell about some of their fights when they were first married. Of course, when people grow closer and closer, some of their rough edges have to get smoothed away. But I don't think who they really are changes, not the basic person inside."

Dorrie lifted her shoulders. "Well, I like the person that Liam is inside."

"So do I," Clem said. "I know you don't believe that, but I really do. I'm just not sure that person is the sort of man you need."

∞

All during the next weeks, while the dark red leaves turned brown and dropped off the oak trees, Dorrie felt Clem's eyes on her whenever she and Liam were together. He stopped at the house after school more and more, and every weekend he and Dorrie went out, then spent Sundays after church together.

Clem seemed quieter than usual, but Dorrie no longer felt she was shutting herself away from Dorrie the way she had before she got sick. She was still not seeing Mason, and Dorrie knew she spent long hours alone, praying for wisdom.

She no longer criticized Liam or questioned his relationship with Dorrie, but Dorrie knew she was watching them, listening to them talk. At last, one Sunday after they had all eaten dinner at the Adams', Clem watched Liam pull out of their driveway and then turned to Dorrie.

"You know," she said, "I think maybe he really does love you."

Dorrie smiled. "I told you."

"I know, I know. But I couldn't help but watch for him to repeat the same old pattern of loving and leaving. But he hasn't. I don't think he's ever gone with a girl this long. Maybe he's finally serious."

"Of course he's serious." *After all, he and I are going to get married, aren't we? It's just a matter of time.* Dorrie looked at her friend's face and then threw up her hands in exasperation. "So why are you frowning now?"

Clem looked at her thoughtfully. "I think maybe Liam loves you. But I'm not sure you love him."

Dorrie laughed. "Don't be silly. Of course I love him."

She was still smiling as she drove to work the next morning. *O God, You've worked everything out just like I dreamed You would. I knew Liam was the man for me. We'll smooth off our rough edges, and then we'll be so happy....* His truck was in the parking lot, and she hurried into the school building, hoping to run into him in the hall.

She lingered by the main office, longing for him to appear, and then went up to her classroom. The room was empty and so was Felix's closet. She sat at her desk, praying for the new day ahead of her, trying to quiet her mind and concentrate on her students, but she was too restless. After a moment she jumped to her feet and ran down the stairs to the gym.

Usually he came to see her in the morning, but today she would seek him out. *What if he feels like Clem, that I may not really love him? I should probably take the initiative more often....* The light was on in his office, the door not quite shut. She smiled and pushed the door open. "Liam—"

Liam's arms were around a woman with long blond hair. Dorrie knew that a moment before, his mouth had been pressed to hers. The woman pulled away and looked at Dorrie; Dorrie saw she was the new third grade teacher who had come to the Home last week.

"I keep forgetting your name," Dorrie said, as though from a great distance. "But I'm sorry to interrupt." She did not look at Liam's face, but she saw his arms drop to his sides.

"I'm sorry, Dorrie," he said quietly. "I really did try."

Chapter 13

Dorrie turned toward Liam. She saw the clear blue blaze of his eyes against his dark hair and beard, the neat, slender bones, the long fingers that were never still. "I loved you," she whispered. She turned blindly away.

She found herself outside her classroom with no memory of how she got there. Through the open door, she could see the light on in the closet. She turned away, knowing she could not face Felix now. Without thinking, she ran down the hallway, stumbling a little, to Alec's room.

When she burst through the door, he stood up and came around his desk toward her. "Dorrie—"

Tears streaming down her face, she flung herself at him. He stood very still for a second and then his arms pulled her close. "Dorrie, what is it?"

She shook her head and pushed her face against his chest. She didn't want to talk or explain, didn't want to think or remember. She only wanted to stay here where she was safe and warm. Her sobs shook her entire body.

"Shh, Sweetheart, shh." She felt his hand against her hair, stroking. He let her cry, saying nothing more while he held her tight.

After a long time, he drew back a little and tried to see into her face. "Dorrie?" He tipped her face up with his fingers. "What is it?"

Dorrie pulled away, suddenly embarrassed. "Liam. He was with— They were—" She gulped and stepped back. "I'm sorry," she muttered. "I'd better get back to my classroom. The kids will be here any minute."

He kept his hands on her shoulders. She knew he was staring into her face, but she could not look at him. "No," he said finally. "I'll get your class and bring them down here with mine. We'll watch that science film we were going to show them tomorrow. You go for a walk. Get yourself calmed down."

She nodded, still not looking at him, and pulled away from his hands. "Dorrie?"

She glanced at him quickly.

"I–I'll be praying for you."

She nodded and hurried away, afraid the students would catch her in the hall. She knew her makeup was ruined, her french braid mussed, and she did not feel strong enough yet to deal with their curiosity. She ducked into the women's room, then slipped out one of the school's back doors and ran across the soccer field into the woods.

The trees were nearly bare now, the wind cold through her sweater. She wrapped her arms around herself and leaned against a beech tree's smooth gray trunk. In the distance she could hear the children's voices as they made their way from the cottages to the school building; close by, the only noise was the wind stirring the few dead leaves that lingered in the trees' limbs. Her tears had dried; she felt still and numb inside, as though her feelings had been frozen. Overhead, the sky was the pale chill gray of metal. Dorrie tipped back her head and looked up through the bare branches, remembering how blue the sky had been, how clear and warm, the day she and Liam had sat on the fallen log by the river. *As blue as Liam's eyes.* She shook her head and walked slowly back to the school building.

∞

At the end of the day, she stuck her head in Alec's room. "Thank you for your help earlier. I really appreciate it."

He stood up and came toward her. She felt his eyes on her face, but she looked away and stared at Felix's mural of the solar system. "How did your day go?" he asked.

She lifted her shoulders. "All right. I was operating on autopilot, but the structure I've been building with the kids seemed firm enough to take that, at least for now." She smiled faintly. "I guess that's good, right?"

He nodded and came closer to her. "How are you?"

"I'm fine."

"Would you—would you like to talk?"

She shook her head. "Thanks, Alec. But I'm okay. I'm going to go home now."

∞

Outside her house, though, she hesitated. Clem was already home. Somehow, Dorrie felt reluctant to face her. She took a breath and opened the door.

Clem was curled up reading in one of the chairs. "Hi," she said without looking up.

"Hi." Dorrie took off her jacket and hung it up. She went to the refrigerator and opened it. "Want me to get supper?"

"Sure." Clem's eyes were still on her book. "I took out a package of hamburg."

Dorrie chopped an onion. She mixed it together with the meat, added an egg and bread crumbs.

"How was your day?" Clem asked.

"All right." Dorrie took a loaf pan out of the cupboard. "Meat loaf sound okay?"

"Sounds fine. I think there's some potatoes left we could bake." Clem closed her book and came to stand beside Dorrie by the kitchen counter. "I'll scrub them."

Dorrie pressed the meat into the pan. "No, I'll do it. You go sit down." She kept her eyes on her work.

Clem didn't move. "What's wrong, Dorrie?" she asked after a moment.

"What makes you think something is wrong?" Dorrie tried to make her voice light.

"You won't look at me. And your eyes look like you've been crying. What is it?" When Dorrie still didn't answer, Clem let the bag of potatoes tumble into the sink. "Is it Liam?"

"I guess you could say that." Dorrie picked up a potato and began to scrub it. "I found him kissing the new third grade teacher this morning." She carefully cut out the potato eyes. "Chances are he doesn't love me after all, don't you think?"

"Oh, Dorrie." Clem took the potato out of Dorrie's hands and put her arms around her. "Oh, Dorrie. I'm sorry."

"You're too short to hug me." Dorrie stepped away from Clem's arms. "I always feel like a giant next to you." She picked up another potato. "Aren't you going to say, I told you so?"

"No," said Clem, "I'm not." She touched Dorrie's arm. "I'm going to pray for you. And then I'm going to give my brother a piece of my mind." Her round eyes flashed.

Dorrie shook her head. "No, you're not. Not if you love me." She set the potato on the counter. "I think I'm going to go lie down for a little while. Call me when supper is ready."

She flung herself on her bed and lay with her face in her pillow. She found herself thinking about the next day's lessons, about the grocery shopping she and Clem needed to do, about anything except Liam. She picked her head up and made herself reach for the Bible she kept on the table beside her bed. Opening it at random, she stared blindly at the fourth chapter of Romans.

After a moment, however, words she had underlined registered in her brain. "God...calls into being that which does not exist. In hope against hope [Abraham] believed.... He did not waver in unbelief, but grew strong in faith...." (NASB)

"Of course," Dorrie whispered. "Of course." She shut the Bible and went back to the kitchen.

"Feel better?" Clem asked.

Dorrie nodded.

While they ate, she felt Clem's eyes studying her. Dorrie only smiled.

⚭

The next Sunday as they drove home from church together, Clem shook her head. "I don't understand this. You're too—serene. You go around with this little smile on your lips, looking like the Mona Lisa. Like you know a secret no one else does."

Dorrie's smile widened. "Maybe I do."

Clem turned her eyes away from the road to look at Dorrie, and then she shook her head again. "I don't get it. You've been infatuated with Liam for years. You finally see him in his true colors—and you act as though nothing has happened. What's up?"

Dorrie hesitated. "I just believe that everything's going to be all right," she said at last.

"Well, of course, it is. But I'm surprised that you've been able to see that so easily. I'm glad of course, but—" Clem looked away from the road again, her eyes narrowed. "Wait a minute. You don't *still* think Liam is the man for you, do you?" She pulled over to the side of the road and turned so she could see into Dorrie's face. "No. You do." She rested her elbow on the steering wheel and put her forehead in her palm. "I don't believe it."

They sat in silence for a moment. "Listen, Clem," Dorrie said finally, "isn't that what faith is all about? Believing something despite the odds against it? So Liam isn't ready yet to make a serious commitment. That doesn't mean he never will be. The Holy Spirit is constantly at work in our hearts. You know that."

Clem pressed her lips together. She turned the key in the ignition, then swung the car out onto the road, heading back in the direction they had come.

"Where are we going?" Dorrie asked.

"To my grandparents'."

"I thought you didn't want to go for dinner today." Dorrie shifted uneasily in her seat. "What made you change your mind?"

Clem looked straight ahead. "Once Liam knew we weren't going to be there, I heard him tell Gram he'd be over. I need to talk to him. And so do you."

She pulled into the Adams' driveway. "Come on."

"Clem, I don't think—" But Clem was already opening the front door. Slowly, Dorrie followed her inside.

"What a lovely surprise, girls," Gram said, coming from the kitchen. She wiped her wet hands on her apron and leaned to kiss them. "I was just making the salad. I'm so glad you changed your minds about coming. I'll just set a couple of extra plates and—"

"I don't think we're staying, Gram," Clem interrupted. "We need to talk to Liam."

Gram opened her mouth and then shut it. "I see," she said at last, her eyes on Dorrie's face. "Well, he's in the living room. I'll just call Grandpop into the kitchen." Her blue eyes crinkled. "I think I need his help cutting those vegetables."

"Thanks, Gram." Clem returned her grandmother's small smile, but Dorrie's lips felt too stiff to curve.

"Come on, Clem," she whispered. "I don't know what you think you're doing, but—"

"I'm changing the station, letting some new voices into that busy little mind of yours, Dorrie Carpenter. I think the volume's been up so high inside your head, playing the same station, the same song for so many years, that you can't hear anything else."

"What do you mean?" But Clem had already gone into the living room.

Dorrie hung back in the hallway, staring at the shiny curve of the stair bannister. She heard Clem's voice and then Liam's answer, she heard Gram and Grandpop's murmur from the kitchen, and then she tiptoed to the front door and quietly let herself out.

She pulled her jacket tighter around her shoulders and hurried across the yard, no goal in her mind except to escape.

"What's up?" Liam called from behind her. "Hey, Dorrie. Clem says you need to talk to me."

She turned around slowly. She shook her head. "I don't need to talk to you. Not right now." She smiled shakily. "You know Clem. She just has an idea in her head."

He nodded and then crossed the distance between them. "About you catching me with Stacey, right?"

Dorrie watched a crow wheel down out of the sky and land on the picket fence that bordered Gram's garden. Nothing grew there now; only a few dead tomato vines still clung to their wire frames, and even the sturdy broccoli plants looked brown and frozen. She could not answer Liam, could not even bring herself to look at him.

"Dorrie?"

"I don't want to do this," she whispered at last, her eyes suddenly burning.

He took a step closer to her. "Clem's right this time, Dorrie. We do need to talk. Come back inside where it's warmer."

Dorrie felt as though a wave that had been frozen at its crest suddenly broke and crashed over her head. She could not keep the tears from streaming out of her eyes. "You said you loved me!"

Liam cocked his head to one side. "No," he said thoughtfully, "I don't think I ever *said* that, did I? I generally try hard not to lie."

Dorrie listened to his words, and she felt as though her feet had been swept out from under her by that raging wave of water. She closed her eyes. "How could you?" she whispered. "You were just playing with me, weren't you?"

"No." Liam's voice was regretful. "This time I wanted to love you. I really did. I tried. It felt so good knowing you loved me. I wanted to convince myself I could change for you." She opened her eyes and saw him shake his head. "But I couldn't. I'm sorry, Dorrie."

"Why didn't you tell me? Why did you let me go on making a fool out of myself? Why—" She heard her voice climbing higher, and she shut her teeth hard. *God calls into being that which does not exist,* she told herself, trying to stem the flood of her emotions. The words seemed suddenly flimsy, though, and they were swept away by the tide of hurt and anger that was spilling out of her. She looked at Liam's narrow, handsome face, and she saw no shame or sorrow there, only a faint regret. "You should have told me," she said between her teeth. "You shouldn't have let me stumble on the truth like that."

"I suppose I should have talked to you." He shrugged. "I hated to hurt you, little Dorrie."

"Don't call me that." She wiped her hand across her eyes and glared at him. "You didn't want to hurt me? How do you think I felt when I walked in on you kissing another woman?"

Liam shrugged. "I thought I could let you down slowly, gently." He smiled wryly. "I have lots of practice at that. I hadn't planned on what happened the other morning with Stacey. I've seen her a couple of times, I admit, but nothing more than coffee and talk. But then she came down to my office, and she was so sweet—" He shrugged again. "I like women. I like it when they like me." Beneath his mustache, his lips quirked. "What else can I say?"

"You can say you're sorry." Clem's voice was hard. She had come across the yard without either Dorrie or Liam noticing, and she came even closer to Liam now, her cheeks bright red, her blue eyes blazing. She looked as though she would like to swing one of her small fists at her brother, and he stepped backward, laughing.

"Hey, Clem, easy now. The last time you came at me looking like that you were ten years old—and I ended up with a black eye. Aren't we all grown up now?"

"Apparently not. Apparently some people never grow up." Clem shook her head. "You make me sick. You stand there and admit that you use women—and you don't even have the grace to be ashamed of yourself."

Liam's brows pulled together, but his voice was still mild when he replied, "We can't all be saints, Clemmie." He turned toward the house and started back across the yard.

"Oh!" For a moment, words seemed to fail Clem. Then she ran after Liam and grabbed his shirt sleeve. "You're the one who pretends to be the saint, not me. All your self-righteous talk, as though you were Mr. Super-Christian. It wouldn't be so bad if you were just a creep. But you're a creep who pretends to be a saint. And you have the nerve to say you try to be honest."

"You must have been eavesdropping for quite some time, Clemmie dear." For the first time, Dorrie saw a hint of red above Liam's dark beard. "Nothing very Christian about listening to other people's private conversations, is there?"

"Oh, for goodness' sake." Clem sighed. "I was standing right there in plain sight, that's hardly eavesdropping. And this isn't about who is worse, me or you, you know."

"No?" Liam raised his brows. "Then what is it about?"

"You!" Clem let go of his sleeve, but she grabbed the front of his shirt and shook him. "You've been doing the same thing ever since Mom and Dad died. Aren't you ever going to stop?"

Liam pried her fingers off his shirt. He took a step backward. "I don't know what you're talking about."

"I'm talking about the way you changed after they died. You wouldn't let me close anymore, you wouldn't let anyone close. And you act as though you're a Christian, when I know you aren't."

"How nice it must be to be omniscient." Liam's cheeks were very red now, his blue eyes blazing as bright as Clem's. Dorrie watched him glare into Clem's eyes for a long moment, and then he sighed and looked away. "You're right, of course. But," his eyes swung back to Clem's face, "I wasn't stupid. I could see the way you got all the attention, all the loving sympathy from Gram and Grandpop. You were the little Christian, and they adored you. So I decided to play the same game."

Clem stared back at him. "And here you are," she said at last, her voice quiet now, "fifteen years later, still playing the same game. Only now you play it with women."

Liam shrugged and looked away. "I don't see how that's really any of your business, Clem."

"I thought the fact that you're my brother and I love you made it my business. But if I'm wrong," Clem's lips tightened, "then when you start playing your games with Dorrie, then it certainly becomes my business. Here she thinks you're going to marry her—"

"Clem!" wailed Dorrie.

Liam's eyes swung briefly to Dorrie. "I never said anything about marriage; I'm sure of that."

"Oh, I'm sure you didn't. You try so hard to be honest." Clem's lip curled. "But poor Dorrie has been in love with you for years. For years and years she's thought you were the man God wanted her to marry." Clem glanced at Dorrie. "I'm sorry, Dorrie. But like I said, it's time to turn the volume down on whatever it is you've been listening to all these years. The only way I know to do that is with a good loud blast of reality."

Liam's eyes were resting curiously on Dorrie. "Why would you think God wanted you to marry me?"

Dorrie could feel her face growing hotter. The heat spread down her neck to her entire body. She shrugged and turned away, unable to look at the cool distance in Liam's eyes.

"Because she's an optimist," Clem said. "She loved you—and so she thought sure that God would give you to her. She literally believed the Bible verse about God being a good Father who gives what we ask for—you know, 'if a son shall ask for a loaf, will he give him a stone? Or if he shall ask for a fish, will he give him a serpent?' She didn't know that what she was asking God for actually *was* a serpent."

Dorrie turned back and saw Liam's face flush still darker, until his skin was the color of bricks. He looked like a stranger, she thought. "How nice," he said.

"How nice to know what my little sister thinks of me." He leaned forward and put his face close to Clem's. "Talk about being self-righteous. Well, while we're quoting Bible verses, what about the one that says to get rid of the beam in your own eye before you start picking at the splinter in someone else's? You take it upon yourself to straighten me out, to straighten Dorrie out—and meanwhile, you're not half so perfect as everyone thinks."

"I never said I was perfect."

"No, but you act as though you think it. What else would give you the right to interfere with me and Dorrie? Little Clementine, God's messenger on earth. But you know what? I'm not fooled by you, any more than you've been fooled by me."

"What do you mean?" Clem's voice was suddenly small. "I'm committed to Christ. I really am."

"Oh, I'm sure you are. But you don't trust God any more than I do, not really. You'd never make Dorrie's mistake, because you know all too well that God does give His children stones and snakes. Why else would He have let Mom and Dad die?"

Clem's eyes were swimming with tears. "God knew what He was doing. He loves us. I trust Him."

"No, you don't. If you did, you'd marry Mason. But you know all too well what can happen. Maybe I'm not honest in my relationships with women— but you're not honest, either, blaming God for your refusal to marry Mason." Liam's voice was no longer angry. He sighed. "You've decided never to put yourself in the position where God can do to you what He did to you when our parents died. I don't blame you. But admit, at least to yourself, that that's what you're doing."

Clem closed her eyes. "They were so happy. We were so happy. We had the perfect life." She opened her eyes. "Didn't we, Liam?"

He nodded. "Close enough."

Clem rubbed her eyes with her fists. "When they died," she whispered, "we lost it all. I thought we were paying the price for being so happy." She looked from Liam to Dorrie. "I didn't want to ever risk being that happy again." She bit her lip, holding back a sob. "The price is just too high."

Dorrie crossed the distance between them and put her arm around her friend. "Talk about listening to the same station for too many years," she said gently. "You were right—we all needed a blast of reality." She looked over Clem's head at Liam and then pushed Clem toward him.

Liam opened his arms and pulled Clem close. "I love you, little sister. I probably haven't told you that for awhile. But I do. And you're wrong—we didn't lose everything when Mom and Dad died. Because we still had each other."

Clem looked up at him. "You were right," she gulped, "I've been a self-righteous little prig, worrying about the specks in everyone else's eyes, when all the time I had a chunk of wood the size of a log in my own. I must have been so obnoxious."

Liam smiled. "You were. But we still love you." He watched Clem's eyes fill up with tears again and shook his head. "I've had enough of this standing out in the cold while we bare our hearts to each other. I'm going inside where it's warm. Gram must have dinner ready by now."

But when they turned back toward the house, they saw Gram sitting on the step, a blue sweater pulled around her shoulders. "I'm sorry," she said, "but I thought that if I pled guilty right away, then maybe listening to you children wouldn't count as eavesdropping. Grandpop probably won't speak to me when we go inside, but I was just too curious about what was going on."

Clem laughed shakily and leaned to hug her grandmother. "We have no secrets from you anyway, Gram."

"How can we?" Liam muttered, but then he grinned at Gram.

She looked back at him soberly. "I never realized before that we had failed you so badly, Liam. When your parents died, Clem was still a child, and it seemed—I don't know—easier somehow to comfort her. You were an adolescent, all cool and prickly. I should have known enough to reach past your defenses to where you were hurting. But I didn't. Will you forgive me?"

Liam opened his mouth as though to deny his grandmother's words. Dorrie saw Gram's eyes, still as bright a blue as Liam's, rest steadily on Liam's face. "Don't worry about it, Gram," Liam said at last and turned away. "I'm going inside. You women can stand out here in the cold all day, nattering and blubbering, if you want to. I can see that if Grandpop and I don't get dinner on the table, we'll all starve."

Gram watched him go inside. "He's not ready to truly forgive me." She sighed, then turned back to Clem and Dorrie. "No matter how old I get, I still find it so difficult to leave things with the Lord. I have a few voices of my own inside my head, and I've paid too much attention to them over the years, just like you girls. Over and over, I have to remind myself of that verse in Isaiah thirty: 'In returning and rest shall ye be saved; in quietness and in confidence shall be your strength.' (KJV) Right now, I have to turn down all the other noise in my heart and just wait upon the Lord."

◆◆◆

"I'm trying to wait upon You, God," Dorrie whispered as she drove to work the next morning. "But it's hard." She felt empty inside, hollow.

After leaving the Adams' house, she had been glad to go home and fall into bed. For once, she was glad that Clem went to bed so early, for Dorrie did not want to talk things over, did not even want to think. And this morning she was glad to be driving to work, glad that she had her class. She thought of Felix waiting in her classroom and smiled. "At least I still have him."

She parked her car and walked toward the school building. A small woman with short dark hair and wire-rimmed glasses was waiting on the step. "Can I help you?" Dorrie asked.

The woman turned to her, her forehead creased. "I want to talk to someone who's in charge. I'm Terri Jones. I've come to take my son Felix home."

Chapter 14

"S he can't just take him home with her, can she?" Mrs. Jones was with Felix now, and Dorrie strode from one end of Margaret Truesdell's office to the other.

"Of course not." Margaret's gray eyes were calm. *Too calm,* Dorrie thought. "But from what she says, the family court judge who placed Felix here has now decided that Mrs. Jones is ready and able to have Felix back in her home. We can't release him to his mother's custody until the necessary paperwork comes through the mail—but if his mother's right, then it's just a matter of time."

Margaret's delicate brows drew together, and she put a hand on Dorrie's shoulder. "This is hard for you, I know. These children need us to care for them, to put our own hearts on the line. The only problem with that is that sooner or later we get hurt."

Dorrie shook her head. "It's not fair. Felix was just starting to respond to me. He asked me for a Bible— He comes in early and we talk— I was so excited about—" She swallowed hard and shook her head again. "The judge is wrong. Felix is so special, so talented. He can't go back into that horrible environment."

Margaret poured a cup of spearmint tea and handed it to Dorrie. "Sit down and drink this. Your class will be ready for you soon, and you need to calm yourself."

Reluctantly, Dorrie sat on the edge of one of the shabby velvet chairs that clustered around Margaret's desk. She sipped the hot tea and took a long, deep breath, but her knees jumped and jiggled, and she longed for Margaret to tell her there was some action she could take to change things. "What can I do? There must be something we can do."

Margaret smiled and shook her head. "I'm afraid not. Mrs. Jones tells me she's been participating in an intensive counseling program. She has a new job, one that she likes and that pays better money. She insists that she's changed— and I must admit, she seems like a different, happier person. She's even taking a night class at the state college."

"That's nice for her." Dorrie's voice was cool. "But that doesn't mean that Felix will be any happier living with her than he was before."

Margaret wrapped her slender fingers around her own cup of tea. "I think it does mean he'll be happier, Dorrie. Felix comes by his intelligence honestly, you know. His mother is very smart—and she was frustrated by her previous low-paying job. When Felix came here, she was beaten down by the pressures of her life, unable to cope with the responsibilities of being a single parent with a dead-end, monotonous job that didn't pay enough to meet their needs—and unfortunately, she was taking her frustrations out on Felix. Neither one of them was functioning well. But that doesn't mean they don't love each other or that they don't belong together."

Margaret took a swallow of her tea and smiled at Dorrie. "Mrs. Jones has apparently gotten some much needed help. In fact, I would call the new life I sense in her remarkable, miraculous perhaps. I'm sure you've been praying for Felix—and I suspect the change in his mother is the answer to those prayers."

"I have been praying for him. But I wasn't praying that—" Dorrie broke off and shut her lips tight, knowing her words would sound bitter and unloving.

Margaret's smile deepened. "I know, Dorrie. I don't always like the way God answers my prayers, either. I have my own ideas about the way things should work out—and then I'm disconcerted by the way God works His will instead." She shook her head. "This business of quieting our hearts so that we're open to what God wants—it's not always easy."

She set her cup on her desk and leaned back. "But, Dorrie, if you love Felix, then I believe you have to accept that being with his mother is the best thing for him. Our students need to get out of their home situations, and that's why they come here—but most of the time, after they've had time to work on their problems and so have their parents, the best thing for them is to go back to the people they love. As hard as we work to make the Home a loving environment, we're just not the same as a family."

Dorrie stared down into the green tea and frowned. "So you believe the Home gives happy endings for these kids?"

Margaret sighed, and once again her brows knit together. "Most of these kids come from homes that are so scarred and damaged that no completely happy ending is possible. But I do believe the Home can open some windows that will let in flickerings of God's grace. I have to trust that somehow, someday that grace will bring healing, whether it's in the ways I imagine and long for or not." The lines between her eyebrows softened. "In the particular case of Felix Jones, I have great hope. And so should you."

She glanced at her watch and got to her feet. "Go on, Dorrie. Get up to your classroom. And don't let your hurt make you afraid to love." Her lips curved. "Christ loved us—and His love made Him vulnerable to hurt, even to the point of death. But look what life came from it!"

∞

"I'm going home pretty soon." Felix sat on his desk after the other students had left for the day. Dorrie glanced at him, trying to read his expression, but his dark hair hung over his glasses, and she could tell nothing from the straight line of his mouth.

"I heard." She turned to stack workbooks in a pile on the corner of her desk. "How do you feel about that?"

Felix snorted. "How do you think I feel? I'm glad. I can't wait to get out of this dump. This place drives me crazy."

Dorrie looked up at him. "I'll miss you," she said quietly.

He shrugged and turned away. "I'm going to clean out my closet," he said over his shoulder.

Dorrie watched him pack his art supplies and books neatly into a cardboard box. Her eyes blurred, and she went to stand by the window so he wouldn't see her tears. "I'll see you tomorrow," she said when he had finished.

"Maybe. If I'm not gone by then." He ran out the door before she could say anything more.

Dorrie sat down at her desk and put her head in her hands. *I don't understand, God. Everything I hope for turns to ashes. I know You alone are all that I truly need. But I'd thought—*

"How're you doing?"

Dorrie raised her head quickly. She rubbed her hand across her eyes and smiled. "Hi, Alec."

He came in and leaned against her desk. As usual, his physical presence overwhelmed her, his size and the warmth that seemed to radiate from his body, but today she found herself comforted rather than repulsed. She got to her feet, however, and crossed the room to the windows; if she didn't put some distance between them, she was afraid she would give in to her longing to reach out and touch him.

"Margaret tells me it's God's will for Felix to go back with his mother," she said, her eyes on the brown line of bare trees that edged the playing field behind the school. "I'm having a hard time accepting that."

"I don't blame you." His voice was quiet. She found herself comparing the deep huskiness to Liam's light tenor and mentally shook herself. *The last thing I need is to imagine myself in love with someone new right now.* She heard him move and sensed he was standing close behind her now; she fought the urge to lean back against his warmth. *Dear Lord, what is wrong with me? How can I feel so attracted to Alec now, when I'm so upset about Felix, when I'm still so confused about Liam?*

"Margaret says his mother's changed," Dorrie said, forcing herself to ignore the excited messages her body was sending her because of Alec's nearness. She turned to look up into his face. "Do you think Felix will be all right?"

Alec shrugged. "I don't think his life will ever be perfect, Dorrie, if that's what you mean. He and his mother will always have to struggle." He stuck his hands in his pockets and lifted his shoulders again, his eyes fastened on her face. "I'm not happy about him leaving, either. But I do think things will be better for him and his mother, at least for now. And I have faith that God will continue to follow Felix throughout his life."

He took a step closer to her. She lowered her eyes from his face and stared at the blue-and-green plaid of his shirt; her hands curled into fists as she fought the urge to feel the soft flannel with her fingertips. He reached out a hand and slid his knuckles along the line of her jaw. She shivered and swallowed hard.

"How are you, Dorrie Carpenter?" he asked softly. "This has been a hard time for you, hasn't it?"

She nodded and smiled faintly, though she could not meet his eyes. "First Liam and now Felix." She shook her head. "Just a few weeks ago I felt as though life was falling into place so neatly. Now I feel as though someone took the pieces of my life and tossed them into the air. The pattern I thought was shaping up so nicely isn't there at all anymore."

Alec smiled. "Maybe you'll find there's a brand-new pattern. Remember what I told you once about God liking to surprise us?"

Dorrie nodded. "You said God was like a jack-in-the-box." She met his eyes and grinned. "I didn't know what you were talking about. All I knew was that it made me feel uncomfortable—and that made me annoyed with you."

"Seemed like most everything I did annoyed you back then." He returned her grin, but she saw the watchfulness in his eyes, as though he feared that reaction from her again.

They looked away from each other and turned toward the windows. Dorrie looked out at the cold, gray sky, but she was very aware of the warm, quiet room around her and of Alec's presence beside her, his shoulder nearly touching hers.

"I feel so stupid about Liam," she said at last, her voice barely more than a whisper. She did not want to tell him this, but something in the quiet room seemed to draw the words from her mouth.

"Stupid? What do you mean?"

"Embarrassed, I guess. Like I made a fool of myself."

From the corner of her eye, she saw Alec shake his head. "We all make fools of ourselves sometimes." He moved, and she felt his shoulder brush hers. "I've been imagining you feeling hurt, heartbroken. But not embarrassed."

"I *was* hurt," she said slowly. "But then when I saw Liam again, it was the strangest thing. Like Paul when the scales fell from his eyes. I looked at Liam, and I realized that the man I had been in love with so long had only existed in my mind. I'd been infatuated with an imaginary person. I felt so silly."

She took a deep breath, trying to ignore the way the warmth of his shoulder was making her heart pound. "Now I keep remembering when Felix accused me of talking to an imaginary friend. When he'd overheard me praying, remember? And I wonder if maybe he was right. Maybe God's been a figment of my imagination, just like Liam was. Like maybe I thought my life was a story I could create all on my own, and God was just one more character in that story."

She moved away from him slightly and put her palms against the cold glass of the window. "That's what scares me the most. And now when Margaret and you tell me to have faith, that God will take care of Felix, I think, 'Of course, that's what would be nice to believe.' But it was nice to believe the fairy tale I'd made up about Liam, too." She looked over her shoulder at him. "How do I dare have faith in anything again?"

He was silent for a moment, his eyes focused beyond her face on the darkening sky outside the window. "Seems to me," he said at last, his voice slow and careful, "that in any relationship there are times when communication breaks down. Our selfishness gets in the way, and we hear what we want to hear, see what we want to see, instead of being truly in touch with the reality of the other person."

She waited for him to continue. When he didn't, she felt her old impatience with him for a moment. "So?" she asked at last.

His gaze focused on her face. "So that's what happened with you and God. You had a communication breakdown. When you realize that's been happening with another person, I don't think you walk away and say, 'I'll never talk to that person again.' Or, 'Because I misunderstood that person once, I'll never believe anything he says again.'"

The curve of his mouth was so tender that she looked away, afraid to believe what she was seeing. She realized she was behaving in almost the way he was describing, and she forced herself to look into his face again.

His smile widened. "God's not your imaginary friend, Dorrie. You may have been treating Him like one. That's why He had to leap out of the box you'd been putting Him in, confront you all over again with the boundlessness of His reality. But He's bigger than you thought—*more* real, not less. He's giving you the chance to grow in faith—you don't have to shrink back out of fear and embarrassment."

He put his hand toward her again, then dropped it before it reached her. "Believe me, I know how scary this is. Like the people who lived with Christ nearly two thousand years ago, we'd all like to put Christ somewhere small and confined, where He won't threaten the way we want our lives to go. Then we'd roll a stone in front of the opening, just like they did, and never realize that we're as guilty as they were of crucifying His life."

Dorrie felt a shiver of joy. "But He won't stay dead, will He?"

Alec shook his head. "Thank God for the Resurrection." He turned and leaned against the windowsill, facing her now. "It's funny," he said. He opened his mouth as though about to say something more, then closed it again. The silence stretched between them, suddenly tense where before it had been peaceful.

"What's funny?" she prodded at last.

He shrugged and she watched, fascinated, as the tips of his ears turned red. He cleared his throat. "I guess," he said at last, "that I've had my own communication breakdown with God. Kind of along the same lines as you. Except," his hands gripped the windowsill behind him until his knuckles whitened, then loosened, "I thought God wanted me to remain single all my life. You know in 1 Corinthians 7 where Paul talks about how if you're single, it's better to stay that way?"

"I guess." Dorrie smiled a little sheepishly. "I have to confess that it's not a passage I've paid a lot of attention to."

"Well, I never had, either. But then a couple of years ago, I was dating this girl. We didn't have a whole lot in common, I suppose, but I'd been lonely and getting involved with her seemed like a good idea at first. But then she started wanting to change me. She'd come over to my house and start sorting through my books." He shook his head and grinned. "She even wanted me to get rid of Esther. She was pushing me for a more serious commitment—but one day when I was praying about our relationship, I opened up the Bible to 1 Corinthians 7, and I thought, 'That's it. God's calling me to be single.' I felt so relieved."

"You—" Dorrie hesitated, not certain what she wanted to say, "you don't think that's what God wants for you after all?" she finished at last.

Alec grimaced and shrugged. "I wish I knew. All I do know is that I was guilty of using the Bible as though it were a fortune cookie. Oh, I believe that God uses Scripture to speak to us. But I see now that I was using the Bible just to support what *I* was already thinking, instead of using it to search for God's thoughts."

Dorrie nodded. "I did that, too, with Liam. Even after what happened the other morning. I opened up to a verse and convinced myself that I would be like Abraham if I continued to have faith that Liam, against all odds, would one day marry me." Alec's dark eyes on her face made her flush. She shook her head. "I see now how silly I was being. But what made you decide you'd been wrong?"

She'd asked the question innocently, truly curious, but something in his face made her breath catch. She saw him suck in a deep breath of his own. "You," he said at last.

"Me?" She didn't understand.

He nodded, and the high planes of his cheeks were now as red as his ears. "You." He looked past her, studying a map of the world she had hung on one wall. "At first I thought it was just because you were so pretty. I'd been feeling lonely again and—" He shrugged. "I figured it was only human to feel attracted to someone now and then. I thought we could be friends, and that would be enough." He smiled faintly, and his eyes flickered toward her, then back to the map. "But you didn't want to be friends. And I couldn't get you out of my mind." His voice was very low. "You finally let me be your friend—and then I realized," his mouth twisted, "that I wanted to be much more than your friend. I don't know anymore what God wants for the future. I only know what I want."

Dorrie found it hard to take a breath. "Well," she said, trying to make her voice light, "I know now how confusing God's will can be."

Alec shook his head. "I said I don't know what God wants for the future. For now, I think I do know."

Dorrie looked out the window. The sky was nearly dark now; Clem would be wondering where she was, she thought absently. "What is it you think He wants?" she whispered at last, still not looking at his face.

He cupped her chin with his hand. "I think God wants me to love you, Dorrie Carpenter," he said. She stared at him, saw him take a breath and swallow hard. "I haven't wanted to. You were so obviously in love with Liam. You didn't even like me. The more I cared about you, the more it hurt." He shook his head. "And yet somehow I felt more alive, more aware of God's presence in my life, than I had in a long time."

She bit her lip, not knowing what to say. His hand dropped from her face. "I'm sorry," he said. "I didn't mean to say all that. I don't want you to feel awkward around me. I truly do want to be your friend." He shook his head and pushed himself away from the windowsill, as though ready to leave. "I'm sorry."

"No—" She put her hand against his chest to stop him. She looked up at him. "I—" She could not continue. He looked down at her, and for once she was grateful that he could read her face so well, that she would not need to find words for the emotions that suddenly threatened to overwhelm her.

"Dorrie?" Very slowly, his hands went to her shoulders and drew her closer. Even more slowly, his mouth lowered to hers. She felt the warm gentleness of his lips, and though her heart continued to pound, she sighed, as though at long last, after the months of turmoil and confusion, she could relax.

A knock at the door made them spring apart. "I'm so glad you're both still here," Margaret Truesdell said when Dorrie opened the door. "Felix Jones has run away."

Chapter 15

D orrie stared at Margaret. "But why would he run away now? He sounded so excited about going home."

Margaret shrugged. "He knows what life was like at home before. Could be he's scared." She shook her head. "His mother's downstairs. When I told her this morning that we couldn't release Felix without the necessary paperwork, seems she drove directly to the judge's office and insisted she give her the papers. She brought them back to me this afternoon after classes were dismissed. Everything looked to be in order, but I called the judge just to double-check. She confirmed that it was okay to send Felix home. I sent word over to Felix's houseparents, and Mrs. Jones and I talked a little more. When we were done, we walked over to Corinthians Cottage—and found that Felix had disappeared." Margaret sighed. "Mrs. Jones is pretty upset."

"He hasn't had time to go far," Alec said quietly. "Let's search the grounds."

∞

An hour later, they still had not found him. "He used to hitchhike sometimes," Terri Jones said. Her face was white and pinched. "If he got a ride with someone, he could be anywhere by now."

Alec and Dorrie exchanged looks. "We'll drive around town and look for him, Mrs. Jones," Alec told her. "Don't worry. We'll find him."

They took Alec's car and drove slowly up and down the streets of the small town. "I'm scared," Dorrie said.

Alec reached over and put his hand on the back of her neck. "He's smart, remember? He won't do anything stupid."

"But he's only eleven years old."

"He's used to taking care of himself. Just keep praying."

Dear Lord, I know You're with Felix right now. She felt the warmth of Alec's hand against the back of her neck; she felt the assurance of God's love like a warmth that touched her heart. Slowly, she relaxed. She let out her breath in a long sigh.

"Do you think he would have gone to the art museum?" she asked Alec.

They drove the hour-long trip into the city, but by the time they got there, the art museum was closed and dark. They parked the car anyway and walked around the building, peering into window wells and behind bushes. At last, they got back in the car and drove to a pay phone.

Dorrie waited while Alec called Margaret back at the Home. He came out of the phone booth and shook his head. "Still no sign of him. Margaret says they've called the police. Mrs. Jones has gone home in case he should show up there. Margaret says we should go home, too."

When at last they reached the turn to their own road, Alec glanced at Dorrie. "Mind leaving your car at the Home overnight? I'll drive you to work tomorrow."

Dorrie nodded.

He pulled into her driveway. After a moment, he turned off the ignition and reached for Dorrie. "Come here a minute."

She slid closer to him, glad for his warmth.

"This isn't the right time to talk," Alec said. "I just wanted to make sure I didn't dream what happened earlier." He turned toward her and hesitated, then gently put his lips against hers. "Get some sleep," he whispered after a moment. "Felix is all right."

She nodded, then opened the car door. She started to swing her legs out, then turned toward Alec again, wanting to feel his warmth one more time. She, too, felt as though she were in some strange dream.

"Looks like I won my bet after all."

Dorrie leapt out of the car. "Felix!"

He was huddled on her doorstep, his arms wrapped around his knees. He shivered. "Where have you been? I've been waiting for you for hours." The light from the car's interior glinted on his glasses; his voice was cross.

"Felix." Dorrie grabbed him and hugged him tight.

"What's the big deal? You into hugging everybody today, or what?" He grinned. "I saw what you and Mr. MacIntyre were doing. So much for Mr. Adams, huh?"

Alec came around the car and looked down at Felix. "Do you know how worried we've been about you?"

Felix shrugged. Dorrie still had her arms around his shoulders, and though he scowled at her, she noticed he did not pull away. "Why did you run away?" she asked him. "Didn't you want to go home with your mother?"

"Of course I want to go home." He did pull away from her then. "I'm not stupid. I wasn't running away. I just wanted to see you before Mom and I took off. I was afraid if I asked her to bring me here, she wouldn't, so I caught a ride here by myself. How was I supposed to know you wouldn't turn up for hours? Off smooching with Mr. MacIntyre probably."

"We've been looking for you," Dorrie said. "All over. We even drove into the city. They've called the police to help search for you. Your mother's worried sick."

Felix shook his head. "Oh, great. Like I need to be in trouble with the police before I even get back home." He shook his hair out of his eyes and looked up at

Alec. "This won't mean they'll change their minds about letting me go home?"

Alec shook his head. "I don't think so. But maybe next time you might think about the consequences a little more before you decide to do something on your own." He reached out and messed Felix's hair. "So what was it you had to see Miss Carpenter about?"

Felix looked down at his sneakers. "I just wanted to say good-bye, I guess." He looked up at her quickly, then shrugged his backpack off his shoulders and reached inside. "And I have something for you."

He pulled out the Bible she had given him. She thought he was going to give it back to her, and she started to shake her head, but instead he pulled a square wrapped in a paper towel from between its pages. He handed it to her.

She unwrapped the paper towel and found a piece of thick drawing paper, covered with the intense jewel colors of markers. She held the paper toward the light from the car and saw a fantastic bird, each feather perfect, blood-red against the glow of a rising sun.

"It's a phoenix," Felix said. "You know, those mythical birds that die and then rise out of the ashes back to life." He pushed his glasses up his nose and looked up at Dorrie quickly. "I've been reading the Bible you gave me. I thought maybe a phoenix would be appropriate for a Christian."

Dorrie blinked the tears out of her eyes. "It's beautiful," she said. "Thank you. I think it's the best gift anyone ever gave me."

"Really?" Felix stared up into her face. "Then how come you're crying?"

"Oh, Felix!" Dorrie hugged him tight again. "I'm going to miss you so much."

Alec put his hand on her shoulder. "This doesn't have to be the last time we see Felix, you know. I seem to remember you made a promise to Felix about going to the art museum again. I think probably your mom wouldn't mind if we kept that promise, would she, Felix?"

Felix grinned and shook his head.

"But not if we don't let her know soon that you're all right. Mind if we come inside and use your phone, Miss Carpenter?"

∞

"I can't believe he was sitting out on our step all evening, and I never knew it," Clem said later that night. Alec and Dorrie had driven Felix back to the Home, where his relieved mother had been waiting. The last Dorrie had seen of him he had been turned toward his mother as they walked to their car, talking quickly, his face flushed and excited.

Dorrie sank down onto the sofa. "What a day!"

Clem looked at her. "Looks like it was a pretty good day for you and Alec."

Dorrie shook her head and grinned. "You don't miss much, do you?"

"Nope." Clem settled cross-legged in one of the deep chairs. "So—tell me what happened between you two."

"I'm not sure." Dorrie looked down at the picture Felix had given her. "I guess—I guess all the while I was so busy thinking about Liam, some hidden, quiet part of me was falling in love with Alec. I didn't want to accept it. I was so used to thinking that Liam was the man for me that it scared me to even think about Alec. The more attracted I felt to Alec, the more I had to insist that Liam was the one I loved. Does that make any sense?"

"Nope." Clem rested her chin in her hand and smiled at Dorrie. "But I understand. I've been just as silly about Mason."

"Have you talked to him yet?"

Clem nodded and her smile widened. "Today wasn't such a bad day for me, either. Mason and I went for a long walk after work today."

"And?"

"And I told him how much I love him. And that no matter how scared I am, I want to marry him." She held out her left hand, and Dorrie saw the gleam and glitter of a diamond ring. "Seems he had faith that I would finally say yes."

"Oh, Clem!" Dorrie leapt across the room and hugged her friend. "Congratulations! I'm so glad you worked things out."

"Me, too. Mason says he would have waited for me no matter how long I took. But I would have been pretty sorry if he'd left for the mission field without me, and I would have had to wait a couple of years before I could see him again." Clem smiled down at the solitaire. "Liam would probably hate to admit it—but God really used him when he confronted me yesterday."

Dorrie nodded. "It's funny," she said slowly. "I was so sure that God was going to give me this tidy, little happy ending with Liam and Felix, just because that's what I thought I wanted most. And you were so sure that God was going to give you a sad ending if you dared marry Mason, just because that's what scared you most. But we were both doing the same thing." She sank down on the floor beside Clem's chair and looked up at her friend. "We were both listening to our own voices instead of God's. The story I was telling myself had God confused with a fairy godmother—and the story you were listening to had God cast as a frightening, punishing ogre."

She reached for Felix's drawing and smiled. "Felix accused me once of living in a fairy tale. Well, I guess he was right. And now I see that God's reality is so much better, so much bigger and more wonderful than the fairy tale."

Gently, Dorrie touched the phoenix's burning colors. "For awhile there, I felt as though everything I'd longed for had turned to ashes. And now—now that our hearts are finally quiet and open to God—look what life has risen from it all!"

⌒⌒

On a Saturday nearly a month later, Alec and Dorrie drove home together from a visit to the Jones' trailer. Alec pulled into Dorrie's driveway and turned to her. "Felix really liked the oil paints you gave him. They were the perfect gift."

"The expression on his face when he saw them—I think he was even more excited than he was when we took him back to the art museum. I'm glad his mother doesn't mind us seeing him."

Alec nodded. "I like Terri. I can see where Felix gets his quirky sense of humor. They both seem pretty happy—and did you notice that Bible you gave Felix was lying on the coffee table? I have a feeling that God's taking good care of Felix and his mom."

Dorrie smiled. She looked out the car window and watched the snowflakes that floated down, drawing white lines along the branches of the oak trees.

After a moment Alec reached out and took her hand in his. "You've been so quiet since we left the trailer court. What are you thinking about?"

Dorrie looked down at his long, wide hand intertwined with hers. She felt her face grow warm, but she lifted her gaze to his and answered honestly. "I was remembering the day when Felix left. When you and I were together in my classroom. You said you didn't know anymore what God wanted for the future—but that you knew what *you* wanted. I was wondering what you meant."

"Nosy, aren't you?" He grinned, but she saw his dark lashes lower, as though he were uncertain of her reaction. His thumb moved back and forth on her hand. "I meant," he said at last, "that I don't know whether or not God wants me to marry. The answer to that depends on you." He looked up and met her eyes. "Because you're the person I want to marry, Dorrie."

She watched the warm blood stain his ears and high cheekbones, and she smiled. His dark eyes studied her face, but he did not return her smile. When he spoke again, his voice was very soft. "I love you, Dorrie Carpenter. How do you feel about me?"

She reached out her free hand and traced the strong lines of his brows and cheeks and nose. He closed his eyes, his face very still, as though he was afraid that if he moved, he would scare her hand away. "Don't you know by now?" she asked. "Can't you read it in my face?"

His mouth curved a little. "I think I can. But I need to hear the words."

She touched his dark hair, then tugged one of the wiry curls until his face came closer to her own. "I'm through making up my own stories about what the future holds. But I hope very much that God does want you to marry." She smiled into his eyes, though for some reason she felt tears pricking beneath her lids. "Because I love you, too, Alec MacIntyre."

"Dorrie," he said and sighed as though he had been holding his breath. His arms went around her. She closed her eyes and felt his warm mouth against her own.

∽∾

After Alec said good-bye at last, Dorrie went inside. Clem and Mason were chaperoning a youth party at the church, and the little house was quiet and empty. Dorrie picked up her briefcase and sat down at the kitchen table to work on the next week's lessons. Her class was a source of joy to her, but they were also a constant challenge; no matter how excited she felt about her growing relationship with Alec, she knew she could not afford to neglect her responsibility to her students.

As she worked, she felt the stillness touching her, like a warm and gentle hand. A verse from Isaiah 32 came into her head: "And the work of righteousness shall be peace; and the effect of righteousness quietness and assurance forever. And my people shall dwell in a peaceable habitation, and in sure dwellings, and in quiet resting places" (KJV). She smiled. The quiet that she had sensed all along in this little house no longer made her uneasy; she knew now that it was God's presence. At last, her heart could hear His quiet voice.

ELLYN SANNA is a prolific author of various books. She has also spent several years editing and proofreading the works of other authors, but this was her first published novel. She and her family make their home in New York.

A Letter to Our Readers

Dear Readers:

In order that we might better contribute to your reading enjoyment, we would appreciate your taking a few minutes to respond to the following questions. When completed, please return to the following: Fiction Editor, Barbour Publishing, Inc., P.O. Box 719, Uhrichsville, OH 44683.

1. Did you enjoy reading *New York?*
   ❑ Very much—I would like to see more books like this.
   ❑ Moderately—I would have enjoyed it more if _____
   _____
   _____

2. What influenced your decision to purchase this book?
   (Check those that apply.)
   ❑ Cover   ❑ Back cover copy   ❑ Title   ❑ Price
   ❑ Friends   ❑ Publicity   ❑ Other

3. Which story was your favorite?
   ❑ *Wait for the Morning*   ❑ *A Touching Performance*
   ❑ *Santanoni Sunrise*   ❑ *The Quiet Heart*

4. Please check your age range:
   ❑ Under 18   ❑ 18–24   ❑ 25–34
   ❑ 35–45   ❑ 46–55   ❑ Over 55

5. How many hours per week do you read? _____

Name _____

Occupation _____

Address _____

City _____ State _____ Zip _____

If you enjoyed
New York
then read:

⌐✧⌐

Ozarks

*The Hills Are Alive with Small Towns
and Big Hearts Revealed
in Four Complete Romances*

The Healing Promise by Hannah Alexander
A Place for Love by Mary Louise Colln
A Sign of Love by Veda Boyd Jones
The Hasty Heart by Helen Spears